UNCLE SILAS

A Tale of Bartram-Haugh

UNCLE SILAS

A Tale of Bartram-Haugh

By

J. S. LeFanu

With a New Introduction by
FREDERICK SHROYER
California State College
at Los Angeles

Dover Publications, Inc.
New York

Published in Canada by General Publishing Company, Ltd., 30 Lesmill Road, Don Mills, Toronto, Ontario.
Published in the United Kingdom by Constable and Company, Ltd., 10 Orange Street, London WC 2.

This Dover edition, first published in 1966, is an unabridged and unaltered republication of the work as published by Macmillan and Co., Ltd. in 1899. This edition contains a new Introduction by Frederick Shroyer.

Standard Book Number: 486-21715-9

Library of Congress Catalog Card Number: 66-13830

Manufactured in the United States of America
Dover Publications, Inc.
180 Varick Street
New York, N.Y. 10014

INTRODUCTION TO
THE DOVER EDITION

Since Joseph Sheridan LeFanu's death in 1873, most of this Victorian Anglo-Irish writer's fourteen novels have been largely forgotten, but not his masterly terror novel, *Uncle Silas*. Rereading it, preparatory to writing this Introduction, I was again reminded of how very good it is, and to me there seems no mystery involved in both its longevity and perennial appeal. Simply, it is one of the most effective, gripping novels of terror —a true Gothic novel—ever written.

Today, as in the past, *Uncle Silas* continues to serve diabolically well to chill the reader's psychic bones. It begins gently and discursively enough as the narration of a lady who remembers what it was that surrounded her as a girl—her isolated home, her dour, withdrawn father, and their servants—and then, little by little, it draws the reader into an insidious, one-way tunnel of fear wherein crouches murder most foul.

Uncle Silas is definitely not a novel to be read alone in a creaking, deserted house late at night. Indeed, in the malign glow of its bloody foxfire, most other novels of terror dim quickly toward extinction. Nor should the reader be comforted overmuch by its relatively quiet, almost prosaic beginning. Rather let him heed the cry of the winter winds outside the ghost-whispering old manse of Knowl, forewarned that it is that, and the encroaching darkness of a winter's night, that most truly presage the true nature of the horror awaiting him at the narrative's next turning.

We are all a little afraid of death, and *Uncle Silas* is, above all, a novel in which death prowls the pages. Maud Ruthyn, the narrator, is peculiarly obsessed with night thoughts, and though she may at times philosophize sentimentally about death, she

v

lives in the awful shadow of its presence and, indeed, at times seems half in love with it. Her death-obsessed father, Austin Ruthyn, a Swedenborgian, knowing that he is a dying man, half-yearns for the opening of the gate through which, he believes, he will pass into a landscape littered with signs and wonders.

But all of this is, in itself, not enough to make *Uncle Silas* the outré experience it is. LeFanu, death-haunted himself, especially after the death of his beloved wife, knew that unrelieved darkness loses in time its effect, and thus all through the novel, as murder and terror accumulate, he scatters small diamonds of wit, sunlight and satire upon the novel's vast shroud. Just as *Macbeth* is made infinitely more terrible by the interpolation of the gate-keeper scene, so is the basic terror of *Uncle Silas* amplified by LeFanu's occasional introductions of warm fireside scenes and episodes which serve, briefly, seemingly to move Maud away from the bloody death for which she is destined. Thus, too, from time to time, pleasant, frequently comic characters are introduced to serve as shafts of sunlight in an ever darkening room: Maud's cousin, Milly, the simple, slangy daughter of Silas Ruthyn; the worldly, witty, heart-of-gold Lady Knollys; and even Silas's son, Dudley, especially when he jigs, smokes his churchwarden and presents Maud with a parrot.

Still, LeFanu does not dally long with the comic and the whimsical. It is a darker, bloodier draught that he brews, and in its making he draws upon the blacker, more disturbing manifestations of nature to froth it with terror. Indeed, *Uncle Silas* begins with a touch of this sort of thing, and in the following quotation from the beginning of the novel, it should be noted that even when he contrasts the wildness of a winter's night outside with the warm candle-lit rooms within Knowl, LeFanu brings something of the external gloom into the rooms by the use of such words as 'sombre,' 'black,' 'ebony,' 'grim,' and 'pale':

> It was winter—that is, about the second week in November—and great gusts were rattling at the windows, and wailing and thundering among our tall trees and ivied chimneys—a very dark night, and a very cheerful fire blazing, a pleasant mixture of good round coal and spluttering dry wood, in a genuine old fireplace, in a sombre old room. Black wainscoting glimmered up to the

ceiling, in small ebony panels; a cheerful clump of wax candles on the tea-table; many old portraits, some grim and pale, others pretty, and some very graceful and charming, hanging from the walls.

On another occasion, after the death of her father, Maud's depression and growing apprehension are orchestrated and amplified again by the seeming shouts of phantom riders galloping through a nighted storm:

> And so it was like the yelling of phantom hounds and hunters, and the thunder of their coursers in the air—a furious, grand, and supernatural music, which in my fancy made a suitable accompaniment to the discussion of that enigmatical person—martyr—angel—demon—Uncle Silas—with whom my fate was now so strangely linked, and whom I had begun to fear.
>
> 'The storm blows from that point,' I said, indicating it with my hand and eye, although the window shutters and curtains were closed. 'I saw all the trees bend that way this evening. That way stands the great lonely wood, where my darling father and mother lie. Oh, how dreadful on nights like this, to think of them—a vault!—damp, and dark, and solitary—under the storm.'

The above description of a storm leads quickly, it will be noted, into gloomy speculations about the finality of death, and, as it has been intimated before, LeFanu comes unerringly to the matter of death to contribute to the horror and accumulating drifts of creeping doom and darkness in his novel. Not infrequently in LeFanu's fiction does death forsake the anonymity of an abstraction to become, in fact, an actual entity. Though it is true that in the following little interpolated essay on death Maud compares that last eternal sleep with the little deaths that round each of our days, and does it with a gentle resignation and wistfulness, the quotation which follows it brings Death directly before the reader as a veritable King of Terrors:

> See how a sleepy child will put off the inevitable departure for bed. The little creature's eyes blink and stare, and it needs constant jogging to prevent his nodding off into the slumber which nature craves. His waking is a pain; he is quite worn out, and peevish, and stupid, and yet he implores a respite, and deprecates repose, and vows he is not sleepy, even to the moment when his mother takes him in her arms, and carries him, in a sweet slumber, to the

nursery. So it is with us old children of earth and the great sleep of
death, and nature our kind mother. Just so reluctantly we part
with consciousness, the picture is, even to the last so interesting;
the bird in the hand, though sick and moulting, so inestimably
better than all the brilliant tenants of the bush. We sit up, yawning, and blinking, and stupid, the whole scene swimming before
us, and the stories and music humming off into the sound of distant winds and waters. It is not time yet; we are not fatigued; we
are good for another hour still, and so protesting against bed, we
falter and drop into the dreamless sleep which nature assigns to
fatigue and satiety.

*　　*　　*

Next day was the funeral, that appalling necessity; smuggled
away in whispers, by black familiars, unresisting, the loved one
leaves home, without a farewell, to darken those doors no more,
henceforward to lie outside, far away and forsaken, through the
drowsy heats of summer, through days of snow and nights of
tempest, without light or warmth, without a voice near. Oh, Death,
king of terrors! The body quakes and the spirit faints before thee.
It is vain, with hands clasped over our eyes, to scream our reclamation; the horrible image will not be excluded.

Finally, in this connection, LeFanu seldom fails to utilize
the supernatural as a device to darken most effectively the atmosphere of terror he creates. *Uncle Silas* is not a novel of the
supernatural, but what is one to make of the gypsy girl's prophetic utterances when she is accosted by Maud on her way to
Uncle Silas's decaying manse? Or of the voice that Maud hears
'near the hearthstone, as I thought, say in a stern whisper, "Fly
the fangs of Belisaurius" '? Or of Lady Knollys's chilling comment upon Uncle Silas when she says, 'Perhaps other souls than
human are sometimes born into the world and clothed in flesh,
venerable, fiery-eyed'?

Indeed, early in *Uncle Silas*, Knowl is described as the habitat
of legendary phantoms which, Maud suggests, may or may not
really exist:

There is not an old house in England of which the servants and
young people who live in it do not cherish some traditions of the
ghostly. Knowl has its shadows, noises, and marvellous records.
Rachel Ruthyn, the beauty of Queen Anne's time, who died of
grief for the handsome Colonel Norbrooke, who was killed in the

Low Countries, walks the house by night, in crisp and sounding silks. She is not seen, only heard. The tapping of her high-heeled shoes, the sweep and rustle of her brocades, her sighs as she pauses in the galleries, near the bed-room doors; and sometimes, on stormy nights, her sobs.

There is, beside the 'link-man,' a lank, dark-faced, black-haired man, in a sable suit, with a link or torch in his hand. It usually only smoulders, with a deep red glow, as he visits his beat. The library is one of the rooms he sees to. Unlike 'Lady Rachel,' as the maids called her, he is seen only, never heard. His steps fall noiseless as shadows on floor and carpet. The lurid glow of his smouldering torch imperfectly lights his figure and face, and, except when much perturbed, his link never blazes. On those occasions, however, as he goes his rounds, he ever and anon whirls it round his head, and it bursts into a dismal flame. This is a fearful omen, and always portends some direful crisis or calamity.

Though later LeFanu's marvellous creation, the grotesque, unforgettable Madame de la Rougierre, who repeatedly asserts that she is in love with death and all of its sombre accoutrements, says that she has seen one of Knowl's ghosts, it is not important really if she has or not. By his descriptions of the ghosts that may or may not haunt Knowl, and by Madame's statement, LeFanu has achieved the effect he sought: he has made us all a little afraid, and like the witty French lady who, when asked if she believed in ghosts, replied, 'No, but I'm afraid of them,' we, too, find ourselves whistling a little too loudly as we glance apprehensively over our shoulders.

Well, you now have *Uncle Silas* in your hands. If you've not read it before, I envy you. You are about to have a first-time reading experience which, I suspect, you will never forget. Though I have read *Uncle Silas* many times, I still remember the unbearable suspense, the tension, that accompanied my first perusal of it. That peculiar, nervous pleasure now awaits you. As the late—one hopes—Count Dracula was wont to greet his guests with the purring invitation, 'Welcome to Castle Dracula,' so do I now say, 'Welcome to Knowl and Bartram-Haugh.'

Uncle Silas was first published in *The Dublin University Magazine* in 1865, under the title *Maud Ruthyn and Uncle Silas.*

It was subsequently published in book form as a 'three-decker' by Richard Bentley of London in December of the same year under its present title, *Uncle Silas.*

While still a young man, LeFanu had begun his professional literary career by writing short stories. In 1839 he published 'A Passage in the Secret History of an Irish Countess,' which, with some minor changes appeared again as 'The Murdered Cousin' in LeFanu's collection of short stories, *Ghost Stories and Tales of Mystery* (1851). This two-titled short story was an early rehearsal for the impressive, extended performance that was to be the novel, *Uncle Silas.* In effect, moving the scene from Ireland to England, LeFanu used the plot of the short story for the novel.

It might be appropriate here to mention that the author, of Anglo-Irish descent, was born in Dublin on August 28, 1814, and that while yet an infant was taken to the adjacent Phoenix Park when his father was appointed Chaplain of the Royal Hibernian Military School located there. When twelve years of age, he moved with his family to Abington in Limerick, where his father assumed another ecclesiastical post. His literary precociousness was early manifested in a number of poetical productions, and in January, 1838, he published his first short story, 'The Ghost and the Bone Setter.' From 1838 until 1839—when he was called to the bar, though he never practiced law—LeFanu published nine short stories and 'Scraps of Hibernian Ballads.'

His first novel, *The Cock and the Anchor,* was published in 1845, one year after his marriage to Susan Bennett, the daughter of a prominent lawyer. *The Cock and the Ancho*r followed in the footsteps of Sir Walter Scott, as did his second novel, *The Fortunes of Colonel Torlough O'Brien.* LeFanu's historical romances, set in Ireland, are chiefly memorable for some effective touches of the supernatural, scenes of unrelieved brutality and some masterly characterizations, especially of minor figures and villains. These early novels were not notably successful, and they are largely forgotten today.

In 1861, LeFanu bought *The Dublin University Magazine,* which no longer had any official connection with that institution. After the death of his wife in 1858, LeFanu had written no further fiction, but with the acquisition of the magazine he began to write again and, until his death in 1873, not a year passed without publication on his part.

In 1861-1862, one of LeFanu's finest novels, *The House by the Churchyard,* appeared serially in the aforementioned *The Dublin University Magazine,* and later in book form. This was followed in 1863-1864 by another superb mystery novel, *Wylder's Hand.* The last of his major novels—and no doubt his best—was *Uncle Silas* (1864). During the time he was writing these three outstanding novels he was also publishing short stories, mostly of the supernatural.

In the years that followed the appearance of his three major novels—all eminently worthy of being read today—LeFanu published a number of other, lesser novels, including *Guy Deverell* (1865), *All in the Dark* (1866), *The Wyvern Mystery* (1869), and the best of these second-rank works, *Checkmate* (1871).

After the death of his wife, LeFanu, living in Dublin, became more and more a recluse. As his years neared their end, they brought terrifying dreams to him. One which came again and again was of an old decayed mansion which was about to topple upon him as he stood transfixed before it. And then on February 7, 1873, shortly after he had published his last significantly titled novel, *Willing to Die,* as his physician metaphorically said, '. . . the house fell at last,' and Joseph Sheridan LeFanu was dead beneath it.

LeFanu made an indelible impression upon many of his distinguished readers, and a number of them, including M. R. James and Henry James, have paid their respects to the man and his work. Arthur Conan Doyle paid the greatest compliment imaginable to *Uncle Silas* when he utilized its basic plot for his own novel, *The Firm of Girdlestone.* Elizabeth Bowen considers *Uncle Silas* to be the first of the psychological thrillers, and Bram Stoker wrote his *Dracula* as a kind of sequel to LeFanu's powerful and innovational vampire story, 'Carmilla.'

The Gothic novel to which LeFanu made major contributions, has had a long and deserved popularity. There is something about the romance, terror and menace which such tales evoke that has a perennial appeal for the reader, especially the modern one, who, often living in a routine, drab IBM world, seeks to escape into calendarless, clockless places where it always is midnight and winter, and where frightened girls tiptoe fearfully down haunted corridors of lightless, decaying, moor-surrounded castles and mansions.

Though Gothic elements appeared in previous English fiction, the first recognized Gothic was *The Castle of Otranto,* written by Horace Walpole in 1764. Inspired by a dream, this short novel established much of the pattern subsequent Gothics were to follow. The setting is an ancient castle; the heroine is pursued by an evil, lecherous nobleman, and supernatural entities and manifestations abound. There is a mystery centered about the identity of a young man of seemingly humble origins who darts through haunted, subterranean passages.

It would not be appropriate here to trace the Gothic novel from its inception in Walpole's work to the present, but surely it is necessary to mention the Queen of Terrors, Mrs. Radcliffe, whose *Mysteries of Udolpho* (1794) is considered one of the greatest of the Gothics. So great was its influence that few of the Gothics written after it fail to show its mark. Indeed, the reader of *Uncle Silas* will note that when Maud is prowling through Bartram-Haugh she thinks immediately of one of Mrs. Radcliffe's haunted settings.

Suffice it to say that early the Gothics fell into two divisions: the rationalized and the unrationalized. The former presented the seemingly supernatural, but explained it naturally before the story ended. The latter presented the genuine supernatural and let it go at that. Rationalized or unrationalized, these early novels usually had medieval settings, and because 'gothic' was then a synonym for 'medieval,' they were called Gothic novels.

During the nineteenth century, especially in England, the Gothic romance took many forms and loosed itself from the bonds of its origins. Increasingly the setting was in the present or the near present, but, though modernized in this respect, the mixture was much as before. In time the rationalized Gothic gave birth to the detective story, and certainly much of modern science fiction owes a considerable debt to the unrationalized Gothics.

The reader will perhaps remember, as an example of a relatively modern rationalized Gothic, Arthur Conan Doyle's *The Hound of the Baskervilles*, in which a supposedly supernatural hound is ultimately revealed to be but a hound, though a most fearsome one. Then, too, Daphne DuMaurier's *Rebecca* comes quickly to mind, carrying as it does a Gothic strain directly traceable to the works of the Brontës.

Today the Gothics are with us in force, and many publishers are issuing series of novels which they so designate. In such a climate it is altogether appropriate that LeFanu—the greatest of them all—should be introduced again to a world that unaccountably for a time almost forgot him.

FREDERICK SHROYER

Palm Desert, California
March, 1966

A PRELIMINARY WORD

The writer of this Tale ventures, in his own person, to address a very few words, chiefly of explanation, to his readers. A leading situation in this ' Story of Bartram-Haugh ' is repeated, with a slight variation, from a short magazine tale of some fifteen pages written by him, and published long ago in a periodical under the title of 'A Passage in the Secret History of an Irish Countess,' and afterwards, still anonymously, in a small volume under an altered title. It is very unlikely that any of his readers should have encountered, and still more so that they should remember, this trifle. The bare possibility, however, he has ventured to anticipate by this brief explanation, lest he should be charged with plagiarism—always a disrespect to a reader.

May he be permitted a few words also of remonstrance against the promiscuous application of the term ' sensation ' to that large school of fiction which transgresses no one of those canons of construction and morality which, in producing the unapproachable ' Waverley Novels,' their great author imposed upon himself ? No one, it is assumed, would describe Sir Walter Scott's romances as 'sensation novels ; ' yet in that marvellous series there is not a single tale in which death, crime, and, in some form, mystery, have not a place.

Passing by those grand romances of ' Ivanhoe,' ' Old Mortality,' and ' Kenilworth,' with their terrible intricacies of crime and bloodshed, constructed with so fine a mastery of the art of exciting suspense and horror, let the reader pick out those two exceptional novels in the series which profess to paint contemporary manners and the scenes of common life ; and remembering in the 'Antiquary' the vision in the tapestried chamber, the duel, the horrible secret, and the death of old Elspeth, the drowned fisherman, and above all the tremendous situation of the tide-bound party under the cliffs ; and in ' St. Ronan's Well,' the long-drawn mystery, the suspicion of insanity, and the catastrophe of suicide ;—determine whether an epithet which it would be a profanation to apply to the structure of any, even the most exciting of Sir Walter Scott's stories, is fairly applicable to tales which, though illimitably inferior in execution, yet observe the same limitations of incident, and the same moral aims.

The author trusts that the Press, to whose masterly criticism and generous encouragement he and other humble labourers in the art owe so much, will insist upon the limitation of that degrading term to the peculiar type of fiction which it was originally intended to indicate, and prevent, as they may, its being made to include the legitimate school of tragic English romance, which has been ennobled, and in great measure founded, by the genius of Sir Walter Scott.

CONTENTS

UNCLE SILAS

A Tale of Bartram-Haugh

CHAPTER I

AUSTIN RUTHYN, OF KNOWL, AND HIS DAUGHTER

It was winter—that is, about the second week in November—and great gusts were rattling at the windows, and wailing and thundering among our tall trees and ivied chimneys—a very dark night, and a very cheerful fire blazing, a pleasant mixture of good round coal and spluttering dry wood, in a genuine old fireplace, in a sombre old room. Black wainscoting glimmered up to the ceiling, in small ebony panels ; a cheerful clump of wax candles on the tea-table ; many old portraits, some grim and pale, others pretty, and some very graceful and charming, hanging from the walls. Few pictures, except portraits long and short, were there. On the whole, I think you would have taken the room for our parlour. It was not like our modern notion of a drawing-room. It was a long room too, and every way capacious, but irregularly shaped.

A girl, of a little more than seventeen, looking, I believe, younger still ; slight and rather tall, with a great deal of golden hair, dark grey-eyed, and with a countenance rather sensitive and melancholy, was sitting at the tea-table, in a reverie. I was that girl.

The only other person in the room—the only person in the house related to me—was my father. He was Mr. Ruthyn, of Knowl, so called in his county, but he had many other places, was of a very ancient lineage, who had refused a baronetage often, and it was said even a viscounty, being of a proud and defiant spirit, and thinking themselves higher in station and purer of blood than two-thirds of the nobility into whose ranks, it was said, they had been invited to enter. Of all this family lore I knew but little and vaguely ; only what is to be gathered from the fireside talk of old retainers in the nursery.

1

I am sure my father loved me, and I know I loved him. With the sure instinct of childhood I apprehended his tenderness, although it was never expressed in common ways. But my father was an oddity. He had been early disappointed in Parliament, where it was his ambition to succeed. Though a clever man, he failed there, where very inferior men did extremely well. Then he went abroad, and became a connoisseur and a collector ; took a part, on his return, in literary and scientific institutions, and also in the foundation and direction of some charities. But he tired of this mimic government, and gave himself up to a country life, not that of a sportsman, but rather of a student, staying sometimes at one of his places and sometimes at another, and living a secluded life.

Rather late in life he married, and his beautiful young wife died, leaving me, their only child, to his care. This bereavement, I have been told, changed him—made him more odd and taciturn than ever, and his temper also, except to me, more severe. There was also some disgrace about his younger brother— my uncle Silas—which he felt bitterly.

He was now walking up and down this spacious old room, which, extending round an angle at the far end, was very dark in that quarter. It was his wont to walk up and down thus, without speaking—an exercise which used to remind me of Chateaubriand's father in the great chamber of the Château de Combourg. At the far end he nearly disappeared in the gloom, and then returning emerged for a few minutes, like a portrait with a background of shadow, and then again in silence faded nearly out of view.

This monotony and silence would have been terrifying to a person less accustomed to it than I. As it was, it had its effect. I have known my father a whole day without once speaking to me. Though I loved him very much, I was also much in awe of him.

While my father paced the floor, my thoughts were employed about the events of a month before. So few things happened at Knowl out of the accustomed routine, that a very trifling occurrence was enough to set people wondering and conjecturing in that serene household. My father lived in remarkable seclusion ; except for a ride, he hardly ever left the grounds of Knowl ;

and I don't think it happened twice in the year that a visitor sojourned among us.

There was not even that mild religious bustle which sometimes besets the wealthy and moral recluse. My father had left the Church of England for some odd sect, I forget its name, and ultimately became, I was told, a Swedenborgian. But he did not care to trouble me upon the subject. So the old carriage brought my governess, when I had one, the old housekeeper, Mrs. Rusk, and myself to the parish church every Sunday. And my father, in the view of the honest rector who shook his head over him— 'a cloud without water, carried about of winds, and a wandering star to whom is reserved the blackness of darkness'—corresponded with the 'minister' of his church, and was provokingly contented with his own fertility and illumination ; and Mrs. Rusk, who was a sound and bitter churchwoman, said he fancied he saw visions and talked with angels like the rest of that 'rubbitch.'

I don't know that she had any better foundation than analogy and conjecture for charging my father with supernatural pretensions ; and in all points when her orthodoxy was not concerned, she loved her master and was a loyal housekeeper.

I found her one morning superintending preparations for the reception of a visitor, in the hunting-room it was called, from the pieces of tapestry that covered its walls, representing scenes à la Wouvermans, of falconry, and the chase, dogs, hawks, ladies, gallants, and pages. In the midst of whom Mrs. Rusk, in black silk, was rummaging drawers, counting linen, and issuing orders.

'Who is coming, Mrs. Rusk ? '

Well, she only knew his name. It was a Mr. Bryerly. My papa expected him to dinner, and to stay for some days.

'I guess he's one of those creatures, dear, for I mentioned his name just to Dr. Clay (the rector), and he says there is a Doctor Bryerly, a great conjurer among the Swedenborg sect—and that's him, I do suppose.'

In my hazy notions of these sectaries there was mingled a suspicion of necromancy, and a weird freemasonry, that inspired something of awe and antipathy.

Mr. Bryerly arrived time enough to dress at his leisure, before dinner. He entered the drawing-room—a tall, lean man, all in ungainly black, with a white choker, with either a black wig, or black hair dressed in imitation of one, a pair of spectacles, and a dark, sharp, short visage, rubbing his large hands together, and with a short brisk nod to me, whom he plainly regarded merely as a child, he sat down before the fire, crossed his legs, and took up a magazine.

This treatment was mortifying, and I remember very well the resentment of which *he* was quite unconscious.

His stay was not very long; not one of us divined the object of his visit, and he did not prepossess us favourably. He seemed restless, as men of busy habits do in country houses, and took walks, and a drive, and read in the library, and wrote half a dozen letters.

His bed-room and dressing-room were at the side of the gallery, directly opposite to my father's, which had a sort of ante-room *en suite,* in which were some of his theological books.

The day after Mr. Bryerly's arrival, I was about to see whether my father's water caraffe and glass had been duly laid on the table in this ante-room, and in doubt whether he was there, I knocked at the door.

I suppose they were too intent on other matters to hear, but receiving no answer, I entered the room. My father was sitting in his chair, with his coat and waistcoat off, Mr. Bryerly kneeling on a stool beside him, rather facing him, his black scratch wig leaning close to my father's grizzled hair. There was a large tome of their divinity lore, I suppose, open on the table close by. The lank black figure of Mr. Bryerly stood up, and he concealed something quickly in the breast of his coat.

My father stood up also, looking paler, I think, than I ever saw him till then, and he pointed grimly to the door, and said, ' Go.'

Mr. Bryerly pushed me gently back with his hands to my shoulders, and smiled down from his dark features with an expression quite unintelligible to me.

I had recovered myself in a second, and withdrew without a word. The last thing I saw at the door was the tall, slim figure in black, and the dark, significant smile following me : and then the door was shut and locked, and the two Swedenborgians were left to their mysteries.

I remember so well the kind of shock and disgust I felt in

the certainty that I had surprised them at some, perhaps, de-
basing incantation—a suspicion of this Mr. Bryerly, of the ill-
fitting black coat, and white choker—and a sort of fear came
upon me, and I fancied he was asserting some kind of mastery
over my father, which very much alarmed me.

I fancied all sorts of dangers in the enigmatical smile of the
lank high-priest. The image of my father, as I had seen him, it
might be, confessing to this man in black, who was I knew not
what, haunted me with the disagreeable uncertainties of a mind
very uninstructed as to the limits of the marvellous.

I mentioned it to no one. But I was immensely relieved when
the sinister visitor took his departure the morning after, and
it was upon this occurrence that my mind was now employed.

Some one said that Dr. Johnson resembled a ghost, who must
be spoken to before it will speak. But my father, in whatever
else he may have resembled a ghost, did not in that particular ;
for no one but I in his household—and I very seldom—dared to
address him until first addressed by him. I had no notion how
singular this was until I began to go out a little among friends
and relations, and found no such rule in force anywhere else.

As I leaned back in my chair thinking, this phantasm of my
father came, and turned, and vanished with a solemn regularity.
It was a peculiar figure, strongly made, thick-set, with a face
large, and very stern ; he wore a loose, black velvet coat and
waistcoat. It was, however, the figure of an elderly rather than
an old man—though he was then past seventy—but firm, and
with no sign of feebleness.

I remember the start with which, not suspecting that he was
close by me, I lifted my eyes, and saw that large, rugged countenance looking fixedly on me, from less than a yard away.

After I saw him, he continued to regard me for a second or
two ; and then, taking one of the heavy candlesticks in his
gnarled hand, he beckoned me to follow him ; which, in silence
and wondering, I accordingly did.

He led me across the hall, where there were lights burning,
and into a lobby by the foot of the back stairs, and so into his
library.

It is a long, narrow room, with two tall, slim windows at the
far end, now draped in dark curtains. Dusky it was with but one
candle; and he paused near the door, at the left-hand side of

which stood, in those days, an old-fashioned press or cabinet of carved oak. In front of this he stopped.

He had odd, absent ways, and talked more to himself, I believe, than to all the rest of the world put together.

'She won't understand,' he whispered, looking at me enquiringly. 'No, she won't. *Will* she?'

Then there was a pause, during which he brought forth from his breast pocket a small bunch of some half-dozen keys, on one of which he looked frowningly, every now and then balancing it a little before his eyes, between his finger and thumb, as he deliberated.

I knew him too well, of course, to interpose a word.

'They are easily frightened—ay, they are. I'd better do it another way.'

And pausing, he looked in my face as he might upon a picture.

'They *are*—yes—I had better do it another way—another way; yes—and she'll not suspect—she'll not suppose.'

Then he looked steadfastly upon the key, and from it to me, suddenly lifting it up, and said abruptly, 'See, child,' and, after a second or two, '*Remember* this key.'

It was oddly shaped, and unlike others.

'Yes, sir.' I always called him 'sir.'

'It opens that,' and he tapped it sharply on the door of the cabinet. 'In the daytime it is always here,' at which word he dropped it into his pocket again. 'You see?—and at night under my pillow—you hear me?'

'Yes, sir.'

'You won't forget this cabinet—oak—next the door—on your left—you won't forget?'

'No, sir.'

'Pity she's a girl, and so young—ay, a girl, and so young—no sense—giddy. You say, you'll *remember*?'

'Yes, sir.'

'It behoves you.'

He turned round and looked full upon me, like a man who has taken a sudden resolution; and I think for a moment he had made up his mind to tell me a great deal more. But if so, he changed it again; and after another pause, he said slowly and sternly—

'You will tell *no*body what I have said, under pain of my displeasure.'

'Oh ! no, sir ! '

'Good child ! '

'*Except,*' he resumed, ' under one contingency ; that is, in case I should be absent, and Dr. Bryerly—you recollect the thin gentleman, in spectacles and a black wig, who spent three days here last month—should come and enquire for the key, you understand, in my absence.'

'Yes, sir.'

So he kissed me on the forehead, and said—

'Let us return.'

Which, accordingly, we did, in silence ; the storm outside, like a dirge on a great organ, accompanying our flitting.

CHAPTER II

UNCLE SILAS

When we reached the drawing-room, I resumed my chair, and my father his slow and regular walk to and fro, in the great room. Perhaps it was the uproar of the wind that disturbed the ordinary tenor of his thoughts ; but, whatever was the cause, certainly he was unusually talkative that night.

After an interval of nearly half an hour, he drew near again, and sat down in a high-backed arm-chair, beside the fire, and nearly opposite to me, and looked at me steadfastly for some time, as was his wont, before speaking ; and said he—

'This won't do—you must have a governess.'

In cases of this kind I merely set down my book or work, as it might be, and adjusted myself to listen without speaking.

'Your French is pretty well, and your Italian ; but you have no German. Your music may be pretty good—I'm no judge— but your drawing might be better—yes—yes. I believe there are accomplished ladies—finishing governesses, they call them—

who undertake more than any one teacher would have professed in my time, and do very well. She can prepare you, and
next winter, then, you shall visit France and Italy, where you
may be accomplished as highly as you please.'

' Thank you, sir.'

' You shall. It is nearly six months since Miss Ellerton left
you—too long without a teacher.'

Then followed an interval.

' Dr. Bryerly will ask you about that key, and what it opens ;
you show all that to *him*, and no one else.'

' But,' I said, for I had a great terror of disobeying him in
ever so minute a matter, ' you will then be absent, sir—how am
I to find the key ?'

He smiled on me suddenly—a bright but wintry smile—it seldom came, and was very transitory, and kindly though mysterious.

' True, child ; I'm glad you are so wise ; *that,* you will find, I
have provided for, and you shall know exactly where to look.
You have remarked how solitarily I live. You fancy, perhaps,
I have not got a friend, and you are nearly right—*nearly,* but
not altogether. I have a very sure friend—*one*—a friend whom I
once misunderstood, but now appreciate.'

I wondered silently whether it could be Uncle Silas.

' He'll make me a call, some day soon ; I'm not quite sure
when. I won't tell you his name—you'll hear that soon enough,
and I don't want it talked of ; and I must make a little journey
with him. You'll not be afraid of being left alone for a time ? '

' And have you promised, sir ? ' I answered, with another question, my curiosity and anxiety overcoming my awe. He took
my questioning very good-humouredly.

' Well—*promise* ?—no, child ; but I'm under condition ; he's not
to be denied. I must make the excursion with him the moment
he calls. I have no choice ; but, on the whole, I rather like it—
remember, I say, I rather *like* it.'

And he smiled again, with the same meaning, that was at once
stern and sad. The exact purport of these sentences remained
fixed in my mind, so that even at this distance of time I am
quite sure of them.

A person quite unacquainted with my father's habitually abrupt
and odd way of talking, would have fancied that he was possibly

a little disordered in his mind. But no such suspicion for a moment troubled me. I was quite sure that he spoke of a real person who was coming, and that his journey was something momentous ; and when the visitor of whom he spoke did come, and he departed with him upon that mysterious excursion, I perfectly understood his language and his reasons for saying so much and yet so little.

You are not to suppose that all my hours were passed in the sort of conference and isolation of which I have just given you a specimen ; and singular and even awful as were sometimes my *tête-a-têtes* with my father, I had grown so accustomed to his strange ways, and had so unbounded a confidence in his affection, that they never depressed or agitated me in the manner you might have supposed. I had a great deal of quite a different sort of chat with good old Mrs. Rusk, and very pleasant talks with Mary Quince, my somewhat ancient maid ; and besides all this, I had now and then a visit of a week or so at the house of some one of our country neighbours, and occasionally a visitor— but this, I must own, very rarely—at Knowl.

There had come now a little pause in my father's revelations, and my fancy wandered away upon a flight of discovery. Who, I again thought, could this intending visitor be, who was to come, armed with the prerogative to make my stay-at-home father forthwith leave his household goods—his books and his child—to whom he clung, and set forth on an unknown knight-errantry ? Who but Uncle Silas, I thought—that mysterious relative whom I had never seen—who was, it had in old times been very darkly hinted to me, unspeakably unfortunate or unspeakably vicious—whom I had seldom heard my father mention, and then in a hurried way, and with a pained, thoughtful look. Once only he had said anything from which I could gather my father's opinion of him, and then it was so slight and enigmatical that I might have filled in the character very nearly as I pleased.

It happened thus. One day Mrs. Rusk was in the oak-room, I being then about fourteen. She was removing a stain from a tapestry chair, and I watched the process with a childish interest. She sat down to rest herself—she had been stooping over her work—and threw her head back, for her neck was weary, and in this position she fixed her eyes on a portrait that hung before her.

It was a full-length, and represented a singularly handsome young man, dark, slender, elegant, in a costume then quite obsolete, though I believe it was seen at the beginning of this century—white leather pantaloons and top-boots, a buff waist-coat, and a chocolate-coloured coat, and the hair long and brushed back.

There was a remarkable elegance and a delicacy in the fea-tures, but also a character of resolution and ability that quite took the portrait out of the category of mere fops or fine men. When people looked at it for the first time, I have so often heard the exclamation—' What a wonderfully handsome man ! ' and then, ' What a clever face ! ' An Italian greyhound stood by him, and some slender columns and a rich drapery in the back-ground. But though the accessories were of the luxurious sort, and the beauty, as I have said, refined, there was a masculine force in that slender oval face, and a fire in the large, shadowy eyes, which were very peculiar, and quite redeemed it from the suspicion of effeminacy.

' Is not that Uncle Silas ? ' said I.

' Yes, dear,' answered Mrs. Rusk, looking, with her resolute little face, quietly on the portrait.

' He must be a very handsome man, Mrs. Rusk. Don't you think so ? ' I continued.

' He *was*, my dear—yes ; but it is forty years since that was painted—the date is there in the corner, in the shadow that comes from his foot, and forty years, I can tell you, makes a change in most of us ; ' and Mrs. Rusk laughed, in cynical good-humour.

There was a little pause, both still looking on the handsome man in top-boots, and I said—

' And why, Mrs. Rusk, is papa always so sad about Uncle Silas ? '

' What's that, child ? ' said my father's voice, very near. I looked round, with a start, and flushed and faltered, receding a step from him.

' No harm, dear. You have said nothing wrong,' he said gently, observing my alarm. ' You said I was always sad, I think, about Uncle Silas. Well, I don't know how you gather that ; but if I were, I will now tell you, it would not be unnatural. Your uncle is a man of great talents, great faults, and great wrongs. His talents have not availed him ; his faults are long ago repented of ; and his wrongs I believe he feels less than I do, but they are deep. Did she say any more, madam ? ' he demanded abruptly of Mrs. Rusk.

' Nothing, sir,' with a stiff little courtesy, answered Mrs. Rusk, who stood in awe of him.

'And there is no need, child,' he continued, addressing himself to me, ' that you should think more of him at present. Clear your head of Uncle Silas. One day, perhaps, you will know him —yes, very well—and understand how villains have injured him.

Then my father retired, and at the door he said—

' Mrs. Rusk, a word, if you please,' beckoning to that lady, who trotted after him to the library.

I think he then laid some injunction upon the housekeeper, which was transmitted by her to Mary Quince, for from that time forth I could never lead either to talk with me about Uncle Silas. They let me talk on, but were reserved and silent themselves, and seemed embarrassed, and Mrs. Rusk sometimes pettish and angry, when I pressed for information.

Thus curiosity was piqued ; and round the slender portrait in the leather pantaloons and top-boots gathered many-coloured circles of mystery, and the handsome features seemed to smile down upon my baffled curiosity with a provoking significance.

Why is it that this form of ambition—curiosity—which entered into the temptation of our first parent, is so specially hard to resist ? Knowledge is power—and power of one sort or another is the secret lust of human souls ; and here is, beside the sense of exploration, the undefinable interest of a story, and above all, something forbidden, to stimulate the contumacious appetite.

CHAPTER III

A NEW FACE

I think it was about a fortnight after that conversation in which my father had expressed his opinion, and given me the mysterious charge about the old oak cabinet in his library, as already detailed, that I was one night sitting at the great drawing-room window, lost in the melancholy reveries of night, and in admiration of the moonlighted scene. I was the only occupant of the room ; and the lights near the fire, at its farther end, hardly reached to the window at which I sat.

The shorn grass sloped gently downward from the windows till it met the broad level on which stood, in clumps, or solitarily scattered, some of the noblest timber in England. Hoar in the moonbeams stood those graceful trees casting their moveless shadows upon the grass, and in the background crowning the undulations of the distance, in masses, were piled those woods among which lay the solitary tomb where the remains of my beloved mother rested.

The air was still. The silvery vapour hung serenely on the far horizon, and the frosty stars blinked brightly. Everyone knows the effect of such a scene on a mind already saddened. Fancies and regrets float mistily in the dream, and the scene affects us with a strange mixture of memory and anticipation, like some sweet old air heard in the distance. As my eyes rested on those, to me, funereal but glorious woods, which formed the background of the picture, my thoughts recurred to my father's mysterious intimations and the image of the approaching visitor ; and the thought of the unknown journey saddened me.

In all that concerned his religion, from very early association, there was to me something of the unearthly and spectral.

When my dear mamma died I was not nine years old ; and I remember, two days before the funeral, there came to Knowl, where she died, a thin little man, with large black eyes, and a very grave, dark face.

He was shut up a good deal with my dear father, who was in deep affliction ; and Mrs. Rusk used to say, ' It is rather odd to see him praying with that little scarecrow from London, and good Mr. Clay ready at call, in the village ; much good that little black whipper-snapper will do him ! '

With that little black man, on the day after the funeral, I was sent out, for some reason, for a walk ; my governess was ill, I know, and there was confusion in the house, and I dare say the maids made as much of a holiday as they could.

I remember feeling a sort of awe of this little dark man ; but I was not afraid of him, for he was gentle, though sad—and seemed kind. He led me into the garden—the Dutch garden, we used to call it—with a balustrade, and statues at the farther front, laid out in a carpet-pattern of brilliantly-coloured flowers. We came down the broad flight of Caen stone steps into this, and we walked in silence to the balustrade. The base was too high at the spot where we reached it for me to see over ; but holding my hand, he said, ' Look through that, my child. Well, you can't ; but *I* can see beyond it—shall I tell you what ? I see ever so much. I see a cottage with a steep roof, that looks like gold in the sunlight ; there are tall trees throwing soft shadows round it, and flowering shrubs, I can't say what, only the colours are beautiful, growing by the walls and windows, and two little children are playing among the stems of the trees, and we are on our way there, and in a few minutes shall be under those trees ourselves, and talking to those little children. Yet now to me it is but a picture in my brain, and to you but a story told by me, which you believe. Come, dear ; let us be going.'

So we descended the steps at the right, and side by side walked along the grass lane between tall trim walls of ever-greens. The way was in deep shadow, for the sun was near the horizon ; but suddenly we turned to the left, and there we stood in rich sunlight, among the many objects he had described.

' Is this your house, my little men ? ' he asked of the children—pretty little rosy boys—who assented ; and he leaned with his open hand against the stem of one of the trees, and with a grave smile he nodded down to me, saying—

' You see now, and hear, and *feel* for yourself that both the vision and the story were quite true ; but come on, my dear, we have further to go.'

And relapsing into silence we had a long ramble through the wood, the same on which I was now looking in the distance. Every now and then he made me sit down to rest, and he in a musing solemn sort of way would relate some little story, reflecting, even to my childish mind, a strange suspicion of a spiritual meaning, but different from what honest Mrs. Rusk used to expound to me from the Parables, and, somehow, startling in its very vagueness.

Thus entertained, though a little awfully, I accompanied the dark mysterious little ' whipper-snapper ' through the woodland glades. We came, to me quite unexpectedly, in the deep sylvan shadows, upon the grey, pillared temple, four-fronted, with a slanting pedestal of lichen-stained steps, the lonely sepulchre in which I had the morning before seen poor mamma laid. At the sight the fountains of my grief reopened, and I cried bitterly, repeating, ' Oh ! mamma, mamma, little mamma ! ' and so went on weeping and calling wildly on the deaf and the silent. There was a stone bench some ten steps away from the tomb.

' Sit down beside me, my child,' said the grave man with the black eyes, very kindly and gently. ' Now, what do you see there ? ' he asked, pointing horizontally with his stick towards the centre of the opposite structure.

' Oh, *that*—that place where poor mamma is ? '

' Yes, a stone wall with pillars, too high for either you or me to see over. But——'

Here he mentioned a name which I think must have been Swedenborg, from what I afterwards learnt of his tenets and revelations ; I only know that it sounded to me like the name of a magician in a fairy tale ; I fancied he lived in the wood which surrounded us, and I began to grow frightened as he proceeded.

' But Swedenborg sees beyond it, over, and *through* it, and has told me all that concerns us to know. He says your mamma is not there.'

' She is taken away ! ' I cried, starting up, and with streaming eyes, gazing on the building which, though I stamped my feet in my distraction, I was afraid to approach. ' Oh, *is* mamma taken away ? Where is she ? Where have they brought her to ? '

I was uttering unconsciously very nearly the question with

which Mary, in the grey of that wondrous morning on which she stood by the empty sepulchre, accosted the figure standing near.

'Your mamma is alive, but too far away to see or hear us ; but Swedenborg, standing here, can see and hear her, and tells me all he sees, just as I told you in the garden about the little boys and the cottage, and the trees and flowers which you could not see, but believed in when *I* told you. So I can tell you now as I did then ; and as we are both, I hope, walking on to the same place, just as we did to the trees and cottage, you will surely see with your own eyes how true is the description which I give you.'

I was very much frightened, for I feared that when he had done his narrative we were to walk on through the wood into that place of wonders and of shadows where the dead were visible.

He leaned his elbow on his knee, and his forehead on his hand, which shaded his downcast eyes, and in that attitude described to me a beautiful landscape, radiant with a wondrous light, in which, rejoicing, my mother moved along an airy path, ascending among mountains of fantastic height, and peaks, melting in celestial colouring into the air, and peopled with human beings translated into the same image, beauty, and splendour. And when he had ended his relation, he rose, took my hand, and smiling gently down on my pale, wondering face, he said the same words he had spoken before—

'Come, dear, let us be going.'

'Oh ! no, no, *no*—not now,' I said, resisting, and very much frightened.

'Home, I mean, dear. We cannot walk to the place I have described. We can only reach it through the gate of death, to which we are all tending, young and old, with sure steps.'

'And where is the gate of death ?' I asked in a sort of whisper, as we walked together, holding his hand very fast, and looking stealthily. He smiled sadly and said—

'When, sooner or later, the time comes, as Hagar's eyes were opened in the wilderness, and she beheld the fountain of water, so shall each of us see the door open before us, and enter in and be refreshed.'

For a long time after this walk I was very nervous ; the more so for the awful manner in which Mrs. Rusk received my statement—with stern lips and upturned hands and eyes, and an angry expostulation : ' I do wonder at you, Mary Quince, letting the child walk into the wood with that limb of darkness. It is a mercy he did not show her the devil, or frighten her out of her senses, in that lonely place ! '

Of these Swedenborgians, indeed, I know no more than I might learn from good Mrs. Rusk's very inaccurate talk. Two or three of them crossed in the course of my early life, like magic-lantern figures, the disk of my very circumscribed observation. All outside was and is darkness. I once tried to read one of their books upon the future state—heaven and hell ; but I grew after a day or two so nervous that I laid it aside. It is enough for me to know that their founder either saw or fancied he saw amazing visions, which, so far from superseding, confirmed and interpreted the language of the Bible ; and as dear papa accepted their ideas, I am happy in thinking that they did not conflict with the supreme authority of holy writ.

Leaning on my hand, I was now looking upon that solemn wood, white and shadowy in the moonlight, where, for a long time after that ramble with the visionary, I fancied the gate of death, hidden only by a strange glamour, and the dazzling land of ghosts, were situate ; and I suppose these earlier associations gave to my reverie about my father's coming visitor a wilder and a sadder tinge.

CHAPTER IV

MADAME DE LA ROUGIERRE

On a sudden, on the grass before me, stood an odd figure—a very tall woman in grey draperies, nearly white under the moon, courtesying extraordinarily low, and rather fantastically.

I stared in something like a horror upon the large and rather hollow features which I did not know, smiling very unpleasantly on me; and the moment it was plain that I saw her, the grey woman began gobbling and cackling shrilly—I could not distinctly hear *what* through the window—and gesticulating oddly with her long hands and arms.

As she drew near the window, I flew to the fireplace, and rang the bell frantically, and seeing her still there, and fearing that she might break into the room, I flew out of the door, very much frightened, and met Branston the butler in the lobby.

' There's a woman at the window ! ' I gasped ; ' turn her away, please.'

If I had said a man, I suppose fat Branston would have summoned and sent forward a detachment of footmen. As it was, he bowed gravely, with a—

' Yes,'m—shall,'m.'

And with an air of authority approached the window.

I don't think that he was pleasantly impressed himself by the first sight of our visitor, for he stopped short some steps of the window, and demanded rather sternly—

' What ye doin' there, woman ? '

To this summons, her answer, which occupied a little time, was inaudible to me. But Branston replied—

' I wasn't aware, ma'am ; I heerd nothin'; if you'll go round *that* way, you'll see the hall-door steps, and I'll speak to the master, and do as he shall order.'

The figure said something and pointed.

' Yes, that's it, and ye can't miss of the door.'

And Mr. Branston returned slowly down the long room, and halted with out-turned pumps and a grave inclination before me, and the faintest amount of interrogation in the announcement—

' Please, 'm, she says she's the governess. '

' The governess ! *What* governess ? '

Branston was too well-bred to smile, and he said thoughtfully—

' P'raps, 'm, I'd best ask the master ? '

To which I assented, and away strode the flat pumps of the butler to the library.

I stood breathless in the hall. Every girl at my age knows how much is involved in such an advent. I also heard Mrs. Rusk, in a minute or two more, emerge I suppose from the study. She walked quickly, and muttered sharply to herself—an

evil trick, in which she indulged when much 'put about.' I
should have been glad of a word with her ; but I fancied she was
vexed, and would not have talked satisfactorily. She did not,
however, come my way ; merely crossing the hall with her quick,
energetic step.

Was it really the arrival of a governess ? Was that apparition
which had impressed me so unpleasantly to take the command of
me—to sit alone with me, and haunt me perpetually with her
sinister looks and shrilly gabble ?

I was just making up my mind to go to Mary Quince, and
learn something definite, when I heard my father's step approaching from the library : so I quietly re-entered the drawing-
room, but with an anxious and throbbing heart.

When he came in, as usual, he patted me on the head gently,
with a kind of smile, and then began his silent walk up and
down the room. I was yearning to question him on the point
that just then engrossed me so disagreeably ; but the awe in
which I stood of him forbade.

After a time he stopped at the window, the curtain of which
I had drawn, and the shutter partly opened, and he looked out,
perhaps with associations of his own, on the scene I had been
contemplating.

It was not for nearly an hour after, that my father suddenly,
after his wont, in a few words, apprised me of the arrival of
Madame de la Rougierre to be my governess, highly recom-
mended and perfectly qualified. My heart sank with a sure
presage of ill. I already disliked, distrusted, and feared her.

I had more than an apprehension of her temper and fear
of possibly abused authority. The large-featured, smirking phantom, saluting me so oddly in the moonlight, retained ever after
its peculiar and unpleasant hold upon my nerves.

'Well, Miss Maud, dear, I hope you'll like your new governess
—for it's more than *I* do, just at present at least,' said Mrs. Rusk,
sharply—she was awaiting me in my room. 'I hate them French-
women ; they're not natural, I think. I gave her her supper in
my room. She eats like a wolf, she does, the great raw-boned
hannimal. I wish you saw her in bed as I did. I put her next
the clock-room—she'll hear the hours betimes, I'm thinking.
You never saw such a sight. The great long nose and hollow

cheeks of her, and oogh ! such a mouth ! I felt a'most like little Red Riding-Hood—I did, Miss.'

Here honest Mary Quince, who enjoyed Mrs. Rusk's satire, a weapon in which she was not herself strong, laughed outright.

' Turn down the bed, Mary. She's very agreeable—she is, just now—all new-comers is ; but she did not get many compliments from me, Miss—no, I rayther think not. I wonder why honest English girls won't answer the gentry for governesses, instead of them gaping, scheming, wicked furriners ? Lord forgi' me, I think they're all alike.'

Next morning I made acquaintance with Madame de la Rougierre. She was tall, masculine, a little ghastly perhaps, and draped in purple silk, with a lace cap, and great bands of black hair, too thick and black, perhaps, to correspond quite naturally with her bleached and sallow skin, her hollow jaws, and the fine but grim wrinkles traced about her brows and eyelids. She smiled, she nodded, and then for a good while she scanned me in silence with a steady cunning eye, and a stern smile.

' And how is she named—what is Mademoiselle's name ? ' said the tall stranger.

' *Maud,* Madame.'

' Maud !—what pretty name ! Eh bien ! I am very sure my dear Maud she will be very good little girl—is not so ?—and I am sure I shall love you vary moche. And what 'av you been learning, Maud, my dear cheaile—music, French, German, eh ? '

' Yes, a little ; and I had just begun the use of the globes when my governess went away.'

I nodded towards the globes, which stood near her, as I said this.

' Oh ! yes—the globes ; ' and she spun one of them with her great hand. 'Je vous expliquerai tout cela à fond.'

Madame da la Rougierre, I found, was always quite ready to explain everything ' à fond ; ' but somehow her ' explications,' as she termed them, were not very intelligible, and when pressed her temper woke up ; so that I preferred, after a while, accepting the expositions just as they came.

Madame was on an unusually large scale, a circumstance which made some of her traits more startling, and altogether rendered her, in her strange way, more awful in the eyes of a nervous *child,* I may say, such as I was. She used to look at me for a long time sometimes, with the peculiar smile I have mentioned, and a great finger upon her lip, like the Eleusinian priestess on the vase.

She would sit, too, sometimes for an hour together, looking into the fire or out of the window, plainly seeing nothing, and with an odd, fixed look of something like triumph—very nearly a smile—on her cunning face.

She was by no means a pleasant *gouvernante* for a nervous girl of my years. Sometimes she had accesses of a sort of hilarity which frightened me still more than her graver moods, and I will describe these by-and-by.

CHAPTER V

SIGHTS AND NOISES

There is not an old house in England of which the servants and young people who live in it do not cherish some traditions of the ghostly. Knowl has its shadows, noises, and marvellous records. Rachel Ruthyn, the beauty of Queen Anne's time, who died of grief for the handsome Colonel Norbrooke, who was killed in the Low Countries, walks the house by night, in crisp and sounding silks. She is not seen, only heard. The tapping of her high-heeled shoes, the sweep and rustle of her brocades, her sighs as she pauses in the galleries, near the bed-room doors; and sometimes, on stormy nights, her sobs.

There is, beside, the 'link-man,' a lank, dark-faced, black-haired man, in a sable suit, with a link or torch in his hand. It usually only smoulders, with a deep red glow, as he visits his beat. The library is one of the rooms he sees to. Unlike 'Lady Rachel,' as the maids called her, he is seen only, never heard. His steps fall noiseless as shadows on floor and carpet. The lurid glow of his smouldering torch imperfectly lights his figure and face, and, except when much perturbed, his link never blazes. On those occasions, however, as he goes his rounds, he ever and anon whirls it round his head, and it bursts into a dismal flame. This is a fearful omen, and always portends some direful crisis or calamity. It occurs, however, only one or twice in a century.

I don't know whether Madame had heard anything of these phenomena; but she did report what very much frightened me and Mary Quince. She asked us who walked in the gallery on which her bed-room opened, making a rustling with her dress, and going down the stairs, and breathing long breaths here and there. Twice, she said, she had stood at her door in the dark, listening to these sounds, and once she called to know who it was. There was no answer, but the person plainly turned back, and hurried towards her with an unnatural speed, which made her jump within her door and shut it.

When first such tales are told, they excite the nerves of the young and the ignorant intensely. But the special effect, I have found, soon wears out, and the tale simply takes its place with the rest. So it was with Madame's narrative.

About a week after its relation, I had my experience of a similar sort. Mary Quince went down-stairs for a night-light, leaving me in bed, a candle burning in the room, and there, being tired, I fell asleep before her return. When I awoke the candle had been extinguished. But I heard a step softly approaching. I jumped up—quite forgetting the ghost, and thinking only of Mary Quince—and opened the door, expecting to see the light of her candle. Instead, all was dark, and near me I heard the fall of a bare foot on the oak floor. It was as if some one had stumbled. I said, ' Mary,' but no answer came, only a rustling of clothes and a breathing at the other side of the gallery, which passed off towards the upper staircase. I turned into my room, freezing with horror, and clapt my door. The noise wakened Mary Quince, who had returned and gone to her bed half an hour before.

About a fortnight after this, Mary Quince, a very veracious spinster, reported to me, that having got up to fix the window, which was rattling, at about four o'clock in the morning, she saw a light shining from the library window. She could swear to its being a strong light, streaming through the chinks of the shutter, and moving, as no doubt the link was waved about his head by the angry ' link-man.'

These strange occurrences helped, I think, just then to make me nervous, and prepared the way for the odd sort of ascendency which, through my sense of the mysterious and supernatural, that repulsive Frenchwoman was gradually, and it seemed without effort, establishing over me.

Some dark points of her character speedily emerged from the prismatic mist with which she had enveloped it.

Mrs. Rusk's observation about the agreeability of new-comers I found to be true ; for as Madame began to lose that character, her good-humour abated very perceptibly, and she began to show gleams of another sort of temper, that was lurid and dangerous.

Notwithstanding this, she was in the habit of always having her Bible open by her, and was austerely attentive at morning and evening services, and asked my father, with great humility, to lend her some translations of Swedenborg's books, which she laid much to heart.

When we went out for our walk, if the weather were bad we generally made our promenade up and down the broad terrace in front of the windows. Sullen and malign at times she used to look, and as suddenly she would pat me on the shoulder caressingly, and smile with a grotesque benignity, asking tenderly, ' Are you fatigue, ma chère ? ' or ' Are you cold-a, dear Maud ? '

At first these abrupt transitions puzzled me, sometimes half frightened me, savouring, I fancied, of insanity. The key, however, was accidentally supplied, and I found that these accesses of demonstrative affection were sure to supervene whenever my father's face was visible through the library windows.

I did not know well what to make of this woman, whom I feared with a vein of superstitious dread. I hated being alone with her after dusk in the school-room. She would sometimes sit for half an hour at a time, with her wide mouth drawn down at the corners, and a scowl, looking into the fire. If she saw me looking at her, she would change all this on the instant, affect a sort of languor, and lean her head upon her hand, and ultimately have recourse to her Bible. But I fancied she did not read, but pursued her own dark ruminations, for I observed that the open book might often lie for half an hour or more under her eyes and yet the leaf never turned.

I should have been glad to be assured that she prayed when

on her knees, or read when that book was before her ; I should
have felt that she was more canny and human. As it was, those
external pieties made a suspicion of a hollow contrast with real-
ities that helped to scare me ; yet it was but a suspicion—I could
not be certain.

Our rector and the curate, with whom she was very gracious,
and anxious about my collects and catechism, had an exalted
opinion of her. In public places her affection for me was always
demonstrative.

In like manner she contrived conferences with my father.
She was always making excuses to consult him about my reading,
and to confide in him her sufferings, as I learned, from my
contumacy and temper. The fact is, I was altogether quiet and
submissive. But I think she had a wish to reduce me to a state
of the most abject bondage. She had designs of domination and
subversion regarding the entire household, I now believe, worthy
of the evil spirit I sometimes fancied her.

My father beckoned me into the study one day, and said he—

'You ought not to give poor Madame so much pain. She is
one of the few persons who take an interest in you ; why should
she have so often to complain of your ill-temper and disobed-
ience ?—why should she be compelled to ask my permission to
punish you ? Don't be afraid, I won't concede that. But in so
kind a person it argues much. Affection I can't command—respect and obedience I may—and I insist on your rendering *both*
to Madame.'

' But sir,' I said, roused into courage by the gross injustice of
the charge, ' I have always done exactly as she bid me, and never
said one disrespectful word to Madame.'

' I don't think, child, *you* are the best judge of that. Go, and
amend.' And with a displeased look he pointed to the door. My
heart swelled with the sense of wrong, and as I reached the door
I turned to say another word, but I could not, and only burst
into tears.

' There—don't cry, little Maud—only let us do better for the
future. There—there—there has been enough.'

And he kissed my forehead, and gently put me out and closed
the door.

In the school-room I took courage, and with some warmth
upbraided Madame.

'Wat wicked cheaile!' moaned Madame, demurely. 'Read aloud those three—yes, *those* three chapters of the Bible, my dear Maud.'

There was no special fitness in those particular chapters, and when they were ended she said in a sad tone—

'Now, dear, you must commit to memory this pretty priaire for umility of art.'

It was a long one, and in a state of profound irritation I got through the task.

Mrs. Rusk hated her. She said she stole wine and brandy whenever the opportunity offered—that she was always asking her for such stimulants and pretending pains in her stomach. Here, perhaps, there was exaggeration; but I knew it was true that I had been at different times despatched on that errand and pretext for brandy to Mrs. Rusk, who at last came to her bedside with pills and a mustard blister only, and was hated irrevocably ever after.

I felt all this was done to torture me. But a day is a long time to a child, and they forgive quickly. It was always with a sense of danger that I heard Madame say she must go and see Monsieur Ruthyn in the library, and I think a jealousy of her growing influence was an ingredient in the detestation in which honest Mrs. Rusk held her.

CHAPTER VI

A WALK IN THE WOOD

Two little pieces of by-play in which I detected her confirmed my unpleasant suspicion. From the corner of the gallery I one day saw her, when she thought I was out and all quiet, with her ear at the keyhole of papa's study, as we used to call the sitting-room next his bed-room. Her eyes were turned in the direction of the stairs, from which only she apprehended surprise. Her great mouth was open, and her eyes absolutely goggled with eagerness. She was devouring all that was passing there. I drew back into the shadow with a kind of disgust and horror. She was transformed into a great gaping reptile. I felt that I could have thrown something at her; but a kind of fear made me recede again toward my room. Indignation, however, quickly returned, and I came back, treading briskly as I did so. When I reached the angle of the gallery again, Madame, I suppose, had heard me, for she was half-way down the stairs.

'Ah, my dear cheaile, I am so glad to find you, and you are dress to come out. We shall have so pleasant walk.'

At that moment the door of my father's study opened, and Mrs. Rusk, with her dark energetic face very much flushed, stepped out in high excitement.

'The Master says you may have the brandy-bottle, Madame and I'm glad to be rid of it—I am.'

Madame courtesied with a great smirk, that was full of intangible hate and insult.

'Better your own brandy, if drink you must !' exclaimed Mrs. Rusk. 'You may come to the store-room now, or the butler can take it.'

And off whisked Mrs. Rusk for the back staircase.

There had been no common skirmish on this occasion, but a pitched battle.

Madame had made a sort of pet of Anne Wixted, an under-chambermaid, and attached her to her interest economically by persuading me to make her presents of some old dresses and other things. Anne was such an angel !

But Mrs. Rusk, whose eyes were about her, detected Anne, with a brandy-bottle under her apron, stealing up-stairs. Anne, in a panic, declared the truth. Madame had commissioned her to buy it in the town, and convey it to her bed-room. Upon this, Mrs. Rusk impounded the flask ; and, with Anne beside her, rather precipitately appeared before 'the Master.' He heard, and summoned Madame. Madame was cool, frank, and fluent. The brandy was purely medicinal. She produced a document in form of a note. Doctor Somebody presented his compliments to Madame de la Rougierre, and ordered her a table-spoonful of brandy and some drops of laudanum whenever the pain of stomach returned. The flask would last a whole year, perhaps two. She claimed her medicine.

Man's estimate of woman is higher than woman's own. Perhaps
in their relations to men they are generally more trustworthy—
perhaps woman's is the juster, and the other an appointed illusion. I don't know ; but so it is ordained.

Mrs. Rusk was recalled, and I saw, as you are aware, Madame's
procedure during the interview.

It was a great battle—a great victory. Madame was in high
spirits. The air was sweet—the landscape charming—I, so good
—everything so beautiful ! Where should we go ? *this* way ?

I had made a resolution to speak as little as possible to
Madame, I was so incensed at the treachery I had witnessed ;
but such resolutions do not last long with very young people,
and by the time we had reached the skirts of the wood we were
talking pretty much as usual.

' I don't wish to go into the wood, Madame.

' And for what ? '

' Poor mamma is buried there.'

' Is *there* the vault ? ' demanded Madame eagerly.

I assented.

' My faith, curious reason ; you say because poor mamma is
buried there you will not approach ! Why, cheaile, what would
good Monsieur Ruthyn say if he heard such thing? You are
surely not so unkain', and I am with you. *Allons.* Let us come
—even a little part of the way.'

And so I yielded, though still reluctant.

There was a grass-grown road, which we easily reached, leading to the sombre building, and we soon arrived before it.

Madame de la Rougierre seemed rather curious. She sat down
on the little bank opposite, in her most languid pose—her head
leaned upon the tips of her fingers.

' How very sad—how solemn ! ' murmured Madame. ' What
noble tomb ! How triste, my dear cheaile, your visit 'ere must
it be, remembering a so sweet maman. There is new inscription
—is it not new ? ' And so, indeed, it seemed.

' I am fatigue—maybe you will read it aloud to me slowly and
solemnly, my dearest Maud ? '

As I approached, I happened to look, I can't tell why, suddenly, over my shoulder ; I was startled, for Madame was grim-
acing after me with a vile derisive distortion. She pretended to

be seized with a fit of coughing. But it would not do : she saw that I had detected her, and she laughed aloud.

'Come here, dear cheaile. I was just reflecting how foolish is all this thing—the tomb—the epitaph. I think I would 'av none —no, no epitaph. We regard them first for the oracle of the dead, and find them after only the folly of the living. So I despise. Do you think your house of Knowl down there is what you call haunt, my dear ?'

'Why ?' said I, flushing and growing pale again. I felt quite afraid of Madame, and confounded at the suddenness of all this.

'Because Anne Wixted she says there is ghost. How dark is this place ! and so many of the Ruthyn family they are buried here—is not so ? How high and thick are the trees all round ! and nobody comes near.'

And Madame rolled her eyes awfully, as if she expected to see something unearthly, and, indeed, looked very like it herself.

'Come away, Madame,' I said, growing frightened, and feeling that if I were once, by any accident, to give way to the panic that was gathering round me, I should instantaneously lose all control of myself. 'Oh, come away ! do, Madame—I'm frightened.'

'No, on the contrary, sit here by me. It is very odd, you will think, ma chêre—un goût bizarre, vraiment !—but I love very much to be near to the dead people—in solitary place like this. I am not afraid of the dead people, nor of the ghosts. 'Av you ever see a ghost, my dear ?'

'Do, Madame, *pray* speak of something else.'

'Wat little fool ! But no, you are not afraid. I'av seen the ghosts myself. I saw one, for example, last night, shape like a monkey, sitting in the corner, with his arms round his knees ; very wicked, old, old man his face was like, and white eyes so large.'

'Come away, Madame ! you are trying to frighten me,' I said, in the childish anger which accompanies fear.

Madame laughed an ugly laugh, and said—

'Eh bien ! little fool !—I will not tell the rest if you are really frightened ; let us change to something else.'

'Yes, yes ! oh, do—pray do.'

'Wat good man is your father !'

'Very—the kindest darling. I don't know why it is, Madame, I am so afraid of him, and never could tell him how much I love him.'

This confidential talking with Madame, strange to say, implied no confidence ; it resulted from fear—it was deprecatory. I treated her as if she had human sympathies, in the hope that they might be generated somehow.

'Was there not a doctor from London with him a few months ago ? Dr. Bryerly, I think they call him.'

'Yes, a Doctor Bryerly, who remained a few days. Shall we begin to walk towards home, Madame ? Do, pray.'

'Immediately, cheaile ; and does your father suffer much ? '

'No—I think not.'

'And what then is his disease ? '

'Disease ! he has *no* disease. Have you heard anything about his health, Madame ? ' I said, anxiously.

'Oh no, ma foi—I have heard nothing ; but if the doctor came, it was not because he was quite well.'

'But that doctor is a doctor in theology, I fancy. I know he is a Swedenborgian ; and papa is so well, he *could* not have come as a physician.'

'I am very glad, ma chère, to hear ; but still you know your father is old man to have so young cheaile as you. Oh, yes—he is old man, and so uncertain life is. 'As he made his will, my dear ? Every man so rich as he, especially so old, aught to 'av made his will.'

'There is no need of haste, Madame ; it is quite time enough when his health begins to fail.'

'But has he really compose no will ? '

'I really don't know, Madame.'

'Ah, little rogue ! you will not tell—but you are not such fool as you feign yourself. No, no ; you know everything. Come, tell me all about—it is for your advantage, you know. What is in his will, and when he wrote ? '

'But, Madame, I really know nothing of it. I can't say whether there is a will or not. Let us talk of something else.'

'But, cheaile, it will not kill Monsieur Ruthyn to make his will ; he will not come to lie here a day sooner by cause of that ; but if he make no will, you may lose a great deal of the property. Would not that be pity ? '

' I really don't know anything of his will. If papa has made one, he has never spoken of it to me. I know he loves me—that is enough.'

' Ah ! you are not such little goose—you do know everything, of course. Come, come, tell me, little obstinate, otherwise I will break your little finger. Tell me everything.'

' I know nothing of papa's will. You don't know, Madame, how you pain me. Do let us speak of something else.'

' You do know, and you must tell, petite dure-tête, or I will break a your leetle finger.'

With which words she seized that joint, and laughing spitefully, she twisted it suddenly back. I screamed ; she continued to laugh.

' Will you tell ? '

' Yes, yes ! let me go,' I shrieked.

She did not release it, however, immediately, but continued her torture and discordant laughter. At last, however, she did release my finger.

' So she is going to be good cheaile, and to tell everything to her affectionate gouvernante. What do you cry for, little fool ? '

' You've hurt me very much—you have broken my finger,' I sobbed.

' Rub it and blow it, and give it a kees, little fool ! what cross girl ! I will never play with you again—never. Let us go home.'

Madame was silent and morose all the way home. She would not answer my questions, and affected to be very lofty and offended.

This did not last very long, however, and she soon resumed her wonted ways. And she returned to the question of the will, but not so directly, and with more art.

Why should this dreadful woman's thoughts be running so continually upon my father's will ? How could it concern her ?

CHAPTER VII

CHURCH SCARSDALE

I think all the females of our household, except Mrs. Rusk, who was at open feud with her, and had only room for the fiercer emotions, were more or less afraid of this inauspicious foreigner.

Mrs. Rusk would say in her confidences in my room—

' Where does she come from ?—is she a French or a Swiss one, or is she a Canada woman ? I remember one of *them* when I was a girl, and a nice limb *she* was, too ! And who did she live with ? Where was her last family ? Not one of us knows nothing about her, no more than a child ; except, of course, the Master—I do suppose he made enquiry. She's always at hugger-mugger with Anne Wixted. I'll pack that *one* about her business, if she don't mind. Tattling and whispering eternally. It's not about her own business she's a-talking. Madame de la Rougepot, *I* call her. She *does* know how to paint up to the ninety-nines—she does, the old cat. I beg your pardon, Miss, but *that* she is —a devil, and no mistake. I found her out first by her thieving the Master's gin, that the doctor ordered him, and filling the decanter up with water—the old villain ; but she'll be found out yet, she will ; and all the maids is afraid on her. She's not right, they think—a witch or a ghost—I should not wonder. Catherine Jones found her in her bed asleep in the morning after she sulked with you, you know, Miss, with all her clothes on, whatever was the meaning ; and I think she has frightened *you*, Miss and has you as nervous as anythink—I do,' and so forth.

It was true. I *was* nervous, and growing rather more so; and I think this cynical woman perceived and intended it, and was pleased. I was always afraid of her concealing herself in my room, and emerging at night to scare me. She began sometimes to mingle in my dreams, too—always awfully ; and this nourished, of course, the kind of ambiguous fear in which, in waking hours, I held her.

I dreamed one night that she led me, all the time whispering something so very fast that I could not understand her, into the library, holding a candle in her other hand above her head. We walked on tiptoe, like criminals at the dead of night, and stopped before that old oak cabinet which my father had indicated in so odd a way to me. I felt that we were about some contraband practice. There was a key in the door, which I experienced a guilty horror at turning, she whispering in the same unintelligible way, all the time, at my ear. I *did* turn it ; the door opened quite softly, and within stood my father, his face white and malignant, and glaring close in mine. He cried in a terrible voice, ' Death ! ' Out went Madame's candle, and at the same moment, with a scream, I waked in the dark—still fancying myself in the library ; and for an hour after I continued in a hysterical state.

Every little incident about Madame furnished a topic of eager discussion among the maids. More or less covertly, they nearly all hated and feared her. They fancied that she was making good her footing with ' the Master ; ' and that she would then oust Mrs. Rusk—perhaps usurp her place—and so make a clean sweep of them all. I fancy the honest little housekeeper did not discourage that suspicion.

About this time I recollect a pedlar—an odd, gipsified-looking man—called in at Knowl. I and Catherine Jones were in the court when he came, and set down his pack on the low balustrade beside the door.

All sorts of commodities he had—ribbons, cottons, silks, stockings, lace, and even some bad jewellry ; and just as he began his display—an interesting matter in a quiet country house—Madame came upon the ground. He grinned a recognition, and hoped ' Madamasel ' was well, and ' did not look to see *her* here.'

' Madamasel ' thanked him. ' Yes, vary well,' and looked for the first time decidedly ' put out.'

' Wat a pretty things ! ' she said. ' Catherine, run and tell Mrs. Rusk. She wants scissars, and lace too—I heard her say.'

So Catherine, with a lingering look, departed ; and Madame said—

' Will you, dear cheaile, be so kind to bring here my purse, I forgot on the table in my room ; also, I advise you, bring *your*.'

Catherine returned with Mrs. Rusk. Here was a man who

could tell them something of the old Frenchwoman, at last !
Slyly they dawdled over his wares, until Madame had made her
market and departed with me. But when the coveted opportunity
came, the pedlar was quite impenetrable. ' He forgot everything ;
he did not believe as he ever saw the lady before. He called a
Frenchwoman, all the world over, Madamasel—that wor the name
on 'em all. He never seed her in partiklar afore, as he could
bring to mind. He liked to see 'em always, 'cause they makes
the young uns buy.'

This reserve and oblivion were very provoking, and neither
Mrs. Rusk nor Catherine Jones spent sixpence with him ;—he
was a stupid fellow, or worse.

Of course Madame had tampered with him. But truth, like
murder, will out some day. Tom Williams, the groom, had seen
her, when alone with him, and pretending to look at his stock,
with her face almost buried in his silks and Welsh linseys, talking as fast as she could all the time, and slipping *money,* he did
suppose, under a piece of stuff in his box.

In the mean time, I and Madame were walking over the
wide, peaty sheep-walks that lie between Knowl and Church
Scarsdale. Since our visit to the mausoleum in the wood, she
had not worried me so much as before. She had been, indeed,
more than usually thoughtful, very little talkative, and troubled
me hardly at all about French and other accomplishments. A
walk was a part of our daily routine. I now carried a tiny
basket in my hand, with a few sandwiches, which were to furnish
our luncheon when we reached the pretty scene, about two
miles away, whither we were tending.

We had started a little too late ; Madame grew unwontedly
fatigued and sat down to rest on a stile before we had got half-
way ; and there she intoned, with a dismal nasal cadence, a
quaint old Bretagne ballad, about a lady with a pig's head :—

' This lady was neither pig nor maid,
And so she was not of human mould ;
Not of the living nor the dead.
Her left hand and foot were warm to touch ;
Her right as cold as a corpse's flesh !
And she would sing like a funeral bell, with a ding-dong tune.
The pigs were afraid, and viewed her aloof ;

And women feared her and stood afar.
She could do without sleep for a year and a day ;
She could sleep like a corpse, for a month and more.
No one knew how this lady fed—
On acorns or on flesh.
Some say that she's one of the swine-possessed,
That swam over the sea of Gennesaret.
A mongrel body and demon soul.
Some say she's the wife of the Wandering Jew,
And broke the law for the sake of pork ;
And a swinish face for a token doth bear,
That her shame is now, and her punishment coming.'

And so it went on, in a gingling rigmarole. The more anxious I
seemed to go on our way, the more likely was she to loiter. I
therefore showed no signs of impatience, and I saw her consult
her watch in the course of her ugly minstrelsy, and slyly glance,
as if expecting something, in the direction of our destination.

When she had sung to her heart's content, up rose Madame,
and began to walk onward silently. I saw her glance once or
twice, as before, toward the village of Trillsworth, which lay in
front, a little to our left, and the smoke of which hung in a
film over the brow of the hill. I think she observed me, for she
enquired—

'Wat is that a smoke there ? '

'That is Trillsworth, Madame ; there is a railway station there.'

'Oh, le chemin de fer, so near ! I did not think. Where it
goes?'

I told her, and silence returned.

Church Scarsdale is a very pretty and odd scene. The slightly
undulating sheep-walk dips suddenly into a wide glen, in the lap
of which, by a bright, winding rill, rise from the sward the ruins
of a small abbey, with a few solemn trees scattered round. The
crows' nests hung untenanted in the trees ; the birds were forag-
ing far away from their roosts. The very cattle had forsaken the
place. It was solitude itself.

Madame drew a long breath and smiled.

'Come down, come down, cheaile—come down to the churchyard.'

As we descended the slope which shut out the surrounding

world, and the scene grew more sad and lonely, Madame's spirits
seemed to rise.

' See 'ow many grave-stones—one, *two* hundred. Don't you love
the dead, cheaile ? I will teach you to love them. You shall see
me die here to-day, for half an hour, and be among them. That
is what I love.'

We were by this time at the little brook's side, and the low
churchyard wall with a stile, reached by a couple of stepping-
stones, across the stream, immediately at the other side.

' Come, now ! ' cried Madame, raising her face, as if to sniff the
air ; ' we are close to them. You will like them soon as I. You
shall see five of them. Ah, ça ira, ça ira, ça ira ! Come cross
quickily ! I am Madame la Morgue—Mrs. Deadhouse ! I will
present you my friends, Monsieur Cadavre and Monsieur Sque-
lette. Come, come, leetle mortal, let us play. Ouaah ! ' And she
uttered a horrid yell from her enormous mouth, and pushing her
wig and bonnet back, so as to show her great, bald head. She was
laughing, and really looked quite mad.

' No, Madame, I will not go with you,' I said, disengaging my
hand with a violent effort, receding two or three steps.

' Not enter the churchyard ! Ma foi—wat mauvais goût ! But
see, we are already in shade. The sun he is setting soon— where
well you remain, cheaile ? I will not stay long.'

' I'll stay here,' I said, a little angrily—for I *was* angry as well
as nervous ; and through my fear was that indignation at her ex-
travagances which mimicked lunacy so unpleasantly, and were, I
knew, designed to frighten me.

Over the stepping-stones, pulling up her dress, she skipped with
her long, lank legs, like a witch joining a Walpurgis. Over the
stile she strode, and I saw her head wagging, and heard her sing
some of her ill-omened rhymes, as she capered solemnly, with
many a grin and courtesy, among the graves and headstones, towards the ruin.

CHAPTER VIII

THE SMOKER

Three years later I learned—in a way she probably little expected, and then did not much care about—what really occurred there. I learned even phrases and looks—for the story was related by one who had heard it told—and therefore I venture to narrate what at the moment I neither saw nor suspected. While I sat, flushed and nervous, upon a flat stone by the bank of the little stream, Madame looked over her shoulder, and perceiving that I was out of sight, she abated her pace, and turned sharply towards the ruin which lay at her left. It was her first visit, and she was merely exploring ; but now, with a perfectly shrewd and businesslike air, turning the corner of the building, she saw, seated upon the edge of a grave-stone, a rather fat and flashily-equipped young man, with large, light whiskers, a jerry hat, green cutaway coat with gilt buttons, and waistcoat and trousers rather striking than elegant in pattern. He was smoking a short pipe, and made a nod to Madame, without either removing it from his lips or rising, but with his brown and rather good-looking face turned up, he eyed her with something of the impudent and sulky expression that was habitual to it.

' Ha, Deedle, you are there ! an' look so well. I am here, too, quite *a*lon ; but my friend, she wait outside the churchyard, byside the leetle river, for she must not think I know you—so I am come *a*lon.'

' You're a quarter late, and I lost a fight by you, old girl, this morning,' said the gay man, and spat on the ground ; ' and I wish you would not call me Diddle. I'll call you Granny if you do.'

' Eh bien ! *Dud,* then. She is vary nice—wat you like. Slim waist, wite teeth, vary nice eyes—dark—wat you say is best—and nice leetle foot and ankle.'

Madame smiled leeringly.

35

Dud smoked on.

'Go on,' said Dud, with a nod of command.

'I am teach her to sing and play—she has such sweet voice !

There was another interval here.

'Well, that isn't much good. I hate women's screechin' about fairies and flowers. Hang her ! there's a scarecrow as sings at Curl's Divan. Such a caterwauling upon a stage ! I'd like to put my two barrels into her.'

By this time Dud's pipe was out, and he could afford to converse.

'You shall see her and decide. You will walk down the river, and pass her by.'

'That's as may be ; howsoever, it would not do, nohow, to buy a pig in a poke, you know. And s'pose I shouldn't like her, arter all ? '

Madame sneered, with a patois ejaculation of derision.

'Vary good ! Then some one else will not be so 'ard to please —as you will soon find.'

'Some one's bin a-lookin' arter her, you mean ? ' said the young man, with a shrewd uneasy glance on the cunning face of the French lady.

'I mean precisely—that which I mean,' replied the lady, with a teazing pause at the break I have marked.

'Come, old 'un, none of your d—— old chaff, if you want me to stay here listening to you. Speak out, can't you ? There's any chap as has bin a-lookin' arter her—is there ? '

'Eh bien ! I suppose some.'

'Well, you *suppose,* and *I* suppose—we may *all* suppose, I guess ; but that does not make a thing be, as wasn't before ; and you tell me as how the lass is kep' private up there, and will be till *you*'re done educating her—a precious good 'un that is ! ' And he laughed a little lazily, with the ivory handle of his cane on his lip, and eyeing Madame with indolent derision.

Madame laughed, but looked rather dangerous.

'I'm only chaffin', you know, old girl. *You*'ve bin chaffin'— w'y shouldn't *I* ? But I don't see why she can't wait a bit ; and what's all the d——d hurry for ? *I*'m in no hurry. I don't want a wife on my back for a while. There's no fellow marries till he's took his bit o' fun, and seen life—is there ! And why should I be driving with her to fairs, or to church, or to meeting, by jingo !—

for they say she's a Quaker—with a babby on each knee, only
to please them as will be dead and rotten when *I'm* only beginning ? '

' Ah, you are such charming fellow ; always the same—always
sensible. So I and my friend we will walk home again, and you
go see Maggie Hawkes. Good-a-by, Dud—good-a-by.'

' Quiet, you fool !—can't ye ? ' said the young gentleman, with
the sort of grin that made his face vicious when a horse vexed
him. ' Who ever said I wouldn't go look at the girl ? Why, you
know that's just what I come here for—don't you ? Only when
I think a bit, and a notion comes across me, why shouldn't I
speak out ? I'm not one o' them shilly-shallies. If I like the girl,
I'll not be mug in and mug out about it. Only mind ye, I'll
judge for myself. Is that her a-coming ? '

' No ; it was a distant sound.'

Madame peeped round the corner. No one was approaching.

' Well, you go round that a-way, and you only look at her, you
know, for she is such fool—so nairvous.'

' Oh, is that the way with her ? ' said Dud, knocking out the
ashes of his pipe on a tombstone, and replacing the Turkish
utensil in his pocket. ' Well, then, old lass, good-bye,' and he
shook her hand. ' And, do ye see, don't ye come up till I pass, for
I'm no hand at play-acting ; an' if you called me " sir," or was
coming it dignified and distant, you know, I'd be sure to laugh,
a'most, and let all out. So good-bye, d'ye see, and if you want me
again be sharp to time, mind.

From habit he looked about for his dogs, but he had not
brought one. He had come unostentatiously by rail, travelling in
a third-class carriage, for the advantage of Jack Briderly's company, and getting a world of useful wrinkles about the steeple-
chase that was coming off next week.

So he strode away, cutting off the heads of the nettles with
his cane as he went ; and Madame walked forth into the open
space among the graves, where I might have seen her, had I
stood up, looking with the absorbed gaze of an artist on the
ruin.

In a little while, along the path, I heard the clank of a step,
and the gentleman in the green cutaway coat, sucking his cane,
and eyeing me with an offensive familiar sort of stare the while,
passed me by, rather hesitating as he did so.

I was glad when he turned the corner in the little hollow close
by, and disappeared. I stood up at once, and was reassured by a
sight of Madame, not very many yards away, looking at the ruin,
and apparently restored to her right mind. The last beams of the
sun were by this time touching the uplands, and I was longing
to recommence our walk home. I was hesitating about calling to
Madame, because that lady had a certain spirit of opposition
within her, and to disclose a small wish of any sort was generally, if it lay in her power, to prevent its accomplishment.

At this moment the gentleman in the green coat returned,
approaching me with a slow sort of swagger.

' I say, Miss, I dropped a glove close by here. May you have
seen it ? '

' No, sir,' I said, drawing back a little, and looking, I dare say,
both frightened and offended.

' I do think I must 'a dropped it close by your foot, Miss.'

' No, sir,' I repeated.

' No offence, Miss, but you're sure you didn't hide it ? '

I was beginning to grow seriously uncomfortable.

' Don't be frightened, Miss ; it's only a bit o' chaff. I'm not
going to search.'

I called aloud, ' Madame, Madame ! ' and he whistled through
his fingers, and shouted, ' Madame, Madame,' and added, ' She's
as deaf as a tombstone, or she'll hear that. Gi'e her my compliments, and say I said you're a beauty, Miss ; ' and with a laugh
and a leer he strode off.

Altogether this had not been a very pleasant excursion.
Madame gobbled up our sandwiches, commending them every
now and then to me. But I had been too much excited to have
any appetite left, and very tired I was when we reached home.

' So, there is lady coming to-morrow ? ' said Madame, who
knew everything. ' Wat is her name ? I forget.'

' Lady Knollys,' I answered.

' Lady Knollys—wat odd name ! She is very young—is she
not ? '

' Past fifty, I think.'

' Hélas ! She's vary old, then. Is she rich ? '

' I don't know. She has a place in Derbyshire.'

' Derbyshire—that is one of your English counties, is it not ? '

' Oh yes, Madame,' I answered, laughing. ' I have said it to you twice since you came ; ' and I gabbled through the chief towns and rivers as catalogued in my geography.

' Bah ! to be sure—of course, cheaile. And is she your relation ? '

' Papa's first cousin.'

' Won't you present-a me, pray ?—I would so like ! '

Madame had fallen into the English way of liking people with titles, as perhaps foreigners would if titles implied the sort of power they do generally with us.

' Certainly, Madame.'

' You will not forget ? '

' Oh no.'

Madame reminded me twice, in the course of the evening, of my promise. She was very eager on this point. But it is a world of disappointment, influenza, and rheumatics; and next morning Madame was prostrate in her bed, and careless of all things but flannel and James's powder.

Madame was *désolée* ; but she could not raise her head. She only murmured a question.

' For 'ow long time, dear, will Lady Knollys remain ? '

' A very few days, I believe.'

' Hélas ! 'ow onlucky ! maybe to-morrow I shall be better Ouah ! my ear. The laudanum, dear cheaile ! '

And so our conversation for that time ended, and Madame buried her head in her old red cashmere shawl.

CHAPTER IX

MONICA KNOLLYS

Punctually Lady Knollys arrived. She was accompanied by her nephew, Captain Oakley.

They arrived a little before dinner ; just in time to get to their rooms and dress. But Mary Quince enlivened my toilet with eloquent descriptions of the youthful Captain whom she had met in the gallery, on his way to his room, with the servant, and told me how he stopped to let her pass, and how 'he smiled so 'ansom.'

I was very young then, you know, and more childish even than my years; but this talk of Mary Quince's interested me, I must confess, considerably. I was painting all sort of portraits of this heroic soldier, while affecting, I am afraid, a hypocritical indifference to her narration, and I know I was very nervous and painstaking about my toilet that evening. When I went down to the drawing-room, Lady Knollys was there, talking volubly to my father as I entered—a woman not really old, but such as very young people fancy aged—energetic, bright, saucy, dressed handsomely in purple satin, with a good deal of lace, and a rich point—I know not how to call it—not a cap, a sort of head-dress —light and simple, but grand withal, over her greyish, silken hair.

Rather tall, by no means stout, on the whole a good firm figure, with something kindly in her look. She got up, quite like a young person, and coming quickly to meet me with a smile—

'My young cousin!' she cried, and kissed me on both cheeks. 'You know who I am? Your cousin Monica—Monica Knollys— and very glad, dear, to see you, though she has not set eyes on you since you were no longer than that paper-knife. Now come here to the lamp, for I must look at you. Who is she like? Let me see. Like your poor mother, I think, my dear; but you've the Aylmer nose—yes—not a bad nose either, and, come! very good eyes, upon my life—yes, certainly something of her poor mother—not a bit like you, Austin.'

My father gave her a look as near a smile as I had seen there for a long time, shrewd, cynical, but kindly too, and said he—

'So much the better, Monica, eh?'

'It was not for me to say—but you know, Austin, you always were an ugly creature. How shocked and indignant the little girl looks! You must not be vexed, you loyal little woman, with Cousin Monica for telling the truth. Papa was and will be ugly all his days. Come, Austin, dear, tell her—is not it so?'

'What! depose against myself! That's not English law, Monica.'

'Well, maybe not; but if the child won't believe her own eyes,

how is she to believe me? She has long, pretty hands—you have
—and very nice feet too. How old is she?'

'How old, child?' said my father to me, transferring the
question.

She recurred again to my eyes.

'That is the true grey—large, deep, soft—very peculiar. Yes,
dear, very pretty—long lashes, and such bright tints! You'll be
in the Book of Beauty, my dear, when you come out, and have
all the poet people writing verses to the tip of your nose—and
a very pretty little nose it is!'

I must mention here how striking was the change in my
father's spirit while talking and listening to his odd and voluble
old Cousin Monica. Reflected from bygone associations, there
had come a glimmer of something, not gaiety, indeed, but like
an appreciation of gaiety. The gloom and inflexibility were
gone, and there was an evident encouragement and enjoyment
of the incessant sallies of his bustling visitor.

How morbid must have been the tendencies of his habitual
solitude, I think, appeared from the evident thawing and bright-
ening that accompanied even this transient gleam of human society. I was not a companion—more childish than most girls of
my age, and trained in all his whimsical ways, never to interrupt a silence, or force his thoughts by unexpected question or
remark out of their monotonous or painful channel.

I was as much surprised at the good-humour with which he
submitted to his cousin's saucy talk; and, indeed, just then
those black-panelled and pictured walls, and that quaint, misshapen room, seemed to have exchanged their stern and awful
character for something wonderfully pleasanter to me, notwithstanding the unpleasantness of the personal criticism to which
the plain-spoken lady chose to subject me.

Just at that moment Captain Oakley joined us. He was my
first actual vision of that awful and distant world of fashion, of
whose splendours I had already read something in the three-
volumed gospel of the circulating library.

Handsome, elegant, with features almost feminine, and soft,
wavy, black hair, whiskers and moustache, he was altogether
such a knight as I had never beheld, or even fancied, at Knowl—
a hero of another species, and from the region of the demigods.
I did not then perceive that coldness of the eye, and cruel curl

of the voluptuous lip—only a suspicion, yet enough to indicate the profligate man, and savouring of death unto death.

But I was young, and had not yet the direful knowledge of good and evil that comes with years ; and he was so very hand-some, and talked in a way that was so new to me, and was so much more charming than the well-bred converse of the hum-drum county families with whom I had occasionally sojourned for a week at a time.

It came out incidentally that his leave of absence was to ex-pire the day after to-morrow. A Lilliputian pang of disappoint-ment followed this announcement. Already I was sorry to lose him. So soon we begin to make a property of what pleases us.

I was shy, but not awkward. I was flattered by the attention of this amusing, perhaps rather fascinating, young man of the world ; and he plainly addressed himself with diligence to amuse and please me. I dare say there was more effort than I fancied in bringing his talk down to my humble level, and in-teresting me and making me laugh about people whom I had never heard of before, than I then suspected.

Cousin Knollys meanwhile was talking to papa. It was just the conversation that suited a man so silent as habit had made him, for her frolic fluency left him little to supply. It was totally impossible, indeed, even in our taciturn household, that conversation should ever flag while she was among us.

Cousin Knollys and I went into the drawing-room together, leaving the gentlemen—rather ill-assorted, I fear—to entertain one another for a time.

'Come here, my dear, and sit near me,' said Lady Knollys, dropping into an easy chair with an energetic little plump, 'and tell me how you and your papa get on. I can remember him quite a cheerful man once, and rather amusing—yes, indeed—and now you see what a bore he is—all by shutting himself up and nursing his whims and fancies. Are those your drawings, dear ?'

'Yes, very bad, I'm afraid ; but there are a few, *better,* I think in the portfolio in the cabinet in the hall.'

'They are by *no* means bad, my dear ; and you play, of course ?'

'Yes—that is, a little—pretty well, I hope.'

'I dare say. I must hear you by-and-by. And how does your papa amuse you ? You look bewildered, dear. Well, I dare say,

amusement is not a frequent word in this house. But you must
not turn into a nun, or worse, into a puritan. What is he ? A
Fifth-Monarchy-man, or something—I forget ; tell me the name,
my dear.'

' Papa is a Swedenborgian, I believe.'

' Yes, yes—I forgot the horrid name—a Swedenborgian, that is
it. I don't know exactly what they think, but everyone knows
they are a sort of pagans, my dear. He's not making one of *you,*
dear—is he ? '

' I go to church every Sunday.'

' Well, that's a mercy ; Swedenborgian is such an ugly name,
and besides, they are all likely to be damned, my dear, and that's
a serious consideration. I really wish poor Austin had hit on
something else ; I'd much rather have no religion, and enjoy
life while I'm in it, than choose one to worry me here and be-
devil me hereafter. But some people, my dear, have a taste for
being miserable, and provide, like poor Austin, for its gratification in the next world as well as here. Ha, ha, ha ! how grave the
little woman looks ! Don't you think me very wicked ? You know
you do ; and very likely you are right. Who makes your dresses,
my dear ? You *are* such a figure of fun ! '

' Mrs. Rusk, I think, ordered *this* dress. I and Mary Quince
planned it. I thought it very nice. We all like it very well.'

There was something, I dare say, very whimsical about it,
probably very absurd, judged at least by the canons of fashion,
and old Cousin Monica Knollys, in whose eye the London fash-
ions were always fresh, was palpably struck by it as if it had
been some enormity against anatomy, for she certainly laughed
very heartily ; indeed, there were tears on her cheeks when she
had done, and I am sure my aspect of wonder and dignity, as
her hilarity proceeded, helped to revive her merriment again
and again as it was subsiding.

' There, you mustn't be vexed with old Cousin Monica,' she
cried, jumping up, and giving me a little hug, and bestowing a
hearty kiss on my forehead, and a jolly little slap on my cheek.
' Always remember your cousin Monica is an outspoken, wicked
old fool, who likes you, and never be offended by her nonsense.
A council of three—you all sat upon it—Mrs. Rusk, you said,
and Mary Quince, and your wise self, the weird sisters ; and
Austin stepped in, as Macbeth, and said, ' What is't ye do ? ' you

all made answer together, ' A something or other without a name ! ' Now, seriously, my dear, it is quite unpardonable in Austin—your papa, I mean—to hand you over to be robed and bedizened according to the whimsies of these wild old women— aren't they old ? If they know better, it's positively *fiendish*. I'll blow him up—I will indeed, my dear. You know you're an heiress, and ought not to appear like a jack-pudding.'

' Papa intends sending me to London with Madame and Mary Quince, and going with me himself, if Doctor Bryerly says he may make the journey, and then I am to have dresses and everything.'

' Well, that is better. And who is Doctor Bryerly—is your papa ill ? '

' Ill ; oh no ; he always seems just the same. You don't think him ill—*looking* ill, I mean ? ' I asked eagerly and frightened.

' No, my dear, he looks very well for his time of life ; but why is Doctor What's-his-name here ? Is he a physician, or a divine, or a horse-doctor ? and why is his leave asked ? '

' I—I really don't understand.'

' Is he a what d'ye call'em—a Swedenborgian ? '

' I believe so.'

' Oh, I see ; ha, ha, ha ! And so poor Austin must ask leave to go up to town. Well, go he shall, whether his doctor likes it or not, for it would not do to send you there in charge of your Frenchwoman, my dear. What's her name ? '

' Madame de la Rougierre.'

CHAPTER X

LADY KNOLLYS REMOVES A COVERLET

Lady Knollys pursued her enquiries.

' And why does not Madame make your dresses, my dear ? I wager a guinea the woman's a milliner. Did not she engage to make your dresses ? '

' I—I really don't know ; I rather think not. She is my governess—a finishing governess, Mrs. Rusk says.'

' Finishing fiddle ! Hoity-toity ! and my lady's too grand to
cut out your dresses and help to sew them ? And what *does* she
do ? I venture to say she's fit to teach nothing but devilment—
not that she has taught *you* much, my dear—*yet* at least. I'll see
her, my dear ; where is she ? Come, let us visit Madame. I
should so like to talk to her a little.'

' But she is ill,' I answered, and all this time I was ready to cry
for vexation, thinking of my dress, which must be very absurd to
elicit so much unaffected laughter from my experienced relative,
and I was only longing to get away and hide myself before that
handsome Captain returned.

' Ill ! is she ? what's the matter ? '

' A cold—feverish and rheumatic, she says.'

' Oh, a cold ; is she up, or in bed ? '

' In her room, but not in bed.'

' I should so like to see her, my dear. It is not mere curiosity,
I assure you. In fact, curiosity has nothing on earth to do with
it. A governess may be a very useful or a very useless person ;
but she may also be about the most pernicious inmate imaginable. She may teach you a bad accent, and worse manners, and
heaven knows what beside. Send the housekeeper, my dear, to
tell her that I am going to see her.'

' I had better go myself, perhaps,' I said, fearing a collision
between Mrs. Rusk and the bitter Frenchwoman.

' Very well, dear.'

And away I ran, not sorry somehow to escape before Captain
Oakley returned.

As I went along the passage, I was thinking whether my dress
could be so very ridiculous as my old cousin thought it, and trying in vain to recollect any evidence of a similar contemptuous
estimate on the part of that beautiful and garrulous dandy. I
could not—quite the reverse, indeed. Still I was uncomfortable
and feverish—girls of my then age will easily conceive how miserable, under similar circumstances, such a misgiving would make
them.

It was a long way to Madame's room. I met Mrs. Rusk bustling
along the passage with a housemaid.

' How is Madame ? ' I asked.

' Quite well, I believe,' answered the housekeeper, drily. ' Nothing the matter that *I* know of. She eat enough for two to-day. I wish *I* could sit in my room doing nothing.'

Madame was sitting, or rather reclining, in a low arm-chair, when I entered the room, close to the fire, as was her wont, her feet extended near to the bars, and a little coffee equipage beside her. She stuffed a book hastily between her dress and the chair, and received me in a state of langour which, had it not been for Mrs. Rusk's comfortable assurances, would have frightened me.

' I hope you are better, Madame,' I said, approaching.

' Better than I deserve, my dear cheaile, sufficiently well. The people are all so good, trying me with every little thing, like a bird ; here is café—Mrs. Rusk-a, poor woman, I try to swallow a little to please her.'

' And your cold, is it better ? '

She shook her head languidly, her elbow resting on the chair, and three finger-tips supporting her forehead, and then she made a little sigh, looking down from the corners of her eyes, in an interesting dejection.

' Je sens des lassitudes in all the members—but I am quaite 'appy, and though I suffer I am console and oblige des bontés, ma chère, que vous avez tous pour moi ; ' and with these words she turned a languid glance of gratitude on me which dropped on the ground.

' Lady Knollys wishes very much to see you, only for a few minutes, if you could admit her.'

' Vous savez les malades see *never* visitors,' she replied with a startled sort of tartness, and a momentary energy. ' Besides, I cannot converse ; je sens de temps en temps des douleurs de tête—of head, and of the ear, the right ear, it is parfois agony absolutely, and now it is here.'

And she winced and moaned, with her eyes closed and her hand pressed to the organ affected.

Simple as I was, I felt instinctively that Madame was shamming. She was over-acting ; her transitions were too violent, and beside she forgot that I knew how well she could speak English, and must perceive that she was heightening the interest of her helplessness by that pretty tessellation of foreign idiom. I therefore said with a kind of courage which sometimes helped me suddenly—

' Oh, Madame, don't you really think you might, without much inconvenience, see Lady Knollys for a very few minutes ? '

' Cruel cheaile ! you know I have a pain of the ear which makes me 'orribly suffer at this moment, and you demand me whether I will not converse with strangers. I did not think you would be so unkain, Maud ; but it is impossible, you must see —quaite impossible. I never, you *know,* refuse to take trouble when I am able—never—*never.*'

And Madame shed some tears, which always came at call, and with her hand pressed to her ear, said very faintly,

' Be so good to tell your friend how you see me, and how I suffer, and leave me, Maud, for I wish to lie down for a little, since the pain will not allow me to remain longer.'

So with a few words of comfort which could not well be refused, but I dare say betraying my suspicion that more was made of her sufferings than need be, I returned to the drawing-room.

' Captain Oakley has been here, my dear, and fancying, I suppose, that you had left us for the evening, has gone to the billiard-room, I think,' said Lady Knollys, as I entered.

That, then, accounted for the rumble and smack of balls which I had heard as I passed the door.

' I have been telling Maud how detestably she is got up.'

' Very thoughtful of you, Monica ! ' said my father.

' Yes, and really, Austin, it is quite clear you ought to marry ; you want some one to take this girl out, and look after her, and who's to do it ? She's a dowdy—don't you see ? Such a dust ! and it *is* really such a pity ; for she's a very pretty creature, and a clever woman could make her quite charming.'

My father took Cousin Monica's sallies with the most wonderful good-humour. She had always, I fancy, been a privileged person, and my father, whom we all feared, received her jolly attacks, as I fancy the grim Front-de-Bœufs of old accepted the humours and personalities of their jesters.

' Am I to accept this as an overture ? ' said my father to his voluble cousin.

' Yes, you may, but not for myself, Austin—I'm not worthy. Do you remember little Kitty Weadon that I wanted you to marry eight-and-twenty years ago, or more, with a hundred and twenty thousand pounds ? Well, you know, she has got ever so much now, and she is really a most amiable old thing, and though *you* would not have her then, she has had her second husband since, I can tell you.'

' I'm glad I was not the first,' said my father.

' Well, they really say her wealth is absolutely immense. Her last husband, the Russian merchant, left her everything. She has not a human relation, and she is in the best set.'

' You were always a match-maker, Monica,' said my father, stopping, and putting his hand kindly on hers. ' But it won't do. No, no, Monica ; we must take care of little Maud some other way.'

I was relieved. We women have all an instinctive dread of second marriages, and think that no widower is quite above or below that danger ; and I remember, whenever my father, which indeed was but seldom, made a visit to town or anywhere else, it was a saying of Mrs. Rusk—

' I shan't wonder, neither need you, my dear, if he brings home a young wife with him.'

So my father, with a kind look at her, and a very tender one on me, went silently to the library, as he often did about that hour.

I could not help resenting my Cousin Knollys' officious recommendation of matrimony. Nothing I dreaded more than a step-mother. Good Mrs. Rusk and Mary Quince, in their several ways, used to enhance, by occasional anecdotes and frequent reflections, the terrors of such an intrusion. I suppose they did not wish a revolution and all its consequences at Knowl, and thought it no harm to excite my vigilance.

But it was impossible long to be vexed with Cousin Monica.

' You know, my dear, your father is an oddity,' she said. ' I don't mind him—I never did. You must not. Cracky, my dear, cracky—decidedly cracky ! '

And she tapped the corner of her forehead, with a look so sly and comical, that I think I should have laughed, if the sentiment had not been so awfully irreverent.

' Well, dear, how is our friend the milliner ? '

' Madame is suffering so much from pain in her ear, that she says it would be quite impossible to have the honour——'

' Honour—fiddle ! I want to see what the woman's like. Pain in her ear, you say ? Poor thing ! Well, dear, I think I can cure that in five minutes. I have it myself, now and then. Come to my room, and we'll get the bottles.

So she lighted her candle in the lobby, and with a light and agile step she scaled the stairs, I following; and having found the remedies, we approached Madame's room together.

I think, while we were still at the end of the gallery, Madame heard and divined our approach, for her door suddenly shut, and there was a fumbling at the handle. But the bolt was out of order.

Lady Knollys tapped at the door, saying—'we'll come in, please, and see you. I've some remedies, which I'm sure will do you good.'

There was no answer ; so she opened the door, and we both entered. Madame had rolled herself in the blue coverlet, and was lying on the bed, with her face buried in the pillow, and enveloped in the covering.

'Perhaps she's asleep ?' said Lady Knollys, getting round to the side of the bed, and stooping over her.

Madame lay still as a mouse. Cousin Monica set down her two little vials on the table, and, stooping again over the bed, began very gently with her fingers to lift the coverlet that covered her face. Madame uttered a slumbering moan, and turned more upon her face, clasping the coverlet faster about her.

'Madame, it is Maud and Lady Knollys. We have come to relieve your ear. Pray let me see it. She can't be asleep, she's holding the clothes so fast. Do, pray, allow me to see it.'

CHAPTER XI

LADY KNOLLYS SEES THE FEATURES

Perhaps, if Madame had murmured, 'It is quite well—pray permit me to sleep,' she would have escaped an awkwardness. But having adopted the rôle of the exhausted slumberer, she could not consistently speak at the moment ; neither would it do by main force, to hold the coverlet about her face : and so her presence of mind forsook her, and Cousin Monica drew it back, and hardly beheld the profile of the sufferer, when her good-humoured face was lined and shadowed with a dark curiosity and a surprise by no means pleasant ; and she stood erect beside the bed, with her mouth firmly shut and drawn down at the corners, in a sort of recoil and perturbation, looking down upon the patient.

' So that's Madame de la Rougierre ? ' at length exclaimed Lady Knollys, with a very stately disdain. I think I never saw anyone look more shocked.

Madame sat up, very flushed. No wonder, for she had been wrapped so close in the coverlet. She did not look quite at Lady Knollys, but straight before her, rather downward, and very luridly.

I was very much frightened and amazed, and felt on the point of bursting into tears.

' So, Mademoiselle, you have married, it seems, since I had last the honour of seeing you ? I did not recognise Mademoiselle under her new name.'

' Yes—I *am* married, Lady Knollys ; I thought everyone who knew me had heard of that. Very respectably married, for a person of my rank. I shall not need long the life of a governess. There is no harm, I hope ? '

' I hope not,' said Lady Knollys, drily, a little pale, and still looking with a dark sort of wonder upon the flushed face and forehead of the governess, who was looking downward, straight before her, very sulkily and disconcerted.

' I suppose you have explained everything satisfactorily to Mr. Ruthyn, in whose house I find you ? ' said Cousin Monica.

' Yes, certainly—everything he requires—in effect there is *nothing* to explain. I am ready to answer to any question. Let *him* demand me.'

' Very good, Mademoiselle.'

' *Madame,* if you please.'

' I forgot—*Madame*—yes. I shall apprise him of everything.'

Madame turned upon her a peaked and malign look, smiling askance with a stealthy scorn.

' For myself, I have nothing to conceal. I have always done my duty. What fine scene about nothing absolutely—what charming remedies for a sick person ! Ma foi ! how much oblige I am for these so amiable attentions ! '

' So far as I can see, Mademoiselle—Madame, I mean—you don't stand very much in need of remedies. Your ear and head don't seem to trouble you just now. I fancy these pains may now be dismissed.'

Lady Knollys was now speaking French.

' Mi ladi has diverted my attention for a moment, but that does not prevent that I suffer frightfully. I am, of course, only poor governess, and such people perhaps ought not to have pain —at least to show when they suffer. It is permitted us to die, but not to be sick.'

' Come, Maud, my dear, let us leave the invalid to her repose and to nature. I don't think she needs my chloroform and opium at present.'

'Mi ladi is herself a physic which chases many things, and powerfully affects the ear. I would wish to sleep, notwithstanding, and can but gain that in silence, if it pleases mi ladi.'

' Come, my dear,' said Lady Knollys, without again glancing at the scowling, smiling, swarthy face in the bed ; ' let us leave your instructress to her *concforto*.'

' The room smells all over of brandy, my dear—does she drink ? ' said Lady Knollys, as she closed the door, a little sharply.

I am sure I looked as much amazed as I felt, at an imputation which then seemed to me so entirely incredible.

' Good little simpleton ! ' said Cousin Monica, smiling in my face, and bestowing a little kiss on my cheek ; ' such a thing as a tipsy lady has never been dreamt of in your philosophy. Well, we live and learn. Let us have our tea in my room—the gentlemen, I dare say, have retired.'

I assented, of course, and we had tea very cosily by her bedroom fire.

' How long have you had that woman ? ' she asked suddenly, after, for her, a very long rumination.

' She came in the beginning of February—nearly ten months ago—is not it ? '

' And who sent her ? '

' I really don't know ; papa tells me so little—he arranged it all himself, I think.'

Cousin Monica made a sound of acquiescence—her lips closed, and a nod, frowning hard at the bars.

'It *is* very odd!' she said; 'how people *can* be such fools!' Here there came a little pause. 'And what sort of person is she—do you like her?'

'Very well—that is, *pretty* well. You won't tell?—but she rather frightens me. I'm sure she does not intend it, but somehow I am very much afraid of her.'

'She does not beat you?' said Cousin Monica, with an incipient frenzy in her face that made me love her.

'Oh no!'

'Nor ill-use you in any way?'

'No.'

'Upon your honour and word, Maud?'

'No, upon my honour.'

'You know I won't tell her anything you say to me; and I only want to know, that I may put an end to it, my poor little cousin.'

'Thank you, Cousin Monica very much; but really and truly she does not ill-use me.'

'Nor threaten you, child?'

'Well, *no*—no, she does not threaten.'

'And how the plague *does* she frighten you, child?'

'Well, I really—I'm half ashamed to tell you—you'll laugh at me—and I don't know that she wishes to frighten me. But there is something, is not there, ghosty, you know, about her?'

'*Ghosty*—is there? well, I'm sure I don't know, but I suspect there's something devilish—I mean, she seems roguish—does not she? And I really think she has had neither cold nor pain, but has just been shamming sickness, to keep out of my way.'

I perceived plainly enough that Cousin Monica's damnatory epithet referred to some retrospective knowledge, which she was not going to disclose to me.

'You knew Madame before,' I said. 'Who is she?'

'She assures me she is Madame de la Rougierre, and, I suppose, in French phrase she so calls herself,' answered Lady Knollys, with a laugh, but uncomfortably, I thought.

'Oh, dear Cousin Monica, do tell me—is she—is she very wicked? I am so afraid of her!'

'How should I know, dear Maud? But I do remember her face, and I don't very much like her, and you may depend on it. I will speak to your father in the morning about her, and don't, darling, ask me any more about her, for I really have not very much to tell that you would care to hear, and the fact is I *won't* say any more about her—there!'

And Cousin Monica laughed, and gave me a little slap on the cheek, and then a kiss.

'Well, just tell me this——'

'Well, I *won't* tell you this, nor anything—not a word, curious little woman. The fact is, I have little to tell, and I mean to speak to your father, and he, I am sure, will do what is right; so don't ask me any more, and let us talk of something pleasanter.'

There was something indescribably winning, it seemed to me, in Cousin Monica. Old as she was, she seemed to me so girlish, compared with those slow, unexceptionable young ladies whom I had met in my few visits at the county houses. By this time my shyness was quite gone, and I was on the most intimate terms with her.

'You know a great deal about her, Cousin Monica, but you won't tell me.'

'Nothing I should like better, if I were at liberty, little rogue; but you know, after all, I don't really say whether I *do* know anything about her or not, or what sort of knowledge it is. But tell me what you mean by ghosty, and all about it.'

So I recounted my experiences, to which, so far from laughing at me, she listened with very special gravity.

'Does she write and receive many letters?'

I had seen her write letters, and supposed, though I could only recollect one or two, that she received in proportion.

'Are *you* Mary Quince?' asked my lady cousin.

Mary was arranging the window-curtains, and turned, dropping a courtesy affirmatively toward her.

'You wait on my little cousin, Miss Ruthyn, don't you?'

'Yes, 'm,' said Mary, in her genteelest way.

'Does anyone sleep in her room?'

'Yes, 'm, *I*—please, my lady.'

'And no one else?'

'No, 'm—please, my lady.'

'Not even the *governess,* sometimes ?

'No, please, my lady.'

'Never, you are quite sure, my dear?' said Lady Knollys, transferring the question to me.

'Oh, no, never,' I answered.

Cousin Monica mused gravely, I fancied even anxiously, into the grate ; then stirred her tea and sipped it, still looking into the same point of our cheery fire.

'I like your face, Mary Quince ; I'm sure you are a good creature,' she said, suddenly turning toward her with a pleasant countenance. 'I'm very glad you have got her, dear. I wonder whether Austin has gone to his bed yet ! '

'I think not. I am certain he is either in the library or in his private room—papa often reads or prays alone at night, and —and he does not like to be interrupted.'

'No, no ; of course not—it will do very well in the morning.'

Lady Knollys was thinking deeply, as it seemed to me.

'And so you are afraid of goblins, my dear,' she said at last, with a faded sort of smile, turning toward me ; 'well, if *I* were, I know what *I* should do—so soon as I, and good Mary Quince here, had got into my bed-chamber for the night, I should stir the fire into a good blaze, and bolt the door—do you see, Mary Quince ?—bolt the door and keep a candle lighted all night. You'll be very attentive to her, Mary Quince, for I—I don't think she is very strong, and she must not grow nervous : so get to bed early, and don't leave her alone—do you see ?—and—and remember to bolt the door, Mary Quince, and I shall be sending a little Christmas-box to my cousin, and I shan't forget you. Good-night.'

And with a pleasant courtesy Mary fluttered out of the room.

CHAPTER XII

A CURIOUS CONVERSATION

We each had another cup of tea, and were silent for awhile.

'We must not talk of ghosts now. You are a superstitious little woman, you know, and you shan't be frightened.'

And now Cousin Monica grew silent again, and looking briskly around the room, like a lady in search of a subject, her eye rested on a small oval portrait, graceful, brightly tinted, in the French style, representing a pretty little boy, with rich golden hair, large soft eyes, delicate features, and a shy, peculiar expression.

'It is odd ; I think I remember that pretty little sketch, very long ago. I think I was then myself a child, but that is a much older style of dress, and of wearing the hair, too, than I ever saw. I am just forty-nine now. Oh dear, yes ; that is a good while before I was *born*. What a strange, pretty little boy ! a mysterious little fellow. Is he quite sincere, I wonder ? What rich golden hair ! It is very clever—a French artist, I dare say— and who *is* that little boy ? '

'I never heard. Some one a hundred years ago, I dare say. But there is a picture down-stairs I am so anxious to ask you about ! '

'Oh ! ' murmured Lady Knollys, still gazing dreamily on the crayon.

'It is the full-length picture of Uncle Silas—I want to ask you about him.'

At mention of his name, my cousin gave me a look so sudden and odd as to amount almost to a start.

'Your uncle Silas, dear ? It is very odd, I was just thinking of him ; ' and she laughed a little.

'Wondering whether that little boy could be he.'

And up jumped active Cousin Monica, with a candle in her

55

hand, upon a chair, and scrutinised the border of the sketch for
a name or a date.

' Maybe on the back ? ' said she.

And so she unhung it, and there, true enough, not on the back
of the drawing, but of the frame, which was just as good, in pen-
and-ink round Italian letters, hardly distinguishable now from
the discoloured wood, we traced—

    ' *Silas Aylmer Ruthyn, Ætate* viii. 15 *May,* 1779.'

' It is very odd I should not have been told or remembered
who it was. I think if I had *ever* been told I *should* have remembered it. I do recollect this picture, though, I am nearly
certain. What a singular child's face ! '

And my cousin leaned over it with a candle on each side, and
her hand shading her eyes, as if seeking by aid of these fair and
half-formed lineaments to read an enigma.

The childish features defied her, I suppose ; their secret was
unfathomable, for after a good while she raised her head, still
looking at the portrait, and sighed.

' A very singular face,' she said, softly, as a person might who
was looking into a coffin. 'Had not we better replace it ?'

So the pretty oval, containing the fair golden hair and large
eyes, the pale, unfathomable sphinx, remounted to its nail, and
the *funeste* and beautiful child seemed to smile down oracularly
on our conjectures.

' So is the face in the large portrait—*very* singular—more, I
think, than that—handsomer too. This is a sickly child, I think ;
but the full-length is so manly, though so slender, and so handsome too. I always think him a hero and a mystery, and they
won't tell me about him, and I can only dream and wonder.'

' He has made more people than you dream and wonder, my
dear Maud. I don't know what to make of him. He is a sort of
idol, you know, of your father's, and yet I don't think he helps
him much. His abilities were singular ; so has been his misfortune ; for the rest, my dear, he is neither a hero nor a wonder.
So far as I know, there are very few sublime men going about
the world.'

' You really must tell me all you know about him, Cousin
Monica. Now don't refuse.'

' But why should you care to hear ? There is really nothing
pleasant to tell.'

' That is just the reason I wish it. If it were at all pleasant, it would be quite commonplace. I like to hear of adventures, dangers, and misfortunes ; and above all, I love a mystery. You know, papa will never tell me, and I dare not ask him ; not that he is ever unkind, but, somehow, I am afraid ; and neither Mrs. Rusk nor Mary Quince will tell me anything, although I suspect they know a good deal.'

' I don't see any good in telling you, dear, nor, to say the truth, any great harm either.'

' No—now that's *quite* true—no harm. There *can't* be, for I *must* know it all some day, you know, and better now, and from *you*, than perhaps from a stranger, and in a less favourable way.'

' Upon my word, it is a wise little woman ; and really, that's not such bad sense after all.'

So we poured out another cup of tea each, and sipped it very comfortably by the fire, while Lady Knollys talked on, and her animated face helped the strange story.

' It is not very much, after all. Your uncle Silas, you know, is living ? '

' Oh yes, in Derbyshire.'

' So I see you do know something of him, sly girl ! but no matter. You know how very rich your father is ; but Silas was the younger brother, and had little more than a thousand a year. If he had not played, and did not care to marry, it would have been quite enough—ever so much more than younger sons of dukes often have ; but he was—well, a *mauvais sujet*—you know what that is. I don't want to say any ill of him—more than I really know—but he was fond of his pleasures, I suppose, like other young men, and he played, and was always losing, and your father for a long time paid great sums for him. I believe he was really a most expensive and vicious young man ; and I fancy he does not deny that now, for they say he would change the past if he could.

I was looking at the pensive little boy in the oval frame—aged eight years—who was, a few springs later, ' a most expensive and vicious young man,' and was now a suffering and outcast old one, and wondering from what a small seed the hemlock or the wallflower grows, and how miscroscopic are the beginnings of

the kingdom of God or of the mystery of iniquity in a human
being's heart.

'Austin—your papa—was very kind to him—*very*; but then,
you know, he's an oddity, dear—he *is* an oddity, though no one
may have told you before—and he never forgave him for his
marriage. Your father, I suppose, knew more about the lady
than I did—I was young then—but there were various reports,
none of them pleasant, and she was not visited, and for some
time there was a complete estrangement between your father
and your uncle Silas ; and it was made up, rather oddly, on the
very occasion which some people said ought to have totally
separated them. Did you ever hear anything—anything *very*
remarkable—about your uncle ? '

'No, never, they would not tell me, though I am sure they
know. Pray go on.'

'Well, Maud, as I have begun, I'll complete the story, though
perhaps it might have been better untold. It was something
rather shocking—indeed, *very* shocking ; in fact, they insisted
on suspecting him of having committed a murder.'

I stared at my cousin for some time, and then at the little boy,
so refined, so beautiful, so *funeste*, in the oval frame.

'Yes, dear,' said she, her eyes following mine ; 'who'd have
supposed he could ever have—have fallen under so horrible a
suspicion ? '

'The wretches ! Of course, Uncle Silas—of course, he's innocent ? ' I said at last.

'Of course, my dear,' said Cousin Monica, with an odd look ;
'but you know there are some things as bad almost to be suspected of as to have done, and the country gentlemen chose to
suspect him. They did not like him, you see. His politics vexed
them ; and he resented their treatment of his wife—though I
really think, poor Silas, he did not care a pin about her—and he
annoyed them whenever he could. Your papa, you know, is very
proud of his family—*he* never had the slightest suspicion of your
uncle.'

'Oh no ! ' I cried vehemently.

'That's right, Maud Ruthyn,' said Cousin Monica, with a sad
little smile and a nod. 'And your papa was, you may suppose,
very angry.'

'Of course he was,' I exclaimed.

'You have no idea, my dear, *how* angry. He directed his attorney to prosecute, by wholesale, all who had said a word affecting your uncle's character. But the lawyers were against it, and then your uncle tried to fight his way through it, but the men would not meet him. He was quite slurred. Your father went up and saw the Minister. He wanted to have him a Deputy-Lieutenant, or something, in his county. Your papa, you know, had a very great influence with the Government. Beside his county influence, he had two boroughs then. But the Minister was afraid, the feeling was so very strong. They offered him something in the Colonies, but your father would not hear of it—that would have been a banishment, you know. They would have given your father a peerage to make it up, but he would not accept it, and broke with the party. Except in that way—which, you know, was connected with the reputation of the family—I don't think, considering his great wealth, he has done very much for Silas. To say truth, however, he was very liberal before his marriage. Old Mrs. Aylmer says he made a vow *then* that Silas should never have more than five hundred a year, which he still allows him, I believe, and he permits him to live in the place. But they say it is in a very wild, neglected state.'

'You live in the same county—have you seen it lately, Cousin Monica ?'

'No, not very lately,' said Cousin Monica, and began to hum an air abstractedly.

CHAPTER XIII

BEFORE AND AFTER BREAKFAST

Next morning early I visited my favourite full-length portrait in the chocolate coat and top-boots. Scanty as had been my cousin Monica's notes upon this dark and eccentric biography, they were everything to me. A soul had entered that enchanted

form. Truth had passed by with her torch, and a sad light
shone for a moment on that enigmatic face.

There stood the *roué*—the duellist—and, with all his faults, the
hero too ! In that dark large eye lurked the profound and fiery
enthusiasm of his ill-starred passion. In the thin but exquisite
lip I read the courage of the paladin, who would have ' fought
his way,' though single-handed, against all the magnates of his
county, and by ordeal of battle have purged the honour of the
Ruthyns. There in that delicate half-sarcastic tracery of the nos-
tril I detected the intellectual defiance which had politically
isolated Silas Ruthyn and opposed him to the landed oligarchy
of his county, whose retaliation had been a hideous slander.
There, too, and on his brows and lip, I traced the patience of a
cold disdain. I could now see him as he was—the prodigal, the
hero, and the martyr. I stood gazing on him with a girlish interest and admiration. There was indignation, there was pity,
there was hope. Some day it might come to pass that I, girl as
I was, might contribute by word or deed towards the vindication
of that long-suffering, gallant, and romantic prodigal. It was a
flicker of the Joan of Arc inspiration, common, I fancy, to many
girls. I little then imagined how profoundly and strangely involved my uncle's fate would one day become with mine.

I was interrupted by Captain Oakley's voice at the window.
He was leaning on the window-sill, and looking in with a smile
—the window being open, the morning sunny, and his cap lifted
in his hand.

' Good-morning, Miss Ruthyn. What a charming old place !
quite the setting for a romance ; such timber, and this really
beautiful house. I *do* so like these white and black houses—
wonderful old things. By-the-by, you treated us very badly last
night—you did, indeed ; upon my word, now, it really was too
bad—running away, and drinking tea with Lady Knollys—so
she says. I really—I should not like to tell you how very savage
I felt, particularly considering how very short my time is.'

I was a shy, but not a giggling country miss. I knew I was an
heiress ; I knew I was somebody. I was not the least bit in the
world conceited, but I think this knowledge helped to give me
a certain sense of security and self-possession, which might have
been mistaken for dignity or simplicity. I am sure I looked at
him with a fearless enquiry, for he answered my thoughts.

'I do really assure you, Miss Ruthyn, I am quite serious;
you have no idea how very much we missed you.'

There was a little pause, and, I believe, like a fool, I lowered my eyes, and blushed.

'I—I was thinking of leaving to-day; I am so unfortunate—
my leave is just out—it *is* so unlucky; but I don't quite know
whether my aunt Knollys will allow me to go.'

'*I*?—certainly, my dear Charlie, *I* don't want you at all,' exclaimed a voice—Lady Knollys's—briskly, from an open window
close by; 'what could put that in your head, dear?'

And in went my cousin's head, and the window shut down.

'She is *such* an oddity, poor dear Aunt Knollys,' murmured
the young man, ever so little put out, and he laughed. 'I never
know quite what she wishes, or how to please her; but she's
so good-natured; and when she goes to town for the season—
she does not always, you know—her house is really very gay—
you can't think——'

Here again he was interrupted, for the door opened, and
Lady Knollys entered. 'And you know, Charles,' she continued,
'it would not do to forget your visit to Snodhurst; you wrote,
you know, and you have only to-night and to-morrow. You are
thinking of nothing but that moor; I heard you talking to the
gamekeeper; I know he is—is not he, Maud, the brown man
with great whiskers, and leggings? I'm very sorry, you know, but
I really must spoil your shooting, for they do expect you at
Snodhurst, Charlie; and do not you think this window a little
too much for Miss Ruthyn? Maud, my dear, the air is very sharp;
shut it down, Charles, and you'd better tell them to get a fly for
you from the town after luncheon. Come, dear,' she said to me.
'Was not that the breakfast bell? Why does not your papa
get a gong?—it is so hard to know one bell from another.'

I saw that Captain Oakley lingered for a last look, but I did
not give it, and went out smiling with Cousin Knollys, and
wondering why old ladies are so uniformly disagreeable.

In the lobby she said, with an odd, goodnatured look—

'Don't allow any of his love-making, my dear. Charles Oakley has not a guinea, and an heiress would be very convenient.
Of course he has his eyes about him. Charles is not by any
means foolish; and I should not be at all sorry to see him well
married, for I don't think he will do much good any other way;

but there are degrees, and his ideas are sometimes very impertinent.'

I was an admiring reader of the *Albums,* the *Souvenirs,* the
Keepsakes, and all that flood of Christmas-present lore which
yearly irrigated England, with pretty covers and engravings;
and floods of elegant twaddle—the milk, not destitute of water,
on which the babes of literature were then fed. On this, my
genius throve. I had a little album, enriched with many gems
of original thought and observation, which I jotted down in
suitable language. Lately, turning over these faded leaves of
rhyme and prose, I lighted, under this day's date, upon the following sage reflection, with my name appended:—

' Is there not in the female heart an ineradicable jealousy,
which, if it sways the passions of the young, rules also the *advice*
of the *aged* ? Do they not grudge to youth the sentiments (though
Heaven knows how *shadowed* with sorrow) which they can *no
longer inspire,* perhaps even *experience* ; and does not youth,
in turn, sigh over the envy which has *power to blight* ?

MAUD AYLMER RUTHYN.'

' He has not been making love to me,' I said rather tartly,
' and he does not seem to me at all impertinent, and I really
don't care the least whether he goes or stays.'

Cousin Monica looked in my face with her old waggish smile,
and laughed.

' You'll understand those London dandies better some day,
dear Maud ; they are very well, but they like money—not to keep,
of course—but still they like it and know its value.'

At breakfast my father told Captain Oakley where he might
have shooting, or if he preferred going to Dilsford, only half
an hour's ride, he might have his choice of hunters, and find
the dogs there that morning.

The Captain smiled archly at me, and looked at his aunt.
There was a suspense. I hope I did not show how much I was
interested—but it would not do. Cousin Monica was inexorable.

' Hunting, hawking, fishing, fiddle-de-dee ! You know, Charlie,
my dear, it is quite out of the question. He is going to Snodhurst this afternoon, and without quite a rudeness, in which

I should be involved too, he really can't—you know you can't, Charles! and—and he *must* go and keep his engagement.'

So papa acquiesced with a polite regret, and hoped another time.

'Oh, leave all that to me. When you want him, only write me a note, and I'll send him or bring him if you let me. I always know where to find him—don't I, Charlie ?—and we shall be only too happy.'

Aunt Monica's influence with her nephew was special, for she 'tipped' him handsomely every now and then, and he had formed for himself agreeable expectations, besides, respecting her will. I felt rather angry at his submitting to this sort of tutelage, knowing nothing of its motive ; I was also disgusted by Cousin Monica's tyranny.

So soon as he had left the room, Lady Knollys, not minding me, said briskly to papa, ' Never let that young man into your house again. I found him making speeches, this morning, to little Maud here ; and he really has not two pence in the world —it is amazing impudence—and you know such absurd things do happen.'

' Come, Maud, what compliments did he pay you ? ' asked my father.

I was vexed, and therefore spoke courageously. ' His compliments were not to me ; they were all to the house,' I said, drily.

' Quite as it should be—the house, of course ; it is that he's in love with,' said Cousin Knollys.

> ' 'Twas on a widow's jointure land,
> The archer, Cupid, took his stand.'

' Hey ! I don't quite understand,' said my father, slily.

' Tut ! Austin ; you forget Charlie is my nephew.'

' So I did,' said my father.

' Therefore the literal widow in this case *can* have no interest in view but one, and that is yours and Maud's. I wish him well, but he shan't put my little cousin and her expectations into his empty pocket—*not* a bit of it. And *there's* another reason, Austin, why you should marry—you have no eye for these things, whereas a clever *woman* would see at a glance and prevent mischief.'

'So she would,' acquiesced my father, in his gloomy, amused way. 'Maud, you must try to be a clever woman.'

'So she will in her time, but that is not come yet ; and I tell you, Austin Ruthyn, if you won't look about and marry some-body, somebody may possibly marry you.'

'You were always an oracle, Monica ; but *here* I am lost in total perplexity,' said my father.

'Yes ; sharks sailing round you, with keen eyes and large throats ; and you have come to the age precisely when men *are* swallowed up alive like Jonah.'

'Thank you for the parallel, but you know that was not a happy union, even for the fish, and there was a separation in a few days ; not that I mean to trust to that ; but there's no one to throw me into the jaws of the monster, and I've no notion of jumping there ; and the fact is, Monica, there's no monster at all.'

'I'm not so sure.'

'But I'm quite sure,' said my father, a little drily. 'You forget how old I am, and how long I've lived alone—I and little Maud ; ' and he smiled and smoothed my hair, and, I thought, sighed.

'No one is ever too old to do a foolish thing,' began Lady Knollys.

'Nor to say a foolish thing, Monica. This has gone on too long. Don't you see that little Maud here is silly enough to be frightened at your fun.'

So I was, but I could not divine how he guessed it.

'And well or ill, wisely or madly, I'll *never* marry ; so put that out of your head.'

This was addressed rather to me, I think, than to Lady Knollys, who smiled a little waggishly on me, and said—

'To be sure, Maud ; maybe you are right ; a stepdame is a risk, and I ought to have asked you first what you thought of it ; and upon my honour,' she continued merrily but kindly, ob-serving that my eyes, I know not exactly from what feeling, filled with tears, 'I'll never again advise your papa to marry, unless you first tell me you wish it.'

This was a great deal from Lady Knollys, who had a taste for advising her friends and managing their affairs.

'I've a great respect for instinct. I believe, Austin, it is truer

than reason, and yours and Maud's are both against me, though
I know I have reason on my side.'

My father's brief wintry smile answered, and Cousin Monica
kissed me, and said—

'I've been so long my own mistress that I sometimes forget
there are such things as fear and jealousy ; and are you going to
your governess, Maud ? '

CHAPTER XIV

ANGRY WORDS

I was going to my governess, as Lady Knollys said ; and so I
went. The undefinable sense of danger that smote me whenever
I beheld that woman had deepened since last night's occurrence,
and was taken out of the region of instinct or prepossession by
the strange though slight indications of recognition and abhor-
rence which I had witnessed in Lady Knollys on that occasion.

The tone in which Cousin Monica had asked, ' are you going
to your governess ? ' and the curious, grave, and anxious look
that accompanied the question, disturbed me ; and there was
something odd and cold in the tone as if a remembrance had
suddenly chilled her. The accent remained in my ear, and the
sharp brooding look was fixed before me as I glided up the
broad dark stairs to Madame de la Rougierre's chamber.

She had not come down to the school-room, as the scene of my
studies was called. She had decided on having a relapse, and accordingly had not made her appearance down-stairs that morning. The gallery leading to her room was dark and lonely, and
I grew more nervous as I approached ; I paused at the door,
making up my mind to knock.

But the door opened suddenly, and, like a magic-lantern
figure, presented with a snap, appeared close before my eyes
the great muffled face, with the forbidding smirk, of Madame de
la Rougierre.

'Wat you mean, my dear cheaile?' she inquired with a malevolent shrewdness in her eyes, and her hollow smile all the time
disconcerting me more even than the suddenness of her appearance; 'wat for you approach so softly? I do not sleep, you see,
but you feared, perhaps, to have the misfortune of wakening me,
and so you came—is it not so?—to leesten, and looke in very
gently; you want to know how I was. Vous êtes bien aimable
d'avoir pensé à moi. Bah!' she cried, suddenly bursting through
her irony. 'Wy could not Lady Knollys come herself and leesten
to the keyhole to make her report? Fi donc! wat is there to
conceal? Nothing. Enter, if you please. Every one they are
welcome!' and she flung the door wide, turned her back upon
me, and, with an ejaculation which I did not understand, strode
into the room.

'I did not come with any intention, Madame, to pry or to
intrude—you don't think so—you *can't* think so— you can't possibly mean to insinuate anything so insulting!'

I was very angry, and my tremors had all vanished now.

'No, not for *you*, dear cheaile; I was thinking to miladi Knollys, who, without cause, is my enemy. Every one has enemy; you
will learn all that so soon as you are little older, and without
cause she is mine. Come, Maud, speak a the truth—was it not
miladi Knollys who sent you here doucement, doucement, so
quaite to my door—is it not so, little rogue?'

Madame had confronted me again, and we were now standing
in the middle of her floor.

I indignantly repelled the charge, and searching me for a moment with her oddly-shaped, cunning eyes, she said—

'That is good cheaile, you speak a so direct—I like that, and
am glad to hear; but, my dear Maud, that woman——'

'Lady Knollys is papa's cousin,' I interposed a little gravely.

'She does hate a me so, you av no idea. She as tryed to injure
me several times, and would employ the most innocent person,
unconsciously you know, my dear, to assist her malice.'

Here Madame wept a little. I had already discovered that she
could shed tears whenever she pleased. I have heard of such persons, but I never met another before or since.

Madame was unusually frank—no one ever knew better when
to be candid. At present I suppose she concluded that Lady
Knollys would certainly relate whatever she knew concerning

her before she left Knowl ; and so Madame's reserves, whatever they might be, were dissolving, and she growing childlike and confiding.

' Et comment va monsieur votre père aujourd'hui ? '

' Very well, ' I thanked her.

' And how long miladi Knollys her visit is likely to be ? '

' I could not say exactly, but for some days. '

' Eh bien, my dear cheaile, I find myself better this morning, and we must return to our lessons. Je veux m'habiller, ma chère Maud ; you will wait me in the school-room. '

By this time Madame, who, though lazy, could make an effort, and was capable of getting into a sudden hurry, had placed herself before her dressing-table, and was ogling her discoloured and bony countenance in the glass.

' Wat horror ! I am so pale. Quel ennui ! wat bore ! Ow weak av I grow in two three days ! '

And she practised some plaintive, invalid glances into the mirror. But on a sudden there came a little sharp inquisitive frown as she looked over the frame of the glass, upon the terrace beneath. It was only a glance, and she sat down languidly in her arm-chair to prepare, I suppose, for the fatigues of the toilet.

My curiosity was sufficiently aroused to induce me to ask—

' But why, Madame, do you fancy that Lady Knollys dislikes you ? '

' 'Tis not fancy, my dear Maud. Ah ha, no ! Mais c'est toute une histoire—too tedious to tell now—some time maybe—and you will learn when you are little older, the most violent hatreds often they are the most without cause. But, my dear cheaile, the hours they are running from us, and I must dress. Vite, vite ! so you run away to the school-room, and I will come after. '

Madame had her dressing-case and her mysteries, and palpably stood in need of repairs ; so away I went to my studies. The room which we called the school-room was partly beneath the floor of Madame's bed-chamber, and commanded the same view ; so, remembering my governess's peering glance from her windows, I looked out, and saw Cousin Monica making a brisk promenade up and down the terrace-walk. Well, that was quite enough to account for it. I had grown very curious, and I resolved when our lessons were over to join her and make another attempt to discover the mystery.

As I sat over my books, I fancied I heard a movement outside the door. I suspected that Madame was listening. I waited for a time, expecting to see the door open, but she did not come ; so I opened it suddenly myself, but Madame was not on the threshold nor on the lobby. I heard a rustling, however, and on the staircase over the banister I saw the folds of her silk dress as she descended.

She is going, I thought, to seek an interview with Lady Knollys. She intends to propitiate that dangerous lady ; so I amused some eight or ten minutes in watching Cousin Monica's quick march and right-about face upon the parade-ground of the terrace. But no one joined her.

' She is certainly talking to papa,' was my next and more probable conjecture. Having the profoundest distrust of Madame, I was naturally extremely jealous of the confidential interviews in which deceit and malice might make their representations plausibly and without answer.

' Yes, I'll run down and see—see *papa ;* she shan't tell lies behind my back, horrid woman ! '

At the study-door I knocked, and forthwith entered. My father was sitting near the window, his open book before him, Madame standing at the other side of the table, her cunning eyes bathed in tears, and her pocket-handkerchief pressed to her mouth. Her eyes glittered stealthily on me for an instant : she was sobbing—*désolée,* in fact—that grim grenadier lady, and her attitude was exquisitely dejected and timid. But she was, notwithstanding, reading closely and craftily my father's face. He was not looking at her, but rather upward toward the ceiling, reflectively leaning on his hand, with an expression, not angry, but rather surly and annoyed.

' I ought to have heard of this before, Madame, ' my father was saying as I came in ; ' not that it would have made any difference—not the least ; mind that. But it was the kind of thing that I ought to have heard, and the omission was not strictly right. '

Madame, in a shrill and lamentable key, opened her voluble reply, but was arrested by a nod from my father, who asked me if I wanted anything.

' Only—only that I was waiting in the school-room for Madame, and did not know where she was.'

'Well, she is here, you see, and will join you up-stairs in a few minutes.'

So back I went again, huffed, angry, and curious, and sat back in my chair with a clouded countenance, thinking very little about lessons.

When Madame entered, I did not lift my head or eyes.

'Good cheaile! reading,' said she, as she approached briskly and reassured.

'No,' I answered tartly; 'not good, nor a child either; I'm not reading, I've been thinking.'

'Très-bien!' she said, with an insufferable smile, ' thinking is very good also; but you look unhappy—very, poor cheaile. Take care you are not grow jealous for poor Madame talking some-time to your papa; you must not, little fool. It is only for a your good, my dear Maud, and I had no objection you should stay.'

'You! Madame!' I said loftily. I was very angry, and showed it through my dignity, to Madame's evident satisfaction.

'No—it was your papa, Mr. Ruthyn, who weesh to speak alone; for me I do not care; there was something I weesh to tell him. I don't care who know, but Mr. Ruthyn he is deefer-ent.'

I made no remark.

'Come, leetle Maud, you are not to be so cross; it will be much better you and I to be good friends together. Why should a we quarrel?—wat nonsense! Do you imagine I would any-where undertake a the education of a young person unless I could speak with her parent?—wat folly! I would like to be your friend, however, my poor Maud, if you would allow—you and I together—wat you say?'

'People grow to be friends by liking, Madame, and liking comes of itself, not by bargain; I like every one who is kind to me.'

'And so I. You are like me in so many things, my dear Maud! Are you quaite well to-day? I think you look fateague; so I feel, too, vary tire. I think we weel put off the lessons to to-morrow. Eh? and we will come to play la grace in the garden.'

Madame was plainly in a high state of exultation. Her audience had evidently been satisfactory, and, like other people, when things went well, her soul lighted up into a sulphureous

good-humour, not very genuine nor pleasant, but still it was
better than other moods.

I was glad when our calisthenics were ended, and Madame
had returned to her apartment, so that I had a pleasant little
walk with Cousin Monica.

We women are persevering when once our curiosity is roused,
but she gaily foiled mine, and, I think, had a mischievous
pleasure in doing so. As we were going in to dress for dinner,
however, she said, quite gravely—

' I am sorry, Maud, I allowed you to see that I have any unpleasant impressions about that governess lady. I shall be at
liberty some day to explain all about it, and, indeed, it will be
enough to tell your father, whom I have not been able to find
all day ; but really we are, perhaps, making too much of the
matter, and I cannot say that I know anything against Madame
that is conclusive, or—or, indeed, at all ; but that there are
reasons, and—you must not ask any more—no, you must not.'

That evening, while I was playing the overture to Cenern-
tola, for the entertainment of my cousin, there arose from the
tea-table, where she and my father were sitting, a spirited and
rather angry harangue from Lady Knollys' lips ; I turned my
eyes from the music towards the speakers ; the overture swooned
away with a little hesitating babble into silence, and I listened.

Their conversation had begun under cover of the music which
I was making, and now they were too much engrossed to perceive its discontinuance. The first sentence I heard seized my
attention ; my father had closed the book he was reading, upon
his finger, and was leaning back in his chair, as he used to do
when at all angry ; his face was a little flushed, and I knew the
fierce and glassy stare which expressed pride, surprise, and
wrath.

' Yes, Lady Knollys, there's an animus ; I know the spirit you
speak in—it does you no honour, ' said my father.

' And I know the spirit *you* speak in, the spirit of *madness*,'
retorted Cousin Monica, just as much in earnest. ' I can't conceive how you *can* be so *demented*, Austin. What has perverted
you ? are you *blind* ? '

' *You* are, Monica ; your own unnatural prejudice—*unnatural*
prejudice, blinds you. What is it all ?—*nothing*. Were I to act
as you say, I should be a *coward* and a traitor. I see, I *do* see,

all that's real. I'm no Quixote, to draw my sword on illusions. '

' There should be no halting here. How *can* you—do you ever *think* ? I wonder you can breathe. I feel as if the evil one were in the house. '

A stern, momentary frown was my father's only answer, as he looked fixedly at her.

' People need not nail up horseshoes and mark their door-stones with charms to keep the evil spirit out, ' ran on Lady Knollys, who looked as pale and angry, in her way, ' but you open your door in the dark and invoke unknown danger. How can you look at that child that's — she's *not* playing, ' said Knollys, abruptly stopping.

My father rose, muttering to himself, and cast a lurid glance at me, as he went in high displeasure to the door. Cousin Monica, now flushed a little, glanced also silently at me, biting the tip of her slender gold cross, and doubtful how much I had heard.

My father opened the door suddenly, which he had just closed, and looking in, said, in a calmer tone—

' Perhaps, Monica, you would come for a moment to the study ; I'm sure you have none but kindly feelings towards me and little Maud, there ; and I thank you for your good-will ; but you must see other things more reasonably, and I think you will. '

Cousin Monica got up silently and followed him, only throwing up her eyes and hands as she did so, and I was left alone, wondering and curious more than ever.

CHAPTER XV

A WARNING

I sat still, listening and wondering, and wondering and listening ; but I ought to have known that no sound could reach me where I was from my father's study. Five minutes passed and they did not return. Ten, fifteen. I drew near the fire and made myself comfortable in a great arm-chair, looking on the embers, but not seeing all the scenery and *dramatis personæ* of my past life or future fortunes, in their shifting glow, as people in romances usually do ; but fanciful castles and caverns in blood-red and golden glare, suggestive of dreamy fairy-land, salamanders, sunsets, and palaces of fire-kings, and all this partly shaping and partly shaped by my fancy, and leading my closing eyes and drowsy senses off into dream-land. So I nodded and dozed, and sank into a deep slumber, from which I was roused by the voice of my cousin Monica. On opening my eyes, I saw nothing but Lady Knollys' face looking steadily into mine, and expanding into a good-natured laugh as she watched the vacant and lack-lustre stare with which I returned her gaze.

' Come, dear Maud, it is late ; you ought to have been in your bed an hour ago. '

Up I stood, and so soon as I had begun to hear and see aright, it struck me that Cousin Monica was more grave and subdued than I had seen her.

' Come, let us light our candles and go together. '

Holding hands, we ascended, I sleepy, she silent ; and not a word was spoken until we reached my room. Mary Quince was in waiting, and tea made.

' Tell her to come back in a few minutes ; I wish to say a word to you, ' said Lady Knollys.

The maid accordingly withdrew.

Lady Knollys' eyes followed her till she closed the door behind her.

' I'm going in the morning. '

' So soon ! '

' Yes, dear ; I could not stay ; in fact, I should have gone to-night, but it was too late, and I leave instead in the morning. '

' I am so sorry—so *very* sorry, ' I exclaimed, in honest disappointment, and the walls seemed to darken round me, and the monotony of the old routine loomed more terrible in prospect.

' So am I, dear Maud. '

' But can't you stay a little longer ; *won't* you ? '

' No, Maud ; I'm vexed with Austin—very much vexed with your father ; in short, I can't conceive anything so entirely preposterous, and dangerous, and insane as his conduct, now that his eyes are quite opened, and I must say a word to you before

I go, and it is just this :—you must cease to be a mere child, you must try and be a woman, Maud : now don't be frightened or foolish, but hear me out. That woman—what does she call herself—Rougierre ? I have reason to believe is—in fact, from circumstances, *must* be your enemy ; you will find her very deep, daring, and unscrupulous, I venture to say, and you can't be too much on your guard. Do you quite understand me, Maud ? '

' I do, ' said I, with a gasp, and my eyes fixed on her with a terrified interest, as if on a warning ghost.

' You must bridle your tongue, mind, and govern your conduct, and command even your features. It is hard to practise reserve ; but you must—you must be secret and vigilant. Try and be in appearance just as usual ; don't quarrel ; tell her nothing, if you do happen to know anything, of your father's business ; be always on your guard when with her, and keep your eye upon her everywhere. Observe everything, disclose nothing—do you see ? '

' Yes,' again I whispered.

' You have good, honest servants about you, and, thank God, they don't like her. But you must not repeat to them one word I am now saying to you. Servants are fond of dropping hints, and letting things ooze out in that way, and in their quarrels with her would compromise you—you understand me ? '

' I do,' I sighed, with a wild stare.

' And—and, Maud, don't let her meddle with your food.'

Cousin Monica gave me a pale little nod, and looked away.

I could only stare at her ; and under my breath I uttered an ejaculation of terror.

' Don't be so frightened ; you must not be foolish ; I only wish you to be upon your guard. I have my suspicions, but I may be quite wrong ; your father thinks I am a fool ; perhaps I am—perhaps not ; maybe he may come to think as I do. But you must not speak to him on the subject ; he's an odd man, and never did and never will act wisely, when his passions and prejudices are engaged.'

' Has she ever committed any great crime ? ' I asked, feeling as if I were on the point of fainting.

' No, dear Maud, I never said anything of the kind ; don't be so frightened : I only said I have formed, from something I know, an ill opinion of her ; and an unprincipled person, under temptation, is capable of a great deal. But no matter how wicked she may be, you may defy her, simply by assuming her to be so, and acting with caution ; she is cunning and selfish, and she'll do nothing desperate. But I would give her no opportunity.'

' Oh, dear ! Oh, Cousin Monica, don't leave me.'

' My dear, I *can't* stay ; your papa and I — we've had a quarrel. I know I'm right, and he's wrong, and he'll come to see it soon, if he's left to himself, and then all will be right. But just now he misunderstands me, and we've not been civil to one another. I could not think of staying, and he would not allow you to come away with me for a short visit, which I wished. It won't last, though ; and I do assure you, my dear Maud, I am quite happy about you now that you are quite on your guard. Just act respecting that person as if she were capable of any treachery, without showing distrust or dislike in your manner, and nothing will remain in her power ; and write to me whenever you wish to hear from me, and if I can be of any real use, I don't care, I'll come : so there's a wise little woman ; do as I've said, and depend upon it everything will go well, and I'll contrive before long to get that nasty creature away.'

Except a kiss and a few hurried words in the morning when she was leaving, and a pencilled farewell for papa, there was nothing more from Cousin Monica for some time.

Knowl was dark again—darker than ever. My father, gentle always to me, was now—perhaps it was contrast with his fitful return to something like the world's ways, during Lady Knollys' stay—more silent, sad, and isolated than before. Of Madame de la Rougierre I had nothing at first particular to remark. Only, reader, if you happen to be a rather nervous and very young girl, I ask you to conceive my fears and imaginings, and the kind of misery which I was suffering. Its intensity I cannot now even myself recall. But it overshadowed me perpetually—a care, an alarm. It lay down with me at night and got up with me in the morning, tinting and disturbing my dreams, and making my daily life terrible. I wonder now that I lived through the ordeal. The torment was secret and incessant, and kept my mind in unintermitting activity.

Externally things went on at Knowl for some weeks in the usual routine. Madame was, so far as her unpleasant ways were concerned, less tormenting than before, and constantly reminded

me of ' our leetle vow of friendship, you remember, dearest
Maud ! ' and she would stand beside me, and looked from the
window with her bony arm round my waist, and my reluctant
hand drawn round in hers ; and thus she would smile, and talk
affectionately and even playfully ; for at times she would grow
quite girlish, and smile with her great carious teeth, and begin
to quiz and babble about the young ' faylows,' and tell bragging
tales of her lovers, all of which were dreadful to me.

She was perpetually recurring, too, to the charming walk we
had had together to Church Scarsdale, and proposing a repetition of that delightful excursion, which, you may be sure, I
evaded, having by no means so agreeable a recollection of our
visit.

One day, as I was dressing to go out for a walk, in came good
Mrs. Rusk, the housekeeper, to my room.

' Miss Maud, dear, is not that too far for you ? It is a long
walk to Church Scarsdale, and you are not looking very well. '

' To Church Scarsdale ? ' I repeated ; ' I'm not going to
Church Scarsdale ; who said I was going to Church Scarsdale ?
There is nothing I should so much dislike.'

' Well, I never ! 'exclaimed she. ' Why, there's old Madame's
been down-stairs with me for fruit and sandwiches, telling me
you were longing to go to Church Scarsdale——'

' It's quite untrue,' I interrupted. ' She knows I hate it.'

' She does ? ' said Mrs. Rusk, quietly ; ' and you did not tell
her nothing about the basket ? Well—if there isn't a story ! Now
what may she be after—what is it—what *is* she driving at ? '

' I can't tell, but I won't go.'

' No, of course, dear, you won't go. But you may be sure
there's some scheme in her old head. Tom Fowkes says she's bin
two or three times to drink tea at Farmer Gray's—now, could it
be she's thinking to marry him ? ' And Mrs. Rusk sat down and
laughed heartily, ending with a crow of derision.

' To think of a young fellow like that, and his wife, poor
thing, not dead a year—maybe she's got money ? '

' I don't know—I don't care—perhaps, Mrs. Rusk, you mistook
Madame. I will go down ; I am going out.'

Madame had a basket in her hand. She held it quietly by her
capacious skirt, at the far side, and made no allusion to the
preparation, neither to the direction in which she proposed

walking, and prattling artlessly and affectionately she marched by my side.

Thus we reached the stile at the sheep-walk, and then I paused.

Now, Madame, have not we gone far enough in this direction ?—suppose we visit the pigeon-house in the park ? '

' Wat folly ! my dear a Maud—you cannot walk so far.'

' Well, towards home, then.'

' And wy not a this way ? We ave not walk enough, and Mr. Ruthyn he will not be pleased if you do not take proper exercise. Let us walk on by the path, and stop when you like.'

' Where do you wish to go, Madame ? '

' Nowhere particular—come along ; don't be fool, Maud.'

' This leads to Church Scarsdale.'

' A yes indeed ! wat sweet place ! bote we need not a walk all the way to there.'

' I'd rather not walk outside the grounds to-day, Madame.'

' Come, Maud, you shall not be fool—wat you mean, Mademoiselle ? ' said the stalworth lady, growing yellow and greenish with an angry mottling, and accosting me very gruffly.

' I don't care to cross the stile, thank you, Madame. I shall remain at this side.'

' You shall do wat I tell you ! ' exclaimed she.

' Let go my arm, Madame, you hurt me,' I cried.

She had griped my arm very firmly in her great bony hand, and seemed preparing to drag me over by main force.

' Let me go,' I repeated shrilly, for the pain increased.

' La ! ' she cried with a smile of rage and a laugh, letting me go and shoving me backward at the same time, so that I had a rather dangerous tumble.

I stood up, a good deal hurt, and very angry, notwithstanding my fear of her.

' I'll ask papa if I am to be so ill-used.'

' Wat av I done ? ' cried Madame, laughing grimly from her hollow jaws ; ' I did all I could to help you over—'ow could I prevent you to pull back and tumble if you would do so ? That is the way wen you petites Mademoiselles are naughty and hurt yourself they always try to make blame other people. Tell a wat you like—you think I care ? '

' Very well, Madame.'

'Are a you coming?'

'No.'

She looked steadily in my face and very wickedly. I gazed at her as with dazzled eyes—I suppose as the feathered prey do at the owl that glares on them by night. I neither moved back nor forward, but stared at her quite helplessly.

'You are nice pupil—charming young person! So polite, so obedient, so amiable! I will walk towards Church Scarsdale,' she continued, suddenly breaking through the conventionalism of her irony, and accosting me in savage accents. 'You weel stay behind if you dare. I tell you to accompany—do you hear?'

More than ever resolved against following her, I remained where I was, watching her as she marched fiercely away, swinging her basket as though in imagination knocking my head off with it.

She soon cooled, however, and looking over her shoulder, and seeing me still at the other side of the stile, she paused, and beckoned me grimly to follow her. Seeing me resolutely maintain my position, she faced about, tossed her head, like an angry beast, and seemed uncertain for a while what course to take with me.

She stamped and beckoned furiously again. I stood firm. I was very much frightened, and could not tell to what violence she might resort in her exasperation. She walked towards me with an inflamed countenance, and a slight angry wagging of the head; my heart fluttered, and I awaited the crisis in extreme trepidation. She came close, the stile only separating us, and stopped short, glaring and grinning at me like a French grenadier who has crossed bayonets, but hesitates to close.

CHAPTER XVI

DOCTOR BRYERLY LOOKS IN

What had I done to excite this ungovernable fury? We had often before had such small differences, and she had contented herself with being sarcastic, teasing, and impertinent.

' So, for future you are gouvernante and I the cheaile for you to command—is not so?—and you must direct where we shall walk. Très-bien! we shall see; Monsieur Ruthyn he shall know everything. For me I do not care—not at all—I shall be rather pleased, on the contrary. Let him decide. If I shall be responsible for the conduct and the health of Mademoiselle his daughter, it must be that I shall have authority to direct her wat she must do—it must be that she or I shall obey. I ask only witch shall command for the future—voilà tout!'

I was frightened, but resolute—I dare say I looked sullen and uncomfortable. At all events, she seemed to think she might possibly succeed by wheedling; so she tried coaxing and cajoling, and patted my cheek, and predicted that I would be ' a good cheaile,' and not ' vex poor Madame,' but do for the future 'wat she tell a me.'

She smiled her wide wet grin, smoothed my hand, and patted my cheek, and would in the excess of her conciliatory paroxysm have kissed me; but I withdrew, and she commented only with a little laugh, and a ' Foolish little thing! but you will be quite amiable just now.'

' Why, Madame,' I asked, suddenly raising my head and looking her straight in the face, ' do you wish me to walk to Church Scarsdale so particularly to-day?'

She answered my steady look with a contracted gaze and an unpleasant frown.

' Wy do I?—I do not understand a you; there is *no* particular day—wat folly! Wy I like Church Scarsdale? Well, it is such

78

pretty place. There is all ! Wat leetle fool ! I suppose you think
I want to keel a you and bury you in the churchyard ? '

And she laughed, and it would not have been a bad laugh for
a ghoul.

' Come, my dearest Maud, you are not a such fool to say, if
you tell me me go thees a way, I weel go that ; and if you say,
go that a way, I weel go thees—you are rasonable leetle girl—
come along—*alons donc*—we shall av soche agreeable walk— weel
a you ? '

But I was immovable. It was neither obstinacy nor caprice,
but a profound fear that governed me. I was then afraid—yes,
afraid. Afraid of *what* ? Well, of going with Madame de la
Rougierre to Church Scarsdale that day. That was all. And I
believe that instinct was true.

She turned a bitter glance toward Church Scarsdale, and bit
her lip. She saw that she must give it up. A shadow hung upon
her drab features. A little scowl—a little sneer—wide lips compressed with a false smile, and a leaden shadow mottling all.
Such was the countenance of the lady who only a minute or two
before had been smiling and murmuring over the stile so am-
iably with her idiomatic ' blarney,' as the Irish call that kind of
blandishment.

There was no mistaking the malignant disappointment that
hooked and warped her features—my heart sank—a tremendous
fear overpowered me. Had she intended poisoning me ? What
was in that basket ? I looked in her dreadful face. I felt for a
minute quite frantic. A feeling of rage with my father, with my
Cousin Monica, for abandoning me to this dreadful rogue, took
possession of me, and I cried, helplessly wringing my hands—

' Oh ! it is a shame—it is a shame—it is a shame ! '

The countenance of the gouvernante relaxed. I think she in
turn was frightened at my extreme agitation. It might have
worked unfavourably with my father.

' Come, Maud, it is time you should try to control your temper. You shall not walk to Church Scarsdale if you do not like—
I only invite. *There !* It is quite as you please, where we shall
walk then ? Here to the peegeon-house ? I think you say.
Tout bien ! Remember I concede you everything. Let us go.'

We went, therefore, towards the pigeon-house, through the
forest trees ; I not speaking as the children in the wood did

with their sinister conductor, but utterly silent and scared ; she
silent also, meditating, and sometimes with a sharp side-glance
gauging my progress towards equanimity. Her own was rapid ;
for Madame was a philosopher, and speedily accommodated
herself to circumstances. We had not walked a quarter of an
hour when every trace of gloom had left her face, which had
assumed its customary brightness, and she began to sing with a
spiteful hilarity as we walked forward, and indeed seemed to be
approaching one of her waggish, frolicsome moods. But her fun
in these moods was solitary. The joke, whatever it was, remained
in her own keeping. When we approached the ruined brick
tower—in old times a pigeon-house—she grew quite frisky, and
twirled her basket in the air, and capered to her own singing.

Under the shadow of the broken wall, and its ivy, she sat
down with a frolicsome *plump*, and opened her basket, inviting
me to partake, which I declined. I must do her justice, however,
upon the suspicion of poison, which she quite disposed of by
gobbling up, to her own share, everything which the basket contained.

The reader is not to suppose that Madame's cheerful de-
meanour indicated that I was forgiven. Nothing of the kind.
One syllable more, on our walk home, she addressed not to me.
And when we reached the terrace, she said—

'You will please, Maud, remain for two—three minutes in the
Dutch garden, while I speak with Mr. Ruthyn in the study.'

This was spoken with a high head and an insufferable smile ;
and I more haughtily, but quite gravely, turned without disputing, and descended the steps to the quaint little garden she
had indicated.

I was surprised and very glad to see my father there. I ran
to him, and began, 'Oh ! papa ! ' and then stopped short, adding
only, ' may I speak to you now ? '

He smiled kindly and gravely on me.

' Well, Maud, say your say.'

' Oh, sir, it is only this : I entreat that our walks, mine and
Madame's may be confined to the grounds.'

' And why ? '

' I—I'm afraid to go with her.'

' *Afraid !* ' he repeated, looking hard at me. ' Have you lately
had a letter from Lady Knollys ? '

'No, papa, not for two months or more.'

There was a pause.

'And why *afraid*, Maud?'

'She brought me one day to Church Scarsdale; you know what a solitary place it is, sir; and she frightened me so that I was afraid to go with her into the churchyard. But she went and left me alone at the other side of the stream, and an impudent man passing by stopped and spoke to me, and seemed inclined to laugh at me, and altogether frightened me very much, and he did not go till Madame happened to return.'

'What kind of man—young or old?'

'A young man; he looked like a farmer's son, but very impudent, and stood there talking to me whether I would or not; and Madame did not care at all, and laughed at me for being frightened; and, indeed, I am very uncomfortable with her.'

He gave me another shrewd look, and then looked down cloudily and thought.

'You say you are uncomfortable and frightened. How is this—what causes these feelings?'

'I don't know, sir; she likes frightening me; I am afraid of her—we are all afraid of her, I think. The servants, I mean, as well as I.'

My father nodded his head contemptuously, twice or thrice, and muttered, 'A pack of fools!'

'And she was so very angry to-day with me, because I would not walk again with her to Church Scarsdale. I am very much afraid of her. I—' and quite unpremeditatedly I burst into tears.

'There, there, little Maud, you must not cry. She is here only for your good. If you are afraid—even *foolishly* afraid—it is enough. Be it as you say; your walks are henceforward confined to the grounds; I'll tell her so.'

I thanked him through my tears very earnestly.

'But, Maud, beware of prejudice; women are unjust and violent in their judgments. Your family has suffered in some of its members by such injustice. It behoves us to be careful not to practise it.'

That evening in the drawing-room my father said, in his usual abrupt way—

'About my departure, Maud: I've had a letter from London this morning, and I think I shall be called away sooner than I

at first supposed, and for a little time we must manage apart
from one another. Do not be alarmed. You shall not be in
Madame de la Rougierre's charge, but under the care of a relation ; but even so, little Maud will miss her old father, I
think.'

His tone was very tender, so were his looks ; he was looking
down on me with a smile, and tears were in his eyes. This
softening was new to me. I felt a strange thrill of surprise,
delight, and love, and springing up, I threw my arms about his
neck and wept in silence. He, I think, shed tears also.

'You said a visitor was coming ; some one, you mean, to go
away with. Ah, yes, you love him better than me.'

'No, dear, no ; but I *fear* him ; and I am sorry to leave you,
little Maud.'

'It won't be very long,' I pleaded.

'No, dear,' he answered with a sigh.

I was tempted almost to question him more closely on the
subject, but he seemed to divine what was in my mind, for he
said—

'Let us speak no more of it, but only bear in mind, Maud,
what I told you about the oak cabinet, the key of which is here,'
and he held it up as formerly : 'you remember what you are to
do in case Doctor Bryerly should come while I am away ? '

'Yes, sir.'

His manner had changed, and I had returned to my accustomed formalities.

It was only a few days later that Dr. Bryerly actually did
arrive at Knowl, quite unexpectedly, except, I suppose, by my
father. He was to stay only one night.

He was twice closeted in the little study up-stairs with my
father, who seemed to me, even for him, unusually dejected,
and Mrs. Rusk inveighing against 'them rubbitch,' as she always
termed the Swedenborgians, told me 'they were making him
quite shaky-like, and he would not last no time, if that lanky,
lean ghost of a fellow in black was to keep prowling in and
out of his room like a tame cat.'

I lay awake that night, wondering what the mystery might be
that connected my father and Dr. Bryerly. There was something
more than the convictions of their strange religion could account
for. There was something that profoundly agitated my father.

It may not be reasonable, but so it is. The person whose presence, though we know nothing of the cause of that effect, is palpably attended with pain to anyone who is dear to us, grows odious, and I began to detest Doctor Bryerly.

It was a grey, dark morning, and in a dark pass in the gallery, near the staircase, I came full upon the ungainly Doctor, in his glossy black suit.

I think, if my mind had been less anxiously excited on the subject of his visit, or if I had not disliked him so much, I should not have found courage to accost him as I did. There was something sly, I thought, in his dark, lean face ; and he looked so low, so like a Scotch artisan in his Sunday clothes, that I felt a sudden pang of indignation, at the thought that a great gentleman, like my father, should have suffered under his influence, and I stopped suddenly, instead of passing him by with a mere salutation, as he expected, ' May I ask a question, Doctor Bryerly ? '

' Certainly.'

' Are you the friend whom my father expects ? '

' I don't quite see.'

' The friend, I mean, with whom he is to make an expedition to some distance, I think, and for some little time ? '

' No,' said the Doctor, with a shake of his head.

' And who is he ? '

' I really have not a notion, Miss.'

' Why, he said that *you knew*,' I replied.

The Doctor looked honestly puzzled.

' Will he stay long away ? pray tell me.'

The Doctor looked into my troubled face with inquiring and darkened eyes, like one who half reads another's meaning ; and then he said a little briskly, but not sharply—

' Well, *I* don't know, I'm sure, Miss ; no, indeed, you must have mistaken ; there's nothing that *I* know.'

There was a little pause, and he added—

' No. He never mentioned any friend to me.' I fancied that he was made uncomfortable by my question, and wanted to hide the truth. Perhaps I was partly right.

' Oh ! Doctor Bryerly, pray, *pray* who is the friend, and where is he going ? '

'I do *assure* you,' he said, with a strange sort of impatience, 'I don't know ; it is all nonsense.'

And he turned to go, looking, I think, annoyed and disconcerted.

A terrific suspicion crossed my brain like lightning.

'Doctor, one word,' I said, I believe, quite wildly. 'Do you—do you think his mind is at all affected ? '

'Insane ? ' he said, looking at me with a sudden, sharp inquisitiveness, that brightened into a smile. 'Pooh, pooh ! Heaven forbid ! not a saner man in England.'

Then with a little nod he walked on, carrying, as I believed, notwithstanding his disclaimer, the secret with him. In the afternoon Doctor Bryerly went away.

CHAPTER XVII

AN ADVENTURE

For many days after our quarrel, Madame hardly spoke to me. As for lessons, I was not much troubled with them. It was plain, too, that my father had spoken to her, for she never after that day proposed our extending our walks beyond the precincts of Knowl.

Knowl, however, was a very considerable territory, and it was possible for a much better pedestrian than I to tire herself effectually, without passing its limits. So we took occasionally long walks.

After some weeks of sullenness, during which for days at a time she hardly spoke to me, and seemed lost in dark and evil abstraction, she once more, and somewhat suddenly, recovered her spirits, and grew quite friendly. Her gaieties and friendliness were not reassuring, and in my mind presaged approaching mischief and treachery. The days were shortening to the wintry span. The edge of the red sun had already touched the horizon as Madame and I, overtaken at the warren by his last beams, were hastening homeward.

A narrow carriage-road traverses this wild region of the park, to which a distant gate gives entrance. On descending into this unfrequented road, I was surprised to see a carriage standing there. A thin, sly postilion, with that pert, turned-up nose which the old caricaturist Woodward used to attribute to the gentlemen of Tewkesbury, was leaning on his horses, and looked hard at me as I passed. A lady who sat within looked out, with an extra-fashionable bonnet on, and also treated us to a stare. Very pink and white cheeks she had, very black glossy hair and bright eyes—fat, bold, and rather cross, she looked—and in her bold way she examined us curiously as we passed.

I mistook the situation. It had once happened before that an intending visitor at Knowl had entered the place by that park-road, and lost several hours in a vain search for the house.

' Ask him, Madame, whether they want to go to the house ; I dare say they have missed their way,' whispered I.

' *Eh bien,* they will find again. I do not choose to talk to post-boys ; *allons* !'

But I asked the man as we passed, ' Do you want to reach the house ? '

By this time he was at the horses' heads, buckling the harness.

' Noa,' he said in a surly tone, smiling oddly on the winkers, but, recollecting his politeness, he added, ' Noa, thankee, misses, it's what they calls a picnic ; we'll be takin' the road now.'

He was smiling now on a little buckle with which he was engaged.

' Come—nonsense ! ' whispered Madame sharply in my ear, and she whisked me by the arm, so we crossed the little stile at the other side.

Our path lay across the warren, which undulates in little hillocks. The sun was down by this time, blue shadows were stretching round us, colder in the splendid contrast of the bur-nished sunset sky.

Descending over these hillocks we saw three figures a little in advance of us, not far from the path we were tracing. Two were standing smoking and chatting at intervals : one tall and slim, with a high chimney-pot, worn a little on one side, and a white

great-coat buttoned up to the chin ; the other shorter and
stouter, with a dark-coloured wrapper. These gentlemen were
facing rather our way as we came over the edge of the eminence,
but turned their backs on perceiving our approach. As they did
so, I remember so well each lowered his cigar suddenly with
the simultaneousness of a drill. The third figure sustained the
picnic character of the group, for he was repacking a hamper.
He stood suddenly erect as we drew near, and a very ill-looking
person he was, low-browed, square-chinned, and with a broad,
broken nose. He wore gaiters, and was a little bandy, very broad,
and had a closely-cropped bullet head, and deep-set little eyes.
The moment I saw him, I beheld the living type of the burglars
and bruisers whom I had so often beheld with a kind of scepticism in *Punch*. He stood over his hamper and scowled sharply
at us for a moment ; then with the point of his foot he jerked
a little fur cap that lay on the ground into his hand, drew it
tight over his lowering brows, and called to his companions,
just as we passed him—' Hallo ! mister. How's this ? '

' All right,' said the tall person in the white great-coat, who,
as he answered, shook his shorter companion by the arm, I
thought angrily.

This shorter companion turned about. He had a muffler loose
about his neck and chin. I thought he seemed shy and irresolute,
and the tall man gave him a great jolt with his elbow, which
made him stagger, and I fancied a little angry, for he said, as it
seemed, a sulky word or two.

The gentleman in the white surtout, however, standing direct
in our way, raised his hat with a mock salutation, placing his
hand on his breast, and forthwith began to advance with an
insolent grin and an air of tipsy frolic.

' Jist in time, ladies ; five minutes more and we'd a bin off.
Thankee, Mrs. Mouser, ma'am, for the honour of the meetin',
and more particular for the pleasure of making your young
lady's acquaintance—niece, ma'am ? daughter, ma'am ? grand-
daughter, by Jove, is it ? Hallo ! there, mild 'n, I say, stop
packin'.' This was to the ill-favoured person with the broken
nose. ' Bring us a couple o' glasses and a bottle o' curaçoa ; what
are you fear'd on, my dear ? this is Lord Lollipop, here, a reg'lar
charmer, wouldn't hurt a fly, hey Lolly ? Isn't he pretty, Miss ?
and I'm Sir Simon Sugarstick—so called after old Sir Simon,

ma'am ; and I'm so tall and straight, Miss, and slim—ain't I ?
and ever so sweet, my honey, when you come to know me, just
like a sugarstick; ain't I, Lolly, boy ? '

' I'm Miss Ruthyn, tell them, Madame,' I said, stamping on
the ground, and very much frightened.

' Be quaite, Maud. If you are angry, they will hurt us ; leave
me to speak,' whispered the gouvernante.

All this time they were approaching from separate points. I
glanced back, and saw the ruffianly-looking man within a yard
or two, with his arm raised and one finger up, telegraphing, as
it seemed, to the gentlemen in front.

' Be quaite, Maud,' whispered Madame, with an awful adjura-
tion, which I do not care to set down. ' They are teepsy ; don't
seem 'fraid.'

I *was* afraid—terrified. The circle had now so narrowed that
they might have placed their hands on my shoulders.

' Pray, gentlemen, wat you want ? *weel* a you 'av the goodness
to permit us to go on ? '

I now observed for the first time, with a kind of shock, that
the shorter of the two men, who prevented our advance, was
the person who had accosted me so offensively at Church Scarsdale. I pulled Madame by the arm, whispering, ' Let us run.'

' Be quaite, my dear Maud,' was her only reply.

' I tell you what,' said the tall man, who had replaced his high
hat more jauntily than before on the side of his head, ' We've
caught you now, fair game, and we'll let you off on conditions.
You must not be frightened, Miss. Upon my honour and soul,
I mean no mischief ; do I, Lollipop ? I call him Lord Lollipop ;
it's only chaff, though; his name's Smith. Now, Lolly, I vote we
let the prisoners go, when we just introduce them to Mrs.
Smith ; she's sitting in the carriage, and keeps Mr. S. here in
precious good order, I promise you. There's easy terms for you,
eh, and we'll have a glass o' curaçoa round, and so part friends.
Is it a bargain ? Come !'

' Yes, Maud, we must go—wat matter ? ' whispered Madame
vehemently.

' You shan't,' I said, instinctively terrified.

' You'll go with Ma'am, young 'un, won't you ? ' said Mr. Smith,
as his companion called him.

Madame was holding my arm, but I snatched it from her, and

would have run ; the tall man, however, placed his arms round me and held me fast with an affectation of playfulness, but his grip was hard enough to hurt me a good deal. Being now thoroughly frightened, after an ineffectual struggle, during which I heard Madame say, ' You fool, Maud, weel you come with me ? see wat you are doing,' I began to scream, shriek after shriek, which the man attempted to drown with loud hooting, peals of laughter, forcing his handkerchief against my mouth, while Madame continued to bawl her exhortations to ' be quaite ' in my ear.

' I'll lift her, I say ! ' said a gruff voice behind me.

But at this instant, wild with terror, I distinctly heard other voices shouting. The men who surrounded me were instantly silent, and all looked in the direction of the sound, now very near, and I screamed with redoubled energy. The ruffian behind me thrust his great hand over my mouth.

' It is the gamekeeper,' cried Madame. ' *Two* gamekeepers— we are safe—thank Heaven !' and she began to call on Dykes by name.

I only remember, feeling myself at liberty—running a few steps—seeing Dykes' white furious face—clinging to his arm, with which he was bringing his gun to a level, and saying, ' Don't fire—they'll murder us if you do.'

Madame, screaming lustily, ran up at the same moment.

' Run on to the gate and lock it—I'll be wi' ye in a minute,' cried he to the other gamekeeper ; who started instantly on this mission, for the three ruffians were already in full retreat for the carriage.

Giddy—wild—fainting—still terror carried me on.

'Now, Madame Rogers—s'pose you take young Misses on— I must run and len' Bill a hand.'

' No, no ; you moste not,' cried Madame. ' I am fainting myself, and more villains they may be near to us.'

But at this moment we heard a shot, and, muttering to himself and grasping his gun, Dykes ran at his utmost speed in the direction of the sound.

With many exhortations to speed, and ejaculations of alarm, Madame hurried me on toward the house, which at length we reached without further adventure.

As it happened, my father met us in the hall. He was perfectly transported with fury on hearing from Madame what had happened, and set out at once, with some of the servants, in the hope of intercepting the party at the park-gate.

Here was a new agitation ; for my father did not return for nearly three hours, and I could not conjecture what might be occurring during the period of his absence. My alarm was greatly increased by the arrival in the interval of poor Bill, the under-gamekeeper, very much injured.

Seeing that he was determined to intercept their retreat, the three men had set upon him, wrested his gun, which exploded in the struggle, from him, and beat him savagely. I mention these particulars, because they convinced everybody that there was something specially determined and ferocious in the spirit of the party, and that the fracas was no mere frolic, but the result of a predetermined plan.

My father had not succeeded in overtaking them. He traced them to the Lugton Station, where they had taken the railway, and no one could tell him in what direction the carriage and posthorses had driven.

Madame was, or affected to be, very much shattered by what had occurred. Her recollection and mine, when my father questioned us closely, differed very materially respecting many details of the *personnel* of the villanous party. She was obstinate and clear ; and although the gamekeeper corroborated my description of them, still my father was puzzled. Perhaps he was not sorry that some hesitation was forced upon him, because although at first he would have gone almost any length to detect the persons, on reflection he was pleased that there was not evidence to bring them into a court of justice, the publicity and annoyance of which would have been inconceivably distressing to me.

Madame was in a strange state—tempestuous in temper, talking incessantly—every now and then in floods of tears, and perpetually on her knees pouring forth torrents of thanksgiving to Heaven for our joint deliverance from the hands of those villains. Notwithstanding our community of danger and her thankfulness on my behalf, however, she broke forth into wrath and railing whenever we were alone together.

' Wat fool you were ! so disobedient and obstinate ; if you 'ad done wat *I* say, then we should av been quaite safe ; those per-

sons they were tipsy, and there is nothing so dangerous as to
quarrel with tipsy persons ; I would 'av brought you quaite
safe—the lady she seem so nice and quaite, and we should 'av
been safe with her—there would 'av been nothing absolutely ;
but instead you would scream and pooshe, and so they grow
quite wild, and all the impertinence and violence follow of
course ; and that a poor Bill—all his beating and danger to his
life it is cause entairely by you.'

And she spoke with more real virulence than that kind of upbraiding generally exhibits.

'The beast ! ' exclaimed Mrs. Rusk, when she, I, and Mary
Quince were in my room together, 'with all her crying and praying, I'd like to know as much as she does, maybe, about them
rascals. There never was sich like about the place, long as I
remember it, till she came to Knowl, old witch ! with them un-
merciful big bones of hers, and her great bald head, grinning
here, and crying there, and her nose everywhere. The old French
hypocrite ! '

Mary Quince threw in an observation, and I believe Mrs.
Rusk rejoined, but I heard neither. For whether the housekeeper spoke with reflection or not, what she said affected me
strangely. Through the smallest aperture, for a moment, I had
had a peep into Pandemonium. Were not peculiarities of Madame's demeanour and advice during the adventure partly accounted for by the suggestion ? Could the proposed excursion to
Church Scarsdale have had any purpose of the same sort ? What
was proposed ? How was Madame interested in it ? Were such
immeasurable treason and hypocrisy possible ? I could not explain nor quite believe in the shapeless suspicion that with
these light and bitter words of the old housekeeper had stolen
so horribly into my mind.

After Mrs. Rusk was gone I awoke from my dismal abstraction with something like a moan and a shudder, with a dreadful sense of danger.

'Oh ! Mary Quince,' I cried, ' do *you* think she really knew ? '
'*Who*, Miss Maud ? '
'Do you think Madame knew of those dreadful people ? Oh,
no—say you don't—you don't believe it—tell me she did not.
I'm distracted, Mary Quince, I'm frightened out of my life.'
'There now, Miss Maud, dear—there now, don't take on so—

why should she ?—no sich a thing. Mrs. Rusk, law bless you, she's no more meaning in what she says than the child unborn.'

But I was really frightened. I was in a horrible state of uncertainty as to Madame de la Rougierre's complicity with the party who had beset us at the warren, and afterwards so murderously beat our poor gamekeeper. How was I ever to get rid of that horrible woman ? How long was she to enjoy her continual opportunities of affrighting and injuring me ?

' She hates me—she hates me, Mary Quince ; and she will never stop until she has done me some dreadful injury. Oh! will no one relieve me—will no one take her away ? Oh, papa, papa, papa ! you will be sorry when it is too late.'

I was crying and wringing my hands, and turning from side to side, at my wits' ends, and honest Mary Quince in vain endevoured to quiet and comfort me.

CHAPTER XVIII

A MIDNIGHT VISITOR

The frightful warnings of Lady Knollys haunted me too. Was there no escape from the dreadful companion whom fate had assigned me ? I made up my mind again and again to speak to my father and urge her removal. In other things he indulged me ; here, however, he met me drily and sternly, and it was plain that he fancied I was under my cousin Monica's influence, and also that he had secret reasons for persisting in an opposite course. Just then I had a gay, odd letter from Lady Knollys, from some country house in Shropshire. Not a word about Captain Oakley. My eye skimmed its pages in search of that charmed name. With a peevish feeling I tossed the sheet upon the table. Inwardly I thought how ill-natured and unwomanly it was.

After a time, however, I read it, and found the letter very good-natured. She had received a note from papa. He had ' had

the impudence to forgive *her* for *his* impertinence.' But for my
sake she meant, notwithstanding this aggravation, really to pardon him ; and whenever she had a disengaged week, to accept
his invitation to Knowl, from whence she was resolved to whisk
me off to London, where, though I was too young to be presented
at Court and come out, I might yet—besides having the best
masters and a good excuse for getting rid of Medusa—see a great
deal that would amuse and surprise me.

' Great news, I suppose, from Lady Knollys ? ' said Madame,
who always knew who in the house received letters by the post,
and by an intuition from whom they came.

' Two letters—you and your papa. She is quite well, I hope ? '

' Quite well, thank you, Madame.'

Some fishing questions, dropped from time to time, fared no
better. And as usual, when she was foiled even in a trifle, she
became sullen and malignant.

That night, when my father and I were alone, he suddenly
closed the book he had been reading, and said—

' I heard from Monica Knollys to-day. I always liked poor
Monnie ; and though she's no witch, and very wrong-headed
at times, yet now and then she does say a thing that's worth
weighing. Did she ever talk to you of a time, Maud, when you
are to be your own mistress ?'

' No,' I answered, a little puzzled, and looking straight in his
rugged, kindly face.

' Well, I thought she might—she's a rattle, you know—always
was a rattle, and that sort of people say whatever comes uppermost. But that's a subject for me, and more than once, Maud,
it has puzzled me.'

He sighed.

' Come with me to the study, little Maud.'

So, he carrying a candle, we crossed the lobby, and marched
together through the passage, which at night always seemed a
little awesome, darkly wainscoted, uncheered by the cross-light
from the hall, which was lost at the turn, leading us away from
the frequented parts of the house to that misshapen and lonely
room about which the traditions of the nursery and the servants'
hall had had so many fearful stories to recount.

I think my father had intended making some disclosure to me

on reaching this room. If so, he changed his mind, or at least postponed his intention.

He had paused before the cabinet, respecting the key of which he had given me so strict a charge, and I think he was going to explain himself more fully than he had done. But he went on, instead, to the table where his desk, always jealously locked, was placed, and having lighted the candles which stood by it, he glanced at me, and said—

'You must wait a little, Maud; I shall have something to say to you. Take this candle and amuse yourself with a book meanwhile.'

I was accustomed to obey in silence. I chose a volume of engravings, and ensconced myself in a favourite nook in which I had often passed a half-hour similarly. This was a deep recess by the fireplace, fenced on the other side by a great old escritoir. Into this I drew a stool, and, with candle and book, I placed myself snugly in the narrow chamber. Every now and then I raised my eyes and saw my father either writing or ruminating, as it seemed to me, very anxiously at his desk.

Time wore on—a longer time than he had intended, and still he continued absorbed at his desk. Gradually I grew sleepy, and as I nodded, the book and room faded away, and pleasant little dreams began to gather round me, and so I went off into a deep slumber.

It must have lasted long, for when I wakened my candle had burnt out; my father, having quite forgotten me, was gone, and the room was dark and deserted. I felt cold and a little stiff, and for some seconds did not know where I was.

I had been wakened, I suppose, by a sound which I now distinctly heard, to my great terror, approaching. There was a rustling; there was a breathing. I heard a creaking upon the plank that always creaked when walked upon in the passage. I held my breath and listened, and coiled myself up in the innermost recess of my little chamber.

Sudden and sharp, a light shone in from the nearly-closed study door. It shone angularly on the ceiling like a letter L reversed. There was a pause. Then some one knocked softly at the door, which after another pause was slowly pushed open. I expected, I think, to see the dreaded figure of the linkman. I was scarcely less frightened to see that of Madame de la Rou-

gierre. She was dressed in a sort of grey silk, which she called
her Chinese silk—precisely as she had been in the daytime. In
fact, I do not think she had undressed. She had no shoes on.
Otherwise her toilet was deficient in nothing. Her wide mouth
was grimly closed, and she stood scowling into the room with
a searching and pallid scrutiny, the candle held high above her
head at the full stretch of her arm.

Placed as I was in a deep recess, and in a seat hardly raised
above the level of the floor, I escaped her, although it seemed to
me for some seconds, as I gazed on this spectre, that our eyes
actually met.

I sat without breathing or winking, staring upon the formidable image which with upstretched arm, and the sharp lights
and hard shadows thrown upon her corrugated features, looked
like a sorceress watching for the effect of a spell.

She was plainly listening intensely. Unconsciously she had
drawn her lower lip altogether between her teeth, and I well
remember what a deathlike and idiotic look the contortion
gave her. My terror lest she should discover me amounted to
positive agony. She rolled her eyes stealthily from corner to
corner of the room, and listened with her neck awry at the
door.

Then to my father's desk she went. To my great relief, her
back was towards me. She stooped over it, with the candle close
by ; I saw her try a key—it could be nothing else—and I heard
her blow through the wards to clear them.

Then, again, she listened at the door, candle in hand, and
then with long tiptoe steps came back, and papa's desk in
another moment was open, and Madame cautiously turning over
the papers it contained.

Twice or thrice she paused, glided to the door, and listened
again intently with her head near the ground, and then returned
and continued her search, peeping into papers one after another,
tolerably methodically, and reading some quite through.

While this felonious business was going on, I was freezing with
fear lest she should accidentally look round and her eyes light
on me; for I could not say what she might not do rather than
have her crime discovered.

Sometimes she would read a paper twice over; sometimes a
whisper no louder than the ticking of a watch, sometimes a brief

chuckle under her breath, bespoke the interest with which here and there a letter or a memorandum was read.

For about half an hour, I think, this went on; but at the time it seemed to me all but interminable. On a sudden she raised her head and listened for a moment, replaced the papers deftly, closed the desk without noise, except for the tiny click of the lock, extinguished the candle, and rustled stealthily out of the room, leaving in the darkness the malign and hag-like face on which the candle had just shone still floating filmy in the dark.

Why did I remain silent and motionless while such an outrage was being committed ? If, instead of being a very nervous girl, preoccupied with an undefinable terror of that wicked woman, I had possessed courage and presence of mind, I dare say I might have given an alarm, and escaped from the room without the slightest risk. But so it was ; I could no more stir than the bird who, cowering under its ivy, sees the white owl sailing back and forward under its predatory cruise.

Not only during her presence, but for more than an hour after, I remained cowering in my hiding-place, and afraid to stir, lest she might either be lurking in the neighborhood, or return and surprise me.

You will not be astonished, that after a night so passed I was ill and feverish in the morning. To my horror, Madame de la Rougierre came to visit me at my bedside. Not a trace of guilty consciousness of what had passed during the night was legible in her face. She had no sign of late watching, and her toilet was exemplary.

As she sat smiling by me, full of anxious and affectionate enquiry, and smoothed the coverlet with her great felonious hand, I could quite comprehend the dreadful feeling with which the deceived husband in the ' Arabian Nights ' met his ghoul wife, after his nocturnal discovery.

Ill as I was, I got up and found my father in that room which adjoined his bedchamber. He perceived, I am sure, by my looks, that something unusual had happened. I shut the door, and came close beside his chair.

' Oh, papa, I have such a thing to tell you ! ' I forgot to call him ' Sir.' ' A secret ; and you won't say who told you ? Will you come down to the study ? '

He looked hard at me, got up, and kissing my forehead, said—

' Don't be frightened, Maud ; I venture to say it is a mare's nest ; at all events, my child, we will take care that no danger reaches you ; come, child.'

And by the hand he led me to the study. When the door was shut, and we had reached the far end of the room next the window, I said, but in a low tone, and holding his arm fast—

' Oh, sir, you don't know what a dreadful person we have living with us—Madame de la Rougierre, I mean. Don't let her in if she comes ; she would guess what I am telling you, and one way or another I am sure she would kill me.'

' Tut, tut, child. You *must* know that's nonsense,' he said, looking pale and stern.

' Oh no, papa. I am horribly frightened, and Lady Knollys thinks so too.'

' Ha ! I dare say ; one fool makes many. We all know what Monica thinks.'

' But I *saw* it, papa. She stole your key last night, and opened your desk, and read all your papers.'

' Stole my key ! ' said my father, staring at me perplexed, but at the same instant producing it. ' Stole it ! Why here it is ! '

' She unlocked your desk ; she read your papers for ever so long. Open it now, and see whether they have not been stirred.'

He looked at me this time in silence, with a puzzled air ; but he did unlock the desk, and lifted the papers curiously and suspiciously. As he did so he uttered a few of those inarticulate interjections which are made with closed lips, and not always intelligible ; but he made no remark.

Then he placed me on a chair beside him, and sitting down himself, told me to recollect myself, and tell him distinctly all I had seen. This accordingly I did, he listening with deep attention.

' Did she remove any paper ? ' asked my father, at the same time making a little search, I suppose, for that which he fancied might have been stolen.

' No ; I did not see her take anything.'

' Well, you are a good girl, Maud. Act discreetly. Say nothing to anyone—not even to your cousin Monica.'

Directions which, coming from another person would have had no great weight, were spoken by my father with an earnest look and a weight of emphasis that made them irresistibly impressive, and I went away with the seal of silence upon my lips.

'Sit down, Maud, *there*. You have not been very happy with Madame de la Rougierre. It is time you were relieved. This occurrence decides it.'

He rang the bell.

'Tell Madame de la Rougierre that I request the honour of seeing her for a few minutes here.'

My father's communications to her were always equally ceremonious. In a few minutes there was a knock at the door, and the same figure, smiling, courtesying, that had scared me on the threshold last night, like the spirit of evil, presented itself.

My father rose, and Madame having at his request taken a chair opposite, looking, as usual in his presence, all amiability, he proceeded at once to the point.

'Madame de la Rougierre, I have to request you that you will give me the key now in your possession, which unlocks this desk of mine.'

With which termination he tapped his gold pencil-case suddenly on it.

Madame, who had expected something very different, became instantly so pale, with a dull purplish hue upon her forehead, that, especially when she had twice essayed with her white lips, in vain, to answer, I expected to see her fall in a fit.

She was not looking in his face; her eyes were fixed lower, and her mouth and cheek sucked in, with a strange distortion at one side.

She stood up suddenly, and staring straight in his face, she succeeded in saying, after twice clearing her throat—

'I cannot comprehend, Monsieur Ruthyn, unless you intend to insult me.'

'It won't do, Madame ; I must have that false key. I give you the opportunity of surrendering it quietly here and now.'

'But who dares to say I possess such thing ?' demanded Madame, who, having rallied from her momentary paralysis, was now fierce and voluble as I had often seen her before.

'You know, Madame, that you can rely on what I say, and I tell you that you were seen last night visiting this room, and with a key in your possession, opening this desk, and reading my letters and papers contained in it. Unless you forthwith give me that key, and any other false keys in your possession—in

which case I shall rest content with dismissing you summarily—
I will take a different course. You know I am a magistrate ;—and
and I shall have you, your boxes, and places up-stairs, searched
forthwith, and I will prosecute you criminally. The thing is
clear ; you aggravate by denying ; you must give me that key,
if you please, instantly, otherwise I ring this bell, and you shall
see that I mean what I say.'

There was a little pause. He rose and extended his hand
towards the bell-rope. Madame glided round the table, extended her hand to arrest his.

' I will do everything, Monsieur Ruthyn—whatever you wish.'

And with these words Madame de la Rougierre broke down
altogether. She sobbed, she wept, she gabbled piteously, all
manner of incomprehensible roulades of lamentation and entreaty ; coyly, penitently, in a most interesting agitation, she
produced the very key from her breast, with a string tied to it.
My father was little moved by this piteous tempest. He coolly
took the key and tried it in the desk, which it locked and unlocked quite freely, though the wards were complicated. He
shook his head and looked her in the face.

' Pray, who made this key ? It is a new one, and made expressly
to pick this lock.'

But Madame was not going to tell any more than she had
expressly bargained for ; so she only fell once more into her
old paroxysm of sorrow, self-reproach, extenuation, and entreaty.

' Well,' said my father, ' I promised that on surrendering the
key you should go. It is enough. I keep my word. You shall
have an hour and a half to prepare in. You must then be ready
to depart. I will send your money to you by Mrs. Rusk ; and if
you look for another situation, you had better not refer to me.
Now be so good as to leave me.'

Madame seemed to be in a strange perplexity. She bridled up,
dried her eyes fiercely, and dropped a great courtesy, and then
sailed away towards the door. Before reaching it she stopped on
the way, turning half round, with a peaked, pallid glance at my
father, and she bit her lip viciously as she eyed him. At the door
the same repulsive pantomime was repeated, as she stood for a
moment with her hand upon the handle. But she changed her
bearing again with a sniff, and with a look of scorn, almost height-

ened to a sneer, she made another very low courtesy and a dis-
dainful toss of her head, and so disappeared, shutting the door
rather sharply behind her.

CHAPTER XIX

AU REVOIR

Mrs. Rusk was fond of assuring me that Madame ' did not like
a bone in my skin.' Instinctively I knew that she bore me no
good-will, although I really believe it was her wish to make me
think quite the reverse. At all events I had no desire to see
Madame again before her departure, especially as she had thrown
upon me one momentary glance in the study, which seemed to
me charged with very peculiar feelings.

You may be very sure, therefore, that I had no desire for a
formal leave-taking at her departure. I took my hat and cloak,
therefore, and stole out quietly.

My ramble was a sequestered one, and well screened, even at
this late season, with foliage ; the pathway devious among the
stems of old trees, and its flooring interlaced and groined with
their knotted roots. Though near the house, it was a sylvan
solitude ; a little brook ran darkling and glimmering through it,
wild strawberries and other woodland plants strewed the ground,
and the sweet notes and flutter of small birds made the shadow
of the boughs cheery.

I had been fully an hour in this picturesque solitude when I
heard in the distance the ring of carriage-wheels, announcing
to me that Madame de la Rougierre had fairly set out upon her
travels. I thanked heaven ; I could have danced and sung with
delight ; I heaved a great sigh and looked up through the
branches to the clear blue sky.

But things are oddly timed. Just at this moment I heard
Madame's voice close at my ear, and her large bony hand was

laid on my shoulder. We were instantly face to face—I recoiling, and for a moment speechless with fright.

In very early youth we do not appreciate the restraints which act upon malignity, or know how effectually fear protects us where conscience is wanting. Quite alone, in this solitary spot, detected and overtaken with an awful instinct by my enemy, what might not be about to happen to me at that moment?

'Frightened as usual, Maud,' she said quietly, and eyeing me with a sinister smile, 'and with cause you think, no doubt. Wat 'av you done to injure poor Madame? Well, I think I know, little girl, and have quite discover the cleverness of my sweet little Maud. Eh—is not so? Petite carogne—ah, ha, ha!'

I was too much confounded to answer.

'You see, my dear cheaile,' she said, shaking her uplifted finger with a hideous archness at me, 'you could not hide what you 'av done from poor Madame. You cannot look so innocent but I can see your pretty little villany quite plain—you dear little diablesse.

'Wat I 'av done I 'av no reproach of myself for it. If I could explain, your papa would say I 'av done right, and you should thank me on your knees; but I cannot explain yet.'

She was speaking, as it were, in little paragraphs, with a momentary pause between each, to allow its meaning to impress itself.

'If I were to choose to explain, your papa he would implore me to remain. But no—I would not—notwithstanding your so cheerful house, your charming servants, your papa's amusing society, and your affectionate and sincere heart, my sweet little maraude.

'I am to go to London first, where I 'av, oh, so good friends! next I will go abroad for some time; but be sure, my sweetest Maud, wherever I may 'appen to be, I will remember you—ah, ha! Yes; *most certainly*, I will remember you.

'And although I shall not be always near, yet I shall know everything about my charming little Maud; you will not know how, but I shall indeed, *everything*. And be sure, my dearest cheaile, I will some time be able to give you the sensible proofs of my gratitude and affection—you understand.

'The carriage is waiting at the yew-tree stile, and I must go on. You did not expect to see me—here; I will appear, per-

haps, as suddenly another time. It is great pleasure to us both—
this opportunity to make our adieux. Farewell ! my dearest little
Maud. I will never cease to think of you, and of some way to
recompense the kindness you 'av shown for poor Madame.'

My hand hung by my side, and she took, not it, but my
thumb, and shook it, folded in her broad palm, and looking on
me as she held it, as if meditating mischief. Then suddenly she
said—

' You will always remember Madame, I *think*, and I will remind you of me beside ; and for the present farewell, and I hope
you may be as 'appy as you deserve.'

The large sinister face looked on me for a second with its latent
sneer, and then, with a sharp nod and a spasmodic shake of my
imprisoned thumb, she turned, and holding her dress together,
and showing her great bony ankles, she strode rapidly away over
the gnarled roots into the perspective of the trees, and I did not
awake, as it were, until she had quite disappeared in the distance.

Events of this kind made no difference with my father ; but
every other face in Knowl was gladdened by the removal. My
energies had returned, my spirits were come again. The sunlight
was happy, the flowers innocent, the songs and flutter of the
birds once more gay, and all nature delightful and rejoicing.

After the first elation of relief, now and then a filmy shadow
of Madame de la Rougierre would glide across the sunlight, and
the remembrance of her menace return with an unexpected pang
of fear.

' Well, if *there* isn't impittens ! ' cried Mrs. Rusk. ' But never
you trouble your head about it, Miss. Them sort's all alike—
you never saw a rogue yet that was found out and didn't
threaten the honest folk as he was leaving behind with all sorts ;
there was Martin the gamekeeper, and Jervis the footman, I
mind well how hard they swore all they would not do when they
was a-going, and who ever heard of them since ? They always
threatens that way—them sort always does, and none ever the
worse—not but she would if she could, mind ye, but there it is ;
she can't do nothing but bite her nails and cuss us—not she—
ha, ha, ha ! '

So I was comforted. But Madame's evil smile, nevertheless,
from time to time, would sail across my vision with a silent

menace, and my spirits sank, and a Fate, draped in black, whose face I could not see, took me by the hand, and led me away, in the spirit, silently, on an awful exploration from which I would rouse myself with a start, and Madame was gone for a while.

She had, however, judged her little parting well. She contrived to leave her glamour over me, and in my dreams she troubled me.

I was, however, indescribably relieved. I wrote in high spirits to Cousin Monica ; and wondered what plans my father might have formed about me, and whether we were to stay at home, or go to London, or go abroad. Of the last—the pleasantest arrangement, in some respects—I had nevertheless an occult horror. A secret conviction haunted me that were we to go abroad, we should there meet Madame, which to me was like meeting my evil genius.

I have said more than once that my father was an odd man ; and the reader will, by this time, have seen that there was much about him not easily understood. I often wonder whether, if he had been franker, I should have found him less odd than I supposed, or more odd still. Things that moved me profoundly did not apparently affect him at all. The departure of Madame, under the circumstances which attended it, appeared to my childish mind an event of the vastest importance. No one was indifferent to the occurrence in the house but its master. He never alluded again to Madame de la Rougierre. But whether connected with her exposure and dismissal, I could not say, there did appear to be some new care or trouble now at work in my father's mind.

'I have been thinking a great deal about you, Maud. I am anxious. I have not been so troubled for years. Why has not Monica Knollys a little more sense ? '

This oracular sentence he spoke, having stopped me in the hall ; and then saying, 'We shall see,' he left me as abruptly as he appeared.

Did he apprehend any danger to me from the vindictiveness of Madame ?

A day or two afterwards, as I was in the Dutch garden, I saw him on the terrace steps. He beckoned to me, and came to meet me as I approached.

'You must be very solitary, little Maud ; it is not good. I

have written to Monica : in a matter of detail she is competent
to advise ; perhaps she will come here for a short visit.'

I was very glad to hear this.

'*You* are more interested than for my time *I* can be, in vindicating his character.'

'Whose character, sir ?' I ventured to enquire during the
pause that followed.

One trick which my father had acquired from his habits of
solitude and silence was this of assuming that the context of his
thoughts was legible to others, forgetting that they had not been
spoken.

'Whose ?—your uncle Silas's. In the course of nature he must
survive me. He will then represent the family name. Would
you make some sacrifice to clear that name, Maud ?'

I answered briefly ; but my face, I believe, showed my enthusiasm.

He turned on me such an approving smile as you might fancy
lighting up the rugged features of a pale old Rembrandt.

'I can tell you, Maud ; if my life could have done it, it should
not have been undone—*ubi lapsus, quid feci*. But I had almost
made up my mind to change my plan, and leave all to time—
edax rerum—to illuminate or to *consume*. But I think little
Maud would like to contribute to the restitution of her family
name. It may cost you something—are you willing to buy it at
a sacrifice ? Is there—I don't speak of fortune, that is not involved—but is there any other honourable sacrifice you would
shrink from to dispel the disgrace under which our most ancient
and honourable name must otherwise continue to languish ?'

'Oh, none—none indeed, sir—I am delighted ! '

Again I saw the Rembrandt smile.

'Well, Maud, I am sure there is *no* risk ; but you are to suppose there is. Are you still willing to accept it ?'

Again I assented.

'You are worthy of your blood, Maud Ruthyn. It will come
soon, and it won't last long. But you must not let people like
Monica Knollys frighten you.'

I was lost in wonder.

'If you allow them to possess you with their follies, you had
better recede in time—they may make the ordeal as terrible as
hell itself. You have zeal—have you nerve ?'

I thought in such a cause I had nerve for anything.

'Well, Maud, in the course of a few months—and it may be sooner—there must be a change. I have had a letter from London this morning that assures me of that. I must then leave you for a time ; in my absence be faithful to the duties that will arise. To whom much is committed, of him will much be required. You shall promise me not to mention this conversation to Monica Knollys. If you are a talking girl, and cannot trust yourself, say so, and we will not ask her to come. Also, don't invite her to talk about your uncle Silas—I have reasons. Do you quite understand my conditions ? '

'Yes, sir.'

'Your uncle Silas,' he said, speaking suddenly in loud and fierce tones that sounded from so old a man almost terrible, 'lies under an intolerable slander. I don't correspond with him ; I don't sympathise with him ; I never quite did. He has grown religious, and that's well ; but there are things in which even religion should not bring a man to acquiesce ; and from what I can learn, he, the person primarily affected—the cause, though the innocent cause—of this great calamity—bears it with an easy apathy which is mistaken, and liable easily to be mistaken, and such as no Ruthyn, under the circumstances, ought to exhibit. I told him what he ought to do, and offered to open my purse for the purpose ; but he would not, or *did* not ; indeed, he *never* took my advice ; he followed his own, and a foul and dismal shoal he has drifted on. It is not for his sake—why should I ?— that I have longed and laboured to remove the disgraceful slur under which his ill-fortune has thrown us. He troubles himself little about it, I believe—he's meek, meeker than I. He cares less about his children than I about you, Maud ; he is selfishly sunk in futurity—a feeble visionary. I am not so. I believe it to be a duty to take care of others beside myself. The character and influence of an ancient family is a peculiar heritage—sacred but destructible ; and woe to him who either destroys or suffers it to perish ! '

This was the longest speech I ever heard my father speak before or after. He abruptly resumed—

'Yes, we will, Maud—you and I—we'll leave one proof on record, which, fairly read, will go far to convince the world.'

He looked round, but we were alone. The garden was nearly

always solitary, and few visitors ever approached the house from that side.

'I have talked too long, I believe ; we are children to the last. Leave me, Maud. I think I know you better than I did, and I am pleased with you. Go, child—I'll sit here.'

If he had acquired new ideas of me, so had I of him from that interview. I had no idea till then how much passion still burned in that aged frame, nor how full of energy and fire that face, generally so stern and ashen, could appear. As I left him seated on the rustic chair, by the steps, the traces of that storm were still discernible on his features. His gathered brows, glowing eyes, and strangely hectic face, and the grim compression of his mouth, still showed the agitation which, somehow, in grey old age, shocks and alarms the young.

CHAPTER XX

AUSTIN RUTHYN SETS OUT ON HIS JOURNEY

The Rev. William Fairfield, Doctor Clay's somewhat bald curate, a mild, thin man, with a high and thin nose, who was preparing me for confirmation, came next day ; and when our catechetical conference was ended, and before lunch was announced, my father sent for him to the study, where he remained until the bell rang out its summons.

'We have had some interesting—I may say *very* interesting— conversation, your papa and I, Miss Ruthyn,' said my reverend *vis-à-vis,* so soon as nature was refreshed, smiling and shining, as he leaned back in his chair, his hand upon the table, and his finger curled gently upon the stem of his wine-glass. 'It never was your privilege, I believe, to see your uncle, Mr. Silas Ruthyn, of Bartram-Haugh ?'

'No—never ; he leads so retired—so *very* retired a life.'

'Oh, no,—of course, no ; but I was going to remark a like-

ness—I mean, of course, a *family* likeness—only *that* sort of
thing—you understand—between him and the profile of Lady
Margaret in the drawing-room—is not it Lady Margaret?—
which you were so good as to show me on Wednesday last. There
certainly *is* a likeness. I *think* you would agree with me, if you
had the pleasure of seeing your uncle.'

' You know him, then ? I have never seen him.'

' Oh dear, yes—I am happy to say, I know him very well. I
have that privilege. I was for three years curate of Feltram, and
I had the honour of being a pretty constant visitor at Bartram-
Haugh during that, I may say, protracted period ; and I think
it really never has been my privilege and happiness, I may say,
to enjoy the acquaintance and society of so very experienced a
Christian, as my admirable friend, I may call him, Mr. Ruthyn,
of Bartram-Haugh. I look upon him, I do assure you, quite in
the light of a saint ; not, of course, in the Popish sense, but in
the very highest, you will understand me, which *our* Church
allows,—a man built up in faith—full of faith—faith and grace—
altogether exemplary ; and I often ventured to regret, Miss
Ruthyn, that Providence in its mysterious dispensations should
have placed him so far apart from his brother, your respected
father. His influence and opportunities would, no doubt, we may
venture to hope, at least have been blessed ; and, perhaps, we—
my valued rector and I—might possibly have seen more of him at
church, than, I deeply regret, we *have* done.' He shook his head
a little, as he smiled with a sad complacency on me through his
blue steel spectacles, and then sipped a little meditative sherry.

' And you saw a good deal of my uncle ? '

' Well, a *good* deal, Miss Ruthyn—I may say a *good* deal—
principally at his own house. His health is wretched—miserable
health—a sadly afflicted man he has been, as, no doubt, you are
aware. But afflictions, my dear Miss Ruthyn, as you remember
Doctor Clay so well remarked on Sunday last, though birds of
ill omen, yet spiritually resemble the ravens who supplied the
prophet ; and when they visit the faithful, come charged with
nourishment for the soul.

' He is a good deal embarrassed pecuniarily, I should say,'
continued the curate, who was rather a good man than a very
well-bred one. ' He found a difficulty—in fact it was not in his
power—to subscribe generally to our little funds, and—and

objects, and I used to say to him, and I really felt it, that it was more gratifying, such were his feeling and his power of expression, to be refused by him than assisted by others.'

' Did papa wish you to speak to me about my uncle ? ' I enquired, as a sudden thought struck me ; and then I felt half ashamed of my question.

He looked surprised.

' No, Miss Ruthyn, certainly not. Oh dear, no. It was merely a conversation between Mr. Ruthyn and me. He never suggested my opening that, or indeed any other point in my interview with you, Miss Ruthyn—not the least.'

' I was not aware before that Uncle Silas was so religious.'

He smiled tranquilly, not quite up to the ceiling, but gently upward, and shook his head in pity for my previous ignorance, as he lowered his eyes—

' I don't say that there may not be some little matters in a few points of doctrine which we could, perhaps, wish otherwise. But these, you know, are speculative, and in all essentials he is Church—not in the perverted modern sense ; far from it— unexceptionably Church, strictly so. Would there were more among us of the same mind that is in him ! Ay, Miss Ruthyn, even in the highest places of the Church herself.'

The Rev. William Fairfield, while fighting against the Dissenters with his right hand, was, with his left, hotly engaged with the Tractarians. A good man I am sure he was, and I dare say sound in doctrine, though naturally, I think, not very wise. This conversation with him gave me new ideas about my uncle Silas. It quite agreed with what my father had said. These principles and his increasing years would necessarily quiet the turbulence of his resistance to injustice, and teach him to acquiesce in his fate.

You would have fancied that one so young as I, born to wealth so vast, and living a life of such entire seclusion, would have been exempt from care. But you have seen how troubled my life was with fear and anxiety during the residence of Madame de la Rougierre, and now there rested upon my mind a vague and awful anticipation of the trial which my father had announced, without defining it.

An ' ordeal ' he called it, requiring not only zeal but nerve, which might possibly, were my courage to fail, become frightful, and even intolerable. What, and of what nature, could it be ? Not designed to vindicate the fair fame of the meek and sub- missive old man — who, it seemed, had ceased to care for his bygone wrongs, and was looking to futurity—but the reputation of our ancient family.

Sometimes I repented my temerity in having undertaken it. I distrusted my courage. Had I not better retreat, while it was yet time ? But there was shame and even difficulty in the thought. How should I appear before my father ? Was it not important— had I not deliberately undertaken it—and was I not bound in conscience ? Perhaps he had already taken steps in the matter which committed *him*. Besides, was I sure that, even were I free again, I would not once more devote myself to the trial, be it what it might ? You perceive I had more spirit than courage. I think I had the mental attributes of courage ; but then I was but a hysterical girl, and in so far neither more nor less than a coward.

No wonder I distrusted myself ; no wonder also my will stood out against my timidity. It was a struggle, then ; a proud, wild resolve against constitutional cowardice.

Those who have ever had cast upon them more than their strength seemed framed to bear—the weak, the aspiring, the ad- venturous and self-sacrificing in will, and the faltering in nerve— will understand the kind of agony which I sometimes endured.

But, again, consolation would come, and it seemed to me that I must be exaggerating my risk in the coming crisis ; and cer- tain at least, if my father believed it attended with real peril, he would never have wished to see me involved in it. But the si- lence under which I was bound was terrifying—double so when the danger was so shapeless and undivulged.

I was soon to understand it all—soon, too, to know all about my father's impending journey, whither, with what visitor, and why guarded from me with so awful a mystery.

That day there came a lively and goodnatured letter from Lady Knollys. She was to arrive at Knowl in two or three days' time. I thought my father would have been pleased, but he seemed apathetic and dejected.

'One does not always feel quite equal to Monica. But for you—yes, thank God. I wish she could only stay, Maud, for a month or two ; I may be going then, and would be glad—provided she talks about suitable things—very glad, Maud, to leave her with you for a week or so.'

There was something, I thought, agitating my father secretly that day. He had the strange hectic flush I had observed when he grew excited in our interview in the garden about Uncle Silas. There was something painful, perhaps even terrible, in the circumstances of the journey he was about to make, and from my heart I wished the suspense were over, the annoyance past, and he returned.

That night my father bid me good-night early and went up-stairs. After I had been in bed some little time, I heard his hand-bell ring. This was not usual. Shortly after I heard his man, Ridley, talking with Mrs. Rusk in the gallery. I could not be mistaken in their voices. I knew not why I was startled and excited, and had raised myself to listen on my elbow. But they were talking quietly, like persons giving or taking an ordinary direction, and not in the haste of an unusual emergency.

Then I heard the man bid Mrs. Rusk good-night and walk down the gallery to the stairs, so that I concluded he was wanted no more, and all must therefore be well. So I laid myself down again, though with a throbbing at my heart, and an ominous feeling of expectation, listening and fancying footsteps.

I was going to sleep when I heard the bell ring again ; and, in a few minutes, Mrs. Rusk's energetic step passed along the gallery ; and, listening intently, I heard, or fancied, my father's voice and hers in dialogue. All this was very unusual, and again I was, with a beating heart, leaning with my elbow on my pillow.

Mrs. Rusk came along the gallery in a minute or so after, and stopping at my door, began to open it gently. I was startled, and challenged my visitor with—

'Who's there ? '

'It's only Rusk, Miss. Dearie me ! and are you awake still ? '

'Is papa ill ? '

'Ill ! not a bit ill, thank God. Only there's a little black book as I took for your prayer-book, and brought in here ; ay, here it is, sure enough, and he wants it. And then I must go down to the study, and look out this one, " C, 15 ; " but I can't read the name, noways ; and I was afraid to ask him again ; if you be so kind to read it, Miss—I suspeck my eyes is a-going.'

I read the name ; and Mrs. Rusk was tolerably expert at finding out books, as she had often been employed in that way before. So she departed.

I suppose that this particular volume was hard to find, for she must have been a long time away, and I had actually fallen into a doze when I was roused in an instant by a dreadful crash and a piercing scream from Mrs. Rusk. Scream followed scream, wilder and more terror-stricken. I shrieked to Mary Quince, who was sleeping in the room with me :—' Mary, do you hear ? what is it ? It is something dreadful.'

The crash was so tremendous that the solid flooring even of my room trembled under it, and to me it seemed as if some heavy man had burst through the top of the window, and shook the whole house with his descent. I found myself standing at my own door, crying, ' Help, help ! murder ! murder ! ' and Mary Quince, frightened half out of her wits, by my side.

I could not think what was going on. It was plainly something most horrible, for Mrs. Rusk's screams pealed one after the other unabated, though with a muffled sound, as if the door was shut upon her ; and by this time the bells of my father's room were ringing madly.

' They are trying to murder him ! ' I cried, and I ran along the gallery to his door, followed by Mary Quince, whose white face I shall never forget, though her entreaties only sounded like unmeaning noises in my ears.

' Here ! help, help, help ! ' I cried, trying to force open the door.

' Shove it, shove it, for God's sake ! he's across it,' cried Mrs. Rusk's voice from within ; ' drive it in. I can't move him.'

I strained all I could at the door, but ineffectually. We heard steps approaching. The men were running to the spot, and shouting as they did so—

' Never mind ; hold on a bit ; here we are ; all right ;' and the like.

We drew back, as they came up. We were in no condition to be seen. We listened, however, at my open door.

Then came the straining and bumping at the door. Mrs. Rusk's voice subsided to a sort of wailing ; the men were talking all together, and I suppose the door opened, for I heard some of the voices, on a sudden, as if in the room ; and then came a

strange lull, and talking in very low tones, and not much even
of that.

'What is it, Mary? what *can* it be?' I ejaculated, not knowing what horror to suppose. And now, with a counterpane about
my shoulders, I called loudly and imploringly, in my horror, to
know what had happened.

But I heard only the subdued and eager talk of men engaged
in some absorbing task, and the dull sounds of some heavy
body being moved.

Mrs. Rusk came towards us looking half wild, and pale as a
spectre, and putting her thin hands to my shoulders, she said—
'Now, Miss Maud, darling, you must go back again; 'tisn't no
place for you; you'll see all, my darling, time enough—you will.
There now, there, like a dear, do get into your room.'

What was that dreadful sound? Who had entered my father's
chamber? It was the visitor whom we had so long expected,
with whom he was to make the unknown journey, leaving me
alone. The intruder was Death!

CHAPTER XXI

ARRIVALS

My father was dead—as suddenly as if he had been murdered.
One of those fearful aneurisms that lie close to the heart, showing no outward sign of giving way in a moment, had been detected a good time since by Dr. Bryerly. My father knew what
must happen, and that it could not be long deferred. He feared
to tell me that he was soon to die. He hinted it only in the alle-
gory of his journey, and left in that sad enigma some words of
true consolation that remained with me ever after. Under his
rugged ways was hidden a wonderful tenderness. I could not
believe that he was actually dead. Most people for a minute or
two, in the wild tumult of such a shock, have experienced the

same skepticism. I insisted that the doctor should be instantly
sent for from the village.

'Well, Miss Maud, dear, I *will* send to please you, but it is
all to no use. If only you saw him yourself you'd know that.
Mary Quince, run you down and tell Thomas, Miss Maud de-
sires he'll go down this minute to the village for Dr. Elweys.'

Every minute of the interval seemed to me like an hour. I
don't know what I said, but I fancied that if he were not already dead, he would lose his life by the delay. I suppose I was
speaking very wildly, for Mrs. Rusk said—

'My dear child, you ought to come in and see him ; indeed
but you should, Miss Maud. He's quite dead an hour ago. You'd
wonder all the blood that's come from him—you would indeed ;
it's soaked through the bed already.'

'Oh, don't, don't, *don't*, Mrs. Rusk.'

'Will you come in and see him, just ?'

'Oh, no, no, no, no !"

'Well, then, my dear, don't of course, if you don't like ;
there's no need. Would not you like to lie down, Miss Maud ?
Mary Quince, attend to her. I must go into the room for a
minute or two.'

I was walking up and down the room in distraction. It was a
cool night ; but I did not feel it. I could only cry :—' Oh, Mary,
Mary ! what shall I do ? Oh, Mary Quince ! what shall I do ? '

It seemed to me it must be near daylight by the time the
Doctor arrived. I had dressed myself. I dared not go into the
room where my beloved father lay.

I had gone out of my room to the gallery, where I awaited
Dr. Elweys, when I saw him walking briskly after the servant,
his coat buttoned up to his chin, his hat in his hand, and his
bald head shining. I felt myself grow cold as ice, and colder and
colder, and with a sudden sten my heart seemed to stand still.

I heard him ask the maid who stood at the door, in that
low, decisive, mysterious tone which doctors cultivate—

'In *here* ? '

And then, with a nod, I saw him enter.

'Would not you like to see the Doctor, Miss Maud ? ' asked
Mary Quince.

The question roused me a little.

'Thank you, Mary ; yes, I must see him.'

And so, in a few minutes, I did. He was very respectful, very sad, semi-undertakerlike, in air and countenance, but quite explicit. I heard that my dear father ' had died palpably from the rupture of some great vessel near the heart.' The disease had, no doubt, been ' long established, and is in its nature incurable.' It is ' consolatory in these cases that in the act of dissolution, which is instantaneous, there can be no suffering.' These, and a few more remarks, were all he had to offer ; and having had his fee fom Mrs. Rusk, he, with a respectful melancholy, vanished.

I returned to my room, and broke into paroxysms of grief, and after an hour or more grew more tranquil.

From Mrs. Rusk I learned that he had seemed very well—better than usual, indeed—that night, and that on her return from the study with the book he required, he was noting down, after his wont, some passages which illustrated the text on which he was employing himself. He took the book, detaining her in the room, and then mounting on a chair to take down another book from a shelf, he had fallen, with the dreadful crash I had heard, dead upon the floor. He fell across the door, which caused the difficulty in opening it. Mrs. Rusk found she had not strength to force it open. No wonder she had given way to terror. I think I should have almost lost my reason.

Everyone knows the reserved aspect and the taciturn mood of the house, one of whose rooms is tenanted by that mysterious guest.

I do not know how those awful days, and more awful nights, passed over. The remembrance is repulsive. I hate to think of them. I was soon draped in the conventional black, with its heavy folds of crape. Lady Knollys came, and was very kind. She undertook the direction of all those details which were to me so inexpressibly dreadful. She wrote letters for me beside, and was really most kind and useful, and her society supported me indescribably. She was odd, but her eccentricity was leavened with strong common sense ; and I have often thought since with admiration and gratitude of the tact with which she managed my grief.

There is no dealing with great sorrow as if it were under the control of our wills. It is a terrible phenomenon, whose laws we must study, and to whose conditions we must submit, if we would mitigate it. Cousin Monica talked a great deal of my father. This was easy to her, for her early recollections were full of him.

One of the terrible dislocations of our habits of mind respecting the dead is that our earthly future is robbed of them, and we thrown exclusively upon retrospect. From the long look forward they are removed, and every plan, imagination, and hope henceforth a silent and empty perspective. But in the past they are all they ever were. Now let me advise all who would comfort people in a new bereavement to talk to them, very freely, all they can, in this way of the dead. They will engage in it with interest, they will talk of their own recollections of the dead, and listen to yours, though they become sometimes pleasant, sometimes even laughable. I found it so. It robbed the calamity of something of its supernatural and horrible abruptness; it prevented that monotony of object which is to the mind what it is to the eye, and prepared the faculty for those mesmeric illusions that derange its sense.

Cousin Monica, I am sure, cheered me wonderfully. I grow to love her more and more, as I think of all her trouble, care, and kindness.

I had not forgotten my promise to dear papa about the key, concerning which he had evinced so great an anxiety. It was found in the pocket where he had desired me to remember he always kept it, except when it was placed, while he slept, under his pillow.

'And so, my dear, that wicked woman was actually found picking the lock of your poor papa's desk. I *wonder* he did not punish her—you know that is *burglary*.'

'Well, Lady Knollys, you know she is gone, and so I care no more about her—that is, I mean, I need not fear her.'

'No, my dear, but you must call me Monica—do you mind— I'm your cousin, and you call me Monica, unless you wish to vex me. No, of course, you need not be afraid of her. And she's gone. But I'm an old thing, you know, and not so tender-hearted as you; and I confess I should have been very glad to hear that the wicked old witch had been sent to prison and hard labour—I should. And what do you suppose she was looking for—what did she want to steal? I think I can guess—what do *you* think?'

' To read the papers ; maybe to take bank-notes—I'm not sure,'
I answered.

' Well, I think most likely she wanted to get at your poor
papa's *will*—that's *my* idea.

' There is nothing surprising in the supposition, dear,' she
resumed. 'Did not you read the curious trial at York, the other
day ? There is nothing so valuable to steal as a will, when a
great deal of property is to be disposed of by it. Why, you would
have given her ever so much money to get it back again. Suppose you go down, dear—I'll go with you, and open the cabinet
in the study.'

' I don't think I can, for I promised to give the key to Dr.
Bryerly, and the meaning was that *he* only should open it.'

Cousin Monica uttered an inarticulate ' H'm ! ' of surprise
or disapprobation.

' Has he been written to ?'

' No, I do not know his address.'

' Not know his address ! come, that is curious,' said Knollys,
a little testily.

I could not—no one now living in the house could furnish
even a conjecture. There was even a dispute as to which train he
had gone by—north or south—they crossed the station at an interval of five minutes. If Dr. Bryerly had been an evil spirit,
evoked by a secret incantation, there could not have been more
complete darkness as to the immediate process of his approach.

' And how long do you mean to wait, my dear ? No matter ;
at all events you may open the *desk* ; you may find papers to
direct you—you may find Dr. Bryerly's address—you may find,
heaven knows what.'

So down we went—I assenting—and we opened the desk. How
dreadful the desecration seems—all privacy abrogated—the shocking compensation for the silence of death !

Henceforward all is circumstantial evidence—all conjectural—
except the *litera scripta,* and to this evidence every note-book,
and every scrap of paper and private letter, must contribute—
ransacked, bare in the light of day—what it can.

At the top of the desk lay two notes sealed, one to Cousin
Monica, the other to me. Mine was a gentle and loving little
farewell — nothing more — which opened afresh the fountains
of my sorrow, and I cried and sobbed over it bitterly and long.

The other was for ' Lady Knollys.' I did not see how she received it, for I was already absorbed in mine. But in awhile she came and kissed me in her girlish, goodnatured way. Her eyes used to fill with tears at sight of my paroxysms of grief. Then she would begin, ' I remember it was a saying of his,' and so she would repeat it—something maybe wise, maybe playful, at all events consolatory—and the circumstances in which she had heard him say it, and then would follow the recollections suggested by these ; and so I was stolen away half by him, and half by Cousin Monica, from my despair and lamentation.

Along with these lay a large envelope, inscribed with the words ' Directions to be complied with immediately on my death.' One of which was, ' Let the event be *forthwith* published in the *county* and principal *London* papers.' This step had been already taken. We found no record of Dr. Bryerly's address.

We made search everywhere, except in the cabinet, which I would on no account permit to be opened except, according to his direction, by Dr. Bryerly's hand. But nowhere was a will, or any document resembling one, to be found. I had now, therefore, no doubt that his will was placed in the cabinet.

In the search among my dear father's papers we found two sheafs of letters, neatly tied up and labelled—these were from my uncle Silas.

My cousin Monica looked down upon these papers with a strange smile ; was it satire—was it that indescribable smile with which a mystery which covers a long reach of years is sometimes approached ?

These were odd letters. If here and there occurred passages that were querulous and even abject, there were also long passages of manly and altogether noble sentiment, and the strangest rodomontade and maunderings about religion. Here and there a letter would gradually transform itself into a prayer, and end with a doxology and no signature ; and some of them expressed such wild and disordered views respecting religion, as I imagine he can never have disclosed to good Mr. Fairfield, and which approached more nearly to the Swedenborg visions than to anything in the Church of England.

I read these with a solemn interest, but my cousin Monica was not similarly moved. She read them with the same smile

—faint, serenely contemptuous, I thought—with which she had first looked down upon them. It was the countenance of a person who amusedly traces the working of a character that is well understood.

'Uncle Silas is very religious ? ' I said, not quite liking Lady Knollys' looks.

'Very,' she said, without raising her eyes or abating her old bitter smile, as she glanced over a passage in one of his letters.

'You don't think he *is*, Cousin Monica ? ' said I. She raised her head and looked straight at me.

'Why do you say that, Maud ? '

'Because you smile incredulously, I think, over his letters.'

'Do I ?' said she ; 'I was not thinking—it was quite an accident. The fact is, Maud, your poor papa quite mistook me. I had no prejudice respecting him—no theory. I never knew what to think about him. I do not think Silas a product of nature, but a child of the Sphinx, and I never could understand him—that's all.'

'I always felt so too ; but that was because I was left to speculation, and to glean conjectures as I might from his portrait, or anywhere. Except what you told me, I never heard more than a few sentences ; poor papa did not like me to ask questions about him, and I think he ordered the servants to be silent.'

'And much the same injunction this little note lays upon me —not quite, but something like it ; and I don't know the meaning of it.'

And she looked enquiringly at me.

'You are not to be *alarmed* about your uncle Silas, because your being afraid would unfit you for an *important service* which you have undertaken for your family, the nature of which I shall soon understand, and which, although it is quite *passive,* would be made very sad if *illusory fears* were allowed to *steal into your mind.*'

She was looking into the letter in poor papa's handwriting, which she had found addressed to her in his desk, and emphasised the words, I suppose, which she quoted from it.

'Have you any idea, Maud, darling, what this *service* may be ? ' she enquired, with a grave and anxious curiosity in her countenance.

'None, Cousin Monica ; but I have thought long over my un-

dertaking to do it, or submit to it, be it what it may ; and I will
keep the promise I voluntarily made, although I know what a
coward I am, and often distrust my courage.'

' Well, I am not to frighten you.'

' How could you ? Why should I be afraid ? *Is* there anything frightful to be disclosed ? Do tell me—you *must* tell me.'

' No, darling, I did not mean *that*—I don't mean that ;—I
could, if I would ; I—I don't know exactly what I meant. But
your poor papa knew him better than I—in fact, I did not know
him at all—that is, ever quite understood him—which your poor
papa, I see, had ample opportunities of doing.' And after a
little pause, she added—' So you do not know what you are
expected to do or to undergo.'

' Oh ! Cousin Monica, I know you think he committed that
murder,' I cried, starting up, I don't know why, and I felt that I
grew deadly pale.

' I don't believe any such thing, you little fool ; you must not
say such horrible things, Maud,' she said, rising also, and looking both pale and angry. ' Shall we go out for a little walk ?
Come, lock up these papers, dear, and get your things on ;
and if that Dr. Bryerly does not turn up to-morrow, you must
send for the Rector, good Doctor Clay, and let him make search
for the will—there may be directions about many things, you
know ; and, my dear Maud, you are to remember that Silas is
my cousin as well as your uncle. Come, dear, put on your hat.'

So we went out together for a little cloistered walk.

CHAPTER XXII

SOMEBODY IN THE ROOM WITH THE COFFIN

When we returned, a ' young ' gentleman had arrived. We saw
him in the parlour as we passed the window. It was simply a
glance, but such a one as suffices to make a photograph, which

we can study afterwards, at our leisure. I remember him at this moment—a man of six-and-thirty—dressed in a grey travelling suit, not over-well made ; light-haired, fat-faced, and clumsy ; and he looked both dull and cunning, and not at all like a gentleman.

Branston met us, announced the arrival, and handed me the stranger's credentials. My cousin and I stopped in the passage to read them.

' *That's* your uncle Silas's,' said Lady Knollys, touching one of the two letters with the tip of her finger.

' Shall we have lunch, Miss ? '

' Certainly.' So Branston departed.

' Read it with me, Cousin Monica,' I said. And a very curious letter it was. It spoke as follows :—

' How can I thank my beloved niece for remembering her aged and forlorn kinsman at such a moment of anguish ? '

I had written a note of a few, I dare say, incoherent words by the next post after my dear father's death.

' It is, however, in the hour of bereavement that we most value the ties that are broken, and yearn for the sympathy of kindred.'

Here came a little distich of French verse, of which I could only read *ciel* and *l'amour*.

' Our quiet household here is clouded with a new sorrow. How inscrutable are the ways of Providence ! I—though a few years younger—how much the more infirm—how shattered in energy and in mind—how mere a burden—how entirely *de trop*—am spared to my sad place in a world where I can be no longer use- ful, where I have but one business—prayer, but one hope—the tomb ; and he—apparently so robust—the centre of so much good—so necessary to you—so necessary, alas ! to me—is taken ! He is gone to his rest—for us, what remains but to bow our heads, and murmur, " His will be done"? I trace these lines with a trembling hand, while tears dim my old eyes. I did not think that any earthly event could have moved me so pro- foundly. From the world I have long stood aloof. I once led a life of pleasure—alas ! of wickedness—as I now do one of aus- terity ; but as I never was rich, so my worst enemy will allow I never was avaricious. My sins, I thank my Maker, have been of

a more reducible kind, and have succumbed to the discipline
which Heaven has provided. To earth and its interests, as well
as to its pleasures, I have long been dead. For the few remaining
years of my life I ask but quiet—an exemption from the agitations and distractions of struggle and care, and I trust to the
Giver of all Good for my deliverance—well knowing, at the
same time, that whatever befalls will, under His direction,
prove best. Happy shall I be, my dearest niece, if in your most
interesting and, in some respects, forlorn situation, I can be of
any use to you. My present religious adviser—of whom I ventured to ask counsel on your behalf—states that I ought to send
some one to represent me at the melancholy ceremony of reading
the will which my beloved and now happy brother has, no doubt,
left behind ; and the idea that the experience and professional
knowledge possessed by the gentleman whom I have selected
may possibly be of use to you, my dearest niece, determines me
to place him at your disposal. He is the junior partner in the
firm of Archer and Sleigh, who conduct any little business which
I may have from time to time ; may I entreat your hospitality
for him during a brief stay at Knowl ? I write, even for a moment, upon these small matters of business with an effort—a
painful one, but necessary. Alas ! my brother ! The cup of bitterness is now full. Few and evil must the remainder of my old
days be. Yet, while they last, I remain always for my beloved
niece, that which all her wealth and splendour cannot purchase
—a loving and faithful kinsman and friend,

                                        SILAS RUTHYN.'

   ' Is not it a kind letter ? ' I said, while tears stood in my eyes.
   ' Yes,' answered Lady Knollys, drily.
   ' But don't you think it so, really ? '
   ' Oh ! kind, very kind,' she answered in the same tone, ' and
perhaps a little cunning.'
   ' Cunning !—how ? '
   ' Well, you know I'm a peevish old Tabby, and of course I
scratch now and then, and see in the dark. I dare say Silas is
sorry, but I don't think he is in sackcloth and ashes. He has
reason to be sorry and anxious, and I say I think he is both ;
and you know he pities you very much, and also himself a good
deal ; and he wants money, and you—his beloved niece—have a

great deal—and altogether it is an affectionate and prudent letter : and he has sent his attorney here to make a note of the
will ; and you are to give the gentleman his meals and lodging ;
and Silas, very thoughtfully, invites you to confide your diffi-
cuties and troubles to *his* solicitor. It is very kind, but not imprudent.'

' Oh, Cousin Monica, don't you think at such a moment it is
hardly natural that he should form such petty schemes, even
were he capable at other times of practising so low ? Is it not
judging him hardly ? and you, you know, so little acquainted
with him.'

' I told you, dear, I'm a cross old thing—and there's an end ;
and I really don't care two pence about him ; and of the two
I'd much rather he were no relation of ours.'

Now, was not this prejudice ? I dare say in part it was. So,
too, was my vehement predisposition in his favour. I am afraid
we women are factionists ; we always take a side, and nature has
formed us for advocates rather than judges ; and I think the
function, if less dignified, is more amiable.

I sat alone at the drawing-room window, at nightfall, awaiting
my cousin Monica's entrance.

Feverish and frightened I felt that night. It was a sympathy,
I fancy, with the weather. The sun had set stormily. Though the
air was still, the sky looked wild and storm-swept. The crowd-
ing clouds, slanting in the attitude of flight, reflected their own
sacred aspect upon my spirits. My grief darkened with a wild
presaging of danger, and a sense of the supernatural fell upon
me. It was the saddest and most awful evening that had come
since my beloved father's death.

All kinds of shapeless fears environed me in silence. For the
first time, dire misgivings about the form of faith affrighted me.
Who were these Swedenborgians who had got about him—no one
could tell how—and held him so fast to the close of his life?
Who was this bilious, bewigged, black-eyed Doctor Bryerly,
whom none of us quite liked and all a little feared ; who seemed
to rise out of the ground, and came and went, no one knew
whence or whither, exercising, as I imagined, a mysterious authority over him ? Was it all good and true, or a heresy and a
witchcraft ? Oh, my beloved father ! was it all well with you ?

When Lady Knollys entered, she found me in floods of tears,

walking distractedly up and down the room. She kissed me in silence ; she walked back and forward with me, and did her best to console me.

' I think, Cousin Monica, I would wish to see him once more. Shall we go up ? '

' Unless you really wish it very much, I think, darling, you had better not mind it. It is happier to recollect them as they were ; there's a change, you know, darling, and there is seldom any comfort in the sight.'

' But I do wish it *very* much. Oh ! won't you come with me ? '

And so I persuaded her, and up we went hand in hand, in the deepening twilight ; and we halted at the end of the dark gallery, and I called Mrs. Rusk, growing frightened.

' Tell her to let us in, Cousin Monica,' I whispered.

' She wishes to see him, my lady—does she ? ' enquired Mrs. Rusk, in an under-tone, and with a mysterious glance at me, as she softly fitted the key to the lock.

' Are you quite sure, Maud, dear ? '

' Yes, yes.'

But when Mrs. Rusk entered bearing the candle, whose beam mixed dismally with the expiring twilight, disclosing a great black coffin standing upon trestles, near the foot of which she took her stand, gazing sternly into it, I lost heart again altogether and drew back.

' No, Mrs. Rusk, she won't ; and I am very glad, dear,' she added to me. ' Come, Mrs. Rusk, come away. Yes, darling,' she continued to me, ' it is much better for you ; ' and she hurried me away, and down-stairs again. But the awful outlines of that large black coffin remained upon my imagination with a new and terrible sense of death.

I had no more any wish to see him. I felt a horror even of the room, and for more than an hour after a kind of despair and terror, such as I have never experienced before or since at the idea of death.

Cousin Monica had had her bed placed in my room, and Mary Quince's moved to the dressing-room adjoining it. For the first time the superstitious awe that follows death, but not immediately, visited me. The idea of seeing my father enter the room, or open the door and look in, haunted me. After Lady Knollys and I were in bed, I could not sleep. The wind sounded mournfully outside, and the small sounds, the rattlings, and strainings that responded from within, constantly startled me, and simulated the sounds of steps, of doors opening, of knockings, and so forth, rousing me with a palpitating heart as often as I fell into a doze.

At length the wind subsided, and these ambiguous noises abated, and I, fatigued, dropped into a quiet sleep. I was awakened by a sound in the gallery—which I could not define. A considerable time had passed, for the wind was now quite lulled. I sat up in my bed a good deal scared, listening breathlessly for I knew not what.

I heard a step moving stealthily along the gallery. I called my cousin Monica softly; and we both heard the door of the room in which my father's body lay unlocked, some one furtively enter, and the door shut.

'What can it be? Good Heavens, Cousin Monica, do you hear it?'

'Yes, dear; and it is two o'clock.'

Everyone at Knowl was in bed at eleven. We knew very well that Mrs. Rusk was rather nervous, and would not, for worlds, go alone, and at such an hour, to the room. We called Mary Quince. We all three listened, but we heard no other sound. I set these things down here because they made so terrible an impression upon me at the time.

It ended by our peeping out, all three in a body, upon the gallery. Through each window in the perspective came its blue sheet of moonshine; but the door on which our attention was fixed was in the shade, and we thought we could discern the glare of a candle through the key-hole. While in whispers we were debating this point together, the door opened, the dusky light of a candle emerged, the shadow of a figure crossed it within, and in another moment the mysterious Doctor Bryerly—angular, ungainly, in the black cloth coat that fitted little better than a coffin—issued from the chamber, candle in hand; murmuring, I suppose, a prayer—it sounded like a farewell—stepped cautiously upon the gallery floor, shutting and locking the door upon the dead; and then having listened for a second, the saturnine figure, casting a gigantic and distorted shadow

upon the ceiling and side-wall from the lowered candle, strode
lightly down the long dark passage, away from us.

I can only speak for myself, and I can honestly say that I felt
as much frightened as if I had just seen a sorcerer stealing
from his unhallowed business. I think Cousin Monica was also
affected in the same way, for she turned the key on the inside
of the door when we entered. I do not think one of us believed
at the moment that what we had seen was a Doctor Bryerly of
flesh and blood, and yet the first thing we spoke of in the
morning was Doctor Bryerly's arrival. The mind is a different
organ by night and by day.

CHAPTER XXIII

I TALK WITH DOCTOR BRYERLY

Doctor Bryerly had, indeed, arrived at half-past twelve o'clock
at night. His summons at the hall-door was little heard at our
remote side of the old house of Knowl ; and when the sleepy,
half-dressed servant opened the door, the lank Doctor, in glossy
black clothing, was standing alone, his portmanteau on its end
upon the steps, and his vehicle disappearing in the shadows of
the old trees.

In he came, sterner and sharper of aspect than usual.

' I've been expected ? I'm Doctor Bryerly. Haven't I ? So,
let whoever is in charge of the body be called. I must visit it
forthwith.'

So the Doctor sat in the back drawing-room, with a solitary
candle ; and Mrs. Rusk was called up, and, grumbling much and
very peevish, dressed and went down, her ill-temper subsiding in
a sort of fear as she approached the visitor.

' How do you do, Madam ? A sad visit this. Is anyone watching in the room where the remains of your late master are
laid ? '

' No.'

' So much the better ; it is a foolish custom. Will you please conduct me to the room ? I must pray where he lies—no longer *he !* And be good enough to show me my bedroom, and so no one need wait up, and I shall find my way.'

Accompanied by the man who carried his valise, Mrs. Rusk showed him to his apartment ; but he only looked in, and then glanced rapidly about to take ' the bearings ' of the door.

' Thank you—yes. Now we'll proceed, here, along here ? Let me see. A turn to the right and another to the left—yes. He has been dead some days. Is he yet in his coffin ? '

' Yes, sir ; since yesterday afternoon.'

Mrs. Rusk was growing more and more afraid of this lean figure sheathed in shining black cloth, whose eyes glittered with a horrible sort of cunning, and whose long brown fingers groped before him, as if indicating the way by guess.

' But, of course, the lid's not on ; you've not screwed him down, hey ? '

' No, sir.'

' That's well. I must look on the face as I pray. He is in his place ; I here on earth. He in the spirit ; I in the flesh. The neutral ground lies there. So are carried the vibrations, and so the light of earth and heaven reflected back and forward—apaugasma, a wonderful though helpless engine, the ladder of Jacob, and behold the angels of God ascending and descending on it. Thanks, I'll take the key. Mysteries to those who *will* live altogether in houses of clay, no mystery to such as will use their eyes and read what is revealed. *This* candle, it is the longer, please ; no—no need of a pair, thanks ; just this, to hold in my hand. And remember, all depends upon the willing mind. Why do you look frightened ? Where is your faith ? Don't you know that spirits are about us at all times ? Why should you fear to be near the body ? The spirit is everything ; the flesh profiteth nothing.'

' Yes, sir,' said Mrs. Rusk, making him a great courtesy in the threshold.

She was frightened by his eerie talk, which grew, she fancied, more voluble and energetic as they approached the corpse.

' Remember, then, that when you fancy yourself alone and wrapt in darkness, you stand, in fact, in the centre of a theatre, as wide as the starry floor of heaven, with an audience, whom no man can number, beholding you under a flood of light. Therefore, though your body be in solitude and your mortal sense in darkness, remember to walk as being in the light, surrounded with a cloud of witnesses. Thus walk ; and when the hour comes, and you pass forth unprisoned from the tabernacle of the flesh, although it still has its relations and its rights '— and saying this, as he held the solitary candle aloft in the doorway, he nodded towards the coffin, whose large black form was faintly traceable against the shadows beyond—' you will rejoice ; and being clothed upon with your house from on high, you will not be found naked. On the other hand, he that loveth corruption shall have enough thereof. Think upon these things. Goodnight. '

And the Swedenborgian Doctor stepped into the room, taking the candle with him, and closed the door upon the shadowy still-life there, and on his own sharp and swarthy visage, leaving Mrs. Rusk in a sort of panic in the dark alone, to find her way to her room the best way she could.

Early in the morning Mrs. Rusk came to my room to tell me that Doctor Bryerly was in the parlour, and begged to know whether I had not a message for him. I was already dressed, so, though it was dreadful seeing a stranger in my then mood, taking the key of the cabinet in my hand, I followed Mrs. Rusk downstairs.

Opening the parlour door, she stepped in, and with a little courtesy said,—

' Please, sir, the young mistress—Miss Ruthyn.'

Draped in black and very pale, tall and slight, ' the young mistress' was ; and as I entered I heard a newspaper rustle, and the sound of steps approaching to meet me.

Face to face we met, near the door ; and, without speaking, I made him a deep courtesy.

He took my hand, without the least indication on my part, in his hard lean grasp, and shook it kindly, but familiarly, peering with a stern sort of curiosity into my face as he continued to hold it. His ill-fitting, glossy black cloth, ungainly presence, and sharp, dark, vulpine features had in them, as I said before, the vulgarity of a Glasgow artisan in his Sabbath suit. I made an instantaneous motion to withdraw my hand, but he held it firmly.

Though there was a grim sort of familiarity, there was also decision, shrewdness, and, above all, kindness, in his dark face —a gleam on the whole of the masterly and the honest—that along with a certain paleness, betraying, I thought, restrained emotion, indicated sympathy and invited confidence.

'I hope, Miss, you are pretty well?' He pronounced 'pretty' as it is spelt. 'I have come in consequence of a solemn promise exacted more than a year since by your deceased father, the late Mr. Austin Ruthyn of Knowl, for whom I cherished a warm esteem, being knit besides with him in spiritual bonds. It has been a shock to you, Miss?'

'It has, indeed, sir.'

'I've a doctor's degree, I have—Doctor of Medicine, Miss. Like St. Luke, preacher and doctor. I was in business once, but this is better. As one footing fails, the Lord provides another. The stream of life is black and angry; how so many of us get across without drowning, I often wonder. The best way is not to look too far before—just from one stepping-stone to another; and though you may wet your feet, He won't let you drown—He has not allowed me.'

And Doctor Bryerly held up his head, and wagged it resolutely.

'You are born to this world's wealth; in its way a great blessing, though a great trial, Miss, and a great trust; but don't suppose you are destined to exemption from trouble on that account, any more than poor Emmanuel Bryerly. As the sparks fly upwards, Miss Ruthyn! Your cushioned carriage may overturn on the highroad, as I may stumble and fall upon the footpath. There are other troubles than debt and privation. Who can tell how long health may last, or when an accident may happen the brain; what mortifications may await you in your own high sphere; what unknown enemies may rise up in your path; or what slanders may asperse your name—ha, ha!' It is a wonderful equilibrium—a marvellous dispensation—ha, ha!' and he laughed with a shake of his head, I thought a little sarcastically, as if he was not sorry my money could not avail to buy immunity from the general curse.

'But what money can't do, *prayer* can—bear that in mind, Miss Ruthyn. We can all pray; and though thorns and snares, and stones of fire lie strewn in our way, we need not fear them. He

will give His angels charge over us, and in their hands they will
bear us up, for He hears and sees everywhere, and His angels
are innumerable.'

He was now speaking gently and solemnly, and paused. But
another vein of thought he had unconsciously opened in my
mind, and I said—

'And had my dear papa no other medical adviser?'

He looked at me sharply, and flushed a little under his dark
tint. His medical skill was, perhaps, the point on which his
human vanity vaunted itself, and I dare say there was something
very disparaging in my tone.

'And if he *had* no other, he might have done worse. I've had
many critical cases in my hands, Miss Ruthyn. I can't charge
myself with any miscarriage through ignorance. My diagnosis
in Mr. Ruthyn's case has been verified by the result. But I was
not alone ; Sir Clayton Barrow saw him, and took my view ;
a note will reach him in London. But this, excuse me, is not
to the present purpose. The late Mr. Ruthyn told me I was to
receive a key from you, which would open a cabinet where he
had placed his will—ha ! thanks,—in his study. And, I think, as
there may be directions about the funeral, it had better be read
forthwith. Is there any gentleman—a relative or man of business
—near here, whom you would wish sent for?'

'No, none, thank you ; I have confidence in you, sir.'

I think I spoke and looked frankly, for he smiled very kindly,
though with closed lips.

'And you may be sure, Miss Ruthyn, your confidence shall not
be disappointed.' Here was a long pause. 'But you are very
young, and you must have some one by in your interest, who
has some experience in business. Let me see. Is not the Rector,
Dr. Clay, at hand ? In the town ?—very good ; and Mr. Danvers,
who manages the estate, *he* must come. And get Grimston—you
see I know all the names—Grimston, the attorney ; for though he
was not employed about this will, he has been Mr. Ruthyn's
solicitor a great many years : we must have Grimston ; for, as I
suppose you know, though it is a short will, it is a very strange
one. I expostulated, but you know he was very decided when
he took a view. He read it to you, eh ?

'No, sir.'

' Oh, but he told you so much as relates to you and your uncle, Mr. Silas Ruthyn, of Bartram-Haugh ? '

' No, indeed, sir.'

' Ha ! I wish he had.'

And with these words Doctor Bryerly's countenance darkened.

' Mr. Silas Ruthyn is a religious man ? '

' Oh, *very* ! ' said I.

' You've seen a good deal of him ? '

' No, I never saw him,' I answered.

' H'm ? Odder and odder ! But he's a good man, isn't he ? '

' Very good, indeed, sir—a very religious man.'

Doctor Bryerly was watching my countenance as I spoke, with a sharp and anxious eye ; and then he looked down, and read the pattern of the carpet like bad news, for a while, and looking again in my face, askance, he said—

' He was very near joining *us*—on the point. He got into correspondence with Henry Voerst, one of our best men. They call us Swedenborgians, you know ; but I dare say that won't go much further, now. I suppose, Miss Ruthyn, one o'clock would be a good hour, and I am sure, under the circumstances, the gentlemen will make a point of attending.'

' Yes, Dr. Bryerly, the notes shall be sent, and my cousin, Lady Knollys, would I am sure attend with me while the will is being read—there would be no objection to her presence ? '

' None in the world. I can't be quite sure who are joined with me as executors. I'm almost sorry I did not decline ; but it is too late regretting. One thing you must believe Miss Ruthyn : in framing the provisions of the will I was never consulted— although I expostulated against the only very unusual one it contains when I heard it. I did so strenuously, but in vain. There was one other against which I protested—having a right to do so—with better effect. In no other way does the will in any respect owe anything to my advice or dissuasion. You will please believe this ; also that I am your friend. Yes, indeed, it is my duty.'

The latter words he spoke looking down again, as it were in soliloquy ; and thanking him, I withdrew.

When I reached the hall, I regretted that I had not asked him to state distinctly what arrangements the will made so nearly affecting, as it seemed, my relations with my uncle Silas, and

for a moment I thought of returning and requesting an explanation. But then, I bethought me, it was not very long to wait
till one o'clock—so *he*, at least, would think. I went up-stairs,
therefore, to the ' school-room,' which we used at present as a
sitting-room, and there I found Cousin Monica awaiting me.

' Are you quite well, dear ? ' asked Lady Knollys, as she came
to meet and kiss me.

' Quite well, Cousin Monica.'

' No nonsense, Maud ! you're as white as that handkerchief—
what's the matter ? Are you ill—are you frightened ? Yes, you're
trembling—you're terrified, child.'

' I believe I *am* afraid. There *is* something in poor papa's will
about Uncle Silas—about *me*. I don't know—Doctor Bryerly says,
and he seems so uncomfortable and frightened himself, I am
sure it is something very bad. I am *very* much frightened—I am
—I *am*. Oh, Cousin Monica ! you won't leave me ?'

So I threw my arms about her neck, clasping her very close,
and we kissed one another, I crying like a frightened child—
and indeed in experience of the world I was no more.

CHAPTER XXIV

THE OPENING OF THE WILL

Perhaps the terror with which I anticipated the hour of one,
and the disclosure of the unknown undertaking to which I had
bound myself, was irrational and morbid. But, honestly, I doubt
it ; my tendency has always been that of many other weak characters, to act impetuously, and afterwards to reproach myself
for consequences which I have, perhaps, in reality, had little or
no share in producing.

It was Doctor Bryerly's countenance and manner in alluding
to a particular provision in my father's will that instinctively
awed me. I have seen faces in a nightmare that haunted me with
an indescribable horror, and yet I could not say wherein lay

the fascination. And so it was with his—an omen, a menace,
lurked in its sallow and dismal glance.

'You must not be so frightened, darling,' said Cousin Monica.
'It is foolish; it *is, really;* they can't cut off your head, you
know : they can't really harm you in any essential way. If it
involved a risk of a little money, you would not mind it; but
men are such odd creatures—they measure all sacrifices by money.
Doctor Bryerly would look just as you describe, if you were
doomed to lose 500*l.*, and yet it would not kill you.'

A companion like Lady Knollys is reassuring; but I could
not take her comfort altogether to heart, for I felt that she had
no great confidence in it herself.

There was a little French clock over the mantelpiece in the
school-room, which I consulted nearly every minute. It wanted
now but ten minutes of one.

'Shall we go down to the drawing-room, dear?' said Cousin
Knollys, who was growing restless like me.

So down-stairs we went, pausing by mutual consent at the
great window at the stair-head, which looks out on the avenue.
Mr. Danvers was riding his tall, grey horse at a walk, under the
wide branches toward the house, and we waited to see him get
off at the door. In his turn he loitered there, for the good
Rector's gig, driven by the Curate, was approaching at a smart
ecclesiastical trot.

Doctor Clay got down, and shook hands with Mr. Danvers;
and after a word or two, away drove the Curate with that upward glance at the windows from which so few can refrain.

I watched the Rector and Mr. Danvers loitering on the steps
as a patient might the gathering of surgeons who are to perform
some unknown operation. They, too, glanced up at the window
as they turned to enter the house, and I drew back. Cousin
Monica looked at her watch.

'Four minutes only. Shall we go to the drawing-room?'

Waiting for a moment to let the gentlemen get by on the
way to the study, we, accordingly, went down, and I heard the
Rector talk of the dangerous state of Grindleston bridge, and
wondered how he could think of such things at a time of sorrow.
Everything about those few minutes of suspense remains fresh
in my recollection. I remember how they loitered and came to
a halt at the corner of the oak passage leading to the study, and

how the Rector patted the marble head and smoothed the inflexible tresses of William Pitt, as he listened to Mr. Danvers'
details about the presentment ; and then, as they went on, I
recollect the boisterous nose-blowing that suddenly resounded
from the passage, and which I then referred, and still refer,
intuitively to the Rector.

We had not been five minutes in the drawing-room when
Branston entered, to say that the gentlemen I had mentioned
were all assembled in the study.

' Come, dear,' said Cousin Monica ; and leaning on her arm I
reached the study door. I entered, followed by her. The gentlemen arrested their talk and stood up, those who were sitting,
and the Rector came forward very gravely, and in low tones, and
very kindly, greeted me. There was nothing emotional in this
salutation, for though my father never quarrelled, yet an immense distance separated him from all his neighbours, and I
do not think there lived a human being who knew him at more
than perhaps a point or two of his character.

Considering how entirely he secluded himself, my father was,
as many people living remember, wonderfully popular in his
county. He was neighbourly in everything except in seeing company and mixing in society. He had magnificent shooting, of
which he was extremely liberal. He kept a pack of hounds at
Dollerton, with which all his side of the county hunted through
the season. He never refused any claim upon his purse which
had the slightest show of reason. He subscribed to every fund,
social, charitable, sporting, agricultural, no matter what, provided the honest people of his county took an interest in it,
and always with a princely hand ; and although he shut himself
up, no one could say that he was inaccessible, for he devoted
hours daily to answering letters, and his checque-book con-
tributed largely in those replies. He had taken his turn long ago
as High Sheriff ; so there was an end of that claim before his
oddity and shyness had quite secluded him. He refused the Lord-
Lieutenancy of his county ; he declined every post of personal
distinction connected with it. He could write an able as well as
a genial letter when he pleased ; and his appearances at public
meetings, dinners, and so forth were made in this epistolary
fashion, and, when occasion presented, by magnificent contributions from his purse.

If my father had been less goodnatured in the sporting relations of his vast estates, or less magnificent in dealing with his
fortune, or even if he had failed to exhibit the intellectual
force which always characterised his letters on public matters, I
dare say that his oddities would have condemned him to rid-
icule, and possibly to dislike. But every one of the principal
gentlemen of his county, whose judgment was valuable, has told
me that he was a remarkably able man, and that his failure in
public life was due to his eccentricities, and in no respect to
deficiency in those peculiar mental qualities which make men
feared and useful in Parliament.

I could not forbear placing on record this testimony to the
high mental and the kindly qualities of my beloved father, who
might have passed for a misanthrope or a fool. He was a man of
generous nature and powerful intellect, but given up to the oddities of a shyness which grew with years and indulgence, and
became inflexible with his disappointments and affliction.

There was something even in the Rector's kind and ceremonious greeting which oddly enough reflected the mixed feelings
in which awe was not without a place, with which his neighbours had regarded my dear father.

Having done the honours—I am sure looking woefully pale—I
had time to glance quietly at the only figure there with which
I was not tolerably familiar. This was the junior partner in the
firm of Archer and Sleigh who represented my uncle Silas—a
fat and pallid man of six-and-thirty, with a sly and evil countenance, and it has always seemed to me, that ill dispositions
show more repulsively in a pale fat face than in any other.

Doctor Bryerly, standing near the window, was talking in a
low tone to Mr. Grimston, our attorney.

I heard good Dr. Clay whisper to Mr. Danvers—

' Is not that Doctor Bryerly—the person with the black—the
black—it's a wig, I think—in the window, talking to Abel Grimston?'

' Yes ; that's he.'

' Odd-looking person—one of the Swedenborg people, is not
he ?' continued the Rector.

' So I am told.'

' Yes,' said the Rector, quietly ; and he crossed one gaitered
leg over the other, and, with fingers interlaced, twiddled his

thumbs, as he eyed the monstrous sectary under his orthodox old brows with a stern inquisitiveness. I thought he was meditating theologic battle.

But Dr. Bryerly and Mr. Grimston, still talking together, began to walk slowly from the window, and the former said in his peculiar grim tones—

' I beg pardon, Miss Ruthyn ; perhaps you would be so good as to show us which of the cabinets in this room your late lamented father pointed out as that to which this key belongs.'

I indicated the oak cabinet.

' Very good, ma'am—very good,' said Doctor Bryerly, as he fumbled the key into the lock.

Cousin Monica could not forbear murmuring—

' Dear ! what a brute ! '

The junior partner, with his dumpy hands in his pocket, poked his fat face over Mr. Grimston's shoulder, and peered into the cabinet as the door opened.

The search was not long. A handsome white paper enclosure, neatly tied up in pink tape, and sealed with large red seals, was inscribed in my dear father's hand :—' Will of Austin R. Ruthyn, of Knowl.' Then, in smaller characters, the date, and in the corner a note—' This will was drawn from my instructions by Gaunt, Hogg, and Hatchett, Solicitors, Great Woburn Street, London, A. R. R.'

' Let *me* have a squint at that indorsement, please, gentlemen,' half whispered the unpleasant person who represented my uncle Silas.

' '*Tisn't* an indorsement. There, look—a memorandum on an envelope,' said Abel Grimston, gruffly.

' Thanks—all right—that will do,' he responded, himself making a pencil-note of it, in a long clasp-book which he drew from his coat-pocket.

The tape was carefully cut, and the envelope removed without tearing the writing, and forth came the will, at sight of which my heart swelled and fluttered up to my lips, and then dropped down dead as it seemed into its place.

' Mr. Grimston, you will please to read it,' said Doctor Bryerly, who took the direction of the process. ' I will sit beside you, and as we go along you will be good enough to help us to understand technicalities, and give us a lift where we want it.'

'It's a short will,' said Mr. Grimston, turning over the sheets
'*very*—considering. Here's a codicil.'

'I did not see that,' said Doctor Bryerly.

'Dated only a month ago.'

'Oh!' said Doctor Bryerly, putting on his spectacles. Uncle
Silas's ambassador, sitting close behind, had insinuated his face
between Doctor Bryerly's and the reader's of the will.

'On behalf of the surviving brother of the testator,' interposed
the delegate, just as Abel Grimston had cleared his voice to begin, 'I take leave to apply for a copy of this instrument. It
will save a deal of trouble, if the young lady as represents the
testator here has no objection.'

'You can have as many copies as you like when the will is
proved,' said Mr. Grimston.

'I know that; but supposing as all's right, where's the objection?'

'Just the objection there always is to acting irregular,' replied
Mr. Grimston.

'You don't object to act disobliging, it seems.'

'You can do as I told you,' replied Mr. Grimston.

'Thank you for nothing,' murmured Mr. Sleigh.

And the reading of the will proceeded, while he made elaborate notes of its contents in his capacious pocket-book.

'I, Austin Alymer Ruthyn Ruthyn, being, I thank God, of
sound mind and perfect recollection,' &c, &c.; and then came a
bequest of all his estates real, chattels real, copyrights, leases,
chattels, money, rights, interests, reversions, powers, plate, pictures, and estates and possessions whatsoever, to four persons—
Lord Ilbury, Mr. Penrose Creswell of Creswell, Sir William Aylmer, Bart., and Hans Emmanuel Bryerly, Doctor of Medicine,
to have and to hold,' &c. &c. Whereupon my Cousin Monica
ejaculated 'Eh?' and Doctor Bryerly interposed—

'Four trustees, ma'am. We take little but trouble—you'll see;
go on.'

Then it came out that all this multifarious splendour was be-
queathed in trust for me, subject to a bequest of 15,000*l.* to his
only brother, Silas Aylmer Ruthyn, and 3,500*l.* each to the two
children of his said brother; and lest any doubt should arise
by reason of his, the testator's decease as to the continuance of
the arrangement by way of lease under which he enjoyed his

present habitation and farm, he left him the use of the mansion-house and lands of Bartram-Haugh, in the county of Derbyshire, and of the lands of so-and-so and so-and-so, adjoining thereto, in the said county, for the term of his natural life, on payment of a rent of 5s. per annum, and subject to the like conditions as to waste, &c., as are expressed in the said lease.

'By your leave, may I ask is them dispositions all the devises to my client, which is his only brother, as it seems to me you've seen the will before?' enquired Mr. Sleigh.

'Nothing more, unless there is something in the codicil,' answered Dr. Bryerly.

But there was no mention of him in the codicil.

Mr. Sleigh threw himself back in his chair, and sneered, with the end of his pencil between his teeth. I hope his disappointment was altogether for his client. Mr. Danvers fancied, he afterwards said, that he had probably expected legacies which might have involved litigation, or, at all events, law costs, and perhaps a stewardship; but this was very barren; and Mr. Danvers also remarked, that the man was a very low practitioner, and wondered how my uncle Silas could have commissioned such a person to represent him.

So far the will contained nothing of which my most partial friend could have complained. The codicil, too, devised only legacies to servants, and a sum of 1,000l., with a few kind words, to Monica, Lady Knollys, and a further sum of 3,000l. to Dr. Bryerly, stating that the legatee had prevailed upon him to erase from the draft of his will a bequest to him to that amount, but that, in consideration of all the trouble devolving upon him as trustee, he made that bequest by his codicil; and with these arrangements the permanent disposition of his property was completed.

But that direction to which he and Doctor Bryerly had darkly alluded, was now to come, and certainly it was a strange one. It appointed my uncle Silas my sole guardian, with full parental authority over me until I should have reached the age of twenty-one, up to which time I was to reside under his care at Bartram-Haugh, and it directed the trustees to pay over to him yearly a sum of 2,000l. during the continuance of the guardianship for my suitable maintenance, education, and expenses.

You have now a sufficient outline of my father's will. The only thing I painfully felt in this arrangement was, the break-up—the dismay that accompanies the disappearance of home. Otherwise, there was something rather pleasurable in the idea. As long as I could remember, I had always cherished the same mysterious curiosity about my uncle, and the same longing to behold him. This was about to be gratified. Then there was my cousin Milicent, about my own age. My life had been so lonely, that I had acquired none of those artificial habits that induce the fine-lady nature—a second, and not always a very amiable one. She had lived a solitary life, like me. What rambles and readings we should have together ! what confidences and castle-buildings ! and then there was a new country and a fine old place, and the sense of interest and adventure that always accompanies change in our early youth.

There were four letters all alike with large, red seals, addressed respectively to each of the trustees named in the will. There was also one addressed to Silas Alymer Ruthyn, Esq., Bartram-Haugh Manor, &c. &c., which Mr. Sleigh offered to deliver. But Doctor Bryerly thought the post-office was the more regular channel. Uncle Silas's representative was questioning Doctor Bryerly in an under-tone.

I turned my eyes on my cousin Monica—I felt so inexpressibly relieved—expecting to see a corresponding expression in her countenance. But I was startled. She looked ghastly and angry. I stared in her face, not knowing what to think. Could the will have personally disappointed her ? Such doubts, though we fancy in after-life they belong to maturity and experience only, do sometimes cross our minds in youth. But the suggestion wronged Lady Knollys, who neither expected nor wanted anything, being rich, childless, generous, and frank. It was the unexpected character of her countenance that scared me, and for a moment the shock called up corresponding moral images.

Lady Knollys, starting up, raised her head, so as to see over Mr. Sleigh's shoulder, and biting her pale lip, she cleared her voice and demanded—

' Doctor Bryerly, pray, sir, is the reading concluded ? '

' Concluded ? Quite. Yes, nothing more,' he answered with a nod, and continued his talk with Mr. Danvers and Abel Grimston.

' And to whom,' said Lady Knollys, with an effort, ' will the property belong, in case—in case my little cousin here should die before she comes of age ? '

' Eh ? Well—wouldn't it go to the heir-at-law and next of kin ? ' said Doctor Bryerly, turning to Abel Grimston.

' Ay—to be sure,' said the attorney, thoughtfully.

' And who is that ? ' pursued my cousin.

' Well, her uncle, Mr. Silas Ruthyn. He's both heir-at-law and next of kin,' pursued Abel Grimston.

' Thank you,' said Lady Knollys.

Doctor Clay came forward, bowing very low, in his standing collar and single-breasted coat, and graciously folded my hand in his soft wrinkled grasp—

' Allow me, my dear Miss Ruthyn, while expressing my regret that we are to lose you from among our little flock—though I trust but for a short, a very short time—to say how I rejoice at the particular arrangement indicated by the will we have just heard read. My curate, William Fairfield, resided for some years in the same spiritual capacity in the neighbourhood of your, I will say, admirable uncle, with occasional intercourse with whom he was favoured—may I not say blessed ?—a true Christian Church-man—a Christian gentleman. Can I say more ? A most happy, happy choice.' A very low bow here, with eyes nearly closed, and a shake of the head. ' Mrs. Clay will do herself the honour of waiting upon you, to pay her respects, before you leave Knowl for your temporary sojourn in another sphere.'

So, with another deep bow—for I had become a great per-sonage all at once—he let go my hand cautiously and delicately, as if he were setting down a curious china tea-cup. And I cour-tesied low to him, not knowing what to say, and then to the assembly generally, who all bowed. And Cousin Monica whis-pered, briskly, ' Come away,' and took my hand with a very cold and rather damp one, and led me from the room.

CHAPTER XXV

I HEAR FROM UNCLE SILAS

Without saying a word, Cousin Monica accompanied me to the school-room, and on entering she shut the door, not with a spirited clang, but quietly and determinedly.

'Well, dear,' she said, with the same pale, excited countenance, ' that certainly is a sensible and charitable arrangement. I could not have believed it possible, had I not heard it with my ears.'

'About my going to Bartram-Haugh?'

' Yes, exactly so, under Silas Ruthyn's guardianship, to spend two—*three*—of the most important years of your education and your life under that roof. Is *that,* my dear, what was in your mind when you were so alarmed about what you were to be called upon to do, or undergo?'

'No, no, indeed. I had no notion what it might be. I was afraid of something serious,' I answered.

'And, my dear Maud, did not your poor father speak to you as if it *was* something serious?' said she. 'And so it *is,* I can tell you, something serious, and *very* serious; and I think it ought to be prevented, and I certainly *will* prevent it if I possibly can.'

I was puzzled utterly by the intensity of Lady Knollys' protest. I looked at her, expecting an explanation of her meaning; but she was silent, looking steadfastly on the jewels on her right-hand fingers, with which she was drumming a staccato march on the table, very pale, with gleaming eyes, evidently thinking deeply. I began to think she *had* a prejudice against my uncle Silas.

'He is not very rich,' I commenced.

'Who?' said Lady Knollys.

'Uncle Silas,' I replied.

'No, certainly; he's in debt,' she answered.

139

'But then, how very highly Doctor Clay spoke of him!' I
pursued.

'Don't talk of Doctor Clay. I do think that man is the greatest goose I ever heard talk. I have no patience with such men,'
she replied.

I tried to remember what particular nonsense Doctor Clay had
uttered, and I could recollect nothing, unless his eulogy upon
my uncle were to be classed with that sort of declamation.

'Danvers is a very proper man and a good accountant, I dare
say ; but he is either a very deep person, or a fool—*I* believe a
fool. As for your attorney, I suppose he knows his business, and
also his interest, and I have no doubt he will consult it. I begin
to think the best man among them, the shrewdest and the most
reliable, is that vulgar visionary in the black wig. I saw him look
at you, Maud, and I liked his face, though it is abominably
ugly and vulgar, and cunning, too ; but I think he's a just man,
and I dare say with right feelings—I'm *sure* he has.'

I was quite at a loss to divine the gist of my cousin's criticism.

'I'll have some talk with Dr. Bryerly ; I feel convinced he
takes my view, and we must really think what had best be
done.'

'Is there anything in the will, Cousin Monica, that does not
appear ?' I asked, for I was growing very uneasy. 'I wish you
would tell me. What view do you mean ?'

'No view in particular ; the view that a desolate old park, and
the house of a *neglected* old man, who is very poor, and has been
desperately foolish, is not the right place for you, particularly
at your years. It is quite shocking, and I *will* speak to Doctor
Bryerly. May I ring the bell, dear ?'

'Certainly ;' and I rang it.

'When does he leave Knowl ?'

I could not tell. Mrs. Rusk, however, was sent for, and she
could tell us that he had announced his intention of taking
the night train from Drackleton, and was to leave Knowl for that
station at half-past six o'clock.

'May Rusk give or send him a message from me, dear ?' asked
Lady Knollys.

Of course she might.

'Then please let him know that I request he will be so good

as to allow me a very few minutes, just to say a word before he goes.'

'You kind cousin!' I said, placing my two hands on her shoulders, and looking earnestly in her face; 'you are anxious about me, more than you say. Won't you tell me why? I am much more unhappy, really, in ignorance, than if I understood the cause.'

'Well, dear, haven't I told you? The two or three years of your life which are to form you are destined to be passed in utter loneliness, and, I am sure, neglect. You can't estimate the disadvantage of such an arrangement. It is full of disadvantages. How it could have entered the head of poor Austin—although I should not say that, for I am sure I do understand it, —but how he could for any purpose have directed such a measure is quite inconceivable. I never heard of anything so foolish and abominable, and I will prevent it if I can.'

At that moment Mrs. Rusk announced that Doctor Bryerly would see Lady Knollys at any time she pleased before his departure.

'It shall be this moment, then,' said the energetic lady, and up she stood, and made that hasty general adjustment before the glass, which, no matter under what circumstances, and before what sort of creature one's appearance is to be made, is a duty that every woman owes to herself. And I heard her a moment after, at the stair-head, directing Branston to let Dr. Bryerly know that she awaited him in the drawing-room.

And now she was gone, and I began to wonder and speculate. Why should my cousin Monica make all this fuss about, after all, a very natural arrangement? My uncle, whatever he might have been, was now a good man—a religious man—perhaps a little severe; and with this thought a dark streak fell across my sky.

A cruel disciplinarian! had I not read of such characters?— lock and key, bread and water, and solitude! To sit locked up all night in a dark out-of-the-way room, in a great, ghosty, old-fashioned house, with no one nearer than the other wing. What years of horror in one such night! Would not this explain my poor father's hesitation, and my cousin Monica's apparently disproportioned opposition? When an idea of terror presents itself to a young person's mind, it transfixes and fills the vision, without respect of probabilities or reason.

My uncle was now a terrible old martinet, with long Bible lessons, lectures, pages of catechism, sermons to be conned by rote, and an awful catalogue of punishments for idleness, and what would seem to him impiety. I was going, then, to a frightful isolated reformatory, where for the first time in my life I should be subjected to a rigorous and perhaps barbarous discipline.

All this was an exhalation of fancy, but it quite overcame me. I threw myself, in my solitude, on the floor, upon my knees, and prayed for deliverance—prayed that Cousin Monica might prevail with Doctor Bryerly, and both on my behalf with the Lord Chancellor, or the High Sheriff, or whoever else my proper deliverer might be ; and when my cousin returned, she found me quite in an agony.

' Why, you little fool ! what fancy has taken possession of you now ? ' she cried.

And when my new terror came to light, she actually laughed a little to reassure me, and she said—

' My dear child, your uncle Silas will never put you through your duty to your neighbour ; all the time you are under his roof you'll have idleness and liberty enough, and too much, I fear. It is neglect, my dear, not discipline, that I'm afraid of.'

' I think, dear Cousin Monica, you are afraid of something more than neglect,' I said, relieved, however.

' I *am* afraid of more than neglect,' she replied promptly ; ' but I hope my fears may turn out illusory, and that possibly they may be avoided. And now, for a few hours at least, let us think of something else. I rather like that Doctor Bryerly. I could not get him to say what I wanted. I don't think he's Scotch, but he is very cautious, and I am sure, though he would not say so, that he thinks of the matter exactly as I do. He says that those fine people, who are named as his co-trustees, won't take any trouble, and will leave everything to him, and I am sure he is right. So we must not quarrel with him, Maud, nor call him hard names, although he certainly is intolerably vulgar and ugly, and at times very nearly impertinent—I suppose without knowing, or indeed very much caring.'

We had a good deal to think of, and talked incessantly. There

I HEAR FROM UNCLE SILAS **143**

were bursts and interruptions of grief, and my kind cousin's
consolations. I have often since been so lectured for giving way
to grief, that I wonder at the patience exercised by her during
this irksome visit. Then there was some reading of that book
whose claims are always felt in the terrible days of affliction.
After that we had a walk in the yew garden, that quaint little
cloistered quadrangle—the most solemn, sad, and antiquated of
gardens.

'And now, my dear, I must really leave you for two or three
hours. I have ever so many letters to write, and my people must
think I'm dead by this time.'

So till tea-time I had poor Mary Quince, with her gushes of
simple prattle and her long fits of vacant silence, for my companion. And such a one, who can con over by rote the old
friendly gossip about the dead, talk about their ways, and looks,
and likings, without much psychologic refinement, but with a
simple admiration and liking that never measured them criti-
cally, but always with faith and love, is in general about as comfortable a companion as one can find for the common moods of
grief.

It is not easy to recall in calm and happy hours the sensations
of an acute sorrow that is past. Nothing, by the merciful ordi-
nance of God, is more difficult to remember than pain. One or
two great agonies of that time I do remember, and they remain
to testify of the rest, and convince me, though I can see it no
more, how terrible all that period was.

Next day was the funeral, that appalling necessity ; smuggled
away in whispers, by black familiars, unresisting, the beloved
one leaves home, without a farewell, to darken those doors no
more ; henceforward to lie outside, far away, and forsaken,
through the drowsy heats of summer, through days of snow and
nights of tempest, without light or warmth, without a voice
near. Oh, Death, king of terrors ! The body quakes and the
spirit faints before thee. It is vain, with hands clasped over our
eyes, to scream our reclamation ; the horrible image will not
be excluded. We have just the word spoken eighteen hundred
years ago, and our trembling faith. And through the broken
vault the gleam of the Star of Bethlehem.

I was glad in a sort of agony when it was over. So long as it remained to be done, something of the catastrophe was still suspended. Now it was all over.

The house so strangely empty. No owner—no master ! I with my strange momentary liberty, bereft of that irreplaceable love, never quite prized until it is lost. Most people have experienced the dismay that underlies sorrow under such circumstances.

The apartment of the poor outcast from life is now dismantled. Beds and curtains taken down, and furniture displaced ; carpets removed, windows open and doors locked ; the bedroom and anteroom were henceforward, for many a day, uninhabited. Every shocking change smote my heart like a reproach.

I saw that day that Cousin Monica had been crying for the first time, I think, since her arrival at Knowl ; and I loved her more for it, and felt consoled. My tears have often been arrested by the sight of another person weeping, and I never could explain why. But I believe that many persons experience the same odd reaction.

The funeral was conducted, in obedience to his brief but peremptory direction, very privately and with little expense. But of course there was an attendance, and the tenants of the Knowl estate also followed the hearse to the mausoleum, as it is called, in the park, where he was laid beside my dear mother. And so the repulsive ceremonial of that dreadful day was over. The grief remained, but there was rest from the fatigue of agitation, and a comparative calm supervened.

It was now the stormy equinoctial weather that sounds the wild dirge of autumn, and marches the winter in. I love, and always did, that grand undefinable music, threatening and bewailing, with its strange soul of liberty and desolation.

By this night's mail, as we sat listening to the storm, in the drawing-room at Knowl, there reached me a large letter with a great black seal, and a wonderfully deep-black border, like a widow's crape. I did not recognise the handwriting ; but on opening the funereal missive, it proved to be from my uncle Silas, and was thus expressed :—

' MY DEAREST NIECE,—This letter will reach you, probably, on the day which consigns the mortal remains of my beloved brother, Austin, your dear father, to the earth. Sad ceremony, from taking my mournful part in which I am excluded by years, distance, and broken health. It will, I trust, at this season of desolation, be not unwelcome to remember that a substitute, imperfect—unworthy—but most affectionately zealous, for the honoured parent whom you have just lost, has been appointed, in me, your uncle, by his will. I am aware that you were present during the reading of it, but I think it will be for our mutual satisfaction that our new and more affectionate relations should be forthwith entered upon. My conscience and your safety, and I trust convenience, will thereby be consulted. You will, my dear niece, remain at Knowl, until a few simple arrangements shall have been completed for your reception at this place. I will then settle the details of your little journey to us, which shall be performed as comfortably and easily as possible. I humbly pray that this affliction may be sanctified to us all, and that in our new duties we may be supported, comforted, and directed. I need not remind you that I now stand to you *in loco parentis*, which means in the relation of father, and you will not forget that you are to remain at Knowl until you hear further from me.

' I remain, my dear niece, your most affectionate uncle and guardian,

SILAS RUTHYN.'

' P.S.—Pray present my respects to Lady Knollys, who, I understand, is sojourning at Knowl. I would observe that a lady who cherishes, I have reason to fear, unfriendly feelings against your uncle, is not the most desirable companion for his ward. But upon the express condition that I am not made the subject of your discussions—a distinction which could not conduce to your forming a just and respectful estimate of me— I do not interpose my authority to bring your intercourse to an immediate close.'

As I read this postscript, my cheek tingled as if I had received a box on the ear. Uncle Silas was as yet a stranger. The menace of authority was new and sudden, and I felt with a pang of mortification the full force of the position in which my dear father's will had placed me.

I was silent, and handed the letter to my cousin, who read it with a kind of smile until she came, as I supposed, to the postscript, when her countenance, on which my eyes were fixed,

changed, and with flushed cheeks she knocked the hand that
held the letter on the table before her, and exclaimed—

' Did I ever hear ! Well, if this isn't impertinence ! *What* an
old man that is ! '

There was a pause, during which Lady Knollys held her head
high with a frown, and sniffed a little.

' I did not intend to talk about him, but now I *will*. I'll talk
away just whatever I like ; and I'll stay here just as long as you
let me, Maud, and you need not be one atom afraid of him. Our
intercourse to an "immediate close," indeed ! I only wish he
were here. He should hear something ! '

And Cousin Monica drank off her entire cup of tea at one
draught, and then she said, more in her own way—

' I'm better ! ' and drew a long breath, and then she laughed
a little in a waggish defiance. ' I wish we had him here, Maud,
and *would* not we give him a bit of our minds ! And this before
the poor will is so much as proved ! '

' I am almost glad he wrote that postscript ; for although I
don't think he has any authority in that matter while I am under
my own roof,' I said, extemporising a legal opinion, ' and, therefore, shan't obey him, it has somehow opened my eyes to my real
situation.'

I sighed, I believe, very desolately, for Lady Knollys came
over and kissed me very gently and affectionately.

' It really seems, Maud, as if he had a supernatural sense, and
heard things through the air over fifty miles of heath and hill.
You remember how, just as he was probably writing that very
postscript yesterday, I was urging you to come and stay with
me, and planning to move Dr. Bryerly in our favour. And so I
will, Maud, and to me you *shall* come—my guest, mind—I should
be so delighted ; and really if Silas is under a cloud, it has been
his own doing, and I don't see that it is your business to fight
his battle. He can't live very long. The suspicion, whatever it is
dies with him, and what could poor dear Austin prove by his
will but what everybody knew quite well before—his own strong
belief in Silas's innocence ? What an awful storm ! The room
trembles. Don't you like the sound ? What they used to call
' wolving ' in the old organ at Dorminster ! '

CHAPTER XXVI

THE STORY OF UNCLE SILAS

And so it was like the yelling of phantom hounds and hunters, and the thunder of their coursers in the air—a furious, grand and supernatural music, which in my fancy made a suitable accompaniment to the discussion of that enigmatical person—martyr—angel—demon—Uncle Silas—with whom my fate was now so strangely linked, and whom I had begun to fear.

'The storm blows from that point,' I said, indicating it with my hand and eye, although the window shutters and curtains were closed. 'I saw all the trees bend that way this evening. That way stands the great lonely wood, where my darling father and mother lie. Oh, how dreadful on nights like this, to think of them—a vault!—damp, and dark, and solitary—under the storm.'

Cousin Monica looked wistfully in the same direction, and with a short sigh she said—

'We think too much of the poor remains, and too little of the spirit which lives for ever. I am sure they are happy.' And she sighed again. 'I wish I dare hope as confidently for myself. Yes, Maud, it is sad. We are such materialists, we can't help feeling so. We forget how well it is for us that our present bodies are not to last always. They are constructed for a time and place of trouble—plainly mere temporary machines that wear out, constantly exhibiting failure and decay, and with such tremendous capacity for pain. The body lies alone, and so it ought, for it is plainly its good Creator's will; it is only the tabernacle, not the person, who is clothed upon after death, Saint Paul says, "with a house which is from heaven." So Maud, darling, although the thought will trouble us again and again, there is nothing in it; and the poor mortal body is only the cold ruin of a habitation which *they* have forsaken before we do. So this great wind,

147

you say, is blowing toward us from the wood there. If so, Maud, it is blowing from Bartram-Haugh, too, over the trees and chimneys of that old place, and the mysterious old man, who is quite right in thinking I don't like him ; and I can fancy him an old enchanter in his castle, waving his familiar spirits on the wind to fetch and carry tidings of our occupations here.'

I lifted my head and listened to the storm, dying away in the distance sometimes—sometimes swelling and pealing around and above us—and through the dark and solitude my thoughts sped away to Bartram-Haugh and Uncle Silas.

'This letter,' I said at last, 'makes me feel differently. I think he is a stern old man—is he ? '

'It is twenty years, now, since I saw him,' answered Lady Knollys. 'I did not choose to visit at his house.'

'Was that before the dreadful occurrence at Bartram-Haugh ? '

'Yes—before, dear. He was not a reformed rake, but only a ruined one then. Austin was very good to him. Mr. Danvers says it is quite unaccountable how Silas can have made away with the immense sums he got from his brother from time to time without benefiting himself in the least. But, my dear, he played ; and trying to help a man who plays, and is unlucky— and some men are, I believe, habitually unlucky—is like trying to fill a vessel that has no bottom. I think, by-the-by, my hopeful nephew, Charles Oakley, plays. Then Silas went most unjustifiably into all manner of speculations, and your poor father had to pay everything. He lost something quite astounding in that bank that ruined so many country gentlemen—poor Sir Harry Shackleton, in Yorkshire, had to sell half his estate. But your kind father went on helping him, up to his marriage—I mean in that extravagant way which was really totally useless.'

'Has my aunt been long dead ? '

'Twelve or fifteen years—more, indeed—she died before your poor mamma. She was very unhappy, and I am sure would have given her right hand she had never married Silas.'

'Did you like her ? '

'No, dear ; she was a coarse, vulgar woman.'

'Coarse and vulgar, and Uncle Silas's wife ! ' I echoed in extreme surprise, for Uncle Silas was a man of fashion—a beau in his day—and might have married women of good birth and fortune, I had no doubt, and so I expressed myself.

'Yes, dear; so he might, and poor dear Austin was very anxious he should, and would have helped him with a handsome settlement, I dare say, but he chose to marry the daughter of a Denbigh innkeeper.'

'How utterly incredible!' I exclaimed.

'Not the least incredible, dear—a kind of thing not at all so uncommon as you fancy.'

'What!—a gentleman of fashion and refinement marry a person ——'

'A barmaid!—just so,' said Lady Knollys. 'I think I could count half a dozen men of fashion who, to my knowledge, have ruined themselves just in a similar way.'

'Well, at all events, it must be allowed that in this he proved himself altogether unworldly.'

'Not a bit unworldly, but very vicious,' replied Cousin Monica, with a careless little laugh. 'She was very beautiful, curiously beautiful, for a person in her station. She was very like that Lady Hamilton who was Nelson's sorceress—elegantly beautiful, but perfectly low and stupid. I believe, to do him justice, he only intended to ruin her; but she was cunning enough to insist upon marriage. Men who have never in all their lives denied themselves the indulgence of a single fancy, cost what it may, will not be baulked even by that condition if the *penchant* be only violent enough.'

I did not half understand this piece of worldly psychology, at which Lady Knollys seemed to laugh.

'Poor Silas, certainly he struggled honestly against the consequences, for he tried after the honeymoon to prove the marriage bad. But the Welsh parson and the innkeeper papa were too strong for him, and the young lady was able to hold her struggling swain fast in that respectable noose—and a pretty prize he proved!'

'And she died, poor thing, broken-hearted, I heard.'

'She died, at all events, about ten years after her marriage; but I really can't say about her heart. She certainly had enough ill-usage, I believe, to kill her; but I don't know that she had feeling enough to die of it, if it had not been that she drank: I am told that Welsh women often do. There was jealousy, of course, and brutal quarrelling, and all sorts of horrid stories. I visited at Bartram-Haugh for a year or two, though no one else would. But when that sort of thing began, of course I gave it up ; it was out of the question. I don't think poor Austin ever knew how bad it was. And then came that odious business about wretched Mr. Charke. You know he—he committed suicide at Bartram.'

' I never heard about that,' I said ; and we both paused, and she looked sternly at the fire, and the storm roared and ha-ha-ed till the old house shook again.

' But Uncle Silas could not help that,' I said at last.

' No, he could not help it,' she acquiesced unpleasantly.

' And Uncle Silas was'—I paused in a sort of fear.

' He was suspected by some people of having killed him'—she completed the sentence.

There was another long pause here, during which the storm outside bellowed and hooted like an angry mob roaring at the windows for a victim. An intolerable and sickening sensation overpowered me.

' But *you* did not suspect him, Cousin Knollys ? ' I said, trembling very much.

' No,' she answered very sharply. ' I told you so before. Of course I did not.'

There was another silence.

' I wish, Cousin Monica,' I said, drawing close to her, 'you had not said *that* about Uncle Silas being like a wizard, and sending his spirits on the wind to listen. But I'm very glad you never suspected him.' I insinuated my cold hand into hers, and looked into her face I know not with what expression. She looked down into mine with a hard, haughty stare, I thought.

' Of *course* I never suspected him ; and *never* ask me *that* question again, Maud Ruthyn.'

Was it family pride, or what was it, that gleamed so fiercely from her eyes as she said this ? I was frightened—I was wounded —I burst into tears.

' What is my darling crying for ? I did not mean to be cross. *Was* I cross ? ' said this momentary phantom of a grim Lady Knollys, in an instant translated again into kind, pleasant Cousin Monica, with her arms about my neck.

' No, no, indeed—only I thought I had vexed you ; and, I believe, thinking of Uncle Silas makes me nervous, and I can't help thinking of him nearly always.'

'Nor can I, although we might both easily find something better to think of. Suppose we try?' said Lady Knollys.

'But, first, I must know a little more about that Mr. Charke, and what circumstances enabled Uncle Silas's enemies to found on his death that wicked slander, which has done no one any good, and caused some persons so much misery. There is Uncle Silas, I may say, ruined by it ; and we all know how it darkened the life of my dear father.'

'People will talk, my dear. Your uncle Silas had injured himself before that in the opinion of the people of his county. He was a black sheep, in fact. Very bad stories were told and believed of him. His marriage certainly was a disadvantage, you know, and the miserable scenes that went on in his disreputable house—all that predisposed people to believe ill of him.'

'How long is it since it happened?'

'Oh, a long time ; I think before you were born,' answered she.

'And the injustice still lives—they have not forgotten it yet?' said I, for such a period appeared to me long enough to have consigned anything in its nature perishable to oblivion.

Lady Knollys smiled.

'Tell me, like a darling cousin, the whole story as well as you can recollect it. Who was Mr. Charke?'

'Mr. Charke, my dear, was a gentleman on the turf—that is the phrase, I think—one of those London men, without birth or breeding, who merely in right of their vices and their money are admitted to associate with young dandies who like hounds and horses, and all that sort of thing. That set knew him very well, but of course no one else. He was at the Matlock races, and your uncle asked him to Bartram-Haugh ; and the creature, Jew or Gentile, whatever he was, fancied there was more honour than, perhaps, there really was in a visit to Bartram-Haugh.'

'For the kind of person you describe, it *was*, I think, a rather unusual honour to be invited to stay in the house of a man of Uncle Ruthyn's birth.'

'Well, so it was perhaps ; for though they knew him very well on the course, and would ask him to their tavern dinners, they would not, of course, admit him to the houses where ladies were. But Silas's wife was not much regarded at Bartram-Haugh.

Indeed, she was very little seen, for she was every evening tipsy in her bedroom, poor woman !'

' How miserable !' I exclaimed.

' I don't think it troubled Silas very much, for she drank gin, they said, poor thing, and the expense was not much ; and, on the whole, I really think he was glad she drank, for it kept her out of his way, and was likely to kill her. At this time your poor father, who was thoroughly disgusted at his marriage, had stopped the supplies, you know, and Silas was very poor, and as hungry as a hawk, and they said he pounced upon this rich London gamester, intending to win his money. I am telling you now all that was said afterwards. The races lasted I forget how many days, and Mr. Charke stayed at Bartram-Haugh all this time and for some days after. It was thought that poor Austin would pay all Silas's gambling debts, and so this wretched Mr. Charke made heavy wagers with him on the races, and they played very deep, besides, at Bartram. He and Silas used to sit up at night at cards. All these particulars, as I told you, came out afterwards, for there was an inquest, you know, and then Silas published what he called his "statement," and there was a great deal of most distressing correspondence in the newspapers.'

' And why did Mr. Charke kill himself ?' I asked.

' Well, I will tell you first what all are agreed about. The second night after the races, your uncle and Mr. Charke sat up till between two and three o'clock in the morning, quite by themselves, in the parlour. Mr. Charke's servant was at the Stag's Head Inn at Feltram, and therefore could throw no light upon what occurred at night at Bartram-Haugh ; but he was there at six o'clock in the morning, and very early at his master's door by his direction. He had locked it, as was his habit, upon the inside, and the key was in the lock, which turned out afterwards a very important point. On knocking he found that he could not awaken his master, because, as it appeared when the door was forced open, his master was lying dead at his bedside, not in a pool, but a perfect pond of blood, as they described it, with his throat cut.'

' How horrible !' cried I.

' So it was. Your uncle Silas was called up, and greatly shocked of course, and he did what I believe was best. He had everything left as nearly as possible in the exact state in which it had been found, and he sent his own servant forthwith for the coroner, and, being himself a justice of the peace, he took the depositions of Mr. Charke's servant while all the incidents were still fresh in his memory.'

'Could anything be more straightforward, more right and wise?' I said.

'Oh, nothing of course,' answered Lady Knollys, I thought a little drily.

CHAPTER XXVII

MORE ABOUT TOM CHARKE'S SUICIDE

So the inquest was held, and Mr. Manwaring, of Wail Forest, was the only juryman who seemed to entertain the idea during the inquiry that Mr. Charke had died by any hand but his own.

'And how *could* he fancy such a thing?' I exclaimed indignantly.

'Well, you will see the result was quite enough to justify them in saying as they did, that he died by his own hand. The window was found fastened with a screw on the inside, as it had been when the chambermaid had arranged it at nine o'-clock; no one could have entered through it. Besides, it was on the third story, and the rooms are lofty, so it stood at a great height from the ground, and there was no ladder long enough to reach it. The house is built in the form of a hollow square, and Mr. Charke's room looked into the narrow court-yard within. There is but one door leading into this, and it did not show any sign of having been open for years. The door was locked upon the inside, and the key in the lock, so that nobody could have made an entrance that way either, for it was impossible, you see, to unlock the door from the outside.'

' And how could they affect to question anything so clear ? ' I asked.

' There did come, nevertheless, a kind of mist over the subject, which gave those who chose to talk unpleasantly an opportunity of insinuating suspicions, though they could not themselves find the clue of the mystery. In the first place, it appeared that he had gone to bed very tipsy, and that he was heard singing and noisy in his room while getting to bed—not the mood in which men make away with themselves. Then, although his own razor was found in that dreadful blood (it is shocking to have to hear all this) near his right hand, the fingers of his left were cut to the bone. Then the memorandum book in which his bets were noted was nowhere to be found. That, you know, was very odd. His keys were there attached to a chain. He wore a great deal of gold and trinkets. I saw him, wretched man, on the course. They had got off their horses. He and your uncle were walking on the course.'

' Did he look like a gentleman ? ' I inquired, as I dare say, other young ladies would.

' He looked like a Jew, my dear. He had a horrid brown coat with a velvet cape, curling black hair over his collar, and great whiskers, very high shoulders, and he was puffing a cigar straight up into the air. I was shocked to see Silas in such company.'

' And did his keys discover anything ? ' I asked.

' On opening his travelling desk and a small japanned box within it a vast deal less money was found than was expected— in fact, very little. Your uncle said that he had won some of it the night before at play, and that Charke complained to him when tipsy of having had severe losses to counterbalance his gains on the races. Besides, he had been paid but a small part of those gains. About his book it appeared that there were little notes of bets on the backs of letters, and it was said that he sometimes made no other memorandum of his wagers—but this was disputed—and among those notes there was not one referring to Silas. But, then, there was an omission of all allusion to his transactions with two other well-known gentlemen. So that was not singular.'

' No, certainly ; that was quite accounted for,' said I.

' And then came the question,' continued she, ' what motive

could Mr. Charke possibly have had for making away with himself.'

'But is not that very difficult to make out in many cases?' I interposed.

'It was said that he had some mysterious troubles in London, at which he used to hint. Some people said that he really was in a scrape, but others that there was no such thing, and that when he talked so he was only jesting. There was no suspicion during the inquest that your uncle Silas was involved, except those questions of Mr. Manwaring's.'

'What were they?' I asked.

'I really forget; but they greatly offended your uncle, and there was a little scene in the room. Mr. Manwaring seemed to think that some one had somehow got into the room. Through the door it could not be, nor down the chimney, for they found an iron bar across the flue, near the top in the masonry. The window looked into a court-yard no bigger than a ball-room. They went down and examined it, but, though the ground beneath was moist, they could not discover the slightest trace of a footprint. So far as they could make out, Mr. Charke had hermetically sealed himself into his room, and then cut his throat with his own razor.'

'Yes,' said I, 'for it was all secured—that is, the window and the door—upon the inside, and no sign of any attempt to get in.'

'Just so; and when the walls were searched, and, as your uncle Silas directed, the wainscoting removed, some months afterwards, when the scandal grew loudest, then it was evident that there was no concealed access to the room.'

'So the answer to all those calumnies was simply that the crime was impossible,' said I. 'How dreadful that such a slander should have required an answer at all!'

'It was an unpleasant affair even then, although I cannot say that anyone supposed Silas guilty; but you know the whole thing was disreputable, that Mr. Charke was a discreditable inmate, the occurrence was horrible, and there was a glare of publicity which brought into relief the scandals of Bartram-Haugh. But in a little time it became, all on a sudden, a great deal worse.'

My cousin paused to recollect exactly.

'There were very disagreeable whispers among the sporting people in London. This person, Charke, had written two letters. Yes—two. They were published about two months after, by the villain to whom they were written ; he wanted to extort money. They were first talked of a great deal among that set in town ; but the moment they were published they produced a sensation in the country, and a storm of newspaper commentary. The first of these was of no great consequence, but the second was very startling, embarrassing, and even alarming.'

'What was it, Cousin Monica ?' I whispered.

'I can only tell you in a general way, it is so very long since I read it ; but both were written in the same kind of slang, and parts as hard to understand as a prize fight. I hope you never read those things.'

I satisfied this sudden educational alarm, and Lady Knollys proceeded.

'I am afraid you hardly hear me, the wind makes such an uproar. Well, listen. The letter said distinctly, that he, Mr. Charke, had made a very profitable visit to Bartram-Haugh, and mentioned in exact figures for how much he held your uncle Silas's I.O.U.'s, for he could not pay him. I can't say what the sum was. I only remember that it was quite frightful. It took away my breath when I read it.'

'Uncle Silas had lost it ?' I asked.

'Yes, and owed it ; and had given him those papers called I.O.U.'s promising to pay, which, of course, Mr. Charke had locked up with his money ; and the insinuation was that Silas had made away with him, to get rid of this debt, and that he had also taken a great deal of his money.

'I just recollect these points which were exactly what made the impression,' continued Lady Knollys, after a short pause ; 'the letter was written in the evening of the last day of the wretched man's life, so that there had not been much time for your uncle Silas to win back his money ; and he stoutly alleged that he did not owe Mr. Charke a guinea. It mentioned an enormous sum as being actually owed by Silas ; and it cautioned the man, an agent, to whom he wrote, not to mention the circumstance, as Silas could only pay by getting the money from his wealthy brother, who would have the management ; and he distinctly said that he had kept the matter very close at Silas's request. That, you know, was a very awkward letter, and all the worse that it was written in brutally high spirits, and not at all like a man meditating an exit from the world. You can't imagine what a sensation the publication of these letters produced. In a moment the storm was up, and certainly Silas did meet it bravely—yes, with great courage and ability. What a pity he did not early enter upon some career of ambition ! Well, well, it is idle regretting. He suggested that the letters were forgeries. He alleged that Charke was in the habit of boasting, and telling enormous falsehoods about his gambling transactions, especially in his letters. He reminded the world how often men affect high animal spirits at the very moment of meditating suicide. He alluded, in a manly and graceful way, to his family and their character. He took a high and menacing tone with his adversaries, and he insisted that what they dared to insinuate against him was physically impossible.'

I asked in what form this vindication appeared.

' It was a letter, printed as a pamphlet ; everybody admired its ability, ingenuity, and force, and it was written with immense rapidity.'

' Was it at all in the style of his letters ? ' I innocently asked. My cousin laughed.

' Oh, dear, no ! Ever since he avowed himself a religious character, he had written nothing but the most vapid and nerveless twaddle. Your poor dear father used to send his letters to me to read, and I sometimes really thought that Silas was losing his faculties ; but I believe he was only trying to write in character.'

' I suppose the general feeling was in his favour ? ' I said.

' I don't think it was, anywhere ; but in his own county it was certainly unanimously against him. There is no use in asking why ; but so it was, and I think it would have been easier for him with his unaided strength to uproot the Peak than to change the convictions of the Derbyshire gentlemen. They were all against him. Of course there were predisposing causes. Your uncle published a very bitter attack upon them, describing himself as the victim of a political conspiracy : and I recollect he mentioned that from the hour of the shocking catastrophe in his house, he had forsworn the turf and all pursuits and amusements connected with it. People sneered, and said he might as well go as wait to be kicked out.'

'Were there law-suits about all this?' I asked.

'Everybody expected that there would, for there were very savage things printed on both sides, and I think, too, that the persons who thought worst of him expected that evidence would yet turn up to convict Silas of the crime they chose to impute; and so years have glided away, and many of the people who remembered the tragedy of Bartram-Haugh, and took the strongest part in the denunciation, and ostracism that followed, are dead, and no new light had been thrown upon the occurrence, and your uncle Silas remains an outcast. At first he was quite wild with rage, and would have fought the whole county, man by man, if they would have met him. But he had since changed his habits and, as he says, his aspirations altogether.'

'He has become religious.'

'The only occupation remaining to him. He owes money; he is poor; he is isolated; and he says, sick and religious. Your poor father, who was very decided and inflexible, never helped him beyond the limit he had prescribed, after Silas's *mésalliance*. He wanted to get him into Parliament, and would have paid his expenses, and made him an allowance; but either Silas had grown lazy, or he understood his position better than poor Austin, or he distrusted his powers, or possibly he really is in ill-health; but he objected his religious scruples. Your poor papa thought self-assertion possible, where an injured man has right to rely upon, but he had been very long out of the world, and the theory won't do. Nothing is harder than to get a person who has once been effectually slurred, received again. Silas, I think, was right. I don't think it was practicable.

'Dear child, how late it is!' exclaimed Lady Knollys suddenly, looking at the Louis Quatorze clock, that crowned the mantel-piece.

It was near one o'clock. The storm had a little subsided, and I took a less agitated and more confident view of Uncle Silas than I had at an earlier hour of that evening.

'And what do you think of him?' I asked.

Lady Knollys drummed on the table with her finger points as she looked into the fire.

'I don't understand metaphysics, my dear, nor witchcraft. I

sometimes believe in the supernatural, and sometimes I don't.
Silas Ruthyn is himself alone, and I can't define him, because
I don't understand him. Perhaps other souls than human are
sometimes born into the world, and clothed in flesh. It is not only
about that dreadful occurrence, but nearly always throughout
his life ; early and late he has puzzled me. I have tried in vain
to understand him. But at one time of his life I am sure he was
awfully wickèd—eccentric indeed in his wickedness—gay, frivo-
lous, secret, and dangerous. At one time I think he could have
made poor Austin do almost anything ; but his influence vanished
with his marriage, never to return again. No ; I don't understand
him. He always bewildered me, like a shifting face, sometimes
smiling, but always sinister, in an unpleasant dream.'

CHAPTER XXVIII

I AM PERSUADED

So now at last I had heard the story of Uncle Silas's mysterious
disgrace. We sat silent for a while, and I, gazing into vacancy,
sent him in a chariot of triumph, chapletted, ringed, and robed
through the city of imagination, crying after him, ' Innocent !
innocent ! martyr and crowned ! ' All the virtues and honesties,
reason and conscience, in myriad shapes—tier above tier of human faces—from the crowded pavement, crowded windows,
crowded roofs, joined in the jubilant acclamation, and trumpe-
ters trumpeted, and drums rolled, and great organs and choirs
through open cathedral gates, rolled anthems of praise and
thanksgiving, and the bells rang out, and cannons sounded, and
the air trembled with the roaring harmony ; and Silas Ruthyn,
the full-length portrait, stood in the burnished chariot, with a
proud, sad, clouded face, that rejoiced not with the rejoicers,
and behind him the slave, thin as a ghost, white-faced, and
sneering something in his ear : while I and all the city went
on crying ' Innocent ! innocent ! martyr and crowned ! ' And now

the reverie was ended ; and there were only Lady Knollys' stern, thoughtful face, with the pale light of sarcasm on it, and the storm outside thundering and lamenting desolately.

It was very good of Cousin Monica to stay with me so long. It must have been unspeakably tiresome. And now she began to talk of business at home, and plainly to prepare for immediate flight, and my heart sank.

I know that I could not then have defined my feelings and agitations. I am not sure that I even now could. Any misgiving about Uncle Silas was, in my mind, a questioning the foundations of my faith, and in itself an impiety. And yet I am not sure that some such misgiving, faint, perhaps, and intermittent, may not have been at the bottom of my tribulation.

I was not very well. Lady Knollys had gone out for a walk. She was not easily tired, and sometimes made a long excursion. The sun was setting now, when Mary Quince brought me a letter which had just arrived by the post. My heart throbbed violently. I was afraid to break the broad black seal. It was from Uncle Silas. I ran over in my mind all the unpleasant mandates which it might contain, to try and prepare myself for a shock. At last I opened the letter. It directed me to hold myself in readiness for the journey to Bartram-Haugh. It stated that I might bring two maids with me if I wished so many, and that his next letter would give me the details of my route, and the day of my departure for Derbyshire ; and he said that I ought to make arrangements about Knowl during my absence, but that he was hardly the person properly to be consulted on that matter. Then came a prayer that he might be enabled to acquit himself of his trust to the full satisfaction of his conscience, and that I might enter upon my new relations in a spirit of prayer.

I looked round my room, so long familiar, and now so endeared by the idea of parting and change. The old house—dear, dear Knowl, how could I leave you and all your affectionate associations, and kind looks and voices, for a strange land !

With a great sigh I took Uncle Silas's letter, and went down stairs to the drawing-room. From the lobby window, where I loitered for a few moments, I looked out upon the well-known forest-trees. The sun was down. It was already twilight, and the white vapours of coming night were already filming their thinned and yellow foliage. Everything looked melancholy. How little did those who envied the young inheritrex of a princely fortune suspect the load that lay at her heart, or, bating the fear of death, how gladly at that moment she would have parted with her life !

Lady Knollys had not yet returned, and it was darkening rapidly ; a mass of black clouds stood piled in the west, through the chasms of which was still reflected a pale metallic lustre.

The drawing-room was already very dark ; but some streaks of this cold light fell upon a black figure, which would otherwise have been unseen, leaning beside the curtains against the window frame.

It advanced abruptly, with creaking shoes ; it was Doctor Bryerly.

I was startled and surprised, not knowing how he had got there. I stood staring at him in the dusk rather awkwardly, I am afraid.

' How do you do, Miss Ruthyn ? ' said he, extending his hand, long, hard, and brown as a mummy's, and stooping a little so as to approach more nearly, for it was not easy to see in the imperfect light. 'You're surprised, I dare say, to see me here so soon again ? '

' I did not know you had arrived. I am glad to see you, Doctor Bryerly. Nothing unpleasant, I hope, has happened ? '

' No, nothing unpleasant, Miss. The will has been lodged, and we shall have probate in due course ; but there has been something on my mind, and I'm come to ask you two or three questions which you had better answer very considerately. Is Miss Knollys still here ? '

' Yes, but she is not returned from her walk.'

' I am glad she is here. I think she takes a sound view, and women understand one another better. As for me, it is plainly my duty to put it before you as it strikes me, and to offer all I can do in accomplishing, should you wish it, a different arrangement. You don't know your uncle, you said the other day ? '

' No, I've never seen him.'

' You understand your late father's intention in making you his ward ? '

' I suppose he wished to show his high opinion of my uncle's fitness for such a trust.'

' That's quite true ; but the nature of the trust in this instance
is extraordinary.'

' I don't understand.'

' Why, if you die before you come to the age of twenty-one,
the entire of the property will go to him—do you see ?—and
he has the custody of your person in the meantime ; you are to
live in his house, under his care and authority. You see now, I
think, how it is ; and I did not like it when your father read
the will to me, and I said so. Do *you* ? '

I hesitated to speak, not sure that I quite comprehended him.

' And the more I think of it, the less I like it, Miss,' said Doctor Bryerly, in a calm, stern tone.

' Merciful Heaven ! Doctor Bryerly, you can't suppose that
I should not be as safe in my uncle's house as in the Lord Chancellor's ? ' I ejaculated, looking full in his face.

' But don't you see, Miss, it is not a fair position to put
your uncle in,' replied he, after a little hesitation.

' But suppose *he* does not think so. You know, if he does, he
may decline it.'

' Well that's true—but he won't. Here is his letter'—and he
produced it—'announcing officially that he means to accept the
office ; but I think he ought to be told it is not *delicate,* under
all circumstances. You know, Miss, that your uncle, Mr. Silas
Ruthyn, was talked about unpleasantly once.'

' You mean '—I began.

' I mean about the death of Mr. Charke, at Bartram-Haugh.'

' Yes, I have heard that,' I said ; he was speaking with a
shocking *aplomb.*

' We assume, of course, *unjustly* ; but there are many who
think quite differently.'

' And possibly, Doctor Bryerly, it was for that very reason that
my dear papa made him my guardian.'

' There can be no doubt of that, Miss ; it was to purge him
of that scandal.'

' And when he has acquitted himself honourably of that trust,
don't you think such a proof of confidence so honourably ful-
filled must go far to silence his traducers ? '

' Why, if all goes well, it may do a little ; but a great deal less
than you fancy. But take it that you happen to *die,* Miss, during
your minority. We are all mortal, and there are three years and

some months to go; how will it be then ? Don't you see ? Just
fancy how people will talk.'

' I think you know that my uncle is a religious man ? ' said
I.

'Well, Miss, what of that ? ' he asked again.

' He is—he has suffered intensely,' I continued. 'He has long
retired from the world ; he is very religious. Ask our curate,
Mr. Fairfield, if you doubt it.'

' But I am not disputing it, Miss ; I'm only supposing what
may happen—an accident, we'll call it small-pox, diphtheria,
that's going very much. Three years and three months, you know,
is a long time. You proceed to Bartram-Haugh, thinking you
have much goods laid up for many years ; but your Creator, you
know, may say, "Thou fool, this day is thy soul required of thee."
You go—and what pray is thought of your uncle, Mr. Silas
Ruthyn, who walks in for the entire inheritance, and who has
long been abused like a pickpocket, or worse, in his own county,
I'm told ? '

' You are a religious man, Doctor Bryerly, according to your
lights ? ' I said.

The Swedenborgian smiled.

' Well, knowing that he is so too, and having yourself experienced the power of religion, do not you think him deserving of
every confidence ? Don't you think it well that he should have
this opportunity of exhibiting both his own character and the
reliance which my dear papa reposed on it, and that we should
leave all consequences and contingencies in the hands of Heaven?'

' It appears to have been the will of Heaven hitherto,' said
Doctor Bryerly—I could not see with what expression of face,
but he was looking down, and drawing little diagrams with
his stick on the dark carpet, and spoke in a very low tone—
' that your uncle should suffer under this ill report. In counter-
vailing the appointment of Providence, we must employ our
reason, with conscientious diligence, as to the means, and if we
find that they are as likely to do mischief as good, we have no
right to expect a special interposition to turn our experiment
into an ordeal. I think you ought to weigh it well—I am sure
there are reasons against it. If you make up your mind that you
would rather be placed under the care, say of Lady Knollys, I
will endeavour all I can to effect it.'

' That could not be done without his consent, could it ? '
said I.

' No, but I don't despair of getting that—on terms, of course,'
remarked he.

' I don't quite understand,' I said.

'I mean, for instance, if he were allowed to keep the allowance
for your maintenance—eh ? '

' I mistake my uncle Silas very much,' I said, 'if that allowance is any object whatever to him compared with the moral
value of the position. If he were deprived of that, I am sure
he would decline the other.'

' We might try him at all events,' said Doctor Bryerly, on
whose dark sinewy features, even in this imperfect light, I
thought I detected a smile.

' Perhaps,' said I, ' I appear very foolish in supposing him
actuated by any but sordid motives ; but he is my near relation,
and I can't help it, sir.'

' That is a very serious thing, Miss Ruthyn,' he replied. ' You
are very young, and cannot see it at present, as you will hereafter.
He is very religious, you say, and all that, but his house is not a
proper place for you. It is a solitude—its master an outcast, and
it has been the repeated scene of all sorts of scandals, and of one
great crime ; and Lady Knollys thinks your having been domesti-
cated there will be an injury to you all the days of your life.'

' So I do, Maud,' said Lady Knollys, who had just entered the
room unperceived,—' How do you do, Doctor Bryerly ?—a serious
injury. You have no idea how entirely that house is condemned
and avoided, and the very name of its inmates tabooed.'

' How monstrous—how cruel ! ' I exclaimed.

' Very unpleasant, my dear, but perfectly natural. You are to
recollect that quite independently of the story of Mr. Charke,
the house was talked about, and the county people had cut your
uncle Silas long before that adventure was dreamed of ; and as to
the circumstance of your being placed in his charge by his
brother, who took, from strong family feeling, a totally one-sided
view of the affair from the first, having the slightest effect in
restoring his position in the county, you must quite give that up.
Except me, if he will allow me, and the clergyman, not a soul
in the country will visit at Bartram-Haugh. They may pity you,
and think the whole thing the climax of folly and cruelty ; but

they won't visit at Bartram, or know Silas, or have anything to do with his household.'

'They will see, at all events, what my dear papa's opinion was.'

'They know that already,' answered she, 'and it has not, and ought not to have, the slightest weight with them. There are people there who think themselves just as great as the Ruthyns, or greater ; and your poor father's idea of carrying it by a demonstration was simply the dream of a man who had forgotten the world, and learned to exaggerate himself in his long seclusion. I know he was beginning himself to hesitate ; and I think if he had been spared another year that provision of his will would have been struck out.'

Doctor Bryerly nodded, and he said—

'And if he had the power to dictate *now*, would he insist on that direction ? It is a mistake every way, injurious to you, his child ; and should you happen to die during your sojourn under your uncle's care, it would woefully defeat the testator's object, and raise such a storm of surmise and inquiry as would awaken all England, and send the old scandal on the wing through the world again.'

'Doctor Bryerly will, I have no doubt, arrange it all. In fact, I do not think it would be very difficult to bring Silas to terms ; and if you do not consent to his trying, Maud, mark my words, you will live to repent it.'

Here were two persons viewing the question from totally different points ; both perfectly disinterested ; both in their different ways, I believe, shrewd and even wise ; and both honourable, urging me against it, and in a way that undefinably alarmed my imagination, as well as moved my reason. I looked from one to the other—there was a silence. By this time the candles had come, and we could see one another.

'I only wait your decision, Miss Ruthyn,' said the trustee, 'to see your uncle. If his advantage was the chief object contemplated in this arrangement, he will be the best judge whether his interest is really best consulted by it or no ; and I think he will clearly see that it is *not* so, and will answer accordingly.'

'I cannot answer now—you must allow me to think it over— I will do my best. I am very much obliged, my dear Cousin Monica, you are so very good, and you too, Doctor Bryerly.'

Doctor Bryerly by this time was looking into his pocket-book, and did not acknowledge my thanks even by a nod.

' I must be in London the day after to-morrow. Bartram-Haugh is nearly sixty miles from here, and only twenty of that by rail, I find. Forty miles of posting over those Derbyshire mountains is slow work ; but if you say *try*, I'll see him to-morrow morning.'

' You must say try—you *must*, my dear Maud.'

' But how can I decide in a moment ? Oh, dear Cousin Monica, I am so distracted ! '

' But *you* need not decide at all ; the decision rests with *him*. Come ; he is more competent than you. You *must* say yes.'

Again I looked from her to Doctor Bryerly, and from him to her again. I threw my arms about her neck, and hugging her closely to me, I cried—

' Oh, Cousin Monica, dear Cousin Monica, advise me. I am a wretched creature. You must advise me.'

I did not know till now how irresolute a character was mine.

I knew somehow by the tone of her voice that she was smiling as she answered—

' Why, dear, I have advised you ; I *do* advise you ; ' and then she added, impetuously, 'I entreat and implore, if you really think I love you, that you will *follow* my advice. It is your duty to leave your uncle Silas, whom you believe to be more competent than you are, to decide, after full conference with Doctor Bryerly, who knows more of your poor father's views and intentions in making that appointment than either you or I.'

' Shall I say, yes ? ' I cried, drawing her close, and kissing her helplessly. ' Oh, tell me—tell me to say, yes.'

' Yes, of course, *yes*. She agrees, Doctor Bryerly, to your kind proposal.'

"I am to understand so ? ' he asked.

' Very well—yes, Doctor Bryerly,' I replied.

' You have resolved wisely and well,' said he, briskly, like a man who has got a care off his mind.

' I forgot to say, Doctor Bryerly—it was very rude—that you must stay here to-night.'

' He *can't*, my dear,' interposed Lady Knolly's ; ' it is a long way.'

' He will dine. Won't you, Doctor Bryerly ? '

'No; he can't. You know you can't, sir,' said my cousin, peremptorily.' You must not worry him, my dear, with civilities he can't accept. He'll bid us good-bye this moment. Good-bye, Doctor Bryerly. You'll write immediately; don't wait till you reach town. Bid him good-bye, Maud. I'll say a word to you in the hall.'

And thus she literally hurried him out of the room, leaving me in a state of amazement and confusion, not able to review my decision—unsatisfied, but still unable to recall it.

I stood where they had left me, looking after them, I suppose, like a fool.

Lady Knollys returned in a few minutes. If I had been a little cooler I was shrewd enough to perceive that she had sent poor Doctor Bryerly away upon his travels, to find board and lodging half-way to Bartram, to remove him forthwith from my presence, and thus to make my decision—if mine it was—irrevocable.

'I applaud you, my dear,' said Cousin Knollys, in her turn embracing me heartily. 'You are a sensible little darling, and have done exactly what you ought to have done.'

'I hope I have,' I faltered.

'Hope? fiddle! stuff! the thing's as plain as a pikestaff.'

And in came Branston to say that dinner was served.

CHAPTER XXIX

HOW THE AMBASSADOR FARED

Lady Knollys, I could plainly see, when we got into the brighter lights at the dinner table, was herself a good deal excited; she was relieved and glad, and was garrulous during our meal, and told me all her early recollections of dear papa. Most of them I had heard before; but they could not be told too often.

Notwithstanding my mind sometimes wandered, *often* indeed, to the conference so unexpected, so suddenly decisive, possibly so

momentous ; and with a dismayed uncertainly, the question—
had I done right ?—was always before me.

I dare say my cousin understood my character better, perhaps,
after all my honest self-study, then I do even now. Irresolute,
suddenly reversing my own decisions, impetuous in action as
she knew me, she feared, I am sure, a revocation of my commission to Doctor Bryerly, and thought of the countermand I might
send galloping after him.

So, kind creature, she laboured to occupy my thoughts, and
when one theme was exhausted found another, and had always
her parry prepared as often as I directed a reflection or an
enquiry to the re-opening of the question which she had taken
so much pains to close.

That night I was troubled. I was already upbraiding myself.
I could not sleep, and at last sat up in bed, and cried. I lamented my weakness in having assented to Doctor Bryerly's and
my cousin's advice. Was I not departing from my engagement
to my dear papa ? Was I not consenting that my Uncle Silas
should be induced to second my breach of faith by a corresponding perfidy ?

Lady Knollys had done wisely in despatching Doctor Bryerly
so promptly ; for, most assuredly, had he been at Knowl next
morning when I came down I should have recalled my commission.

That day in the study I found four papers which increased
my perturbation. They were in dear papa's handwriting, and
had an indorsement in these words—' Copy of my letter addressed to ——— , one of the trustees named in my will.' Here,
then, were the contents of those four sealed letters which had
excited mine and Lady Knollys' curiosity on the agitating day
on which the will was read.

It contained these words :—

' I name my oppressed and unhappy brother, Silas Ruthyn,
residing at my house of Bartram-Haugh, as guardian of the
person of my beloved child, to convince the world if possible,
and failing that, to satisfy at least all future generations of our
family, that his brother, who knew him best, had implicit confidence in him, and that he deserved it. A cowardly and preposterous slander, originating in political malice, and which

would never have been whispered had he not been poor and imprudent, is best silenced by this ordeal of purification. All I possess goes to him if my child dies under age ; and the custody of her person I commit meanwhile to him alone, knowing that she is as safe in his as she could have been under my own care. I rely upon your remembrance of our early friendship to make this known wherever an opportunity occurs, and also to say what your sense of justice may warrant.'

The other letters were in the same spirit. My heart sank like lead as I read them. I quaked with fear. What had I done ? My father's wise and noble vindication of our dishonoured name I had presumed to frustrate. I had, like a coward, receded from my easy share in the task ; and, merciful Heaven, I had broken my faith with the dead !

a troubled conscience

With these letters in my hand, white with fear, I flew like a shadow to the drawing-room where Cousin Monica was, and told her to read them. I saw by her countenance how much alarmed she was by my looks, but she said nothing, only read the letters hurriedly, and then exclaimed—

' Is this all, my dear child ? I really fancied you had found a second will, and had lost everything. Why, my dearest Maud, we knew all this before. We quite understood poor dear Austin's motive. Why are you so easily disturbed ? '

' Oh, Cousin Monica, I think he was right ; it all seems quite reasonable now ; and I—oh, what a crime !—it must be stopped.'

' My dear Maud, listen to reason. Doctor Bryerly has seen your uncle at Bartram at least two hours ago. You *can't* stop it, and why on earth should you if you could ? Don't you think your uncle should be consulted ? ' said she.

' But he has *decided*. I have his letter speaking of it as settled ; and Doctor Bryerly—oh, Cousin Monica, he's gone *to tempt him*.'

' Nonsense, girl ! Doctor Bryerly is a good and just man, I do believe, and has, beside, no imaginable motive to pervert either his conscience or his judgment. He's not gone to tempt him—stuff !—but to unfold the facts and invite his consideration ; and I say, considering how thoughtlessly such duties are often undertaken, and how long Silas has been living in lazy solitude, shut out from the world, and unused to discuss anything, I do think it only conscientious and honourable that he should have a fair and distinct view of the matter in all its bearings submitted to him before he indolently incurs what may prove the worst danger he was ever involved in.'

So Lady Knollys argued, with feminine energy, and I must confess, with a good deal of the repetition which I have sometimes observed in logicians of my own sex, and she puzzled without satisfying me.

' I don't know why I went to that room,' I said, quite frightened ; ' or why I went to that press ; how it happened that these papers, which we never saw there before, were the first things to strike my eye to-day.'

' What do you mean, dear ? ' said Lady Knollys.

' I mean this—I think I was *brought* there, and that *there* is poor papa's appeal to me, as plain as if his hand came and wrote it upon the wall. ' I nearly screamed the conclusion of this wild confession.

' You are nervous, my darling ; your bad nights have worn you out. Let us go out ; the air will do you good ; and I do assure you that you will very soon see that we are quite right, and rejoice conscientiously that you have acted as you did.'

But I was not to be satisfied, although my first vehemence was quieted. In my prayers that night my conscience upbraided me. When I lay down in bed my nervousness returned fourfold. Everybody at all nervously excitable has suffered some time or another by the appearance of ghastly features presenting themselves in every variety of contortion, one after another, the moment the eyes are closed. This night my dear father's face troubled me—sometimes white and sharp as ivory, sometimes strangely transparent like glass, sometimes all hanging in cadaverous folds, always with the same unnatural expression of diabolical fury.

From this dreadful vision I could only escape by sitting up and staring at the light. At length, worn out, I dropped asleep, and in a dream I distinctly heard papa's voice say sharply outside the bed-curtain :—' Maud, we shall be late at Bartram-Haugh. '

And I awoke in a horror, the wall, as it seemed, still ringing with the summons, and the speaker, I fancied, standing at the other side of the curtain.

A miserable night I passed. In the morning, looking myself like a ghost, I stood in my night-dress by Lady Knollys' bed.

' I have had my warning,' I said. ' Oh, Cousin Monica, papa has been with me, and ordered me to Bartram-Haugh ; and go I will.'

She stared in my face uncomfortably, and then tried to laugh the matter off ; but I know she was troubled at the strange state to which agitation and suspense had reduced me.

' You're taking too much for granted, Maud,' said she ; ' Silas Ruthyn, most likely, will refuse his consent, and insist on your going to Bartram-Haugh. '

' Heaven grant ! ' I exclaimed ; ' but if he doesn't, it is all the same to me, go I will. He may turn me out, but I'll go, and try to expiate the breach of faith that I fear is so horribly wicked. '

We had several hours still to wait for the arrival of the post. For both of us the delay was a suspense ; for me an almost ago-nising one. At length, at an unlooked-for moment, Branston did enter the room with the post-bag. There was a large letter, with the Feltram post-mark, addressed to Lady Knollys—it was Doctor Bryerly's despatch ; we read it together. It was dated on the day before, and its purport was thus :—

' RESPECTED MADAM,—I this day saw Mr. Silas Ruthyn at Bartram-Haugh, and he peremptorily refuses, on any terms, to vacate the guardianship, or to consent to Miss Ruthyn's residing anywhere but under his own immediate care. As he bases his refusal, first upon a conscientious difficulty, declaring that he has no right, through fear of personal contingencies, to abdicate an office imposed in so solemn a way, and so naturally devolv-ing on him as only brother to the deceased ; and secondly upon the effect such a withdrawal, at the instance of the acting trustee, would have upon his own character, amounting to a public self-condemnation ; and as he refused to discuss these positions with me, I could make no way whatsoever with him. Finding, therefore, that his mind was quite made up, after a short time I took my leave. He mentioned that preparations for his niece's reception are being completed, and that he will send for her in a few days ; so that I think it will be advisable that I should go down to Knowl, to assist Miss Ruthyn with any advice she may require before her departure, to discharge servants, get inven-

tories made, and provide for the care of the place and grounds
during her minority.

> 'I am, respected Madam, yours truly,
>   HANS E. BRYERLY.'

I can't describe to you how chapfallen and angry my cousin
looked. She sniffed once or twice, and then said, rather bitterly,
in a subdued tone :—

'Well, *now ;* I hope you are pleased ? '

'No, no, no ; you *know* I'm not—grieved to the heart, my
only friend, my dear Cousin Monica ; but my conscience is at
rest ; you don't know what a sacrifice it is ; I am a most unhappy creature. I feel an indescribable foreboding. I am frightened ; but you won't forsake me, Cousin Monica.'

'No, darling, never,' she said, sadly.

'And you'll come and see me, won't you, as often as you
can ? '

'Yes, dear ; that is if Silas allows me ; and I'm sure he will,'
she added hastily, seeing, I suppose, my terror in my face. 'All
I can do, you may be sure I will, and perhaps he will allow you
to come to me, now and then, for a short visit. You know I am
only six miles away—little more than half an hour's drive,
and though I hate Bartram, and detest Silas—Yes, I *detest Silas,*'
she repeated in reply to my surprised gaze—'I *will* call at Bartram—that is, I say, if he allows me ; for, you know, I haven't
been there for a quarter of a century ; and though I never understood Silas, I fancy he forgives no sins, whether of omission
or commission.'

I wondered what old grudge could make my cousin judge
Uncle Silas always so hardly—I could not suppose it was justice.
I had seen my hero indeed lately so disrespectfully handled
before my eyes, that he had, as idols will, lost something of his
sacredness. But as an article of faith, I still cultivated my trust
in his divinity, and dismissed every intruding doubt with an
exorcism, as a suggestion of the evil one. But I wronged Lady
Knollys in suspecting her of pique, or malice, or anything more
than that tendency to take strong views which some persons
attribute to my sex.

So, then, the little project of Cousin Monica's guardianship,
which, had it been poor papa's wish, would have made me so

very happy, was quite knocked on the head, to revive no more. I
comforted myself, however, with her promise to re-open communications with Bartram-Haugh, and we grew resigned.

I remember, next morning, as we sat at a very late breakfast, Lady Knollys, reading a letter, suddenly made an exclamation and a little laugh, and read on with increased interest
for a few minutes, and then, with another little laugh, she
looked up, placing her hand, with the open letter in it, beside
her tea-cup.

' You'll not guess whom I've been reading about,' said she,
with her head the least thing on one side, and an arch smile.

I felt myself blushing—cheeks, forehead, even down to the tips
of my fingers. I anticipated the name I was to hear. She looked
very much amused. Was it possible that Captain Oakley was
married ?

' I really have not the least idea,' I replied, with that kind of
overdone carelessness which betrays us.

' No, I see quite plainly you have not ; but you can't think
how prettily you blush,' answered she, very much diverted.

' I really don't care,' I replied, with some little dignity, and
blushing deeper and deeper.

' Will you make a guess ?' she asked.

' I *can't* guess.'

' Well, shall I tell you ? '

' Just as you please.'

' Well, I will—that is, I'll read a page of my letter, which tells
it all. Do you know Georgina Fanshawe ? ' she asked.

' Lady Georgina ? No.'

' Well, no matter ; she's in Paris now, and this letter is from
her, and she says—let me see the place—"Yesterday, what do you
think ?—quite an apparition ! — you shall hear. My brother
Craven yesterday insisted on my accompanying him to Le Bas'
shop in that odd little antique street near the Grève ; it is a
wonderful old curiosity shop. I forget what they call them here.
When we went into this place it was very nearly deserted, and
there were so many curious things to look at all about, that for
a minute or two I did not observe a tall woman, in a grey silk
and a black velvet mantle, and quite a nice new Parisian bonnet. You will be *charmed*, by-the-by, with the new shape—it is
only out three weeks, and is quite *indescribably* elegant, *I*

think, at least. They have them, I am sure, by this time at Mol-
nitz's, so I need say no more. And now that I am on this subject
of dress, I have got your lace ; and I think you will be very ungrateful if you are not *charmed* with it." Well, I need not read
all that—here is the rest ; ' and she read—

'"But you'll ask about my mysterious *dame* in the new bonnet and velvet mantle ; she was sitting on a stool at the counter,
not buying, but evidently selling a quantity of stones and trinkets which she had in a card-box, and the man was picking them
up one by one, and, I suppose, valuing them. I was near enough
to see such a darling little pearl cross, with at least half a dozen
really good pearls in it, and had begun to covet them for my
set, when the lady glanced over my shoulder, and she knew me
—in fact, we knew one another—and who do you think she was ?
Well—you'll not guess in a week, and I can't wait so long ; so
I may as well tell you at once—she was that horrid old Mademoiselle Blassemare whom you pointed out to me at Elverston ;
and I never forgot her face since—nor she, it seems, mine, for
she turned away very quickly, and when I next saw her, her
veil was down." '

'Did not you tell me, Maud, that you had lost your pearl
cross while that dreadful Madame de la Rougierre was here ? '

'Yes ; but——'

'I know ; but what has she to do with Mademoiselle de Blassemare, you were going to say—they are one and the same person.'

'Oh, I perceive,' answered I, with that dim sense of danger
and dismay with which one hears suddenly of an enemy of whom
one has lost sight for a time.

'I'll write and tell Georgie to buy that cross. I wager my life
it is yours,' said Lady Knollys, firmly.

The servants, indeed, made no secret of their opinion of
Madame de la Rougierre, and frankly charged her with a long
list of larcenies. Even Anne Wixted, who had enjoyed her barren favour while the gouvernante was here, hinted privately that
she had bartered a missing piece of lace belonging to me with a
gipsy pedlar, for French gloves and an Irish poplin.

'And so surely as I find it is yours, I'll set the police in pursuit.'

'But you must not bring me into court,' said I, half amused
and half alarmed.

' No occasion, my dear ; Mary Quince and Mrs. Rusk can prove it perfectly.'

' And why do you dislike her so very much ? ' I asked.

Cousin Monica leaned back in her chair, and searched the cornice from corner to corner with upturned eyes for the reason, and at last laughed a little, amused at herself.

' Well, really, it is not easy to define, and, perhaps, it is not quite charitable ; but I know I hate her, and I know, you little hypocrite, you hate her as much as I ;' and we both laughed a little.

' But you must tell me all you know of her history.'

' Her history ? ' echoed she. ' I really know next to nothing about it ; only that I used to see her sometimes about the place that Georgina mentions, and there were some unpleasant things said about her ; but you know they may be all lies. The worst I *know* of her is her treatment of you, and her robbing the desk'—(Cousin Monica always called it her *robbery*—'and I think that's enough to hang her. Suppose we go out for a walk ? '

So together we went, and I resumed about Madame ; but no more could I extract—perhaps there was not much more to hear.

CHAPTER XXX

ON THE ROAD

All at Knowl was indicative of the break-up that was so near at hand. Doctor Bryerly arrived according to promise. He was in a whirl of business all the time. He and Mr. Danvers conferred about the management of the estate. It was agreed that the grounds and gardens should be let, but not the house, of which Mrs. Rusk was to take the care. The gamekeeper remained in office, and some out-door servants. But the rest were to go, except Mary Quince, who was to accompany me to Bartram-Haugh as my maid.

' Don't part with Quince,' said Lady Knollys, peremptorily
' they'll want you, but *don't.*'

She kept harping on this point, and recurred to it half a
dozen times every day.

' They'll say, you know, that she is not fit for a lady's maid,
as she certainly is *not,* if it in the least signified in such a wilderness as Bartram-Haugh ; but she is attached, trustworthy, and
honest ; and those are qualities valuable everywhere, especially
in a solitude. Don't allow them to get you a wicked young
French milliner in her stead.'

Sometimes she said things that jarred unpleasantly on my
nerves, and left an undefined sense of danger. Such as :—

' I know she's true to you, and a good creature ; but is she
shrewd enough ? '

Or, with an anxious look :—

' I hope Mary Quince is not easily frightened.'

Or, suddenly :—

' Can Mary Quince write, in case you were ill ?

Or,

' Can she take a message exactly ? '

Or,

' Is she a person of any enterprise and resource, and cool in
an emergency ? '

Now, these questions did not come all in a string, as I write
them down here, but at long intervals, and were followed
quickly by ordinary talk ; but they generally escaped from my
companion after silence and gloomy thought ; and though I
could extract nothing more defined than these questions, yet
they seemed to me to point at some possible danger contemplated in my good cousin's dismal ruminations.

Another topic that occupied my cousin's mind a good deal
was obviously the larceny of my pearl cross. She made a note of
the description furnished by the recollection, respectively, of
Mary Quince, Mrs. Rusk, and myself. I had fancied her little
vision of the police was no more than the result of a momentary impulse ; but really, to judge by her methodical examin-
ations of us, I should have fancied that she had taken it up in
downright earnest.

Having learned that my departure from Knowl was to be
so very soon, she resolved not to leave me before the day of my

journey to Bartram-Haugh ; and as day after day passed by, and the hour of our leave-taking approached, she became more and more kind and affectionate. A feverish and sorrowful interval it was to me.

Of Doctor Bryerly, though staying in the house, we saw almost nothing, except for an hour or so at tea-time. He breakfasted very early, and dined solitarily, and at uncertain hours, as business permitted.

The second evening of his visit, Cousin Monica took occasion to introduce the subject of his visit to Bartram-Haugh.

'You saw him, of course?' said Lady Knollys.

'Yes, he saw me ; he was not well. On hearing who I was, he asked me to go to his room, where he sat in a silk dressing-gown and slippers.'

'About business principally,' said Cousin Monica, laconically.

'That was despatched in very few words ; for he was quite resolved, and placed his refusal upon grounds which it was difficult to dispute. But difficult or no, mind you, he intimated that he would hear nothing more on the subject—so that was closed.'

'Well ; and what is his religion now?' inquired she, irreverently.

'We had some interesting conversation on the subject. He leans much to what we call the doctrine of correspondents. He is read rather deeply in the writings of Swedenborg, and seemed anxious to discuss some points with one who professes to be his follower. To say truth, I did not expect to find him either so well read or so deeply interested in the subject.'

'Was he angry when it was proposed that he should vacate the guardianship?'

'Not at all. Contrariwise, he said he had at first been so minded himself. His years, his habits, and something of the unfitness of the situation, the remoteness of Bartram-Haugh from good teachers, and all that, had struck him, and nearly determined him against accepting the office. But then came the views which I stated in my letter, and they governed him ; and nothing could shake them, he said, or induce him to re-open the question in his own mind.'

All the time Doctor Bryerly was relating his conference with the head of the family at Bartram-Haugh my cousin commented on the narrative with a variety of little 'pishes' and sneers, which I thought showed more of vexation than contempt.

I was glad to hear all that Doctor Bryerly related. It gave me a kind of confidence ; and I experienced a momentary reaction. After all, could Bartram-Haugh be more lonely than I had found Knowl ? Was I not sure of the society of my Cousin Millicent, who was about my own age ? Was it not quite possible that my sojourn in Derbyshire might turn out a happy though very quiet remembrance through all my after-life ? Why should it not ? What time or place would be happy if we gave ourselves over to dismal imaginations ?

So the summons reached me from Uncle Silas. The hours at Knowl were numbered.

The evening before I departed I visited the full-length portrait of Uncle Silas, and studied it for the last time carefully, with deep interest, for many minutes ; but with results vaguer than ever.

With a brother so generous and so wealthy, always ready to help him forward ; with his talents ; with his lithe and gorgeous beauty, the shadow of which hung on that canvas—what might he not have accomplished ? whom might he not have captivated ? And yet where and what was he ? A poor and shunned old man, occupying a lonely house and place that did not belong to him, married to degradation, with a few years of suspected and solitary life before him, and then swift oblivion his best portion.

I gazed on the picture, to fix it well and vividly in my remembrance. I might still trace some of its outlines and tints in its living original, whom I was next day to see for the first time in my life.

So the morning came—my last for many a day at Knowl—a day of partings, a day of novelty and regrets. The travelling carriage and post horses were at the door. Cousin Monica's carriage had just carried her away to the railway. We had embraced with tears ; and her kind face was still before me, and her words of comfort and promise in my ears. The early sharpness of morning was still in the air ; the frosty dew still glistened on the window-panes. We had made a hasty breakfast, my share of which was a single cup of tea. The aspect of the house how strange ! Uncarpeted, uninhabited, doors for the most part

locked, all the servants but Mrs. Rusk and Branston departed.
The drawing-room door stood open, and a charwoman was wash-
ing the bare floor. I was looking my last—for who could say how
long?—on the old house, and lingered. The luggage was all up.
I made Mary Quince get in first, for every delay was precious;
and now the moment was come. I hugged and kissed Mrs. Rusk
in the hall.

' God bless you, Miss Maud, darling. You must not fret;
mind, the time won't be long going over—*no* time at all; and
you'll be bringing back a fine young gentleman—who knows?
as great as the Duke of Wellington, for your husband; and I'll
take the best of care of everything, and the birds and the dogs,
till you come back; and I'll go and see you and Mary, if you'll
allow, in Derbyshire;' and so forth.

I got into the carriage, and bid Branston, who shut the door,
good-bye, and kissed hands to Mrs. Rusk, who was smiling and
drying her eyes and courtesying on the hall-door steps. The
dogs, who had started gleefully with the carriage, were called
back by Branston, and driven home, wondering and wistful,
looking back with ears oddly cocked and tails dejected. My
heart thanked them for their kindness, and I felt like a stranger,
and very desolate.

It was a bright, clear morning. It had been settled that it was
not worth the trouble changing from the carriage to the railway
for sake of five-and-twenty miles, and so the entire journey of
sixty miles was to be made by the post road—the pleasantest
travelling, if the mind were free. The grander and more distant features of the landscape we may see well enough from
the window of the railway-carriage; but it is the foreground
that interests and instructs us, like a pleasant gossiping history;
and *that* we had, in old days, from the post-chaise window. It
was more than travelling picquet. Something of all conditions of
life—luxury and misery—high spirits and low;—all sorts of costume, livery, rags, millinery; faces buxom, faces wrinkled,
faces kind, faces wicked;—no end of interest and suggestion,
passing in a procession silent and vivid, and all in their proper
scenery. The golden corn-sheafs—the old dark-alleyed orchards,
and the high streets of antique towns. There were few dreams
brighter, few books so pleasant.

We drove by the dark wood—it always looked dark to me—

where the ' mausoleum ' stands—where my dear parents both lay now. I gazed on its sombre masses not with a softened feeling, but a peculiar sense of pain, and was glad when it was quite past.

All the morning I had not shed a tear. Good Mary Quince cried at leaving Knowl ; Lady Knollys' eyes were not dry as she kissed and blessed me, and promised an early visit ; and the dark, lean, energetic face of the housekeeper was quivering, and her cheeks wet, as I drove away. But I, whose grief was sorest, never shed a tear. I only looked about from one familiar object to another, pale, excited, not quite apprehending my departure, and wondering at my own composure.

But when we reached the old bridge, with the tall osiers standing by the buttress, and looked back at poor Knowl—the places we love and are leaving look so fairy-like and so sad in the clear distance, and this is the finest view of the gabled old house, with its slanting meadow-lands and noble timber reposing in solemn groups—I gazed at the receding vision, and the tears came at last, and I wept in silence long after the fair picture was hidden from view by the intervening uplands.

I was relieved, and when we had made our next change of horses, and got into a country that was unknown to me, the new scenery and the sense of progress worked their accustomed effects on a young traveller who had lived a particularly secluded life, and I began to experience, on the whole, a not unpleasurable excitement.

Mary Quince and I, with the hopefulness of inexperienced travellers, began already to speculate about our proximity to Bartram-Haugh, and were sorely disappointed when we heard from the nondescript courier—more like a ostler than a servant, who sat behind in charge of us and the luggage, and represented my guardian's special care—at nearly one o'clock, that we had still forty miles to go, a considerable portion of which was across the high Derbyshire mountains, before we reached Bartram-Haugh.

The fact was, we had driven at a pace accommodated rather to the convenience of the horses than to our impatience ; and finding, at the quaint little inn where we now halted, that we must wait for a nail or two in a loose shoe of one of our relay, we consulted, and being both hungry, agreed to beguile the time

with an early dinner, which we enjoyed very sociably in a queer
little parlour with a bow window, and commanding, with a
litle garden for foreground, a very pretty landscape.

Good Mary Quince, like myself, had quite dried her tears
by this time, and we were both highly interested, and I a little
nervous, too, about our arrival and reception at Bartram. Some
time, of course, was lost in this pleasant little parlour, before
we found ourselves once more pursuing our way.

The slowest part of our journey was the pull up the long
mountain road, ascending zig-zag, as sailors make way against
a head-wind, by tacking. I forget the name of the pretty little
group of houses—it did not amount to a village—buried in trees,
where we got our *four* horses and two postilions, for the work
was severe. I can only designate it as the place where Mary
Quince and I had our tea, very comfortably, and bought some
gingerbread, very curious to look upon, but quite uneatable.

The greater portion of the ascent, when we were fairly upon
the mountain, was accomplished at a walk, and at some particularly steep points we had to get out and go on foot. But
this to me was quite delightful. I had never scaled a mountain
before, and the ferns and heath, the pure boisterous air, and
above all the magnificent view of the rich country we were
leaving behind, now gorgeous and misty in sunset tints, stretching in gentle undulations far beneath us, quite enchanted me.

We had just reached the summit when the sun went down.
The low grounds at the other side were already lying in cold
grey shadow, and I got the man who sat behind to point out as
well as he could the site of Bartram-Haugh. But mist was gathering over all by this time. The filmy disk of the moon which
was to light us on, so soon as twilight faded into night, hung
high in air. I tried to see the sable mass of wood which he
described. But it was vain, and to acquire a clear idea of the
place, as of its master, I must only wait that nearer view which
an hour or two more would afford me.

And now we rapidly descended the mountain side. The scenery was wilder and bolder than I was accustomed to. Our road
skirted the edge of a great heathy moor. The silvery light of the
moon began to glimmer, and we passed a gipsy bivouac with
fires alight and caldrons hanging over them. It was the first I
had seen. Two or three low tents ; a couple of dark, withered

crones, veritable witches ; a graceful girl standing behind, gazing
after us ; and men in odd-shaped hats, with gaudy waistcoats and
bright-coloured neck-handkerchiefs and gaitered legs, stood
lazily in front. They had all a wild tawdry display of colour ;
and a group of alders in the rear made a background of shade
for tents, fires, and figures.

I opened a front window of the chariot, and called to the
postboys to stop. The groom from behind came to the window.

'Are not those gipsies ? ' I enquired.

'Yes, please'm, them's gipsies, sure, Miss,' he answered, glancing with that odd smile, half contemptuous, half superstitious,
with which I have since often observed the peasants of Derbyshire eyeing those thievish and uncanny neighbours.

CHAPTER XXXI

BARTRAM-HAUGH

In a moment a tall, lithe girl, black-haired, black-eyed, and, as
I thought, inexpressibly handsome, was smiling, with such beautiful rings of pearly teeth, at the window ; and in her peculiar
accent, with a suspicion of something foreign in it, proposing
with many courtesies to tell the lady her fortune.

I had never seen this wild tribe of the human race before—
children of mystery and liberty. Such vagabondism and beauty
in the figure before me ! I looked at their hovels and thought
of the night, and wondered at their independence, and felt my
inferiority. I could not resist. She held up her slim oriental
hand.

'Yes, I'll hear my fortune,' I said, returning the sibyl's smile
instinctively.

'Give me some money, Mary Quince. No, *not* that,' I said,
rejecting the thrifty sixpence she tendered, for I had heard that
the revelations of this weird sisterhood were bright in proportion to the kindness of their clients, and was resolved to ap-

proach Bartram with cheerful auguries. 'That five-shilling piece,' I insisted ; and honest Mary reluctantly surrendered the coin.

So the feline beauty took it, with courtesies and 'thankees,' smiling still, and hid it away as if she stole it, and looked on my open palm still smiling ; and told me, to my surprise, that there was *somebody* I liked very much, and I was almost afraid she would name Captain Oakley ; that he would grow very rich, and that I should marry him ; that I should move about from place to place a great deal for a good while to come. That I had some enemies, who should be sometimes so near as to be in the same room with me, and yet they should not be able to hurt me. That I should see blood spilt and yet not my own, and finally be very happy and splendid, like the heroine of a fairy tale.

Did this strange, girlish charlatan see in my face some signs of shrinking when she spoke of enemies, and set me down for a coward whose weakness might be profitable ? Very likely. At all events she plucked a long brass pin, with a round bead for a head, from some part of her dress, and holding the point in her fingers, and exhibiting the treasure before my eyes, she told me that I must get a charmed pin like that, which her grandmother had given to her, and she ran glibly through a story of all the magic expended on .it, and told me she could not part with it ; but its virtue was that you were to stick it through the blanket, and while it was there neither rat, nor cat, nor snake—and then came two more terms in the catalogue, which I suppose belonged to the gipsy dialect, and which she explained to mean, as well as I could understand, the first a malevolent spirit, and the second 'a cove to cut your throat,' could approach or hurt you.

A charm like that, she gave me to understand, I must by hook or by crook obtain. She had not a second. None of her people in the camp over there possessed one. I am ashamed to confess that I actually paid her a pound for this brass pin ! The purchase was partly an indication of my temperament, which could never let an opportunity pass away irrevocably without a struggle, and always apprehended 'Some day or other I'll reproach myself for having neglected it !' and partly a record of the trepidations of that period of my life. At all events I had her pin, and she my pound, and I venture to say I was the gladder of the two.

She stood on the road-side bank courtseying and smiling, the first enchantress I had encountered, and I watched the receding picture, with its patches of firelight, its dusky groups and donkey carts, white as skeletons in the moonlight, as we drove rapidly away.

They, I suppose, had a wild sneer and a merry laugh over my purchase, as they sat and ate their supper of stolen poultry, about their fire, and were duly proud of belonging to the superior race.

Mary Quince, shocked at my prodigality, hinted a remonstrance.

'It went to my heart, Miss, it did. They're such a lot, young and old, all alike thieves and vagabonds, and many a poor body wanting.'

'Tut, Mary, never mind. Everyone has her fortune told some time in her life, and you can't have a good one without paying. I think, Mary, we must be near Bartram now.'

The road now traversed the side of a steep hill, parallel to which, along the opposite side of a winding river, rose the dark steeps of a corresponding upland, covered with forest that looked awful and dim in the deep shadow, while the moonlight rippled fitfully upon the stream beneath.

'It seems to be a beautiful country,' I said to Mary Quince, who was munching a sandwich in the corner, and thus appealed to, adjusted her bonnet, and made an inspection from *her* window, which, however, commanded nothing but the heathy slope of the hill whose side we were traversing.

'Well, Miss, I suppose it is; but there's a deal o' mountains— is not there?'

And so saying, honest Mary leaned back again, and went on with her sandwich.

We were now descending at a great pace. I knew we were coming near. I stood up as well as I could in the carriage, to see over the postilions' heads. I was eager, but frightened too; agitated as the crisis of the arrival and meeting approached. At last, a long stretch of comparatively level country below us, with masses of wood as well as I could see irregularly overspreading

it, became visible as the narrow valley through which we were
speeding made a sudden bend.

Down we drove, and now I did perceive a change. A great
grass-grown park-wall, overtopped with mighty trees ; but still
on and on we came at a canter that seemed almost a gallop. The
old grey park-wall flanking us at one side, and a pretty pastoral
hedgerow of ash-trees, irregularly on the other.

At last the postilions began to draw bridle, and at a slight
angle, the moon shining full upon them, we wheeled into a wide
semicircle formed by the receding park-walls, and halted before
a great fantastic iron gate, and a pair of tall fluted piers, of
white stone, all grass-grown and ivy-bound, with great cornices,
surmounted with shields and supporters, the Ruthyn bearings
washed by the rains of Derbyshire for many a generation of
Ruthyns, almost smooth by this time, and looking bleached and
phantasmal, like giant sentinels, with each a hand clasped in
his comrade's, to bar our passage to the enchanted castle—the
florid tracery of the iron gate showing like the draperies of white
robes hanging from their extended arms to the earth.

Our courier got down and shoved the great gate open, and we
entered, between sombre files of magnificent forest trees, one of
those very broad straight avenues whose width measures the
front of the house. This was all built of white stone, resembling
that of Caen, which parts of Derbyshire produce in such abundance.

So this was Bartram, and here was Uncle Silas. I was almost
breathless as I approached. The bright moon shining full on the
white front of the old house revealed not only its highly dec-
orated style, its fluted pillars and doorway, rich and florid
carving, and balustraded summit, but also its stained and moss-
grown front. Two giant trees, overthrown at last by the recent
storm, lay with their upturned roots, and their yellow foliage
still flickering on the sprays that were to bloom no more, where
they had fallen, at the right side of the court-yard, which, like
the avenue, was studded with tufted weeds and grass.

All this gave to the aspect of Bartram a forlorn character of
desertion and decay, contrasting almost awfully with the gran-
deur of its proportions and richness of its architecture.

There was a ruddy glow from a broad window in the
second row, and I thought I saw some one peep from it and dis-

appear; at the same moment there was a furious barking of
dogs, some of whom ran scampering into the court-yard from
a half-closed side door ; and amid their uproar, the bawling of
the man in the back seat, who jumped down to drive them off,
and the crack of the postilions' whips, who struck at them, we
drew up before the lordly door-steps of this melancholy mansion.

Just as our attendant had his hand on the knocker the door
opened, and we saw, by a not very brilliant candle-light, three
figures—a shabby little old man, thin, and very much stooped,
with a white cravat, and looking as if his black clothes were too
large, and made for some one else, stood with his hand upon the
door ; a young, plump, but very pretty female figure, in unusually short petticoats, with fattish legs, and nice ankles, in boots,
stood in the centre ; and a dowdy maid, like an old charwoman,
behind her.

The household paraded for welcome was not certainly very
brilliant. Amid the riot the trunks were deliberately put down
by our attendant, who kept shouting to the old man at the door,
and to the dogs in turn ; and the old man was talking and
pointing stiffly and tremulously, but I could not hear what he
said.

' Was it possible—could that mean-looking old man be Uncle
Silas ? '

The idea stunned me ; but I almost instantly perceived that he
was much too small, and I was relieved, and even grateful. It
was certainly an odd mode of procedure to devote primary attention to the trunks and boxes, leaving the travellers still
shut up in the carriage, of which they were by this time pretty
well tired. I was not sorry for the reprieve, however : being nervous about first impressions, and willing to defer mine, I sat
shyly back, peeping at the candle and moonlight picture before
me, myself unseen.

' Will you tell—yes or no—is my cousin in the coach ? '
screamed the plump young lady, stamping her stout black boot,
in a momentary lull.

Yes, I was there, sure.

' And why the puck don't you let her out, you stupe, you ? '

' Run down, Giblets, you never do nout without driving, and
let Cousin Maud out. You're very welcome to Bartram.' This
greeting was screamed at an amazing pitch, and repeated before

I had time to drop the window, and say ' thank you.' ' I'd a let you out myself—there's a good dog, you would na' bite Cousin ' (the parenthesis was to a huge mastiff, who thrust himself beside her, by this time quite pacified)—' only I daren't go down the steps, for the governor said I shouldn't.'

The venerable person who went by the name of Giblets had by this time opened the carriage door, and our courier, or ' boots '—he looked more like the latter functionary—had lowered the steps, and in greater trepidation than I experienced when in after-days I was presented to my sovereign, I glided down, to offer myself to the greeting and inspection of the plain-spoken young lady who stood at the top of the steps to receive me.

She welcomed me with a hug and a hearty buss, as she called that salutation, on each cheek, and pulled me into the hall, and was evidently glad to see me.

' And you're tired a bit, I warrant ; and who 's the old 'un, who ? ' she asked eagerly, in a stage whisper, which made my ear numb for five minutes after. ' Oh, oh, the maid ! and a precious old 'un—ha, ha, ha ! But lawk ! how grand she is, with her black silk, cloak and crape, and I only in twilled cotton, and rotten old Coburg for Sundays. Odds ! it's a shame ; but you'll be tired, you will. It's a smartish pull, they do say, from Knowl. I know a spell of it, only so far as the " Cat and Fiddle," near the Lunnon-road. Come up, will you ? Would you like to come in first and talk a bit wi' the governor ? Father, you know, he's a bit silly, he is, this while.' I found that the phrase meant only *bodily* infirmity. ' He took a pain o' Friday, newralgie—something or other he calls it—rheumatics it is when it takes old " Giblets " there ; and he's sitting in his own room ; or maybe you'd like better to come to your bedroom first, for it is dirty work travelling, they do say.'

Yes ; I preferred the preliminary adjustment. Mary Quince was standing behind me ; and as my voluble kinswoman talked on, we had each ample time and opportunity to observe the personnel of the other ; and she made no scruple of letting me perceive that she was improving it, for she stared me full in the face, taking in evidently feature after feature ; and she felt the material of my mantle pretty carefully between her finger and thumb, and manually examined my chain and trinkets, and picked up my hand as she might a glove, to con over my rings.

I can't say, of course, exactly what impression I may have produced on her. But in my cousin Milly I saw a girl who looked younger than her years, plump, but with a slender waist, with light hair, lighter than mine, and very blue eyes, rather round ; on the whole very good-looking. She had an odd swaggering walk, a toss of her head, and a saucy and imperious, but rather good-natured and honest countenance. She talked rather loud, with a good ringing voice, and a boisterous laugh when it came.

If *I* was behind the fashion, what would Cousin Monica have thought of her ? She was arrayed, as she had stated, in black twilled cotton expressive of her affliction ; but it was made almost as short in the skirt as that of the prints of the Bavarian broom girls. She had white cotton stockings, and a pair of black leather boots, with leather buttons, and, for a lady, prodigiously thick soles, which reminded me of the navvy boots I had so often admired in *Punch*. I must add that the hands with which she assisted her scrutiny of my dress, though pretty, were very much sunburnt indeed.

' And what's *her* name ? ' she demanded, nodding to Mary Quince, who was gazing on her awfully, with round eyes, as an inland spinster might upon a whale beheld for the first time.

Mary courtesied, and I answered.

' Mary Quince,' she repeated. ' You're welcome, Quince. What shall I call her ? I've a name for all o' them. Old Giles there, is Giblets. He did not like it first, but he answers quick enough now ; and Old Lucy Wyat there,' nodding toward the old woman, ' is Lucia de l'Amour.' A slightly erroneous reading of Lammermoor, for my cousin sometimes made mistakes, and was not much versed in the Italian opera. ' You know it's a play, and I call her L'Amour for shortness ; ' and she laughed hilariously, and I could not forbear joining ; and, winking at me, she called aloud, ' L'Amour.'

To which the crone, with a high-cauled cap, resembling Mother Hubbard, responded with a courtesy and ' Yes, 'm.'

' Are all the trunks and boxes took up ? '

They were.

' Well, we'll come now ; and what shall I call you, Quince ? Let me see.'

'According to your pleasure, Miss,' answered Mary, with dignity, and a dry courtesy.

'Why, you're as hoarse as a frog, Quince. We'll call you Quinzy for the present. That'll do. Come along, Quinzy.'

So my Cousin Milly took me under the arm, and pulled me forward; but as we ascended, she let me go, leaning back to make inspection of my attire from a new point of view.

'Hallo, cousin,' she cried, giving my dress a smack with her open hand. 'What a plague do you want of all that bustle; you'll leave it behind, lass, the first bush you jump over.'

I was a good deal astounded. I was also very near laughing, for there was a sort of importance in her plump countenance, and an indescribable grotesqueness in the fashion of her garments, which heightened the outlandishness of her talk, in a way which I cannot at all describe.

What palatial wide stairs those were which we ascended, with their prodigious carved banisters of oak, and each huge pillar on the landing-place crowned with a shield and carved heraldic supporters; florid oak panelling covered the walls. But of the house I could form no estimate, for Uncle Silas's housekeeping did not provide light for hall and passages, and we were dependent on the glimmer of a single candle; but there would be quite enough of this kind of exploration in the daylight.

So along dark oak flooring we advanced to my room, and I had now an opportunity of admiring, at my leisure, the lordly proportions of the building. Two great windows, with dark and tarnished curtains, rose half as high again as the windows of Knowl; and yet Knowl, in its own style, is a fine house. The door-frames, like the window-frames, were richly carved; the fireplace was in the same massive style, and the mantelpiece projected with a mass of very rich carving. On the whole I was surprised. I had never slept in so noble a room before.

The furniture, I must confess, was by no means on a par with the architectural pretensions of the apartment. A French bed, a piece of carpet about three yards square, a small table, two chairs, a toilet table—no wardrobe—no chest of drawers. The furniture painted white, and of the light and diminutive kind, was particularly ill adapted to the scale and style of the apartment, one end only of which it occupied, and that but sparsely, leaving the rest of the chamber in the nakedness of a stately desolation.

My cousin Milly ran away to report progress to 'the Governor,' as she termed Uncle Silas.

'Well, Miss Maud, I never did expect to see the like o' that!' exclaimed honest Mary Quince. 'Did you ever see such a young lady? She's no more like one o' the family than I am. Law bless us! and what's she dressed like? Well, well, well!' And Mary, with a rueful shake of her head, clicked her tongue pathetically to the back of her teeth, while I could not forbear laughing.

'And such a scrap o' furniture! Well, well, well!' and the same ticking of the tongue followed.

But, in a few minutes, back came Cousin Milly, and, with a barbarous sort of curiosity, assisted in unpacking my trunks, and stowing away the treasures, on which she ventured a variety of admiring criticisms, in the presses which, like cupboards, filled recesses in the walls, with great oak doors, the keys of which were in them.

As I was making my hurried toilet, she entertained me now and then with more strictly personal criticisms.

'Your hair's a shade darker than mine—it's none the better o' that though—is it? Mine's said to be the right shade. I don't know—what do you say?'

I conceded the point with a good grace.

'I wish my hands was as white though—you do lick me there; but it's all gloves, and I never could abide 'em. I think I'll try though—they *are* very white, sure.'

'I wonder which is the prettiest, you or me? *I* don't know, *I*'m sure—which do *you* think?'

I laughed outright at this challenge, and she blushed a little, and for the first time seemed for a moment a little shy.

'Well, you *are* a half an inch longer than me, I think—don't you?'

I was fully an inch taller, so I had no difficulty in making the proposed admission.

'Well, you do look handsome! doesn't she, Quinzy, lass? but your frock comes down almost to your heels—it does.'

And she glanced from mine to hers, and made a little kick up with the heel of the navvy boot to assist her in measuring the comparative distance.

'Maybe mine's a thought too short?' she suggested. 'Who's

there ? Oh ! it's you, is it ? ' she cried as Mother Hubbard appeared at the door. ' Come in, L'Amour—don't you know, lass, you're always welcome ? '

She had come to let us know that Uncle Silas would be happy to see me whenever I was ready ; and that my cousin Millicent would conduct me to the room where he awaited me.

In an instant all the comic sensations awakened by my singular cousin's eccentricities vanished, and I was thrilled with awe. I was about to see in the flesh—faded, broken, aged, but still identical—that being who had been the vision and the problem of so many years of my short life.

CHAPTER XXXII

UNCLE SILAS

I thought my odd cousin was also impressed with a kind of awe, though different in degree from mine, for a shade overcast her face, and she was silent as we walked side by side along the gallery, accompanied by the crone who carried the candle which lighted us to the door of that apartment which I may call Uncle Silas's presence chamber.

Milly whispered to me as we approached—

' Mind how you make a noise ; the governor's as sharp as a weasel, and nothing vexes him like that.'

She was herself toppling along on tiptoe. We paused at a door near the head of the great staircase, and L'Amour knocked timidly with her rheumatic knuckles.

A voice, clear and penetrating, from within summoned us to enter. The old woman opened the door, and the next moment I was in the presence of Uncle Silas.

At the far end of a handsome wainscoted room, near the hearth in which a low fire was burning, beside a small table on which stood four waxlights, in tall silver candlesticks, sat a singular-looking old man.

The dark wainscoting behind him, and the vastness of the room, in the remoter parts of which the light which fell strongly upon his face and figure expended itself with hardly any effect, exhibited him with the forcible and strange relief of a finely painted Dutch portrait. For some time I saw nothing but him.

A face like marble, with a fearful monumental look, and, for an old man, singularly vivid strange eyes, the singularity of which rather grew upon me as I looked ; for his eyebrows were still black, though his hair descended from his temples in long locks of the purest silver and fine as silk, nearly to his shoulders.

He rose, tall and slight, a little stooped, all in black, with an ample black velvet tunic, which was rather a gown than a coat, with loose sleeves, showing his snowy shirt some way up the arm, and a pair of wrist buttons, then quite out of fashion, which glimmered aristocratically with diamonds.

I know I can't convey in words an idea of this apparition, drawn as it seemed in black and white, venerable, bloodless, fiery-eyed, with its singular look of power, and an expression so bewildering—was it derision, or anguish, or cruelty, or patience ?

The wild eyes of this strange old man were fixed upon me as he rose ; an habitual contraction, which in certain lights took the character of a scowl, did not relax as he advanced toward me with his thin-lipped smile. He said something in his clear, gentle, but cold voice, the import of which I was too much agitated to catch, and he took both my hands in his, welcomed me with a courtly grace which belonged to another age, and led me affectionately, with many inquiries which I only half comprehended, to a chair near his own.

' I need not introduce my daughter ; she has saved me that mortification. You'll find her, I believe, good-natured and affectionate ; *au reste,* I fear a very rustic Miranda, and fitted rather for the society of Caliban than of a sick old Prospero. Is it not so, Millicent ? '

The old man paused sarcastically for an answer, with his eyes fixed severely on my odd cousin, who blushed and looked uneasily to me for a hint.

' I don't know who they be—neither one nor t'other.'

' Very good, my dear,' he replied, with a little mocking bow. ' You see, my dear Maud, what a Shakespearean you have got for a cousin. It's plain, however, she has made acquaintance with some of our dramatists : she has studied the rôle of *Miss Hoyden* so perfectly.'

It was not a reasonable peculiarity of my uncle that he resented, with a good deal of playful acrimony, my poor cousin's want of education, for which, if he were not to blame, certainly neither was she.

' You see her, poor thing, a result of all the combined disadvantages of want of refined education, refined companionship, and, I fear, naturally, of refined tastes ; but a sojourn at a good French conventual school will do wonders, and I hope to manage by-and-by. In the meantime we jest at our misfortunes, and love one another, I hope, cordially.'

He extended his thin, white hand with a chilly smile towards Milly, who bounced up, and took it with a frightened look ; and he repeated, holding her hand rather slightly I thought, ' Yes, I hope, very cordially,' and then turning again to me, he put it over the arm of his chair, and let it go, as a man might drop something he did not want from a carriage window.

Having made this apology for poor Milly, who was plainly bewildered, he passed on, to her and my relief, to other topics, every now and then expressing his fears that I was fatigued, and his anxiety that I should partake of some supper or tea ; but these solicitudes somehow seemed to escape his remembrance almost as soon as uttered ; and he maintained the conversation, which soon degenerated into a close, and to me a painful examination, respecting my dear father's illness and its symptoms, upon which I could give no information, and his habits, upon which I could.

Perhaps he fancied that there might be some family predisposition to the organic disease of which his brother died, and that his questions were directed rather to the prolonging of his own life than to the better understanding of my dear father's death.

How little was there left to this old man to make life desirable, and yet how keenly, I afterwards found, he clung to it. Have we not all of us seen those to whom life was not only *undesirable,* but positively painful—a mere series of bodily torments, yet hold to it with a desperate and pitiable tenacity—old children or young, it is all the same.

See how a sleepy child will put off the inevitable departure for bed. The little creature's eyes blink and stare, and it needs constant jogging to prevent his nodding off into the slumber which nature craves. His waking is a pain ; he is quite worn out, and peevish, and stupid, and yet he implores a respite, and deprecates repose, and vows he is not sleepy, even to the moment when his mother takes him in her arms, and carries him, in a sweet slumber, to the nursery. So it is with us old children of earth and the great sleep of death, and nature our kind mother. Just so reluctantly we part with consciousness, the picture is, even to the last, so interesting ; the bird in the hand, though sick and môulting, so inestimably better than all the brilliant tenants of the bush. We sit up, yawning, and blinking, and stupid, the whole scene swimming before us, and the stories and music humming off into the sound of distant winds and waters. It is not time yet ; we are not fatigued ; we are good for another hour still, and so protesting against bed, we falter and drop into the dreamless sleep which nature assigns to fatigue and satiety.

He then spoke a little eulogy of his brother, very polished, and, indeed, in a kind of way, eloquent. He possessed in a high degree that accomplishment, too little cultivated, I think, by the present generation, of expressing himself with perfect precision and fluency. There was, too, a good deal of slight illustrative quotation, and a sprinkling of French flowers, over his conversation, which gave to it a character at once elegant and artificial. It was all easy, light, and pointed, and being quite new to me, had a wonderful fascination.

He then told me that Bartram was the temple of liberty, that the health of a whole life was founded in a few years of youth, air, and exercise, and that accomplishments, at least, if not education, should wait upon health. Therefore, while at Bartram, I should dispose of my time quite as I pleased, and the more I plundered the garden and gipsied in the woodlands, the better.

Then he told me what a miserable invalid he was, and how the doctors interfered with his frugal tastes. A glass of beer and a mutton chop—his ideal of a dinner—he dared not touch. They made him drink light wines, which he detested, and live upon those artificial abominations all liking for which vanishes with youth.

There stood on a side-table, in its silver coaster, a long-necked Rhenish bottle, and beside it a thin pink glass, and he quivered his fingers in a peevish way toward them.

But unless he found himself better very soon, he would take his case into his own hands, and try the dietary to which nature pointed.

He waved his fingers toward his bookcases, and told me his books were altogether at my service during my stay; but this promise ended, I must confess, disappointingly. At last, remarking that I must be fatigued, he rose, and kissed me with a solemn tenderness, placed his hand upon what I now perceived to be a large Bible, with two broad silk markers, red and gold, folded in it—the one, I might conjecture, indicating the place in the Old, the other in the New Testament. It stood on the small table that supported the waxlights, with a handsome cut bottle of eau-de-cologne, his gold and jewelled pencil-case, and his chased repeater, chain, and seals, beside it. There certainly were no indications of poverty in Uncle Silas's room; and he said impressively—

'Remember that book; in it your father placed his trust, in it he found his reward, in it lives my only hope; consult it, my beloved niece, day and night, as the oracle of life.'

Then he laid his thin hand on my head, and blessed me, and then kissed my forehead.

'No—a!' exclaimed Cousin Milly's lusty voice. I had quite forgotten her presence, and looked at her with a little start. She was seated on a very high old-fashioned chair; she had palpably been asleep; her round eyes were blinking and staring glassily at us; and her white legs and navvy boots were dangling in the air.

'Have you anything to remark about Noah?' enquired her father, with a polite inclination and an ironical interest.

'No—a,' she repeated in the same blunt accents; 'I didn't snore; did I? No—a.'

The old man smiled and shrugged a little at me—it was the smile of disgust.

'Good night, my dear Maud;' and turning to her, he said,

with a peculiar gentle sharpness, ' Had not you better wake, my
dear, and try whether your cousin would like some supper ? '

So he accompanied us to the door, outside which we found
L'Amour's candle awaiting us.

' I'm awful afraid of the Governor, I am. Did I snore that
time ? '

' No, dear ; at least, I did not hear it,' I said, unable to repress
a smile.

' Well, if I didn't, I was awful near it,' she said, reflectively.

We found poor Mary Quince dozing over the fire ; but we
soon had tea and other good things, of which Milly partook
with a wonderful appetite.

' I *was* in a qualm about it,' said Milly, who by this time was
quite herself again. ' When he spies me a-napping, maybe he
don't fetch me a prod with his pencil-case over the head. Odd !
girl, it *is* sore.'

When I contrasted the refined and fluent old gentleman whom
I had just left, with this amazing specimen of young ladyhood, I
grew sceptical almost as to the possibility of her being his child.

I was to learn, however, how little she had, I won't say of his
society, but even of his presence—that she had no domestic companion of the least pretensions to education—that she ran wild
about the place—never, except in church, so much as saw a person of that rank to which she was born—and that the little she
knew of reading and writing had been picked up, in desultory
half-hours, from a person who did not care a pin about her manners or decorum, and perhaps rather enjoyed her grotesqueness—
and that no one who was willing to take the least trouble about
her was competent to make her a particle more refined than
I saw her—the wonder ceased. We don't know how little is
heritable, and how much simply training, until we encounter
some·such spectacle as that of my poor cousin Milly.

When I lay down in my bed and reviewed the day, it seemed
like a month of wonders. Uncle Silas was always before me ; the
voice so silvery for an old man—so preternaturally soft ; the manners so sweet, so gentle ; the aspect, smiling, suffering, spectral.
It was no longer a shadow ; I had now seen him in the flesh.
But, after all, was he more than a shadow to me ? When I closed
my eyes I saw him before me still, in necromantic black, ashy
with a pallor on which I looked with fear and pain, a face so

dazzlingly pale, and those hollow, fiery, awful eyes ! It sometimes seemed as if the curtain opened, and I had seen a ghost.

I had seen him ; but he was still an enigma and a marvel.
The living face did not expound the past, any more than the
portrait portended the future. He was still a mystery and a
vision ; and thinking of these things I fell asleep.

Mary Quince, who slept in the dressing-room, the door of
which was close to my bed, and lay open to secure me against
ghosts, called me up ; and the moment I knew where I was I
jumped up, and peeped eagerly from the window. It commanded
the avenue and court-yard ; but we were many windows removed from that over the hall-door, and immediately beneath
ours lay the two giant lime trees, prostrate and uprooted,
which I had observed as we drove up the night before.

I saw more clearly in the bright light of morning the signs
of neglect and almost of dilapidation which had struck me as I
approached. The court-yard was tufted over with grass, seldom
from year to year crushed by the carriage-wheels, or trodden by
the feet of visitors. This melancholy verdure thickened where
the area was more remote from the centre ; and under the windows, and skirting the walls to the left, was reinforced by a
thick grove of nettles. The avenue was all grass-grown, except
in the very centre, where a narrow track still showed the road-
way. The handsome carved balustrade of the court-yard was
discoloured with lichens, and in two places gapped and broken ;
and the air of decay was heightened by the fallen trees, among
whose sprays and yellow leaves the small birds were hopping.

Before my toilet was completed, in marched my cousin Milly.
We were to breakfast alone that morning, ' and so much the
better,' she told me. Sometimes the Governor ordered her to
breakfast with him, and ' never left off chaffing her ' till his
newspaper came, and ' sometimes he said such things he made
her cry,' and then he only ' boshed her more,' and packed her
away to her room ; but she was by chalks nicer than him, talk
as he might. ' *Was* not she nicer ? was not she ? was not she ? '
Upon this point she was so strong and urgent that I was obliged
to reply by a protest against awarding the palm of elegance
between parent and child, and declaring I liked her very much,
which I attested by a kiss.

' I know right well which of us you do think's the nicest, and no mistake, only you're afraid of him ; and he had no business boshing me last night before you. I knew he was at it, though I couldn't twig him altogether ; but wasn't he a sneak, now, wasn't he ? '

This was a still more awkward question ; so I kissed her again, and said she must never ask me to say of my uncle in his absence anything I could not say to his face.

At which speech she stared at me for a while, and then treated me to one of her hearty laughs, after which she seemed happier, and gradually grew into better humour with her father.

' Sometimes, when the curate calls, he has me up—for he's as religious as six, he is—and they read Bible and prays, ho—don't they ? You'll have that, lass, like me, to go through ; and maybe I don't hate it ; oh, no ! '

We breakfasted in a small room, almost a closet, off the great parlour, which was evidently quite disused. Nothing could be homelier than our equipage, or more shabby than the furniture of the little apartment. Still, somehow, I liked it. It was a total change ; but one likes ' roughing it ' a little at first.

CHAPTER XXXIII

THE WINDMILL WOOD

I had not time to explore this noble old house as my curiosity prompted ; for Milly was in such a fuss to set out for the ' blackberry dell ' that I saw little more than just so much as I necessarily traversed in making my way to and from my room.

The actual decay of the house had been prevented by my dear father ; and the roof, windows, masonry, and carpentry had all been kept in repair. But short of indications of actual ruin, there are many manifestations of poverty and neglect which impress with a feeling of desolation. It was plain that not nearly a tithe of this great house was inhabited ; long corridors and galleries stretched away in dust and silence, and were crossed by others, whose dark arches inspired me in the distance with an awful sort of sadness. It was plainly one of those great structures in which you might easily lose yourself, and with a pleasing terror it reminded me of that delightful old abbey in Mrs. Radcliffe's romance, among whose silent staircases, dim passages, and long suites of lordly, but forsaken chambers, begirt without by the sombre forest, the family of La Mote secured a gloomy asylum.

My cousin Milly and I, however, were bent upon an open-air ramble, and traversing several passages, she conducted me to a door which led us out upon a terrace overgrown with weeds, and by a broad flight of steps we descended to the level of the grounds beneath. Then on, over the short grass, under the noble trees, we walked ; Milly in high good-humour, and talking away volubly, in her short garment, navvy boots, and a weather-beaten hat. She carried a stick in her gloveless hand. Her conversation was quite new to me, and resembled very much what I would have fancied the holiday recollections of a schoolboy ; and the language in which it was sustained was sometimes so outlandish, that I was forced to laugh outright—a demonstration which she plainly did not like.

Her talk was about the great jumps she had made—how she snow-balled the chaps' in winter—how she could slide twice the length of her stick beyond ' Briddles, the cow-boy.'

With this and similar conversation she entertained me.

The grounds were delightfully wild and neglected. But we had now passed into a vast park beautifully varied with hollows and uplands, and such glorious old timber massed and scattered over its slopes and levels. Among these, we got at last into a picturesque dingle ; the grey rocks peeped from among the ferns and wild flowers, and the steps of soft sward along its sides were dark in the shadows of silver-stemmed birch, and russet thorn, and oak, under which, in the vaporous night, the Erl-king and his daughter might glide on their aërial horses.

In the lap of this pleasant dell were the finest blackberry bushes, I think, I ever saw, bearing fruit quite fabulous ; and plucking these, and chatting, we rambled on very pleasantly.

I had first thought of Milly's absurdities, to which, in description, I cannot do justice, simply because so many details have, by distance of time, escaped my recollection. But her ways and

her talk were so indescribably grotesque that she made me
again and again quiver with suppressed laughter.

But there was a pitiable and even a melancholy meaning un-
derlying the burlesque.

This creature, with no more education than a dairy-maid, I
gradually discovered had fine natural aptitudes for accomplishment—a very sweet voice, and wonderfully delicate ear, and a
talent for drawing which quite threw mine into the shade. It was
really astonishing.

Poor Milly, in all her life, had never read three books, and
hated to think of them. One, over which she was wont to yawn
and sigh, and stare fatiguedly for an hour every Sunday, by command of the Governor, was a stout volume of sermons of the
earlier school of George III., and a drier collection you can't
fancy. I don't think she read anything else. But she had, notwithstanding, ten times the cleverness of half the circulating
library misses one meets with. Besides all this, I had a long
sojourn before me at Bartram-Haugh, and I had learned from
Milly, as I had heard before, what a perennial solitude it was,
with a ludicrous fear of learning Milly's preposterous dialect,
and turning at last into something like her. So I resolved to do
all I could for her—teach her whatever I knew, if she would
allow me—and gradually, if possible, effect some civilising
changes in her language, and, as they term it in boarding-
schools, her demeanour.

But I must pursue at present our first day's ramble in what
was called Bartram Chase. People can't go on eating blackberries
always ; so after a while we resumed our walk along this pretty
dell, which gradually expanded into a wooded valley—level
beneath and enclosed by irregular uplands, receding, as it were,
in mimic bays and harbours at some points, and running out at
others into broken promontories, ending in clumps of forest
trees.

Just where the glen which we had been traversing expanded
into this broad, but wooded valley, it was traversed by a high
and close paling, which, although it looked decayed, was still
very strong.

In this there was a wooden gate, rudely but strongly constructed, and at the side we were approaching stood a girl, who

was leaning against the post, with one arm resting on the top of the gate.

This girl was neither tall nor short—taller than she looked at a distance ; she had not a slight waist ; sooty black was her hair, with a broad forehead, perpendicular but low ; she had a pair of very fine, dark, lustrous eyes, and no other good feature—unless I may so call her teeth, which were very white and even. Her face was rather short, and swarthy as a gipsy's ; observant and sullen too ; and she did not move, only eyed us negligently from under her dark lashes as we drew near. Altogether a not unpicturesque figure, with a dusky, red petticoat of drugget, and tattered jacket of bottle-green stuff, with short sleeves, which showed her brown arms from the elbow.

' That's Pegtop's daughter,' said Milly.

' Who is Pegtop ? ' I asked.

' He's the miller—see, yonder it is,' and she pointed to a very pretty feature in the landscape, a windmill, crowning the summit of a hillock which rose suddenly above the level of the tree-tops, like an island in the centre of the valley.

' The mill not going to-day, Beauty ? ' bawled Milly.

' No—a, Beauty ; it baint,' replied the girl, loweringly, and without stirring.

' And what's gone with the stile ? ' demanded Milly, aghast. ' It's tore away from the paling ! '

' Well, so it be, ' replied the wood nymph in the red petticoat, showing her fine teeth with a lazy grin.

' Who's a bin and done all that ? ' demanded Milly.

' Not you nor me, lass,' said the girl.

' 'Twas old Pegtop, your father, did it,' cried Milly, in rising wrath.

' 'Appen it wor,' she replied.

' And the gate locked.'

' That's it—the gate locked,' she repeated, sulkily, with a defiant side-glance at Milly.

' And where's Pegtop ? '

' At t'other side, somewhere ; how should I know where he be ? ' she replied.

' Who's got the key ? '

' Here it be, lass,' she answered, striking her hand on her pocket.

' And how durst you stay us here ? Unlock it, huzzy, this minute ! ' cried Milly, with a stamp.

Her answer was a sullen smile.

' Open the gate this instant ! ' bawled Milly.

' Well, I *won't*.'

I expected that Milly would have flown into a frenzy at this direct defiance, but she looked instead puzzled and curious—the girl's unexpected audacity bewildered her.

' Why, you fool, I could get over the paling as soon as look at you, but I won't. What's come over you ? Open the gate, I say, or I'll make you.'

' Do let her alone, dear,' I entreated, fearing a mutual assault. ' She has been ordered, may be, not to open it. Is it so, my good girl ? '

' Well, thou'rt not the biggest fool o' the two,' she observed, commendatively, ' thou'st hit it, lass.'

' And who ordered you ? ' exclaimed Milly.

' Fayther.'

' Old Pegtop. Well, *that's* summat to laugh at, it is—our servant a-shutting us out of our own grounds.'

' No servant o' yourn ! '

' Come, lass, what do you mean ? '

'He be old Silas's miller, and what's that to thee?'

With these words the girl made a spring on the hasp of the padlock, and then got easily over the gate.

' Can't you do that, cousin ? ' whispered Milly to me, with an impatient nudge. ' I *wish* you'd try.'

' No, dear—come away, Milly,' and I began to withdraw.

' Lookee, lass, 'twill be an ill day's work for thee when I tell the Governor,' said Milly, addressing the girl, who stood on a log of timber at the other side, regarding us with a sullen composure.

' We'll be over in spite o' you,' cried Milly.

' You lie ! ' answered she.

' And why not, huzzy ? ' demanded my cousin, who was less incensed at the affront than I expected. All this time I was urging Milly in vain to come away.

' Yon lass is no wild cat, like thee—that's why,' said the sturdy portress.

' If I cross, I'll give you a knock,' said Milly.

'And I'll gi' thee another,' she answered, with a vicious wag of the head.

'Come, Milly, *I'll* go if *you* don't,' I said.

'But we must not be beat,' whispered she, vehemently, catching my arm ; 'and ye *shall* get over, and *see* what I will gi' her ! '

'I'll *not* get over.'

'Then I'll break the door, for ye *shall* come through,' exclaimed Milly, kicking the stout paling with her ponderous boot.

'Purr it, purr it, purr it ! ' cried the lass in the red petticoat with a grin.

'Do you know who this lady is ? ' cried Milly, suddenly.

'She is a prettier lass than thou,' answered Beauty.

'She's *my* cousin Maud—Miss Ruthyn of Knowl—and she's a deal richer than the Queen ; and the Governor's taking care of her ; and he'll make old Pegtop bring you to reason.'

The girl eyed me with a sulky listlessness, a little inquisitively, I thought.

'See if he don't,' threatened Milly.

'You positively *must* come,' I said, drawing her away with me.

'Well, shall we come in ? ' cried Milly, trying a last summons.

'You'll not come in that much,' she answered, surlily, measuring an infinitesimal distance on her finger with her thumb, which she pinched against it, the gesture ending with a snap of defiance, and a smile that showed her fine teeth.

'I've a mind to shy a stone at you,' shouted Milly.

'Faire away ; I'll shy wi' ye as long as ye like, lass ; take heed o' yerself ; ' and Beauty picked up a round stone as large as a cricket ball.

With difficulty I got Milly away without an exchange of missiles, and much disgusted at my want of zeal and agility.

'Well, come along, cousin, I know an easy way by the river, when it's low,' answered Milly. 'She's a brute—is not she ? '

As we receded, we saw the girl slowly wending her way towards the old thatched cottage, which showed its gable from the side of a little rugged eminence embowered in spreading trees, and dangling and twirling from its string on the end of her finger the key for which a battle had so nearly been fought.

The stream was low enough to make our flank movement round the end of the paling next it quite easy, and so we pursued our way, and Milly's equanimity returned, and our ramble grew very pleasant again.

Our path lay by the river bank, and as we proceeded, the dwarf timber was succeeded by grander trees, which crowded closer and taller, and, at last, the scenery deepened into solemn forest, and a sudden sweep in the river revealed the beautiful ruin of a steep old bridge, with the fragments of a gate-house on the farther side.

' Oh, Milly darling ! ' I exclaimed, ' what a beautiful drawing this would make ! I should so like to make a sketch of it.'

' So it would. *Make* a picture—*do* !—here's a stone that's pure and flat to sit upon, and you look very tired. Do make it, and I'll sit by you.'

' Yes, Milly, I *am* tired, a little, and I *will* sit down ; but we must wait for another day to make the picture, for we have neither pencil nor paper. But it is much too pretty to be lost ; so let us come again to-morrow.'

' To-morrow be hanged ! you'll do it to-day, bury-me-wick, but you *shall*; I'm wearying to see you make a picture, and I'll fetch your conundrums out o' your drawer, for do't you shall.'

CHAPTER XXXIV

ZAMIEL

It was all vain my remonstrating. She vowed that by crossing the stepping-stones close by she could, by a short cut, reach the house, and return with my pencils and block-book in a quarter of an hour. Away then, with many a jump and fling, scampered Milly's queer white stockings and navvy boots across the irregular and precarious stepping-stones, over which I dared not follow her ; so I was fain to return to the stone so ' pure and flat,' on which I sat, enjoying the grand sylvan solitude, the dark background and the grey bridge mid-way, so tall and slim, across whose ruins a sunbeam glimmered, and the gigantic forest trees that slumbered round, opening here and there in dusky vistas, and breaking in front into detached and solemn groups. It was the setting of a dream of romance.

It would have been the very spot in which to read a volume of German folk-lore, and the darkening colonnades and silent nooks of the forest seemed already haunted with the voices and shadows of those charming elves and goblins.

As I sat here enjoying the solitude and my fancies among the low branches of the wood, at my right I heard a crashing, and saw a squat broad figure in a stained and tattered military coat, and loose short trousers, one limb of which flapped about a wooden leg. He was forcing himself through. His face was rugged and wrinkled, and tanned to the tint of old oak ; his eyes black, beadlike, and fierce, and a shock of sooty hair escaped from under his battered wide-awake nearly to his shoulders. This forbidding-looking person came stumping and jerking along toward me, whisking his stick now and then viciously in the air, and giving his fell of hair a short shake, like a wild bull preparing to attack.

I stood up involuntarily with a sense of fear and surprise, almost fancying I saw in that wooden-legged old soldier, the forest demon who haunted Der Freischütz.

So he approached shouting—

' Hollo ! you—how came you here ? Dost 'eer ? '

And he drew near panting, and sometimes tugging angrily in his haste at his wooden leg, which sunk now and then deeper than was convenient in the sod. This exertion helped to anger him, and when he halted before me, his dark face smirched with smoke and dust, and the nostrils of his flat drooping nose expanded and quivered as he panted, like the gills of a fish ; an angrier or uglier face it would not be easy to fancy.

' Ye'll all come when ye like, will ye ? and do nout but what pleases yourselves, won't you ? And who'rt thou ? Dost 'eer— who *are* ye, I say ; and what the deil seek ye in the woods here ? Come, bestir thee ! '

If his wide mouth and great tobacco-stained teeth, his scowl, and loud discordant tones were intimidating, they were also extremely irritating. The moment my spirit was roused, my courage came.

' I am Miss Ruthyn of Knowl, and Mr. Silas Ruthyn, your master, is my uncle.'

' Hoo ! ' he exclaimed more gently, ' an' if Silas be thy uncle thou'lt be come to live wi' him, and thou'rt she as come over-night—eh ? '

I made no answer, but I believe I looked both angrily and disdainfully.

' And what make ye alone here ? and how was I to know't, an' Milly not wi' ye, nor no one ? But Maud or no Maud, I wouldn't let the Dooke hisself set foot inside the palin' without Silas said let him. And you may tell Silas them's the words o' Dickon Hawkes, and I'll stick to 'm—and what's more I'll tell him *myself*—I will ; I'll tell him there be no use o' my striving and straining hee, day an' night and night and day, watchin' again poachers, and thieves, and gipsies, and they robbing lads, if rules won't be kep, and folk do jist as they pleases. Dang it, lass, thou'rt in luck I didn't heave a brick at thee when I saw thee first.'

' I'll complain of you to my uncle,' I replied.

' So do, and and 'appen thou'lt find thyself in the wrong box, lass ; thou canst na' say I set the dogs arter thee, nor cau'd thee so much as a wry name, nor heave a stone at thee—did I ? Well ? and where's the complaint then ? '

I simply answered, rather fiercely,

' Be good enough to leave me.'

' Well, I make no objections, mind. I'm takin' thy word— thou'rt Maud Ruthyn—'appen thou be'st and 'appen thou baint. I'm not aweer on't, but I takes thy word, and all I want to know's just this, did Meg open the gate to thee ? '

I made him no answer, and to my great relief I saw Milly striding and skipping across the unequal stepping-stones.

' Hallo, Pegtop ! what are you after now ? ' she cried, as she drew near.

' This man has been extremely impertinent. You know him, Milly ? ' I said.

' Why that's Pegtop Dickon. Dirty old Hawkes that never was washed. I tell you, lad, ye'll see what the Governor thinks o't—a-ha ! He'll talk to you.'

' I done or said nout—not but I *should,* and there's the fack— she can't deny't ; she hadn't a hard word from I ; and I don't care the top o' that thistle what no one says—not I. But I tell thee, Milly, I stopped *some* o' thy pranks, and I'll stop more. Ye'll be shying no more stones at the cattle.'

'Tell your tales, and welcome, cried Milly. 'I wish I was here when you jawed cousin. If Winny was here she'd catch you by the timber toe and put you on your back.'

'Ay, she'll be a good un yet if she takes arter thee,' retorted the old man with a fierce sneer.

'Drop it, and get away wi' ye,' cried she, 'or maybe I'd call Winny to smash your timber leg for you.'

'A-ha! there's more on't. She's a sweet un. Isn't she?' he replied sardonically.

'You did not like it last Easter, when Winny broke it with a kick.'

''Twas a kick o' a horse,' he growled with a glance at me.

''Twas no such thing—'twas Winny did it—and he laid on his back for a week while carpenter made him a new one.' And Milly laughed hilariously.

'I'll fool no more wi' ye, losing my time; I won't; but mind ye, I'll speak wi' Silas.' And going away he put his hand to his crumpled wide-awake, and said to me with a surly difference—

'Good evening, Miss Ruthyn—good evening, ma'am—and ye'll please remember, I did not mean nout to vex thee.'

And so he swaggered away, jerking and waddling over the sward, and was soon lost in the wood.

'It's well he's a little bit frightened—I never saw him so angry, I think; he is awful mad.'

'Perhaps he really is not aware how very rude he is,' I suggested.

'I hate him. We were twice as pleasant with poor Tom Driver —he never meddled with any one, and was always in liquor; Old Gin was the name he went by. But this brute—I do hate him—he comes from Wigan, I think, and he's always spoiling sport—and he whops Meg—that's Beauty, you know, and I don't think she'd be half as bad only for him. Listen to him whistlin'.'

'I did hear whistling at some distance among the trees.'

'I declare if he isn't callin' the dogs! Climb up here, I tell ye,' and we climbed up the slanting trunk of a great walnut tree, and strained our eyes in the direction from which we expected the onset of Pegtop's vicious pack.

But it was a false alarm.

' Well, I don't think he *would* do that, after all—*hardly* ; but he is a brute, sure ! '

' And that dark girl who would not let us through, is his daughter, is she ? '

' Yes, that's Meg—Beauty, I christened her, when I called him Beast ; but I call him Pegtop now, and she's Beauty still, and that's the way o't.'

' Come, sit down now, an' make your picture,' she resumed so soon as we had dismounted from our position of security.

' I'm afraid I'm hardly in the vein. I don't think I could draw a straight line. My hand trembles.'

' I wish you could, Maud,' said Milly, with a look so wistful and entreating, that considering the excursion she had made for the pencils, I could not bear to disappoint her.

' Well, Milly, we must only try ; and if we fail we can't help it. Sit you down beside me and I'll tell you why I begin with one part and not another, and you'll see how I make trees and the river, and—yes, *that* pencil, it is hard and answers for the fine light lines ; but we must begin at the beginning, and learn to copy drawings before we attempt real views like this. And if you wish it, Milly, I'm resolved to teach you everything I know, which, after all, is not a great deal, and we shall have such fun making sketches of the same landscapes, and then comparing.'

And so on, Milly, quite delighted, and longing to begin her course of instruction, sat down beside me in a rapture, and hugged and kissed me so heartily that we were very near rolling together off the stone on which we were seated. Her boisterous delight and good-nature helped to restore me, and both laughing heartily together, I commenced my task.

' Dear me ! who's that ? ' I exclaimed suddenly, as looking up from my block-book I saw the figure of a slight man in the careless morning-dress of a gentleman, crossing the ruinous bridge in our direction, with considerable caution, upon the precarious footing of the battlement, which alone offered an unbroken passage.

This was a day of apparitions ! Milly recognised him instantly. The gentleman was Mr. Carysbroke. He had taken The

Grange only for a year. He lived quite to himself, and was very good to the poor, and was the only gentleman, for ever so long, who had visited at Bartram, and oddly enough nowhere else. But he wanted leave to cross through the grounds, and having obtained it, had repeated his visit, partly induced, no doubt, by the fact that Bartram boasted no hospitalities, and that there was no risk of meeting the county folk there.

With a stout walking-stick in his hand, and a short shooting-coat, and a wide-awake hat in much better trim than Zamiel's, he emerged from the copse that covered the bridge, walking at a quick but easy pace.

'He'll be goin' to see old Snoddles, I guess,' said Milly, looking a little frightened and curious ; for Milly, I need not say, was a bumpkin, and stood in awe of this gentleman's good-breeding, though she was as brave as a lion, and would have fought the Philistines at any odds, with the jawbone of an ass.

' 'Appen he won't see us,' whispered Milly, hopefully.

But he did, and raising his hat, with a cheerful smile, that showed very white teeth, he paused.

'Charming day, Miss Ruthyn.'

I raised my head suddenly as he spoke, from habit appropriating the address ; it was so marked that he raised his hat respectfully to me, and then continued to Milly—

'Mr. Ruthyn, I hope, quite well ? but I need hardly ask, you seem so happy. Will you kindly tell him, that I expect the book I mentioned in a day or two, and when it comes I'll either send or bring it to him immediately ? '

Milly and I were standing, by this time, but she only stared at him, tongue-tied, her cheeks rather flushed, and her eyes very round, and to facilitate the dialogue, as I suppose, he said again—

'He's quite well, I hope ? '

Still no response from Milly, and I, provoked, though myself a little shy, made answer—

'My uncle, Mr. Ruthyn, is very well, thank you,' and I felt that I blushed as I spoke.

'Ah, pray excuse me, may I take a great liberty ? you are Miss Ruthyn, of Knowl ? Will you think me very impertinent—I'm afraid you will—if I venture to introduce myself ? My name is Carysbroke, and I had the honour of knowing poor Mr. Ruthyn when I was quite a little boy, and he has shown a kindness for me since, and I hope you will pardon the liberty I fear I've taken. I think my friend, Lady Knollys, too, is a relation of yours ; what a charming person she is ! '

' Oh, is not she ? such a darling ! ' I said, and then blushed at my outspoken affection.

But he smiled kindly, as if he liked me for it ; and he said—

' You know whatever I think, I dare not quite say that ; but frankly I can quite understand it. She preserves her youth so wonderfully, and her fun and her good-nature are so entirely girlish. What a sweet view you have selected,' he continued, changing all at once. ' I've stood just at this point so often to look back at that exquisite old bridge. Do you observe—you're an artist, I see—something very peculiar in that tint of the grey, with those odd cross stains of faded red and yellow ? '

' I do, indeed ; I was just remarking the peculiar beauty of the colouring—was not I, Milly ? '

Milly stared at me, and uttered an alarmed ' Yes,' and looked as if she had been caught in a robbery.

' Yes, and you have so very peculiar a background,' he resumed. ' It was better before the storm though ; but it is very good still.'

Then a little pause, and ' Do you know this country at all ?' rather suddenly.

' No, not in the least—that is, I've only had the drive to this place ; but what I did see interested me very much.'

' You will be charmed with it when you know it better—the very place for an artist. I'm a wretched scribbler myself, and I carry this little book in my pocket,' and he laughed deprecatingly while he drew forth a thin fishing-book, as it looked. ' They are mere memoranda, you see. I walk so much and come unexpectedly on such pretty nooks and studies, I just try to make a note of them, but it is really more writing than sketching ; my sister says it is a cipher which nobody but myself understands. However, I'll try and explain just two—because you really ought to go and see the places. Oh, no ; not that,' he laughed, as accidentally the page blew over, ' that's the Cat and Fiddle, a curious little pot-house, where they gave me some very good ale one day.'

Milly at this exhibited some uneasy tokens of being about to speak, but not knowing what might be coming, I hastened to observe on the spirited little sketches to which he meant to draw my attention.

' I want to show you only the places within easy reach—a short ride or drive.'

So he proceeded to turn over two or three, in addition to the two he had at first proposed, and then another ; then a little sketch just tinted, and really quite a charming little gem, of Cousin Monica's pretty gabled old house ; and every subject had its little criticism, or its narrative, or adventure.

As he was about returning this little sketch-book to his pocket, still chatting to me, he suddenly recollected poor Milly, who was looking rather lowering ; but she brightened a good deal as he presented it to her, with a little speech which she palpably mis-understood, for she made one of her odd courtesies, and was about, I thought, to put it into her large pocket, and accept it as a present.

' Look at the drawings, Milly, and then return it,' I whis-pered.

At his request I allowed him to look at my unfinished sketch of the bridge, and while he was measuring distances and propor-tions with his eye, Milly whispered rather angrily to me,

' And why should I ? '

' Because he wants it back, and only meant to lend it to you,' whispered I.

'*Lend* it to me—and after you ! Bury-me-wick if I look at a leaf of it,' she retorted in high dudgeon. ' Take it, lass ; give it him yourself—I'll not,' and she popped it into my hand, and made a sulky step back.

' My cousin is very much obliged,' I said, returning the book, and smiling for her, and he took it smiling also and said—

' I think if I had known how very well you draw, Miss Ruthyn, I should have hesitated about showing you my poor scrawls. But these are not my best, you know ; Lady Knollys will tell you that I can really do better—a great deal better, I think.'

And then with more apologies for what he called his imperti-nence, he took his leave, and I felt altogether very much pleased and flattered.

He could not be more than twenty-nine or thirty, I thought, and he was decidedly handsome—that is, his eyes and teeth, and clear brown complexion were—and there was something distinguished and graceful in his figure and gesture ; and altogether there was the indescribable attraction of intelligence ; and I fancied—though this, of course, was a secret—that from the moment he spoke to us he felt an interest in me. I am not going to be vain. It was a *grave* interest, but still an interest, for I could see him studying my features while I was turning over his sketches, and he thought I saw nothing else. It was flattering, too, his anxiety that I should think well of his drawing, and referring me to Lady Knollys. Carysbroke—had I ever heard my dear father mention that name ? I could not recollect it. But then he was habitually so silent, that his not doing so argued nothing.

CHAPTER XXXV

WE VISIT A ROOM IN THE SECOND STOREY

Mr. Carysbroke amused my fancy sufficiently to prevent my observing Milly's silence, till we had begun our return homeward.

' The Grange must be a pretty house, if that little sketch be true ; is it far from this ? '

' 'Twill be two mile.'

' Are you vexed, Milly ? ' I asked, for both her tone and looks were angry.

' Yes, I am vexed ; and why not lass ? '

' What has happened ? '

' Well, now, that is rich ! Why, look at that fellow, Carysbroke : he took no more notice to me than a dog, and kep' talking to you all the time of his pictures, and his walks, and his people. Why, a pig's better manners than that.'

' But, Milly dear, you forget, he tried to talk to you, and you would not answer him,' I expostulated.

' And is not that just what I say—I can't talk like other folk—

ladies, I mean. Every one laughs at me ; an' I'm dressed like a show, I am. It's a shame ! I saw Polly Shives—what a lady she is, my eyes !—laughing at me in church last Sunday. I was minded to give her a bit of my mind. An' I know I'm queer. It's a shame, it is. Why should *I* be so rum ? it is a shame ! I don't want to be so, nor it isn't my fault.'

And poor Milly broke into a flood of tears, and stamped on the ground, and buried her face in her short frock, which she whisked up to her eyes ; and an odder figure of grief I never beheld.

' And I could not make head or tail of what he was saying,' cried poor Milly through her buff cotton, with a stamp ; 'and you twigged every word o't. An' why am I so ? It's a shame—a shame ! Oh, ho, ho ! it's a shame ! '

' But, my dear Milly, we were talking of *drawing,* and you have not learned yet, but you shall—I'll teach you ; and then you'll understand all about it.'

' An' every one laughs at me—even you ; though you try, Maud, you can scarce keep from laughing sometimes. I don't blame you, for I know I'm queer ; but I can't help it ; and it's a shame.'

' Well, my dear Milly, listen to me : if you allow me, I assure you, I'll teach you all the music and drawing I know. You have lived very much alone ; and, as you say, ladies have a way of speaking of their own that is different from the talk of other people.'

' Yes, that they have, an' gentlemen too—like the Governor, and that Carysbroke ; and a precious lingo it is—dang it—why, the devil himself could not understand it ; an' I'm like a fool among you. I could 'most drown myself. It's a shame ! It is— you know it is.—It's a shame ! '

' But I'll teach you that lingo too, if you wish it, Milly ; and you shall know everything that I know ; and I'll manage to have your dresses better made.'

By this time she was looking very ruefully, but attentively, in my face, her round eyes and nose swelled, and her cheeks all wet.

' I think if they were a little longer—yours is longer, you know ; ' and the sentence was interrupted by a sob.

' Now, Milly, you must not be crying ; if you choose you

may be just as the same as any other lady—and you shall ; and
you will be very much admired, I can tell you, if only you will
take the trouble to quite unlearn all your odd words and ways,
and dress yourself like other people ; and I will take care of
that if you let me ; and I think you are very clever, Milly ; and
I know you are very pretty.'

Poor Milly's blubbered face expanded into a smile in spite
of herself ; but she shook her head, looking down.

' Noa, noa, Maud, I fear 'twon't be.' And indeed it seemed I
had proposed to myself a labour of Hercules.

But Milly was really a clever creature, could see quickly, and
when her ungainly dialect was mastered, describe very pleasantly ; and if only she would endure the restraint and possessed
the industry requisite, I did not despair, and was resolved at
least to do my part.

Poor Milly ! she was really very grateful, and entered into the
project of her education with great zeal, and with a strange
mixture of humility and insubordination.

Milly was in favour of again attacking ' Beauty's' position on
her return, and forcing a passage from this side ; but I insisted
on following the route by which we had arrived, and so we got
round the paling by the river, and were treated to a provoking
grin of defiance by ' Beauty,' who was talking across the gate to
a slim young man, arrayed in fustian, and with an odd-looking
cap of rabbit-skin on his head, which, on seeing us, he pulled
sheepishly to the side of his face next to us, as he lounged, with
his arm under his chin, on the top bar of the gate.

After our encounter of to-day, indeed, it was Miss ' Beauty's '
wont to exhibit a kind of jeering disdain in her countenance
whenever we passed.

I think Milly would have engaged her again, had I not reminded her of her undertaking, and exerted my new authority.

' Look at that sneak, Pegtop, there, going up the path to the
mill. He makes belief now he does not see us ; but he does,
though, only he's afraid we'll tell the Governor, and he thinks
Governor won't give him his way with you. I hate that Pegtop :
he stopped me o' riding the cows a year ago, he did.'

I thought Pegtop might have done worse. Indeed it was plain
that a total reformation was needed here ; and I was glad to
find that poor Milly seemed herself conscious of it ; and that

her resolution to become more like other people of her station was not a mere spasm of mortification and jealousy, but a genuine and very zealous resolve.

I had not half seen this old house of Bartram-Haugh yet. At first, indeed, I had but an imperfect idea of its extent. There was a range of rooms along one side of the great gallery, with closed window-shutters, and the doors generally locked. Old L'Amour grew cross when we went into them, although we could see nothing ; and Milly was afraid to open the windows —not that any Bluebeard revelations were apprehended, but simply because she knew that Uncle Silas's order was that things should be left undisturbed ; and this boisterous spirit stood in awe of him to a degree which his gentle manners and apparent quietude rendered quite surprising.

There were in this house, what certainly did not exist at Knowl, and what I have never observed, thought they may possibly be found in other old houses—I mean, here and there, very high hatches, which we could only peep over by jumping in the air. They crossed the long corridors and great galleries ; and several of them were turned across and locked, so as to intercept the passage, and interrupt our explorations.

Milly, however, knew a queer little, very steep and dark back stair, which reached the upper floor ; so she and I mounted, and made a long ramble through rooms much lower and ruder in finish than the lordly chambers we had left below. These commanded various views of the beautiful though neglected grounds; but on crossing a gallery we entered suddenly a chamber, which looked into a small and dismal quadrangle, formed by the inner walls of this great house, and of course designed only by the architect to afford the needful light and air to portions of the structure.

I rubbed the window-pane with my handkerchief and looked out. The surrounding roof was steep and high. The walls looked soiled and dark. The windows lined with dust and dirt, and the window-stones were in places tufted with moss, and grass, and groundsel. An arched doorway had opened from the house into this darkened square, but it was soiled and dusty ; and the damp weeds that overgrew the quadrangle drooped undisturbed against it. It was plain that human footsteps tracked it little,

and I gazed into that blind and sinister area with a strange
thrill and sinking.

'This is the second floor—there is the enclosed court-yard'—
I, as it were, soliloquised.

'What are you afraid of, Maud? you look as ye'd seen a
ghost,' exclaimed Milly, who came to the window and peeped
over my shoulder.

'It reminded me suddenly, Milly, of that frightful business.'

'What business, Maud?—what a plague are ye thinking on?'
demanded Milly, rather amused.

'It was in one of these rooms—maybe this—yes, it certainly
was this—for see, the panelling has been pulled off the wall—
that Mr. Charke killed himself.'

I was staring ruefully round the dim chamber, in whose corners the shadows of night were already gathering.

'Charke!—what about him?—who's Charke?' asked Milly.

'Why, you must have heard of him,' said I.

'Not as I'm aware on,' answered she. 'And he killed himself,
did he, hanged himself, eh, or blowed his brains out?'

'He cut his throat in one of these rooms—*this* one, I'm sure—
for your papa had the wainscoting stripped from the wall to
ascertain whether there was any second door through which a
murderer could have come; and you see these walls are stripped,
and bear the marks of the woodwork that has been removed,' I
answered.

'Well, that *was* awful! I don't know how they have pluck to
cut their throats; if I was doing it, I'd like best to put a pistol
to my head and fire, like the young gentleman did, they say, in
Deadman's Hollow. But the fellows that cut their throats, they
must be awful game lads, I'm thinkin', for it's a long slice, you
know.'

'Don't, don't, Milly dear. Suppose we come away,' I said, for
the evening was deepening rapidly into night.

'Hey and bury-me-wick, but here's the blood; don't you see a
big black cloud all spread over the floor hereabout, don't ye
see?' Milly was stooping over the spot, and tracing the outline
of this, perhaps, imaginary mapping, in the air with her finger.

'No, Milly, you could not see it: the floor is too dark, and
it's all in shadow. It must be fancy; and perhaps, after all, this
is not the room.'

'Well—I think, I'm *sure* it *is*. Stand—just look.'

'We'll come in the morning, and if you are right we can see it better then. Come away,' I said, growing frightened.

And just as we stood up to depart, the white high-cauled cap and large sallow features of old L'Amour peeped in at the door.

'Lawk! what brings you here?' cried Milly, nearly as much startled as I at the intrusion.

'What brings *you* here, miss?' whistled L'Amour through her gums.

'We're looking where Charke cut his throat,' replied Milly.

'Charke the devil!' said the old woman, with an odd mixture of scorn and fury. ''Tisn't his room; and come ye out of it, please. Master won't like when he hears how you keep pulling Miss Maud from one room to another, all through the house, up and down.'

She was gabbling sternly enough, but dropped a low courtesy as I passed her, and with a peaked and nodding stare round the room, the old woman clapped the door sharply, and locked it.

'And who has been a talking about Charke—a pack o lies, I warrant. I s'pose you want to frighten Miss Maud here' (another crippled courtesy) 'wi' ghosts and like nonsense.'

'You're out there: 'twas she told me; and much about it. Ghosts, indeed! I don't vally them, not I; if I did, I know who'd frighten me,' and Milly laughed.

The old woman stuffed the key in her pocket, and her wrinkled mouth pouted and receded with a grim uneasiness.

'A harmless brat, and kind she is; but wild—wild—she will be wild.'

So whispered L'Amour in my ear, during the silence that followed, nodding shakily toward Milly over the banister, and she courtesied again as we departed, and shuffled off toward Uncle Silas's room.

The Governor is queerish this evening,' said Milly, when we were seated at our tea. 'You never saw him queerish, did you?'

'You must say what you mean, more plainly, Milly. You don't mean ill, I hope?'

'Well! I don't know what it is; but he does grow very queer sometimes—you'd think he was dead a'most, maybe two or three days and nights together. He sits all the time like an old woman in a swound. Well, well, it is awful!'

' Is he insensible when in that state ? ' I asked, a good deal
alarmed.

' I don't know ; but it never signifies anything. It won't kill
him, I do believe ; but old L'Amour knows all about it. I
hardly ever go into the room when he's so, only when I'm sent
for ; and he sometimes wakes up and takes a fancy to call for
this one or that. One day he sent for Pegtop all the way to the
mill ; and when he came, he only stared at him for a minute
or two, and ordered him out o' the room. He's like a child
a'most, when he's in one o' them dazes.'

I always knew when Uncle Silas was ' queerish,' by the in-
junctions of old L'Amour, whistled and spluttered over the
banister as we came up-stairs, to mind how we made a noise
passing master's door ; and by the sound of mysterious to-ings
and fro-ings about his room.

I saw very little of him. He sometimes took a whim to have
us breakfast with him, which lasted perhaps for a week ; and
then the order of our living would relapse into its old routine.

I must not forget two kind letters from Lady Knollys, who
was detained away, and delighted to hear that I enjoyed my
quiet life ; and promised to apply, in person, to Uncle Silas, for
permission to visit me.

She was to be for the Christmas at Elverston, and that was
only six miles away from Bartram-Haugh, so I had the excitement of a pleasant look forward.

She also said that she would include poor Milly in her invitation ; and a vision of Captain Oakley rose before me, with his
handsome gaze turned in wonder on poor Milly, for whom I
had begun to feel myself responsible.

CHAPTER XXXVI

AN ARRIVAL AT DEAD OF NIGHT

I have sometimes been asked why I wear an odd little turquois ring—which to the uninstructed eye appears quite valueless and altogether an unworthy companion of those jewels which flash insultingly beside it. It is a little keepsake, of which I became possessed about this time.

' Come, lass, what name shall I give you ? ' cried Milly, one morning, bursting into my room in a state of alarming hilarity.

' My own, Milly.'

' No, but you must have a nickname, like every one else.'

' Don't mind it, Milly.'

' Yes, but I will. Shall I call you Mrs. Bustle ? '

' You shall do no such thing.'

' But you must have a name.'

' I refuse a name.'

' But I'll give you one, lass.'

' And *I* won't have it.'

' But you can't help me christening you.'

' I can decline answering.'

' But I'll make you,' said Milly, growing very red.

Perhaps there was something provoking in my tone, for I certainly was very much disgusted at Milly's relapse into barbarism.

' You can't,' I retorted quietly.

' See if I don't, and I'll give ye one twice as ugly.'

I smiled, I fear, disdainfully.

' And I think you're a minx, and a slut, and a fool,' she broke out, flushing scarlet.

I smiled in the same unchristian way.

' And I'd give ye a smack o' the cheek as soon as look at you.'

And she gave her dress a great slap, and drew near me, in her

219

wrath. I really thought she was about tendering the ordeal of single combat.

I made her, however, a paralysing courtesy, and, with immense dignity, sailed out of the room, and into Uncle Silas's study, where it happened we were to breakfast that morning, and for several subsequent ones.

During the meal we maintained the most dignified reserve ; and I don't think either so much as looked at the other.

We had no walk together that day.

I was sitting in the evening, quite alone, when Milly entered the room. Her eyes were red, and she looked very sullen.

' I want your hand, cousin,' she said, at the same time taking it by the wrist, and administering with it a sudden slap on her plump cheek, which made the room ring, and my fingers tingle ; and before I had recovered from my surprise, she had vanished.

I called after her, but no answer ; I pursued, but she was running too ; and I quite lost her at the cross galleries.

I did not see her at tea, nor before going to bed ; but after I had fallen asleep I was awakened by Milly, in floods of tears.

' Cousin Maud, will ye forgi' me—you'll never like me again, will ye ? No—I know ye won't—I'm such a brute—I hate it— it's a shame. And here's a Banbury cake for you—I sent to the town for it, and some taffy—won't ye eat it ? and here's a little ring—'tisn't as pretty as your own rings ; and ye'll wear it, maybe, for my sake—poor Milly's sake, before I was so bad to ye —if ye forgi' me ; and I'll look at breakfast, and if it's on your finger I'll know you're friends wi' me again ; and if ye don't, I won't trouble you no more ; and I think I'll just drown myself out o' the way, and you'll never see wicked Milly no more.'

And without waiting a moment, leaving me only half awake, and with the sensations of dreaming, she scampered from the room, in her bare feet, with a petticoat about her shoulders.

She had left her candle by my bed, and her little offerings on the coverlet by me. If I had stood an atom less in terror of goblins than I did, I should have followed her, but I was afraid. I stood in my bare feet at my bedside, and kissed the poor little ring and put it on my finger, where it has remained ever since and always shall. And when I lay down, longing for morning, the image of her pale, imploring, penitential face was before me for hours ; and I repented bitterly of my cool provoking ways, and thought myself, I dare say justly, a thousand times more to blame than Milly.

I searched in vain for her before breakfast. At that meal, however, we met, but in the presence of Uncle Silas, who, though silent and apathetic, was formidable ; and we, sitting at a table disproportionably large, under the cold, strange gaze of my guardian, talked only what was inevitable, and that in low tones ; for whenever Milly for a moment raised her voice, Uncle Silas would wince, place his thin white fingers quickly over his ear, and look as if a pain had pierced his brain, and then shrug and smile piteously into vacancy. When Uncle Silas, therefore, was not in the talking vein himself—and that was not often—you may suppose there was very little spoken in his presence.

When Milly, across the table, saw the ring upon my finger, she, drawing in her breath, said, ' Oh ! ' and, with round eyes and mouth, she looked so delighted ; and she made a little motion, as if she was on the point of jumping up ; and then her poor face quivered, and she bit her lip ; and staring imploringly at me, her eyes filled fast with tears, which rolled down her round penitential cheeks.

I am sure I felt more penitent than she. I know I was crying and smiling, and longing to kiss her. I suppose we were very absurd ; but it is well that small matters can stir the affections so profoundly at a time of life when great troubles seldom approach us.

When at length the opportunity did come, never was such a hug out of the wrestling ring as poor Milly bestowed on me, swaying me this way and that, and burying her face in my dress, and blubbering—

' I was so lonely before you came, and you so good to me, and I such a devil ; and I'll never call you a name, but Maud—my darling Maud.'

' You must, Milly—Mrs. Bustle. I'll be Mrs. Bustle, or anything you like. You must.' I was blubbering like Milly, and hugging my best ; and, indeed, I wonder how we kept our feet.

So Milly and I were better friends than ever.

Meanwhile, the winter deepened, and we had short days and long nights, and long fireside gossipings at Bartram-Haugh. I was frightened at the frequency of the strange collapses to which

Uncle Silas was subject. I did not at first mind them much, for I naturally fell into Milly's way of talking about them.

But one day, while in one of his ' queerish ' states, he called for me, and I saw him, and was unspeakably scared.

In a white wrapper, he lay coiled in a great easy chair. I should have thought him dead, had I not been accompanied by old L'Amour, who knew every gradation and symptom of these strange affections.

She winked and nodded to me with a ghastly significance, and whispered—

' Don't make no noise, miss, till he talks ; he'll come to for a bit, anon.'

Except that there was no sign of convulsions, the countenance was like that of an epileptic arrested in one of his contortions.

There was a frown and smirk like that of idiotcy, and a strip of white eyeball was also disclosed.

Suddenly, with a kind of chilly shudder, he opened his eyes wide, and screwed his lips together, and blinked and stared on me with a fatuised uncertainty, that gradually broke into a feeble smile.

' Ah ! the girl—Austin's child. Well, dear, I'm hardly able—I'll speak to-morrow—next day—it is tic—neuralgia, or something —*torture*—tell her.'

So, huddling himself together, he lay again in his great chair, with the same inexpressible helplessness in his attitude, and gradually his face resumed its dreadful cast.

' Come away, miss : he's changed his mind ; he'll not be fit to talk to you noways all day, maybe,' said the old woman, again in a whisper.

So forth we stole from the room, I unspeakably shocked. In fact, he looked as if he were dying, and so, in my agitation, I told the crone, who, forgetting the ceremony with which she usually treated me, chuckled out derisively,

' A-dying is he ? Well, he be like Saint Paul—he's bin a-dying daily this many a day.'

I looked at her with a chill of horror. She did not care, I sup-pose, what sort of feelings she might excite, for she went on mumbling sarcastically to herself. I had paused, and overcame my reluctance to speak to her again, for I was really very much frightened.

' Do you think he is in danger ? Shall we send for a doctor ? '
I whispered.

' Law bless ye, the doctor knows all about it, miss.' The old
woman's face had a gleam of that derision which is so shocking
in the features of feebleness and age.

' But it is a *fit*, it is paralytic, or something horrible—it can't
be *safe* to leave him to chance or nature to get through these
terrible attacks.'

' There's no fear of him, 'tisn't no fits at all, he's nout the
worse o't. Jest silly a bit now and again. It's been the same a
dozen year and more ; and the doctor knows all about it,' answered the old woman sturdily. ' And ye'll find he'll be as mad
as bedlam if ye make any stir about it.'

That night I talked the matter over with Mary Quince.

' They're very dark, miss ; but I think he takes a deal too
much laudlum,' said Mary.

To this hour I cannot say what was the nature of those periodical seizures. I have often spoken to medical men about
them, since, but never could learn that excessive use of opium
could altogether account for them. It was, I believe, certain,
however, that he did use that drug in startling quantities. It was,
indeed, sometimes a topic of complaint with him that his neuralgia imposed this sad necessity upon him.

The image of Uncle Silas, as I had seen him that day, troubled and affrighted my imagination, as I lay in my bed ; I had
slept very well since my arrival at Bartram. So much of the day
was passed in the open air, and in active exercise, that this
was but natural. But that night I was nervous and wakeful,
and it was past two o'clock when I fancied I heard the sound of
horses and carriage-wheels on the avenue.

Mary Quince was close by, and therefore I was not afraid to
get up and peep from the window. My heart beat fast as I saw
a post-chaise approach the court-yard. A front window was let
down, and the postilion pulled up for a few seconds.

In consequence of some directions received by him, I fancied
he resumed his route at a walk, and so drew up at the hall-door,
on the steps of which a figure awaited his arrival. I think it was
old L'Amour, but I could not be quite certain. There was a
lantern on the top of the balustrade, close by the door. The
chaise-lamps were lighted, for the night was rather dark.

A bag and valise, as well as I could see, were pulled from the interior by the post-boy, and a box from the top of the vehicle, and these were carried into the hall.

I was obliged to keep my cheek against the window-pane to command a view of the point of debarkation, and my breath upon the glass, which dimmed it again almost as fast as I wiped it away, helped to obscure my vision. But I saw a tall figure, in a cloak, get down and swiftly enter the house, but whether male or female I could not discern.

My heart beat fast. I jumped at once to a conclusion. My uncle was worse—was, in fact, dying ; and this was the physician, too late summoned to his bedside.

I listened for the ascent of the doctor, and his entrance at my uncle's door, which, in the stillness of the night, I thought I might easily hear, but no sound reached me. I listened so for fully five minutes, but without result. I returned to the window, but the carriage and horses had disappeared.

I was strongly tempted to wake Mary Quince, and take counsel with her, and persuade her to undertake a reconnoissance. The fact is, I was persuaded that my uncle was in extremity, and I was quite wild to know the doctor's opinion. But, after all, it would be cruel to summon the good soul from her refreshing nap. So, as I began to feel very cold, I returned to my bed, where I continued to listen and conjecture until I fell asleep.

In the morning, as was usual, before I was dressed, in came Milly.

' How is Uncle Silas ? ' I eagerly enquired.

' Old L'Amour says he's queerish still ; but he's not so dull as yesterday,' answered she.

' Was not the doctor sent for ? ' I asked.

' Was he ? Well, that's odd ; and she said never a word o't to me,' answered she.

' I'm asking only,' said I.

' I don't know whether he came or no,' she replied ; 'but what makes you take that in your head ? '

' A chaise arrived here between two and three o'clock last night.'

' Hey ! and who told you ? ' Milly seemed all on a sudden highly interested.

' I saw it, Milly ; and some one, I fancy the doctor, came from it into the house.'

' Fudge, lass ! who'd send for the doctor ? 'Twasn't he, I tell you. What was he like ?' said Milly.

' I could only see clearly that he, or *she,* was tall, and wore a cloak,' I replied.

' Then 'twasn't him nor t'other I was thinking on, neither ; and I'll be hanged but I think it will be Cormoran,' cried Milly, with a thoughtful rap with her knuckle on the table.

Precisely at this juncture a tapping came to the door.

' Come in,' said I.

And old L'Amour entered the room, with a courtesy.

' I came to tell Miss Quince her breakfast's ready,' said the old lady.

' Who came in the chaise, L'Amour ?' demanded Milly.

' What chaise ? ' spluttered the beldame tartly.

' The chaise that came last night, past two o'clock,' said Milly.

' That's a lie, and a damn lie ! ' cried the beldame. ' There worn't no chaise at the door since Miss Maud there come from Knowl.'

I stared at the audacious old menial who could utter such language.

' Yes, there was a chaise, and Cormoran, as I think, be come in it,' said Milly, who seemed accustomed to L'Amour's daring address.

' And there's another damn lie, as big as the t'other,' said the crone, her haggard and withered face flushing orange all over.

' I beg you will not use such language in my room,' I replied, very angrily. 'I *saw* the chaise at the door ; your untruth sig- nifies very little, but your impertinence here I will not permit. Should it be repeated, I will assuredly complain to my uncle.'

The old woman flushed more fiercely as I spoke, and fixed her bleared glare on me, with a compression of her mouth that amounted to a wicked grimace. She resisted her angry impulse, however, and only chuckled a little spitefully, saying,

' No offence, miss : it be a way we has in Derbyshire o' speak- ing our minds. No offence, miss, were meant, and none took, as I hopes,' and she made me another courtesy.

'And I forgot to tell you, Miss Milly, the master wants you this minute.'

So Milly, in mute haste, withdrew, followed closely by L'-Amour.

CHAPTER XXXVII

DOCTOR BRYERLY EMERGES

When Milly joined me at breakfast, her eyes were red and swollen. She was still sniffing with that little sobbing hiccough, which betrays, even were there no other signs, recent violent weeping. She sat down quite silent.

'Is he worse, Milly?' I enquired, anxiously.

'No, nothing's wrong wi' him; he's right well,' said Milly, fiercely.

'What's the matter then, Milly dear?'

'The poisonous old witch! 'Twas just to tell the Gov'nor how I'd said 'twas Cormoran that came by the po'shay last night.'

'And who is Cormoran?' I enquired.

'Ay, there it is; I'd like to tell, and you want to hear—and I just daren't, for he'll send me off right to a French school—hang it—hang them all!—if I do.'

'And why should Uncle Silas care?' said I, a good deal surprised.

'They're a-tellin' lies.'

'Who?' said I.

'L'Amour—that's who. So soon as she made her complaint of me, the Gov'nor asked her, sharp enough, did anyone come last night, or a po'shay; and she was ready to swear there was no one. Are ye quite sure, Maud, you really did see aught, or 'appen 'twas all a dream?'

'It was no dream, Milly; so sure as you are there, I saw exactly what I told you,' I replied.

'Gov'nor won't believe it anyhow; and he's right mad wi''

me ; and he threatens me he'll have me off to France ; I wish
'twas under the sea. I hate France—I do—like the devil. Don't
you ? They're always a-threatening me wi' France, if I dare say
a word more about the po'shay, or—or anyone.'

I really was curious about Cormoran ; but Cormoran was not
to be defined to me by Milly ; nor did she, in reality, know
more than I respecting the arrival of the night before.

One day I was surprised to see Doctor Bryerly on the stairs.
I was standing in a dark gallery as he walked across the floor
of the lobby to my uncle's door, his hat on, and some papers
in his hand.

He did not see me ; and when he had entered Uncle Silas's
door, I went down and found Milly awaiting me in the hall.

' So Doctor Bryerly is here,' I said.

' That's the thin fellow, wi' the sharp look, and the shiny
black coat, that went up just now ? ' asked Milly.

' Yes, he's gone into your papa's room,' said I.

' 'Appen 'twas he come 'tother night. He may be staying
here, though we see him seldom, for it's a barrack of a house—
it is.'

The same thought had struck me for a moment, but was
dismissed immediately. It certainly was *not* Doctor Bryerly's
figure which I had seen.

So, without any new light gathered from this apparition, we
went on our way, and made our little sketch of the ruined
bridge. We found the gate locked as before ; and, as Milly
could not persuade me to climb it, we got round the paling by
the river's bank.

While at our drawing, we saw the swarthy face, sooty locks,
and old weather-stained red coat of Zamiel, who was glowering
malignly at us from among the trunks of the forest trees, and
standing motionless as a monumental figure in the side aisle of
a cathedral. When we looked again he was gone.

Although it was a fine mild day for the wintry season, we yet,
cloaked as we were, could not pursue so still an occupation as
sketching for more than ten or fifteen minutes. As we returned,
in passing a clump of trees, we heard a sudden outbreak of
voices, angry and expostulatory ; and saw, under the trees, the
savage old Zamiel strike his daughter with his stick two great
blows, one of which was across the head. ' Beauty ' ran only a

short distance away, while the swart old wood-demon stumped lustily after her, cursing and brandishing his cudgel.

My blood boiled. I was so shocked that for a moment I could not speak ; but in a moment more I screamed—

'You brute ! How dare you strike the poor girl ? '

She had only run a few steps, and turned about confronting him and us, her eyes gleaming fire, her features pale and quivering to suppress a burst of weeping. Two little rivulets of blood were trickling over her temple.

' I say, fayther, look at that,' she said, with a strange tremulous smile, lifting her hand, which was smeared with blood.

Perhaps he was ashamed, and the more enraged on that account, for he growled another curse, and started afresh to reach her, whirling his stick in the air. Our voices, however, arrested him.

' My uncle shall hear of your brutality. The poor girl ! '

' Strike him, Meg, if he does it again ; and pitch his leg into the river to-night, when he's asleep.'

' I'd serve *you* the same ; ' and out came an oath. ' You'd have her lick her fayther, would ye ? Look out ! '

And he wagged his head with a scowl at Milly, and a flourish of his cudgel.

' Be quiet, Milly,' I whispered, for Milly was preparing for battle ; and I again addressed him with the assurance that, on reaching home, I would tell my uncle how he had treated the poor girl.

' 'Tis you she may thank for't, a wheedling o' her to open that gate,' he snarled.

' That's a lie ; we went round by the brook,' cried Milly.

I did not think proper to discuss the matter with him ; and looking very angry, and, I thought, a little put out, he jerked and swayed himself out of sight. I merely repeated my promise of informing my uncle as he went, to which, over his shoulder, he bawled—

' Silas won't mind ye *that* ; ' snapping his horny finger and thumb.

The girl remained where she had stood, wiping the blood off roughly with the palm of her hand, and looking at it before she rubbed it on her apron.

' My poor girl,' I said, ' you must not cry. I'll speak to my uncle about you.'

But she was not crying. She raised her head, and looked at us a little askance, with a sullen contempt, I thought.

' And you must have these apples—won't you ? ' We had brought in our basket two or three of those splendid apples for which Bartram was famous.

I hesitated to go near her, these Hawkeses, Beauty and Pegtop, were such savages. So I rolled the apples gently along the ground to her feet.

She continued to look doggedly at us with the same expression, and kicked away the apples sullenly that approached her feet. Then, wiping her temple and forehead in her apron, without a word, she turned and walked slowly away.

' Poor thing ! I'm afraid she leads a hard life. What strange, repulsive people they are ! '

When we reached home, at the head of the great staircase old L'Amour was awaiting me ; and with a courtesy, and very respectfully, she informed me that the Master would be happy to see me.

Could it be about my evidence as to the arrival of the mysterious chaise that he summoned me to this interview ? Gentle as were his ways, there was something undefinable about Uncle Silas which inspired fear ; and I should have liked few things less than meeting his gaze in the character of a culprit.

There was an uncertainty, too, as to the state in which I might find him, and a positive horror of beholding him again in the condition in which I had last seen him.

I entered the room, then, in some trepidation, but was instantly relieved. Uncle Silas was in the same health apparently, and, as nearly as I could recollect it, in precisely the same rather handsome though negligent garb in which I had first seen him.

Doctor Bryerly—what a marked and vulgar contrast, and yet, somehow, how reassuring !—sat at the table near him, and was tying up papers. His eyes watched me, I thought, with an anxious scrutiny as I approached ; and I think it was not until I had saluted him that he recollected suddenly that he had not seen me before at Bartram, and stood up and greeted me in his usual abrupt and somewhat familiar way. It was vulgar and not cordial, and yet it was honest and indefinably kind.

Up rose my uncle, that strangely venerable, pale portrait, in his loose Rembrandt black velvet. How gentle, how benignant, how unearthly, and inscrutable!

' I need not say how she is. Those lilies and roses, Doctor Bryerly, speak their own beautiful praises of the air of Bartram. I almost regret that her carriage will be home so soon. I only hope it may not abridge her rambles. It positively does me good to look at her. It is the glow of flowers in winter, and the fragrance of a field which the Lord hath blessed.'

' Country air, Miss Ruthyn, is a right good kitchen to country fare. I like to see young women eat heartily. You have had some pounds of beef and mutton since I saw you last,' said Dr. Bryerly.

And this sly speech made, he scrutinised my countenance in silence rather embarrassingly.

' My system, Doctor Bryerly, as a disciple of Æsculapius you will approve—health first, accomplishment afterwards. The Continent is the best field for elegant instruction, and we must see the world a little, by-and-by, Maud ; and to me, if my health be spared, there would be an unspeakable though a melancholy charm in the scenes where so many happy, though so many wayward and foolish, young days were passed ; and I think I should return to these picturesque solitudes with, perhaps, an increased relish. You remember old Chaulieu's sweet lines—

> Désert, aimable solitude,
> Séjour du calme et de la paix,
> Asile où n'entrèrent jamais
> Le tumulte et l'inquiétude.

I can't say that care and sorrow have not sometimes penetrated these sylvan fastnesses ; but the tumults of the world, thank Heaven !—never.'

There was a sly scepticism, I thought, in Doctor Bryerly's sharp face ; and hardly waiting for the impressive ' never,' he said—

' I forgot to ask, who is your banker ? '

' Oh ! Bartlet and Hall, Lombard Street,' answered Uncle Silas, dryly and shortly.

Dr. Bryerly made a note of it, with an expression of face

which seemed, with a sly resolution, to say, 'You shan't come the anchorite over me.'

I saw Uncle Silas's wild and piercing eye rest suspiciously on me for a moment, as if to ascertain whether I felt the spirit of Doctor Bryerly's almost interruption ; and, nearly at the same moment, stuffing his papers into his capacious coat pockets, Doctor Bryerly rose and took his leave.

When he was gone, I bethought me that now was a good opportunity of making my complaint of Dickon Hawkes. Uncle Silas having risen, I hesitated, and began,

'Uncle, may I mention an occurrence—which I witnessed ? '

'Certainly, child,' he answered, fixing his eye sharply on me. I really think he fancied that the conversation was about to turn upon the phantom chaise.

So I described the scene which had shocked Milly and me, an hour or so ago, in the Windmill Wood.

'You see, my dear child, they are rough persons ; their ideas are not ours ; their young people must be chastised, and in a way and to a degree that we would look upon in a serious light. I've found it a bad plan interfering in strictly domestic mis-understandings, and should rather not.'

'But he struck her violently on the head, uncle, with a heavy cudgel, and she was bleeding very fast.'

'Ah ? ' said my uncle, dryly.

'And only that Milly and I deterred him by saying that we would certainly tell you, he would have struck her again ; and I really think if he goes on treating her with so much violence and cruelty he may injure her seriously, or perhaps kill her.'

'Why, you romantic little child, people in that rank of life think absolutely nothing of a broken head,' answered Uncle Silas, in the same way.

'But is it not horrible brutality, uncle ? '

'To be sure it is brutality ; but then you must remember they are brutes, and it suits them,' said he.

I was disappointed. I had fancied that Uncle Silas's gentle nature would have recoiled from such an outrage with horror and indignation ; and instead, here he was, the apologist of that savage ruffian, Dickon Hawkes.

'And he is always so rude and impertinent to Milly and to me,' I continued.

'Oh! impertinent to you—that's another matter. I must see to that. Nothing more, my dear child?'

'Well, there *was* nothing more.'

'He's a useful servant, Hawkes; and though his looks are not prepossessing, and his ways and language rough, yet he is a very kind father, and a most honest man—a thoroughly moral man, though severe—a very rough diamond though, and has no idea of the refinements of polite society. I venture to say he honestly believes that he has been always unexceptionably polite to you, so we must make allowances.'

And Uncle Silas smoothed my hair with his thin aged hand, and kissed my forehead.

'Yes, we must make allowances; we must be kind. What says the Book?—"Judge not, that ye be not judged." Your dear father acted upon that maxim—so noble and so awful—and I strive to do so. Alas! dear Austin, *longo intervallo*, far behind! and you are removed—my example and my help; you are gone to your rest, and I remain beneath my burden, still marching on by bleak and alpine paths, under the awful night.

> O nuit, nuit douloureuse! O toi, tardive aurore!
> Viens-tu? vas-tu venir? es-tu bien loin encore?

And repeating these lines of Chenier, with upturned eyes, and one hand lifted, and an indescribable expression of grief and fatigue, he sank stiffly into his chair, and remained mute, with eyes closed for some time. Then applying his scented hand-kerchief to them hastily, and looking very kindly at me, he said—

'Anything more, dear child?'

'Nothing, uncle, thank you, very much, only about that man, Hawkes; I dare say that he does not mean to be so uncivil as he is, but I am really afraid of him, and he makes our walks in that direction quite unpleasant.'

'I understand quite, my dear. I will see to it; and you must remember that nothing is to be allowed to vex my beloved niece and ward during her stay at Bartram—nothing that her old kinsman, Silas Ruthyn, can remedy.'

So with a tender smile, and a charge to shut the door 'perfectly, but without clapping it,' he dismissed me.

Doctor Bryerly had not slept at Bartram, but at the little inn in Feltram, and he was going direct to London, as I afterwards learned.

'Your ugly doctor's gone away in a fly,' said Milly, as we met on the stairs, she running up, I down.

On reaching the little apartment which was our sitting-room, however, I found that she was mistaken; for Doctor Bryerly, with his hat and a great pair of woollen gloves on, and an old Oxford grey surtout that showed his lank length to advantage, buttoned all the way up to his chin, had set down his black leather bag on the table, and was reading at the window a little volume which I had borrowed from my uncle's library.

It was Swedenborg's account of the other worlds, Heaven and Hell.

He closed it on his finger as I entered, and without recollecting to remove his hat, he made a step or two towards me with his splay, creaking boots. With a quick glance at the door, he said—

'Glad to see you alone for a minute—very glad.'

But his countenance, on the contrary, looked very anxious.

CHAPTER XXXVIII

A MIDNIGHT DEPARTURE

'I'm going this minute—I—I want to know'—another glance at the door—'are you really quite comfortable here?'

'Quite,' I answered promptly.

'You have only your cousin's company?' he continued, glancing at the table, which was laid for two.

'Yes; but Milly and I are very happy together.'

'That's very nice; but I think there are no teachers, you see—painters, and singers, and that sort of thing that is usual with young ladies. No teachers of that kind—of *any* kind—are there?'

' No ; my uncle thinks it better I should lay in a store of health, he says.'

' I know ; and the carriage and horses have not come ; how soon are they expected ? '

' I really can't say, and I assure you I don't much care. I think running about great fun.'

' You walk to church ? '

' Yes ; Uncle Silas's carriage wants a new wheel, he told me.'

' Ay, but a young woman of your rank, you know, it is not usual she should be without the use of a carriage. Have you horses to ride ? '

I shook my head.

' Your uncle, you know, has a very liberal allowance for your maintenance and education.'

I remembered something in the will about it, and Mary Quince was constantly grumbling that ' he did not spend a pound a week on our board.'

I answered nothing, but looked down.

Another glance at the door from Doctor Bryerly's sharp black eyes.

' Is he kind to you ? '

' Very kind—most gentle and affectionate.'

' Why doesn't he keep company with you ? Does he ever dine with you, or drink tea, or talk to you ? Do you see much of him ? '

' He is a miserable invalid—his hours and regimen are peculiar. Indeed I wish very much you would consider his case ; he is, I believe, often insensible for a long time, and his mind in a strange feeble state sometimes.'

' I dare say—worn out in his young days ; and I saw that preparation of opium in his bottle—he takes too much.'

' Why do you think so, Doctor Bryerly ? '

' It's made on water : the spirit interferes with the use of it beyond a certain limit. You have no idea what those fellows can swallow. Read the " Opium Eater." I knew two cases in which the quantity exceeded De Quincy's. Aha ! it's new to you ? ' and he laughed quietly at my simplicity.

' And what do you think his complaint is ? ' I asked.

' Pooh ! I haven't a notion ; but, probably, one way or another, he has been all his days working on his nerves and his brain. These men of pleasure, who have no other pursuit, use themselves up mostly, and pay a smart price for their sins. And so he's kind and affectionate, but hands you over to your cousin and the servants. Are his people civil and obliging?'

'Well, I can't say much for them; there is a man named Hawkes, and his daughter, who are very rude, and even abusive sometimes, and say they have orders from my uncle to shut us out from a portion of the grounds; but I don't believe that, for Uncle Silas never alluded to it when I was making my complaint of them to-day.'

'From what part of the grounds is that?' asked Doctor Bryerly, sharply.

I described the situation as well as I could.

'Can we see it from this?' he asked, peeping from the window.

'Oh, no.'

Doctor Bryerly made a note in his pocket-book here, and I said—

'But I am really quite sure it was a story of Dickon's, he is such a surly, disobliging man.'

'And what sort is that old servant that came in and out of his room?'

'Oh, that is old L'Amour,' I answered, rather indirectly, and forgetting that I was using Milly's nickname.

'And is *she* civil?' he asked.

No, she certainly was not; a most disagreeable old woman, with a vein of wickedness. I thought I had heard her swearing.

'They don't seem to be a very engaging lot,' said Doctor Bryerly; 'but where there's one, there will be more. See here, I was just reading a passage,' and he opened the little volume at the place where his finger marked it, and read for me a few sentences, the purport of which I well remember, although, of course, the words have escaped me.

It was in that awful portion of the book which assumes to describe the condition of the condemned; and it said that, independently of the physical causes in that state operating to enforce community of habitation, and an isolation from superior spirits, there exist sympathies, aptitudes, and necessities which would, of themselves, induce that depraved gregariousness, and isolation too.

'And what of the rest of the servants, are they better?' he resumed.

We saw little or nothing of the others, except of old 'Giblets,' the butler, who went about like a little automaton of dry bones, poking here and there, and whispering and smiling to himself as he laid the cloth; and seeming otherwise quite unconscious of an external world.

'This room is not got up like Mr. Ruthyn's: does he talk of furnishings and making things a little smart? No! Well, I must say, I think he might.'

Here there was a little silence, and Doctor Bryerly, with his accustomed simultaneous glance at the door, said in low, cautious tones, very distinctly—

'Have you been thinking at all over that matter again, I mean about getting your uncle to forego his guardianship? I would not mind his first refusal. You could make it worth his while, unless he—that is—unless he's very unreasonable indeed; and I think you would consult your interest, Miss Ruthyn, by doing so and, if possible, getting out of this place.'

'But I have not thought of it at all; I am much happier here than I had at all expected, and I am very fond of my cousin Milly.'

'How long have you been here exactly?'

I told him. It was some two or three months.

'Have you seen your other cousin yet—the young gentleman?'

'No.'

'H'm! Aren't you very lonely?' he enquired.

'We see no visitors here; but that, you know, I was prepared for.'

Doctor Bryerly read the wrinkles on his splay boot intently and peevishly, and tapped the sole lightly on the ground.

'Yes, it is very lonely, and the people a bad lot. You'd be pleasanter somewhere else—with Lady Knollys, for instance, eh?'

'Well, *there* certainly. But I am very well here: really the time passes very pleasantly; and my uncle is so kind. I have only to mention anything that annoys me, and he will see that it is remedied: he is always impressing that on me.'

'Yes, it is not a fit place for you,' said Doctor Bryerly. 'Of course, about your uncle,' he resumed, observing my surprised look, 'it is all right: but he's quite helpless, you know. At all events, *think* about it. Here's my address—Hans Emmanuel Bryerly, M. D., 17 King Street, Covent Garden, London—don't lose it, mind,' and he tore the leaf out of his note-book.

' Here's my fly at the door, and you must—you must' (he was looking at his watch)—' mind you *must* think of it seriously ; and so, you see, don't let anyone see that. You'll be sure to leave it throwing about. The best way will be just to scratch it on the door of your press, inside, you know ; and don't put my name— you'll remember that—only the rest of the address ; and burn this. Quince is with you ? '

' Yes,' I answered, glad to have a satisfactory word to say.

' Well, don't let her go ; it's a bad sign if they wish it. Don't consent, mind ; but just tip me a hint and you'll have me down. And any letters you get from Lady Knollys, you know, for she's very plain-spoken, you'd better burn them off-hand. And I've stayed too long, though ; mind what I say, scratch it with a pin, and burn that, and not a word to a mortal about it. Good-bye ; oh, I was taking away your book.'

And so, in a fuss, with a slight shake of the hand, getting up his umbrella, his bag, and tin box, he hurried from the room ; and in a minute more, I heard the sound of his vehicle as it drove away.

I looked after it with a sigh ; the uneasy sensations which I had experienced respecting my sojourn at Bartram-Haugh were re-awakened.

My ugly, vulgar, true friend was disappearing beyond those gigantic lime trees which hid Bartram from the eyes of the outer world. The fly, with the doctor's valise on top, vanished, and I sighed an anxious sigh. The shadow of the over-arching trees contracted, and I felt helpless and forsaken ; and glancing down the torn leaf, Doctor Bryerly's address met my eye, between my fingers.

I slipt it into my breast, and ran up-stairs stealthily, trembling lest the old woman should summon me again, at the head of the stairs, into Uncle Silas's room, where under his gaze, I fancied, I should be sure to betray myself.

But I glided unseen and safely by, entered my room, and shut my door. So listening and working, I, with my scissors' point, scratched the address where Doctor Bryerly had advised. Then, in positive terror, lest some one should even knock during the operation, I, with a match, consumed to ashes the tell-tale bit of paper.

Now, for the first time, I experienced the unpleasant sensations of having a secret to keep. I fancy the pain of this solitary liability was disproportionately acute in my case, for I was naturally very open and very nervous. I was always on the point of betraying it *apropos des bottes*—always reproaching myself for my duplicity ; and in constant terror when honest Mary Quince approached the press, or good-natured Milly made her occasional survey of the wonders of my wardrobe. I would have given anything to go and point to the tiny inscription, and say :—
' This is Doctor Bryerly's address in London. I scratched it with my scissors' point, taking every precaution lest anyone—you, my good friends, included—should surprise me. I have ever since kept this secret to myself, and trembled whenever your frank kind faces looked into the press. There—you at last know all about it. Can you ever forgive my deceit ? '

But I could not make up my mind to reveal it ; nor yet to erase the inscription, which was my alternative thought. Indeed I am a wavering, irresolute creature as ever lived, in my ordinary mood. High excitement or passion only can inspire me with decision. Under the inspiration of either, however, I am transformed, and often both prompt and brave.

' Some one left here last night, I think, Miss,' said Mary Quince, with a mysterious nod, one morning. ' 'Twas two o'clock, and I was bad with the toothache, and went down to get a pinch o' red pepper—leaving the candle a-light here lest you should awake. When I was coming up—as I was crossing the lobby, at the far end of the long gallery—what should I hear, but a horse snorting, and some people a-talking, short and quiet like. So I looks out o' the window ; and there surely I did see two horses yoked to a shay, and a fellah a-pullin' a box up o' top ; and out comes a walise and a bag ; and I think it was old Wyat, please'm, that Miss Milly calls L'Amour, that stood in the doorway a-talking to the driver.'

' And who got into the chaise, Mary ? ' I asked.

' Well, Miss, I waited as long as I could ; but the pain was bad, and me so awful cold ; I gave it up at last, and came back to bed, for I could not say how much longer they might wait. And you'll find, Miss, 'twill be kep' a secret, like the shay as you saw'd, Miss, last week. I hate them dark ways, and secrets ; and old Wyat—she does tell stories, don't she ?—and she as ought to be partickler, seein' her time be short now, and she so old. It is awful, an old un like that telling such crams as she do.'

Milly was as curious as I, but could throw no light on this. We both agreed, however, that the departure was probably that of the person whose arrival I had accidentally witnessed. This time the chaise had drawn up at the side door, round the corner of the left side of the house ; and, no doubt, driven away by the back road.

Another accident had revealed this nocturnal move. It was very provoking, however, that Mary Quince had not had resolution to wait for the appearance of the traveller. We all agreed, however, that we were to observe a strict silence, and that even to Wyat—L'Amour I had better continue to call her— Mary Quince was not to hint what she had seen. I suspect, however, that injured curiosity asserted itself, and that Mary hardly adhered to this self-denying resolve.

But cheerful wintry suns and frosty skies, long nights, and brilliant starlight, with good homely fires in our snuggery— gossipings, stories, short readings now and then, and brisk walks through the always beautiful scenery of Bartram-Haugh, and, above all, the unbroken tenor of our life, which had fallen into a serene routine, foreign to the idea of danger or misadventure, gradually quieted the qualms and misgivings which my interview with Doctor Bryerly had so powerfully resuscitated.

My cousin Monica, to my inexpressible joy, had returned to her country-house ; and an active diplomacy, through the post-office, was negotiating the re-opening of friendly relations between the courts of Elverston and of Bartram.

At length, one fine day, Cousin Monica, smiling pleasantly, with her cloak and bonnet on, and her colour fresh from the shrewd air of the Derbyshire hills, stood suddenly before me in our sitting-room. Our meeting was that of two school-companions long separated. Cousin Monica was always a girl in my eyes.

What a hug it was ; what a shower of kisses and ejaculations, enquiries and caresses ! At last I pressed her down into a chair, and, laughing, she said—

'You have no idea what self-denial I have exercised to bring this visit about. I, who detest writing, have actually written five letters to Silas ; and I don't think I said a single impertinent thing in one of them ! What a wonderful little old thing your butler is ! I did not know what to make of him on the steps. Is he a struldbrug, or a fairy, or only a ghost ? Where on earth did your uncle pick him up ? I'm sure he came in on All Hallows E'en, to answer an incantation—not your future husband, I hope—and he'll vanish some night into gray smoke, and whisk sadly up the chimney. He's the most venerable little thing I ever beheld in my life. I leaned back in the carriage and thought I should absolutely die of laughing. He's gone up to prepare your uncle for my visit ; and I really am very glad, for I'm sure I shall look as young as Hebe after *him*. But who is this ? Who are you, my dear ? '

This was addressed to poor Milly, who stood at the corner of the chimney-piece, staring with her round eyes and plump cheeks in fear and wonder upon the strange lady.

'How stupid of me,' I exclaimed. 'Milly, dear, this is your cousin, Lady Knollys.'

'And so *you* are Millicent. Well, dear, I am very glad to see you.' And Cousin Monica was on her feet again in an instant, with Milly's hand very cordially in hers ; and she gave her a kiss upon each cheek, and patted her head.

Milly, I must mention, was a much more presentable figure than when I first encountered her. Her dresses were at least a quarter of a yard longer. Though very rustic, therefore, she was not so barbarously grotesque, by any means.

CHAPTER XXXIX

COUSIN MONICA AND
UNCLE SILAS MEET

Cousin Monica, with her hands upon Milly's shoulders, looked amusedly and kindly in her face. 'And,' said she, 'we must be very good friends—you funny creature, you and I. I'm allowed to be the most saucy old woman in Derbyshire—quite incorrigibly privileged ; and nobody is ever affronted with me, so I say the most shocking things constantly.'

'I'm a bit that way, myself ; and I think,' said poor Milly, making an effort, and growing very red ; she quite lost her head at that point, and was incompetent to finish the sentiment she had prefaced.

'You think ? Now, take my advice, and never wait to think my dear ; talk first, and think afterwards, that is my way ; though, indeed, I can't say I ever think at all. It is a very cowardly habit. Our cold-blooded cousin Maud, there, thinks sometimes ; but it is always such a failure that I forgive her. I wonder when your little pre-Adamite butler will return. He speaks the language of the Picts and Ancient Britons, I dare say, and your father requires a little time to translate him. And, Milly dear, I am very hungry, so I won't wait for your butler, who would give me, I suppose, one of the cakes baked by King Alfred, and some Danish beer in a skull ; but I'll ask you for a little of that nice bread and butter.'

With which accordingly Lady Knollys was quickly supplied; but it did not at all impede her utterance.

'Do you think, girls, you could be ready to come away with me, if Silas gives leave, in an hour or two ? I should so like to take you both home with me to Elverston.'

'How delightful ! you darling,' cried I, embracing and kissing her ; 'for my part, I should be ready in five minutes ; what do you say, Milly ? '

Poor Milly's wardrobe, I am afraid, was more portable than handsome ; and she looked horribly affrighted, and whispered in my ear—

' My best petticoat is away at the laundress ; say in a week, Maud.'

' What does she say ? ' asked Lady Knollys.

' She fears she can't be ready,' I answered, dejectedly.

' There's a deal of my slops in the wash,' blurted out poor Milly, staring straight at Lady Knollys.

' In the name of wonder, what does my cousin mean ? ' asked Lady Knollys.

' Her things have not come home yet from the laundress,' I replied ; and at this moment our wondrous old butler entered to announce to Lady Knollys that his master was ready to receive her, whenever she was disposed to favour him ; and also to make polite apologies for his being compelled, by his state of health, to give her the trouble of ascending to his room.

So Cousin Monica was at the door in a moment, over her shoulder calling to us, ' Come, girls.'

' Please, not yet, my lady—you alone ; and he requests the young ladies will be in the way, as he will send for them presently.'

I began to admire poor ' Giblets ' as the wreck of a tolerably respectable servant.

' Very good ; perhaps it *is* better we should kiss and be friends in private first,' said Cousin Knollys, laughing ; and away she went under the guidance of the mummy.

I had an account of this *tête-à-tête* afterwards from Lady Knollys.

' When I saw him, my dear,' she said, ' I could hardly believe my eyes : such white hair—such a white face—such mad eyes— such a death-like smile. When I saw him last, his hair was dark ; he dressed himself like a modern Englishman ; and he really preserved a likeness to the full-length portrait at Knowl, that you fell in love with, you know ; but, angels and ministers of grace ! such a spectre ! I asked myself, is it necromancy, or is it delirium tremens that has reduced him to this ? And said he, with that odious smile, that made me fancy myself half insane—

' " You see a change, Monica."

' What a sweet, gentle, insufferable voice he has ! Somebody once told me about the tone of a glass flute that made some people hysterical to listen to, and I was thinking of it all the time. There was always a peculiar quality in his voice.

' "I do see a change, Silas," I said at last ; "and, no doubt, so do you in me—a great change."

' " There has been time enough to work a greater than I observe in you since you last honoured me with a visit," said he.

' I think he was at his old sarcasms, and meant that I was the same impertinent minx he remembered long ago, uncorrected by time ; and so I am, and he must not expect compliments from old Monica Knollys.

' " It is a long time, Silas ; but that, you know, is not my fault," said I.

' "Not your fault, my dear—your instinct. We are all imitative creatures: the great people ostracised me, and the small ones followed. We are very like turkeys, we have so much good sense and so much generosity. Fortune, in a freak, wounded my head, and the whole brood were upon me, pecking and gobbling, gobbling and pecking, and you among them, dear Monica. It wasn't your fault, only your instinct, so I quite forgive you ; but no wonder the peckers wear better than the pecked. You are robust ; and I, what I am."

' " Now, Silas, I have not come here to quarrel. If we quarrel now, mind, we can never make it up—we are too old, so let us forget all we can, and try to forgive something ; and if we can do neither, at all events let there be truce between us while I am here."

' " My personal wrongs I can quite forgive, and I do, Heaven knows, from my heart ; but there are things which ought not to be forgiven. My children have been ruined by it. I may, by the mercy of Providence, be yet set right in the world, and so soon as that time comes, I will remember, and I will act ; but my children—you will see that wretched girl, my daughter—education, society, all would come too late—my children have been ruined by it."

' " I have not done it ; but I know what you mean," I said. " You menace litigation whenever you have the means ; but you forget that Austin placed you under promise, when he gave you the use of this house and place, never to disturb my title to Elverston. So there is my answer, if you mean that."

' " I mean what I mean," he replied, with his old smile.

' " You mean then," said I, "that for the pleasure of vexing me with litigation, you are willing to forfeit your tenure of this house and place."

' " Suppose I *did* mean precisely that, why should I forfeit anything ? My beloved brother, by his will, has given me a right to the use of Bartram-Haugh for my life, and attached no absurd condition of the kind you fancy to his gift."

' Silas was in one of his vicious old moods, and liked to menace me. His vindictiveness got the better of his craft ; but he knows as well as I do that he never could succeed in disturbing the title of my poor dear Harry Knollys ; and I was not at all alarmed by his threats ; and I told him so, as coolly as I speak to you now.

' " Well, Monica," he said, "I have weighed you in the balance, and you are not found wanting. For a moment the old man possessed me : the thought of my children, of past unkindness, and present affliction and disgrace, exasperated me, and I was mad. It was but for a moment—the galvanic spasm of a corpse. Never was breast more dead than mine to the passions and ambitions of the world. They are not for white locks like these, nor for a man who, for a week in every month, lies in the gate of death. Will you shake hands ? *Here*—I *do* strike a truce ; and I *do* forget and forgive *everything*."

' I don't know what he meant by this scene. I have no idea whether he was acting, or lost his head, or, in fact, why or how it occurred ; but I am glad, darling, that, unlike myself, I was calm, and that a quarrel has not been forced upon me.'

When our turn came and we were summoned to the presence, Uncle Silas was quite as usual ; but Cousin Monica's heightened colour, and the flash of her eyes, showed plainly that something exciting and angry had occurred.

Uncle Silas commented in his own vein upon the effect of Bartram air and liberty, all he had to offer ; and called on me to say how I liked them. And then he called Milly to him, kissed her tenderly, smiled sadly upon her, and turning to Cousin Monica, said—

' This is my daughter Milly—oh ! she has been presented to

you down-stairs, has she ? You have, no doubt, been interested
by her. As I told her cousin Maud, though I am not yet quite
a Sir Tunbelly Clumsy, she is a very finished Miss Hoyden. Are
not you, my poor Milly ? You owe your distinction, my dear, to
that line of circumvallation which has, ever since your birth, in-
tercepted all civilisation on its way to Bartram. You are much
obliged, Milly, to everybody who, whether naturally or *un*-natu-
rally, turned a sod in that invisible, but impenetrable, work. For
your accomplishments—rather singular than fashionable—you
are indebted, in part, to your cousin, Lady Knollys. Is not she,
Monica ? *Thank* her, Milly.'

' This is your *truce*, Silas,' said Lady Knollys, with a quiet
sharpness. ' I think, Silas Ruthyn, you want to provoke me to
speak in a way before these young creatures which we should all
regret.'

' So my badinage excites your temper, Monnie. Think how
you would feel, then, if I had found you by the highway side,
mangled by robbers, and set my foot upon your throat, and spat
in your face. But—stop this. Why have I said this ? simply to
emphasize my forgiveness. See, girls, Lady Knollys and I, cousins
long estranged, forget and forgive the past, and join hands over
its buried injuries.'

' Well, *be* it so ; only let us have done with ironies and covert
taunts.'

And with these words their hands were joined ; and Uncle
Silas, after he had released hers, patted and fondled it with
his, laughing icily and very low all the time.

' I wish so much, dear Monica,' he said, when this piece of
silent by-play was over, ' that I could ask you to stay to-night ;
but absolutely I have not a bed to offer, and even if I had, I
fear my suit would hardly prevail.'

Then came Lady Knollys' invitation for Milly and me. He
was very much obliged ; he smiled over it a great deal, meditating. I thought he was puzzled ; and amid his smiles, his wild
eyes scanned Cousin Monica's frank face once or twice suspiciously.

There was a difficulty—an *undefined* difficulty—about letting
us go that day ; but on a future one—soon—*very* soon—he would
be most happy.

Well, there was an end of that little project, for to-day at least ; and Cousin Monica was too well-bred to urge it beyond a certain point.

' Milly, my dear, will you put on your hat and show me the grounds about the house ? May she, Silas ? I should like to renew my acquaintance.'

' You'll see them sadly neglected, Monnie. A poor man's pleasure grounds must rely on Nature, and trust to her for effects. Where there is fine timber, however, and abundance of slope, and rock, and hollow, we sometimes gain in picturesqueness what we lose by neglect in luxury.'

Then, as Cousin Monica said she would cross the grounds by a path, and meet her carriage at a point to which we would accompany her, and so make her way home, she took leave of Uncle Silas ; a ceremony whereat—without, I thought, much zeal at either side—a kiss took place.

' Now, girls ! ' said Cousin Knollys, when we were fairly in motion over the grass, ' what do you say—will he let you come—yes or no ? I can't say, but I think, dear,'—this to Milly—' he ought to let you see a little more of the world than appears among the glens and bushes of Bartram. Very pretty they are, like yourself ; but very wild, and very little seen. Where is your brother, Milly ; is not he older than you ? '

' I don't know where ; and he is older by six years and a bit.'

By-and-by, when Milly was gesticulating to frighten some herons by the river's brink into the air, Cousin Monica said confidentially to me—

' He has run away, I'm told—I wish I could believe it—and enlisted in a regiment going to India, perhaps the best thing for him. Did you see him here before his judicious self-banishment ? '

' No.'

' Well, I suppose you have had no loss. Doctor Bryerly says from all he can learn he is a very bad young man. And now tell me, dear, is Silas kind to you ? '

' Yes, always gentle, just as you saw him to-day ; but we don't see a great deal of him—very little, in fact.'

' And how do you like your life and the people ? ' she asked.

' My life, very well ; and the people, pretty well. There's an old women we don't like, old Wyat, she is cross and mysterious and tells untruths ; but I don't think she is dishonest—so Mary

Quince says—and that, you know, is a point ; and there is a family, father and daughter, called Hawkes, who live in the Windmill Wood, who are perfect savages, though my uncle says they don't mean it ; but they are very disagreeable, rude people ; and except them we see very little of the servants or other people. But there has been a mysterious visit ; some one came late at night, and remained for some days, though Milly and I never saw them, and Mary Quince saw a chaise at the side-door at two o'clock at night.'

Cousin Monica was so highly interested at this that she arrested her walk and stood facing me, with her hand on my arm, questioning and listening, and lost, as it seemed, in dismal conjecture.

' It is not pleasant, you know,' I said.

' No, it is not pleasant,' said Lady Knollys, very gloomily.

And just then Milly joined us, shouting to us to look at the herons flying ; so Cousin Monica did, and smiled and nodded in thanks to Milly, and was again silent and thoughtful as we walked on.

' You are to come to me, mind, both of you girls,' she said, abruptly ; ' you *shall*. I'll manage it.'

When silence returned, and Milly ran away once more to try whether the old gray trout was visible in the still water under the bridge, Cousin Monica said to me in a low tone, looking hard at me—

' You've not seen anything to frighten you, Maud ? Don't look so alarmed, dear,' she added with a little laugh, which was not very merry, however. ' I don't mean frighten in any awful sense —in fact, I did not mean frighten at all. I meant—I can't exactly express it—anything to vex, or make you uncomfortable ; have you ? '

' No, I can't say I have, except that room in which Mr. Charke was found dead.'

' Oh ! you saw that, did you ?—I should like to see it so much. Your bedroom is not near it ? '

' Oh, no ; on the floor beneath, and looking to the front. And Doctor Bryerly talked a little to me, and there seemed to be something on his mind more than he chose to tell me ; so that for some time after I saw him I really was, as you say, fright-

ened ; but, except that, I really have had no cause. And what was
in your mind when you asked me ? '

'Well, you know, Maud, you are afraid of ghosts, banditti,
and *every*thing ; and I wished to know whether you were uncomfortable, and what your particular bogle was just now—that, I
assure you, was all ; and I know,' she continued, suddenly changing her light tone and manner for one of pointed entreaty,
'what Doctor Bryerly said ; and I *implore* of you, Maud, to
think of it seriously ; and when you come to me, you shall do so
with the intention of remaining at Elverston.'

'Now, Cousin Monica, is this fair ? You and Doctor Bryerly
both talk in the same awful way to me ; and I assure you, you
don't know how nervous I am sometimes, and yet you won't,
either of you, say what you mean. Now, Monica, dear cousin,
won't you tell me ? '

'You see, dear, it is so lonely ; it's a strange place, and he
so odd. I don't like the place, and I don't like him. I've tried,
but I can't, and I think I never shall. He may be a very—what
was it that good little silly curate at Knowl used to call him ?
—a very advanced Christian—that is it, and I hope he is ; but if
he is only what he used to be, his utter seclusion from society
removes the only check, except personal fear—and he never had
much of that—upon a very bad man. And you must know, my
dear Maud, what a prize you are, and what an immense trust
it is.'

Suddenly Cousin Monica stopped short, and looked at me as if
she had gone too far.

'But, you know, Silas may be very good *now,* although he was
wild and selfish in his young days. Indeed I don't know what
to make of him ; but I am sure when you have thought it over,
you will agree with me and Doctor Bryerly, that you must not
stay here.'

It was vain trying to induce my cousin to be more explicit.

'I hope to see you at Elverston in a very few days. I will
shame Silas into letting you come. I don't like his reluctance.'

'But don't you think he must know that Milly would require
some little outfit before her visit ? '

'Well, I can't say. I hope that is all ; but be it what it may,
I'll *make* him let you come, and *immediately,* too.'

After she had gone, I experienced a repetition of those un-defined doubts which had tortured me for some time after my conversation with Dr. Bryerly. I had truly said, however, I was well enough contented with my mode of life here, for I had been trained at Knowl to a solitude very nearly as profound.

CHAPTER XL

IN WHICH I MAKE ANOTHER COUSIN'S ACQUAINTANCE

My correspondence about this time was not very extensive. About once a fortnight a letter from honest Mrs. Rusk conveyed to me how the dogs and ponies were, in queer English, oddly spelt ; some village gossip, a critique upon Doctor Clay's or the Curate's last sermon, and some severities generally upon the Dis-senters' doings, with loves to Mary Quince, and all good wishes to me. Sometimes a welcome letter from cheerful Cousin Mon-ica ; and now, to vary the series, a copy of complimentary verses, without a signature, very adoring—very like Byron, I then fan-cied, and now, I must confess, rather vapid. Could I doubt from whom they came ?

I had received, about a month after my arrival, a copy of verses in the same hand, in a plaintive ballad style, of the sol-dierly sort, in which the writer said, that as living his sole object was to please me, so dying I should be his latest thought ; and some more poetic impieties, asking only in return that when the storm of battle had swept over, I should ' shed a tear ' on seeing ' the *oak lie,* where it fell.' Of course, about this lugubrious pun, there could be no misconception. The Captain was unmis-takably indicated ; and I was so moved that I could no longer retain my secret ; but walking with Milly that day, confided the little romance to that unsophisticated listener, under the chestnut trees. The lines were so amorously dejected, and yet so heroically redolent of blood and gunpowder, that Milly and

I agreed that the writer must be on the verge of a sanguinary campaign.

It was not easy to get at Uncle Silas's ' Times ' or ' Morning Post,' which we fancied would explain these horrible allusions ; but Milly bethought her of a sergeant in the militia, resident in Feltram, who knew the destination and quarters of every regiment in the service ; and circuitously, from this authority, we learned, to my infinite relief, that Captain Oakley's regiment had still two years to sojourn in England.

I was summoned one evening by old L'Amour, to my uncle's room. I remember his appearance that evening so well, as he lay back in his chair ; the pillow ; the white glare of his strange eye ; his feeble, painful smile.

' You'll excuse my not rising, dear Maud, I am so miserably ill this evening.'

I expressed my respectful condolence.

' Yes ; I *am* to be pitied ; but pity is of no use, dear,' he murmured, peevishly. ' I sent for you to make you acquainted with your cousin, my son. Where are you Dudley ? '

A figure seated in a low lounging chair, at the other side of the fire, and which till then I had not observed, at these words rose up a little slowly, like a man stiff after a day's hunting ; and I beheld with a shock that held my breath, and fixed my eyes upon him in a stare, the young man whom I had encountered at Church Scarsdale, on the day of my unpleasant excursion there with Madame, and who, to the best of my belief, was also one of that ruffianly party who had so unspeakably terrified me in the warren at Knowl.

I suppose I looked very much affrighted. If I had been looking at a ghost I could not have felt much more scared and incredulous.

When I was able to turn my eyes upon my uncle he was not looking at me ; but with a glimmer of that smile with which a father looks on a son whose youth and comeliness he admires, his white face was turned towards the young man, in whom I beheld nothing but the image of odious and dreadful associations.

' Come, sir,' said my uncle, we must not be too modest. Here's your cousin Maud—what do you say ? '

'How are ye, Miss ? ' he said, with a sheepish grin.

'Miss! Come, come. Miss us, no Misses,' said my uncle; 'she is Maud, and you Dudley, or I mistake; or we shall have you calling Milly, madame. She'll not refuse you her hand, I venture to think. Come, young gentleman, speak for yourself.'

'How are ye, Maud?' he said, doing his best, and drawing near, he extended his hand. 'You're welcome to Bartram-Haugh, Miss.'

'Kiss your cousin, sir. Where's your gallantry? On my honour, I disown you,' exclaimed my uncle, with more energy than he had shown before.

With a clumsy effort, and a grin that was both sheepish and impudent, he grasped my hand and advanced his face. The imminent salute gave me strength to spring back a step or two, and he hesitated.

My uncle laughed peevishly.

'Well, well, that will do, I suppose. In my time first-cousins did not meet like strangers; but perhaps we were wrong; we are learning modesty from the Americans, and old English ways are too gross for us.'

'I have—I've seen him before—that is;' and at this point I stopped.

My uncle turned his strange glare, in a sort of scowl of enquiry, upon me.

'Oh!—hey! why this is news. You never told me. Where have you met—eh, Dudley?'

'Never saw her in my days, so far as I'm aweer on,' said the young man.

'No! Well, then, Maud, will *you* enlighten us?' said Uncle Silas, coldly.

'I *did* see that young gentleman before,' I faltered.

'Meaning *me*, ma'am?' he asked, coolly.

'Yes—certainly *you*. I *did*, uncle,' answered I.

'And where was it, my dear? Not at Knowl, I fancy. Poor dear Austin did not trouble me or mine much with his hospitalities.'

This was not a pleasant tone to take in speaking of his dead brother and benefactor; but at the moment I was too much engaged upon the one point to observe it.

'I met'—I could not say my cousin—'I met him, uncle—your son—that young gentleman—I *saw* him, I should say, at Church

Scarsdale, and afterwards with some other persons in the warren at Knowl. It was the night our gamekeeper was beaten.'

'Well, Dudley, what do you say to that?' asked Uncle Silas.

'I never *was* at them places, so help me. I don't know where they be; and I never set eyes on the young lady before, as I hope to be saved, in all my days,' said he, with a countenance so unchanged and an air so confident that I began to think I must be the dupe of one of those strange resemblances which have been known to lead to positive identification in the witness-box, afterwards proved to be utterly mistaken.

'You look so—so *uncomfortable*, Maud, at the idea of having seen him before, that I hardly wonder at the vehemence of his denial. There was plainly something disagreeable; but you see as respects him it is a total mistake. My boy was always a truth-telling fellow—you may rely implicitly on what he says. You were *not* at those places?'

'I wish I may——,' began the ingenuous youth, with increased vehemence.

'There, there—that will do; your honour and word as a gentleman—and *that* you are, though a poor one—will quite satisfy your cousin Maud. Am I right, my dear? I do assure you, as a gentleman, I never knew him to say the thing that was not.'

So Mr. Dudley Ruthyn began, not to curse, but to swear, in the prescribed form, that he had never seen me before, or the places I had named, 'since I was weaned, by——'

'That's enough—now shake hands, if you won't kiss, like cousins,' interrupted my uncle.

And very uncomfortably I did lend him my hand to shake.

'You'll want some supper, Dudley, so Maud and I will excuse your going. Good-night, my dear boy,' and he smiled and waved him from the room.

'That's as fine a young fellow, I think, as any English father can boast for his son—true, brave, and kind, and quite an Apollo. Did you observe how finely proportioned he is, and what exquisite features the fellow has? He's rustic and rough, as you see; but a year or two in the militia—I've a promise of a commission for him—he's too old for the line—will form and polish him. He wants nothing but manner; and I protest when he has

had a little drilling of that kind, I do believe he'll be as pretty
a fellow as you'd find in England.'

I listened with amazement. I could discover nothing but what
was disagreeable in the horrid bumpkin, and thought such
an instance of the blindness of parental partiality was hardly
credible.

I looked down, dreading another direct appeal to my judgment ; and Uncle Silas, I suppose, referred those downcast looks
to maiden modesty, for he forbore to task mine by any new
interrogatory.

Dudley Ruthyn's cool and resolute denial of ever having
seen me or the places I had named, and the inflexible serenity
of his countenance while doing so, did very much shake my
confidence in my own identification of him. I could not be
quite certain that the person I had seen at Church Scarsdale
was the very same whom I afterwards saw at Knowl. And now,
in this particular instance, after the lapse of a still longer period,
could I be perfectly certain that my memory, deceived by some
accidental points of resemblance, had not duped me, and
wronged my cousin, Dudley Ruthyn ?

I suppose my uncle had expected from me some signs of ac-
quiesence in his splendid estimate of his cub, and was nettled at
my silence. After a short interval he said—

' I've seen something of the world in my day, and I can say
without a misgiving of partiality, that Dudley is the material
of a perfect English gentleman. I am not blind, of course—the
training must be supplied ; a year or two of good models, active self-criticism, and good society. I simply say that the *material* is there.'

Here was another interval of silence.

' And now tell me, child, what these recollections of Church
—Church—*what* ? '

' Church Scarsdale,' I replied.

' Yes, thank you—Church Scarsdale and Knowl—are ? '

So I related my stories as well as I could.

' Well, dear Maud, the adventure of Church Scarsdale is
hardly so terrific as I expected,' said Uncle Silas with a cold
little laugh ; ' and I don't see, if he had really been the hero of
it, why he should shrink from avowing it. I know I should not.
And I really can't say that your pic-nic party in the grounds of

Knowl has frightened me much more. A lady waiting in the
carriage, and two or three tipsy young men. Her presence seems
to me a guarantee that no mischief was meant ; but champagne
is the soul of frolic, and a row with the gamekeepers a natural
consequence. It happened to me once—forty years ago, when
I was a wild young buck—one of the worst rows I ever was in.'

And Uncle Silas poured some eau-de-cologne over the corner
of his handkerchief, and touched his temples with it.

' If my boy had been there, I do assure you—and I know him
—he would say so at once. I fancy he would rather *boast* of it.
I never knew him utter an untruth. When you know him a
little you'll say so.'

With these words Uncle Silas leaned back exhausted, and
languidly poured some of his favourite eau-de-cologne over
the palms of his hands, nodded a farewell, and, in a whisper,
wished me good-night.

' Dudley's come,' whispered Milly, taking me under the arm
as I entered the lobby. ' But I don't care : he never gives me
nout ; and he gets money from Governor, as much as he likes,
and I never a sixpence. It's a shame ! '

So there was no great love between the only son and only
daughter of the younger line of the Ruthyns.

I was curious to learn all that Milly could tell me of this
new inmate of Bartram-Haugh ; and Milly was communicative
without having a great deal to relate, and what I heard from her
tended to confirm my own disagreeable impressions about him.
She was afraid of him. He was a ' woundy ugly customer in a
wax, she could tell me.' He was the only one 'she ever knowed as
had pluck to jaw the Governor.' But he was ' afeard on the
Governor, too.'

His visits to Bartram-Haugh, I heard, were desultory ; and
this, to my relief, would probably not outlast a week or a fortnight. ' He *was* such a fashionable cove : ' he was always ' a
gadding about, mostly to Liverpool and Birmingham, and sometimes to Lunnun, itself.' He was ' keeping company one time
with Beauty, Governor thought, and he was awfully afraid he'd
a married her ; but that was all bosh and nonsense ; and Beauty
would have none of his chaff and wheedling, for she liked
Tom Brice ; ' and Milly thought that Dudley never ' cared a
crack of a whip for her.' He used to go to the Windmill to

have 'a smoke with Pegtop;' and he was a member of the Feltram Club, that met at the 'Plume o' Feathers.' He was 'a rare good shot,' she heard; and 'he was before the justices for poaching, but they could make nothing of it.' And the Governor said 'it was all through spite of him—for they hate us for being better blood than they.' And 'all but the squires and those upstart folk loves Dudley, he is so handsome and gay— though he be a bit cross at home.' And, 'Governor says, he'll be a Parliament man yet, spite o' them all.'

Next morning, when our breakfast was nearly ended, Dudley tapped at the window with the end of his clay pipe—a 'church-warden' Milly called it—just such a long curved pipe as Joe Willet is made to hold between his lips in those charming illustrations of 'Barnaby Rudge'—which we all know so well— and lifting his 'wide-awake' with a burlesque salutation, which, I suppose, would have charmed the 'Plume of Feathers,' he dropped, kicked and caught his 'wide-awake,' with an agility and gravity, as he replaced it, so inexpressibly humorous, that Milly went off in a loud fit of laughter, with the ejaculation—

'Did you ever?'

It was odd how repulsively my confidence in my original identification always revived on unexpectedly seeing Dudley after an interval.

I could perceive that this piece of comic by-play was meant to make a suitable impression on me. I received it, however, with a killing gravity; and after a word or two to Milly, he lounged away, having first broken his pipe, bit by bit, into pieces, which he balanced in turn on his nose and on his chin, from which features he jerked them into his mouth, with a precision which, along with his excellent pantomime of eating them, highly excited Milly's mirth and admiration.

CHAPTER XLI

MY COUSIN DUDLEY

Greatly to my satisfaction, this engaging person did not appear again that day. But next day Milly told me that my uncle had taken him to task for the neglect with which he was treating us.

'He did pitch into him, sharp and short, and not a word from him, only sulky like ; and I so frightened, I durst not look up almost ; and they said a lot I could not make head or tail of ; and Governor ordered me out o' the room, and glad I was to go ; and so they had it out between them.'

Milly could throw no light whatsoever upon the adventures at Church Scarsdale and Knowl ; and I was left still in doubt, which sometimes oscillated one way and sometimes another. But, on the whole, I could not shake off the misgivings which constantly recurred and pointed very obstinately to Dudley as the hero of those odious scenes.

Oddly enough, though, I now felt far less confident upon the point than I did at first sight. I had begun to distrust my memory, and to suspect my fancy ; but of this there could be no question, that between the person so unpleasantly linked in my remembrance with those scenes, and Dudley Ruthyn, a striking, though possibly only a general resemblance did exist.

Milly was certainly right as to the gist of Uncle Silas's injunction, for we saw more of Dudley henceforward.

He was shy ; he was impudent ; he was awkward ; he was conceited ;—altogether a most intolerable bumpkin. Though he sometimes flushed and stammered, and never for a moment was at his ease in my presence, yet, to my inexpressible disgust, there was a self-complacency in his manner, and a kind of triumph in his leer, which very plainly told me how satisfied he was as to the nature of the impression he was making upon me.

I would have given worlds to tell him how odious I thought

him. Probably, however, he would not have believed me. Perhaps he fancied that 'ladies' affected airs of indifference and repulsion to cover their real feelings. I never looked at or spoke to him when I could avoid either, and then it was as briefly as I could. To do him justice, however, he seemed to have no liking for our society, and certainly never seemed altogether comfortable in it.

I find it hard to write quite impartially even of Dudley Ruthyn's personal appearance; but, with an effort, I confess that his features were good, and his figure not amiss, though a little fattish. He had light whiskers, light hair, and a pink complexion, and very good blue eyes. So far my uncle was right; and if he had been perfectly gentlemanlike, he really might have passed for a handsome man in the judgment of some critics.

But there was that odious mixture of *mauvaise honte* and impudence, a clumsiness, a slyness, and a consciousness in his bearing and countenance, not distinctly boorish, but *low,* which turned his good looks into an ugliness more intolerable than that of feature; and a corresponding vulgarity pervading his dress, his demeanour, and his very walk, marred whatever good points his figure possessed. If you take all this into account, with the ominous and startling misgivings constantly recurring, you will understand the mixed feelings of anger and disgust with which I received the admiration he favoured me with.

Gradually he grew less constrained in my presence, and certainly his manners were not improved by his growing ease and confidence.

He came in while Milly and I were at luncheon, jumped up, with a 'right-about face' performed in the air, sitting on the sideboard, whence grinning slyly and kicking his heels, he leered at us.

'Will you have something, Dudley?' asked Milly.

'No, lass; but I'll look at ye, and maybe drink a drop for company.'

And with these words, he took a sportsman's flask from his pocket; and helping himself to a large glass and a decanter, he compounded a glass of strong brandy-and-water, as he talked, and refreshed himself with it from time to time.

'Curate's up wi' the Governor,' he said, with a grin. 'I

wanted a word wi' him ; but I s'pose I'll hardly git in this hour
or more ; they're a praying and disputing, and a Bible-chopping,
as usual. Ha, ha ! But 'twon't hold much longer, old Wyat says,
now that Uncle Austin's dead ; there's nout to be made o' praying and that work no longer, and it don't pay of itself.'

' O fie ! For shame, you sinner ! ' laughed Milly. ' He wasn't
in a church these five years, he says, and then only to meet a
young lady. Now, isn't he a sinner, Maud—isn't he ? '

Dudley, grinning, looked with a languishing slyness at me,
biting the edge of his wide-awake, which he held over his breast.

Dudley Ruthyn probably thought there was a manly and
desperate sort of fascination in the impiety he professed.

' I wonder, Milly,' said I, ' at your laughing. How *can* you
laugh ? '

' You'd have me cry, would ye ? ' answered Milly.

' I certainly would not have you laugh,' I replied.

' I know I wish *some* one 'ud cry for me, and I know who,'
said Dudley, in what he meant for a very engaging way, and he
looked at me as if he thought I must feel flattered by his caring
to have my tears.

Instead of crying, however, I leaned back in my chair, and
began quietly to turn over the pages of Walter Scott's poems,
which I and Milly were then reading in the evenings.

The tone in which this odious young man spoke of his father,
his coarse mention of mine, and his low boasting of his irreli-
gion, disgusted me more than ever with him.

' They parsons be slow coaches—awful slow. I'll have a good
bit to wait, I s'pose. I should be three miles away and more by
this time—drat it ! ' He was eyeing the legging of the foot
which he held up while he spoke, as if calculating how far away
that limb should have carried him by this time. ' Why can't folk
do their Bible and prayers o' Sundays, and get it off their
stomachs ? I say, Milly lass, will ye see if Governor be done
wi' the Curate ? Do. I'm a losing the whole day along o' him.'

Milly jumped up, accustomed to obey her brother, and as she
passed me, whispered, with a wink—

' Money.'

And away she went. Dudley whistled a tune, and swung his
foot like a pendulum, as he followed her with his side-glance.

' I say, it is a hard case, Miss, a lad o' spirit should be kept so tight. I haven't a shilling but what comes through his fingers ; an' drat the tizzy he'll gi' me till he knows the reason why.'

' Perhaps,' I said, ' my uncle thinks you should earn some for yourself.'

' I'd like to know how a fella 's to earn money now-a-days. You wouldn't have a gentleman to keep a shop, I fancy. But I'll ha' a fistful jist now, and no thanks to he. Them executors, you know, owes me a deal o' money. Very honest chaps, of course ; but they're cursed slow about paying, I know.'

I made no remark upon this elegant allusion to the executors of my dear father's will.

' An' I tell ye, Maud, when I git the tin, I know who I'll buy a farin' for. I do, lass.'

The odious creature drawled this with a sidelong leer, which, I suppose, he fancied quite irresistible.

I am one of those unfortunate persons who always blushed when I most wished to look indifferent ; and now, to my inexpressible chagrin, with its accustomed perversity, I felt the blush mount to my cheeks, and glow even on my forehead.

I saw that he perceived this most disconcerting indication of a sentiment the very idea of which was so detestable, that, equally enraged with myself and with him, I did not know how to exhibit my contempt and indignation.

Mistaking the cause of my discomposure, Mr. Dudley Ruthyn laughed softly, with an insufferable suavity.

' And there's some'at, lass, I must have in return. Honour thy father, you know ; you would not ha' me disobey the Governor ? No, you wouldn't—would ye ? '

I darted at him a look which I hoped would have quelled his impertinence ; but I blushed most provokingly—more violently than ever.

' I'd back them eyes again' the county, I would,' he exclaimed, with a condescending enthusiasm. ' You're awful pretty, you are, Maud. I don't know what came over me t'other night when Governor told me to buss ye ; but dang it, ye shan't deny me now, and I'll have a kiss, lass, in spite o' thy blushes.'

He jumped from his elevated seat on the sideboard, and came swaggering toward me, with an odious grin, and his arms extended. I started to my feet, absolutely transported with fury.

' Drat me, if she baint a-going to fight me ! ' he chuckled humorously.

' Come, Maud, you would not be ill-natured, sure ? Arter all, it's only our duty. Governor bid us kiss, didn't he ? '

' Don't—*don't*, sir. Stand back, or I'll call the servants.'

And as it was I began to scream for Milly.

' There's how it is wi' all they cattle ! You never knows your own mind—ye don't,' he said, surlily. ' You make such a row about a bit o' play. Drop it, will you ? There's no one a-harming you—is there ? *I'm* not, for sartain.'

And, with an angry chuckle, he turned on his heel, and left the room.

I think I was perfectly right to resist, with all the vehemence of which I was capable, this attempt to assume an intimacy which, notwithstanding my uncle's opinion to the contrary, seemed to me like an outrage.

Milly found me alone—not frightened, but very angry. I had quite made up my mind to complain to my uncle, but the Curate was still with him ; and, by the time he had gone, I was cooler. My awe of my uncle had returned. I fancied that he would treat the whole affair as a mere playful piece of gallantry. So, with the comfortable conviction that he had had a lesson, and would think twice before repeating his impertinence, I re- solved, with Milly's approbation, to leave matters as they were.

Dudley, greatly to my comfort, was huffed with me, and hardly appeared, and was sulky and silent when he did. I lived then in the pleasant anticipation of his departure, which, Milly thought, would be very soon.

My uncle had his Bible and his consolations ; but it cannot have been pleasant to this old *roué*, converted though he was— this refined man of fashion—to see his son grow up an outcast, and a Tony Lumpkin ; for whatever he may have thought of his natural gifts, he must have known how mere a boor he was.

I try to recall my then impressions of my uncle's character. Grizzly and chaotic the image rises—silver head, feet of clay. I as yet knew little of him.

I began to perceive that he was what Mary Quince used to call ' dreadful particular '—I suppose a little selfish and impa- tient. He used to get cases of turtle from Liverpool. He drank claret and hock for his health, and ate woodcock and other light and salutary dainties for the same reason ; and was petulant and vicious about the cooking of these, and the flavour and clearness of his coffee.

His conversation was easy, polished, and, with a sentimental glazing, cold; but across this artificial talk, with its French rhymes, racy phrases, and fluent eloquence, like a streak of angry light, would, at intervals, suddenly gleam some dismal thought of religion. I never could quite satisfy myself whether they were affectations or genuine, like intermittent thrills of pain.

The light of his large eyes was very peculiar. I can liken it to nothing but the sheen of intense moonlight on burnished metal. But that cannot express it. It glared white and suddenly —almost fatuous. I thought of Moore's lines whenever I looked on it :—

Oh, ye dead ! oh, ye dead ! whom we know by the light you give
From your cold gleaming eyes, though you move like men who live.

I never saw in any other eye the least glimmer of the same baleful effulgence. His fits, too—his hoverings between life and death—between intellect and insanity—a dubious, marsh-fire existence, horrible to look on !

I was puzzled even to comprehend his feelings toward his children. Sometimes it seemed to me that he was ready to lay down his soul for them ; at others, he looked and spoke almost as if he hated them. He talked as if the image of death was always before him, yet he took a terrible interest in life, while seemingly dozing away the dregs of his days in sight of his coffin.

Oh ! Uncle Silas, tremendous figure in the past, burning always in memory in the same awful lights ; the fixed white face of scorn and anguish ! It seems as if the Woman of Endor had led me to that chamber and showed me a spectre.

Dudley had not left Bartram-Haugh when a little note reached me from Lady Knollys. It said—

'DEAREST MAUD,—I have written by this post to Silas, beseeching a loan of you and my Cousin Milly. I see no reason your uncle can possibly have for refusing me ; and, therefore, I count confidently on seeing you both at Elverston to-morrow, to stay for at least a week. I have hardly a creature to meet you. I have been disappointed in several visitors ; but another time we shall have a gayer house. Tell Milly—with my love—that I will not forgive her if she fails to accompany you.

> ' Believe me ever your affectionate cousin,
>
> 'MONICA KNOLLYS.'

Milly and I were both afraid that Uncle Silas would refuse his consent, although we could not divine any sound reason for his doing so, and there were many in favour of his improving the opportunity of allowing poor Milly to see some persons of her own sex above the rank of menials.

At about twelve o'clock my uncle sent for us, and, to our great delight, announced his consent, and wished us a very happy excursion.

CHAPTER XLII

ELVERSTON AND ITS PEOPLE

So Milly and I drove through the gabled high street of Feltram next day. We saw my gracious cousin smoking with a man like a groom, at the door of the ' Plume of Feathers.' I drew myself back as we passed, and Milly popped her head out of the window.

' I'm blessed,' said she, laughing, 'if he hadn't his thumb to his nose, and winding up his little finger, the way he does with old Wyat—L'Amour, ye know ; and you may be sure he said something funny, for Jim Jolliter was laughin', with his pipe in his hand.'

' I wish I had not seen him, Milly. I feel as if it were an ill omen. He always looks so cross ; and I dare say he wished us some ill,' I said.

' No, no, you don't know Dudley : if he were angry, he'd say nothing that's funny ; no, he's not vexed, only shamming vexed.'

The scenery through which we passed was very pretty. The road brought us through a narrow and wooded glen. Such studies of ivied rocks and twisted roots ! A little stream tinkled lonely through the hollow. Poor Milly ! In her odd way she made herself companionable. I have sometimes fancied an enjoyment of natural scenery not so much a faculty as an acquirement. It is so exquisite in the instructed, so strangely absent in uneducated humanity. But certainly with Milly it was inborn and hearty ; and so she could enter into my raptures, and requite them.

Then over one of those beautiful Derbyshire moors we drove, and so into a wide wooded hollow, where was our first view of Cousin Monica's pretty gabled house, beautified with that indescribable air of shelter and comfort which belongs to an old English residence, with old timber grouped round it, and something in its aspect of the quaint old times and bygone merrymakings, saying sadly, but genially, ' Come in : I bid you welcome. For two hundred years, or more, have I been the home of this beloved old family, whose generations I have seen in the cradle and in the coffin, and whose mirth and sorrows and hospitalities I remember. All their friends, like you, were welcome ; and you, like them, will here enjoy the warm illusions that cheat the sad conditions of mortality ; and like them you will go your way, and others succeed you, till at last I, too, shall yield to the general law of decay, and disappear.'

By this time poor Milly had grown very nervous ; a state which she described in such very odd phraseology as threw me, in spite of myself—for I affected an impressive gravity in lecturing her upon her language—into a hearty fit of laughter.

I must mention, however, that in certain important points Milly was very essentially reformed. Her dress, though not very fashionable, was no longer absurd. And I had drilled her into speaking and laughing quietly ; and for the rest I trusted to the indulgence which is always, I think, more honestly and easily obtained from well-bred than from under-bred people.

Cousin Monica was out when we arrived ; but we found that she had arranged a double-bedded room for me and Milly, greatly to our content ; and good Mary Quince was placed in the dressing-room beside us.

We had only just commenced our toilet when our hostess entered, as usual in high spirits, welcomed and kissed us both again and again. She was, indeed, in extraordinary delight, for she had anticipated some stratagem or evasion to prevent our visit ; and in her usual way she spoke her mind as frankly about Uncle Silas to poor Milly as she used to do of my dear father to me.

'I did not think he would let you come without a battle ; and you know if he chose to be obstinate it would not have been easy to get you out of the enchanted ground, for so it seems to be with that awful old wizard in the midst of it. I mean, Silas, your papa, my dear. Honestly, is not he very like Michael Scott ? '

'I never saw him,' answered poor Milly. 'At least, that I'm aware of,' she added, perceiving us smile. 'But I do think he's a thought like old Michael Dobbs, that sells the ferrets, maybe you mean him ? '

'Why, you told me, Maud, that you and Milly were reading Walter Scott's poems. Well, no matter. Michael Scott, my dear, was a dead wizard, with ever so much silvery hair, lying in his grave for ever so many years, with just life enough to scowl when they took his book ; and you'll find him in the "Lay of the Last Minstrel," exactly like your papa, my dear. And my people tell me that your brother Dudley has been seen drinking and smoking about Feltram this week. How long does he remain at home ? Not very long, eh ? And, Maud, dear, he has not been making love to you ? Well, I see ; of course he has. And *apropos* of love-making, I hope that impudent creature, Charles Oakley, has not been teasing you with notes or verses.'

'Indeed but he has though,' interposed Miss Milly ; a good deal to my chagrin, for I saw no particular reason for placing his verses in Cousin Monica's hands. So I confessed the two little copies of verses, with the qualification, however, that I did not know from whom they came.

'Well now, dear Maud, have not I told you fifty times over to have nothing to say to him ? I've found out, my dear, he plays, and he is very much in debt. I've made a vow to pay no more for him. I've been such a fool, you have no notion; and I'm speaking, you know, against myself ; it would be such a relief if he were to find a wife to support him ; and he has been, I'm told, very sweet upon a rich old maid—a button-maker's sister, in Manchester.'

This arrow was well shot.

' But don't be frightened : you are richer as well as younger ;
and, no doubt, will have your chance first, my dear ; and in the
meantime, I dare say, those verses, like Falstaff's *billet-doux,* you
know, are doing double duty.'

I laughed, but the button-maker was a secret trouble to me ;
and I would have given I know not what that Captain Oakley
were one of the company, that I might treat him with the refined
contempt which his deserts and my dignity demanded.

Cousin Monica busied herself about Milly's toilet, and was a
very useful lady's maid, chatting in her own way all the time ;
and, at last, tapping Milly under the chin with her finger, she
said, very complacently—

' I think I have succeeded, Miss Milly ; look in the glass. She
really is a very pretty creature.'

And Milly blushed, and looked with a shy gratification, which
made her still prettier, on the mirror.

Milly indeed was very pretty. She looked much taller now
that her dresses were made of the usual length. A little plump
she was, beautifully fair, with such azure eyes, and rich hair.

' The more you laugh the better, Milly, for you've got very
pretty teeth—very pretty ; and if you were my daughter, or if
your father would become president of a college of magicians,
and give you up to me, I venture to say I would place you very
well ; and even as it is we must try, my dear.'

So down to the drawing-room we went ; and Cousin Monica
entered, leading us both by the hands.

By this time the curtains were closed, and the drawing-room
dependent on the pleasant glow of the fire, and the slight pro-
visional illumination usual before dinner.

' Here are my two cousins,' began Lady Knollys : ' this is Miss
Ruthyn, of Knowl, whom I take the liberty of calling Maud ;
and this is Miss Millicent Ruthyn, Silas's daughter, you know,
whom I venture to call Milly ; and they are very pretty, as you
will see, when we get a little more light, and they know it very
well themselves.'

And as she spoke, a frank-eyed, gentle, prettyish lady, not so
tall as I, but with a very kind face, rose up from a book of prints,
and, smiling, took our hands.

She was by no means young, as I then counted youth—past
thirty, I suppose—and with an air that was very quiet, and

friendly, and engaging. She had never been a mere fashionable woman plainly; but she had the ease and polish of the best society, and seemed to take a kindly interest both in Milly and me; and Cousin Monica called her Mary, and sometimes Polly. That was all I knew of her for the present.

So very pleasantly the time passed by till the dressing-bell rang, and we ran away to our room.

'Did I say anything very bad?' asked poor Milly, standing exactly before me, so soon as our door was shut.

'Nothing, Milly; you are doing admirably.'

'And I do look a great fool, don't I?' she demanded.

'You look extremely pretty, Milly; and not a bit like a fool.'

'I watch everything. I think I'll learn it at last; but it comes a little troublesome at first; and they do talk different from what I used—you were quite right there.'

When we returned to the drawing-room, we found the party already assembled, and chatting, evidently with spirit.

The village doctor, whose name I forget, a small man, grey, with shrewd grey eyes, sharp and mulberry nose, whose conflagration extended to his rugged cheeks, and touched his chin and forehead, was conversing, no doubt agreeably, with Mary, as Cousin Monica called her guest.

Over my shoulder, Milly whispered—

'Mr. Carysbroke.'

And Milly was quite right: that gentleman chatting with Lady Knollys, his elbow resting on the chimney-piece, was, indeed, our acquaintance of the Windmill Wood. He instantly recognised us, and met us with his pleased and intelligent smile.

'I was just trying to describe to Lady Knollys the charming scenery of the Windmill Wood, among which I was so fortunate as to make your acquaintance, Miss Ruthyn. Even in this beautiful county I know of nothing prettier.'

Then he sketched it, as it were, with a few light but glowing words.

'What a sweet scene!' said Cousin Monica: 'only think of her never bringing me through it. She reserves it, I fancy, for her romantic adventures; and you, I know, are very benevolent, Ilbury, and all that kind of thing; but I am not quite certain that you would have walked along that narrow parapet, over a river, to visit a sick old woman, if you had not happened to see two very pretty demoiselles on the other side.'

'What an ill-natured speech ! I must either forfeit my charac- ter for disinterested benevolence, so justly admired, or disavow a motive that does such infinite credit to my taste,' exclaimed Mr. Carysbroke. 'I think a charitable person would have said that a philanthropist, in prosecuting his virtuous, but perilous vocation, was unexpectedly *rewarded* by a vision of angels.'

'And with these angels loitered away the time which ought to have been devoted to good Mother Hubbard, in her fit of lum- bago, and returned without having set eyes on that afflicted Christian, to amaze his worthy sister with poetic babblings about wood-nymphs and such pagan impieties,' rejoined Lady Knollys.

'Well, be just,' he replied, laughing ; 'did not I go next day and see the patient ? '

'Yes ; next day you went by the same route—in quest of the dryads, I am afraid—and were rewarded by the spectacle of Mother Hubbard.'

'Will nobody help a humane man in difficulties ? ' Mr. Carys- broke appealed.

'I do believe,' said the lady whom as yet I knew only as Mary, 'that every word that Monica says is perfectly true.'

'And if it be so, am I not all the more in need of help ? Truth is simply the most dangerous kind of defamation, and I really think I'm most cruelly persecuted.'

At this moment dinner was announced, and a meek and dap- per little clergyman, with smooth pink cheeks, and tresses parted down the middle, whom I had not seen before, emerged from shadow.

This little man was assigned to Milly, Mr. Carysbroke to me, and I know not how the remaining ladies divided the doctor between them.

That dinner, the first at Elverston, I remember as a very pleasant repast. Everyone talked—it was impossible that conver- sation should flag where Lady Knollys was ; and Mr. Carys- broke was very agreeable and amusing. At the other side of the table, the little pink curate, I was happy to see, was prattling away, with a modest fluency, in an under-tone to Milly, who was following my instructions most conscientiously, and speak-

ing in so low a key that I could hardly hear at the opposite side
one word she was saying.

That night Cousin Monica paid us a visit, as we sat chatting
by the fire in our room ; and I told her—

' I have just been telling Milly what an impression she has
made. The pretty little clergyman—*il en est épris*—he has evidently quite lost his heart to her. I dare say he'll preach next
Sunday on some of King Solomon's wise sayings about the irresistible strength of women.'

' Yes,' said Lady Knollys, ' or maybe on the sensible text,
" Whoso findeth a wife findeth a good thing, and obtaineth favour," and so forth. At all events, I may say, Milly, whoso
findeth a husband such as he, findeth a tolerably good thing. He
is an exemplary little creature, second son of Sir Harry Biddlepen, with a little independent income of his own, beside his
church revenues of ninety pounds a year ; and I don't think a
more harmless and docile little husband could be found anywhere ; and I think, Miss Maud, *you* seemed a good deal interested, too.'

I laughed and blushed, I suppose ; and Cousin Monica, skipping after her wont to quite another matter, said in her odd
frank way—

' And how has Silas been ?—not cross, I hope, or very odd.
There was a rumour that your brother, Dudley, had gone a sol-
diering to India, Milly, or somewhere ; but that was all a story,
for he has turned up, just as usual. And what does he mean to
do with himself ? He has got some money now—your poor
father's will, Maud. Surely he doesn't mean to go on lounging
and smoking away his life among poachers, and prize-fighters,
and worse people. He ought to go to Australia, like Thomas
Swain, who, they say, is making a fortune—a great fortune—and
coming home again. That's what your brother Dudley should
do, if he has either sense or spirit ; but I suppose he won't—
too long abandoned to idleness and low company—and he'll not
have a shilling left in a year or two. Does he know, I wonder,
that his father has served a notice or something on Dr. Bryerly,
telling him to pay sixteen hundred pounds of poor Austin's legacy to *him,* and saying that he has paid debts of the young man,
and holds his acknowledgments to that amount ? He won't have
a guinea in a year if he stays here. I'd give fifty pounds he

was in Van Diemen's Land—not that I care for the cub, Milly, any more than you do ; but I really don't see any honest business he has in England.'

Milly gaped in a total puzzle as Lady Knollys rattled on.

' You know, Milly, you must not be talking about this when you go home to Bartram, because Silas would prevent your coming to me any more if he thought I spoke so freely ; but I can't help it : so you must promise to be more discreet than I. And I am told that all kinds of claims are about to be pressed against him, now that he is thought to have got some money ; and he has been cutting down oak and selling the bark, Doctor Bryerly has been told, in that Windmill Wood ; and he has kilns there for burning charcoal, and got a man from Lancashire who understands it—Hawk, or something like that.'

' Ay, Hawkes—Dickon Hawkes ; that's Pegtop, you know, Maud,' said Milly.

' Well, I dare say ; but a man of very bad character, Dr. Bryerly says ; and he has written to Mr. Danvers about it—for that is what they call waste, cutting down and selling the timber, and the oakbark, and burning the willows, and other trees that are turned into charcoal. It is all *waste,* and Dr. Bryerly is about to put a stop to it.'

' Has he got your carriage for you, Maud, and your horses ? ' asked Cousin Monica, suddenly.

' They have not come yet, but in a few weeks, Dudley says, positively——'

Cousin Monica laughed a little and shook her head.

' Yes, Maud, the carriage and horses will always be coming in a few weeks, till the time is over ; and meanwhile the old travelling chariot and post-horses will do very well ; ' and she laughed a little again.

' That's why the stile's pulled away at the paling, I suppose ; and Beauty—Meg Hawkes, that is—is put there to stop us going through ; for I often spied the smoke beyond the windmill,' observed Milly.

Cousin Monica listened with interest, and nodded silently.

I was very much shocked. It seemed to me quite incredible. I think Lady Knollys read my amazement and my exalted estimate of the heinousness of the procedure in my face, for she said—

'You know we can't quite condemn Silas till we have heard what he has to say. He may have done it in ignorance; or, it is just possible, he may have the right.'

'Quite true. He may have the right to cut down trees at Bartram-Haugh. At all events, I am sure he thinks he has,' I echoed.

The fact was, that I would not avow to myself a suspicion of Uncle Silas. Any falsehood there opened an abyss beneath my feet into which I dared not look.

'And now, dear girls, good-night. You must be tired. We breakfast at a quarter past nine—not too early for you, I know.'

And so saying, she kissed us, smiling, and was gone.

I was so unpleasantly occupied, for some time after her departure, with the knaveries said to be practised among the dense cover of the Windmill Wood, that I did not immediately recollect that we had omitted to ask her any particulars about her guests.

'Who can Mary be?' asked Milly.

'Cousin Monica says she's engaged to be married, and I think I heard the Doctor call her *Lady* Mary, and I intended asking her ever so much about her; but what she told us about cutting down the trees, and all that, quite put it out of my head. We shall have time enough to-morrow, however, to ask questions. I like her very much, I know.'

'And I think,' said Milly, 'it is to Mr. Carysbroke she's to be married.'

'Do you?' said I, remembering that he had sat beside her for more than a quarter of an hour after tea in very close and low-toned conversation; 'and have you any particular reason?' I asked.

'Well, I heard her once or twice call him "dear," and she called him his Christian name, just like Lady Knollys did— Ilbury, I think—and I saw him gi' her a sly kiss as she was going up-stairs.'

I laughed.

'Well, Milly,' I said, 'I remarked something myself, I thought, like confidential relations; but if you really saw them kiss on the staircase, the question is pretty well settled.'

'Ay, lass.'

'You're not to say *lass*.'

'Well, *Maud*, then. I did see them with the corner of my eye, and my back turned, when they did not think I could spy anything, as plain as I see you now.'

I laughed again ; but I felt an odd pang—something of mortification—something of regret ; but I smiled very gaily, as I stood before the glass, un-making my toilet preparatory to bed.

'Maud—Maud—fickle Maud !—What, Captain Oakley already superseded ! and Mr. Carysbroke—oh ! humiliation—engaged.' So I smiled on, very much vexed ; and being afraid lest I had listened with too apparent an interest to this impostor, I sang a verse of a gay little chanson, and tried to think of Captain Oakley, who somehow had become rather silly.

CHAPTER XLIII

NEWS AT BARTRAM GATE

Milly and I, thanks to our early Bartram hours, were first down next morning ; and so soon as Cousin Monica appeared we attacked her.

'So Lady Mary is the *fiancée* of Mr. Carysbroke,' said I, very cleverly ; 'and I think it was very wicked of you to try and involve me in a flirtation with him yesterday.'

'And who told you that, pray ?' asked Lady Knollys, with a pleasant little laugh.

'Milly and I discovered it, simple as we stand here,' I answered.

'But you did not flirt with Mr. Carysbroke, Maud, did you ?' she asked.

'No, certainly not ; but that was not your doing, wicked woman, but my discretion. And now that we know your secret, you must tell us all about her, and all about him ; and in the first place, what is her name—Lady Mary what ?' I demanded.

'Who would have thought you so cunning ? Two country misses—two little nuns from the cloisters of Bartram ! Well, I suppose I must answer. It is vain trying to hide anything from you ; but how on earth did you find it out ? '

' We'll tell you that presently, but you shall first tell us who she is,' I persisted.

' Well, that I will, of course, without compulsion. She is Lady Mary Carysbroke,' said Lady Knollys.

' A relation of Mr. Carysbroke's,' I asserted.

' Yes, a relation ; but who told you he was Mr. Carysbroke ? ' asked Cousin Monica.

' Milly told me, when we saw him in the Windmill Wood.'

' And who told you, Milly ? '

' It was L'Amour,' answered Milly, with her blue eyes very wide open.

' What does the child mean ? L'Amour ! You don't mean *love* ? ' exclaimed Lady Knollys, puzzled in her turn.

' I mean old Wyat ; *she* told me and the Governor.'

' You're *not* to say that,' I interposed.

' You mean your father ? ' suggested Lady Knollys.

' Well, yes ; father told her, and so I knew him.'

' What could he mean ? ' exclaimed Lady Knollys, laughing, as it were, in soliloquy ; ' and I did not mention his name, I recollect now. He recognised you, and you him, when you came into the room yesterday ; and now you must tell me how you discovered that he and Lady Mary were to be married.'

So Milly restated her evidence, and Lady Knollys laughed unaccountably heartily ; and she said—

' They *will* be *so* confounded ! but they deserve it ; and, remember, *I* did not say so.'

' Oh ! we acquit you.'

' All I say is, such a deceitful, dangerous pair of girls—all things considered—I never heard of before,' exclaimed Lady Knollys. ' There's no such thing as conspiring in your presence.'

' Good morning. I hope you slept well.' She was addressing the lady and gentleman who were just entering the room from the conservatory. ' You'll hardly sleep so well to-night, when you have learned what eyes are upon you. Here are two very pretty detectives who have found out your secret, and entirely by your imprudence and their own cleverness have discovered that you are a pair of betrothed lovers, about to ratify your vows at the hymeneal altar. I assure you I did not tell of you ; you betrayed yourselves. If you will talk in that confidential way on sofas, and call one another stealthily by your Christian names, and actually kiss at the foot of the stairs, while a clever detective is scaling them, apparently with her back toward you, you must only take the consequences, and be known prematurely as the hero and heroine of the forthcoming paragraph in the "Morning Post." '

Milly and I were horribly confounded, but Cousin Monica was resolved to place us all upon the least formal terms possible, and I believe she had set about it in the right way.

' And now, girls, I am going to make a counter-discovery, which, I fear, a little conflicts with yours. This Mr. Carysbroke is Lord Ilbury, brother of this Lady Mary; and it is all my fault for not having done my honours better ; but you see what clever match-making little creatures they are.'

' You can't think how flattered I am at being made the subject of a theory, even a mistaken one, by Miss Ruthyn.'

And so, after our modest fit was over, Milly and I were very merry, like the rest, and we all grew a great deal more intimate that morning.

I think altogether those were the pleasantest and happiest days of my life : gay, intelligent, and kindly society at home ; charming excursions—sometimes riding—sometimes by carriage—to distant points of beauty in the county. Evenings varied with music, reading, and spirited conversation. Now and then a visitor for a day or two, and constantly some neighbour from the town, or its dependencies, dropt in. Of these I but remember tall old Miss Wintletop, most entertaining of rustic old maids, with her nice lace and thick satin, and her small, kindly round face—pretty, I dare say, in other days, and now frosty, but kindly—who told us such delightful old stories of the county in her father's and grandfather's time ; who knew the lineage of every family in it, and could recount all its duels and elopements ; give us illustrative snatches from old election squibs, and lines from epitaphs, and tell exactly where all the old-world highway robberies had been committed : how it fared with the chief delinquents after the assizes ; and, above all, where, and of what sort, the goblins and elves of the county had made themselves seen, from the phantom post-boy, who every third night crossed Windale Moor, by the old coach-road, to the fat old ghost, in mulberry velvet,

who showed his great face, crutch, and ruffles, by moonlight, at
the bow window of the old court-house that was taken down in
1803.

You cannot imagine what agreeable evenings we passed in
this society, or how rapidly my good Cousin Milly improved in
it. I remember well the intense suspense in which she and I
awaited the answer from Bartram-Haugh to kind Cousin Monica's application for an extension of our leave of absence.

It came, and with it a note from Uncle Silas, which was curious, and, therefore, is printed here :—

' MY DEAR LADY KNOLLYS,—To your kind letter I say yes
(that is, for another week, not a fortnight), with all my heart. I
am glad to hear that my starlings chatter so pleasantly ; at all
events the refrain is not that of Sterne's. They can get out ; and
do get out ; and shall get out as much as they please. I am no
gaoler, and shut up nobody but myself. I have always thought
that young people have too little liberty. My principle has been
to make little free men and women of them from the first. In
morals, altogether—in intellect, more than we allow—self-educa-
tion is that which abides ; and it only begins where constraint
ends. Such is my theory. My practice is consistent. Let them remain for a week longer, as you say. The horses shall be at Elverston on Tuesday, the 7th. I shall be more than usually sad
and solitary till their return ; so pray, I selfishly entreat, do not
extend their absence. You will smile, remembering how little
my health will allow me to see of them, even when at home ;
but as Chaulieu so prettily says—I stupidly forget the words,
but the sentiment is this—" although concealed by a sylvan wall
of leaves, impenetrable— (he is pursuing his favourite nymphs
through the alleys and intricacies of a rustic labyrinth)—yet,
your songs, your prattle, and your laughter, faint and far away,
inspire my fancy ; and, through my ears, I see your unseen
smiles, your blushes, your floating tresses, and your ivory feet ;
and so, though sad, am happy ; though alone, in company ;"
—and such is my case.

' One only request, and I have done. Pray remind them of a
promise made to me. The Book of Life—the fountain of life—
it must be drunk of, night and morning, or their spiritual life
expires.

' And now, Heaven bless and keep you, my dear cousin ; and
with all assurances of affection to my beloved niece and my
child, believe me ever yours affectionately.

SILAS RUTHYN.'

Said Cousin Monica, with a waggish smile—
' And so, girls, you have Chaulieu and the evangelists ; the
French rhymester in his alley, and Silas in the valley of the
shadow of death ; perfect liberty, and a peremptory order to
return in a week ;—all illustrating one another. Poor Silas ! old
as he is, I don't think his religion fits him.'
I really rather liked his letter. I was struggling hard to think
well of him, and Cousin Monica knew it ; and I really think if
I had not been by, she would often have been less severe on him.

As we were all sitting pleasantly about the breakfast table a
day or two after, the sun shining on the pleasant wintry landscape, Cousin Monica suddenly exclaimed—
' I quite forgot to tell you that Charles Oakley has written
to say he is coming on Wednesday. I really don't want him. Poor
Charlie ! I wonder how they manage those doctors' certificates.
I know nothing ails him, and he'd be much better with his
regiment.'
Wednesday !—how odd. Exactly the day after my departure.
I tried to look perfectly unconcerned. Lady Knollys had addressed herself more to Lady Mary and Milly than to me, and
nobody in particular was looking at me. Notwithstanding, with
my usual perversity, I felt myself blushing with a brilliancy that
may have been very becoming, but which was so intolerably provoking that I would have risen and left the room but that matters would have been so infinitely worse. I could have boxed my
odious ears. I could almost have jumped from the window.
I felt that Lord Ilbury saw it. I saw Lady Mary's eyes for a
moment resting gravely on my tell-tale—my lying cheeks—for I
really had begun to think much less celestially of Captain Oakley. I was angry with Cousin Monica, who, knowing my blushing infirmity, had mentioned her nephew so suddenly while I
was strapped by etiquette in my chair, with my face to the
window, and two pair of most disconcerting eyes, at least, opposite. I was angry with myself—generally angry—refused more
tea rather dryly, and was laconic to Lord Ilbury, all which, of

course, was very cross and foolish ; and afterwards, from my
bed-room window, I saw Cousin Monica and Lady Mary among
the flowers, under the drawing-room window, talking, as I
instinctively knew, of that little incident. I was standing at the
glass.

' My odious, stupid, *perjured* face,' I whispered, furiously, at
the same time stamping on the floor, and giving myself quite a
smart slap on the cheek. ' I *can't* go down—I'm ready to cry—
I've a mind to return to Bartram to-day ; I am *always* blushing ;
and I wish that impudent Captain Oakley was at the bottom of
the sea.'

I was, perhaps, thinking more of Lord Ilbury than I was
aware ; and I am sure if Captain Oakley had arrived that day,
I should have treated him with most unjustifiable rudeness.

Notwithstanding this unfortunate blush, the remainder of
our visit passed very happily for me. No one who has not experienced it can have an idea how intimate a small party, such
as ours, will grow in a short time in a country house.

Of course, a young lady of a well-regulated mind cannot possibly care a pin about any one of the opposite sex until she is
well assured that he is beginning, at least, to like her better than
all the world beside ; but I could not deny to myself that I was
rather anxious to know more about Lord Ilbury than I actually
did know.

There was a ' Peerage,' in its bright scarlet and gold uniform,
corpulent and tempting, upon the little marble table in the
drawing-room. I had many opportunities of consulting it, but
I never could find courage to do so.

For an inexperienced person it would have been a matter of
several minutes, and during those minutes what awful risk of
surprise and detection. One day, all being quiet, I did venture,
and actually, with a beating heart, got so far as to find out the
letter ' Il,' when I heard a step outside the door, which opened
a little bit, and I heard Lady Knollys, luckily arrested at
the entrance, talk some sentences outside, her hand still upon
the door-handle. I shut the book, as Mrs. Bluebeard might the
door of the chamber of horrors at the sound of her husband's
step, and skipped to a remote part of the room, where Cousin
Knollys found me in a mysterious state of agitation.

On any other subject I would have questioned Cousin Monica

unhesitatingly ; upon this, somehow, I was dumb. I distrusted myself, and dreaded my odious habit of blushing, and knew that I should look so horribly guilty, and become so agitated and odd, that she would have reasonably concluded that I had quite lost my heart to him.

After the lesson I had received, and my narrow escape of detection in the very act, you may be sure I never trusted myself in the vicinity of that fat and cruel ' Peerage,' which possessed the secret, but would not disclose without compromising me.

In this state of tantalizing darkness and conjecture I should have departed, had not Cousin Monica quite spontaneously relieved me.

The night before our departure she sat with us in our room, chatting a little farewell gossip.

' And what do you think of Ilbury ? ' she asked.

' I think him clever and accomplished, and amusing ; but he sometimes appears to me very melancholy—that is, for a few minutes together—and then, I fancy, with an effort, re-engages in our conversation.'

' Yes, poor Ilbury ! He lost his brother only about five months since, and is only beginning to recover his spirits a little. They were very much attached, and people thought that he would have succeeded to the title, had he lived, because Ilbury is *difficile*—or a philosopher—or a *Saint Kevin* ; and, in fact, has begun to be treated as a premature old bachelor.'

' What a charming person his sister, Lady Mary, is. She has made me promise to write to her,' I said, I suppose—such hypocrites are we—to prove to Cousin Knollys that I did not care particularly to hear anything more about him.

' Yes, and so devoted to him. He came down here, and took The Grange, for change of scene and solitude—of all things the worst for a man in grief—a morbid whim, as he is beginning to find out ; for he is very glad to stay here, and confesses that he is much better since he came. His letters are still addressed to him as Mr. Carysbroke ; for he fancied if his rank were known, that the county people would have been calling upon him, and so he would have found himself soon involved in a tiresome round of dinners, and must have gone somewhere else. You saw him, Milly, at Bartram, before Maud came ? '

Yes, she had, when he called there to see her father.

' He thought, as he had accepted the trusteeship, that he could hardly, residing so near, omit to visit Silas. He was very much struck and interested by him, and he has a better opinion of him—you are not angry, Milly—than some ill-natured people I could name ; and he says that the cutting down of the trees will turn out to have been a mere slip. But these slips don't occur with clever men in other things ; and some persons have a way of always making them in their own favour. And, to talk of other things, I suspect that you and Milly will probably see Ilbury at Bartram ; for I think he likes you very much.'

You ; did she mean *both*, or only me ?

So our pleasant visit was over. Milly's good little curate had been much thrown in her way by our deep and dangerous cousin Monica. He was most laudably steady ; and his flirtation advanced upon the field of theology, where, happily, Milly's little reading had been concentrated. A mild and earnest interest in poor, pretty Milly's orthodoxy was the leading feature of his case ; and I was highly amused at her references to me, when we had retired at night, upon the points which she had disputed with him, and her anxious reports of their low-toned conferences, carried on upon a sequestered ottoman, where he patted and stroked his crossed leg, as he smiled tenderly and shook his head at her questionable doctrine. Milly's reverence for her instructor, and his admiration, grew daily ; and he was known among us as Milly's confessor.

He took luncheon with us on the day of our departure, and with an adroit privacy, which in a layman would have been sly, presented her, in right of his holy calling, with a little book, the binding of which was mediæval and costly, and whose letter-press dealt in a way which he commended, with some points on which she was not satisfactory ; and she found on the fly-leaf this little inscription :—' Presented to Miss Millicent Ruthyn by an earnest well-wisher, 1st December 1844.' A text, very neatly penned, followed this ; and the ' presentation ' was made unctiously indeed, but with a blush, as well as the accustomed smile, and with eyes that were lowered.

The early crimson sun of December had gone down behind the hills before we took our seats in the carriage.

Lord Ilbury leaned with his elbow on the carriage window, looking in, and he said to me—

'I really don't know what we shall do, Miss Ruthyn; we shall all feel so lonely. For myself, I think I shall run away to Grange.'

This appeared to me as nearly perfect eloquence as human lips could utter.

His hand still rested on the window, and the Rev. Sprigge Biddlepen was standing with a saddened smirk on the door steps, when the whip smacked, the horses scrambled into motion, and away we rolled down the avenue, leaving behind us the pleasantest house and hostess in the world, and trotting fleetly into darkness towards Bartram-Haugh.

We were both rather silent. Milly had her book in her lap, and I saw her every now and then try to read her 'earnest well-wisher's' little inscription, but there was not light to read by.

When we reached the great gate of Bartram-Haugh it was dark. Old Crowl, who kept the gate, I heard enjoining the postilion to make no avoidable noise at the hall-door, for the odd but startling reason that he believed my uncle 'would be dead by this time.'

Very much shocked and frightened, we stopped the carriage, and questioned the tremulous old porter.

Uncle Silas, it seemed, had been 'silly-ish' all yesterday, and 'could not be woke this morning,' and 'the doctor had been here twice, being now in the house.'

'Is he better?' I asked, tremblingly.

'Not as I'm aweer on, Miss; he lay at God's mercy two hours agone; 'appen he's in heaven be this time.'

'Drive on—drive fast,' I said to the driver. 'Don't be frightened, Milly; please Heaven we shall find all going well.'

After some delay, during which my heart sank, and I quite gave up Uncle Silas, the aged little servant-man opened the door, and trotted shakily down the steps to the carriage side.

Uncle Silas had been at death's door for hours; the question of life had trembled in the scale; but now the doctor said 'he might do.'

'Where was the doctor?'

'In master's room; he blooded him three hours agone.'

I don't think that Milly was so frightened as I. My heart beat, and I was trembling so that I could hardly get upstairs.

CHAPTER XLIV

A FRIEND ARISES

At the top of the great staircase I was glad to see the friendly face of Mary Quince, who stood, candle in hand, greeting us with many little courtesies, and a very haggard and pallid smile.

'Very welcome, Miss, hoping you are very well.'

'All well, and you are well, Mary? and oh! tell us quickly how is Uncle Silas?'

'We thought he was gone, Miss, this morning, but doing fairly now; doctor says in a trance like. I was helping old Wyat most of the day, and was there when doctor blooded him, an' he spoke at last; but he must be awful weak, he took a deal o' blood from his arm, Miss; I held the basin.'

'And he's better—decidedly better?' I asked.

'Well, he's better, doctor says; he talked some, and doctor says if he goes off asleep again, and begins a-snoring like he did before, we're to loose the bandage, and let him bleed till he comes to his self again; which, it seems to me and Wyat, is the same thing a'most as saying he's to be killed off-hand, for I don't believe he has a drop to spare, as you'll say likewise, Miss, if you'll please look in the basin.'

This was not an invitation with which I cared to comply. I thought I was going to faint. I sat on the stairs and sipped a little water, and Quince sprinkled a little in my face, and my strength returned.

Milly must have felt her father's danger more than I, for she was affectionate, and loved him from habit and relation, although he was not kind to her. But I was more nervous and more impetuous, and my feelings both stimulated and overpowered me more easily. The moment I was able to stand I said— thinking of nothing but the one idea—

'We must see him—*come*, Milly.'

I entered his sitting-room; a common 'dip' candle hanging

like the tower of Pisa all to one side, with a dim, long wick, in a greasy candlestick, profaned the table of the fastidious invalid. The light was little better than darkness, and I crossed the room swiftly, still transfixed by the one idea of seeing my uncle.

His bed-room door beside the fireplace stood partly open, and I looked in.

Old Wyat, a white, high-cauled ghost, was pottering in her slippers in the shadow at the far side of the bed. The doctor, a stout little bald man, with a paunch and a big bunch of seals, stood with his back to the fireplace, which corresponded with that in the next room, eyeing his patient through the curtains of the bed with a listless sort of importance.

The head of the large four-poster rested against the opposite wall. Its foot was presented toward the fireplace ; but the curtains at the side, which alone I could see from my position, were closed.

The little doctor knew me, and thinking me, I suppose, a person of consequence, removed his hands from behind him, suffering the skirts of his coat to fall forward, and with great celerity and gravity made me a low but important bow ; then choosing more particularly to make my acquaintance he further advanced, and with another reverence he introduced himself as Doctor Jolks, in a murmured diapason. He bowed me back again into my uncle's study, and the light of old Wyat's dreadful candle.

Doctor Jolks was suave and pompous. I longed for a fussy practitioner who would have got over the ground in half the time.

Coma, madam ; coma. Miss Ruthyn, your uncle, I may tell you, has been in a very critical state ; highly so. Coma of the most obstinate type. He would have sunk—he must have gone, in fact, had I not resorted to a very extreme remedy, and bled him freely, which happily told precisely as we could have wished. A wonderful constitution—a marvellous constitution— prodigious nervous fibre ; the greatest pity in the world he won't give himself fair play. His habits, you know, are quite, I may say, destructive. We do our best—we do all we can, but if the patient won't cooperate it can't possibly end satisfactorily.'

And Jolks accompanied this with an awful shrug. ' Is there

anything? Do you think change of air? What an awful complaint it is,' I exclaimed.

He smiled, mysteriously looking down, and shook his head undertaker-like.

' Why, we can hardly call it a *complaint*, Miss Ruthyn. I look upon it he has been poisoned—he has had, you understand me,' he pursued, observing my startled look, ' an overdose of opium ; you know he takes opium habitually ; he takes it in laudanum, he takes it in water, and, most dangerous of all, he takes it solid, in lozenges. I've known people take it moderately. I've known people take it to excess, *but* they all were particular as to *measure*, and *that* is exactly the point I've tried to impress upon him. The habit, of course, you understand is formed, there's no uprooting that ; but he won't *measure*—he goes by the eye and by sensation, which I need not tell you, Miss Ruthyn, is going by *chance* ; and opium, as no doubt you are aware, is strictly a poison ; a poison, no doubt, which habit will enable you to partake of, I may say, in considerable quantities, without fatal consequences, but still a poison ; and to exhibit a poison *so*, is, I need scarcely tell you, to trifle with death. He has been so threatened, and for a time he changes his haphazard mode of dealing with it, and then returns ; he may escape—of course, that is possible—but he may any day overdo the thing. I don't think the present crisis will result seriously. I am very glad, independently of the honour of making your acquaintance, Miss Ruthyn, that you and your cousin have returned ; for, however zealous, I fear the servants are deficient in intelligence ; and as in the event of a recurrence of the symptoms— which, however, is not probable—I would beg to inform you of their nature, and how exactly best to deal with them.'

So upon these points he delivered us a pompous little lecture, and begged that either Milly or I would remain in the room with the patient until his return at two or three o'clock in the morning ; a reappearance of the coma ' might be very bad indeed.'

Of course Milly and I did as we were directed. We sat by the fire, scarcely daring to whisper. Uncle Silas, about whom a new and dreadful suspicion began to haunt me, lay still and motionless as if he were actually dead.

' Had he attempted to poison himself ?'

If he believed his position to be as desperate as Lady Knollys had described it, was this, after all, improbable ? There were strange wild theories, I had been told, mixed up in his religion.

Sometimes, at an hour's interval, a sign of life would come— a moan from that tall sheeted figure in the bed—a moan and a pattering of the lips. Was it prayer—*what* was it ? who could guess what thoughts were passing behind that white-fillited forehead ?

I had peeped at him : a white cloth steeped in vinegar and water was folded round his head ; his great eyes were closed, so were his marble lips ; his figure straight, thin, and long, dressed in a white dressing-gown, looked like a corpse ' laid out' in the bed ; his gaunt bandaged arm lay outside the sheet that covered his body.

With this awful image of death we kept our vigil, until poor Milly grew so sleepy that old Wyat proposed that she should take her place and watch with me.

Little as I liked the crone with the high-cauled cap, she would, at all events, keep awake, which Milly could not. And so at one o'clock this new arrangement began.

' Mr. Dudley Ruthyn is not at home ? ' I whispered to old Wyat.

' He went away wi' himself yesternight, to Cloperton, Miss, to see the wrestling ; it was to come off this morning.'

' Was he sent for ? '

' Not he.'

' And why not ? '

' He would na' leave the sport for this, I'm thinking,' and the old woman grinned uglily.

' When is he to return ? '

' When he wants money.'

So we grew silent, and again I thought of suicide, and of the unhappy old man, who just then whispered a sentence or two to himself with a sigh.

For the next hour he had been quite silent, and old Wyat informed me that she must go down for candles. Ours were already burnt down to the sockets.

' There's a candle in the next room,' I suggested, hating the idea of being left alone with the patient.

' Hoot ! Miss. I *dare* na' set a candle but wax in his presence,' whispered the old woman, scornfully.

' I think if we were to stir the fire, and put on a little more coal, we should have a great deal of light.'

' He'll ha' the candles,' said Dame Wyat, doggedly ; and she tottered from the chamber, muttering to herself ; and I heard her take her candle from the next room and depart, shutting the outer door after her.

Here was I then alone, but for this unearthly companion, whom I feared inexpressibly, at two o'clock, in the vast old house of Bartram.

I stirred the fire. It was low, and would not blaze. I stood up, and, with my hand on the mantelpiece, endeavoured to think of cheerful things. But it was a struggle against wind and tide— vain ; and so I drifted away into haunted regions.

Uncle Silas was perfectly still. I would not suffer myself to think of the number of dark rooms and passages which now separated me from the other living tenants of the house. I awaited with a false composure the return of old Wyat.

Over the mantelpiece was a looking-glass. At another time this might have helped to entertain my solitary moments, but now I did not like to venture a peep. A small thick Bible lay on the chimneypiece, and leaning its back against the mirror, I began to read in it with a mind as attentively directed as I could. While so engaged in turning over the leaves, I lighted upon two or three odd-looking papers, which had been folded into it. One was a broad printed thing, with names and dates written into blank spaces, and was about the size of a quarter of a yard of very broad ribbon. The others were mere scraps, with ' Dudley Ruthyn' penned in my cousin's vulgar round-hand at the foot. While I folded and replaced these, I really don't know what caused me to fancy that something was moving behind me, as I stood with my back toward the bed. I do not recollect any sound whatever ; but instinctively I glanced into the mirror, and my eyes were instantly fixed by what I saw.

The figure of Uncle Silas rose up, and dressed in a long white morning gown, slid over the end of the bed, and with two or three swift noiseless steps, stood behind me, with a death-like scowl and a simper. Preternaturally tall and thin, he stood for a moment almost touching me, with the white bandage pinned across his forehead, his bandaged arm stiffly by his side, and diving over my shoulder, with his long thin hand he snatched the Bible, and whispered over my head—' The serpent beguiled her and she did eat ;' and after a momentary pause, he glided to the farthest window, and appeared to look out upon the midnight prospect.

It was cold, but he did not seem to feel it. With the same inflexible scowl and smile, he continued to look out for several minutes, and then with a great sigh, he sat down on the side of his bed, his face immovably turned towards me, with the same painful look.

It seemed to me an hour before old Wyat came back ; and never was lover made happier at sight of his mistress than I to behold that withered crone.

You may be sure I did not prolong my watch. There was now plainly no risk of my uncle's relapsing into lethargy. I had a long hysterical fit of weeping when I got into my room, with honest Mary Quince by my side.

Whenever I closed my eyes, the face of Uncle Silas was before me, as I had seen it reflected in the glass. The sorceries of Bartram were enveloping me once more.

Next morning the doctor said he was quite out of danger, but very weak. Milly and I saw him ; and again in our afternoon walk we saw the doctor marching under the trees in the direction of the Windmill Wood.

' Going down to see that poor girl there ? ' he said, when he had made his salutation, prodding with his levelled stick in the direction. ' Hawke, or Hawkes, I think.'

' Beauty's sick, Maud,' exclaimed Milly.

' *Hawkes*. She's upon my dispensary list. Yes,' said the doctor, looking into his little note-book—' Hawkes.'

' And what is her complaint ? '

' Rheumatic fever.'

' Not infectious ? '

' Not the least—no more, as we say, Miss Ruthyn, than a broken leg,' and he laughed obligingly.

So soon as the doctor had departed, Milly and I agreed to follow to Hawkes' cottage and enquire more particularly how she was. To say truth, I am afraid it was rather for the sake of giving our walk a purpose and a point of termination, than for any very charitable interest we might have felt in the patient.

Over the inequalities of the upland slope, clumped with trees, we reached the gabled cottage, with its neglected little farm-yard. A rheumatic old woman was the only attendant ; and, having turned her ear in an attitude of attention, which induced us in gradually exalted keys to enquire how Meg was, she informed us in very loud tones that she had long lost her hearing and was perfectly deaf. And added considerately—

' When the man comes in, 'appen he'll tell ye what ye want.'

Through the door of a small room at the further end of that in which we were, we could see a portion of the narrow apartment of the patient, and hear her moans and the doctor's voice.

' We'll see him, Milly, when he comes out. Let us wait here.'

So we stood upon the door-stone awaiting him. The sounds of suffering had moved my compassion and interested us for the sick girl.

' Blest if here isn't Pegtop,' said Milly.

And the weather-stained red coat, the swarthy forbidding face and sooty locks of old Hawkes loomed in sight, as he stumped, steadying himself with his stick, over the uneven pavement of the yard. He touched his hat gruffly to me, but did not seem half to like our being where we were, for he looked surlily, and scratched his head under his wide-awake.

' Your daughter is very ill, I'm afraid,' said I.

' Ay—she'll be costin' me a handful, like her mother did,' said Pegtop.

' I hope her room is comfortable, poor thing.'

' Ay, that's it ; she be comfortable enough, I warrant—more nor I. It be all Meg, and nout o' Dickon.'

' When did her illness commence ? ' I asked.

' Day the mare wor shod—*Saturday*. I talked a bit wi' the workus folk, but they won't gi'e nout—dang 'em—an' how be *I* to do't ? It be all'ays hard bread wi' Silas, an' a deal harder now she' ta'en them pains. I won't stan' it much longer. Gammon ! If she keeps on that way I'll just cut. See how the workus fellahs 'ill like *that* ! '

' The Doctor gives his services for nothing,' I said.

' An' *does* nothin', bless him ! ha, ha. No more nor that old deaf gammon there that costs me three tizzies a week, and haint worth a h'porth—no more nor Meg there, that's making all she can o' them pains. They be all a foolin' o' me, an' thinks I don't know't. Hey? we'll see.'

All this time he was cutting a bit of tobacco into shreds on the window-stone.

' A workin' man be same as a hoss ; if he baint cared, he can't work—'tisn't in him : ' and with these words, having by this time stuffed his pipe with tobacco, he poked the deaf lady, who was pattering about with her back toward him, rather viciously with the point of his stick, and signed for a light.

' It baint in him, you can't get it out o' 'im, no more nor ye'll draw smoke out o' this,' and he raised his pipe an inch or two, with his thumb on the bowl, 'without backy and fire. 'Tisn't in it.'

' Maybe I can be of some use ? ' I said, thinking.

' Maybe,' he rejoined.

By this time he received from the old deaf abigail a flaming roll of brown paper, and, touching his hat to me, he withdrew, lighting his pipe and sending up little white puffs, like the salute of a departing ship.

So he did not care to hear how his daughter was, and had only come here to light his pipe !

Just then the Doctor emerged.

' We have been waiting to hear how your poor patient is to-day ? ' I said.

' Very ill, indeed, and utterly neglected, I fear. If she were equal to it—but she's not—I think she ought to be removed to the hospital immediately.'

' That poor old woman is quite deaf, and the man is so surly and selfish ! Could you recommend a nurse who would stay here till she's better ? I will pay her with pleasure, and anything you think might be good for the poor girl.'

So this was settled on the spot. Doctor Jolks was kind, like most men of his calling, and undertook to send the nurse from Feltram with a few comforts for the patient ; and he called Dickon to the yard-gate, and I suppose told him of the arrangement ; and Milly and I went to the poor girl's door and asked, ' May we come in ? '

There was no answer. So, with the conventional construction of silence, we entered. Her looks showed how ill she was. We

adjusted her bed-clothes, and darkened the room, and did what
we could for her—noting, beside, what her comfort chiefly required. She did not answer any questions. She did not thank us.
I should almost have fancied that she had not perceived our
presence, had I not observed her dark, sunken eyes once or
twice turned up towards my face, with a dismal look of wonder
and enquiry.

The girl was very ill, and we went every day to see her.
Sometimes she would answer our questions—sometimes not.
Thoughtful, observant, surly, she seemed ; and as people like to
be thanked, I sometimes wonder that we continued to throw our
bread upon these ungrateful waters. Milly was specially impatient under this treatment, and protested against it, and
finally refused to accompany me into poor Beauty's bed-room.

' I think, my good Meg,' said I one day, as I stood by her bed
—she was now recovering with the sure reascent of youth—
' that you ought to thank Miss Milly.'

' I'll *not* thank her,' said Beauty, doggedly.

' Very well, Meg ; I only thought I'd ask you, for I think you
ought.'

As I spoke, she very gently took just the tip of my finger,
which hung close to her coverlet, in her fingers, and drew it
beneath, and before I was aware, burying her head in the
clothes, she suddenly clasped my hand in both hers to her lips,
and kissed it passionately, again and again, sobbing. I felt her
tears.

I tried to withdraw my hand, but she held it with an angry
pull, continuing to weep and kiss it.

' Do you wish to say anything, my poor Meg ? ' I asked.

' Nout, Miss,' she sobbed gently ; and she continued to kiss
my hand and weep. But suddenly she said, ' I won't thank Milly,
for it's a' *you* ; it baint her, she hadn't the thought—no, no, it's
a' you, Miss. I cried hearty in the dark last night, thinkin' o'
the apples, and the way I knocked them awa' wi' a pur o' my
foot, the day father rapped me ower the head wi' his stick ; it
was kind o' you and very bad o' me. I wish you'd beat me, Miss ;
ye're better to me than father or mother—better to me than a' ;
an' I wish I could die for you, Miss, for I'm not fit to look at
you.'

I was surprised. I began to cry. I could have hugged poor Meg.

I did not know her history. I have never learned it since. She used to talk with the most utter self-abasement before me. It was no religious feeling—it was a kind of expression of her love and worship of me—all the more strange that she was naturally very proud. There was nothing she would not have borne from me except the slightest suspicion of her entire devotion, or that she could in the most trifling way wrong or deceive me.

I am not young now. I have had my sorrows, and with them all that wealth, virtually unlimited, can command; and through the retrospect a few bright and pure lights quiver along my life's dark stream—dark, but for them; and these are shed, not by the splendour of a splendid fortune, but by two or three of the simplest and kindest remembrances, such as the poorest and homeliest life may count up, and beside which, in the quiet hours of memory, all artificial triumphs pale, and disappear, for they are never quenched by time or distance, being founded on the affections, and so far heavenly.

CHAPTER XLV

A CHAPTER-FULL OF LOVERS

We had about this time a pleasant and quite unexpected visit from Lord Ilbury. He had come to pay his respects, understanding that my uncle Silas was sufficiently recovered to see visitors. 'And I think I'll run up-stairs first, and see him, if he admits me, and then I have ever so long a message from my sister, Mary, for you and Miss Millicent; but I had better dispose of my business first—don't you think so?—and I shall return in a few minutes.'

And as he spoke our tremulous old butler returned to say that Uncle Silas would be happy to see him. So he departed;

and you can't think how pleasant our homely sitting-room looked with his coat and stick in it—guarantees of his return.

'Do you think, Milly, he is going to speak about the timber, you know, that Cousin Knollys spoke of ? I do hope not.'

'So do I,' said Milly. 'I wish he'd stayed a bit longer with us first, for if he does, father will sure to turn him out of doors, and we'll see no more of him.'

'Exactly, my dear Milly; and he's so pleasant and good-natured.'

'And he likes you awful well, he does.'

'I'm sure he likes us both equally, Milly; he talked a great deal to you at Elverston, and used to ask you so often to sing those two pretty Lancashire ballads," I said; 'but you know when you were at your controversies and religious exercises in the window, with that pillar of the church, the Rev. Spriggs Biddlepen——'

'Get awa' wi' your nonsense, Maud; how could I help answering when he dodged me up and down my Testament and catechism ?—an I 'most hate him, I tell you, and Cousin Knollys, you're such fools, I do. And whatever you say, the lord likes you uncommon, and well you know it, ye hussy.'

'I know no such thing; and you don't think it, *you* hussy, and I really don't care who likes me or who doesn't, except my relations; and I make the lord a present to you, if you'll have him.'

In this strain were we talking when he re-entered the room, a little sooner than we had expected to see him.

Milly, who, you are to recollect, was only in process of reformation, and still retained something of the Derbyshire dairy-maid, gave me a little clandestine pinch on the arm just as he made his appearance.

'I just refused a present from her,' said odious Milly, in answer to his enquiring look, 'because I knew she could not spare it.'

The effect of all this was that I blushed one of my overpowering blushes. People told me they became me very much; I hope so, for the misfortune was frequent; and I think nature owed me that compensation.

'It places you both in a most becoming light,' said Lord

Ilbury, quite innocently. 'I really don't know which most to admire—the generosity of the offer or of the refusal.'

'Well, it *was* kind, if you but knew. I'm 'most tempted to tell him,' said Milly.

I checked her with a really angry look, and said, 'Perhaps you have not observed it; but I really think, for a sensible person, my cousin Milly here talks more nonsense than any twenty other girls.'

'A twenty-girl power! That's an immense compliment. I've the greatest respect for nonsense, I owe it so much; and I really think if nonsense were banished, the earth would grow insupportable.'

'Thank you, Lord Ilbury,' said Milly, who had grown quite easy in his company during our long visit at Elverston; 'and I tell you, Miss Maud, if you grow saucy, I'll accept your present, and what will you say then?'

'I really don't know; but just now I want to ask Lord Ilbury how he thinks my uncle looks; neither I nor Milly have seen him since his illness.'

'Very much weaker, I think; but he may be gaining strength. Still, as my business was not quite pleasant, I thought it better to postpone it, and if you think it would be right, I'll write to Doctor Bryerly to ask him to postpone the discussion for a little time.'

I at once assented, and thanked him; indeed, if I had had my way, the subject should never have been mentioned, I felt so hardhearted and rapacious; but Lord Ilbury explained that the trustees were constrained by the provisions of the will, and that I really had no power to release them; and I hoped that Uncle Silas also understood all this.

'And now,' said he, 'we've returned to Grange, my sister and I, and it is nearer than Elverston, so that we are really neighbours; and Mary wants Lady Knollys to fix a time she owes us a visit, you know—and you really must come at the same time; it will be so very pleasant, the same party exactly meeting in a new scene; and we have not half explored our neighbourhood; and I've got down all those Spanish engravings I told you of, and the Venetian missals, and all the rest. I think I remember very accurately the things you were most interested by, and they're all there; and really you must promise, you and Miss

Millicent Ruthyn. And I forgot to mention—you know you
complained that you were ill supplied with books, so Mary
thought you would allow her to share her supply—they are the
new books, you know—and when you have read yours, you and
she can exchange.'

What girl was ever quite frank about her likings? I don't
think I was more of a cheat than others; but I never could
tell of myself. It is quite true that this duplicity and reserve
seldom deceives. Our hypocrisies are forced upon some of our
sex by the acuteness and vigilance of all in this field of enquiry;
but if we are sly, we are also lynx-eyed, capital detectives, most
ingenious in fitting together the bits and dovetails of a cumu-
lative case; and in those affairs of love and liking, have a terrible exploratory instinct, and so, for the most part, when
detected we are found out not only to be in love, but to be
rogues moreover.

Lady Mary was very kind; but had Lady Mary of her own
mere motion taken all this trouble? Was there no more energetic influence at the bottom of that welcome chest of books,
which arrived only half an hour later? The circulating library
of those days was not the epidemic and ubiquitous influence
to which it has grown; and there were many places where it
could not find you out.

Altogether that evening Bartram had acquired a peculiar
beauty—a bright and mellow glow, in which even its gate-posts
and wheelbarrow were interesting, and next day came a little
cloud—Dudley appeared.

'You may be sure he wants money,' said Milly. 'He and
father had words this morning.'

He took a chair at our luncheon, found fault with everything
in his own laconic dialect, ate a good deal notwithstanding, and
was sulky, and with Milly snappish. To me, on the contrary,
when Milly went into the hall, he was mild and whimpering,
and disposed to be confidential.

'There's the Governor says he hasn't a bob! Danged if I
know how an old fellah in his bed-room muddles away money
at that rate. I don't suppose he thinks I can git along without
tin, and he knows them trustees won't gi'e me a tizzy till they
get what they calls an opinion—dang 'em! Bryerly says he
doubts it must all go under settlement. They'll settle me nicely

if they do ; and Governor knows all about it, and won't gi'e me a danged brass farthin', an' me wi' bills to pay, an' lawyers—dang 'em — writing letters. He knows summat o' that hisself, does Governor ; and he might ha' consideration a bit for his own flesh and blood, I say. But he never does nout for none but hisself. I'll sell his books and his jewels next fit he takes—that's how I'll fit him.'

This amiable young man, glowering, with his elbows on the table and his fingers in his great whiskers, followed his homily, where clergymen append the blessing, with a muttered variety of very different matter.

'Now, Maud,' said he, pathetically, leaning back suddenly in his chair, with all his conscious beauty and misfortunes in his face, ' is not it hard lines ?'

I thought the appeal was going to shape itself into an application for money ; but it did not.

' I never know'd a reel beauty—first-chop, of course, I mean—that wasn't kind along of it, and I'm a fellah as can't git along without sympathy—that's why I say it—an' isn't it hard lines ? Now, *say* it's hard lines—*haint* it, Maud ? '

I did not know exactly what hard lines meant, but I said—

' I suppose it is very disagreeable.'

And with this concession, not caring to hear any more in the same vein, I rose, intending to take my departure.

' No, that's jest it. I knew ye'd say it, Maud. Ye're a kind lass—ye be—'tis in yer pretty face. I like ye awful, I do—there's not a handsomer lass in Liverpool nor Lunnon itself—*no* where.'

He had seized my hand, and trying to place his arm about my waist, essayed that salute which I had so narrowly escaped on my first introduction.

' *Don't*, sir,' I exclaimed in high indignation, escaping at the same moment from his grasp.

' No offence, lass ; no harm, Maud ; you must not be so shy—we're cousins, you know—an' I wouldn't hurt ye, Maud, no more nor I'd knock my head off. I wouldn't.'

I did not wait to hear the rest of his tender protestations, but, without showing how nervous I was, I glided out of the room quietly, making an orderly retreat, the more meritorious as I heard him call after me persuasively—

'Come back, Maud. What are ye afeard on, lass ? Come back,
I say—do now ; there's a good wench.'

As Milly and I were taking our walk that day, in the direction of the Windmill Wood, to which, in consequence perhaps
of some secret order, we had now free access, we saw Beauty,
for the first time since her illness, in the little yard, throwing
grain to the poultry.

'How do you find yourself to-day, Meg ? I am *very* glad to
see you able to be about again ; but I hope it is not too soon.'

We were standing at the barred gate of the little enclosure,
and quite close to Meg, who, however, did not choose to raise
her head, but, continuing to shower her grain and potato-skins
among her hens and chickens, said in a low tone—

'Father baint in sight ? Look jist round a bit and say if ye
see him.'

But Dickon's dusky red costume was nowhere visible.

So Meg looked up, pale and thin, and with her old grave,
observant eyes, and she said quietly—

' 'Tisn't that I'm not glad to see ye ; but if father was to spy
me talking friendly wi' ye, now that I'm hearty, and you havin'
no more call to me, he'd be all'ays a watching and thinkin' I
was tellin' o' tales, and 'appen he'd want me to worrit ye for
money, Miss Maud ; an' 'tisn't here he'd spend it, but in the
Feltram pottusses, he would, and we want for nothin' that's good
for us. But that's how 'twould be, an' he'd all'ays be a jawing
and a lickin' of I ; so don't mind me, Miss Maud, and 'appen I
might do ye a good turn some day.'

A few days after this little interview with Meg, as Milly and
I were walking briskly—for it was a clear frosty day—along the
pleasant slopes of the sheep-walk, we were overtaken by Dudley
Ruthyn. It was not a pleasant surprise. There was this mitiga-
tion, however : we were on foot, and he driving in a dog-cart
along the track leading to the moor, with his dogs and gun.
He brought his horse for a moment to a walk, and with a careless nod to me, removing his short pipe from his mouth, he
said—

'Governor's callin' for ye, Milly ; and he told me to send you
slick home to him if I saw you, and I think he'll gi'e ye some
money ; but ye better take him while he's in the humour, lass,
or mayhap ye'll go long without.'

And with those words, apparently intent on his game, he nodded again, and, pipe in mouth, drove at a quick trot over the slope of the hill, and disappeared.

So I agreed to await Milly's return while she ran home, and rejoined me where I was. Away she ran, in high spirits, and I wandered listlessly about in search of some convenient spot to sit down upon, for I was a little tired.

She had not been gone five minutes, when I heard a step approaching, and looking round, saw the dog-cart close by, the horse browsing on the short grass, and Dudley Ruthyn within a few paces of me.

' Ye see, Maud, I've bin thinkin' why you're so vexed wi' me, an' I thought I'd jest come back an' ask ye what I may a' done to anger ye so ; there's no sin in that, I think—is there ? '

' I'm not angry. I did not say so. I hope that's enough,' I said, startled ; and, notwithstanding my speech, *very* angry, for I felt instinctively that Milly's despatch homeward was a mere trick, and I the dupe of this coarse stratagem.

' Well then, if ye baint angry, so much the better, Maud. I only want to know why you're afeard o' me. I never struck a man foul, much less hurt a girl, in my days ; besides, Maud, I likes ye too well to hurt ye. Dang it, lass, you're my cousin, ye know, and cousins is all'ays together and lovin' like, an' none says again' it.'

' I've nothing to explain—there *is* nothing to explain. I've been quite friendly,' I said, hurriedly.

' *Friendly* ! Well, if there baint a cram ! How can ye think it friendly, Maud, when ye won't a'most shake hands wi' me ? It's enough to make a fellah sware, or cry a'most. Why d'ye like aggravatin' a poor devil ? Now baint ye an ill-natured little puss, Maud, an' I likin' ye so well ? You're the prettiest lass in Derbyshire ; there's nothin' I wouldn't do for ye.'

And he backed his declaration with an oath.

' Be so good, then, as to re-enter your dog-cart and drive away,' I replied, very much incensed.

' Now, there it is again ! Ye can't speak me civil. Another fellah'd fly out, an' maybe kiss ye for spite ; but I baint that sort, I'm all for coaxin' and kindness, an' ye won't let me. What *be* you drivin' at, Maud ? '

' I think I've said very plainly, sir, that I wish to be alone.

You've *nothing* to say, except utter nonsense, and I've heard quite enough. Once for all, I beg, sir, that you will be so good as to leave me.'

' Well, now, look here, Maud ; I'll do anything you like—burn me if I don't—if you'll only jest be kind to me, like cousins should. What did I ever do to vex you ? If you think I like any lass better than you—some fellah at Elverston's bin talkin', maybe—it's nout but lies an' nonsense. Not but there's lots o' wenches likes me well enough, though I be a plain lad, and speaks my mind straight out.'

' I can't see that you are so frank, sir, as you describe ; you have just played a shabby trick to bring about this absurd and most disagreeable interview.'

' And supposin' I did send that fool, Milly, out o' the way, to talk a bit wi' you here, where's the harm ? Dang it, lass, ye mustn't be too hard. Didn't I say I'd do whatever ye wished ? '

' And you *won't,*' said I.

' Ye mean to get along out o' this ? Well, now, I *will.* There ! No use, of course, askin' you to kiss and be friends, before I go, as cousins should. Well, don't be riled, lass, I'm not askin' it ; only mind, I do like you awful, and 'appen I'll find ye in better humour another time. Good-bye, Maud ; I'll make ye like me at last.'

And with these words, to my comfort, he addressed himself to his horse and pipe, and was soon honestly on his way to the moor.

CHAPTER XLVI

THE RIVALS

All the time that Dudley chose to persecute me with his odious society, I continued to walk at a brisk pace toward home, so that I had nearly reached the house when Milly met me, with a note which had arrived for me by the post, in her hand.

'Here, Milly, are more verses. He is a very persevering poet, whoever he is.' So I broke the seal ; but this time it was prose. And the first words were 'Captain Oakley !'

I confess to an odd sensation as these remarkable words met my eye. It might possibly be a proposal. I did not wait to specu- late, however, but read these sentences traced in the identical handwriting which had copied the lines with which I had been twice favoured.

'Captain Oakley presents his compliments to Miss Ruthyn, and trusts she will excuse his venturing to ask whether, during his short stay in Feltram, he might be permitted to pay his respects at Bartram-Haugh. He has been making a short visit to his aunt, and could not find himself so near without at least attempting to renew an acquaintance which he has never ceased to cherish in memory. If Miss Ruthyn would be so very good as to favour him with ever so short a reply to the question he ven- tures most respectfully to ask, her decision would reach him at the Hall Hotel, Feltram.'

'Well, he's a roundabout fellah, anyhow. Couldn't he come up and see you if he wanted to ? They poeters, they do love writing long yarns—don't they ?' And with this reflection, Milly took the note and read it through again.

'It's jolly polite anyhow, isn't it Maud ?' said Milly, who had conned it over, and accepted it as a model composition.

I must have been, I think, naturally a rather shrewd girl ; and considering how very little I had seen of the world—nothing in fact—I often wonder now at the sage conclusions at which I arrived.

Were I to answer this handsome and cunning fool according to his folly, in what position should I find myself ? No doubt my reply would induce a rejoinder, and that compel another note from me, and that invite yet another from him ; and how- ever his might improve in warmth, they were sure not to abate. Was it his impertinent plan, with this show of respect and ceremony, to drag me into a clandestine correspondence ? In- experienced girl as I was, I fired at the idea of becoming his dupe, and fancying, perhaps, that there was more in merely an- swering his note than it would have amounted to, I said—

'That kind of thing may answer very well with button- makers, but ladies don't like it. What would your papa think

of it if he found that I had been writing to him, and seeing
him without his permission? If he wanted to see me he could
have '— (I really did not know exactly what he could have
done)—' he could have timed his visit to Lady Knollys differently; at all events, he has no right to place me in an embarrassing situation, and I am certain Cousin Knollys would say
so; and I think his note both shabby and impertinent.'

Decision was not with me an intellectual process. When quite
cool I was the most undecided of mortals, but once my feelings
were excited I was prompt and bold.

'I'll give the note to Uncle Silas,' I said, quickening my pace
toward home; he'll know what to do.'

But Milly, who, I fancy, had no objection to the little romance which the young officer proposed, told me that she could
not see her father, that he was ill, and not speaking to anyone.

'And arn't ye making a plaguy row about nothin'? I lay a
guinea if ye had never set eyes on Lord Ilbury you'd a told him
to come, and see ye, an' welcome.'

'Don't talk like a fool, Milly. You never knew me do anything deceitful. Lord Ilbury has no more to do with it, you
know very well, than the man in the moon.'

I was altogether very indignant. I did not speak another word
to Milly. The proportions of the house are so great, that it is a
much longer walk than you would suppose from the hall-door
to Uncle Silas's room. But I did not cool all that way; and it
was not till I had just reached the lobby, and saw the sour,
jealous face, and high caul of old Wyat, and felt the influence
of that neighbourhood, that I paused to reconsider. I fancied
there was a cool consciousness of success behind all the deferen-
tial phraseology of Captain Oakley, which nettled me extremely.
No; there could be no doubt. I tapped softly at the door.

'What is it *now*, Miss?' snarled the querulous old woman,
with her shrivelled fingers on the door-handle.

'Can I see my uncle for a moment?'

'He's tired, and not a word from him all day long.'

'Not ill, though?'

'Awful bad in the night,' said the old crone, with a sudden
savage glare in my face, as if *I* had brought it about.

'Oh! I'm very sorry. I had not heard a word of it.'

'No one does but old Wyat. There's Milly there never asks neither—his own child!'

'Weakness, or what?'

'One o' them fits. He'll slide awa' in one o' them some day, and no one but old Wyat to know nor ask word about it; that's how 'twill be.'

'Will you please hand him this note, if he is well enough to look at it, and say I am at the door?'

She took it with a peevish nod and a grunt, closing the door in my face, and in a few minutes returned—

'Come in wi' ye,' said Dame Wyat, and I appeared.

Uncle Silas, who, after his nightly horror or vision, lay extended on a sofa, with his faded yellow silk dressing-gown about him, his long white hair hanging toward the ground, and that wild and feeble smile lighting his face—a glimmer I feared to look upon—his long thin arms lay by his sides, with hands and fingers that stirred not, except when now and then, with a feeble motion, he wet his temples and forehead with eau de Cologne from a glass saucer placed beside him.

'Excellent girl! dutiful ward and niece!' murmured the oracle; 'heaven reward you—your frank dealing is your own safety and my peace. Sit you down, and say who is this Captain Oakley, when you made his acquaintance, what his age, fortune, and expectations, and who the aunt he mentions.'

Upon all these points I satisfied him as fully as I was able.

'Wyat—the white drops,' he called, in a thin, stern tone. 'I'll write a line presently. I can't see visitors, and, of course, you can't receive young captains before you've come out. Farewell! God bless you, dear.'

Wyat was dropping the 'white' restorative into a wine-glass and the room was redolent of ether. I was glad to escape. The figures and whole *mise en scène* were unearthly.

'Well, Milly,' I said, as I met her in the hall, 'your papa is going to write to him.'

I sometimes wonder whether Milly was right, and how I should have acted a few months earlier.

Next day whom should we meet in the Windmill Wood but Captain Oakley. The spot where this interesting *rencontre* occurred was near that ruinous bridge on my sketch of which I had received so many compliments. It was so great a surprise that I had not time to recollect my indignation, and, having received him very affably, I found it impossible, during our brief interview, to recover my lost altitude.

After our greetings were over, and some compliments neatly made, he said—

' I had such a curious note from Mr. Silas Ruthyn. I am sure he thinks me a very impertinent fellow, for it was really anything but inviting—extremely rude, in fact. But I could not quite see that because he does not want me to invade his bedroom—an incursion I never dreamed of—I was not to present myself to you, who had already honoured me with your acquaintance, with the sanction of those who were most interested in your welfare, and who were just as well qualified as he, I fancy, to say who were qualified for such an honour.'

' My uncle, Mr. Silas Ruthyn, you are aware, is my guardian ; and this is my cousin, his daughter.'

This was an opportunity of becoming a little lofty, and I improved it. He raised his hat and bowed to Milly.

' I'm afraid I've been very rude and stupid. Mr. Ruthyn, of course, has a perfect right to—to—in fact, I was not the least aware that I had the honour of so near a relation's—a—a— and what exquisite scenery you have ! I think this country round Feltram particularly fine ; and this Bartram-Haugh is, I venture to say, about the very most beautiful spot in this beautiful region. I do assure you I am tempted beyond measure to make Feltram and the Hall Hotel my head-quarters for at least a week. I only regret the foliage ; but your trees show wonderfully, even in winter, so many of them have got that ivy about them. They say it spoils trees, but it certainly beautifies them. I have just ten days' leave unexpired ; I wish I could induce you to advise me how to apply them. What shall I do, Miss Ruthyn ? '

' I am the worst person in the world to make plans, even for myself, I find it so troublesome. What do you say ? Suppose you try Wales or Scotland, and climb up some of those fine mountains that look so well in winter ? '

' I should much prefer Feltram. I so wish you would recommend *it*. What is this pretty plant ? '

' We call that Maud's myrtle. She planted it, and it's very pretty when it's full in blow,' said Milly.

Our visit to Elverston had been of immense use to us both.
'Oh! planted by *you*?' he said, very softly, with a momentary
corresponding glance. 'May I—ever so little—just a leaf?'

And without waiting for permission, he held a sprig of it
next his waistcoat.

'Yes, it goes very prettily with those buttons. They are *very*
pretty buttons; are not they, Milly? A present, a souvenir, I
dare say?'

This was a terrible hit at the button-maker, and I thought he
looked a little oddly at me, but my countenance was so 'be-
witchingly simple' that I suppose his suspicions were allayed.

Now, it was very odd of me, I must confess, to talk in this
way, and to receive all those tender allusions from a gentleman
about whom I had spoken and felt so sharply only the evening
before. But Bartram was abominably lonely. A civilised person
was a valuable waif or stray in that region of the picturesque
and the brutal; and to my lady reader especially, because
she will probably be hardest upon me, I put it—can you not
recollect any such folly in your own past life? Can you not in
as many minutes call to mind at least six similar inconsistencies
of your own practising? For my part, I really can't see the advantage of being the weaker sex if we are always to be as strong
as our masculine neighbours.

There was, indeed, no revival of the little sentiment which
I had once experienced. When these things once expire, I do
believe they are as hard to revive as our dead lap-dogs, guinea-
pigs, and parrots. It was my perfect coolness which enabled me
to chat, I flatter myself, so agreeably with the refined Captain,
who plainly thought me his captive, and was probably now and
then thinking what was to be done to utilise that little bit of
Bartram, or to beautify some other, when he should see fit to
become its master, as we rambled over these wild but beautiful
grounds.

It was just about then that Milly nudged me rather vehemently, and whispered 'Look there!'

I followed with mine the direction of her eyes, and saw my
odious cousin, Dudley, in a flagrant pair of cross-barred peg-
tops, and what Milly before her reformation used to call other
'slops' of corresponding atrocity, approaching our refined little
party with great strides. I really think that Milly was very

nearly ashamed of him. I certainly was. I had no apprehension, however, of the scene which was imminent.

The charming Captain mistook him probably for some rustic servant of the place, for he continued his agreeable remarks up to the very moment when Dudley, whose face was pale with anger, and whose rapid advance had not served to cool him, without recollecting to salute either Milly or me, accosted our elegant companion as follows :—

'By your leave, master, baint you summat in the wrong box here, don't you think ? '

He had planted himself directly in his front, and looked unmistakably menacing.

'May I speak to him ? Will you excuse me ? ' said the Captain blandly.

'Ow—ay, they'll excuse ye ready enough, I dessay ; you're to deal wi' me though. Baint ye in the wrong box now ? '

'I'm not conscious, sir, of being in a box at all,' replied the Captain, with severe disdain. 'It strikes me you are disposed to get up a row. Let us, if you please, get a little apart from the ladies if that is your purpose.'

'I mean to turn you out o' this the way ye came. If you make a row, so much the wuss for you, for I'll lick ye to fits.'

'Tell him not to fight,' whispered Milly ; 'he'll a no chance wi' Dudley.'

I saw Dickon Hawkes grinning over the paling on which he leaned.

'Mr. Hawkes,' I said, drawing Milly with me toward that unpromising mediator, 'pray prevent unpleasantness and go between them.'

'An' git licked o' both sides ? Rather not, Miss, thank ye,' grinned Dickon, tranquilly.

'Who are you, sir ? ' demanded our romantic acquaintance, with military sternness.

'I'll tell you who you are—you're Oakley, as stops at the Hall, that Governor wrote, over-night, not to dare show your nose inside the grounds. You're a half-starved cappen, come down here to look for a wife, and——'

Before Dudley could finish his sentence, Captain Oakley, than whose face no regimentals could possibly have been more scarlet, at that moment, struck with his switch at Dudley's handsome features.

I don't know how it was done—by some 'devilish cantrip slight.' A smack was heard, and the Captain lay on his back on the ground, with his mouth full of blood.

'How do ye like the taste o' that?' roared Dickon, from his post of observation.

In an instant Captain Oakley was on his feet again, hatless, looking quite frantic, and striking out at Dudley, who was ducking and dipping quite coolly, and again the same horrid sound, only this time it was double, like a quick postman's knock, and Captain Oakley was on the grass again.

'Tapped his smeller, by——!' thundered Dickon, with a roar of laughter.

'Come away, Milly—I'm growing ill,' said I.

'Drop it, Dudley, I tell ye; you'll kill him,' screamed Milly.

But the devoted Captain, whose nose, and mouth, and shirt-front formed now but one great patch of blood, and who was bleeding beside over one eye, dashed at him again.

I turned away. I felt quite faint, and on the point of crying, with mere horror.

'Hammer away at his knocker,' bellowed Dickon, in a frenzy of delight.

'He'll break it now, if it ain't already,' cried Milly, alluding, as I afterwards understood, to the Captain's Grecian nose.

'Brayvo, little un!' The Captain was considerably the taller.

Another smack, and, I suppose, Captain Oakley fell once more.

'Hooray! the dinner-service again, by ——,' roared Dickon. 'Stick to that. Over the same ground—subsoil, I say. He han't enough yet.'

In a perfect tremor of disgust, I was making as quick a retreat as I could, and as I did, I heard Captain Oakley shriek hoarsely —

'You're a d——prizefighter; I can't box you.'

'I told ye I'd lick ye to fits,' hooted Dudley.

'But you're the son of a gentleman, and by —— you shall fight me *as* a gentleman.'

A yell of hooting laughter from Dudley and Dickon followed this sally.

' Gi'e my love to the Colonel, and think o' me when ye look in the glass—won't ye ? An' so you're goin' arter all ; well, follow what's left o' yer nose. Ye forgot some o' yer ivories, didn't ye, on th' grass ? '

These and many similar jibes followed the mangled Captain in his retreat.

CHAPTER XLVII

DOCTOR BRYERLY REAPPEARS

No one who has not experienced it can imagine the nervous disgust and horror which such a spectacle as we had been forced in part to witness leaves upon the mind of a young person of my peculiar temperament.

It affected ever after my involuntary estimate of the principal actors in it. An exhibition of such thorough inferiority, accompanied by such a shock to the feminine sense of elegance, is not forgotten by any woman. Captain Oakley had been severely beaten by a smaller man. It was pitiable, but also undignified ; and Milly's anxieties about his teeth and nose, though in a certain sense horrible, had also a painful suspicion of the absurd.

People say, on the other hand, that superior prowess, even in such barbarous contests, inspires in our sex an interest akin to admiration. I can positively say in my case it was quite the reverse. Dudley Ruthyn stood lower than ever in my estimation ; for though I feared him more, it was by reason of these brutal and cold-blooded associations.

After this I lived in constant apprehension of being summoned to my uncle's room, and being called on for an explanation of my meeting with Captain Oakley, which, notwithstanding my perfect innocence, looked suspicious, but no such inquisition resulted. Perhaps he did not suspect me ; or, perhaps, he thought, not in his haste, all women are liars, and did not

care to hear what I might say. I rather lean to the latter interpretation.

The exchequer just now, I suppose, by some means, was
replenished, for next morning Dudley set off upon one of his
fashionable excursions, as poor Milly thought them, to Wolverhampton. And the same day Dr. Bryerly arrived.

Milly and I, from my room window, saw him step from his
vehicle to the court-yard.

A lean man, with sandy hair and whiskers, was in the chaise
with him. Dr. Bryerly descended in the unchangeable black suit
that always looked new and never fitted him.

The Doctor looked careworn, and older, I thought, by several years, than when I last saw him. He was not shown up to
my uncle's room ; on the contrary, Milly, who was more actively
curious than I, ascertained that our tremulous butler informed
him that my uncle was not sufficiently well for an interview.
Whereupon Dr. Bryerly had pencilled a note, the reply to which
was a message from Uncle Silas, saying that he would be happy
to see him in five minutes.

As Milly and I were conjecturing what it might mean, and
before the five minutes had expired, Mary Quince entered.

' Wyat bid me tell you, Miss, your uncle wants you *this minute.*'

When I entered his room, Uncle Silas was seated at the table,
with his desk before him. He looked up. Could anything be
more dignified, suffering, and venerable ?

' I sent for you, dear,' he said very gently, extending his thin,
white hand, and taking mine, which he held affectionately
while he spoke, ' because I desire to have no secrets, and wish
you thoroughly to know all that concerns your own interests
while subject to my guardianship ; and I am happy to think,
my beloved niece, that you requite my candour. Oh, here is the
gentleman. Sit down, dear.'

Doctor Bryerly was advancing, as it seemed, to shake hands
with Uncle Silas, who, however, rose with a severe and haughty
air, not the least over-acted, and made him a slow, ceremonious
bow. I wondered how the homely Doctor could confront so tranquilly that astounding statue of hauteur.

A faint and weary smile, rather sad than comtemptuous, was
the only sign he showed of feeling his repulse.

' How do *you* do, Miss ? ' he said, extending his hand, and greeting me after his ungallant fashion, as if it were an after-thought.

' I think I may as well take a chair, sir,' said Doctor Bryerly, sitting down serenely, near the table, and crossing his ungainly legs.

My uncle bowed.

' You understand the nature of the business, sir. Do you wish Miss Ruthyn to remain ? ' asked Doctor Bryerly.

' I *sent* for her, sir,' replied my uncle, in a very gentle and sar-castic tone, a smile on his thin lips, and his strangely-contorted eyebrows raised for a moment contemptuously. ' This gentle-man, my dear Maud, thinks proper to insinuate that I am rob-bing you. It surprises me a little, and, no doubt, you—I've nothing to conceal, and wished you to be present while he favours me more particularly with his views. I'm right, I think, in describing it as *robbery,* sir ? '

' Why,' said Doctor Bryerly thoughtfully, for he was treating the matter as one of right, and not of feeling, ' it would be, certainly, taking that which does not belong to you, and con-verting it to your own use ; but, at the worst, it would more re-semble *thieving,* I think, than robbery.'

I saw Uncle Silas's lip, eyelid, and thin cheek quiver and shrink, as if with a thrill of tic-douloureux, as Doctor Bryerly spoke this unconsciously insulting answer. My uncle had, how-ever, the self-command which is learned at the gaming-table. He shrugged, with a chilly, sarcastic, little laugh, and a glance at me.

' Your note says *waste,* I think, sir ? '

' Yes, waste—the felling and sale of timber in the Windmill Wood, the selling of oak bark and burning of charcoal, as I'm informed,' said Bryerly, as sadly and quietly as a man might relate a piece of intelligence from the newspaper.

' Detectives ? or private spies of your own ?—or, perhaps, my servants, bribed with my poor brother's money ? A very high-minded procedure.'

' Nothing of the kind, sir.'

My uncle sneered.

' I mean, sir, there has been no undue canvass for evidence, and the question is simply one of right ; and it is our duty to see that this inexperienced young lady is not defrauded.'

' By her own uncle ? '

' By anyone,' said Doctor Bryerly, with a natural impenetrability that excited my admiration.

' Of course you come armed with an opinion ? ' said my smiling uncle, insinuatingly.

' The case is before Mr. Serjeant Grinders. These bigwigs don't return their cases sometimes so quickly as we could wish.'

' Then you have *no* opinion ? ' smiled my uncle.

' My solicitor is quite clear upon it ; and it seems to me there can be no question raised, but for form's sake.'

' Yes, for form's sake you take one, and in the meantime, upon a nice question of law, the surmises of a thick-headed attorney and of an ingenious apoth—I beg pardon, physician—are sufficient warrant for telling my niece and ward, in my presence, that I am defrauding her ! '

My uncle leaned back in his chair, and smiled with a contemptuous patience over Doctor Bryerly's head, as he spoke.

' I don't know whether I used that expression, sir, but I am speaking merely in a technical sense. I mean to say, that, whether by mistake or otherwise, you are exercising a power which you don't lawfully possess, and that the effect of that is to impoverish the estate, and, by so much as it benefits you, to wrong this young lady.'

' I'm a technical defrauder, I see, and your manner conveys the rest. I thank my God, sir, I am a *very* different man from what I once was.' Uncle Silas was speaking in a low tone, and with extraordinary deliberation. ' I remember when I should have certainly knocked you down, sir, or *tried* it, at least, for a great deal less.'

' But seriously, sir, what *do* you propose ? ' asked Doctor Bryerly, sternly and a little flushed, for I think the old man was stirred within him ; and though he did not raise his voice, his manner was excited.

' I propose to defend my rights, sir,' murmured Uncle Silas, very grim. ' I'm not without an opinion, though you are.'

' You seem to think, sir, that I have a pleasure in annoying you ; you are quite wrong. I hate annoying anyone—constitutionally—I *hate* it ; but don't you see, sir, the position I'm placed in ? I wish I could please everyone, and do my duty.'

Uncle Silas bowed and smiled.

' I've brought with me the Scotch steward from Tolkingden, *your* estate, Miss, and if you let us we will visit the spot and make a note of what we observe, that is, assuming that you admit waste, and merely question our law.'

' If you please, sir, you and your Scotchman shall do *no such thing* ; and, bearing in mind that I neither deny nor admit anything, you will please further never more to present yourself, under any pretext whatsoever, either in this house or on the grounds of Bartram-Haugh, during my lifetime.'

Uncle Silas rose up with the same glassy smile and scowl, in token that the interview was ended.

' Good-bye, sir,' said Doctor Bryerly, with a sad and thoughtful air, and hesitating for a moment, he said to me, ' Do you think, Miss, you could afford me a word in the hall ? '

' Not a word, sir,' snarled Uncle Silas, with a white flash from his eyes.

There was a pause.

' Sit where you are, Maud.'

Another pause.

' If you have anything to say to my ward, sir, you will please to say it *here*.'

Doctor Bryerly's dark and homely face was turned on me with an expression of unspeakable compassion.

' I was going to say, that if you think of any way in which I can be of the least service, Miss, I'm ready to act, that's all ; mind, *any* way.'

He hesitated, looking at me with the same expression as if he had something more to say ; but he only repeated—

' That's all, Miss.'

' Won't you shake hands, Doctor Bryerly, before you go ? ' I said, eagerly approaching him.

Without a smile, with the same sad anxiety in his face, with his mind, as it seemed to me, on something else, and irresolute whether to speak it or be silent, he took my fingers in a very cold hand, and holding it so, and slowly shaking it, his grave and troubled glance unconsciously rested on Uncle Silas's face, while in a sad tone and absent way he said—

' Good-bye, Miss.'

From before that sad gaze my uncle averted his strange eyes quickly, and looked, oddly, to the window.

In a moment more Doctor Bryerly let my hand go with a sigh, and with an abrupt little nod to me, he left the room ; and I heard that dismallest of sounds, the retreating footsteps of a true friend, *lost*.

' Lead us not into temptation ; if we pray so, we must not mock the eternal Majesty of Heaven by walking into temptation of our own accord.'

This oracular sentence was not uttered by my uncle until Doctor Bryerly had been gone at least five minutes.

' I've forbid him my house, Maud—first, because his perfectly unconscious insolence tries my patience nearly beyond endurance ; and again, because I have heard unfavourable reports of him. On the question of right which he disputes, I am perfectly informed. I am your tenant, my dear niece ; when I am gone you will learn how *scrupulous* I have been ; you will see how, under the pressure of the most agonising pecuniary difficulties, the terrific penalty of a misspent youth, I have been careful never by a hair's breadth to transgress the strict line of my legal privileges ; alike, as your tenant, Maud, and as your guardian ; how, amid frightful agitations, I have kept myself, by the miraculous strength and grace vouchsafed me—*pure*.

' The world,' he resumed after a short pause, ' has no faith in any man's conversion ; it never forgets what he was, it never believes him anything better, it is an inexorable and stupid judge. What I was I will describe in blacker terms, and with more heartfelt detestation, than my traducers—a reckless prodigal, a godless profligate. Such I was ; what I am, I am. If I had no hope beyond this world, of all men most miserable ; but with that hope, a sinner saved.'

Then he waxed eloquent and mystical. I think his Swedenborgian studies had crossed his notions of religion with strange lights. I never could follow him quite in these excursions into the region of symbolism. I only recollect that he talked of the deluge and the waters of Mara, and said, ' I am washed—I am sprinkled,' and then, pausing, bathed his thin temples and forehead with eau de Cologne ; a process which was, perhaps, suggested by his imagery of sprinkling and so forth.

Thus refreshed, he sighed and smiled, and passed to the subject of Doctor Bryerly.

' Of Doctor Bryerly, I know that he is sly, that he loves money, was born poor, and makes nothing by his profession. But he possesses many thousand pounds, under my poor brother's will, of *your money ;* and he has glided with, of course a modest "nolo episcopari," into the acting trusteeship, with all its multitudinous opportunities, of your immense property. That is not doing so badly for a visionary Swedenborgian. Such a man *must* prosper. But if he expected to make money of me, he is disappointed. Money, however, he will make of his trusteeship, as you will see. It is a dangerous resolution. But if he will seek the life of Dives, the worst I wish him is to find the death of Lazarus. But whether, like Lazarus, he be borne of angels into Abraham's bosom, or, like the rich man, only dies and is buried, and *the rest,* neither living nor dying do I desire his company.'

Uncle Silas here seemed suddenly overtaken by exhaustion. He leaned back with a ghastly look, and his lean features glistened with the dew of faintness. I screamed for Wyat. But he soon recovered sufficiently to smile his odd smile, and with it and his frown, nodded and waved me away.

CHAPTER XLVIII

QUESTION AND ANSWER

My uncle, after all, was not ill that day, after the strange fashion of his malady, be it what it might. Old Wyat repeated in her sour laconic way that there was ' nothing to speak of amiss with him.' But there remained with me a sense of pain and fear. Doctor Bryerly, notwithstanding my uncle's sarcastic reflections, remained, in my estimation, a true and wise friend. I had all my life been accustomed to rely upon others, and here, haunted by many unavowed and ill-defined alarms and doubts, the disappearance of an active and able friend caused my heart to sink.

Still there remained my dear Cousin Monica, and my pleasant and trusted friend, Lord Ilbury ; and in less than a week arrived an invitation from Lady Mary to the Grange, for me and Milly, to meet Lady Knollys. It was accompanied, she told me, by a note from Lord Ilbury to my uncle, supporting her request ; and in the afternoon I received a message to attend my uncle in his room.

' An invitation from Lady Mary Carysbroke for you and Milly to meet Monica Knollys ; have you received it ? ' asked my uncle, so soon as I was seated. Answered in the affirmative, he continued —

' Now, Maud Ruthyn, I expect the truth from you ; I have been frank, so shall you. Have you ever heard me spoken ill of by Lady Knollys ? '

I was quite taken aback.

I felt my cheeks flushing. I was returning his fierce cold gaze with a stupid stare, and remained dumb.

' Yes, Maud, you *have*.'

I looked down in silence.

' I *know* it ; but it is right you should answer ; have you or have you not ? '

I had to clear my voice twice or thrice. There was a kind of spasm in my throat.

' I am trying to recollect,' I said at last.

' *Do* recollect,' he replied imperiously.

There was a little interval of silence. I would have given the world to be, on any conditions, anywhere else in the world.

' Surely, Maud, you don't wish to deceive your guardian ? Come, the question is a plain one, and I know the truth already. I ask you again—have you ever heard me spoken ill of by Lady Knollys ? '

' Lady Knollys,' I said, half articulately, ' speaks very freely, and often half in jest ; but,' I continued, observing something menacing in his face, ' I have heard her express disapprobation of some things you have done.'

' Come, Maud,' he continued, in a stern, though still a low key, 'did she not insinuate that charge—then, I suppose, in a state of incubation, the other day presented here full-fledged,

with beak and claws, by that scheming apothecary—the statement that I was defrauding you by cutting down timber upon
the grounds ?'

'She certainly did mention the circumstance ; but she also
argued that it might have been through ignorance of the extent
of your rights.'

'Come, come, Maud, you must not prevaricate, girl. I *will*
have it. Does she not habitually speak disparagingly of me, in
your presence, and *to* you ? *Answer.*'

I hung my head.

'Yes or no ?'

'Well, perhaps so—yes,' I faltered, and burst into tears.

'There, don't cry ; it may well shock you. Did she not, to your
knowledge, say the same things in presence of my child Millicent ? I know it, I repeat—there is no use in hesitating ; and
I command you to answer.'

Sobbing, I told the truth.

'Now sit still, while I write my reply.'

He wrote, with the scowl and smile so painful to witness, as
he looked down upon the paper, and then he placed the note
before me—

'Read that, my dear.'

It began—

'MY DEAR LADY KNOLLYS.—You have favoured me with a note,
adding your request to that of Lord Ilbury, that I should permit my ward and my daughter to avail themselves of Lady
Mary's invitation. Being perfectly cognisant of the ill-feeling
you have always and unaccountably cherished toward me, and
also of the terms in which you have had the delicacy and the
conscience to speak of me before and to my child and my ward,
I can only express my amazement at the modesty of your request, while peremptorily refusing it. And I shall conscientiously
adopt effectual measures to prevent your ever again having an
opportunity of endeavouring to destroy my influence and authority over my ward and my child, by direct or insinuated
slander.

'Your defamed and injured kinsman,
SILAS RUTHYN.'

I was stunned ; yet what could I plead against the blow that was to isolate me ? I wept aloud, with my hands clasped, looking on the marble face of the old man.

Without seeming to hear, he folded and sealed his note, and then proceeded to answer Lord Ilbury.

When that note was written, he placed it likewise before me, and I read it also through. It simply referred him to Lady Knollys ' for an explanation of the unhappy circumstances which compelled him to decline an invitation which it would have made his niece and his daughter so happy to accept.'

' You see, my dear Maud, how frank I am with you,' he said, waving the open note, which I had just read, slightly before he folded it. ' I think I may ask you to reciprocate my candour.'

Dismissed from this interview, I ran to Milly, who burst into tears from sheer disappointment, so we wept and wailed together. But in my grief I think there was more reason.

I sat down to the dismal task of writing to my dear Lady Knollys. I implored her to make her peace with my uncle. I told her how frank he had been with me, and how he had shown me his sad reply to her letter. I told her of the interview to which he had himself invited me with Dr. Bryerly ; how little disturbed he was by the accusation—no sign of guilt ; quite the contrary, perfect confidence. I implored of her to think the best, and remembering my isolation, to accomplish a reconciliation with Uncle Silas. ' Only think,' I wrote, ' I only nineteen, and two years of solitude before me. What a separation ! ' No broken merchant ever signed the schedule of his bankruptcy with a heavier heart than did I this letter.

The griefs of youth are like the wounds of the gods—there is an ichor which heals the scars from which it flows : and thus Milly and I consoled ourselves, and next day enjoyed our ramble, our talk and readings, with a wonderful resignation to the inevitable.

Milly and I stood in the relation of *Lord Duberly* to *Doctor Pangloss*. I was to mend her ' cackleology,' and the occupation amused us both. I think at the bottom of our submission to destiny lurked a hope that Uncle Silas, the inexorable, would relent, or that Cousin Monica, that siren, would win and melt him to her purpose.

Whatever comfort, however, I derived from the absence of

Dudley was not to be of very long duration ; for one morning,
as I was amusing myself alone, with a piece of worsted work,
thinking, and just at that moment not unpleasantly, of many
things, my cousin Dudley entered the room.

'Back again, like a bad halfpenny, ye see. And how a' ye bin
ever since, lass ? Purely, I warrant, be your looks. I'm jolly glad
to see ye, I am ; no cattle going like ye, Maud.'

'I think I must ask you to let go my hand, as I can't continue
my work,' I said, very stiffly, hoping to chill his enthusiasm a
little.

'Anything to pleasure ye, Maud, 'tain't in my heart to refuse
ye nout. I a'bin to Wolverhampton, lass—jolly row there—and
run over to Leamington ; a'most broke my neck, faith, wi' a
borrowed horse arter the dogs ; ye would na care, Maud, if I
broke my neck, would ye ? Well, 'appen, jest a little,' he good-
naturedly supplied, as I was silent.

'Little over a week since I left here, by George ; and to me
it's half the almanac like ; can ye guess the reason, Maud ?'

'Have you seen your sister, Milly, or your father, since your
return ?' I asked coldly.

'*They'll* keep, Maud, never mind 'em ; it be you I want to see
—it be you I wor thinkin' on a' the time. I tell ye, lass, I'm
all'ays a thinkin' on ye.'

'I think you ought to go and see your father ; you have been
away, you say, some time. I don't think it is respectful,' I said, a
little sharply.

'If ye bid me go I'd a'most go, but I could na quite ; there's
nout on earth I would na do for you, Maud, excep' leaving
you.'

'And that,' I said, with a petulant flush, 'is the only thing on
earth I would ask you to do.'

'Blessed if you baint a blushin', Maud,' he drawled, with an
odious grin.

His stupidity was proof against everything.

'It is *too* bad!' I muttered, with an indignant little pat of
my foot and mimic stamp.

'Well, you lasses be queer cattle ; ye're angry wi' me now,
cos ye think I got into mischief—ye do, Maud ; ye know't, ye
buxsom little fool, down there at Wolverhampton ; and jest for

that ye're ready to turn me off again the minute I come back ;
'tisn't fair.'

' I don't *understand* you, sir ; and I *beg* that you'll leave me.'

' Now, didn't I tell ye about leavin' ye, Maud ? 'tis the only
thing I can't compass for yer sake. I'm jest a child in yere hands,
I am, ye know. I can lick a big fellah to pot as limp as a rag,
by George ! '—(his oaths were not really so mild)—' ye see summat o' that t'other day. Well, don't be vexed, Maud ; 'twas all
along o' you ; ye know, I wor a bit jealous, 'appen ; but anyhow
I can do it ; and look at me here, jest a child, I say, in yer
hands.'

' I wish you'd go away. Have you nothing to do, and no one
to see ? Why *can't* you leave me alone, sir ? '

' 'Cos I can't, Maud, that's jest why ; and I wonder, Maud,
how can you be so ill-natured, when you see me like this ; how
can ye ? '

' I wish Milly would come,' said I peevishly, looking toward
the door.

' Well, I'll tell you how it is, Maud. I may as well have it out.
I like you better than any lass that ever I saw, a deal ; you're
nicer by chalks ; there's none like ye—there isn't ; and I wish
you'd have me. I ha'n't much tin—father's run through a deal,
he's pretty well up a tree, ye know ; but though I baint so rich
as some folk, I'm a better man, 'appen ; and if ye'd take a tidy
lad, that likes ye awful, and 'id die for your sake, why here he
is.'

' What can you mean, sir ? ' I exclaimed, rising in indignant
bewilderment.

' I mean, Maud, if ye'll marry me, you'll never ha' cause to
complain ; I'll never let ye want for nout, nor gi'e ye a wry
word.'

' Actually a proposal ! ' I ejaculated, like a person speaking in
a dream.

I stood with my hand on the back of a chair, staring at Dudley ; and looking, I dare say, as stupefied as I felt.

' There's a good lass, ye would na deny me,' said the odious
creature, with one knee on the seat of the chair behind which I
was standing, and attempting to place his arm lovingly round
my neck.

This effectually roused me, and starting back, I stamped upon the ground with actual fury.

' What has there ever been, sir, in my conduct, words, or looks, to warrant this unparalleled audacity ? But that you are as stupid as you are impertinent, brutal, and ugly, you must, long ago, sir, have seen how I dislike you. How dare you, sir ? Don't presume to obstruct me ; I'm going to my uncle.'

I had never spoken so violently to mortal before.

He in turn looked a little confounded ; and I passed his extended but motionless arm with a quick and angry step.

He followed me a pace or two, however, before I reached the door, looking horridly angry, but stopped, and only swore after me some of those ' wry words' which I was never to have heard. I was myself, however, too much incensed, and moving at too rapid a pace, to catch their import ; and I had knocked at my uncle's door before I began to collect my thoughts.

' Come in,' replied my uncle's voice, clear, thin, and peevish.

I entered and confronted him.

' Your son, sir, has insulted me.'

He looked at me with a cold curiosity steadly for a few seconds, as I stood panting before him with flaming cheeks.

' Insulted you ? ' repeated he. ' Egad, you surprise me ! '

The ejaculation savoured of ' the old man,' to borrow his scriptural phrase, more than anything I had heard from him before.

'*How* ? ' he continued ; ' how has Dudley *insulted* you, my dear child ? Come, you're excited ; sit down ; take time, and tell me all about it. I did not know that Dudley was here.'

' I—he—it *is* an insult. He knew very well—he *must* know I dislike him ; and he presumed to make a proposal of marriage to me.'

' O—o—oh ! ' exclaimed my uncle, with a prolonged intonation which plainly said, Is that the mighty matter ?

He looked at me as he leaned back with the same steady curiosity, this time smiling, which somehow frightened me, and his countenance looked to me wicked, like the face of a witch, with a guilt I could not understand.

' And that is the amount of your complaint. He made you a formal proposal of marriage ! '

' Yes ; he proposed for me.'

As I cooled, I began to feel just a very little disconcerted, and a suspicion was troubling me that possibly an indifferent person might think that, having no more to complain of, my language was perhaps a little exaggerated, and my demeanour a little too tempestuous.

My uncle, I dare say, saw some symptoms of this misgiving, for, smiling still, he said—

'My dear Maud, however just, you appear to me a little cruel ; you don't seem to remember how much you are yourself to blame ; you have one faithful friend at least, whom I advise your consulting—I mean your looking-glass. The foolish fellow is young, quite ignorant in the world's ways. He is in love—desperately enamoured.

> Aimer c'est craindre, et craindre c'est souffrir.

And suffering prompts to desperate remedies. We must not be too hard on a rough but romantic young fool, who talks according to his folly and his pain.'

CHAPTER XLIX

AN APPARITION

'But, after all,' he suddenly resumed, as if a new thought had struck him, ' is it quite such folly, after all ? It really strikes me, dear Maud, that the subject may be worth a second thought. No, no, you won't refuse to hear me,' he said, observing me on the point of protesting. ' I am, of course, assuming that you are fancy free. I am assuming, too, that you don't care twopence about Dudley, and even that you fancy you dislike him. You know in that pleasant play, poor Sheridan—delightful fellow !—all our fine spirits are dead—he makes Mrs. Malaprop say there is nothing like beginning with a little aversion. Now, though in matrimony, of course, that is only a joke, yet in love, believe me, it is no such thing. His own marriage with Miss Ogle, I *know*, was a case in point. She expressed a positive horror of him at their first acquaintance ; and yet, I believe, she would, a few months later, have died rather than not have married him.'

I was again about to speak, but with a smile he beckoned me into silence.

' There are two or three points you must bear in mind. One of the happiest privileges of your fortune is that you may, without imprudence, marry simply for love. There are few men in England who could offer you an estate comparable with that you already possess ; or, in fact, appreciably increase the splendour of your fortune. If, therefore, he were in all other respects eligible, I can't see that his poverty would be an objection to weigh for one moment. He is quite a rough diamond. He has been, like many young men of the highest rank, too much given up to athletic sports—to that society which constitutes the aristocracy of the ring and the turf, and all that kind of thing. You see, I am putting all the worst points first. But I have known so many young men in my day, after a madcap career of a few years among prizefighters, wrestlers, and jockeys—learning their slang and affecting their manners—take up and cultivate the graces and the decencies. There was poor dear Newgate, many degrees lower in that kind of frolic, who, when he grew tired of it, became one of the most elegant and accomplished men in the House of Peers. Poor Newgate, he's gone, too ! I could reckon up fifty of my early friends who all began like Dudley, and all turned out, more or less, like Newgate.'

At this moment came a knock at the door, and Dudley put in his head most inopportunely for the vision of his future graces and accomplishments.

' My good fellow,' said his father, with a sharp sort of playfulness, ' I happen to be talking about my son, and should rather not be overheard ; you will, therefore, choose another time for your visit.'

Dudley hesitated gruffly at the door, but another look from his father dismissed him.

' And now, my dear, you are to remember that Dudley has fine qualities—the most affectionate son in his rough way that ever father was blessed with ; most admirable qualities—indomitable courage, and a high sense of honour ; and lastly, that he has the Ruthyn blood—the purest blood, I maintain it, in England.'

My uncle, as he said this, drew himself up a little, unconsciously, his thin hand laid lightly over his heart with a little patting motion, and his countenance looked so strangely dignified and melancholy, that in admiring contemplation of it I lost some sentences which followed next.

'Therefore, dear, naturally anxious that my boy should not be dismissed from home—as he must be, should you persevere in rejecting his suit—I beg that you will reserve your decision to this day fortnight, when I will with much pleasure hear what you may have to say on the subject. But till then, observe me, not a word.'

That evening he and Dudley were closeted for a long time. I suspect that he lectured him on the psychology of ladies ; for a bouquet was laid beside my plate every morning at breakfast, which it must have been troublesome to get, for the conservatory at Bartram was a desert. In a few days more an anonymous green parrot arrived, in a gilt cage, with a little note in a clerk's hand, addressed to 'Miss Ruthyn (of Knowl), Bartram-Haugh,' &c. It contained only 'Directions for caring green parrot,' at the close of which, *underlined*, the words appeared—' The bird's name is Maud.'

The bouquets I invariably left on the table-cloth, where I found them—the bird I insisted on Milly's keeping as her property. During the intervening fortnight Dudley never appeared, as he used sometimes to do before, at luncheon, nor looked in at the window as we were at breakfast. He contented himself with one day placing himself in my way in the hall in his shooting accoutrements, and, with a clumsy, shuffling kind of respect, and hat in hand, he said—

'I think, Miss, I must a spoke uncivil t'other day. I was so awful put about, and didn't know no more nor a child what I was saying ; and I wanted to tell ye I'm sorry for it, and I beg your pardon—very humble, I do.'

I did not know what to say. I therefore said nothing, but made a grave inclination, and passed on.

Two or three times Milly and I saw him at a little distance in our walks. He never attempted to join us. Once only he passed so near that some recognition was inevitable, and he stopped and in silence lifted his hat with an awkward respect. But although he did not approach us, he was ostentatious with a kind of telegraphic civility in the distance. He opened gates, he

whistled his dogs to 'heel,' he drove away cattle, and then himself withdrew. I really think he watched us occasionally to
render these services, for in this distant way we encountered
him decidedly oftener than we used to do before his flattering
proposal of marriage.

You may be sure that we discussed, Milly and I, that occurrence pretty constantly in all sorts of moods. Limited as had
been her experience of human society, she very clearly saw
now how far below its presentable level was her hopeful brother.

The fortnight sped swiftly, as time always does when something we dislike and shrink from awaits us at its close. I never
saw Uncle Silas during that period. It may seem odd to those
who merely read the report of our last interview, in which his
manner had been more playful and his talk more trifling than
in any other, that from it I had carried away a profounder
sense of fear and insecurity than from any other. It was with a
foreboding of evil and an awful dejection that on a very dark
day, in Milly's room, I awaited the summons which I was sure
would reach me from my punctual guardian.

As I looked from the window upon the slanting rain and
leaden sky, and thought of the hated interview that awaited me,
I pressed my hand to my trouble heart, and murmured, 'O
that I had wings like a dove ! then would I flee away, and be at
rest.'

Just then the prattle of the parrot struck my ear. I looked
round on the wire cage, and remembered the words, ' The bird's
name is Maud.'

' Poor bird ! ' I said. ' I dare say, Milly, it longs to get out. If
it were a native of this country, would not you like to open the
window, and then the door of that cruel cage, and let the poor
thing fly away ? '

' Master wants Miss Maud,' said Wyat's disagreeable tones,
at the half-open door.

I followed in silence, with the pressure of a near alarm at my
heart, like a person going to an operation.

When I entered the room, my heart beat so fast that I could
hardly speak. The tall form of Uncle Silas rose before me, and
I made him a faltering reverence.

He darted from under his brows a wild, fierce glance at old

Wyat, and pointed to the door imperiously with his skeleton finger. The door shut, and we were alone.

'A chair ?' he said, pointing to a seat.

'Thank you, uncle, I prefer standing,' I faltered.

He also stood—his white head bowed forward, the phosphoric glare of his strange eyes shone upon me from under his brows—his finger-nails just rested on the table.

'You saw the luggage corded and addressed, as it stands ready for removal in the hall ?' he asked.

I had. Milly and I had read the cards which dangled from the trunk-handles and gun-case. The address was—' Mr. Dudley R. Ruthyn, Paris, *viâ* Dover.'

'I am old—agitated—on the eve of a decision on which much depends. Pray relieve my suspense. Is my son to leave Bartram to-day in sorrow, or to remain in joy ? Pray answer quickly.'

I stammered I know not what. I was incoherent—wild, perhaps ; but somehow I expressed my meaning—my unalterable decision. I thought his lips grew whiter and his eyes shone brighter as I spoke.

When I had quite made an end, he heaved a great sigh, and turning his eyes slowly to the right and the left, like a man in a helpless distraction, he whispered—

'God's will be done.'

I thought he was upon the point of fainting—a clay tint darkened the white of his face ; and, seeming to forget my presence, he sat down, looking with a despairing scowl on his ashy old hand, as it lay upon the table.

I stood gazing at him, feeling almost as if I had murdered the old man—he still gazing askance, with an imbecile scowl, upon his hand.

'Shall I go, sir ?' I at length found courage to whisper.

'Go ?' he said, looking up suddenly ; and it seemed to me as if a stream of cold sheet-lightning had crossed and enveloped me for a moment.

'Go ?—oh !—a—yes—*yes*, Maud—go. I must see poor Dudley before his departure,' he added, as it were, in soliloquy.

Trembling lest he should revoke his permission to depart, I glided quickly and noiselessly from the room.

Old Wyat was prowling outside, with a cloth in her hand, pretending to dust the carved doorcase. She frowned a stare of en-

quiry over her shrunken arm on me, as I passed. Milly, who
had been on the watch, ran and met me. We heard my uncle's
voice, as I shut the door, calling Dudley. He had been waiting,
probably, in the adjoining room. I hurried into my chamber,
with Milly at my side, and there my agitation found relief in
tears, as that of girlhood naturally does.

A little while after we saw from the window Dudley, looking,
I thought, very pale, get into a vehicle, on the top of which his
luggage lay, and drive away from Bartram.

I began to take comfort. His departure was an inexpressible
relief. His final departure ! a distant journey !

We had tea in Milly's room that night. Firelight and candles
are inspiring. In that red glow I always felt and feel more safe,
as well as more comfortable, than in the daylight—quite ir-
rationally, for we know the night is the appointed day of such
as love the darkness better than light, and evil walks thereby.
But so it is. Perhaps the very consciousness of external danger
enhances the enjoyment of the well-lighted interior, just as the
storm does that roars and hurtles over the roof.

While Milly and I were talking, very cosily, a knock came to
the room-door, and, without waiting for an invitation to enter,
old Wyat came in, and glowering at us, with her brown claw
upon the door-handle, she said to Milly—

'Ye must leave your funnin', Miss Milly, and take your turn
in your father's room.'

'Is he ill ? ' I asked.

She answered, addressing not me, but Milly—

'A wrought two hours in a fit arter Master Dudley went.
'Twill be the death o' him, I'm thinkin', poor old fellah. I wor
sorry myself when I saw Master Dudley a going off in the moist
to-day, poor fellah. There's trouble enough in the family without a' that ; but 'twon't be a family long, I'm thinkin'. Nout but
trouble, nout but trouble, since late changes came.'

Judging by the sour glance she threw on me as she said this,
I concluded that I represented those ' late changes' to which all
the sorrows of the house were referred.

I felt unhappy under the ill-will even of this odious old
woman, being one of those unhappily constructed mortals who
cannot be indifferent when they reasonably ought, and always
yearn after kindness, even that of the worthless.

' I must go. I wish you'd come wi' me, Maud, I'm so afraid all alone,' said Milly, imploringly.

' Certainly, Milly,' I answered, not liking it, you may be sure ; ' you shan't sit there alone.'

So together we went, old Wyat cautioning us for our lives to make no noise.

We passed through the old man's sitting-room, where that day had occurred his brief but momentous interview with me, and his parting with his only son, and entered the bed-room at the farther end.

A low fire burned in the grate. The room was in a sort of twilight. A dim lamp near the foot of the bed at the farther side was the only light burning there. Old Wyat whispered an injunction not to speak above our breaths, nor to leave the fireside unless the sick man called or showed signs of weariness. These were the directions of the doctor, who had been there.

So Milly and I sat ourselves down near the hearth, and old Wyat left us to our resources. We could hear the patient breathe ; but he was quite still. In whispers we talked ; but our conversation flagged. I was, after my wont, upbraiding myself for the suffering I had inflicted. After about half an hour's desultory whispering, and intervals, growing longer and longer, of silence, it was plain that Milly was falling asleep.

She strove against it, and I tried hard to keep her talking ; but it would not do—sleep overcame her ; and I was the only person in that ghastly room in a state of perfect consciousness.

There were associations connected with my last vigil there to make my situation very nervous and disagreeable. Had I not had so much to occupy my mind of a distinctly practical kind —Dudley's audacious suit, my uncle's questionable toleration of it, and my own conduct throughout that most disagreeable period of my existence,—I should have felt my present situation a great deal more.

As it was, I thought of my real troubles, and something of Cousin Knollys, and, I confess, a good deal of Lord Ilbury. When looking towards the door, I thought I saw a human face, about the most terrible my fancy could have called up, looking fixedly into the room. It was only a 'three-quarter,' and not the whole figure—the door hid that in a great measure, and I fancied I saw, too, a portion of the fingers. The face gazed toward the bed, and in the imperfect light looked like a livid mask, with chalky eyes.

I had so often been startled by similar apparitions formed by accidental lights and shadows disguising homely objects, that I stooped forward, expecting, though tremulously, to see this tremendous one in like manner dissolve itself into its harmless elements ; and now, to my unspeakable terror, I became perfectly certain that I saw the countenance of Madame de la Rougierre.

With a cry, I started back, and shook Milly furiously from her trance.

' Look ! look ! ' I cried. But the apparition or illusion was gone.

I clung so fast to Milly's arm, cowering behind her, that she could not rise.

' Milly ! Milly ! Milly ! Milly ! ' I went on crying, like one struck with idiotcy, and unable to say anything else.

In a panic, Milly, who had seen nothing, and could conjecture nothing of the cause of my terror, jumped up, and clinging to one another, we huddled together into the corner of the room, I still crying wildly, ' Milly ! Milly ! *Milly* ! ' and nothing else.

' What is it—where is it—what do you see ?' cried Milly, clinging to me as I did to her.

' It will come again ; it will come ; oh, heaven ! '

' What—what is it, Maud ? '

' The face ! the face ! ' I cried. ' Oh, Milly ! Milly ! Milly !'

We heard a step softly approaching the open door, and, in a horrible *sauve qui peut,* we rushed and stumbled together toward the light by Uncle Silas's bed. But old Wyat's voice and figure reassured us.

' Milly,' I said, so soon as, pale and very faint, I reached my apartment, ' no power on earth shall ever tempt me to enter that room again after dark.'

' Why, Maud dear, what, in Heaven's name, did you see ? ' said Milly, scarcely less terrified.

' Oh, I can't ; I can't ; I *can't,* Milly. Never ask me. It is haunted. The room is haunted *horribly.*'

' Was it Charke ? ' whispered Milly, looking over her shoulder, all aghast.

' No, no—don't ask me ; a fiend in a worse shape.' I was

relieved at last by a long fit of weeping; and all night good Mary Quince sat by me, and Milly slept by my side. Starting and screaming, and drugged with sal-volatile, I got through that night of supernatural terror, and saw the blessed light of heaven again.

Doctor Jolks, when he came to see my uncle in the morning, visited me also. He pronounced me very hysterical, made minute enquiries respecting my hours and diet, asked what I had had for dinner yesterday. There was something a little comforting in his cool and confident pooh-poohing of the ghost theory. The result was, a regimen which excluded tea, and imposed chocolate and porter, earlier hours, and I forget all beside; and he undertook to promise that, if I would but observe his directions, I should never see a ghost again.

CHAPTER L

MILLY'S FAREWELL

A few days' time saw me much better. Doctor Jolks was so contemptuously sturdy and positive on the point, that I began to have comfortable doubts about the reality of my ghost; and having still a horror indescribable of the illusion, if such it were, the room in which it appeared, and everything concerning it, I would neither speak, nor, so far as I could, think of it.

So, though Bartram-Haugh was gloomy as well as beautiful, and some of its associations awful, and the solitude that reigned there sometimes almost terrible, yet early hours, bracing exercise, and the fine air that predominates that region, soon restored my nerves to a healthier tone.

But it seemed to me that Bartram-Haugh was to be to me a vale of tears; or rather, in my sad pilgrimage, that valley of the shadow of death through which poor Christian fared alone and in the dark.

One day Milly ran into the parlour, pale, with wet cheeks, and, without saying a word, threw her arms about my neck, and burst into a paroxysm of weeping.

'What is it, Milly—what's the matter, dear—what is it?' I cried aghast, but returning her close embrace heartily.

'Oh! Maud—Maud darling, he's going to send me away.'

'Away, dear! *where* away? And leave me alone in this dreadful solitude, where he knows I shall die of fear and grief without you? Oh! no—no, it *must* be a mistake.'

'I'm going to France, Maud—I'm going away. Mrs. Jolks is going to London, day ar'ter to-morrow, and I'm to go wi' her; and an old French lady, he says, from the school will meet me there, and bring me the rest o' the way.'

'Oh—ho—ho—ho—ho—o—o—o!' cried poor Milly, hugging me closer still, with her head buried in my shoulder, and swaying me about like a wrestler, in her agony.

'I never wor away from home afore, except that little bit wi' you over there at Elverston; and you wor wi' me then, Maud; an' I love ye—better than Bartram—better than a'; an' I think I'll die, Maud, if they take me away.'

I was just as wild in my woe as poor Milly; and it was not until we had wept together for a full hour—sometimes standing —sometimes walking up and down the room—sometimes sitting and getting up in turns to fall on one another's necks,—that Milly, plucking her handkerchief from her pocket, drew a note from it at the same time, which, as it fell upon the floor, she at once recollected to be one from Uncle Silas to me.

It was to this effect :—

'I wish to apprise my dear niece and ward of my plans. Milly proceeds to an admirable French school, as a pensionnaire, and leaves this on Thursday next. If after three months' trial she finds it in any way objectionable, she returns to us. If, on the contrary, she finds it in all respects the charming residence it has been presented to me, you, on the expiration of that period, join her there, until the temporary complication of my affairs shall have been so far adjusted as to enable me to receive you once more at Bartram. Hoping for happier days, and wishing to assure you that three months is the extreme limit of your sep-

aration from my poor Milly, I have written this, feeling alas !
unequal to seeing you at present.
  ' Bartram, Tuesday.

  ' P.S.—I can have no objection to your apprising Monica
Knollys of these arrangements. You will understand, of course,
not a copy of this letter, but its substance.'

  Over this document, scanning it as lawyers do a new Act of
Parliament, we took comfort. After all, it was limited ; a separation not to exceed three months, possibly much shorter. On the
whole, too, I pleased myself with thinking Uncle Silas's note,
though peremptory, was kind.
  Our paroxysms subsided into sadness ; a close correspondence
was arranged. Something of the bustle and excitement of change
supervened. If it turned out to be, in truth, a ' charming residence,' how very delightful our meeting in France, with the
interest of foreign scenery, ways, and faces, would be !
  So Thursday arrived—a new gush of sorrow—a new brighten-
ing up—and, amid regrets and anticipations, we parted at the
gate at the farther end of the Windmill Wood. Then, of course,
were more good-byes, more embraces, and tearful smiles. Good
Mrs. Jolks, who met us there, was in a huge fuss ; I believe it
was her first visit to the metropolis, and she was in proportion
heated and important, and terrified about the train, so we had
not many last words.
  I watched poor Milly, whose head was stretched from the window, her hand waving many adieux, until the curve of the
road, and the clump of old ash-trees, thick with ivy, hid Milly,
carriage and all, from view. My eyes filled again with tears. I
turned towards Bartram. At my side stood honest Mary Quince.
  ' Don't take on so, Miss ; 'twon't be no time passing ; three
months is nothing at all,' she said, smiling kindly.
  I smiled through my tears and kissed the good creature, and
so side by side we re-entered the gate.
  The lithe young man in fustian, whom I had seen talking
with Beauty on the morning of our first encounter with that
youthful Amazon, was awaiting our re-entrance with the key
in his hand. He stood half behind the open wicket. One lean
brown cheek, one shy eye, and his sharp upturned nose, I saw

as we passed. He was treating me to a stealthy scrutiny, and seemed to shun my glance, for he shut the door quickly, and busied himself locking it, and then began stubbing up some thistles which grew close by, with the toe of his thick shoe, his back to us all the time.

It struck me that I recognised his features, and I asked Mary Quince.

'Have you seen that young man before, Quince?'

'He brings up game for your uncle, sometimes, Miss, and lends a hand in the garden, I believe.'

'Do you know his name, Mary?'

'They call him Tom, I don't know what more, Miss.'

'Tom,' I called; 'please, Tom, come here for a moment.'

Tom turned about, and approached slowly. He was more civil than the Bartram people usually were, for he plucked off his shapeless cap of rabbit-skin with a clownish respect.

'Tom, what is your other name,—Tom *what*, my good man?' I asked.

'Tom Brice, ma'am.'

'Haven't I seen you before, Tom Brice?' I pursued, for my curiosity was excited, and with it much graver feelings; for there certainly *was* a resemblance in Tom's features to those of the postilion who had looked so hard at me as I passed the carriage in the warren at Knowl, on the evening of the outrage which had scared that quiet place.

''Appen you may have, ma'am,' he answered, quite coolly, looking down the buttons of his gaiters.

'Are you a good whip—do you drive well?'

'I'll drive a plough wi' most lads hereabout,' answered Tom.

'Have you ever been to Knowl, Tom?'

Tom gaped very innocently.

'Anan,' he said.

'Here, Tom, is half-a-crown.'

He took it readily enough.

'That be very good,' said Tom, with a nod, having glanced sharply at the coin.

I can't say whether he applied that term to the coin, or to his luck, or to my generous self.

'Now, Tom, you'll tell me, have you ever been to Knowl?'

'Maught a' bin, ma'am, but I don't mind no sich place—no.'

As Tom spoke this with great deliberation, like a man who loves truth, putting a strain upon his memory for its sake, he spun the silver coin two or three times into the air and caught it, staring at it the while, with all his might.

'Now, Tom, recollect yourself, and tell me the truth, and I'll be a friend to you. Did you ride postilion to a carriage having a lady in it, and, I think, several gentlemen, which came to the grounds of Knowl, when the party had their luncheon on the grass, and there was a—a quarrel with the gamekeepers? Try, Tom, to recollect; you shall, upon my honour, have no trouble about it, and I'll try to serve you.'

Tom was silent, while with a vacant gape he watched the spin of his half-crown twice, and then catching it with a smack in his hand, which he thrust into his pocket, he said, still looking in the same direction—

'I never rid postilion in my days, ma'am. I know nout o' sich a place, though 'appen I maught a' bin there; Knowl, ye ca't. I was ne'er out o' Derbyshire but thrice to Warwick fair wi' horses be rail, an' twice to York.'

'You're certain, Tom?'

'Sartin sure, ma'am.'

And Tom made another loutish salute, and cut the conference short by turning off the path and beginning to hollo after some trespassing cattle.

I had not felt anything like so nearly sure in this essay at identification as I had in that of Dudley. Even of Dudley's identity with the Church Scarsdale man, I had daily grown less confident; and, indeed, had it been proposed to bring it to the test of a wager, I do not think I should, in the language of sporting gentlemen, have cared to 'back' my original opinion. There was, however, a sufficient uncertainty to make me uncomfortable; and there was another uncertainty to enhance the unpleasant sense of ambiguity.

On our way back we passed the bleaching trunks and limbs of several ranks of barkless oaks lying side by side, some squared by the hatchet, perhaps sold, for there were large letters and Roman numerals traced upon them in red chalk. I sighed as I passed them by, not because it was wrongfully done, for I really rather leaned to the belief that Uncle Silas was well advised in point of law. But, alas! here lay low the grand old family

decorations of Bartram-Haugh, not to be replaced for centuries
to come, under whose spreading boughs the Ruthyns of three
hundred years ago had hawked and hunted !

On the trunk of one of these I sat down to rest, Mary Quince
meanwhile pattering about in unmeaning explorations. While
thus listlessly seated, the girl Meg Hawkes, walked by, carrying
a basket.

' Hish ! ' she said quickly, as she passed, without altering a
pace or raising her eyes ; ' don't ye speak nor look—fayther
spies us ; I'll tell ye next turn.'

' Next turn'—when was that ? Well, she might be returning ;
and as she could not then say more than she had said, in merely
passing without a pause, I concluded to wait for a short time
and see what would come of it.

After a short time I looked about me a little, and I saw
Dickon Hawkes—Pegtop, as poor Milly used to call him—with
an axe in his hand, prowling luridly among the timber.

Observing that I saw him, he touched his hat sulkily, and
by-and-by passed me, muttering to himself. He plainly could
not understand what business I could have in that particular
part of the Windmill Wood, and let me see it in his countenance.

His daughter did pass me again ; but this time he was near,
and she was silent. Her next transit occurred as he was questioning Mary Quince at some little distance ; and as she passed
precisely in the same way, she said—

' Don't you be alone wi' Master Dudley nowhere for the
world's worth.'

The injunction was so startling that I was on the point of
questioning the girl. But I recollected myself, and waited in the
hope that in her future transits she might be more explicit. But
one word more she did not utter, and the jealous eye of old
Pegtop was so constantly upon us that I refrained.

There was vagueness and suggestion enough in the oracle to
supply work for many an hour of anxious conjecture, and many
a horrible vigil by night. Was I never to know peace at Bartram-
Haugh ?

Ten days of poor Milly's absence, and of my solitude, had
already passed, when my uncle sent for me to his room.

When old Wyat stood at the door, mumbling and snarling her message, my heart died within me.

It was late—just that hour when dejected people feel their anxieties most—when the cold grey of twilight has deepened to its darkest shade, and before the cheerful candles are lighted, and the safe quiet of the night sets in.

When I entered my uncle's sitting-room—though his window-shutters were open and the wan streaks of sunset visible through them, like narrow lakes in the chasms of the dark western clouds—a pair of candles were burning; one stood upon the table by his desk, the other on the chimneypiece, before which his tall, thin figure stooped. His hand leaned on the mantelpiece, and the light from the candle just above his bowed head touched his silvery hair. He was looking, as it seemed, into the subsiding embers of the fire, and was a very statue of forsaken dejection and decay.

' Uncle ! ' I ventured to say, having stood for some time unperceived near his table.

' Ah, yes, Maud, my dear child—my *dear* child.'

He turned, and with the candle in his hand, smiling his silvery smile of suffering on me. He walked more feebly and stiffly, I thought, than I had ever seen him move before.

' Sit down, Maud—pray sit there.'

I took the chair he indicated.

' In my misery and my solitude, Maud, I have invoked you like a spirit, and you appear.'

With his two hands leaning on the table, he looked across at me, in a stooping attitude ; he had not seated himself. I continued silent until it should be his pleasure to question or address me.

At last he said, raising himself and looking upward, with a wild adoration—his finger-tips elevated and glimmering in the faint mixed light—

' No, I thank my Creator, I am not quite forsaken.'

Another silence, during which he looked steadfastly at me, and muttered, as if thinking aloud—

' My guardian angel !—my guardian angel ! Maud, *you* have a heart.' He addressed me suddenly—' Listen, for a few moments, to the appeal of an old and broken-hearted man—your guardian—your uncle—your *suppliant*. I had resolved never to speak to you more on this subject. But I was wrong. It was pride that inspired me—mere pride.'

I felt myself growing pale and flushed by turns during the pause that followed.

'I'm very miserable—very nearly desperate. What remains for me—what remains? Fortune has done her worst—thrown in the dust, her wheels rolled over me; and the servile world, who follow her chariot like a mob, stamp upon the mangled wretch. All this had passed over me, and left me scarred and bloodless in this solitude. It was not my fault, Maud—I say it was no fault of mine; I have no remorse, though more regrets than I can count, and all scored with fire. As people passed by Bartram, and looked upon its neglected grounds and smokeless chimneys, they thought my plight, I dare say, about the worst a proud man could be reduced to. They could not imagine one half its misery. But this old hectic—this old epileptic—this old spectre of wrongs, calamities, and follies, had still one hope— my manly though untutored son—the last male scion of the Ruthyns. Maud, have I lost him? His fate—my fate—I may say *Milly's fate*;—we all await your sentence. He loves you, as none but the very young can love, and that once only in a life. He loves you desperately—a most affectionate nature—a Ruthyn, the best blood in England—the last man of the race; and I—if I lose him I lose all; and you will see me in my coffin, Maud, before many months. I stand before you in the attitude of a suppliant—shall I kneel?'

His eyes were fixed on me with the light of despair, his knotted hands clasped, his whole figure bowed toward me. I was inexpressibly shocked and pained.

'Oh, uncle! uncle!' I cried, and from very excitement I burst into tears.

I saw that his eyes were fixed on me with a dismal scrutiny. I think he divined the nature of my agitation; but he determined, notwithstanding, to press me while my helpless agitation continued.

'You see my suspense — you see my miserable and frightful suspense. You are kind, Maud; you love your father's memory; your pity your father's brother; you would not say no, and place a pistol at his head?'

'Oh! I must—I must—I *must* say no. Oh! spare me, uncle,

for Heaven's sake. Don't question me—don't press me. I could not—I *could* not do what you ask.'

'I yield, Maud—I yield, my dear. I will *not* press you; you shall have time, your *own* time, to think. I will accept *no* answer now—no, *none*, Maud.'

He said this, raising his thin hand to silence me.

'There, Maud, enough. I have spoken, as I always do to you, frankly, perhaps too frankly; but agony and despair will speak out, and plead, even with the most obdurate and cruel.'

With these words Uncle Silas entered his bed-chamber, and shut the door, not violently, but with a resolute hand, and I thought I heard a cry.

I hastened to my own room. I threw myself on my knees, and thanked Heaven for the firmness vouchsafed me; I could not believe it to have been my own.

I was more miserable in consequence of this renewed suit on behalf of my odious cousin than I can describe. My uncle had taken such a line of importunity that it became a sort of agony to resist. I thought of the possibility of my hearing of his having made away with himself, and was every morning relieved when I heard that he was still as usual. I have often wondered since at my own firmness. In that dreadful interview with my uncle I had felt, in the whirl and horror of my mind, on the very point of submitting, just as nervous people are said to throw themselves over precipices through sheer dread of falling.

CHAPTER LI

SARAH MATILDA COMES TO LIGHT

Some time after this interview, one day as I sat, sad enough, in my room, looking listlessly from the window, with good Mary Quince, whom, whether in the house or in my melancholy rambles, I always had by my side, I was startled by the sound of a loud and shrill female voice, in violent hysterical action, gabbling with great rapidity, sobbing, and very nearly screaming in a sort of fury.

I started up, staring at the door.

'Lord bless us!' cried honest Mary Quince, with round eyes and mouth agape, staring in the same direction.

'Mary—Mary, what can it be?'

'Are they beating some one down yonder? I don't know where it comes from,' gasped Quince.

'I will—I will—I'll see her. It's her I want. Oo—hoo—hoo—hoo —oo—o—Miss Maud Ruthyn of Knowl. Miss Ruthyn of Knowl. Hoo—hoo—hoo—hoo—oo!'

'What on earth can it be?' I exclaimed, in great bewilderment and terror.

It was now plainly very near indeed, and I heard the voice of our mild and shaky butler evidently remonstrating with the distressed damsel.

'I'll see her,' she continued, pouring a torrent of vile abuse upon me, which stung me with a sudden sense of anger. What had I done to be afraid of anyone? How dared anyone in my uncle's house—in *my* house—mix my name up with her detestable scurrilities?

'For Heaven's sake, Miss, don't ye go out,' cried poor Quince; 'it's some drunken creature.'

But I was very angry, and, like a fool as I was, I threw open the door, exclaiming in a loud and haughty key—

'Here is Miss Ruthyn of Knowl. Who wants to see her?'

A pink and white young lady, with black tresses, violent, weeping, shrill, voluble, was flouncing up the last stair, and shook her dress out on the lobby; and poor old Giblets, as Milly used to call him, was following in her wake, with many small remonstrances and entreaties, perfectly unheeded.

The moment I looked at this person, it struck me that she was the identical lady whom I had seen in the carriage at Knowl Warren. The next moment I was in doubt; the next, still more so. She was decidedly thinner, and dressed by no means in such lady-like taste. Perhaps she was hardly like her at all. I began to distrust all these resemblances, and to fancy, with a shudder, that they originated, perhaps, only in my own sick brain.

On seeing me, this young lady—as it seemed to me, a good

deal of the barmaid or lady's-maid species—dried her eyes
fiercely, and, with a flaming countenance, called upon me peremptorily to produce her 'lawful husband.' Her loud, insolent,
outrageous attack had the effect of enhancing my indignation,
and I quite forget what I said to her, but I well remember that
her manner became a good deal more decent. She was plainly
under the impression that I wanted to appropriate her husband,
or, at least, that he wanted to marry me ; and she ran on at
such a pace, and her harangue was so passionate, incoherent,
and unintelligible, that I thought her out of her mind : she was
far from it, however. I think if she had allowed me even a
second for reflection, I should have hit upon her meaning. As
it was, nothing could exceed my perplexity, until, plucking a
soiled newspaper from her pocket, she indicated a particular
paragraph, already sufficiently emphasised by double lines of
red ink at its sides. It was a Lancashire paper, of about six
weeks since, and very much worn and soiled for its age. I remember in particular a circular stain from the bottom of a
vessel, either of coffee or brown stout. The paragraph was as
follows, recording an event a year or more anterior to the date
of the paper :—

'MARRIAGE.—On Tuesday, August 7, 18—, at Leatherwig
Church, by the Rev. Arthur Hughes, Dudley R. Ruthyn, Esq.,
only son and heir of Silas Ruthyn, Esq., of Bartram-Haugh, Derbyshire, to Sarah Matilda, second daughter of John Mangles,
Esq., of Wiggan, in this county.'

At first I read nothing but amazement in this announcement,
but in another moment I felt how completely I was relieved ;
and showing, I believe, my intense satisfaction in my countenance—for the young lady eyed me with considerable surprise
and curiosity—I said—
' This is extremely important. You must see Mr. Silas Ruthyn
this moment. I am certain he knows nothing of it. I will conduct you to him.'
' No more he does—I know that myself,' she replied, following me with a self-asserting swagger, and a great rustling of
cheap silk.

As we entered, Uncle Silas looked up from his sofa, and closed his *Revue des Deux Mondes.*

' What is all this ? ' he enquired, drily.

' This lady has brought with her a newspaper containing an extraordinary statement which affects our family,' I answered.

Uncle Silas raised himself, and looked with a hard, narrow scrutiny at the unknown young lady.

' A libel, I suppose, in the paper ? ' he said, extending his hand for it.

' No, uncle—no ; only a marriage,' I answered.

' Not Monica ? ' he said, as he took it. ' Pah, it smells all over of tobacco and beer,' he added, throwing a little eau de Cologne over it.

He raised it with a mixture of curiosity and disgust, saying again ' pah,' as he did so.

He read the paragraph, and as he did his face changed from white, all over, to lead colour. He raised his eyes, and looked steadily for some seconds at the young lady, who seemed a little awed by his strange presence.

' And you are, I suppose, the young lady, Sarah Matilda *née* Mangles, mentioned in this little paragraph ? ' he said, in a tone you would have called a sneer, were it not that it trembled.

Sarah Matilda assented.

' My son is, I dare say, within reach. It so happens that I wrote to arrest his journey, and summon him here, some days since— some days since—some days since,' he repeated slowly, like a person whose mind has wandered far away from the theme on which he is speaking.

He had rung his bell, and old Wyat, always hovering about his rooms, entered.

' I want my son, immediately. If not in the house, send Harry to the stables ; if not there, let him be followed, instantly. Brice is an active fellow, and will know where to find him. If he is in Feltram, or at a distance, let Brice take a horse, and Master Dudley can ride it back. He must be here without the loss of one moment.'

There intervened nearly a quarter of an hour, during which whenever he recollected her, Uncle Silas treated the young lady with a hyper-refined and ceremonious politeness, which appeared to make her uneasy, and even a little shy, and certainly pre-

vented a renewal of those lamentations and invectives which he
had heard faintly from the stair-head.

But for the most part Uncle Silas seemed to forget us and
his book, and all that surrounded him, lying back in the corner
of his sofa, his chin upon his breast, and such a fearful shade
and carving on his features as made me prefer looking in any
direction but his.

At length we heard the tread of Dudley's thick boots on the
oak boards, and faint and muffled the sound of his voice as he
cross-examined old Wyat before entering the chamber of audience.

I think he suspected quite another visitor, and had no expectation of seeing the particular young lady, who rose from her
chair as he entered, in an opportune flood of tears, crying—

'Oh, Dudley, Dudley!—oh, Dudley, could you? Oh, Dudley,
your own poor Sal! You could not—you would not—your lawful
wife!'

This and a good deal more, with cheeks that streamed like a
window-pane in a thunder-shower, spoke Sarah Matilda with all
her oratory, working his arm, which she clung to, up and down
all the time, like the handle of a pump. But Dudley was, mani-
festly, confounded and dumbfoundered. He stood for a long time
gaping at his father, and stole just one sheepish glance at me;
and, with red face and forehead, looked down at his boots, and
then again at his father, who remained just in the attitude I
have described, and with the same forbidding and dreary intensity in his strange face.

Like a quarrelsome man worried in his sleep by a noise, Dudley suddenly woke up, as it were, with a start, in a half-sup-
pressed exasperation, and shook her off with a jerk and a
muttered curse, as she whisked involuntarily into a chair, with
more violence than could have been pleasant.

'Judging by your looks and demeanour, sir, I can almost anticipate your answers,' said my uncle, addressing him suddenly.
'Will you be good enough—pray, madame (parenthetically to
our visitor), command yourself for a few moments. Is this young
person the daughter of a Mr. Mangles, and is her name Sarah
Matilda?'

'I dessay,' answered Dudley, hurriedly.

'Is she your wife?'

'Is she my wife?' repeated Dudley, ill at ease.

'Yes, sir ; it is a plain question.'

All this time Sarah Matilda was perpetually breaking into talk, and with difficulty silenced by my uncle.

'Well, 'appen she says I am—does she?' replied Dudley.

'Is she your wife, sir?'

'Mayhap she so considers it, after a fashion,' he replied, with an impudent swagger, seating himself as he did so.

'What do *you* think, sir?' persisted Uncle Silas.

'I don't think nout about it,' replied Dudley, surlily.

'Is that account true?' said my uncle, handing him the paper.

'They wishes us to believe so, at any rate.'

'Answer directly, sir. We have our thoughts upon it. If it be true, it is capable of *every* proof. For expedition's sake I ask you. There is no use in prevaricating.'

'Who wants to deny it? It *is* true—there!'

'*There!* I knew he would,' screamed the young woman, hysterically, with a laugh of strange joy.

'Shut up, will ye?' growled Dudley, savagely.

'Oh, Dudley, Dudley, darling! what have I done?'

'Bin and ruined me, jest—that's all.'

'Oh! no, no, no, Dudley. Ye know I wouldn't. I could not—*could* not hurt ye, Dudley. No, no, no!'

He grinned at her, and, with a sharp side-nod, said—

'Wait a bit.'

'Oh, Dudley, don't be vexed, dear. I did not mean it. I would not hurt ye for all the world. Never.'

'Well, never mind. You and yours tricked me finely ; and now you've got me—that's all.'

My uncle laughed a very odd laugh.

'I knew it, of course ; and upon my word, madame, you and he make a very pretty couple,' sneered Uncle Silas.

Dudley made no answer, looking, however, very savage.

And with this poor young wife, so recently wedded, the low villain had actually solicited me to marry him!

I am quite certain that my uncle was as entirely ignorant as I of Dudley's connection, and had, therefore, no participation in this appalling wickedness.

'And I have to congratulate you, my good fellow, on having

secured the affections of a very suitable and vulgar young woman.'

'I baint the first o' the family as a' done the same,' retorted
Dudley.

At this taunt the old man's fury for a moment overpowered
him. In an instant he was on his feet, quivering from head to
foot. I never saw such a countenance—like one of those demon-
grotesques we see in the Gothic side-aisles and groinings—a
dreadful grimace, monkey-like and insane—and his thin hand
caught up his ebony stick, and shook it paralytically in the
air.

'If ye touch me wi' that, I'll smash ye, by ——— ! ' shouted
Dudley, furious, raising his hands and hitching his shoulder,
just as I had seen him when he fought Captain Oakley.

For a moment this picture was suspended before me, and I
screamed, I know not what, in my terror. But the old man, the
veteran of many a scene of excitement, where men disguise their
ferocity in calm tones, and varnish their fury with smiles, had
not quite lost his self-command. He turned toward me and
said—

'Does he know what he's saying ? '

And with an icy laugh of contempt, his high, thin forehead
still flushed, he sat down trembling.

'If you want to say aught, I'll hear ye. Ye may jaw me all ye
like, and I'll stan' it.'

'Oh, I may speak ? Thank you,' sneered Uncle Silas, glancing
slowly round at me, and breaking into a cold laugh.

'Ay, I don't mind cheek, not I ; but you must not go for to do
that, ye know. Gammon. I won't stand a blow—I won't fro *no*
one.

'Well, sir, availing myself of your permission to speak, I may
remark, without offence to the young lady, that I don't happen
to recollect the name Mangles among the old families of England. I presume you have chosen her chiefly for her virtues and
her graces.'

Mrs. Sarah Matilda, not apprehending this compliment quite
as Uncle Silas meant it, dropped a courtesy, notwithstanding
her agitation, and, wiping her eyes, said, with a blubbered
smile—

'You're very kind, sure.'

'I hope, for both your sakes, she has got a little money. I
don't see how you are to live else. You're too lazy for a gamekeeper; and I don't think you could keep a pot-house, you are
so addicted to drinking and quarrelling. The only thing I am
quite clear upon is, that you and your wife must find some other
abode than this. You shall depart this evening: and now, Mr.
and Mrs. Dudley Ruthyn, you may quit this room, if you
please.'

Uncle Silas had risen, and made them one of his old courtly
bows, smiling a death-like sneer, and pointing to the door with
his trembling fingers.

'Come, will ye?' said Dudley, grinding his teeth. 'You're
pretty well done here.'

Not half understanding the situation, but looking woefully
bewildered, she dropped a farewell courtesy at the door.

'Will ye *cut*?' barked Dudley, in a tone that made her jump;
and suddenly, without looking about, he strode after her from
the room.

'Maud, how shall I recover this? The vulgar *villain*—the *fool*!
What an abyss were we approaching! and for me the last hope
gone—and for me utter, utter, irretrievable ruin.'

He was passing his fingers tremulously back and forward along
the top of the mantelpiece, like a man in search of something,
and continued so, looking along it, feebly and vacantly, although
there was nothing there.

'I wish, uncle—you do not know how much I wish—I could
be of any use to you. Maybe I can?'

He turned, and looked at me sharply.

'Maybe you can,' he echoed slowly. 'Yes, maybe you can,' he
repeated more briskly. 'Let us—let us see—let us think—that
d—— fellow!—my head!'

'You're not well, uncle?'

'Oh! yes, very well. We'll talk in the evening—I'll send for
you.'

I found Wyat in the next room, and told her to hasten, as I
thought he was ill. I hope it was not very selfish, but such had
grown to be my horror of seeing him in one of his strange seizures, that I hastened from the room precipitately—partly to
escape the risk of being asked to remain.

The walls of Bartram House are thick, and the recess at the

doorway deep. As I closed my uncle's door, I heard Dudley's voice on the stairs. I did not wish to be seen by him or by his ' lady,' as his poor wife called herself, who was engaged in vehement dialogue with him as I emerged, and not caring either to re-enter my uncle's room, I remained quietly ensconced within the heavy door-case, in which position I overheard Dudley say with a savage snarl—

' You'll jest go back the way ye came. I'm not goin' wi' ye, if that's what ye be drivin' at—dang your impitins ! '

' Oh ! Dudley, dear, what have I done—what have I done—ye hate me so ? '

' What a' ye done ? ye vicious little beast, ye ! You've got us turned out an' disinherited wi' yer d——d bosh, that's all ; don't ye think it's enough ? '

I could only hear her sobs and shrill tones in reply, for they were descending the stairs ; and Mary Quince reported to me, in a horrified sort of way, that she saw him bundle her into the fly at the door, like a truss of hay into a hay-loft. And he stood with his head in at the window, scolding her, till it drove away.

' I knew he wor jawing her, poor thing ! by the way he kep' waggin' his head—an' he had his fist inside, a shakin' in her face I'm sure he looked wicked enough for anything ; an' she a crying like a babby, an' lookin' back, an' wavin' her wet hankicher to him—poor thing !—and she so young ! 'Tis a pity. Dear me ! I often think, Miss, 'tis well for me I never was married. And see how we all would like to get husbands for all that, though so few is happy together. 'Tis a queer world, and them that's single is maybe the best off after all.'

CHAPTER LII

THE PICTURE OF A WOLF

I went down that evening to the sitting-room which had been assigned to Milly and me, in search of a book—my good Mary Quince always attending me. The door was a little open, and I was startled by the light of a candle proceeding from the fire-side, together with a considerable aroma of tobacco and brandy.

On my little work-table, which he had drawn beside the hearth, lay Dudley's pipe, his brandy-flask, and an empty tumbler ; and he was sitting with one foot on the fender, his elbow on his knee, and his head resting in his hand, weeping. His back being a little toward the door, he did not perceive us ; and we saw him rub his knuckles in his eyes, and heard the sounds of his selfish lamentation.

Mary and I stole away quietly, leaving him in possession, wondering when he was to leave the house, according to the sentence which I had heard pronounced upon him.

I was delighted to see old 'Giblets' quietly strapping his luggage in the hall, and heard from him in a whisper that he was to leave that evening by rail—he did not know whither.

About half an hour afterwards, Mary Quince, going out to reconnoitre, heard from old Wyat in the lobby that he had just started to meet the train.

Blessed be heaven for that deliverance ! An evil spirit had been cast out, and the house looked lighter and happier. It was not until I sat down in the quiet of my room that the scenes and images of that agitating day began to move before my memory in orderly procession, and for the first time I appreciated, with a stunning sense of horror and a perfect rapture of thanksgiving, the value of my escape and the immensity of the danger which had threatened me. It may have been miserable weakness—I think it was. But I was young, nervous, and afflicted with a troublesome sort of conscience, which occasionally went mad, and insisted, in small things as well as great, upon sacrifices which my reason now assures me were absurd. Of Dudley I had a perfect horror ; and yet had that system of solicitation, that dreadful and direct appeal to my compassion, that placing of my feeble girlhood in the seat of the arbiter of my aged uncle's hope or despair, been long persisted in, my resistance might have been worn out—who can tell ?— and I self-sacrificed ! Just as criminals in Germany are teased, and watched, and cross-examined, year after year, incessantly, into a sort of madness ; and worn out with the suspense, the iteration, the self-restraint, and insupportable fatigue, they at last cut all short, accuse themselves, and go infinitely relieved to the scaffold—you may guess, then, for me, nervous, self-diffident, and alone, how intense was the comfort of knowing that Dudley was actually married, and the harrowing importunity which had just commenced for ever silenced.

That night I saw my uncle. I pitied him, though I feared him. I was longing to tell him how anxious I was to help him, if only he could point out the way. It was in substance what I had already said, but now strongly urged. He brightened ; he sat up perpendicularly in his chair with a countenance, not weak or fatuous now, but resolute and searching, and which contracted into dark thought or calculation as I talked.

I dare say I spoke confusedly enough. I was always nervous in his presence ; there was, I fancy, something mesmeric in the odd sort of influence which, without effort, he exercised over my imagination.

Sometimes this grew into a dismal panic, and Uncle Silas— polished, mild—seemed unaccountably horrible to me. Then it was no longer an accidental fascination of electro-biology. It was something more. His nature was incomprehensible by me. He was without the nobleness, without the freshness, without the softness, without the frivolities of such human nature as I had experienced, either within myself or in other persons. I instinctively felt that appeals to sympathies or feelings could no more affect him than a marble monument. He seemed to accommodate his conversation to the moral structure of others, just as spirits are said to assume the shape of mortals. There were the sensualities of the gourmet for his body, and there ended his human nature, as it seemed to me. Through that semi-transparent structure I thought I could now and then discern the light or the glare of his inner life. But I understood it not.

He never scoffed at what was good or noble—his hardest critic could not nail him to one such sentence ; and yet, it seemed somehow to me that his unknown nature was a systematic blasphemy against it all. If fiend he was, he was yet something higher than the garrulous, and withal feeble, demon of Goethe. He assumed the limbs and features of our mortal nature. He shrouded his own, and was a profoundly reticent Mephistopheles. Gentle he had been to me—kindly he had nearly always spoken ; but it seemed like the mild talk of one of those goblins of the desert, whom Asiatic superstition tells of, who appear in friendly shapes to stragglers from the caravan, beckon to them from afar, call them by their names, and lead them where they are found no more. Was, then, all his kindness but a phosphoric radiance covering something colder and more awful than the grave ?

' It is very noble of you, Maud—it is angelic ; your sympathy with a ruined and despairing old man. But I fear you will recoil. I tell you frankly that less than twenty thousand pounds will not extricate me from the quag of ruin in which I am entangled—lost ! '

' Recoil ! Far from it. I'll do it. There must be some way.'

' Enough, my fair young protectress—celestial enthusiast, enough. Though you do not, yet I recoil. I could not bring myself to accept this sacrifice. What signifies, even to me, my extrication ? I lie a mangled wretch, with fifty mortal wounds on my crown; what avails the healing of one wound, when there are so many beyond all cure ? Better to let me perish where I fall ; and reserve your money for the worthier objects whom, perhaps, hereafter may avail to save.'

' But I *will* do this. I must. I cannot see you suffer with the power in my hands unemployed to help you,' I exclaimed.

' Enough, dear Maud ; the will is here—enough : there is balm in your compassion and good-will. Leave me, ministering angel ; for the present I cannot. If you *will*, we can talk of it again. Good-night.'

And so we parted.

The attorney from Feltram, I afterwards heard, was with him nearly all that night, trying in vain to devise by their joint ingenuity any means by which I might tie myself up. But there were none. I could not bind myself.

I was myself full of the hope of helping him. What was this sum to me, great as it seemed? Truly nothing. I could have spared it, and never felt the loss.

I took up a large quarto with coloured prints, one of the few books I had brought with me from dear old Knowl. Too much excited to hope for sleep in bed, I opened it, and turned over the leaves, my mind still full of Uncle Silas and the sum I hoped to help him with.

Unaccountably one of those coloured engravings arrested my attention. It represented the solemn solitude of a lofty forest; a girl, in Swiss costume, was flying in terror, and as she fled flinging a piece of meat behind her which she had taken from a little market-basket hanging upon her arm. Through the glade a pack of wolves were pursuing her.

The narrative told, that on her return homeward with her marketing, she had been chased by wolves, and barely escaped by flying at her utmost speed, from time to time retarding, as she did so, the pursuit, by throwing, piece by piece, the contents of her basket, in her wake, to be devoured and fought for by the famished beasts of prey.

This print had seized my imagination. I looked with a curious interest on the print: something in the disposition of the trees, their great height, and rude boughs, interlacing, and the awful shadow beneath, reminded me of a portion of the Windmill Wood where Milly and I had often rambled. Then I looked at the figure of the poor girl, flying for her life, and glancing terrified over her shoulder. Then I gazed on the gaping, murderous pack, and the hoary brute that led the van; and then I leaned back in my chair, and I thought—perhaps some latent association suggested what seemed a thing so unlikely—of a fine print in my portfolio from Vandyke's noble picture of Belisarius. Idly I traced with my pencil, as I leaned back, on an envelope that lay upon the table, this little inscription. It was mere fiddling; and, absurd as it looked, there was nothing but an honest meaning in it:—' 20,000*l.* Date Obolum Belisario!' My dear father had translated the little Latin inscription for me, and I had written it down as a sort of exercise of memory; and also, perhaps, as expressive of that sort of compassion which my

uncle's fall and miserable fate excited invariably in me. So I
threw this queer little memorandum upon the open leaf of the
book, and again the flight, the pursuit, and the bait to stay it,
engaged my eye. And I heard a voice near the hearthstone, as
I thought, say, in a stern whisper, ' Fly the fangs of Belisarius ! '

' What's that ? ' said I, turning sharply to Mary Quince.

Mary rose from her work at the fireside, staring at me with
that odd sort of frown that accompanies fear and curiosity.

' You spoke ? Did you speak ? ' I said, catching her by the
arm, very much frightened myself.

' No, Miss ; no, dear ! ' answered she, plainly thinking that I
was a little wrong in my head.

There could be no doubt it was a trick of the imagination, and
yet to this hour I could recognise that clear stern voice among a
thousand, were it to speak again.

Jaded after a night of broken sleep and much agitation, I was
summoned next morning to my uncle's room.

He received me *oddly,* I thought. His manner had changed,
and made an uncomfortable impression upon me. He was gentle,
kind, smiling, submissive, as usual ; but it seemed to me that
he experienced henceforth toward me the same half-superstitous
repulsion which I had always felt from him. Dream, or voice,
or vision—which had done it ? There seemed to be an unconscious antipathy and fear. When he thought I was not looking,
his eyes were sometimes grimly fixed for a moment upon me.
When I looked at him, his eyes were upon the book before him ;
and when he spoke, a person not heeding what he uttered
would have fancied that he was reading aloud from it.

There was nothing tangible but this shrinking from the encounter of our eyes. I said he was kind as usual. He was even
more so. But there was this new sign of our silently repellant
natures. Dislike it could not be. He knew I longed to serve him.
Was it shame ? Was there not a shade of horror in it ?

' I have not slept,' said he. ' For me the night has passed in
thought, and the fruit of it is this—I *cannot,* Maud, accept your
noble offer.'

' I am *very* sorry,' exclaimed I, in all honesty.

' I know it, my dear niece, and appreciate your goodness ; but
there are many reasons—none of them, I trust, ignoble—and

which together render it impossible. No. It would be misunderstood—my honour shall not be impugned.'

' But, sir, that could not be ; you have never proposed it. It would be all, from first to last, *my* doing.'

' True, dear Maud, but I know, alas ! more of this evil and slanderous world than your happy inexperience can do. Who will receive our testimony ? None—no, not one. The difficulty— the insuperable moral difficulty is this—that I should expose myself to the plausible imputation of having worked upon you, unduly, for this end ; and more, that I could not hold myself quite free from blame. It is your voluntary goodness, Maud. But you are young, inexperienced ; and it is, I hold it, my duty to stand between you and any dealing with your property at so unripe an age. Some people may call this Quixotic. In my mind it is an imperious mandate of conscience ; and I peremptorily refuse to disobey it, although within three weeks an execution will be in this house !'

I did not quite know what an execution meant ; but from two harrowing novels, with whose distresses I was familiar, I knew that it indicated some direful process of legal torture and spoilation.

' Oh, uncle !—oh, sir !—you cannot allow this to happen. What will people say of me ? And—and there is poor Milly—and *everything* ! Think what it will be.'

' It cannot be helped—*you* cannot help it, Maud. Listen to me. There will be an execution here, I cannot say exactly how soon, but, I think, in a little more than a fortnight. I must provide for your comfort. You must leave. I have arranged that you shall join Milly, for the present, in France, till I have time to look about me. You had better, I think, write to your cousin, Lady Knollys. She, with all her oddities, has a heart. Can you say, Maud, that I have been kind ? '

' You have never been anything but kind,' I exclaimed.

' That I've been self-denying when you made me a generous offer ? ' he continued. ' That I now act to spare you pain ? You may tell her, not as a message from me, but as a fact, that I am seriously thinking of vacating my guardianship—that I feel I have done her an injustice, and that, so soon as my mind is a little less tortured, I shall endeavour to effect a reconciliation with her, and would wish ultimately to transfer the care of your person and education to *her*. You may say I have no longer an interest even in vindicating my name. My son has wrecked himself by a marriage. I forgot to tell you he stopped at Feltram, and this morning wrote to pray a parting interview. If I grant it, it shall be the last. I shall never see him or correspond with him more.'

The old man seemed much overcome, and held his hankerchief to his eyes.

' He and his wife are, I understand, about to emigrate ; the sooner the better,' he resumed, bitterly. ' Deeply, Maud, I regret having tolerated his suit to you, even for a moment. Had I thought it over, as I did the whole case last night, nothing could have induced me to permit it. But I have lived for so long like a monk in his cell, my wants and observation limited to the narrow compass of this chamber, that my knowledge of the world has died out with my youth and my hopes : and I did not, as I ought to have done, consider many objections. Therefore, dear Maud, on this one subject, I entreat, be silent ; its discussion can effect nothing now. I was wrong, and frankly ask you to forget my mistake.'

I had been on the point of writing to Lady Knollys on this odious subject, when, happily, it was set at rest by the disclosure of yesterday ; and being so, I could have no difficulty in acceding to my uncle's request. He was conceding so much that I could not withhold so trifling a concession in return.

' I hope Monica will continue to be kind to poor Milly after I am gone.'

Here there were a few seconds of meditation.

' Maud, you will not, I think, refuse to convey the substance of what I have just said in a letter to Lady Knollys, and perhaps you would have no objection to let me see it when it is written. It will prevent the possibility of its containing any misconception of what I have just spoken : and, Maud, you won't forget to say whether I have been kind. It would be a satisfaction to me to know that Monica was assured that I never either teased or bullied my young ward.'

With these words he dismissed me ; and forthwith I completed such a letter as would quite embody what he had said ; and in my own glowing terms, being in high good-humour with Uncle Silas, recorded my estimate of his gentleness and good-nature ;

and when I submitted it to him, he expressed his admiration of
what he was pleased to call my cleverness in so exactly con-
veying what he wished, and his gratitude for the handsome
terms in which I had spoken of my old guardian.

CHAPTER LIII

AN ODD PROPOSAL

As I and Mary Quince returned from our walk that day, and
had entered the hall, I was surprised most disagreeably by
Dudley's emerging from the vestibule at the foot of the great
staircase. He was, I suppose, in his travelling costume—a rather
soiled white surtout, a great coloured muffler in folds about his
throat, his 'chimney-pot' on, and his fur cap sticking out from
his pocket. He had just descended, I suppose, from my uncle's
room. On seeing me he stepped back, and stood with his shoulders to the wall, like a mummy in a museum.

I pretended to have a few words to say to Mary before leaving
the hall, in the hope that, as he seemed to wish to escape me, he
would take the opportunity of getting quickly off the scene.

But he had changed his mind, it would seem, in the interval ;
for when I glanced in that direction again he had moved toward us, and stood in the hall with his hat in his hand. I must
do him the justice to say he looked horribly dismal, sulky, and
frightened.

' Ye'll gi'e me a word, Miss—only a thing I ought to say—for
your good ; by ——, mind, it's for *your* good, Miss.'

Dudley stood a little way off, viewing me, with his hat in
both hands and a 'glooming' countenance.

I detested the idea of either hearing or speaking to him ; but
I had no resolution to refuse, and only saying ' I can't imagine
what you can wish to speak to me about,' I approached him.
' Wait there at the banister, Quince.'

There was a fragrance of alcohol about the flushed face and

gaudy muffler of this odious cousin, which heightened the effect
of his horribly dismal features. He was speaking, besides, a little
thickly ; but his manner was dejected, and he was treating me
with an elaborate and discomfited respect which reassured me.

' I'm a bit up a tree, Miss,' he said shuffling his feet on the oak
floor. ' I behaved a d—— fool ; but I baint one o' they sort.
I'm a fellah as 'ill fight his man, an' stan' up to 'm fair, don't
ye see ? An' I *baint* one o' they sort—no, *dang* it, I baint.'

Dudley delivered his puzzling harangue with a good deal of
undertoned vehemence, and was strangely agitated. He, too, had
got an unpleasant way of avoiding my eye, and glancing along
the floor from corner to corner as he spoke, which gave him a
very hang-dog air.

He was twisting his fingers in his great sandy whisker, and
pulling it roughly enough to drag his cheek about by that savage purchase ; and with his other hand he was crushing and
rubbing his hat against his knee.

' The old boy above there be half crazed, I think ; he don't
mean half as he says thof, not he. But I'm in a bad fix anyhow
—a regular sell it's been, and I can't get a tizzy out of him. So,
ye see, I'm up a tree, Miss ; and he sich a one, he'll make it a
wuss mull if I let him. He's as sharp wi' me as one o' them lawyer chaps, dang 'em, and he's a lot of I O's and rubbitch o' mine ;
and Bryerly writes to me he can't gi'e me my legacy, 'cause he's
got a notice from Archer and Sleigh a warnin' him not to gi'e
me as much as a bob ; for I signed it away to governor, he says—
which I believe's a lie. I may a' signed some writing—'appen
I did—when I was a bit cut one night. But that's no way to
catch a gentleman, and 'twon't stand. There's justice to be had,
and 'twon't *stand,* I say ; and I'm not in 'is hands that way. Thof
I may be a bit up the spout, too, I don't deny ; only I baint a-
goin' the whole hog all at once. I'm none o' they sort. He'll
find I baint.'

Here Mary Quince coughed demurely from the foot of the
stair, to remind me that the conversation was protracted.

' I don't very well understand,' I said gravely ; ' and I am now
going upstairs.'

' Don't jest a minute, Miss ; it's only a word, ye see. We'll be
goin' t' Australia, Sary Mangles, an' me, aboard the *Seamew,* on
the 5th. I'm for Liverpool to-night, and she'll meet me there,

an'—an', please God Almighty, ye'll never see me more ; an I'd rather gi'e ye a lift, Maud, before I go : an' I tell ye what, if ye'll just gi'e me your written promise ye'll gi'e me that twenty thousand ye were offering to gi'e the Governor, I'll take ye cleverly out o' Bartram, and put ye wi' your cousin Knollys, or anywhere ye like best.'

'Take me from Bartram—for twenty thousand pounds ! Take me away from my guardian ! You seem to forget, sir,' my indignation rising as I spoke, 'that I can visit my cousin, Lady Knollys, whenever I please.'

'Well, that is as it may be,' he said, with a sulky deliberation, scraping about a little bit of paper that lay on the floor with the toe of his boot.

'It *is* as it may be, and that is as I say, sir ; and considering how you have treated me—your mean, treacherous, and infamous suit, and your cruel treason to your poor wife, I am amazed at your effrontery.'

I turned to leave him, being, in truth, in one of my passions.

'Don't ye be a flying' out,' he said peremptorily, and catching me roughly by the wrist, 'I baint a-going to vex ye. What a mouth you be, as can't see your way ! Can't ye speak wi' common sense, like a woman—dang it—for once, and not keep brawling like a brat—can't ye see what I'm saying ? I'll take ye out o' all this, and put ye wi' your cousin, or wheresoever you list, if ye'll gi'e me what I say.'

He was, for the first time, looking me in the face, but with contracted eyes, and a countenance very much agitated.

'Money ?' said I, with a prompt disdain.

'Ay, money—twenty thousand pounds—*there*. On or off ?' he replied, with an unpleasant sort of effort.

'You ask my promise for twenty thousand pounds, and you shan't have it.'

My cheeks were flaming, and I stamped on the ground as I spoke.

If he had known how to appeal to my better feelings, I am sure I should have done, perhaps not quite that, all at once at least, but something handsome, to assist him. But this application was so shabby and insolent ! What could he take me for ? That I should suppose his placing me with Cousin Monica constituted her my guardian ? Why, he must fancy me the merest baby. There was a kind of stupid cunning in this that disgusted my good-nature and outraged my self-importance.

'You won't gi'e me that, then?' he said, looking down again, with a frown, and working his mouth and cheeks about as I could fancy a man rolling a piece of tobacco in his jaw.

'Certainly *not*, sir,' I replied.

'*Take* it, then,' he replied, still looking down, very black and discontented.

I joined Mary Quince, extremely angry. As I passed under the carved oak arch of the vestibule, I saw his figure in the deepening twilight. The picture remains in its murky halo fixed in memory. Standing where he last spoke in the centre of the hall, not looking after me, but downward, and, as well as I could see, with the countenance of a man who has lost a game, and a ruinous wager too—that is black and desperate. I did not utter a syllable on the way up. When I reached my room, I began to reconsider the interview more at my leisure. I was, such were my ruminations, to have agreed at once to his preposterous offer, and to have been driven, while he smirked and grimaced behind my back at his acquaintances, through Feltram in his dog-cart to Elverston; and then, to the just indignation of my uncle, to have been delivered up to Lady Knolly's guardianship, and to have handed my driver, as I alighted, the handsome fare of 20,000*l*. It required the impudence of Tony Lumpkin, without either his fun or his shrewdness, to have conceived such a prodigious practical joke.

'Maybe you'd like a little tea, Miss?' insinuated Mary Quince.

'What impertinence!' I exclaimed, with one of my angry stamps on the floor. 'Not you, dear old Quince,' I added. 'No —no tea just now.'

And I resumed my ruminations, which soon led me to this train of thought—'Stupid and insulting as Dudley's proposition was, it yet involved a great treason against my uncle. Should I be weak enough to be silent, may he not, wishing to forestal me, misrepresent all that has passed, so as to throw the blame altogether upon me?'

This idea seized upon me with a force which I could not withstand; and on the impulse of the moment I obtained admission to my uncle, and related exactly what had passed. When I had finished my narrative, which he listened to without once raising his eyes, my uncle cleared his throat once or twice, as if to speak. He was smiling—I thought with an effort, and with elevated brows. When I concluded, he hummed one of those sliding notes, which a less refined man might have expressed by a whistle of surprise and contempt, and again he essayed to speak, but continued silent. The fact is, he seemed to me very much disconcerted. He rose from his seat, and shuffled about the room in his slippers, I believe affecting only to be in search of something, opening and shutting two or three drawers, and turning over some books and papers ; and at length, taking up some loose sheets of manuscript, he appeared to have found what he was looking for, and began to read them carelessly, with his back towards me, and with another effort to clear his voice, he said at last—

'And pray, what could the fool mean by all that ? '

'I think he must have taken me for an idiot, sir,' I answered.

'Not unlikely. He has lived in a stable, among horses and ostlers ; he has always seemed to me something like a centaur—that is a centaur composed not of man and horse, but of an ape and an ass.'

And upon this jibe he laughed, not coldly and sarcastically, as was his wont, but, I thought, flurriedly. And, continuing to look into his papers, he said, his back still toward me as he read—

'And he did not favour you with an exposition of his meaning, which, except in so far as it estimated his deserts at the modest sum you have named, appears to me too oracular to be interpreted without a kindred inspiration ? '

And again he laughed. He was growing more like himself.

'As to your visiting your cousin, Lady Knollys, the stupid rogue had only five minutes before heard me express my wish that you should do so before leaving this. I am quite resolved you shall—that is, unless, dear Maud, you should yourself object ; but, of course, we must wait for an invitation, which, I conjecture, will not be long in coming. In fact, your letter will naturally bring it about, and, I trust, open the way to a permanent residence with her. The more I think it over, the more am I convinced, dear niece, that as things are likely to turn out, my roof would be no desirable shelter for you ; and that, under all circumstances, hers would. Such were my motives, Maud, in opening, through your letter, a door of reconciliation between us.'

I felt that I ought to have kissed his hand—that he had indicated precisely the future that I most desired ; and yet there was within me a vague feeling, akin to suspicion—akin to dismay which chilled and overcast my soul.

'But, Maud,' he said, 'I am disquieted to think of that stupid jackanapes presuming to make you such an offer ! A creditable situation truly—arriving in the dark at Elverston, under the solitary escort of that wild young man, with whom you would have fled from my guardianship ; and, Maud, I tremble as I ask myself the question, would he have conducted you to Elverston at all ? When you have lived as long in the world as I, you will appreciate its wickedness more justly.' Here there was a little pause.

'I know, my dear, that were he convinced of his legal marriage with that young woman,' he resumed, perceiving how startled I looked, 'such an idea, of course, would not have entered his head ; but he does not believe any such thing. Contrary to fact and logic, he does honestly think that his hand is still at his disposal ; and I certainly do suspect that he would have employed that excursion in endeavouring to persuade you to think as he does. Be that how it may, however, it is satisfactory to me to know that you shall never more be troubled by one word from that ill-regulated young man. I made him my adieux, such as they were, this evening ; and never more shall he enter the walls of Bartram-Haugh while we two live.'

Uncle Silas replaced the papers which had ostensibly interested him so much, and returned. There was a vein which was visible near the angle of his lofty temple, and in moments of agitation stood out against the surrounding pallor in a knotted blue cord ; and as he came back smiling askance, I saw this sign of inward tumult.

'We can, however, afford to despise the follies and knaveries of the world, Maud, as long as we act, as we have hitherto done, with perfect confidence in each other. Heaven bless you, dear Maud ! Your report troubled me, I believe, more than it need—troubled me a good deal ; but reflection assures me it is nothing. He is gone. In a few days' time he will be on the sea. I will issue my orders to-morrow morning, and he will never more, during his brief stay in England, gain admission to Bartram-Haugh. Good-night, my good niece ; I thank you.'

And so I returned to Mary Quince, on the whole happier than I had left her, but still with the confused and jarring vision I could not interpret perpetually rising before me ; and as, from time to time, shapeless anxieties agitated me, relieving them by appeals to Him who alone is wise and strong.

Next day brought me a goodnatured gossiping letter from dear Milly, written in compulsory French, which was, in some places, very difficult to interpret. She gave me a very pleasant account of the place, and her opinion of the girls who were inmates, and mentioned some of the nuns with high commendation. The language plainly cramped poor Milly's genius ; but although there was by no means so much fun as an honest English letter would have brought me, there could be no mistake about her liking the place, and she expressed her honest longing to see me in the most affectionate terms.

This letter came enclosed in one to my uncle, from the proper authority in the convent ; and as there was neither address within, nor post-mark without, I was as much in the dark as ever as to poor Milly's whereabouts.

Pencilled across the envelope of this letter, in my uncle's hand, were the words, ' Let me have your answer when sealed, and I will transmit it.—S. R.'

When, accordingly, some days later, I did place my letter to Milly in my uncle's hands, he told me the reason of his reserves on the subject.

' I thought it best, dear Maud, not to plague you with a secret, and Milly's present address is one. It will in a few weeks become the rallying-point of our diverse routes, when you shall meet her, and I join you both. Nobody, until the storm shall have blown over, must know where I am to be found, except my lawyer ; and I think you would prefer ignorance to the trouble of keeping a secret on which so much may depend.'

This being reasonable, and even considerate, I acquiesced.

In that interval there reached me such a charming, gay, and affectionate letter—a very *long* letter, too—though the writer was scarcely seven miles away, from dear Cousin Monica, full of pleasant gossip, and rose-coloured and golden castles in the air, and the kindest interest in poor Milly, and the warmest affection for me.

One other incident varied that interval, if possible more pleasantly than those. It was the announcement, in a Liverpool paper, of the departure of the *Seamew,* bound for Melbourne ; and among the passengers were reported ' Dudley Ruthyn, Esquire, of Bartram-H., and Mrs. D. Ruthyn.'

And now I began to breathe freely, I plainly saw the end of my probation approaching : a short excursion to France, a happy meeting with Milly, and then a delightful residence with Cousin Monica for the remainder of my nonage.

You will say then that my spirits and my serenity were quite restored. Not quite. How marvellously lie our anxieties, in filmy layers, one over the other ! Take away that which has lain on the upper surface for so long—the care of cares—the only one, as it seemed to you, between your soul and the radiance of Heaven—and straight you find a new stratum there. As physical science tells us no fluid is without its skin, so does it seem with this fine medium of the soul, and these successive films of care that form upon its surface on mere contact with the upper air and light.

What was my new trouble ? A very fantastic one, you will say —the illusion of a self-tormentor. It was the face of Uncle Silas which haunted me. Notwithstanding the old pale smile, there was a shrinking grimness, and the always-averted look.

Sometimes I fancied his mind was disordered. I could not account for the eerie lights and shadows that flickered on his face, except so. There was a look of shame and fear of me, amazing as that seems, in the sheen of his peaked smile.

I thought, ' Perhaps he blames himself for having tolerated Dudley's suit—for having urged it on grounds of personal distress —for having altogether lowered, though under sore temptation, both himself and his office ; and he thinks that he has forfeited my respect.'

Such was my analysis ; but in the *coup-d'œil* of that white face that dazzled me in darkness, and haunted my daily reveries with a faded light, there was an intangible character of the insidious and the terrible.

CHAPTER LIV

IN SEARCH OF MR. CHARKE'S SKELETON

On the whole, however, I was unspeakably relieved. Dudley Ruthyn, Esq., and Mrs. D. Ruthyn, were now skimming the blue waves on the wings of the *Seamew*, and every morning widened the distance between us, which was to go on increasing until it measured a point on the antipodes. The Liverpool paper containing this golden line was carefully preserved in my room ; and like the gentleman who, when much tried by the shrewish heiress whom he had married, used to retire to his closet and read over his marriage settlement, I used, when blue devils haunted me, to unfold my newspaper and read the paragraph concerning the *Seamew*.

The day I now speak of was a dismal one of sleety snow. My own room seemed to me cheerier than the lonely parlour, where I could not have had good Mary Quince so decorously.

A good fire, that kind and trusty face, the peep I had just indulged in at my favourite paragraph, and the certainty of soon seeing my dear cousin Monica, and afterwards affectionate Milly, raised my spirits.

' So,' said I, ' as old Wyat, you say, is laid up with rheumatism, and can't turn up to scold me, I think I'll run up stairs and make an exploration, and find poor Mr. Charke's skeleton in a closet.'

' Oh, law, Miss Maud, how can you say such things ! ' exclaimed good old Quince, lifting up her honest grey head and round eyes from her knitting.

I had grown so familiar with the frightful tradition of Mr. Charke and his suicide, that I could now afford to frighten old Quince with him.

' I am quite serious. I am going to have a ramble up-stairs

and down-stairs, like goosey-goosey-gander ; and if I do light upon
his chamber, it is all the more interesting. I feel so like Adelaide,
in the "Romance of the Forest," the book I was reading to you
last night, when she commenced her delightful rambles through
the interminable ruined abbey in the forest.'

' Shall I go with you, Miss ? '

' No, Quince ; stay there ; keep a good fire, and make some
tea. I suspect I shall lose heart and return very soon ; ' and with
a shawl about me, cowl fashion, over my head, I stole up-stairs.

I shall not recount with the particularity of the conscientious
heroine of Mrs. Ann Radcliffe, all the suites of apartments, corridors, and lobbies, which I threaded in my ramble. It will be
enough to mention that I lighted upon a door at the end of a
long gallery, which, I think, ran parallel with the front of the
house ; it interested me because it had the air of having been
very long undisturbed. There were two rusty bolts, which did
not evidently belong to its original securities, and had been,
though very long ago, somewhat clumsily superadded. Dusty and
rusty they were, but I had no difficulty in drawing them back.
There was a rusty key, I remember it well, with a crooked
handle in the lock ; I tried to turn it, but could not. My curiosity was piqued. I was thinking of going back and getting Mary
Quince's assistance. It struck me, however, that possibly it was
not locked, so I pulled the door and it opened quite easily. I
did not find myself in a strangely-furnished suite of apartments,
but at the entrance of a gallery, which diverged at right angles
from that through which I had just passed ; it was very imperfectly lighted, and ended in total darkness.

I began to think how far I had already come, and to consider
whether I could retrace my steps with accuracy in case of a
panic, and I had serious thoughts of returning.

The idea of Mr. Charke was growing unpleasantly sharp and
menacing ; and as I looked down the long space before me, losing itself among ambiguous shadows, lulled in a sinister silence,
and as it were inviting my entrance like a trap, I was very near
yielding to the cowardly impulse.

But I took heart of grace and determined to see a little more.
I opened a side-door, and entered a large room, where were, in
a corner, some rusty and cobwebbed bird-cages, but nothing
more. It was a wainscoted room, but a white mildew stained the

panels. I looked from the window : it commanded that dismal, weed-choked quadrangle into which I had once looked from another window. I opened a door at its farther end, and entered another chamber, not quite so large, but equally dismal, with the same prison-like look-out, not very easily discerned through the grimy panes and the sleet that was falling thickly outside. The door through which I had entered made a little accidental creak, and, with my heart at my lips, I gazed at it, expecting to see Charke, or the skeleton of which I had talked so lightly, stalk in at the half-open aperture. But I had an odd sort of courage which was always fighting against my cowardly nerves, and I walked to the door, and looking up and down the dismal passage, was reassured.

Well, one room more—just that whose deep-set door fronted me, with a melancholy frown, at the opposite end of the chamber. So to it I glided, shoved it open, advancing one step, and the great bony figure of Madame de la Rougierre was before me.

I could see nothing else.

The drowsy traveller who opens his sheets to slip into bed, and sees a scorpion coiled between them, may have experienced a shock the same in kind, but immeasurably less in degree.

She sat in a clumsy old arm-chair, with an ancient shawl about her, and her bare feet in a delft tub. She looked a thought more withered. Her wig shoved back disclosed her bald wrinkled forehead, and enhanced the ugly effect of her exaggerated features and the gaunt hollows of her face. With a sense of incredulity and terror I gazed, freezing, at this evil phantom, who returned my stare for a few seconds with a shrinking scowl, dismal and grim, as of an evil spirit detected.

The meeting, at least then and there, was as complete a surprise for her as for me. She could not tell how I might take it ; but she quickly rallied, burst into a loud screeching laugh, and, with her old Walpurgis gaiety, danced some fantastic steps in her bare wet feet, tracking the floor with water, and holding out with finger and thumb, in dainty caricature, her slammakin old skirt, while she sang some of her nasal patois with an abominable hilarity and emphasis.

With a gasp, I too recovered from the fascination of the surprise. I could not speak though for some seconds, and Madame was first.

'Ah, dear Maud, what surprise! Are we not overjoy, dearest, and cannot speak? I am full of joy—quite charmed—*ravie*—of seeing you. So are you of me, your face betray. Ah! yes, thou dear little baboon! here is poor Madame once more! Who could have imagine?'

'I thought you were in France, Madame,' I said, with a dismal effort.

'And so I was, dear Maud; I 'av just arrive. Your uncle Silas he wrote to the superioress for gouvernante to accompany a young lady—that is you, Maud—on her journey, and she send me; and so, ma chère, here is poor Madame arrive to charge herself of that affair.'

'How soon do we leave for France, Madame?' I asked.

'I do not know, but the old women—wat is her name?'

'Wyat,' I suggested.

'Oh! oui, Waiatt;—she says two, three week. And who conduct you to poor Madame's apartment, my dear Maud?' She inquired insinuatingly.

'No one, I answered promptly: 'I reached it quite accidentally, and I can't imagine why you should conceal yourself.' Something like indignation kindled in my mind as I began to wonder at the sly strategy which had been practised upon me.

'I 'av not conceal myself, Mademoiselle,' retorted the governness. 'I 'av act precisally as I 'av been ordered. Your uncle, Mr. Silas Ruthyn, he is afraid, Waiatt says, to be interrupted by his creditors, and everything must be done very quaitly. I have been commanded to avoid *me faire voir*, you know, and I must obey my employer—voilà tout!'

'And for how long have you been residing here?' I persisted, in the same resentful vein.

''Bout a week. It is soche triste place! I am so glad to see you, Maud! I've been so isolée, you dear leetle fool!'

'You are *not* glad, Madame; you don't love me—you never did,' I exclaimed with sudden vehemence.

'Yes, I am *very* glad; you know not, chère petite *niaise*, how I 'av desire to educate you a leetle more. Let us understand one another. You think I do not love you, Mademoiselle, because you have mentioned to your poor papa that little *dérèglement* in his library. I have repent very often that so great indiscretion of my life. I thought to find some letters of Dr. Braierly. I think that man was trying to get your property, my dear Maud, and if I had found something I would tell you all about. But it was very great *sottise,* and you were very right to denounce me to Monsieur. Je n'ai point de rancune contre vous. No, no, none at all. On the contrary, I shall be your *gardienne tutelaire* —wat you call ?—guardian angel—ah, yes, that is it. You think I speak *par dérision ;* not at all. No, my dear cheaile, I do not speak *par moquerie,* unless perhaps the very least degree in the world.'

And with these words Madame laughed unpleasantly, showing the black caverns at the side of her mouth, and with a cold, steady malignity in her gaze.

' Yes,' I said ; ' I know what you mean, Madame— you *hate* me.'

' Oh ! wat great ogly word ! I am shock ! *vous me faites honte.* Poor Madame, she never hate any one ; she loves all her friends, and her enemies she leaves to Heaven ; while I am, as you see, more gay, more *joyeuse* than ever, they have not been 'appy— no, they have not been fortunate these others. Wen I return, I find always some of my enemy they 'av die, and some they have put themselves into embarrassment, or there has arrived to them some misfortune ; ' and Madame shrugged and laughed a little scornfully.

A kind of horror chilled my rising anger, and I was silent.

' You see, my dear Maud, it is very natural you should think I hate you. When I was with Mr. Austin Ruthyn, at Knowl, you know you did not like a me—never. But in consequence of our intimacy I confide you that which I 'av of most dear in the world, my reputation. It is always so. The pupil can *calomniate,* without been discover, the gouvernante. 'Av I not been always kind to you, Maud ? Which 'av I use of violence or of sweet-ness the most ? I am, like other persons, *jalouse de ma réputa-tion ;* and it was difficult to suffer with patience the banishment which was invoked by you, because chiefly for your good, and for an indiscretion to which I was excited by motives the most pure and laudable. It was you who spied so cleverly—eh ! and denounce me to Monsieur Ruthyn ? Helas ! wat bad world it is ! '

' I do not mean to speak at all about that occurrence, Mad-ame ; I will not discuss it. I dare say what you tell me of the cause of your engagement here is true, and I suppose we must

travel, as you say, in company ; but you must know that the less
we see of each other while in this house the better.'

' I am not so sure of that, my sweet little *béte* ; your education
has been neglected, or rather entirely abandoned, since you 'av
arrive at this place, I am told. You must not be a *bestiole*. We
must do, you and I, as we are ordered. Mr. Silas Ruthyn he will
tell us.'

All this time Madame was pulling on her stockings, getting
her boots on, and otherwise proceeding with her dowdy toilet.
I do not know why I stood there talking to her. We often act
very differently from what we would have done upon reflection.
I had involved myself in a dialogue, as wiser generals than I
have entangled themselves in a general action when they meant
only an affair of outposts. I had grown a little angry, and would
not betray the least symptom of fear, although I felt that sensation profoundly.

' My beloved father thought you so unfit a companion for me
that he dismissed you at an hour's notice, and I am very sure
that my uncle will think as he did ; you are *not* a fit companion
for me, and had my uncle known what had passed he would
never have admitted you to this house—never ! '

' Helas ! *Quelle disgrace* ! And you really think so, my dear
Maud,' exclaimed Madame, adjusting her wig before her glass, in
the corner of which I could see half of her sly, grinning face,
as she ogled herself in it.

' I do, and so do you, Madame,' I replied, growing more
frightened.

' It may be—we shall see ; but everyone is not so cruel as you,
ma chère petite calomniatrice.'

' You shan't call me those names,' I said, in an angry tremor.

' What name, dearest cheaile ? '

' *Calomniatrice*—that is an insult.'

' Why, my most foolish little Maud, we may say rogue, and
a thousand other little words in play which we do not say
seriously.

' You are not playing—you never play—you are angry, and you
hate me,' I exclaimed, vehemently.

' Oh, fie !—wat shame ! Do you not perceive, dearest cheaile,
how much education you still need ? You are proud, little de-
moiselle ; you must become, on the contrary, quaite humble. Je

ferai baiser le babouin à vous—ha, ha, ha ! I weel make a you
to kees the monkey. You are too proud, my dear cheaile.'

'I am not such a fool as I was at Knowl,' I said ; 'you shall
not terrify me here. I will tell my uncle the whole truth,' I
said.

'Well, it may be that is the best,' she replied, with provoking
coolness.

'You think I don't mean it ?'

'Of course you *do*,' she replied.

'And we shall see what my uncle thinks of it.'

'We shall see, my dear," she replied, with an air of mock
contrition.

'Adieu, Madame ! '

'You are going to Monsieur Ruthyn ?—very good ! '

I made her no answer, but more agitated than I cared to show
her, I left the room. I hurried along the twilight passage, and
turned into the long gallery that opened from it at right angles.
I had not gone half-a-dozen steps on my return when I heard a
heavy tread and a rustling behind me.

'I am ready, my dear ; I weel accompany you,' said the smirking phantom, hurrying after me.

'Very well,' was my reply ; and threading our way, with a few
hesitations and mistakes, we reached and descended the stairs,
and in a minute more stood at my uncle's door.

My uncle looked hard and strangely at us as we entered. He
looked, indeed, as if his temper was violently excited, and glared
and muttered to himself for a few seconds ; and treating Madame
to a stare of disgust, he asked peevishly—

'Why am I disturbed, pray ? '

'Miss Maud a Ruthyn, she weel explain, ' replied Madame,
with a great courtesy, like a boat going down in a ground swell.

'*Will* you explain, my dear ? ' he asked, in his coldest and
most sarcastic tone.

I was agitated, and I am sure my statement was confused. I
succeeded, however, in saying what I wanted.

'Why, Madame, this is a grave charge ! Do you admit it,
pray ?'

Madame, with the coolest possible effrontery, denied it all ;
with the most solemn asseverations, and with streaming eyes
and clasped hands, conjured me melodramatically to withdraw

that intolerable story, and to do her justice. I stared at her for
a while astounded, and turning suddenly to my uncle, as vehemently asserted the truth of every syllable I had related.

'You hear, my dear child, you hear her deny everything ; what
am I to think ? You must excuse the bewilderment of my old
head. Madame de la—that lady has arrived excellently recom-
mended by the superioress of the place where dear Milly awaits
you, and such persons are particular. It strikes me, my dear niece,
that you must have made a mistake.'

I protested here. But he went on without seeming to hear
the parenthesis—

'I know, my dear Maud, that you are quite incapable of wil-
fully deceiving anyone ; but you are liable to be deceived like
other young people. You were, no doubt, very nervous, and but
half awake when you fancied you saw the occurrence you describe ; and Madame de—de ——'

'De la Rougierre,' I supplied.

'Yes, thank you—Madame de la Rougierre, who has arrived
with excellent testimonials, strenuously denies the whole thing.
Here is a conflict, my dear—in my mind a presumption of mistake. I confess I should prefer that theory to a peremptory as-
sumption of guilt.'

I felt incredulous and amazed ; it seemed as if a dream were
being enacted before me. A transaction of the most serious import, which I had witnessed with my own eyes, and described
with unexceptionable minuteness and consistency, is discredited
by that strange and suspicious old man with an imbecile coolness.
It was quite in vain my reiterating my statement, backing it
with the most earnest asseverations. I was beating the air. It did
not seem to reach his mind. It was all received with a simper of
feeble incredulity.

He patted and smoothed my head—he laughed gently, and
shook his while I insisted ; and Madame protested her purity in
now tranquil floods of innocent tears, and murmured mild and
melancholy prayers for my enlightenment and reformation. I
felt as if I should lose my reason.

'There now, dear Maud, we have heard enough ; it is, I do
believe, a delusion. Madame de la Rougierre will be your companion, at the utmost, for three or four weeks. Do exercise a
little of your self-command and good sense—you know how I am

tortured. Do not, I entreat, add to my perplexities. You may make yourself very happy with Madame if you will, I have no doubt.'

'I propose to Mademoiselle,' said Madame, drying her eyes with a gentle alacrity, 'to profit of my visit for her education. But she does not seem to weesh wat I think is so useful.'

'She threatened me with some horrid French vulgarism—*de faire baiser le babouin à moi,* whatever that means; and I know she hates me,' I replied, impetuously.

'Doucement—doucement!' said my uncle, with a smile at once amused and compassionate. 'Doucement! ma chère.'

With great hands and cunning eyes uplifted, Madame tearfully—for her tears came on short notice—again protested her absolute innocence. She had never in all her life so much as heard one so villain phrase.

'You see, my dear, you have misheard; young people never attend. You will do well to take advantage of Madame's short residence to get up your French a little, and the more you are with her the better.'

'I understand then, Mr. Ruthyn, you weesh I should resume my instructions?' asked Madame.

'Certainly; and converse all you can in French with Mademoiselle Maud. You will be glad, my dear, that I've insisted on it,' he said, turning to me, 'when you have reached France, where you will find they speak nothing else. And now, dear Maud—no, not a word more—you must leave me. Farewell, Madame!'

And he waved us out a little impatiently; and I, without one look toward Madame de la Rougierre, stunned and incensed, walked into my room and shut the door.

CHAPTER LV

THE FOOT OF HERCULES

I stood at the window—still the same leaden sky and feathery sleet before me—trying to estimate the magnitude of the discovery I had just made. Gradually a kind of despair seized me, and I threw myself passionately on my bed, weeping aloud.

Good Mary Quince was, of course, beside me in a moment, with her pale, concerned face.

' Oh, Mary, Mary, she's come—that dreadful woman, Madame de la Rougierre, has come to be my governess again ; and Uncle Silas won't hear or believe anything about her. It is vain talking ; he is prepossessed. Was ever so unfortunate a creature as I ? Who could have fancied or feared such a thing ? Oh, Mary, Mary, what am I to do ? what is to become of me ? Am I never to shake off that vindictive, terrible woman ? '

Mary said all she could to console me. I was making too much of her. What was she, after all, more than a governess ?—she could not hurt me. I was not a child no longer—she could not bully me now ; and my uncle, though he might be deceived for a while, would not be long finding her out.

Thus and soforth did good Mary Quince declaim, and at last she did impress me a little, and I began to think that I had, perhaps, been making too much of Madame's visit. But still imagination, that instrument and mirror of prophecy, showed her formidable image always on its surface, with a terrible moving background of shadows.

In a few minutes there was a knock at my door, and Madame herself entered. She was in walking costume. There had been a brief clearing of the weather, and she proposed our making a promenade together.

On seeing Mary Quince she broke into a rapture of compliment and greeting, and took what Mr. Richardson would have called her passive hand, and pressed it with wonderful tenderness.

Honest Mary suffered all this somewhat reluctantly, never smiling, and, on the contrary, looking rather ruefully at her feet.

'Weel you make a some tea? When I come back, dear Mary Quince, I 'av so much to tell you and dear Miss Maud of all my adventures while I 'av been away; it will make a you laugh ever so much. I was—what you theenk?—near, ever so near to be married!' And upon this she broke into a screeching laugh, and shook Mary Quince merrily by the shoulder.

I sullenly declined going out, or rising; and when she had gone away, I told Mary that I should confine myself to my room while Madame stayed.

But self-denying ordinances self-imposed are not always long observed by youth. Madame de la Rougierre laid herself out to be agreeable; she had no end of stories—more than half, no doubt, pure fictions—to tell, but all, in that triste place, amusing. Mary Quince began to entertain a better opinion of her. She actually helped to make beds, and tried to be in every way of use, and seemed to have quite turned over a new leaf; and so gradually she moved me, first to listen, and at last to talk.

On the whole, these terms were better than a perpetual skirmish; but, notwithstanding all her gossip and friendliness, I continued to have a profound distrust and even terror of her.

She seemed curious about the Bartram-Haugh family, and all their ways, and listened darkly when I spoke. I told her, bit by bit, the whole story of Dudley, and she used, whenever there was news of the *Seamew,* to read the paragraph for my benefit; and in poor Milly's battered little Atlas she used to trace the ship's course with a pencil, writing in, from point to point, the date at which the vessel was 'spoken' at sea. She seemed amused at the irrepressible satisfaction with which I received these minutes of his progress; and she used to calculate the distance;—on such a day he was two hundred and sixty miles, on such another five hundred; the last point was more than eight hundred—good, better, best—best of all would be those 'deleecious antipode, w'ere he would so soon promener on his head twelve thousand mile away;' and at the conceit she would fall into screams of laughter.

Laugh as she might, however, there was substantial comfort
in thinking of the boundless stretch of blue wave that rolled between me and that villainous cousin.

I was now on very odd terms with Madame. She had not
relapsed into her favourite vein of oracular sarcasm and menace ;
she had, on the contrary, affected her good-humoured and genial vein. But I was not to be deceived by this. I carried in my
heart that deep-seated fear of her which her unpleasant good-
humour and gaiety never disturbed for a moment. I was very
glad, therefore, when she went to Todcaster by rail, to make
some purchases for the journey which we were daily expecting to
commence ; and happy in the opportunity of a walk, good old
Mary Quince and I set forth for a little ramble.

As I wished to make some purchases in Feltram, I set out,
with Mary Quince for my companion. On reaching the great gate
we found it locked. The key, however, was in it, and as it required more than the strength of my hand to turn, Mary tried
it. At the same moment old Crowle came out of the sombre
lodge by its side, swallowing down a mouthful of his dinner in
haste. No one, I believe, liked the long suspicious face of the
old man, seldom shorn or washed, and furrowed with great,
grimy perpendicular wrinkles. Leering fiercely at Mary, not pretending to see me, he wiped his mouth hurriedly with the back
of his hand, and growled—

'Drop it.'

'Open it, please, Mr. Crowle,' said Mary, renouncing the
task.

Crowle wiped his mouth as before, looking inauspicious ; shuffling to the spot, and muttering to himself, he first satisfied
himself that the lock was fast, and then lodged the key in his
coat-pocket, and still muttering, retraced his steps.

'We want the gate open, please,' said Mary.

No answer.

'Miss Maud wants to go into the town,' she insisted.

'We wants many a thing we can't get,' he growled, stepping
into his habitation.

'Please open the gate,' I said, advancing.

He half turned on his threshold, and made a dumb show of
touching his hat, although he had none on.

' Can't, ma'am ; without an order from maister, no one goes
out here.'

' You won't allow me and my maid to pass the gate ? ' I said.

' 'Tisn't *me,* ma'am,' said he ; ' but I can't break orders, and no
one goes out without the master allows.'

And without awaiting further parley, he entered, shutting
his hatch behind him.

So Mary and I stood, looking very foolish at one another.
This was the first restraint I had experienced since Milly and I
had been refused a passage through the Windmill paling. The
rule, however, on which Crowle insisted I felt confident could
not have been intended to apply to me. A word to Uncle Silas
would set all right ; and in the meantime I proposed to Mary
that we should take a walk—my favourite ramble—into the
Windmill Wood.

I looked toward Dickon's farmstead as we passed, thinking
that Beauty might have been there. I did see the girl, who was
plainly watching us. She stood in the doorway of the cottage,
withdrawn into the shade, and, I fancied, anxious to escape observation. When we had passed on a little, I was confirmed
in that belief by seeing her run down the footpath which led
from the rear of the farmyard in the direction contrary to that
in which we were moving.

' So,' I thought, ' poor Meg falls from me ! '

Mary Quince and I rambled on through the wood, till we
reached the windmill itself, and seeing its low arched door open,
we entered the chiaro-oscuro of its circular basement. As we
did so I heard a rush and the creak of a plank, and looking up,
I saw just a foot—no more—disappearing through the trap-door.

In the case of one we love or fear intensely, what feats of comparative anatomy will not the mind unconsciously perform ? con-
structing the whole living animal from the turn of an elbow,
the curl of a whisker, a segment of a hand. How instantaneous
and unerring is the instinct !

' Oh, Mary, what have I seen ! ' I whispered, recovering from
the fascination that held my gaze fast to the topmost rounds of
the ladder, that disappeared in the darkness above the open door
in the loft. ' Come, Mary—come away.'

At the same instant appeared the swarthy, sullen face of
Dickon Hawkes in the shadow of the aperture. Having but one

serviceable leg, his descent was slow and awkward, and having
got his head to the level of the loft he stopped to touch his hat
to me, and to hasp and lock the trap-door.

When this was done, the man again touched his hat, and
looked steadily and searchingly at me for a second or so, while
he got the key into his pocket.

'These fellahs stores their flour too long 'ere, ma'am. There's
a deal o' trouble a-looking arter it. I'll talk wi' Silas, and settle
that.'

By this time he had got upon the worn-tiled floor, and touching his hat again, he said—

'I'm a-goin' to lock the door, ma'am!'

So with a start, and again whispering—

'Come, Mary—come away'—

With my arm fast in hers, we made a swift departure.

'I feel very faint, Mary,' said I. 'Come quickly. There's nobody following us?'

'No, Miss, dear. That man with the wooden leg is putting a
padlock on the door.'

'Come *very* fast,' I said; and when we had got a little farther,
I said, 'Look again, and see whether anyone is following.'

'No one, Miss,' answered Mary, plainly surprised. 'He's putting the key in his pocket, and standin' there a-lookin' after us.'

'Oh, Mary, did not you see it?'

'What, Miss?' asked Mary, almost stopping.

'Come on, Mary. Don't pause. They will observe us,' I whispered, hurrying her forward.

'What did you see, Miss?' repeated Mary.

'*Mr. Dudley*,' I whispered, with a terrified emphasis, not daring to turn my head as I spoke.

'Lawk, Miss!' remonstrated honest Quince, with a protracted
intonation of wonder and incredulity, which plainly implied a
suspicion that I was dreaming.

'Yes, Mary. When we went into that dreadful room—that
dark, round place—I saw his foot on the ladder. *His* foot, Mary
I can't be mistaken. *I won't be questioned.* You'll *find* I'm right.
He's *here*. He never went in that ship at all. A fraud has been
practised on me—it is infamous—it is terrible. I'm frightened out
of my life. For heaven's sake, look back again, and tell me what
you see.'

'*Nothing*, Miss,' answered Mary, in contagious whispers, 'but that wooden-legged chap, standin' hard by the door.'

'And no one with him?'

'No one, Miss.'

We got without pursuit through the gate in the paling. I drew breath so soon as we had reached the cover of the thicket near the chestnut hollow, and I began to reflect that whoever the owner of the foot might be—and I was still instinctively certain that it was no other than Dudley—concealment was plainly his object. I need not, then, be at all uneasy lest he should pursue us.

As we walked slowly and in silence along the grassy footpath, I heard a voice calling my name from behind. Mary Quince had not heard it at all, but I was quite certain.

It was repeated twice or thrice, and, looking in considerable doubt and trepidation under the hanging boughs, I saw Beauty, not ten yards away, standing among the underwood.

I remember how white the eyes and teeth of the swarthy girl looked, as with hand uplifted toward her ear, she watched us while, as it seemed, listening for more distant sounds.

Beauty beckoned eagerly to me, advancing, with looks of great fear and anxiety, two or three short steps toward me.

'*She* baint to come,' said Beauty, under her breath, so soon as I had nearly reached her, pointing without raising her hand at Mary Quince.

'Tell her to sit on the ash-tree stump down yonder, and call ye as loud as she can if she sees any fellah a-comin' this way, an' rin ye back to me;' and she impatiently beckoned me away on her errand.

When I returned, having made this dispositions, I perceived how pale the girl was.

'Are you ill, Meg?' I asked.

'Never ye mind. Well enough. Listen, Miss; I must tell it all in a crack, an' if she calls, rin awa' to her, and le' me to myself, for if fayther or t'other un wor to kotch me here, I think they'd kill me a'most. Hish!'

She paused a second, looking askance, in the direction where she fancied Mary Quince was. Then she resumed in a whisper—

'Now, lass, mind ye, ye'll keep what I say to yourself. You're

not to tell that un nor any other for your life, mind, a word o'
what I'm goin' to tell ye.'

'I'll not say a word. Go on.'

'Did ye see Dudley?'

'I think I saw him getting up the ladder.'

'In the mill? Ha! that's him. He never went beyond Todcaster. He staid in Feltram arter.'

It was my turn to look pale now. My worst conjecture was
established.

CHAPTER LVI

I CONSPIRE

'That's a bad un, he is—oh, Miss, Miss Maud! It's nout that's
good as keeps him an' fayther—(mind, lass, ye promised you
would not tell no one)—as keeps them two a-talkin' and a-
smokin' secret-like together in the mill. An' fayther don't know I
found him out. They don't let me into the town, but Brice tells
me, and he knows it's Dudley; and it's nout that's good, but
summat very bad. An' I reckon, Miss, it's all about you. Be ye
frightened, Miss Maud?'

I felt on the point of fainting, but I rallied.

'Not much, Meg. Go on, for Heaven's sake. Does Uncle Silas
know he is here?'

'Well, Miss, they were with him, Brice told me, from eleven
o'clock to nigh one o' Tuesday night, an' went in and come out
like thieves, 'feard ye'd see 'em.'

'And how does Brice know anything bad?' I asked, with a
strange freezing sensation creeping from my heels to my head
and down again—I am sure deadly pale, but speaking very col-
lectedly.

'Brice said, Miss, he saw Dudley a-cryin' and lookin' awful
black, and says he to fayther, " 'Tisn't in my line nohow, an' I
can't;" and says fayther to he, "No one likes they soart o'

things, but how can ye help it ? The old boy's behind ye wi'
his pitchfork, and ye canna stop." An' wi' that he bethought
him o' Brice, and says he, " What be ye a-doin' there ? Get
ye down wi' the nags to blacksmith, do ye." An' oop gits Dudley,
pullin' his hat ower his brows, an' says he, "I wish I was in the
Seamew. I'm good for nout wi' this thing a-hangin' ower me."
An' that's all as Brice heard. An' he's afeard o' fayther and
Dudley awful. Dudley could lick him to pot if he crossed him,
and he and fayther 'ud think nout o' havin' him afore the
justices for poachin', and swearin' him into gaol."

' But why does he think it's about *me*?'

' Hish ! ' said Meg, who fancied she heard a sound, but all was
quiet. ' I can't say—we're in danger, lass. I don't know why—
but *he* does, an' so do I, an', for that matter, so do *ye*.'

' Meg, I'll leave Bartram.'

' Ye can't.'

' Can't. What do you mean, girl ? '

' They won't let ye oot. The gates is all locked. They've dogs
—they've bloodhounds, Brice says. Ye *can't* git oot, mind ; put
that oot o' your head.

' I tell ye what ye'll do. Write a bit o' a note to the lady
yonder at Elverston ; an' though Brice be a wild fellah, and
'appen not ower good sometimes, he likes me, an' I'll make him
take it. Fayther will be grindin' at mill to-morrow. Coom ye
here about one o'clock—that's if ye see the mill-sails a-turnin'—
and me and Brice will meet ye here. Bring that old lass wi' ye.
There's an old French un, though, that talks wi' Dudley. Mind
ye, that un knows nout o' the matter. Brice be a kind lad to me,
whatsoe'er he be wi' others, and I think he won't split. Now,
lass, I must go. God help ye ; God bless ye; an', for the world's
wealth, don't ye let one o' them see ye've got ought in your head,
not even that un.'

Before I could say another word, the girl had glided from me,
with a wild gesture of silence, and a shake of her head.

I can't at all account for the state in which I was. There are
resources both of energy and endurance in human nature which
we never suspect until the tremendous voice of necessity summons them into play. Petrified with a totally new horror, but
with something of the coldness and impassiveness of the trans-

formation, I stood, spoke, and acted—a wonder, almost a terror, to myself.

I met Madame on my return as if nothing had happened. I heard her ugly gabble, and looked at the fruits of her hour's shopping, as I might hear, and see, and talk, and smile, in a dream.

But the night was dreadful. When Mary Quince and I were alone, I locked the door. I continued walking up and down the room, with my hands clasped, looking at the inexorable floor, the walls, the ceiling, with a sort of imploring despair. I was afraid to tell my dear old Mary. The least indiscretion would be failure, and failure destruction.

I answered her perplexed solicitudes by telling her that I was not very well—that I was uneasy ; but I did not fail to extract from her a promise that she would not hint to mortal, either my suspicions about Dudley, or our rencontre with Meg Hawkes.

I remember how, when, after we had got, late at night, into bed, I sat up, shivering with horror, in mine, while honest Mary's tranquil breathing told how soundly she slept. I got up, and looked from the window, expecting to see some of those wolfish dogs which they had brought to the place prowling about the court-yard. Sometimes I prayed, and felt tranquil-lised, and fancied that I was perhaps to have a short interval of sleep. But the serenity was delusive, and all the time my nerves were strung hysterically. Sometimes I felt quite wild, and on the point of screaming. At length that dreadful night passed away. Morning came, and a less morbid, though hardly a less terrible state of mind. Madame paid me an early visit. A thought struck me. I knew that she loved shopping, and I said, quite carelessly—

' Your yesterday's shopping tempts me, Madame, and I must get a few things before we leave for France. Suppose we go into Feltram to-day, and make my purchases, you and I ? '

She looked from the corner of her cunning eye in my face without answering. I did not blench, and she said—

' Vary good. I would be vary 'appy,' and again she looked oddly at me.

' Wat hour, my dear Maud ? One o'clock ? I think that weel de very well, eh ? '

I assented, and she grew silent.

I wonder whether I did look as careless as I tried. I do not know. Through the whole of this awful period I was, I think, supernatural ; and I even now look back with wonder upon my strange self-command.

Madame, I hoped, had heard nothing of the order which pro-hibited my exit from the place. She would herself conduct me to Feltram, and secure, by accompanying me, my free egress.

Once in Feltram, I would assert my freedom, and manage to reach my dear cousin Knollys. Back to Bartram no power should convey me. My heart swelled and fluttered in the awful sus-pense of that hour.

Oh, Bartram-Haugh ! how came you by those lofty walls ? Which of my ancestors had begirt me with an impassable barrier in this horrible strait ?

Suddenly I remembered my letter to Lady Knollys. If I were disappointed in effecting my escape through Feltram, all would depend upon it.

Having locked my door, I wrote as follows :—

' Oh, my beloved cousin, as you hope for comfort in *your* hour of fear, aid me now. Dudley has returned, and is secreted somewhere about the grounds. It is a *fraud.* They all pretend to me that he is gone away in the *Seamew* ; and he or they had his name published as one of the passengers. Madame de la Rougierre has appeared ! She is here, and my uncle insists on making her my close companion. I am at my wits' ends. I can-not escape—the walls are a prison ; and I believe the eyes of my gaolers are always upon me. Dogs are kept for pursuit—yes, *dogs* ! and the gates are locked against my escape. God help me ! I don't know where to look, or whom to trust. I fear my uncle more than all. I think I could bear this better if I knew what their plans are, even the worst. If ever you loved or pitied me, dear cousin, I conjure you, help me in this extremity. Take me away from this. Oh, darling, for God's sake take me away !

' Your distracted and terrified cousin,
MAUD '

' Bartram-Haugh.'

I sealed this letter jealously, as if the inanimate missive would burst its cerements, and proclaim my desperate appeal through all the chambers and passages of silent Bartram.

Old Quince, greatly to cousin Monica's amusement, persisted in furnishing me with those capacious pockets which belonged to a former generation. I was glad of this old-world eccentricity now, and placed my guilty letter, that, amidst all my hypocrisies, spoke out with terrible frankness, deep in this receptacle, and having hid away the pen and ink, my accomplices, I opened the door, and resumed my careless looks, awaiting Madame's return.

' I was to demand to Mr. Ruthyn the permission to go to Feltram, and I think he will allow. He want to speak to you.'

With Madame I entered my uncle's room. He was reclining on a sofa, his back towards us, and his long white hair, as fine as spun glass, hung over the back of the couch.

' I was going to ask you, dear Maud, to execute two or three little commissions for me in Feltram.'

My dreadful letter felt lighter in my pocket, and my heart beat violently.

' But I have just recollected that this is a market-day, and Feltram will be full of doubtful characters and tipsy persons, so we must wait till to-morrow ; and Madame says, very kindly, that she will, as she does not so much mind, make any little purchases to-day which cannot conveniently wait.'

Madame assented with a courtesy to Uncle Silas, and a great hollow smile to me.

By this time Uncle Silas had raised himself from his reclining posture, and was sitting, gaunt and white, upon the sofa.

' News of my prodigal to-day,' he said, with a peevish smile, drawing the newspaper towards him. ' The vessel has been spoken again. How many miles away, do you suppose ? '

He spoke in a plaintive key, looking at me, with hungry eyes, and a horribly smiling countenance.

' How far do you suppose Dudley is to-day ? ' and he laid the palm of his hand on the paragraph as he spoke. *Guess* ! '

For a moment I fancied this was a theatric preparation to give point to the disclosure of Dudley's real whereabouts.

' It was a very long way. Guess ! ' he repeated.

So, stammering a little and pale, I performed the required hypocrisy, after which my uncle read aloud for my benefit the line or two in which were recorded the event, and the latitude and longitude of the vessel at the time, of which Madame made a note in her memory, for the purpose of making her usual tracing in poor Milly's Atlas.

I cannot say how it really was, but I fancied that Uncle Silas was all the time reading my countenance, with a grim and practised scrutiny; but nothing came of it, and we were dismissed.

Madame loved shopping, even for its own sake, but shopping with opportunities of peculation still more. She she had had her luncheon, and was dressed for the excursion, she did precisely what I now most desired—she proposed to take charge of my commissions and my money; and thus entrusted, left me at liberty to keep tryst at the Chestnut Hollow.

So soon as I had seen Madame fairly off, I hurried Mary Quince, and got my things on quickly. We left the house by the side entrance, which I knew my uncle's windows did not command. Glad was I to feel a slight breeze, enough to make the mill-sails revolve; and as we got further into the grounds, and obtained a distant view of the picturesque old windmill, I felt inexpressibly relieved on seeing that it was actually working.

We were now in the Chestnut Hollow, and I sent Mary Quince to her old point of observation, which commanded a view of the path in the direction of the Windmill Wood, with her former order to call 'I've found it,' as loudly as she could, in case she should see anyone approaching.

I stopped at the point of our yesterday's meeting. I peered under the branches, and my heart beat fast as I saw Meg Hawkes awaiting me.

CHAPTER LVII

THE LETTER

'Come away, lass,' whispered Beauty, very pale; 'he's here —Tom Brice.'

And she led the way, shoving aside the leafless underwood, and we reached Tom. The slender youth, groom or poacher— he might answer for either—with his short coat and gaitered legs, was sitting on a low horizontal bough, with his shoulder against the trunk.

'*Don't* ye mind; sit ye still, lad,' said Meg, observing that he was preparing to rise, and had entangled his hat in the boughs. 'Sit ye still, and hark to the lady. He'll take it, Miss Maud, if he can; wi' na ye, lad?'

'E'es, I'll take it,' he replied, holding out his hand.

'Tom Brice, you won't deceive me?'

'Noa, sure,' said Tom and Meg nearly in the same breath.

'You are an honest English lad, Tom—you would not betray me?' I was speaking imploringly.

'Noa, sure,' repeated Tom.

There was something a little unsatisfactory in the countenance of this light-haired youth, with the sharpish up-turned nose. Throughout our interview he said next to nothing, and smiled lazily to himself, like a man listening to a child's solemn nonsense, and leading it on, with an amused irony, from one wise sally to another.

Thus it seemed to me that this young clown, without in the least intending to be offensive, was listening to me with a profound and lazy mockery.

I could not choose, however; and, such as he was, I must employ him or none.

'Now, Tom Brice, a great deal depends on this.'

' That's true for her, Tom Brice,' said Meg, who now and then confirmed my asseverations.

' I'll give you a pound *now*, Tom,' and I placed the coin and the letter together in his hand. ' And you are to give this letter to Lady Knollys, at Elverston ; you know Elverston, don't you ? '

' He does, Miss. Don't ye, lad ? '

' E'es.'

' Well, do so, Tom, and I'll be good to you so long as I live.'

' D'ye hear, lad ? '

' E'es,' said Tom ; ' it's very good.'

' You'll take the letter, Tom ? ' I said, in much greater trepidation as to his answer than I showed.

' E'es, I'll take the letter,' said he, rising, and turning it about in his fingers under his eye, like a curiosity.

' Tom Brice,' I said, ' If you can't be true to me, say so ; but don't take the letter except to give it to Lady Knollys, at Elverston. If you won't promise that, let me have the note back. Keep the pound ; but tell me that you won't mention my having asked you to carry a letter to Elverston to anyone.'

For the first time Tom looked perfectly serious. He twiddled the corner of my letter between his finger and thumb, and wore very much the countenance of a poacher about to be committed.

' I don't want to chouce ye, Miss ; but I must take care o' myself, ye see. The letters goes all through Silas's fingers to the post, and he'd know damn well this worn't among 'em. They do say he opens 'em, and reads 'em before they go ; an' that's his diversion. I don't know ; but I do believe that's how it be ; an' if this one turned up, they'd all know it went be hand, and I'd be spotted for't.'

' But you know who I am, Tom, and I'd save you,' said I, eagerly.

' Ye'd want savin' yerself, I'm thinkin', if that feel oot,' said Tom, cynically. I don't say, though, I'll not take it—only this— I won't run my head again a wall for no one.'

' Tom,' I said, with a sudden inspiration, ' give me back the letter, and take me out of Bartram ; take me to Elverston ; it will be the best thing—for *you*, Tom, I mean—it will indeed— that ever befell you.'

With this clown I was pleading, as for my life ; my hand was on his sleeve. I was gazing imploringly in his face.

But it would not do ; Tom Brice looked amused again, swung his head a little on one side, grinning sheepishly over his shoulder on the roots of the trees beside him, as if he were striving to keep himself from an uncivil fit of laughter.

' I'll do what a wise lad may, Miss ; but ye don't know they lads ; they bain't that easy come over ; and I won't get knocked on the head, nor sent to gaol 'appen, for no good to thee nor me. There's Meg there, she knows well enough I could na' manage that ; so I won't try it, Miss, by no chance ; no offence, Miss ; but I'd rayther not, an' I'll just try what I can make o'this ; that's all I can do for ye.'

Tom Brice, with these words, stood up, and looked uneasily in the direction of the Windmill Wood.

' Mind ye, Miss, coom what will, ye'll not tell o' me ? '

' Whar 'ill ye go now, Tom ? ' inquired Meg, uneasily.

' Never ye mind, lass,' answered he, breaking his way through the thicket, and soon disappearing.

' E'es that 'ill be it—he'll git into the sheepwalk behind the mound. They're all down yonder ; git ye back, Miss, to the hoose —be the side-door ; mind ye, don't go round the corner ; and I'll jest sit awhile among the bushes, and wait a good time for a start. And good-bye, Miss ; and don't ye show like as if there was aught out o' common on your mind. Hish ! '

There was a distant hallooing.

' That be fayther ! ' she whispered, with a very blank countenance, and listened with her sunburnt hand to her ear.

' Tisn't me, only Davy he'll be callin',' she said, with a great sigh, and a joyless smile. ' Now git ye away i' God's name.'

So running lightly along the path, under cover of this thick wood, I recalled Mary Quince, and together we hastened back again to the house, and entered, as directed, by the side-door, which did not expose us to be seen from the Windmill Wood, and, like two criminals, we stole up by the backstairs, and so through the side-gallery to my room ; and there sat down to collect my wits, and try to estimate the exact effect of what had just occurred.

Madame had not returned. That was well ; she always visited my room first, and everything was precisely as I had left it—a certain sign that her prying eyes and busy fingers had not been at work during my absence.

When she did appear, strange to say, it was to bring me unexpected comfort. She had in her hand a letter from my dear Lady Knollys—a gleam of sunlight from the free and happy outer world entered with it. The moment Madame left me to myself, I opened it and read as follows :—

' I am so happy, my dearest Maud, in the immediate prospect of seeing you. I have had a really kind letter from poor Silas——poor I say, for I really compassionate his situation, about which he has been, I do believe, quite frank—at least Ilbury says so, and somehow he happens to know. I have had quite an affecting, changed letter. I will tell you all when I see you. He wants me ultimately to undertake that which would afford me the most unmixed happiness—I mean the care of you, my dear girl. I only fear lest my too eager acceptance of the trust should excite that vein of opposition which is in most human beings, and induce him to think over his offer less favourably again. He says I must come to Bartram, and stay a night, and promises to lodge me comfortably ; about which last I honestly do not care a pin, when the chance of a comfortable evening's gossip with you is in view. Silas explains his sad situation, and must hold himself in readiness for early flight, if he would avoid the risk of losing his personal liberty. It is a sad thing that he should have so irretrievably ruined himself, that poor Austin's liberality seems to have positively precipitated his extremity. His great anxiety is that I should see you before you leave for your short stay in France. He thinks you must leave before a fortnight. I am thinking of asking you to come over here ; I know you would be just as well at Elverston as in France ; but perhaps, as he seems disposed to do what we all wish, it may be safer to let him set about it in his own way. The truth is, I have so set my heart upon it that I fear to risk it by crossing him even in a trifle. He says I must fix an early day next week, and talks as if he meant to urge me to make a longer visit than he defined. I shall be only too happy. I begin, my dear Maud, to think that there is no use in trying to control events, and that things often turn out best, and most exactly to our wishes, by being left quite to themselves. I think it was Talleyrand who praised the talent of *waiting* so much. In high spirits, and with

my head brimful of plans, I remain, dearest Maud, ever your
affectionate cousin,

MONICA.'

Here was an inexplicable puzzle ! A faint radiance of hope,
however, began to overspread a landscape only a few minutes
before darkened by total eclipse ; but construct what theory I
might, all were inconsistent with many well-established and
awful incongruities, and their wrecks lay strown over the troubled waters of the gulf into which I gazed.

Why was Madame here ? Why was Dudley concealed about
the place ? Why was I a prisoner within the walls ? What were
those dangers which Meg Hawkes seemed to think so great and
so imminent as to induce her to risk her lover's safety for my
deliverance ? All these menacing facts stood grouped together
against the dark certainty that never were men more deeply interested in making away with one human being, than were Uncle
Silas and Dudley in removing me.

Sometimes to these dreadful evidences I abandoned my soul.
Sometimes, reading Cousin Monica's sunny letter, the sky would
clear, and my terrors melt away like nightmares in the morning.
I never repented, however, that I had sent my letter by Tom
Brice. Escape from Bartram-Haugh was my hourly longing.

That evening Madame invited herself to tea with me. I did
not object. It was better just then to be on friendly relations
with everybody, if possible, even on their own terms. She was in
one of her boisterous and hilarious moods, and there was a per-
fume of brandy.

She narrated some compliments paid her that morning in Feltram by that ' good crayature' Mrs. Litheways, the silk-mercer,
and what ' 'ansom faylow ' was her new foreman— (she intended
plainly that I should ' queez' her)—and how ' he follow' her
with his eyes wherever she went. I thought, perhaps, he fancied
she might pocket some of his lace or gloves. And all the time
her great wicked eyes were rolling and glancing according to her
ideas of fascination, and her bony face grinning and flaming
with the ' strong drink' in which she delighted. She sang twad-
dling chansons, and being, as was her wont under such exhil-
arating influences, in a vapouring mood, she vowed that I should
have my carriage and horses immediately.

' I weel try what I can do weeth your Uncle Silas. We are
very good old friends, Mr. Ruthyn and I,' she said with a leer
which I did not understand, and which yet frightened me.

I never could quite understand why these Jezebels like to insinuate the dreadful truth against themselves ; but they do. Is
it the spirit of feminine triumph overcoming feminine shame,
and making them vaunt their fall as an evidence of bygone fascination and existing power ? Need we wonder ? Have not women
preferred hatred to indifference, and the reputation of witchcraft, with all its penalties, to absolute insignificance ? Thus,
as they enjoyed the fear inspired among simple neighbours by
their imagined traffic with the father of ill, did Madame, I
think, relish with a cynical vainglory the suspicion of her sa-
tanic superiority.

Next morning Uncle Silas sent for me. He was seated at his
table, and spoke his little French greeting, smiling as usual,
pointing to a chair opposite.

' How far, I forget,' he said, carelessly laying his newspaper on
the table, ' did you yesterday guess Dudley to be ? '

' Eleven hundred miles I thought it was.'

' Oh yes, so it was ; ' and then there was an abstracted pause.
' I have been writing to Lord Ilbury, your trustee,' he resumed.
I ventured to say, my dear Maud— (for having thoughts of a
different arrangement for you, more suitable under my distressing circumstances, I do not wish to vacate without some expression of your estimate of my treatment of you while under my
roof) —I ventured to say that you thought me kind, considerate,
indulgent,—may I say so ? '

I assented. What could I say ?

' I said you had enjoyed our poor way of living here—our
rough ways and liberty. Was I right ? '

Again I assented.

' And, in fact, that you had nothing to object against your
poor old uncle, except indeed his poverty, which you forgave. I
think I said truth. Did I, dear Maud ? '

Again I acquiesced.

All this time he was fumbling among the papers in his coat-
pocket.

' That is satisfactory. So I expected you to say,' he murmured.
' I expected no less.'

On a sudden a frightful change spread across his face. He
rose like a spectre with a white scowl.

'Then how do you account for that?' he shrieked in a voice
of thunder, and smiting my open letter to Lady Knollys, face upward, upon the table.

I stared at my uncle, unable to speak, until I seemed to lose
sight of him; but his voice, like a bell, still yelled in my ears.

'There! young hypocrite and liar! explain that farrago of
slander which you bribed my servant to place in the hands of my
kinswoman, Lady Knollys.'

And so on and on it went, I gazing into darkness, until the
voice itself became indistinct, grew into a buzz, and hummed
away into silence.

I think I must have had a fit.

When I came to myself I was drenched with water, my hair,
face, neck, and dress. I did not in the least know where I was. I
thought my father was ill, and spoke to him. Uncle Silas was
standing near the window, looking unspeakably grim. Madame
was seated beside me, and an open bottle of ether, one of Uncle
Silas's restoratives, on the table before me.

'Who's that—who's ill—is anyone dead?' I cried.

At last I was relieved by long paroxysms of weeping. When I
was sufficiently recovered, I was conveyed into my own room.

CHAPTER LVIII

LADY KNOLLYS' CARRIAGE

Next morning—it was Sunday—I lay on my bed in my dressing-
gown, dull, apathetic, with all my limbs sore, and, as I thought,
rheumatic, and feeling so ill that I did not care to speak or lift
my head. My recollection of what had passed in Uncle Silas's
room was utterly confused, and it seemed to me as if my poor
father had been there and taken a share—I could not remember
how—in the conference.

I was too exhausted and stupid to clear up this horrible muddle, and merely lay with my face toward the wall, motionless and silent, except for a great sigh every now and then.

Good Mary Quince was in the room—there was some comfort in that ; but I felt quite worn out, and had rather she did not speak to me ; and indeed for the time I felt absolutely indifferent as to whether I lived or died.

Cousin Monica this morning, at pleasant Elverston, all-unconscious of my sad plight, proposed to Lady Mary Carysbroke and Lord Ilbury, her guests, to drive over to church at Feltram, and then pay us a visit at Bartram-Haugh, to which they readily agreed.

Accordingly, at about two o'clock, this pleasant party of three arrived at Bartram. They walked, having left the carriage to follow when the horses were fed ; and Madame de la Rougierre, who was in my uncle's room when little Giblets arrived to say that the party were in the parlour, whispered for' a little with my uncle, who then said—

' Miss Maud Ruthyn has gone out to drive, but I shall be happy to see Lady Knollys here, if she will do me the favour to come upstairs and see me for a few moments ; and you can mention that I am very far from well.'

Madame followed him out upon the lobby, and added, holding him by the collar, and whispering earnestly in his ear—

' Bring hair ladysheep up by the backstairs—mind, the *back*-stairs.'

And the next moment Madame entered my room, with long tiptoe steps, and looking, Mary Quince said, as if she were going to be hanged.

On entering she looked sharply round, and being satisfied of Mary Quince's presence, she turned the key in the door, and made some affectionate enquiries about me in a whisper ; and then she stole to the window and peeped out, standing back some way ; after which she came to my bedside, murmured some tender sentences, drew the curtain a little, and making some little fidgety adjustments about the room ; among the rest she took the key from the lock, quietly, and put it into her pocket.

This was so odd a procedure that honest Mary Quince rose stoutly from her chair, pointing to the lock, with her frank little blue eyes fixed on Madame, and she whispered—

'Won't you put the key in the lock, please?'

'Oh, certainly, Mary Queence; but it is better it shall be locked, for I think her uncle he is coming to see her, and I am sure she would be very much frightened, for he is very much displease, don't you see? and we can tell him she is not well enough, or asleep, and so he weel go away again, without any trouble.'

I heard nothing of this, which was conducted in close whispers; and Mary, although she did not give Madame credit for caring whether I was frightened or not, and suspected her motives in everything, acquiesced grudgingly, fearing lest her alleged reason might possibly be the true one.

So Madame hovered about the door, uneasily; and of what went on elsewhere during that period Lady Knollys afterwards gave me the following account:—

'We were very much disappointed; but of course I was glad to see Silas, and your little hobgoblin butler led me upstairs to his room a different way, I think, from that I came before; but I don't know the house of Bartram well enough to speak positively. I only know that I was conducted quite across his bedroom, which I had not seen on my former visit, and so into his sitting-room, where I found him.

'He seemed very glad to see me, came forward smiling—I disliked his smile always—with both hands out, and shook mine with more warmth than I ever remembered in his greeting before, and said—

'"My dear, *dear* Monica, how *very* good of you—the very person I longed to see! I have been miserably ill, the sad consequence of still more miserable anxiety. Sit down, pray, for a moment."

'And he paid me some nice little French compliment in verse.

'"And where is Maud?" said I.

'"I think Maud is by this time about halfway to Elverston," said the old gentleman. "I persuaded her to take a drive, and advised a call there, which seemed to please her, so I conjecture she obeyed."

'"How *very* provoking!" cried I.

'"My poor Maud will be sadly disappointed, but you will console her by a visit—you have promised to come, and I shall try to make you comfortable. I shall be happier, Monica, with this proof of our perfect reconciliation. You won't deny me ? "

' "Certainly not. I am only too glad to come," said I ; "and I want to thank you, Silas."

' " For what ? " said he.

' " For wishing to place Maud in my care. I am very much obliged to you."

' " I did not suggest it, I must say, Monica, with the least intention of obliging *you*," said Silas.

' I thought he was going to break into one of his ungracious moods.

' " But I *am* obliged to you— very much obliged to you, Silas ; and you sha'n't refuse my thanks."

' " I am happy, at all events, Monica, in having won your good-will ; we learn at last that in the affections only are our capacities for happiness ; and how true is St. Paul's preference of love—the principle that abideth ! The affections, dear Monica, are eternal ; and being so, celestial, divine, and consequently happy, deriving happiness, and bestowing it."

' I was always impatient of his or anybody else's metaphysics ; but I controlled myself, and only said, with my customary impudence—

' " Well, dear Silas, and when do you wish me to come ? "

' " The earlier the better," said he.

' " Lady Mary and Ilbury will be leaving me on Tuesday morning. I can come to you in the afternoon, if you think Tuesday a good day."

' " Thank you, dear Monica. I shall be, I trust, enlightened by that day as to my enemies' plans. It is a humiliating confession, Monica, but I am past feeling that. It is quite possible that an execution may be sent into this house to-morrow, and an end of all my schemes. It is not likely, however—hardly possible—before three weeks, my attorney tells me. I shall hear from him to-morrow morning, and then I shall ask you to name a very early day. If we are to have an unmolested fortnight certain, you shall hear, and name your own day."

' Then he asked me who had accompanied me, and lamented ever so much his not being able to go down to receive them ; and he offered luncheon, with a sort of Ravenswood smile, and a shrug, and I declined, telling him that we had but a few minutes, and that my companions were walking in the grounds near the house.

'I asked whether Maud was likely to return soon?

'"Certainly not before five o'clock." He thought we should probably meet her on our way back to Elverston ; but could not be certain, as she might have changed her plans.

'So then came—no more remaining to be said—a very affectionate parting. I believe all about his legal dangers was strictly true. How he could, unless that horrid woman had deceived him, with so serene a countenance tell me all those gross untruths about Maud, I can only admire.'

In the meantime, as I lay in my bed, Madame, gliding hither and thither, whispering sometimes, listening at others, I suddenly startled them both by saying—

'Whose carriage?'

'What carriage, dear?' inquired Quince, whose ears were not so sharp as mine.

Madame peeped from the window.

''Tis the physician, Doctor Jolks. He is come to see your uncle, my dear,' said Madame.

'But I hear a female voice,' I said, sitting up.

'No, my dear ; there is only the doctor,' said Madame. 'He is come to your uncle. I tell you he is getting out of his carriage,' and she affected to watch the doctor's descent.

'The carriage is driving away!' I cried.

'Yes, it is draiving away,' she echoed.

But I had sprung from my bed, and was looking over her shoulder, before she perceived me.

'It is Lady Knollys!' I screamed, seizing the window-frame to force it up, and, vainly struggling to open it, I cried—

'I'm here, Cousin Monica. For God's sake, Cousin Monica—Cousin Monica!'

'You are mad, Meess—go back,' screamed Madame, exerting her superior strength to force me back.

But I saw deliverance and escape gliding away from my reach, and, strung to unnatural force by desperation, I pushed past her, and beat the window wildly with my hands, screaming—

'Save me—save me! Here, here, Monica, here! Cousin, cousin, oh! save me!'

Madame had seized my wrists, and a wild struggle was going

on. A window-pane was broken, and I was shrieking to stop the
carriage. The Frenchwoman looked black and haggard as a
fury, as if she could have murdered me.

Nothing daunted—frantic—I screamed in my despair, seeing
the carriage drive swiftly away—seeing Cousin Monica's bonnet,
as she sat chatting with her *vis-à-vis.*

'Oh, oh, oh!' I shrieked, in vain and prolonged agony, as
Madame, exerting her strength and matching her fury against
my despair, forced me back in spite of my wild struggles, and
pushed me sitting on the bed, where she held me fast, glaring
in my face, and chuckling and panting over me.

I think I felt something of the despair of a lost spirit.

I remember the face of poor Mary Quince—its horror, its
wonder—as she stood gaping into my face, over Madame's
shoulder, and crying—

'What is it, Miss Maud? What is it, dear?' And turning
fiercely on Madame, and striving to force her grasp from my
wrists, 'Are you hurting the child? Let her go—let her go.'

'I *weel* let her go. Wat old fool are you, Mary Queence! She
is mad, I think. She 'as lost hair head.'

'Oh, Mary, cry from the window. Stop the carriage!' I cried.

Mary looked out, but there was by this time, of course, nothing in sight.

'Why don't a you stop the carriage?' sneered Madame. 'Call
a the coachman and the postilion. W'ere is the footman? Bah!
elle a le cerveau mal timbré.'

'Oh, Mary, Mary, is it gone—is it gone? Is there nothing
there?' cried I, rushing to the window; and turning to Madame, after a vain straining of my eyes, my face against the
glass—

'Oh, cruel, cruel, wicked woman! why have you done this?
What was it to you? Why do you persecute me? What good
can you gain by my ruin?'

'Rueen! Par bleu! ma chère, you talk too fast. Did not a you
see it, Mary Queence? It was the doctor's carriage, and Mrs.
Jolks, and that eempudent faylow, young Jolks, staring up to
the window, and Mademoiselle she come in soche shocking
déshabille to show herself knocking at the window. 'Twould be
very nice thing, Mary Queence, don't you think?'

I was sitting now on the bedside, crying in mere despair. I

did not care to dispute or to resist. Oh ! why had rescue come so
near, only to prove that it could not reach me ? So I went on crying, with a clasping of my hands and turning up of my eyes, in
incoherent prayer. I was not thinking of Madame, or of Mary
Quince, or any other person, only babbling my anguish and despair helplessly in the ear of heaven.

' I did not think there was soche fool. Wat *enfant gaté* ! My
dear cheaile, wat a can you *mean* by soche strange language and
conduct ? Wat for should a you weesh to display yourself in the
window in soche 'orrible déshabille to the people in the doctor's
coach ? '

' It was *Cousin Knollys*—Cousin Knollys. Oh, Cousin Knollys !
You're gone—you're gone—you're *gone* ! '

' And if it was Lady Knollys' coach, there was certainly a
coachman and a footman ; and whoever has the coach there
was young gentlemen in it. If it was Lady Knollys' carriage it
would 'av been *worse* than the doctor.'

' It is no matter—it is all over. Oh, Cousin Monica, your poor
Maud—where is she to turn ? Is there no help ? '

That evening Madame visited me again, in one of her sedate
and moral moods. She found me dejected and passive, as she had
left me.

' I think, Maud, there is news ; but I am not certain.'

I raised my head and looked at her wistfully.

' I think there is letter of *bad* news from the attorney in
London.'

' Oh ! ' I said, in a tone which I am sure implied the absolute
indifference of dejection.

' But, my dear Maud, if 't be so, we shall go at once, you and
me, to join Meess Millicent in France. La belle France ! You
weel like so moche ! We shall be so gay. You cannot imagine
there are such naice girl there. They all love a me so moche,
you will be delight.'

' How soon do we go ? ' I asked.

' I do not know. Bote I was to bring in a case of eau de
cologne that came this evening, and he laid down a letter and
say :—" The blow has descended, Madame ! My niece must hold
herself in readiness." I said, " For what, Monsieur ? " *twice* ;
bote he did not answer. I am sure it is *un procès*. They 'av ruin
him. Eh bien, my dear. I suppose we shall leave this triste place

immediately. I am so rejoice. It appears to me *un cimetière !* '

' Yes, I should like to leave it,' I said, sitting up, with a great sigh and sunken eyes. It seemed to me that I had quite lost all sense of resentment towards Madame. A debility of feeling had supervened—the fatigue, I suppose, and prostration of the passions.

' I weel make excuse to go into his room again,' said Madame ; ' and I weel endeavor to learn something more from him, and I weel come back again to you in half an hour.'

She departed. But in half an hour did not return. I had a dull longing to leave Bartram-Haugh. For me, since the departure of poor Milly, it had grown like the haunt of evil spirits, and to escape on any terms from it was a blessing unspeakable.

Another half-hour passed, and another, and I grew insufferably feverish. I sent Mary Quince to the lobby to try and see Madame, who, I feared, was probably to-ing and fro-ing in and out of Uncle Silas's room.

Mary returned to tell me that she had seen old Wyat, who told her that she thought Madame had gone to her bed half an hour before.

CHAPTER LIX

A SUDDEN DEPARTURE

' Mary,' said I, ' I am miserably anxious to hear what Madame may have to tell ; she knows the state I am in, and she would not like so much trouble as to look in at my door to say a word. Did you hear what she told me ? '

' No, Miss Maud,' she answered, rising and drawing near.

' She thinks we are going to France immediately, and to leave this place perhaps for ever.'

' Heaven be praised for that, if it be so, Miss ! ' said Mary, with more energy than was common with her, ' for there is no luck about it, and I don't expect to see you ever well or happy in it.'

'You must take your candle, Mary, and make out her room, upstairs; I found it accidentally myself one evening.'

'But Wyat won't let us upstairs.'

'Don't mind her, Mary; I tell you to go. You must try. I can't sleep till we hear.'

'What direction is her room in, Miss?' asked Mary.

'Somewhere in *that* direction, Mary,' I answered, pointing. 'I cannot describe the turns; but I think you will find it if you go along the great passage to your left, on getting to the top of the stairs, till you come to the cross-galleries, and then turn to your left; and when you have passed four or perhaps five doors, you must be very near it, and I am sure she will hear if you call.'

'But will she tell me—she *is* such a rum un, Miss?' suggested Mary.

'Tell her exactly what I have said to you, and when she learns that you already know as much as I do, she may—unless, indeed, she wishes to torture me. If she won't, perhaps at least you can persuade her to come to me for a moment. Try, dear Mary; we can but fail.'

'Will you be very lonely, Miss, while I am away?' asked Mary, uneasily, as she lighted her candle.

'I can't help it, Mary. Go. I think if I heard we were going, I could almost get up and dance and sing. I can't bear this dreadful uncertainty any longer.'

'If old Wyat is outside, I'll come back and wait here a bit, till she's out o' the way,' said Mary; 'and, anyhow, I'll make all the haste I can. The drops and the sal-volatile is here, Miss, by your hand.'

And with an anxious look at me, she made her exit, softly, and did not immediately return, by which I concluded that she had found the way clear, and had gained the upper story without interruption.

This little anxiety ended, its subsidence was followed by a sense of loneliness, and with it, of vague insecurity, which increased at last to such a pitch, that I wondered at my own madness in sending my companion away; and at last my terrors so grew, that I drew back into the farthest corner of the bed, with my shoulders to the wall, and my bed-clothes huddled about me, with only a point open to peep at.

At last the door opened gently.

' Who's there ? ' I cried, in extremity of horror, expecting I knew not whom.

' Me, Miss,' whispered Mary Quince, to my unutterable relief ; and with her candle flared, and a wild and pallid face, Mary Quince glided into the room, locking the door as she entered.

I do not know how it was, but I found myself holding Mary fast with both my hands as we stood side by side on the floor.

' Mary, you are terrified ; for God's sake, what is the matter ? ' I cried.

' No, Miss,' said Mary, faintly, ' not much.'

' I see it in your face. What is it ? '

' Let me sit down, Miss. I'll tell you what I saw ; only I'm just a bit queerish.'

Mary sat down by my bed.

' Get in, Miss ; you'll take cold. Get into bed, and I'll tell you. It is not much.'

I did get into bed, and gazing on Mary's frightened face, I felt a corresponding horror.

' For mercy's sake, Mary, say what it is ? '

So again assuring me ' it was not much,' she gave me in a somewhat diffuse and tangled narrative the following facts :—

On closing my door, she raised her candle above her head and surveyed the lobby, and seeing no one there she ascended the stairs swiftly. She passed along the great gallery to the left, and paused a moment at the cross gallery, and then recollected my directions clearly, and followed the passage to the right.

There are doors at each side, and she had forgotten to ask me at which Madame's was. She opened several. In one room she was frightened by a bat, which had very nearly put her candle out. She went on a little, paused, and began to lose heart in the dismal solitude, when on a sudden, a few doors farther on, she thought she heard Madame's voice.

She said that she knocked at the door, but receiving no answer, and hearing Madame still talking within, she opened it.

There was a candle on the chimneypiece, and another in a stable lantern near the window. Madame was conversing volubly on the hearth, with her face toward the window, the entire frame of which had been taken from its place : Dickon Hawkes, the Zamiel of the wooden leg, was supporting it with one hand, as it leaned imperfectly against the angle of the recess. There was a third figure standing, buttoned up in a surtout, with a bundle of tools under his arm, like a glazier, and, with a silent thrill of fear, she distinctly recognised the features as those of Dudley Ruthyn.

' 'Twas him, Miss, so sure as I sit here ! Well, like that, they were as mute as mice ; three pairs of eyes were on me. I don't know what made me so study like, but som'at told me I should not make as though I knew any but Madame ; and so I made a courtesy, as well as I could, and I said, " Might I speak a word wi' ye, please, on the lobby ? "

' Mr. Dudley was making belief be this time to look out at window, wi' his back to me, and I kept looking straight on Madame, and she said, " They're mendin' my broken glass, Mary," walking between them and me, and coming close up to me very quick ; and so she marched me backward out o' the door, prating all the time.

' When we were on the lobby, she took my candle from my hand, shutting the door behind her, and she held the light a bit behind her ear ; so 'twas full on my face, as she looked sharp into it ; and, after a bit, she said again, in her queer lingo— there was two panes broke in her room, and men sent for to mend it.

' I was awful frightened when I saw Mr. Dudley, for I could not believe any such thing before, and I don't know how I could look her in the face as I did and not show it. I was as smooth and cool as yonder chimneypiece, and she has an awful evil eye to stan' against ; but I never flinched, and I think she's puzzled, for as cunning as she is, whether I believe all she said, or knowed 'twas a pack o' stories. So I told her your message, and she said she had not heard another word since ; but she did believe we had not many more days here, and would tell you if she heard to-night, when she brought his soup to your uncle, in half an hour's time.'

I asked her, as soon as I could speak, whether she was perfectly certain as to the fact that the man in the surtout was Dudley, and she made answer—

'I'd swear to him on that Bible, Miss.'

So far from any longer wishing Madame's return that night, I trembled at the idea of it. Who could tell who might enter the room with her when the door opened to admit her ?

Dudley, so soon as he recovered the surprise, had turned about, evidently anxious to prevent recognition ; Dickon Hawkes stood glowering at her. Both might have hope of escaping recognition in the imperfect light, for the candle on the chimneypiece was flaring in the air, and the light from the lantern fell in spots, and was confusing.

What could that ruffian, Hawkes, be doing in the house ? Why was Dudley there ? Could a more ominous combination be imagined ? I puzzled my distracted head over all Mary Quince's details, but could make nothing of their occupation. I know of nothing so terrifying as this kind of perpetual puzzling over ominous problems.

You may imagine how the long hours of that night passed, and how my heart beat at every fancied sound outside my door.

But morning came, and with its light some reassurance. Early, Madame de la Rougierre made her appearance ; she searched my eyes darkly and shrewdly, but made no allusion to Mary Quince's visit. Perhaps she expected some question from me, and, hearing none, thought it as well to leave the subject at rest.

She had merely come in to say that she had heard nothing since, but was now going to make my uncle's chocolate ; and that so soon as her interview was ended she would see me again, and let me hear anything she should have gleaned.

In a little while a knock came to my door, and Mary Quince was ordered by old Wyat into my uncle's room. She returned flushed, in a huge fuss, to say that I was to be up and dressed for a journey in half an hour, and to go straight, when dressed, to my uncle's room.

It was good news ; at the same time it was a shock. I was glad. I was stunned. I jumped out of bed, and set about my toilet with an energy quite new to me. Good Mary Quince was busily packing my boxes, and consulting as to what I should take with me, and what not.

Was Mary Quince to accompany me ? He had not said a word on that point ; and I feared from his silence she was to remain. There was comfort, however, in this—that the separation would not be for long ; I felt confident of that ; and I was about to

join Milly, whom I loved better than I could have believed
before our separation ; but whatsoever the conditions might be,
it was an indescribable relief to have done with Bartram-Haugh,
and leave behind me its sinister lines of circumvallation, its
haunted recesses, and the awful spectres that had lately appeared
within its walls.

I stood too much in awe of my uncle to fail in presenting myself punctually at the close of the half-hour. I entered his sitting-
room under the shadow of sour old Wyat's high-cauled cap ; she
closed the door behind me, and the conference commenced.

Madame de la Rougierre sat there, dressed and draped for a
journey, and with a thick black lace veil on. My uncle rose,
gaunt and venerable, and with a harsh and severe countenance.
He did not offer his hand ; he made me a kind of bow, more of
repulsion than of respect. He remained in a standing position,
supporting his crooked frame by his hand, which he leaned on
a despatch-box ; he glared on me steadily with his wild phosphoric eyes, from under the dark brows I have described to you,
now corrugated in lines indescribably stern.

'You shall join my daughter at the Pension, in France ;
Madame de la Rougierre shall accompany you,' said my uncle,
delivering his directions with the stern monotony and the
measured pauses of a person dictating an important despatch
to a secretary. 'Old Mrs. Quince shall follow with me, or, if alone,
in a week. You shall pass to-night in London ; to-morrow night
you proceed thence to Dover, and cross by the mail-packet.
You shall now sit down and write a letter to your cousin Monica
Knollys, which I will first read and then despatch. To-morrow
you shall write a note to Lady Knollys, from *London,* telling
her how you have got over so much of your journey, and that
you cannot write from Dover, as you must instantly start by the
packet on reaching it ; and that until my affairs are a little
settled, you cannot write to her from France, as it is of high
importance to my safety that no clue should exist as to our address. Intelligence, however, shall reach her through my attorn-
eys, Archer and Sleigh, and I trust we shall soon return. You
will, please, submit that latter note to Madame de la Rougierre,
who has my directions to see that it contains no *libels* upon
my character. Now, sit down.'

So, with those unpleasant words tingling in my ears, I obeyed.

'*Write*,' said he, when I was duly placed. 'You shall convey the substance of what I say in your own language. The imminent danger this morning announced of an execution—remember the word,' and he spelled it for me—'being put into this house either this afternoon or to-morrow, compels me to anticipate my plans, and despatch you for France this day. That you are starting with an attendant.' Here an uneasy movement from Madame, whose dignity was perhaps excited. 'An *attendant*,' he repeated, with a discordant emphasis ; 'and you can, if you please—but I don't *solicit* that justice— say that you have been as kindly treated here as my unfortunate circumstances would permit. That is all. You have just fifteen minutes to write. Begin.'

I wrote accordingly. My hysterical state had made me far less combative than I might have proved some months since, for there was much that was insulting as well as formidable in his manner. I completed my letter, however, to his satisfaction in the prescribed time ; and he said, as he laid it and its envelope on the table—

'Please to remember that this lady is not your attendant only, but that she has authority to direct every detail respecting your journey, and will make all the necessary payments on the way. You will please, then, implicitly to comply with her directions. The carriage awaits you at the hall-door.'

Having thus spoken, with another grim bow, and 'I wish you a safe and pleasant journey,' he receded a step or two, and I, with an undefinable kind of melancholy, though also with a sense of relief, withdrew.

My letter, I afterwards found, reached Lady Knollys, accompanied by one from Uncle Silas, who said—'Dear Maud apprises me that she has written to tell you something of our movements. A sudden crisis in my miserable affairs compels a break-up as sudden here. Maud joins my daughter at the Pension, in France. I purposely omit the address, because I mean to reside in its vicinity until this storm shall have blown over ; and as the consequences of some of my unhappy entanglements might pursue me even there, I must only for the present spare you the pain and trouble of keeping a secret. I am sure that for some little time you will excuse the girl's silence ; in the meantime you shall hear of them, and perhaps circuitously, from me. Our dear

Maud started this morning *en route* for her destination, very
sorry, as am I, that she could not enjoy first a flying visit to
Elverston, but in high spirits, notwithstanding, at the new life
and sights before her.'

At the door my beloved old friend, Mary Quince, awaited me.

' Am I going with you, Miss Maud ? '

I burst into tears and clasped her in my arms.

' I'm not,' said Mary, very sorrowfully ; ' and I never was
from you yet, Miss, since you wasn't the length of my arm.'

And kind old Mary began to cry with me.

' Bote you are coming in a few days, Mary Quince,' expostulated Madame. ' I wonder you are soche fool. What is two, three
days ? Bah ! nonsense, girl.'

Another farewell to poor Mary Quince, quite bewildered at
the suddenness of her bereavement. A serious and tremulous
bow from our little old butler on the steps. Madame bawling
through the open window to the driver to make good speed, and
remember that we had but nineteen minutes to reach the station. Away we went. Old Crowle's iron *grille* rolled back before
us. I looked on the receding landscape, the giant trees—the
palatial, time-stained mansion. A strange conflict of feelings,
sweet and bitter, rose and mingled in the reverie. Had I been
too hard and suspicious with the inhabitants of that old house
of my family ? Was my uncle *justly* indignant ? Was I ever
again to know such pleasant rambles as some of those I had
enjoyed with dear Millicent through the wild and beautiful
woodlands I was leaving behind me ? And there, with my
latest glimpse of the front of Bartram-Haugh, I beheld dear
old Mary Quince gazing after us. Again my tears flowed. I waved
my handkerchief from the window ; and now the park-wall hid
all from view, and at a great pace, through the steep wooded
glen, with the rocky and precipitous character of a ravine, we
glided ; and when the road next emerged, Bartram-Haugh was
a misty mass of forest and chimneys, slope and hollow, and we
within a few minutes of the station.

CHAPTER LX

THE JOURNEY

Waiting for the train, as we stood upon the platform, I looked back again toward the wooded uplands of Bartram; and far behind, the fine range of mountains, azure and soft in the distance, beyond which lay beloved old Knowl, and my lost father and mother, and the scenes of my childhood, never embittered except by the sibyl who sat beside me.

Under happier circumstances I should have been, at my then early age, quite wild with pleasurable excitement on entering London for the first time. But black Care sat by me, with her pale hand in mine: a voice of fear and warning, whose words I could not catch, was always in my ear. We drove through London, amid the glare of lamps, toward the West-end, and for a little while the sense of novelty and curiosity overcame my despondency, and I peeped eagerly from the window; while Madame, who was in high good-humour, spite of the fatigues of our long railway flight, screeched scraps of topographic information in my ear; for London was a picture-book in which she was well read.

'That is Euston Square, my dear—Russell Square. Here is Oxford Street—Haymarket. See, there is the Opera House—Hair Majesty's Theatre. See all the carriages waiting;' and so on, till we reached at length a little narrow street, which she told me was off Piccadilly, where we drew up before a private house, as it seemed to me—a family hotel—and I was glad to be at rest for the night.

Fatigued with the peculiar fatigue of railway travelling, dusty, a little chilly, with eyes aching and wearied, I ascended the stairs silently, our garrulous and bustling landlady leading the way, and telling her oft-told story of the house, its noble owner in old time, and how those fine drawing-rooms were taken every

year during the Session by the Bishop of Rochet-on-Copeley, and
at last into our double-bedded room.

I would fain have been alone, but I was too tired and dejected
to care very much for anything.

At tea, Madame expanded in spirit, like a giant refreshed,
and chattered and sang ; and at last, seeing that I was nodding,
advised my going to bed, while she ran across the street to see
' her dear old friend, Mademoiselle St. Eloi, who was sure to be
up, and would be offended if she failed to make her ever so
short a call.'

I cared little what she said, and was glad to be rid of her even
for a short time, and was soon fast asleep.

I saw her, I know not how much later, poking about the
room, like a figure in a dream, and taking off her things.

She had her breakfast in bed next morning, and I was, to my
comfort, left to take mine in solitary possession of our sitting-
room ; where I began to wonder how little annoyance I had as
yet suffered from her company, and began to speculate upon the
chances of my making the journey with tolerable comfort.

Our hostess gave me five minutes of her valuable time. Her
talk ran chiefly upon nuns and convents, and her old acquaintance with Madame ; and it seemed to me that she had at one
time driven a kind of trade, no doubt profitable enough, in
escorting young ladies to establishments on the Continent ; and
although I did not then quite understand the tone in which
she spoke to me, I often thought afterwards that Madame had
represented me as a young person destined for the holy vocation
of the veil.

When she was gone, I sat listlessly looking out of the window,
and saw some chance equipages drive by, and now and then a
fashionable pedestrian ; and wondered if this quiet thorough-
fare could really be one of the arteries so near the heart of the
tumultuous capital.

I think my nervous vitality must have burnt very low just
then, for I felt perfectly indifferent about all the novelty and
world of wonders beyond, and should have hated to leave the
dull tranquillity of my window for an excursion through the
splendours of the unseen streets and palaces that surrounded me.

It was one o'clock before Madame joined me ; and finding me

in this dull mood, she did not press me to accompany her in her drive, no doubt well pleased to be rid of me.

After tea that evening, as we sat alone in our room, she entertained me with some very odd conversation—at the time unintelligible—but which acquired a tolerably distinct meaning from the events that followed.

Two or three times that day Madame appeared to me on the point of saying something of grave import, as she scanned me with her bleak wicked stare.

It was a peculiarity of hers, that whenever she was pressed upon by an anxiety that really troubled her, her countenance did not look sad or solicitous, as other people's would, but simply wicked. Her great gaunt mouth was compressed and drawn down firmly at the corners, and her eyes glared with a dismal scowl.

At last she said suddenly—

'Are you ever grateful, Maud?'

'I hope so, Madame,' I answered.

'And how do you show your gratitude? For instance, would you do great deal for a person who would run *risque* for your sake?'

It struck me all at once that she was sounding me about poor Meg Hawkes, whose fidelity, notwithstanding the treason or cowardice of her lover, Tom Brice, I never doubted; and I grew at once wary and reserved.

'I know of no opportunity, thank Heaven, for any such service, Madame. How can anyone serve me at present, by themselves incurring danger? What do you mean?'

'Do you like, for example, to go to that French Pension? Would you not like better some other arrangement?'

'Of course there are other arrangements I should like better; but I see no use in talking of them; they are not to be,' I answered.

'What other arrangements do you mean, my dear cheaile?' enquired Madame. 'You mean, I suppose, you would like better to go to Lady Knollys?'

'My uncle does not choose it at present; and except with his consent nothing can be done!'

'He weel never consent, dear cheaile.'

'But he *has* consented—not immediately indeed, but in a short time, when his affairs are settled.'

'*Lanternes!* They will never be settle,' said Madame.

'At all events, for the present I am to go to France. Milly seems very happy, and I dare say I shall like it too. I am very glad to leave Bartram-Haugh, at all events.'

'But your uncle weel bring you back there,' said Madame, drily.

'It is doubtful whether he will ever return to Bartram himself,' I said.

'Ah!' said Madame, with a long-drawn nasal intonation, 'you theenk I hate you. You are quaite wrong, my dear Maud. I am, on the contrary, very much interested for you—I am, I assure you, dear a cheaile.'

And she laid her great hand, with joints misshapen by old chilblains, upon the back of mine. I looked up in her face. She was not smiling. On the contrary, her wide mouth was drawn down at the corners ruefully, as before, and she gazed on my face with a scowl from her abysmal eyes.

I used to think the flare of that irony which lighted her face so often immeasurably worse than any other expression she could assume; but this lack-lustre stare and dismal collapse of feature was more wicked still.

'Suppose I should bring you to Lady Knollys, and place you in her charge, what would a you do then for poor Madame?' said this dark spectre.

I was inwardly startled at these words. I looked into her unsearchable face, but could draw thence nothing but fear. Had she made the same overture only two days since, I think I would have offered her half my fortune. But circumstances were altered. I was no longer in the panic of despair. The lesson I had received from Tom Brice was fresh in my mind, and my profound distrust of her was uppermost. I saw before me only a tempter and betrayer, and said—

'Do you mean to imply, Madame, that my guardian is not to be trusted, and that I ought to make my escape from him, and that you are really willing to aid me in doing so?'

This, you see, was turning the tables upon her. I looked her steadily in the face as I spoke. She returned my gaze with a strange stare and a gape, which haunted me long after; and it seemed as we sat in utter silence that each was rather horribly fascinated by the other's gaze.

At last she shut her mouth sternly, and eyed me with a more determined and meaning scowl, and then said in a low tone—

'I believe, Maud, that you are a cunning and wicked little thing.'

'Wisdom is not cunning, Madame; nor is it wicked to ask your meaning in explicit language,' I replied.

'And so, you clever cheaile, we two sit here, playing at a game of chess, over this little table, to decide which shall destroy the other—is it not so?'

'I will not allow you to destroy me,' I retorted, with a sudden flash.

Madame stood up, and rubbed her mouth with her open hand. She looked to me like some evil being seen in a dream. I was frightened.

'You are going to hurt me!' I ejaculated, scarce knowing what I said.

'If I were, you deserve it. You are very *malicious*, ma chêre: or, it may be, only very stupid.'

A knock came to the door.

'Come in,' I cried, with a glad sense of relief.

A maid entered.

'A letter, please, 'm,' she said, handing it to me.

'For *me*,' snarled Madame, snatching it.

I had seen my uncle's hand, and the Feltram post-mark.

Madame broke the seal, and read. It seemed but a word, for she turned it about after the first momentary glance, and examined the interior of the envelope, and then returned to the line she had already read.

She folded the letter again, drawing her nails in a sharp pinch along the creases, as she stared in a blank, hesitating way at me.

'You are stupid little ingrate, I am employ by Monsieur Ruthyn, and of course I am faithful to my employer. I do not want to talk to you. *There*, you may read that.'

She jerked the letter before me on the table. It contained but these words:—

Bartram-Haugh:
'*30th January, 1845.*

' MY DEAR MADAME,

' Be so good as to take the half-past eight o'clock train to
Dover to-night. Beds are prepared.—Yours very truly,

SILAS RUTHYN.'

I cannot say what it was in this short advice that struck me
with fear. Was it the thick line beneath the word ' Dover,' that
was so uncalled for, and gave me a faint but terrible sense of
something preconcerted ?

I said to Madame—

' Why is " Dover" underlined ? '

' I do not know, little fool, no more than you. How can I tell
what is passing in your oncle's head when he make that a
mark ? '

' Has it not a meaning, Madame ? '

' How can you talk like that ? ' she answered, more in her old
way. 'You are either mocking of me, or you are becoming truly
a fool ! '

She rang the bell, called for our bill, saw our hostess ; while
I made a few hasty preparations in my room.

' You need not look after the trunks—they will follow us all
right. Let us go, cheaile—we 'av half an hour only to reach the
train.'

No one ever fussed like Madame when occasion offered. There
was a cab at the door, into which she hurried me. I assumed
that she would give all needful directions, and leaned back, very
weary and sleepy already, though it was so early, listening to her
farewell screamed from the cab-step, and seeing her black cloak
flitting and flapping this way and that, like the wings of a raven
disturbed over its prey.

In she got, and away we drove through a glare of lamps, and
shop-windows, still open ; gas everywhere, and cabs, busses, and
carriages, still thundering through the streets. I was too tired
and too depressed to look at those things. Madame, on the contrary, had her head out of the window till we reached the station.

' Where are the rest of the boxes ? ' I asked, as Madame placed

me in charge of her box and my bag in the office of the ter-
minus.

' They will follow with Boots in another cab, and will come
safe with us in this train. Mind those two, we weel bring in the
carriage with us.'

So into a carriage we got ; in came Madame's box and my
bag ; Madame stood at the door, and, I think, frightened away
intending passengers, by her size and shrillness.

At last the bell rang her into her place, the door clapt, the
whistle sounded, and we were off.

CHAPTER LXI

OUR BED-CHAMBER

I had passed a miserable night, and, indeed, for many nights had
not had my due proportion of sleep. Still I sometimes fancy that
I may have swallowed something in my tea that helped to make
me so irresistibly drowsy. It was a very dark night—no moon,
and the stars soon hid by the gathering clouds. Madame sat
silent, and ruminating in her place, with her rugs about her. I,
in my corner similarly enveloped, tried to keep awake. Madame
plainly thought I was asleep already, for she stole a leather flask
from her pocket, and applied it to her lips, causing an aroma of
brandy.

But it was vain struggling against the influence that was
stealing over me, and I was soon in a profound and dreamless
slumber.

Madame awoke me at last, in a huge fuss. She had got out all
our things and hurried them away to a close carriage which was
awaiting us. It was still dark and starless. We got along the
platform, I half asleep, the porter carrying our rugs, by the glare
of a pair of gas-jets in the wall, and out by a small door at
the end.

I remember that Madame, contrary to her wont, gave the man

some money. By the puzzling light of the carriage-lamps we got
in and took our seats.

'Go on,' screamed Madame, and drew up the window with a
great chuck; and we were enclosed in darkness and silence, the
most favourable conditions for thought.

My sleep had not restored me as it might; I felt feverish,
fatigued, and still very drowsy, though unable to sleep as I had
done.

I dozed by fits and starts, and lay awake, or half-awake, sometimes, not thinking but in a way imagining what kind of a place
Dover would be; but too tired and listless to ask Madame any
questions, and merely seeing the hedges, grey in the lamplight,
glide backward into darkness, as I leaned back.

We turned off the main road, at right angles, and drew up.

'Get down and poosh it, it is open,' screamed Madame from
the window.

A gate, I suppose, was thus passed; for when we resumed our
brisk trot, Madame bawled across the carriage—

'We are now in the 'otel grounds.'

And so all again was darkness and silence, and I fell into another doze, from which, on waking, I found that we had come to
a standstill, and Madame was standing on the low step of an
open door, paying the driver. She, herself, pulled her box and
the bag in. I was too tired to care what had become of the rest
of our luggage.

I descended, glancing to the right and left, but there was
nothing visible but a patch of light from the lamps on a paved
ground and on the wall.

We stepped into the hall or vestibule, and Madame shut the
door, and I thought I heard the key turn in it. We were in total
darkness.

'Where are the lights, Madame—where are the people?' I
asked, more awake than I had been.

''Tis pass three o'clock, cheaile, bote there is always light
here.' She was groping at the side; and in a moment more
lighted a lucifer match, and so a bedroom candle.

We were in a flagged lobby, under an archway at the right,
and at the left of which opened long flagged passages, lost in
darkness; a winding stair, barely wide enough to admit Mad-

ame, dragging her box, led upward under a doorway, in a corner at the right.

'Come, dear cheaile, take a your bag; don't mind the rugs, they are safe enough.'

'But where are we to go? There is no one!' I said, looking round in wonder. It certainly was a strange reception at an hotel.

'Never mind, my dear cheaile. They know me here, and I have always the same room ready when I write for it. Follow me quaitely.'

So she mounted, carrying the candle. The stair was steep, and the march long. We halted at the second landing, and entered a gaunt, grimy passage. All the way up we had not heard a single sound of life, nor seen a human being, nor so much as passed a gaslight.

'Violà! here 'tis, my dear old room. Enter, dearest Maud.'

And so I did. The room was large and lofty, but shabby and dismal. There was a tall four-post bed, with its foot beside the window, hung with dark-green curtains, of some plush or velvet texture, that looked like a dusty pall. The remaining furniture was scant and old, and a ravelled square of threadbare carpet covered a patch of floor at the bedside. The room was grim and large, and had a cold, vault-like atmosphere, as if long uninhabited; but there were cinders in the grate and under it. The imperfect light of our mutton-fat candle made all this look still more comfortless.

Madame placed the candle on the chimneypiece, locked the door, and put the key in her pocket.

'I always do so in 'otel,' said she, with a wink at me.

And, then with a long 'ha!' expressive of fatigue and relief, she threw herself into a chair.

'So 'ere we are at last!' said she; 'I'm glad. *There's* your bed, Maud. *Mine* is in the dressing-room.'

She took the candle, and I went in with her. A shabby press-bed, a chair, and table were all its furniture; it was rather a closet than a dressing-room, and had no door except that through which we had entered. So we returned, and very tired, wondering, I sat down on the side of my bed and yawned.

'I hope they will call us in time for the packet,' I said.

' Oh yes, they never fail,' she answered, looking steadfastly on
her box, which she was diligently uncording.

Uninviting as was my bed, I was longing to lie down in it ;
and having made those ablutions which our journey rendered
necessary, I at length lay down, having first religiously stuck my
talismanic pin, with the head of sealing-wax, into the bolster.

Nothing escaped the restless eye of Madame.

' Wat is that, dear cheaile ?' she enquired, drawing near and
scrutinising the head of the gipsy charm, which showed like a
little ladybird newly lighted on the sheet.

' Nothing—a charm—folly. Pray, Madame, allow me to go to
sleep.'

So, with another look and a little twiddle between her finger
and thumb, she seemed satisfied ; but, unhappily for me, she did
not seem at all sleepy. She busied herself in unpacking and dis-
playing over the back of the chair a whole series of London
purchases—silk dresses, a shawl, a sort of lace demi-coiffure then
in vogue, and a variety of other articles.

The vainest and most slammakin of women—the merest slut
at home, a milliner's lay figure out of doors—she had one square
foot of looking-glass upon the chimneypiece, and therein tried
effects, and conjured up grotesque simpers upon her sinister and
weary face.

I knew that the sure way to prolong this worry was to express my uneasiness under it, so I bore it as quietly as I could ;
and at last fell fast asleep with the gaunt image of Madame, with
a festoon of grey silk with a cerise stripe, pinched up in her
finger and thumb, and smiling over her shoulder across it into
the little shaving-glass that stood on the chimney.

I awoke suddenly in the morning, and sat up in my bed, having for a moment forgotten all about our travelling. A moment
more, however, brought all back again.

' Are we in time, Madame ? '

' For the packet ? ' she enquired, with one of her charming
smiles, and cutting a caper on the floor. ' To be sure ; you don't
suppose they would forget. We have two hours yet to wait.'

' Can we see the sea from the window ? '

' No, dearest cheaile ; you will see't time enough.

' I'd like to get up,' I said.

' Time enough, my dear Maud ; you are fatigue ; are you sure you feel quite well ? '

' Well enough to get up ; I should be better, I think, out of bed.'

' There is no hurry, you know ; you need not even go by the next packet. Your uncle, he tell me, I may use my discretion.'

' Is there any water ? '

' They will bring some.'

' Please, Madame, ring the bell.'

She pulled it with alacrity. I afterwards learnt that it did not ring.

' What has become of my gipsy pin ? ' I demanded, with an unaccountable sinking of the heart.

' Oh ! the little pin with the red top ? maybe it 'as fall on the ground ; we weel find when you get up.'

I suspected that she had taken it merely to spite me. It would have been quite the thing she would have liked. I cannot describe to you how the loss of this little ' charm ' depressed and excited me. I searched the bed ; I turned over all the bed-clothes ; I searched in and outside ; at last I gave up.

' How odious ! ' I cried ; ' somebody has stolen it merely to vex me.'

And, like a fool as I was, I threw myself on my face on the bed and wept, partly in anger, partly in dismay.

After a time, however, this blew over. I had a hope of re-covering it. If Madame had stolen it, it would turn up yet. But in the meantime its disappearance troubled me like an omen.

' I am afraid, my dear cheaile, you are not very well. It is really very odd you should make such fuss about a pin ! Nobody would believe ! Do you not theenk it would be a good plan to take a your breakfast in your bed ?

She continued to urge this point for some time. At last, how-ever, having by this time quite recovered my self-command, and resolved to preserve ostensibly fair terms with Madame, who could contribute so essentially to make me wretched during the rest of my journey, and possibly to prejudice me very ser-iously on my arrival, I said quietly—

' Well, Madame, I know it is very silly ; but I had kept that foolish little pin so long and so carefully, that I had grown quite fond of it ; but I suppose it is lost, and I must content myself, though I cannot laugh as you do. So I will get up now, and dress.'

'I think you will do well to get all the repose you can,' answered Madame ; 'but as you please,' she added, observing that I was getting up.

So soon as I had got some of my things on, I said—

'Is there a pretty view from the window ?'

'No,' said Madame.

I looked out and saw a dreary quadrangle of cut stone, in one side of which my window was placed. As I looked a dream rose up before me.

'This hotel,' I said, in a puzzled way. '*Is* it a hotel ? Why this is just like—it *is* the inner court of Bartram-Haugh !'

Madame clapped her large hands together, made a fantastic *chassé* on the floor, burst into a great nasal laugh like the scream of a parrot, and then said—

'Well, dearest Maud, is not clever trick ?'

I was so utterly confounded that I could only stare about me in stupid silence, a spectacle which renewed Madame's peals of laughter.

'We are at Bartram-Haugh !' I repeated, in utter consternation. 'How was this done ?'

I had no reply but shrieks of laughter, and one of those Walpurgis dances in which she excelled.

'It is a mistake—is it ? *What* is it ?'

'All a mistake, of course. Bartram-Haugh, it is so like Dover, as all philosophers know.'

I sat down in total silence, looking out into the deep and dark enclosure, and trying to comprehend the reality and the meaning of all this.

'Well, Madame, I suppose you will be able to satisfy my uncle of your fidelity and intelligence. But to me it seems that his money has been ill-spent, and his directions anything but well observed.'

'Ah, ha ! Never mind ; I think he will forgive me,' laughed Madame.

Her tone frightened me. I began to think, with a vague but overpowering sense of danger, that she had acted under the Machiavellian directions of her superior.

'You have brought me back, then, by my uncle's orders ?'

' Did I say so ? '

' No ; but what you have said can have no other meaning, though I can't believe it. And why have I been brought here ? What is the object of all this duplicity and trick. I *will* know. It is not possible that my uncle, a gentleman and a kinsman, can be privy to so disreputable a manœuvre.'

' First you will eat your breakfast, dear Maud ; next you can tell your story to your uncle, Monsieur Ruthyn ; and then you shall hear what he thinks of my so terrible misconduct. What nonsense, cheaile ! Can you not think how many things may 'appen to change a your uncle's plans ? Is he not in danger to be arrest ? Bah ! You are cheaile still ; you cannot have intelligence more than a cheaile. Dress yourself, and I will order breakfast.'

I could not comprehend the strategy which had been practised on me. Why had I been so shamelessly deceived ? If it were decided that I should remain here, for what imaginable reason had I been sent so far on my journey to France ? Why had I been conveyed back with such mystery ? Why was I removed to this uncomfortable and desolate room, on the same floor with the apartment in which Charke had met his death, and with no window commanding the front of the house, and no view but the deep and weed-choked court, that looked like a deserted churchyard in a city ?

' I suppose I may go to my own room ? ' I said.

' Not to-day, my dear cheaile, for it was all disarrange when we go 'way ; 'twill be ready again in two three days.'

' Where is Mary Quince ? ' I asked.

' Mary Quince !—she has follow us to France,' said Madame, making what in Ireland they call a bull.

' They are not sure where they will go or what will do for day or two more. I will go and get breakfast. Adieu for a moment.'

Madame was out of the door as she said this, and I thought I heard the key turn in the lock.

CHAPTER LXII

A WELL-KNOWN FACE LOOKS IN

You who have never experienced it can have no idea how angry and frightened you become under the sinister insult of being locked into a room, as on trying the door I found I was.

The key was in the lock; I could see it through the hole. I called after Madame, I shook at the solid oak-door, beat upon it with my hands, kicked it—but all to no purpose.

I rushed into the next room, forgetting—if indeed I had observed it, that there was no door from it upon the gallery. I turned round in an angry and dismayed perplexity, and, like prisoners in romances, examined the windows.

I was shocked and affrighted on discovering in reality what they occasionally find—a series of iron bars crossing the window! They were firmly secured in the oak woodwork of the window-frame, and each window was, besides, so compactly screwed down that it could not open. This bedroom was converted into a prison. A momentary hope flashed on me—perhaps all the windows were secured alike! But it was no such thing: these gaol-like precautions were confined to the windows to which I had access.

For a few minutes I felt quite distracted; but I bethought me that I must now, if ever, control my terrors and exert whatever faculties I possessed.

I stood upon a chair and examined the oak-work. I thought I detected marks of new chiselling here and there. The screws, too, looked new; and they and the scars on the woodwork were freshly smeared over with some coloured stuff by way of disguise.

While I was making these observations, I heard the key stealthily stirred. I suspect that Madame wished to surprise me. Her approaching step, indeed, was seldom audible; she had the soft tread of the feline tribe.

I was standing in the centre of the room confronting her when she entered.

' Why did you lock the door, Madame ? ' I demanded.

She slipped in suddenly with an insidious smirk, and locked the door hastily.

' Hish ! ' whispered Madame, raising her broad palm ; and then screwing in her cheeks, she made an ogle over her shoulder in the direction of the passage.

' Hish ! be quaite, cheaile, weel you, and I weel tale you everything presently.'

She paused, with her ear laid to the door.

' Now I can speak, ma chère ; I weel tale a you there is bailiff in the house, two, three, four soche impertinent fallows ! They have another as bad as themselve to make a leest of the furniture : we most keep them out of these rooms, dear Maud.'

' You left the key in the door on the outside,' I retorted ; ' that was not to keep them out, but me in, Madame.'

' *Deed* I leave the key in the door ? ' ejaculated Madame, with both hands raised, and such a genuine look of consternation as for a moment shook me.

It was the nature of this woman's deceptions that they often puzzled though they seldom convinced me.

' I re-ally think, Maud, all those so frequent changes and excite-ments they weel overturn my poor head.'

' And the windows are secured with iron bars—what are they for ? ' I whispered sternly, pointing with my finger at these grim securities.

' That is for more a than forty years, when Sir Phileep Aylmer was to reside here, and had this room for his children's nursery, and was afraid they should fall out.'

' But if you look you will find these bars have been put here very recently : the screws and marks are quite new.'

' *Eendeed* ! ' ejaculated Madame, with prolonged emphasis, in precisely the same consternation. ' Why, my dear, they told a me down stair what I have tell a you, when I ask the reason ! Late a me see.'

And Madame mounted on a chair, and made her scrutiny with much curiosity, but could not agree with me as to the very recent date of the carpentry.

There is nothing, I think, so exasperating as that sort of false-hood which affects not to see what is quite palpable.

'Do you mean to say, Madame, that you really think those chisellings and screws are forty years old?'

'How can I tell, cheaile? What does signify whether it is forty or only fourteen years? Bah! we av other theeng to theenk about. Those villain men! I am glad to see bar and bolt, and lock and key, at least, to our room, to keep soche faylows out!'

At that moment a knock came to the door, and Madame's nasal 'in moment' answered promptly, and she opened the door, stealthily popping out her head.

'Oh, that is all right; go you long, no ting more, go way.'

'Who's there?' I cried.

'Hold a your tongue,' said Madame imperiously to the vis-itor, whose voice I fancied I recognised—'go way.'

Out slipped Madame again, locking the door; but this time she returned immediately, bearing a tray with breakfast.

I think she fancied that I would perhaps attempt to break away and escape; but I had no such thought at that moment. She hastily set down the tray on the floor at the threshold, lock-ing the door as before.

My share of breakfast was a little tea; but Madame's diges-tion was seldom disturbed by her sympathies, and she ate vo-raciously. During this process there was a silence unusual in her company; but when her meal was ended she proposed a reconnaissance, professing much uncertainty as to whether my Uncle had been arrested or not.

'And in case the poor old gentleman be poot in what you call stone jug, where are we to go my dear Maud—to Knowl or to Elverston? You must direct.'

And so she disappeared, turning the key in the door as be-fore. It was an old custom of hers, locking herself in her room, and leaving the key in the lock; and the habit prevailed, for she left it there again.

With a heavy heart I completed my simple toilet, wonder-ing all the while how much of Madame's story might be false and how much, if any, true. Then I looked out upon the dingy courtyard below, in its deep damp shadow, and thought, 'How could an assassin have scaled that height in safety, and entered so noiselessly as not to awaken the slumbering gamester?' Then there were the iron bars across my window. What a fool had I been to object to that security !

I was labouring hard to reassure myself, and keep all ghastly suspicions at arm's length. But I wished that my room had been to the front of the house, with some view less dismal.

Lost in these ruminations of fear, as I stood at the window I was startled by the sound of a sharp tread on the lobby, and by the key turning in the lock of my door.

In a panic I sprang back into the corner, and stood with my eyes fixed upon the door. It opened a little, and the black head of Meg Hawkes was introduced.

' Oh, Meg ! ' I cried ; ' thank God ! '

' I guessed 'twas you, Miss Maud. I am feared, Miss.'

The miller's daughter was pale, and her eyes, I thought, were red and swollen.

'Oh, Meg ! for God's sake, what is it all ? '

' I darn't come in. The old un's gone down, and locked the cross-door, and left me to watch. They think I care nout about ye, no more nor themselves. I donna know all, but summat more nor her. They tell her nout, she's so gi'n to drink ; they say she's not safe, an' awful quarrelsome. I hear a deal when fay-ther and Master Dudley be a-talkin' in the mill. They think, comin' in an' out, I don't mind ; but I put one think an' t'other together. An' don't ye eat nor drink nout here, Miss ; hide away this ; it's black enough, but wholesome anyhow ! ' and she slipt a piece of a coarse loaf from under her apron. ' *Hide* it mind. Drink nout but the water in the jug there—it's clean spring.'

' Oh, Meg ! Oh, Meg ! I know what you mean,' said I, faintly.

' Ay, Miss, I'm feared they'll try it ; they'll try to make away wi' ye somehow. I'm goin' to your friends arter dark ; I darn't try it no sooner. I'll git awa to Ellerston, to your lady-cousin, and I'll bring 'em back wi' me in a rin ; so keep a good hairt, lass. Meg Hawkes will stan' to ye. Ye were better to me than fayther and mother, and a' ; ' and she clasped me round the waist, and buried her head in my dress ; ' an I'll gie my life for ye, darling, and if they hurt ye I'll kill myself.'

She recovered her sterner mood quickly—

' Not a word, lass,' she said, in her old tone. ' Don't ye try to git away—they'll *kill* ye—ye *can't* do't. Leave a' to me. It won't be, whatever it is, till two or three o'clock in the morning. I'll ha'e them a' here long afore ; so keep a brave heart—there's a darling.'

I suppose she heard, or fancied she heard, a step approaching, for she said—

'Hish !'

Her pale wild face vanished, the door shut quickly and softly, and the key turned again in the lock.

Meg, in her rude way, had spoken softly—almost under her breath; but no prophecy shrieked by the Pythoness ever thundered so madly in the ears of the hearer. I dare say that Meg fancied I was marvellously little moved by her words. I felt my gaze grow intense, and my flesh and bones literally freeze. She did not know that every word she spoke seemed to burst like a blaze in my brain. She had delivered her frightful warning, and told her story coarsely and bluntly, which, in effect, means distinctly and concisely ; and, I dare say, the announcement so made, like a quick bold incision in surgery, was more tolerable than the slow imperfect mangling, which falters and recedes and equivocates with torture. Madame was long away. I sat down at the window, and tried to appreciate my dreadful situation. I was stupid—the imagery was all frightful ; but I beheld it as we sometimes see horrors—heads cut off and houses burnt—in a dream, and without the corresponding emotions. It did not seem as if all this were really happening to me. I remember sitting at the window, and looking and blinking at the opposite side of the building, like a person unable but striving to see an object distinctly, and every minute pressing my hand to the side of my head and saying—

'Oh, it won't be—it won't be—Oh no !—never !—it could not be !' And in this stunned state Madame found me on her return.

But the valley of the shadow of death has its varieties of dread. The 'horror of great darkness' is disturbed by voices and illumed by sights. There are periods of incapacity and collapse, followed by paroxysms of active terror. Thus in my journey during those long hours I found it—agonies subsiding into lethargies, and these breaking again into frenzy. I sometimes wonder how I carried my reason safely through the ordeal.

Madame locked the door, and amused herself with her own

business, without minding me, humming little nasal snatches
of French airs, as she smirked on her silken purchases displayed
in the daylight. Suddenly it struck me that it was very dark,
considering how early it was. I looked at my watch; it seemed
to me a great effort of concentration to understand it. Four
o'clock, it said. Four o'clock! It would be dark at five—*night
in one hour!*

'Madame, what o'clock is it? Is it evening?' I cried with
my hand to my forehead, like a person puzzled.

'Two three minutes past four. It had five minutes to four
when I came upstairs,' answered she, without interrupting her
examination of a piece of darned lace which she was holding
close to her eyes at the window.

'Oh, Madame! *Madame!* I'm frightened,' cried I, with a wild
and piteous voice, grasping her arm, and looking up, as ship-
wrecked people may their last to heaven, into her inexorable
eyes. Madame looked frightened too, I thought, as she stared
into my face. At last she said, rather angrily, and shaking her
arm loose—

'What you mean, cheaile?'

'Oh save me, Madame!—oh save me!—oh save me, Madame!'
I pleaded, with the wild monotony of perfect terror, grasping
and clinging to her dress, and looking up, with an agonised
face, into the eyes of that shadowy Atropos.

'Save a you, indeed! Save! What *niaiserie!*'

'Oh, Madame! Oh, *dear* Madame! for God's sake, only get
me away—get me from this, and I'll do everything you ask me
all my life—I will—*indeed*, Madame, I will! Oh save me! save
me! *save* me!'

I was clinging to Madame as to my guardian angel in my
agony.

'And who told you, cheaile, you are in any danger?' demanded Madame, looking down on me with a black and witch-
like stare.

'I am, Madame—I am—in great danger! Oh, Madame, think
of me—take pity on me! I have none to help me—there is no
one but God and you!'

Madame all this time viewed me with the same dismal stare,
like a sorceress reading futurity in my face.

'Well, maybe you are—how can I tell? Maybe your uncle is

mad—maybe you are mad. You have been my enemy always—
why should I care ? '

Again I burst into wild entreaty, and, clasping her fast,
poured forth my supplications with the bitterness of death.

' I have no confidence in you, little Maud ; you are little
rogue—petite traitresse ! Reflect, if you can, how you 'av always
treat Madame. You 'av attempt to ruin me—you conspire with
the bad domestics at Knowl to destroy me—and you expect me
here to take a your part ! You would never listen to me—you 'ad no
mercy for me—you join to hunt me away from your house like
wolf. Well, what you expect to find me now ? *Bah !* '

This terrific ' Bah ! ' with a long nasal yell of scorn, rang in
my ears like a clap of thunder.

' I say you are mad, petite insolente, to suppose I should care
for you more than the poor hare it will care for the hound—
more than the bird who has escape will love the oiseleur. I do
not care—I ought not care. It is your turn to suffer. Lie down
on your bed there, and suffer quaitely. '

CHAPTER LXIII

SPICED CLARET

I did not lie down ; but I despaired. I walked round and round
the room, wringing my hands in utter distraction. I threw myself at the bedside on my knees. I could not pray ; I could only
shiver and moan, with hands clasped, and eyes of horror turned
up to heaven. I think Madame was, in her malignant way, perplexed. That some evil was intended me I am sure she was persuaded ; but I dare say Meg Hawkes had said rightly in telling
me that she was not fully in their secrets.

The first paroxysm of despair subsided into another state. All
at once my mind was filled with the idea of Meg Hawkes, her
enterprise, and my chances of escape. There is one point at
which the road to Elverston makes a short ascent : there is a sud-

den curve there, two great ash-trees, with a roadside stile between, at the right side, covered with ivy. Driving back and
forward, I did not recollect having particularly remarked this
point in the highway; but now it was before me, in the thin
light of the thinnest segment of moon, and the figure of Meg
Hawkes, her back toward me, always ascending towards Elverston. It was constantly the same picture—the same motion without progress—the same dreadful suspense and impatience.

I was now sitting on the side of the bed, looking wistfully
across the room. When I did not see Meg Hawkes, I beheld
Madame darkly eyeing first one then another point of the chamber, evidently puzzling over some problem, and in one of her
most savage moods—sometimes muttering to herself, sometimes
protruding, and sometimes screwing up her great mouth.

She went into her own room, where she remained, I think,
nearly ten minutes, and on her return there was that in the flash
of her eyes, the glow of her face, and the peculiar fragrance that
surrounded her, that showed she had been partaking of her
favourite restorative.

I had not moved since she left my room.

She paused about the middle of the floor, and looked at me
with what I can only describe as her wild-beast stare.

'You are a very secrete family, you Ruthyns—you are so coning. I hate the coning people. By my faith, I weel see Mr. Silas
Ruthyn, and ask wat he mean. I heard him tell old Wyat that
Mr. Dudley is gone away to-night. He shall tell me everything,
or else I weel make echec et mat aussi vrai que je vis.'

Madame's words had hardly ceased, when I was again watching Meg Hawkes on the steep road, mounting, but never reaching, the top of the acclivity, on the way to Elverston, and mentally
praying that she might be brought safely there. Vain prayer
of an agonised heart! Meg's journey was already frustrated:
she was not to reach Elverston in time.

Madame revisited her apartment, and returned, not, I think,
improved in temper. She walked about the room, hustling the
scanty furniture hither and thither as she encountered it. She
kicked her empty box out of her way, with a horrid crash, and
a curse in French. She strode and swaggered round the room,
muttering all the way, and turning the corners of her course
with a furious whisk. At last, out of the door she went. I think

she fancied she had not been sufficiently taken into confidence as to what was intended for me.

It was now growing late, and yet no succour! I was seized, I remember, with a dreadful icy shivering.

I was listening for signals of deliverance. At every distant sound, half stifled with a palpitation, these sounds piercing my ear with a horrible and exaggerated distinctness—'Oh Meg!—Oh cousin Monica!—Oh come! Oh Heaven, have mercy!—Lord, have mercy!' I thought I heard a roaring and jangle of voices. Perhaps it came from Uncle Silas's room. It might be the tipsy violence of Madame. It might—merciful Heaven!—be the arrival of friends. I started to my feet; I listened, quivering with attention. Was it in my brain?—was it real? I was at the door, and it seemed to open of itself. Madame had forgotten to lock it; she was losing her head a little by this time. The key stood in the gallery door beyond; it too, was open. I fled wildly. There was a subsiding sound of voices in my uncle's room. I was, I know not how, on the lobby at the great stair-head outside my uncle's apartment. My hand was on the banisters, my foot on the first step, when below me and against the faint light that glimmered through the great window on the landing I saw a bulky human form ascending, and a voice said 'Hush!' I staggered back, and at that instant fancied, with a thrill of conviction, I heard Lady Knollys's voice in Uncle Silas' room.

I don't know how I entered the room; I was there like a ghost. I was frightened at my own state.

Lady Knollys was not there—no one but Madame and my guardian.

I can never forget the look that Uncle Silas fixed on me as he cowered, seemingly as appalled as I.

I think I must have looked like a phantom newly risen from the grave.

'What's that?—where do you come from?' whispered he.

'Death! death!' was my whispered answer, as I froze with terror where I stood.

'What does she mean?—what does all this mean?' said Uncle Silas, recovering wonderfully, and turning with a withering sneer on Madame. 'Do you think it right to disobey my plain directions, and let her run about the house at this hour?'

'Death! death! Oh, pray to God for you and me!' I whispered in the same dreadful tones.

My uncle stared strangely at me again; and after several horrible seconds, in which he seemed to have recovered himself, he said, sternly and coolly—

'You give too much place to your imagination, niece. Your spirits are in an odd state—you ought to have advice.'

'Oh, uncle, pity me! Oh, uncle, you are good! you're kind; you're kind when you think. You could not—you could not— could not! Oh, think of your brother that was always so good to you! He sees me here. He sees us both. Oh, save me, uncle— save me!—and I'll give up everything to you. I'll pray to God to bless you—I'll never forget your goodness and mercy. But don't keep me in doubt. If I'm to go, oh, for God's sake, shoot me now!'

'You were always odd, niece; I begin to fear you are insane,' he replied, in the same stern icy tone.

'Oh, uncle—oh!—am I? Am I *mad*?'

'I hope not; but you'll conduct yourself like a sane person if you wish to enjoy the privileges of one.'

Then, with his finger pointing at me, he turned to Madame, and said, in a tone of suppressed ferocity—

'What's the meaning of this?—why is she here?'

Madame was gabbling volubly, but to me it was only a shrilly noise. My whole soul was concentrated in my uncle, the arbiter of my life, before whom I stood in the wildest agony of supplication.

That night was dreadful. The people I saw dizzily, made of smoke or shining vapour, smiling or frowning, I could have passed my hand through them. They were evil spirits.

'There's no ill intended you; by —— there's none,' said my uncle, for the first time violently agitated. 'Madame told you why we've changed your room. You told her about the bailiffs, did not you?' with a stamp of fury he demanded of Madame, whose nasal roullades of talk were running on like a accompaniment all the time. She had told me indeed only a few hours since, and now it sounded to me like the echo of something heard a month ago or more.

'You can't go about the house, d—n it, with bailiffs in occupation. There now—there's the whole thing. Get to your room, Maud, and don't vex me. There's a good girl.'

He was trying to smile as he spoke these last words, and, with quavering soft tones, to quiet me ; but the old scowl was there, the smile was corpse-like and contorted, and the softness of his tones was more dreadful than another man's ferocity.

'There, Madame, she'll go quite gently, and you can call if you want help. Don't let it happen again.'

'Come, Maud,' said Madame, encircling but not hurting my arm with her grip ; 'let us go, my friend.'

I did go, you will wonder, as well you may—as you may wonder at the docility with which strong men walk through the press-room to the drop, and thank the people of the prison for their civility when they bid them good-bye, and facilitate the fixing of the rope and adjusting of the cap. Have you never wondered that they don't make a last battle for life with the unscrupulous energy of terror, instead of surrendering it so gently in cold blood, on a silent calculation, the arithmetic of despair ?

I went upstairs with Madame like a somnambulist. I rather quickened my step as I drew near my room. I went in, and stood a phantom at the window, looking into the dark quadrangle. A thin glimmering crescent hung in the frosty sky, and all heaven was strewn with stars. Over the steep roof at the other side spread on the dark azure of the night this glorious blazonry of the unfathomable Creator. To me a dreadful scroll —inexorable eyes—the cloud of cruel witnesses looking down in freezing brightness on my prayers and agonies.

I turned about and sat down, leaning my head upon my arms. Then suddenly I sat up, as for the first time the picture of Uncle Silas's littered room, and the travelling bags and black boxes plied on the floor by his table—the desk, hat-case, umbrella, coats, rugs, and mufflers, all ready for a journey— reached my brain and suggested thought. The *mise en scène* had remained in every detail fixed upon my retina ; and how I wondered—'When is he going—how soon ? Is he going to carry me away and place me in a madhouse ? '

'Am I—am I mad ? ' I began to think. 'Is this all a dream, or is it real ? '

I remembered how a thin polite gentleman, with a tall griz-

zled head and a black velvet waistcoat, came into the carriage
on our journey, and said a few words to me ; how Madame
whispered him something, and he murmured ' Oh ! ' very gently,
with raised eyebrows, and a glance at me, and thenceforward
spoke no more to me, only to Madame, and at the next station
carried his hat and other travelling chattels into another carriage. Had she told him I was mad ?

These horrid bars ! Madame always with me ! The direful
hints that dropt from my uncle ! My own terrific sensations !—
All these evidences revolved in my brain, and presented themselves in turn like writings on a wheel of fire.

There came a knock to the door—

Oh, Meg ! Was it she ? No ; old Wyat whispered Madame
something about her room.

So Madame re-entered, with a little silver tray and flagon in
her hands, and a glass. Nothing came from Uncle Silas in un-
gentlemanlike fashion.

' Drink, Maud,' said Madame, raising the cover, and evidently
enjoying the fragrant steam.

I could not. I might have done so had I been able to swallow
anything—for I was too distracted to think of Meg's warning.

Madame suddenly recollected her mistake of that evening, and
tried the door ; but it was duly locked. She took the key from
her pocket and placed it in her breast.

' You weel 'av these rooms to yourself, ma chère. I shall sleep
downstairs to-night.'

She poured out some of the hot claret into the glass abstractedly, and drank it off.

' 'Tis very good—I drank without theenk. Bote 'tis very good.
Why don't you drink some ? '

' I could not,' I repeated. And Madame boldly helped herself.

' Vary polite, certally, to Madame was it to send nothing at
all for *hair*' (so she pronounced ' her ') ; ' bote is all same thing.'
And so she ran on in her tipsy vein, which was loud and sarcastic, with a fierce laugh now and then.

Afterwards I heard that they were afraid of Madame, who was
given to cross purposes, and violent in her cups. She had been
noisy and quarrelsome downstairs. She was under the delusion
that I was to be conveyed away that night to a remote and safe

place, and she was to be handsomely compensated for services
and evidence to be afterwards given. She was not to be trusted,
however, with the truth. That was to be known but to three
persons on earth.

I never knew, but I believe that the spiced claret which
Madame drank was drugged. She was a person who could, I
have been told, drink a great deal without exhibiting any
change from it but an inflamed colour and furious temper. I
can only state for certain what I saw, and that was, that shortly
after she had finished the claret she lay down upon my bed,
and, I now know, fell asleep. I then thought she was *feigning*
sleep only, and that she was really watching me.

About an hour after this I suddenly heard a little *clink* in
the yard beneath. I peeped out, but saw nothing. The sound was
repeated, however—sometimes more frequently, sometimes at
long intervals. At last, in the deep shadow next the farther wall,
I thought I could discover a figure, sometimes erect, sometimes
stooping and bowing toward the earth. I could see this figure
only in the rudest outline mingling with the dark.

Like a thunderbolt it smote my brain. ' They are making my
grave ! '

After the first dreadful stun I grew quite wild, and ran up and
down the room wringing my hands and gasping prayers to
heaven. Then a calm stole over me—such a dreadful calm as I
could fancy glide over one who floated in a boat under the
shadow of the ' Traitor's Gate,' leaving life and hope and
trouble behind.

Shortly after there came a very low tap at my door ; then
another, like a tiny post-knock. I could never understand why
it was I made no answer. Had I done so, and thus shown that
I was awake, it might have sealed my fate. I was standing in the
middle of the floor staring at the door, which I expected to see
open, and admit I knew not what troop of spectres.

CHAPTER LXIV

THE HOUR OF DEATH

It was a very still night and frosty. My candle had long burnt out. There was still a faint moonlight, which fell in a square of yellow on the floor near the window, leaving the rest of the room in what to an eye less accustomed than mine had become to that faint light would have been total darkness. Now, I am sure, I heard a soft whispering outside my door. I knew that I was in a state of siege ! The crisis was come, and strange to say, I felt myself grow all at once resolute and self-possessed. It was not a subsidence, however, of the dreadful excitement, but a sudden screwing-up of my nerves to a pitch such as I cannot describe.

I suppose the people outside moved with great caution ; and the perfect solidity of the floor, which had not anywhere a creaking board in it, favoured their noiseless movements. It was well for me that there were in the house three persons whom it was part of their plan to mystify respecting my fate. This alone compelled the extreme caution of their proceedings. They suspected that I had placed furniture against the door, and were afraid to force it, lest a crash, a scream, perhaps a long and shrilly struggle, might follow.

I remained for a space which I cannot pretend to estimate in the same posture, afraid to stir—afraid to move my eye from the door.

A very peculiar grating sound above my head startled me from my watch — something of the character of sawing, only more crunching, and with a faint continued rumble in it— utterly inexplicable. It sounded over that portion of the roof which was farthest from the door, toward which I now glided ; and as I took my stand under cover of the projecting angle of a clumsy old press that stood close by it, I perceived the room a little darkened, and I saw a man descend and take his stand upon the window-stone. He let go a rope, which, however, was still fast round his body, and employed both his hands, with apparently some exertion, about something at the side of the window, which in a moment more, in one mass, bars and all, swung noiselessly open, admitting the frosty night-air ; and the man, whom I now distinctly saw to be Dudley Ruthyn, kneeled on the sill, and stept, after a moment's listening, into the room. His foot made no sound upon the floor ; his head was bare, and he wore his usual short shooting-jacket.

I cowered to the ground in my post of observation. He stood, as it seemed to me irresolutely for a moment, and then drew from his pocket an instrument which I distinctly saw against the faint moonlight. Imagine a hammer, one end of which had been beaten out into a longish tapering spike, with a handle something longer than usual. He drew stealthily to the window, and seemed to examine this hurriedly, and tested its strength with a twist or two of his hand. And then he adjusted it very carefully in his grasp, and made two or three little experimental picks with it in the air.

I remained perfectly still, with a terrible composure, crouched in my hiding-place, my teeth clenched, and prepared to struggle like a tigress for my life when discovered. I thought his next measure would be to light a match. I saw a lantern, I fancied, on the window-sill. But this was not his plan. He stole, in a groping way, which seemed strange to me, who could distinguish objects in this light, to the side of my bed, the exact position of which he evidently knew ; he stooped over it. Madame was breathing in the deep respiration of heavy sleep. Suddenly but softly he laid, as it seemed to me, his left hand over her face, and nearly at the same instant there came a scrunching blow ; an unnatural shriek, beginning small and swelling for two or three seconds into a yell such as are imagined in haunted houses, accompanied by a convulsive sound, as of the motion of running, and the arms drumming on the bed ; and then another blow— and with a horrid gasp he recoiled a step or two, and stood perfectly still. I heard a horrible tremor quivering through the joints and curtains of the bedstead—the convulsions of the murdered woman. It was a dreadful sound, like the shaking of a tree and rustling of leaves. Then once more he steps to the side of the bed, and I heard another of those horrid blows—and silence—and another—and more silence—and the diabolical surgery was ended. For a few seconds, I think, I was on the point of fainting ; but a gentle stir outside the door, close to my ear, startled me, and proved that there had been a watcher posted outside. There was a little tapping at the door.

'Who's that ? ' whispered Dudley, hoarsely.

'A friend,' answered a sweet voice.

And a key was introduced, the door quickly unlocked, and Uncle Silas entered. I saw that frail, tall, white figure, the venerable silver locks that resembled those upon the honoured head of John Wesley, and his thin white hand, the back of which hung so close to my face that I feared to breathe. I could see his fingers twitching nervously. The smell of perfumes and of ether entered the room with him.

Dudley was trembling now like a man in an ague-fit.

'Look what you made me do ! ' he said, maniacally.

'Steady, sir ! ' said the old man, close beside me.

'Yes, you damned old murderer ! I've a mind to do for you.'

'There, Dudley, like a dear boy, don't give way ; it's done. Right or wrong, we can't help it. You must be quiet,' said the old man, with a stern gentleness.

Dudley groaned.

'Whoever advised it, you're a gainer, Dudley,' said Uncle Silas.

Then there was a pause.

'I hope that was not heard,' said Uncle Silas.

Dudley walked to the window and stood there.

'Come, Dudley, you and Hawkes must use expedition. You know you must get that out of the way.'

'I've done too much. I won't do nout ; I'll not touch it. I wish my hand was off first ; I wish I was a soger. Do as ye like, you an' Hawkes. I won't go nigh it ; damn ye both — and *that* ! ' and he hurled the hammer with all his force upon the floor.

'Come, come, be reasonable, Dudley, dear boy. There's nothing to fear but your own folly. You won't make a noise ? '

'Oh, oh, my God ! ' said Dudley, hoarsely, and wiped his forehead with his open hand.

'There now, you'll be all well in a minute,' continued the old man.

'You said 'twouldn't hurt her. If I'd a known she'd a screeched like that I'd never a done it. 'Twas a damn lie. You're the damndest villain on earth.'

'Come, Dudley!' said the old man under his breath, but very sternly, 'make up your mind. If you don't choose to go on, it can't be helped ; only it's a pity you began. For *you* it is a good deal—it does not much matter for *me*.'

'Ay, for *you* !' echoed Dudley, through his set teeth. 'The old talk !'

'Well, sir,' snarled the old man, in the same low tones, 'you should have thought of all this before. It's only taking leave of the world a year or two sooner, but a year or two's something. I'll leave you to do as you please.'

'Stop, will you ? Stop here. I know it's a fixt thing now. If a fella does a thing he's damned for, you might let him talk a bit anyhow. I don't care much if I was shot.'

'There now—*there*—just stick to that, and don't run off again. There's a box and a bag here ; we must change the direction, and take them away. The box has some jewels. Can you see them ? I wish we had a light.'

'No, I'd rayther not ; I can see well enough. I wish we were out o' this. *Here's* the box.'

'Pull it to the window,' said the old man, to my inexpressible relief advancing at last a few steps.

Coolness was given me in that dreadful moment, and I knew that all depended on my being prompt and resolute. I stood up swiftly. I often thought if I had happened to wear silk instead of the cachmere I had on that night, its rustle would have betrayed me.

I distinctly saw the tall stooping figure of my uncle, and the outline of his venerable tresses, as he stood between me and the dull light of the window, like a shape cut in card.

He was saying 'just to *there*,' and pointing with his long arm at that contracting patch of moonlight which lay squared upon the floor. The door was about a quarter open, and just as Dudley began to drag Madame's heavy box, with my jewel-case in it, across the floor from her room, inhaling a great breath—with a mental prayer for help—I glided on tiptoe from the room and found myself on the gallery floor.

I turned to my right, simply by chance, and followed a long

gallery in the dark, not running—I was too fearful of making
the least noise—but walking with the tiptoe-swiftness of terror.
At the termination of this was a cross-gallery, one end of which
—that to my left—terminated in a great window, through which
the dusky night-view was visible. With the instinct of terror I
chose the darker, and turned again to my right; hurrying
through this long and nearly dark passage, I was terrified by a
light, about thirty feet before me, emerging from the ceiling.
In spotted patches this light fell through the door and sides of
a stable lantern, and showed me a ladder, down which, from an
open skylight I suppose for the cool night-air floated in my face,
came Dickon Hawkes notwithstanding his maimed condition,
with so much celerity as to leave me hardly a moment for consideration.

He sat on the last round of the ladder, and tightened the
strap of his wooden leg.

At my left was a door-case open, but no door. I entered;
it was a short passage about six feet long, leading perhaps to
a backstair, but the door at the end was locked.

I was forced to stand in this recess, then, which afforded no
shelter, while Pegtop stumped by with his lantern in his hand.
I fancy he had some idea of listening to his master unperceived,
for he stopped close to my hiding-place, blew out the candle,
and pinched the long snuff with his horny finger and thumb.

Having listened for a few seconds, he stumped stealthily along
the gallery which I had just traversed, and turned the corner in
the direction of the chamber where the crime had just been
committed, and the discovery was impending. I could see him
against the broad window which in the daytime lighted this long
passage, and the moment he had passed the corner I resumed my
flight.

I descended a stair corresponding with that backstair, as I am
told, up which Madame had led me only the night before. I
tried the outer door. To my wild surprise it was open. In a
moment I was upon the step, in the free air, and as instantaneously was seized by the arm in the grip of a man.

It was Tom Brice, who had already betrayed me, and who
was now, in surtout and hat, waiting to drive the carriage with
the guilty father and son from the scene of their abhorred outrage.

CHAPTER LXV

IN THE OAK PARLOUR

So it was vain : I was trapped, and all was over.

I stood before him on the step, the white moon shining on my face. I was trembling so that I wonder I could stand, my helpless hands raised towards him, and I looked up in his face. A long shuddering moan—' Oh—oh—oh ! ' was all I uttered.

The man, still holding my arm, looked, I thought frightened, into my white dumb face.

Suddenly he said, in a wild, fierce whisper—

' Never say another word ' (I had not uttered one). ' They shan't hurt ye, Miss ; git ye in ; I don't care a damn ! '

It was an uncouth speech. To me it was the voice of an angel. With a burst of gratitude that sounded in my own ears like a laugh, I thanked God for those blessed words.

In a moment more he had placed me in the carriage, and almost instantly we were in motion—very cautiously while crossing the court, until he had got the wheels upon the grass, and then at a rapid pace, improving his speed as the distance increased. He drove along the side of the back-approach to the house, keeping on the grass ; so that our progress, though swaying like that of a ship in a swell, was very nearly as noiseless.

The gate had been left unlocked—he swung it open, and remounted the box. And we were now beyond the spell of Bartram-Haugh, thundering—Heaven be praised !—along the Queen's highway, right in the route to Elverston. It was literally a gallop. Through the chariot windows I saw Tom stand as he drove, and every now and then throw an awful glance over his shoulder. Were we pursued ? Never was agony of prayer like mine, as with clasped hands and wild stare I gazed through the windows on the road, whose trees and hedges and gabled cottages were chasing one another backward at so giddy a speed.

We were now ascending that identical steep, with the giant ash-trees at the right and the stile between, which my vision of Meg Hawkes had presented all that night, when my excited eye detected a running figure within the hedge. I saw the head of some one crossing the stile in pursuit, and I heard Brice's name shrieked.

'Drive on—on—on!' I screamed.

But Brice pulled up. I was on my knees on the floor of the carriage, with clasped hands, expecting capture, when the door opened, and Meg Hawkes, pale as death, her cloak drawn over her black tresses, looked in.

'Oh! — ho! — ho! —thank God!' she screamed. 'Shake hands, lass. Tom, yer a good un! He's a good lad, Tom.'

'Come in, Meg—you must sit by me,' I said, recovering all at once.

Meg made no demur. 'Take my hand,' I said offering mine to her disengaged one.

'I can't, Miss—my arm's broke.'

And so it was, poor thing! She had been espied and overtaken in her errand of mercy for me, and her ruffian father had felled her with his cudgel, and then locked her into the cottage, whence, however, she had contrived to escape, and was now flying to Elverston, having tried in vain to get a hearing in Feltram, whose people had been for hours in bed.

The door being shut upon Meg, the steaming horses were instantly at a gallop again.

Tom was still watching as before, with many an anxious glance to rearward, for pursuit. Again he pulled up, and came to the window.

'Oh, what is it?' cried I.

''Bout that letter, Miss; I couldn't help. 'Twas Dickon, he found it in my pocket. That's a'.'

'Oh yes!—no matter—thank you—thank Heaven! Are we near Elverston?'

''Twill be a mile, Miss: and please'm to mind I had no finger in't.'

'Thanks—thank you—you're very good—I shall *always* thank you, Tom, as long as I live!'

At length we entered Elverston. I think I was half wild. I don't know how I got into the hall. I was in the oak-parlour, I believe, when I saw cousin Monica. I was standing, my arms extended. I could not speak ; but I ran with a loud long scream into her arms. I forget a great deal after that.

CONCLUSION

Oh, my beloved cousin Monica ! Thank Heaven, you are living still, and younger, I think, than I in all things but in years.

And Milly, my dear companion, she is now the happy wife of that good little clergyman, Sprigge Biddlepen. It has been in my power to be of use to them, and he shall have the next presentation to Dawling.

Meg Hawkes, proud and wayward, and the most affectionate creature on earth, was married to Tom Brice a few months after these events ; and, as both wished to emigrate, I furnished them with the capital, and I am told they are likely to be rich. I hear from my kind Meg often, and she seems very happy.

My dear old friends, Mary Quince and Mrs. Rusk, are, alas ! growing old, but living with me, and very happy. And after long solicitation, I persuaded Doctor Bryerly, the best and truest of ministers, with my dearest friend's concurrence, to undertake the management of the Derbyshire estates. In this I have been most fortunate. He is the very person for such a charge—so punctual, so laborious, so kind, and so shrewd.

In compliance with medical advice, cousin Monica hurried me away to the Continent, where she would never permit me to allude to the terrific scenes which remain branded so awfully on my brain. It needed no constraint. It is a sort of agony to me even now to think of them.

The plan was craftily devised. Neither old Wyat nor Giles, the butler, had a suspicion that I had returned to Bartram. Had I been put to death, the secret of my fate would have been deposited in the keeping of four persons only—the two Ruthyns, Hawkes, and ultimately Madame. My dear cousin Monica had been artfully led to believe in my departure for France, and prepared for my silence. Suspicion might not have been excited for a year after my death, and then would never, in all probability, have pointed to Bartram as the scene of the crime. The weeds would have grown over me, and I should have lain in that deep grave where the corpse of Madame de la Rougierre was unearthed in the darksome quadrangle of Bartram-Haugh.

It was more than two years after that I heard what had befallen at Bartram after my flight. Old Wyat, who went early to Uncle Silas's room, to her surprise—for he had told her that he was that night to accompany his son, who had to meet the mail-train to Derby at five o'clock in the morning—saw her old master lying on the sofa, much in his usual position.

'There was nout much strange about him,' old Wyat said, 'but that his scent-bottle was spilt on its side over on the table, and he dead.'

She thought he was not quite cold when she found him, and she sent the old butler for Doctor Jolks, who said he died of too much 'loddlum.'

Of my wretched uncle's religion what am I to say? Was it utter hypocrisy, or had it at any time a vein of sincerity in it? I cannot say. I don't believe that he had any heart left for religion, which is the highest form of affection, to take hold of. Perhaps he was a sceptic with misgivings about the future, but past the time for finding anything reliable in it. The devil approached the citadel of his heart by stealth, with many zigzags and parallels. The idea of marrying me to his son by fair means, then by foul, and, when that wicked chance was gone, then the design of seizing all by murder, supervened. I dare say that Uncle Silas thought for a while that he was a righteous man. He wished to have heaven and to escape hell, if there were such places. But there were other things whose existence was not speculative, of which some he coveted, and some he dreaded more, and temptation came. 'Now if any man build upon this foundation, gold, silver, precious stones, wood, hay, stubble, every man's work shall be made manifest; for the day shall declare it, because it shall be revealed by fire; and the fire shall try every man's work of what sort it is.' There comes with old age a time when the heart is no longer fusible or malleable, and must retain the form in which it has cooled down. 'He

that is unjust, let him be unjust still ; he which is filthy, let him
be filthy still.'

Dudley had disappeared ; but in one of her letters, Meg, writing from her Australian farm, says : ' There's a fella in toon as
calls hisself Colbroke, wi' a good hoose o' wood, 15 foot length,
and as hy 'bout as silling o' the pearler o' Bartram—only lots
o' rats, they do say, my lady—a bying and sellin' of goold back
and forred wi' the diggin foke and the marchants. His chick
and mouth be wry wi' scar o' burns or vitterel, an' no wiskers,
bless you ; but my Tom ee tolt him he knowed him for Master
Doodley. I ant seed him ; but he sade ad shute Tom soon is
look at 'im, an' denide it, wi' mouthful o' curses and oaf. Tom
baint right shure ; if I seed un wons i'd no for sartin ; but
'appen, 'twil best be let be.' This was all.

Old Hawkes stood his ground, relying on the profound cunning with which their actual proceedings had been concealed,
even from the suspicions of the two inmates of the house, and
on the mystery that habitually shrouded Bartram-Haugh and all
its belongings from the eyes of the outer world.

Strangely enough, he fancied that I had made my escape long
before the room was entered ; and, even if he were arrested,
there was no evidence, he was certain, to connect *him* with the
murder, all knowledge of which he would stoutly deny.

There was an inquest on the body of my uncle, and Dr. Jolks
was the chief witness. They found that his death was caused by
' an excessive dose of laudanum, accidentally administered by
himself.'

It was not until nearly a year after the dreadful occurrences
at Bartram that Dickon Hawkes was arrested on a very awful
charge, and placed in gaol. It was an old crime, committed in
Lancashire, that had found him out. After his conviction, as a
last chance, he tried a disclosure of all the circumstances of the
unsuspected death of the Frenchwoman. Her body was discovered buried where he indicated, in the inner court of Bartram-Haugh, and, after due legal enquiry, was interred in the
churchyard of Feltram.

Thus I escaped the horrors of the witness-box, or the far
worse torture of a dreadful secret.

Doctor Bryerly, shortly after Lady Knollys had described to

him the manner in which Dudley entered my room, visited the
house of Bartram-Haugh, and minutely examined the windows
of the room in which Mr. Charke had slept on the night of his
murder. One of these he found provided with powerful steel
hinges, very craftily sunk and concealed in the timber of the
window-frame, which was secured by an iron pin outside, and
swung open on its removal. This was the room in which they
had placed me, and this the contrivance by means of which the
room had been entered. The problem of Mr. Charke's murder
was solved.

I have penned it. I sit for a moment breathless. My hands are
cold and damp. I rise with a great sigh, and look out on the
sweet green landscape and pastoral hills, and see the flowers and
birds and the waving boughs of glorious trees—all images of liberty and safety ; and as the tremendous nightmare of my youth
melts into air, I lift my eyes in boundless gratitude to the God
of all comfort, whose mighty hand and outstretched arm delivered me. When I lower my eyes and unclasp my hands, my
cheeks are wet with tears. A tiny voice is calling me ' Mamma ! '
and a beloved smiling face, with his dear father's silken brown
tresses, peeps in.

' Yes, darling, our walk. Come away ! '

I am Lady Ilbury, happy in the affection of a beloved and
noblehearted husband. The shy useless girl you have known is
now a mother—trying to be a good one ; and this, the last
pledge, has lived.

I am not going to tell of sorrows—how brief has been my
pride of early maternity, or how beloved were those whom
the Lord gave and the Lord has taken away. But sometimes as,
smiling on my little boy, the tears gather in my eyes, and he
wonders, I can see, why they come, I am thinking—and trembling while I smile—to think, how strong is love, how frail is
life ; and rejoicing while I tremble that, in the deathless love
of those who mourn, the Lord of Life, who never gave a pang
in vain, conveys the sweet and ennobling promise of a compensation by eternal reunion. So, through my sorrows, I have heard
a voice from heaven say, ' Write, from hencefore blessed are the
dead that die in the Lord ! '

This world is a parable—the habitation of symbols—the phantoms of spiritual things immortal shown in material shape. May the blessed second-sight be mine—to recognise under these beautiful forms of earth the ANGELS who wear them ; for I am sure we may walk with them if we will, and hear them speak !

A CATALOGUE OF SELECTED DOVER BOOKS
IN ALL FIELDS OF INTEREST

A CATALOGUE OF SELECTED DOVER
BOOKS IN ALL FIELDS OF INTEREST

CONDITIONED REFLEXES, Ivan P. Pavlov. Full translation of most complete statement of Pavlov's work; cerebral damage, conditioned reflex, experiments with dogs, sleep, similar topics of great importance. 430pp. 5⅜ x 8½. 60614-7 Pa. $4.50

NOTES ON NURSING: WHAT IT IS, AND WHAT IT IS NOT, Florence Nightingale. Outspoken writings by founder of modern nursing. When first published (1860) it played an important role in much needed revolution in nursing. Still stimulating. 140pp. 5⅜ x 8½. 22340-X Pa. $3.00

HARTER'S PICTURE ARCHIVE FOR COLLAGE AND ILLUSTRATION, Jim Harter. Over 300 authentic, rare 19th-century engravings selected by noted collagist for artists, designers, decoupeurs, etc. Machines, people, animals, etc., printed one side of page. 25 scene plates for backgrounds. 6 collages by Harter, Satty, Singer, Evans. Introduction. 192pp. 8⅞ x 11¾. 23659-5 Pa. $5.00

MANUAL OF TRADITIONAL WOOD CARVING, edited by Paul N. Hasluck. Possibly the best book in English on the craft of wood carving. Practical instructions, along with 1,146 working drawings and photographic illustrations. Formerly titled *Cassell's Wood Carving*. 576pp. 6½ x 9¼. 23489-4 Pa. $7.95

THE PRINCIPLES AND PRACTICE OF HAND OR SIMPLE TURNING, John Jacob Holtzapffel. Full coverage of basic lathe techniques—history and development, special apparatus, softwood turning, hardwood turning, metal turning. Many projects—billiard ball, works formed within a sphere, egg cups, ash trays, vases, jardiniers, others—included. 1881 edition. 800 illustrations. 592pp. 6⅛ x 9¼. 23365-0 Clothbd. $15.00

THE JOY OF HANDWEAVING, Osma Tod. Only book you need for hand weaving. Fundamentals, threads, weaves, plus numerous projects for small board-loom, two-harness, tapestry, laid-in, four-harness weaving and more. Over 160 illustrations. 2nd revised edition. 352pp. 6½ x 9¼. 23458-4 Pa. $6.00

THE BOOK OF WOOD CARVING, Charles Marshall Sayers. Still finest book for beginning student in wood sculpture. Noted teacher, craftsman discusses fundamentals, technique; gives 34 designs, over 34 projects for panels, bookends, mirrors, etc. "Absolutely first-rate"—E. J. Tangerman. 33 photos. 118pp. 7¾ x 10⅝. 23654-4 Pa. $3.50

THE PHILOSOPHY OF HISTORY, Georg W. Hegel. Great classic of Western thought develops concept that history is not chance but a rational process, the evolution of freedom. 457pp. 5⅜ x 8½.   20112-0 Pa. $4.50

LANGUAGE, TRUTH AND LOGIC, Alfred J. Ayer. Famous, clear introduction to Vienna, Cambridge schools of Logical Positivism. Role of philosophy, elimination of metaphysics, nature of analysis, etc. 160pp. 5⅜ x 8½. (Available in U.S. only)   20010-8 Pa. $2.00

A PREFACE TO LOGIC, Morris R. Cohen. Great City College teacher in renowned, easily followed exposition of formal logic, probability, values, logic and world order and similar topics; no previous background needed. 209pp. 5⅜ x 8½.   23517-3 Pa. $3.50

REASON AND NATURE, Morris R. Cohen. Brilliant analysis of reason and its multitudinous ramifications by charismatic teacher. Interdisciplinary, synthesizing work widely praised when it first appeared in 1931. Second (1953) edition. Indexes. 496pp. 5⅜ x 8½.   23633-1 Pa. $6.50

AN ESSAY CONCERNING HUMAN UNDERSTANDING, John Locke. The only complete edition of enormously important classic, with authoritative editorial material by A. C. Fraser. Total of 1176pp. 5⅜ x 8½.
                    20530-4, 20531-2 Pa., Two-vol. set $16.00

HANDBOOK OF MATHEMATICAL FUNCTIONS WITH FORMULAS, GRAPHS, AND MATHEMATICAL TABLES, edited by Milton Abramowitz and Irene A. Stegun. Vast compendium: 29 sets of tables, some to as high as 20 places. 1,046pp. 8 x 10½.   61272-4 Pa. $14.95

MATHEMATICS FOR THE PHYSICAL SCIENCES, Herbert S. Wilf. Highly acclaimed work offers clear presentations of vector spaces and matrices, orthogonal functions, roots of polynomial equations, conformal mapping, calculus of variations, etc. Knowledge of theory of functions of real and complex variables is assumed. Exercises and solutions. Index. 284pp. 5⅝ x 8¼.   63635-6 Pa. $5.00

THE PRINCIPLE OF RELATIVITY, Albert Einstein et al. Eleven most important original papers on special and general theories. Seven by Einstein, two by Lorentz, one each by Minkowski and Weyl. All translated, unabridged. 216pp. 5⅜ x 8½.   60081-5 Pa. $3.50

THERMODYNAMICS, Enrico Fermi. A classic of modern science. Clear, organized treatment of systems, first and second laws, entropy, thermodynamic potentials, gaseous reactions, dilute solutions, entropy constant. No math beyond calculus required. Problems. 160pp. 5⅜ x 8½.
                    60361-X Pa. $3.00

ELEMENTARY MECHANICS OF FLUIDS, Hunter Rouse. Classic undergraduate text widely considered to be far better than many later books. Ranges from fluid velocity and acceleration to role of compressibility in fluid motion. Numerous examples, questions, problems. 224 illustrations. 376pp. 5⅝ x 8¼.   63699-2 Pa. $5.00

THE COMPLETE BOOK OF DOLL MAKING AND COLLECTING, Catherine Christopher. Instructions, patterns for dozens of dolls, from rag doll on up to elaborate, historically accurate figures. Mould faces, sew clothing, make doll houses, etc. Also collecting information. Many illustrations. 288pp. 6 x 9. 22066-4 Pa. $4.50

THE DAGUERREOTYPE IN AMERICA, Beaumont Newhall. Wonderful portraits, 1850's townscapes, landscapes; full text plus 104 photographs. The basic book. Enlarged 1976 edition. 272pp. 8¼ x 11¼. 23322-7 Pa. $7.95

CRAFTSMAN HOMES, Gustav Stickley. 296 architectural drawings, floor plans, and photographs illustrate 40 different kinds of "Mission-style" homes from The Craftsman (1901-16), voice of American style of simplicity and organic harmony. Thorough coverage of Craftsman idea in text and picture, now collector's item. 224pp. 8⅛ x 11. 23791-5 Pa. $6.00

PEWTER-WORKING: INSTRUCTIONS AND PROJECTS, Burl N. Osborn. & Gordon O. Wilber. Introduction to pewter-working for amateur craftsman. History and characteristics of pewter; tools, materials, step-by-step instructions. Photos, line drawings, diagrams. Total of 160pp. 7⅞ x 10¾. 23786-9 Pa. $3.50

THE GREAT CHICAGO FIRE, edited by David Lowe. 10 dramatic, eye-witness accounts of the 1871 disaster, including one of the aftermath and rebuilding, plus 70 contemporary photographs and illustrations of the ruins—courthouse, Palmer House, Great Central Depot, etc. Introduction by David Lowe. 87pp. 8¼ x 11. 23771-0 Pa. $4.00

SILHOUETTES: A PICTORIAL ARCHIVE OF VARIED ILLUSTRATIONS, edited by Carol Belanger Grafton. Over 600 silhouettes from the 18th to 20th centuries include profiles and full figures of men and women, children, birds and animals, groups and scenes, nature, ships, an alphabet. Dozens of uses for commercial artists and craftspeople. 144pp. 8⅜ x 11¼. 23781-8 Pa. $4.50

ANIMALS: 1,419 COPYRIGHT-FREE ILLUSTRATIONS OF MAMMALS, BIRDS, FISH, INSECTS, ETC., edited by Jim Harter. Clear wood engravings present, in extremely lifelike poses, over 1,000 species of animals. One of the most extensive copyright-free pictorial sourcebooks of its kind. Captions. Index. 284pp. 9 x 12. 23766-4 Pa. $8.95

INDIAN DESIGNS FROM ANCIENT ECUADOR, Frederick W. Shaffer. 282 original designs by pre-Columbian Indians of Ecuador (500-1500 A.D.). Designs include people, mammals, birds, reptiles, fish, plants, heads, geometric designs. Use as is or alter for advertising, textiles, leathercraft, etc. Introduction. 95pp. 8¾ x 11¼. 23764-8 Pa. $3.50

SZIGETI ON THE VIOLIN, Joseph Szigeti. Genial, loosely structured tour by premier violinist, featuring a pleasant mixture of reminiscenes, insights into great music and musicians, innumerable tips for practicing violinists. 385 musical passages. 256pp. 5⅝ x 8¼. 23763-X Pa. $4.00

ART FORMS IN NATURE, Ernst Haeckel. Multitude of strangely beautiful natural forms: Radiolaria, Foraminifera, jellyfishes, fungi, turtles, bats, etc. All 100 plates of the 19th-century evolutionist's *Kunstformen der Natur* (1904). 100pp. 9⅜ x 12¼. 22987-4 Pa. $5.00

CHILDREN: A PICTORIAL ARCHIVE FROM NINETEENTH-CENTURY SOURCES, edited by Carol Belanger Grafton. 242 rare, copyright-free wood engravings for artists and designers. Widest such selection available. All illustrations in line. 119pp. 8⅜ x 11¼. 23694-3 Pa. $4.00

WOMEN: A PICTORIAL ARCHIVE FROM NINETEENTH-CENTURY SOURCES, edited by Jim Harter. 391 copyright-free wood engravings for artists and designers selected from rare periodicals. Most extensive such collection available. All illustrations in line. 128pp. 9 x 12. 23703-6 Pa. $4.50

ARABIC ART IN COLOR, Prisse d'Avennes. From the greatest ornamentalists of all time—50 plates in color, rarely seen outside the Near East, rich in suggestion and stimulus. Includes 4 plates on covers. 46pp. 9⅜ x 12¼. 23658-7 Pa. $6.00

AUTHENTIC ALGERIAN CARPET DESIGNS AND MOTIFS, edited by June Beveridge. Algerian carpets are world famous. Dozens of geometrical motifs are charted on grids, color-coded, for weavers, needleworkers, craftsmen, designers. 53 illustrations plus 4 in color. 48pp. 8¼ x 11. (Available in U.S. only) 23650-1 Pa. $1.75

DICTIONARY OF AMERICAN PORTRAITS, edited by Hayward and Blanche Cirker. 4000 important Americans, earliest times to 1905, mostly in clear line. Politicians, writers, soldiers, scientists, inventors, industrialists, Indians, Blacks, women, outlaws, etc. Identificatory information. 756pp. 9¼ x 12¾. 21823-6 Clothbd. $40.00

HOW THE OTHER HALF LIVES, Jacob A. Riis. Journalistic record of filth, degradation, upward drive in New York immigrant slums, shops, around 1900. New edition includes 100 original Riis photos, monuments of early photography. 233pp. 10 x 7⅞. 22012-5 Pa. $7.00

NEW YORK IN THE THIRTIES, Berenice Abbott. Noted photographer's fascinating study of city shows new buildings that have become famous and old sights that have disappeared forever. Insightful commentary. 97 photographs. 97pp. 11⅜ x 10. 22967-X Pa. $5.00

MEN AT WORK, Lewis W. Hine. Famous photographic studies of construction workers, railroad men, factory workers and coal miners. New supplement of 18 photos on Empire State building construction. New introduction by Jonathan L. Doherty. Total of 69 photos. 63pp. 8 x 10¾. 23475-4 Pa. $3.00

THE AMERICAN SENATOR, Anthony Trollope. Little known, long unavailable Trollope novel on a grand scale. Here are humorous comment on American vs. English culture, and stunning portrayal of a heroine/villainess. Superb evocation of Victorian village life. 561pp. 5⅜ x 8½.
23801-6 Pa. $6.00

WAS IT MURDER? James Hilton. The author of *Lost Horizon* and *Goodbye, Mr. Chips* wrote one detective novel (under a pen-name) which was quickly forgotten and virtually lost, even at the height of Hilton's fame. This edition brings it back—a finely crafted public school puzzle resplendent with Hilton's stylish atmosphere. A thoroughly English thriller by the creator of Shangri-la. 252pp. 5⅜ x 8. (Available in U.S. only)
23774-5 Pa. $3.00

CENTRAL PARK: A PHOTOGRAPHIC GUIDE, Victor Laredo and Henry Hope Reed. 121 superb photographs show dramatic views of Central Park: Bethesda Fountain, Cleopatra's Needle, Sheep Meadow, the Blockhouse, plus people engaged in many park activities: ice skating, bike riding, etc. Captions by former Curator of Central Park, Henry Hope Reed, provide historical view, changes, etc. Also photos of N.Y. landmarks on park's periphery. 96pp. 8½ x 11. 23750-8 Pa. $4.50

NANTUCKET IN THE NINETEENTH CENTURY, Clay Lancaster. 180 rare photographs, stereographs, maps, drawings and floor plans recreate unique American island society. Authentic scenes of shipwreck, lighthouses, streets, homes are arranged in geographic sequence to provide walking-tour guide to old Nantucket existing today. Introduction, captions. 160pp. 8⅞ x 11¾. 23747-8 Pa. $6.95

STONE AND MAN: A PHOTOGRAPHIC EXPLORATION, Andreas Feininger. 106 photographs by *Life* photographer Feininger portray man's deep passion for stone through the ages. Stonehenge-like megaliths, fortified towns, sculpted marble and crumbling tenements show textures, beauties, fascination. 128pp. 9¼ x 10¾. 23756-7 Pa. $5.95

CIRCLES, A MATHEMATICAL VIEW, D. Pedoe. Fundamental aspects of college geometry, non-Euclidean geometry, and other branches of mathematics: representing circle by point. Poincare model, isoperimetric property, etc. Stimulating recreational reading. 66 figures. 96pp. 5⅝ x 8¼.
63698-4 Pa. $2.75

THE DISCOVERY OF NEPTUNE, Morton Grosser. Dramatic scientific history of the investigations leading up to the actual discovery of the eighth planet of our solar system. Lucid, well-researched book by well-known historian of science. 172pp. 5⅜ x 8½. 23726-5 Pa. $3.50

THE DEVIL'S DICTIONARY. Ambrose Bierce. Barbed, bitter, brilliant witticisms in the form of a dictionary. Best, most ferocious satire America has produced. 145pp. 5⅜ x 8½. 20487-1 Pa. $2.25

HISTORY OF BACTERIOLOGY, William Bulloch. The only comprehensive history of bacteriology from the beginnings through the 19th century. Special emphasis is given to biography-Leeuwenhoek, etc. Brief accounts of 350 bacteriologists form a separate section. No clearer, fuller study, suitable to scientists and general readers, has yet been written. 52 illustrations. 448pp. 5⅝ x 8¼. 23761-3 Pa. $6.50

THE COMPLETE NONSENSE OF EDWARD LEAR, Edward Lear. All nonsense limericks, zany alphabets, Owl and Pussycat, songs, nonsense botany, etc., illustrated by Lear. Total of 321pp. 5⅜ x 8½. (Available in U.S. only) 20167-8 Pa. $3.95

INGENIOUS MATHEMATICAL PROBLEMS AND METHODS, Louis A. Graham. Sophisticated material from Graham *Dial,* applied and pure; stresses solution methods. Logic, number theory, networks, inversions, etc. 237pp. 5⅜ x 8½. 20545-2 Pa. $4.50

BEST MATHEMATICAL PUZZLES OF SAM LOYD, edited by Martin Gardner. Bizarre, original, whimsical puzzles by America's greatest puzzler. From fabulously rare *Cyclopedia,* including famous 14-15 puzzles, the Horse of a Different Color, 115 more. Elementary math. 150 illustrations. 167pp. 5⅜ x 8½. 20498-7 Pa. $2.75

THE BASIS OF COMBINATION IN CHESS, J. du Mont. Easy-to-follow, instructive book on elements of combination play, with chapters on each piece and every powerful combination team—two knights, bishop and knight, rook and bishop, etc. 250 diagrams. 218pp. 5⅜ x 8½. (Available in U.S. only) 23644-7 Pa. $3.50

MODERN CHESS STRATEGY, Ludek Pachman. The use of the queen, the active king, exchanges, pawn play, the center, weak squares, etc. Section on rook alone worth price of the book. Stress on the moderns. Often considered the most important book on strategy. 314pp. 5⅜ x 8½. 20290-9 Pa. $4.50

LASKER'S MANUAL OF CHESS, Dr. Emanuel Lasker. Great world champion offers very thorough coverage of all aspects of chess. Combinations, position play, openings, end game, aesthetics of chess, philosophy of struggle, much more. Filled with analyzed games. 390pp. 5⅜ x 8½. 20640-8 Pa. $5.00

500 MASTER GAMES OF CHESS, S. Tartakower, J. du Mont. Vast collection of great chess games from 1798-1938, with much material nowhere else readily available. Fully annotated, arranged by opening for easier study. 664pp. 5⅜ x 8½. 23208-5 Pa. $7.50

A GUIDE TO CHESS ENDINGS, Dr. Max Euwe, David Hooper. One of the finest modern works on chess endings. Thorough analysis of the most frequently encountered endings by former world champion. 331 examples, each with diagram. 248pp. 5⅜ x 8½. 23332-4 Pa. $3.75

CATALOGUE OF DOVER BOOKS

SECOND PIATIGORSKY CUP, edited by Isaac Kashdan. One of the greatest tournament books ever produced in the English language. All 90 games of the 1966 tournament, annotated by players, most annotated by both players. Features Petrosian, Spassky, Fischer, Larsen, six others. 228pp. 5⅜ x 8½.   23572-6 Pa. $3.50

ENCYCLOPEDIA OF CARD TRICKS, revised and edited by Jean Hugard. How to perform over 600 card tricks, devised by the world's greatest magicians: impromptus, spelling tricks, key cards, using special packs, much, much more. Additional chapter on card technique. 66 illustrations. 402pp. 5⅜ x 8½. (Available in U.S. only)   21252-1 Pa. $4.95

MAGIC: STAGE ILLUSIONS, SPECIAL EFFECTS AND TRICK PHOTOGRAPHY, Albert A. Hopkins, Henry R. Evans. One of the great classics; fullest, most authorative explanation of vanishing lady, levitations, scores of other great stage effects. Also small magic, automata, stunts. 446 illustrations. 556pp. 5⅜ x 8½.   23344-8 Pa. $6.95

THE SECRETS OF HOUDINI, J. C. Cannell. Classic study of Houdini's incredible magic, exposing closely-kept professional secrets and revealing, in general terms, the whole art of stage magic. 67 illustrations. 279pp. 5⅜ x 8½.   22913-0 Pa. $4.00

HOFFMANN'S MODERN MAGIC, Professor Hoffmann. One of the best, and best-known, magicians' manuals of the past century. Hundreds of tricks from card tricks and simple sleight of hand to elaborate illusions involving construction of complicated machinery. 332 illustrations. 563pp. 5⅜ x 8½.   23623-4 Pa. $6.00

MADAME PRUNIER'S FISH COOKERY BOOK, Mme. S. B. Prunier. More than 1000 recipes from world famous Prunier's of Paris and London, specially adapted here for American kitchen. Grilled tournedos with anchovy butter, Lobster a la Bordelaise, Prunier's prized desserts, more. Glossary. 340pp. 5⅜ x 8½. (Available in U.S. only)   22679-4 Pa. $3.00

FRENCH COUNTRY COOKING FOR AMERICANS, Louis Diat. 500 easy-to-make, authentic provincial recipes compiled by former head chef at New York's Fitz-Carlton Hotel: onion soup, lamb stew, potato pie, more. 309pp. 5⅜ x 8½.   23665-X Pa. $3.95

SAUCES, FRENCH AND FAMOUS, Louis Diat. Complete book gives over 200 specific recipes: bechamel, Bordelaise, hollandaise, Cumberland, apricot, etc. Author was one of this century's finest chefs, originator of vichyssoise and many other dishes. Index. 156pp. 5⅜ x 8.   23663-3 Pa. $2.75

TOLL HOUSE TRIED AND TRUE RECIPES, Ruth Graves Wakefield. Authentic recipes from the famous Mass. restaurant: popovers, veal and ham loaf, Toll House baked beans, chocolate cake crumb pudding, much more. Many helpful hints. Nearly 700 recipes. Index. 376pp. 5⅜ x 8½.   23560-2 Pa. $4.50

THE CURVES OF LIFE, Theodore A. Cook. Examination of shells, leaves, horns, human body, art, etc., in *"the* classic reference on how the golden ratio applies to spirals and helices in nature . . . ."—Martin Gardner. 426 illustrations. Total of 512pp. 5⅜ x 8½. 23701-X Pa. $5.95

AN ILLUSTRATED FLORA OF THE NORTHERN UNITED STATES AND CANADA, Nathaniel L. Britton, Addison Brown. Encyclopedic work covers 4666 species, ferns on up. Everything. Full botanical information, illustration for each. This earlier edition is preferred by many to more recent revisions. 1913 edition. Over 4000 illustrations, total of 2087pp. 6⅛ x 9¼. 22642-5, 22643-3, 22644-1 Pa., Three-vol. set $25.50

MANUAL OF THE GRASSES OF THE UNITED STATES, A. S. Hitchcock, U.S. Dept. of Agriculture. The basic study of American grasses, both indigenous and escapes, cultivated and wild. Over 1400 species. Full descriptions, information. Over 1100 maps, illustrations. Total of 1051pp. 5⅜ x 8½. 22717-0, 22718-9 Pa., Two-vol. set $15.00

THE CACTACEAE,, Nathaniel L. Britton, John N. Rose. Exhaustive, definitive. Every cactus in the world. Full botanical descriptions. Thorough statement of nomenclatures, habitat, detailed finding keys. The one book needed by every cactus enthusiast. Over 1275 illustrations. Total of 1080pp. 8 x 10¼. 21191-6, 21192-4 Clothbd., Two-vol. set $35.00

AMERICAN MEDICINAL PLANTS, Charles F. Millspaugh. Full descriptions, 180 plants covered: history; physical description; methods of preparation with all chemical constituents extracted; all claimed curative or adverse effects. 180 full-page plates. Classification table. 804pp. 6½ x 9¼. 23034-1 Pa. $12.95

A MODERN HERBAL, Margaret Grieve. Much the fullest, most exact, most useful compilation of herbal material. Gigantic alphabetical encyclopedia, from aconite to zedoary, gives botanical information, medical properties, folklore, economic uses, and much else. Indispensable to serious reader. 161 illustrations. 888pp. 6½ x 9¼. (Available in U.S. only) 22798-7, 22799-5 Pa., Two-vol. set $13.00

THE HERBAL or GENERAL HISTORY OF PLANTS, John Gerard. The 1633 edition revised and enlarged by Thomas Johnson. Containing almost 2850 plant descriptions and 2705 superb illustrations, Gerard's *Herbal* is a monumental work, the book all modern English herbals are derived from, the one herbal every serious enthusiast should have in its entirety. Original editions are worth perhaps $750. 1678pp. 8½ x 12¼. 23147-X Clothbd. $50.00

MANUAL OF THE TREES OF NORTH AMERICA, Charles S. Sargent. The basic survey of every native tree and tree-like shrub, 717 species in all. Extremely full descriptions, information on habitat, growth, locales, economics, etc. Necessary to every serious tree lover. Over 100 finding keys. 783 illustrations. Total of 986pp. 5⅜ x 8½. 20277-1, 20278-X Pa., Two-vol. set $11.00

THE DEPRESSION YEARS AS PHOTOGRAPHED BY ARTHUR ROTHSTEIN, Arthur Rothstein. First collection devoted entirely to the work of outstanding 1930s photographer: famous dust storm photo, ragged children, unemployed, etc. 120 photographs. Captions. 119pp. 9¼ x 10¾.

23590-4 Pa. $5.00

CAMERA WORK: A PICTORIAL GUIDE, Alfred Stieglitz. All 559 illustrations and plates from the most important periodical in the history of art photography, *Camera Work* (1903-17). Presented four to a page, reduced in size but still clear, in strict chronological order, with complete captions. Three indexes. Glossary. Bibliography. 176pp. 8⅜ x 11¼.

23591-2 Pa. $6.95

ALVIN LANGDON COBURN, PHOTOGRAPHER, Alvin L. Coburn. Revealing autobiography by one of greatest photographers of 20th century gives insider's version of Photo-Secession, plus comments on his own work. 77 photographs by Coburn. Edited by Helmut and Alison Gernsheim. 160pp. 8⅛ x 11.

23685-4 Pa. $6.00

NEW YORK IN THE FORTIES, Andreas Feininger. 162 brilliant photographs by the well-known photographer, formerly with *Life* magazine, show commuters, shoppers, Times Square at night, Harlem nightclub, Lower East Side, etc. Introduction and full captions by John von Hartz. 181pp. 9¼ x 10¾.

23585-8 Pa. $6.95

GREAT NEWS PHOTOS AND THE STORIES BEHIND THEM, John Faber. Dramatic volume of 140 great news photos, 1855 through 1976, and revealing stories behind them, with both historical and technical information. Hindenburg disaster, shooting of Oswald, nomination of Jimmy Carter, etc. 160pp. 8¼ x 11.

23667-6 Pa. $5.00

THE ART OF THE CINEMATOGRAPHER, Leonard Maltin. Survey of American cinematography history and anecdotal interviews with 5 masters—Arthur Miller, Hal Mohr, Hal Rosson, Lucien Ballard, and Conrad Hall. Very large selection of behind-the-scenes production photos. 105 photographs. Filmographies. Index. Originally *Behind the Camera*. 144pp. 8¼ x 11.

23686-2 Pa. $5.00

DESIGNS FOR THE THREE-CORNERED HAT (LE TRICORNE), Pablo Picasso. 32 fabulously rare drawings—including 31 color illustrations of costumes and accessories—for 1919 production of famous ballet. Edited by Parmenia Migel, who has written new introduction. 48pp. 9⅜ x 12¼. (Available in U.S. only)

23709-5 Pa. $5.00

NOTES OF A FILM DIRECTOR, Sergei Eisenstein. Greatest Russian filmmaker explains montage, making of *Alexander Nevsky*, aesthetics; comments on self, associates, great rivals (Chaplin), similar material. 78 illustrations. 240pp. 5⅜ x 8½.

22392-2 Pa. $4.50

YUCATAN BEFORE AND AFTER THE CONQUEST, Diego de Landa. First English translation of basic book in Maya studies, the only significant account of Yucatan written in the early post-Conquest era. Translated by distinguished Maya scholar William Gates. Appendices, introduction, 4 maps and over 120 illustrations added by translator. 162pp. 5⅜ x 8½.
23622-6 Pa. $3.00

THE MALAY ARCHIPELAGO, Alfred R. Wallace. Spirited travel account by one of founders of modern biology. Touches on zoology, botany, ethnography, geography, and geology. 62 illustrations, maps. 515pp. 5⅜ x 8½.
20187-2 Pa. $6.95

THE DISCOVERY OF THE TOMB OF TUTANKHAMEN, Howard Carter, A. C. Mace. Accompany Carter in the thrill of discovery, as ruined passage suddenly reveals unique, untouched, fabulously rich tomb. Fascinating account, with 106 illustrations. New introduction by J. M. White. Total of 382pp. 5⅜ x 8½. (Available in U.S. only)   23500-9 Pa. $4.00

THE WORLD'S GREATEST SPEECHES, edited by Lewis Copeland and Lawrence W. Lamm. Vast collection of 278 speeches from Greeks up to present. Powerful and effective models; unique look at history. Revised to 1970. Indices. 842pp. 5⅜ x 8½.   20468-5 Pa. $8.95

THE 100 GREATEST ADVERTISEMENTS, Julian Watkins. The priceless ingredient; His master's voice; 99 44/100% pure; over 100 others. How they were written, their impact, etc. Remarkable record. 130 illustrations. 233pp. 7⅞ x 10 3/5.   20540-1 Pa. $5.95

CRUICKSHANK PRINTS FOR HAND COLORING, George Cruickshank. 18 illustrations, one side of a page, on fine-quality paper suitable for watercolors. Caricatures of people in society (c. 1820) full of trenchant wit. Very large format. 32pp. 11 x 16.   23684-6 Pa. $5.00

THIRTY-TWO COLOR POSTCARDS OF TWENTIETH-CENTURY AMERICAN ART, Whitney Museum of American Art. Reproduced in full color in postcard form are 31 art works and one shot of the museum. Calder, Hopper, Rauschenberg, others. Detachable. 16pp. 8¼ x 11.
23629-3 Pa. $3.00

MUSIC OF THE SPHERES: THE MATERIAL UNIVERSE FROM ATOM TO QUASAR SIMPLY EXPLAINED, Guy Murchie. Planets, stars, geology, atoms, radiation, relativity, quantum theory, light, antimatter, similar topics. 319 figures. 664pp. 5⅜ x 8½.
21809-0, 21810-4 Pa., Two-vol. set $11.00

EINSTEIN'S THEORY OF RELATIVITY, Max Born. Finest semi-technical account; covers Einstein, Lorentz, Minkowski, and others, with much detail, much explanation of ideas and math not readily available elsewhere on this level. For student, non-specialist. 376pp. 5⅜ x 8½.
60769-0 Pa. $4.50

THE ANATOMY OF THE HORSE, George Stubbs. Often considered the great masterpiece of animal anatomy. Full reproduction of 1766 edition, plus prospectus; original text and modernized text. 36 plates. Introduction by Eleanor Garvey. 121pp. 11 x 14¾.   23402-9 Pa. $6.00

BRIDGMAN'S LIFE DRAWING, George B. Bridgman. More than 500 illustrative drawings and text teach you to abstract the body into its major masses, use light and shade, proportion; as well as specific areas of anatomy, of which Bridgman is master. 192pp. 6½ x 9¼. (Available in U.S. only)
                                                      22710-3 Pa. $3.50

ART NOUVEAU DESIGNS IN COLOR, Alphonse Mucha, Maurice Verneuil, Georges Auriol. Full-color reproduction of *Combinaisons ornementales* (c. 1900) by Art Nouveau masters. Floral, animal, geometric, interlacings, swashes—borders, frames, spots—all incredibly beautiful. 60 plates, hundreds of designs. 9⅜ x 8-1/16.   22885-1 Pa. $4.00

FULL-COLOR FLORAL DESIGNS IN THE ART NOUVEAU STYLE, E. A. Seguy. 166 motifs, on 40 plates, from *Les fleurs et leurs applications decoratives* (1902): borders, circular designs, repeats, allovers, "spots." All in authentic Art Nouveau colors. 48pp. 9⅜ x 12¼.
                                                      23439-8 Pa. $5.00

A DIDEROT PICTORIAL ENCYCLOPEDIA OF TRADES AND IN-DUSTRY, edited by Charles C. Gillispie. 485 most interesting plates from the great French Encyclopedia of the 18th century show hundreds of working figures, artifacts, process, land and cityscapes; glassmaking, paper-making, metal extraction, construction, weaving, making furniture, clothing, wigs, dozens of other activities. Plates fully explained. 920pp. 9 x 12.
                              22284-5, 22285-3 Clothbd., Two-vol. set $40.00

HANDBOOK OF EARLY ADVERTISING ART, Clarence P. Hornung. Largest collection of copyright-free early and antique advertising art ever compiled. Over 6,000 illustrations, from Franklin's time to the 1890's for special effects, novelty. Valuable source, almost inexhaustible.
Pictorial Volume. Agriculture, the zodiac, animals, autos, birds, Christmas, fire engines, flowers, trees, musical instruments, ships, games and sports, much more. Arranged by subject matter and use. 237 plates. 288pp. 9 x 12.
                                                 20122-8 Clothbd. $14.50

Typographical Volume. Roman and Gothic faces ranging from 10 point to 300 point, "Barnum," German and Old English faces, script, logotypes, scrolls and flourishes, 1115 ornamental initials, 67 complete alphabets, more. 310 plates. 320pp. 9 x 12.   20123-6 Clothbd. $15.00

CALLIGRAPHY (CALLIGRAPHIA LATINA), J. G. Schwandner. High point of 18th-century ornamental calligraphy. Very ornate initials, scrolls, borders, cherubs, birds, lettered examples. 172pp. 9 x 13.
                                                      20475-8 Pa. $7.00

THE COMPLETE WOODCUTS OF ALBRECHT DURER, edited by Dr. W. Kurth. 346 in all: "Old Testament," "St. Jerome," "Passion," "Life of Virgin," Apocalypse," many others. Introduction by Campbell Dodgson. 285pp. 8½ x 12¼. 21097-9 Pa. $7.50

DRAWINGS OF ALBRECHT DURER, edited by Heinrich Wolfflin. 81 plates show development from youth to full style. Many favorites; many new. Introduction by Alfred Werner. 96pp. 8⅛ x 11. 22352-3 Pa. $5.00

THE HUMAN FIGURE, Albrecht Dürer. Experiments in various techniques—stereometric, progressive proportional, and others. Also life studies that rank among finest ever done. Complete reprinting of *Dresden Sketchbook*. 170 plates. 355pp. 8⅜ x 11¼. 21042-1 Pa. $7.95

OF THE JUST SHAPING OF LETTERS, Albrecht Dürer. Renaissance artist explains design of Roman majuscules by geometry, also Gothic lower and capitals. Grolier Club edition. 43pp. 7⅞ x 10¾ 21306-4 Pa. $3.00

TEN BOOKS ON ARCHITECTURE, Vitruvius. The most important book ever written on architecture. Early Roman aesthetics, technology, classical orders, site selection, all other aspects. Stands behind everything since. Morgan translation. 331pp. 5⅜ x 8½. 20645-9 Pa. $4.50

THE FOUR BOOKS OF ARCHITECTURE, Andrea Palladio. 16th-century classic responsible for Palladian movement and style. Covers classical architectural remains, Renaissance revivals, classical orders, etc. 1738 Ware English edition. Introduction by A. Placzek. 216 plates. 110pp. of text. 9½ x 12¾. 21308-0 Pa. $10.00

HORIZONS, Norman Bel Geddes. Great industrialist stage designer, "father of streamlining," on application of aesthetics to transportation, amusement, architecture, etc. 1932 prophetic account; function, theory, specific projects. 222 illustrations. 312pp. 7⅞ x 10¾. 23514-9 Pa. $6.95

FRANK LLOYD WRIGHT'S FALLINGWATER, Donald Hoffmann. Full, illustrated story of conception and building of Wright's masterwork at Bear Run, Pa. 100 photographs of site, construction, and details of completed structure. 112pp. 9¼ x 10. 23671-4 Pa. $5.50

THE ELEMENTS OF DRAWING, John Ruskin. Timeless classic by great Viltorian; starts with basic ideas, works through more difficult. Many practical exercises. 48 illustrations. Introduction by Lawrence Campbell. 228pp. 5⅜ x 8½. 22730-8 Pa. $3.75

GIST OF ART, John Sloan. Greatest modern American teacher, Art Students League, offers innumerable hints, instructions, guided comments to help you in painting. Not a formal course. 46 illustrations. Introduction by Helen Sloan. 200pp. 5⅜ x 8½. 23435-5 Pa. $4.00

HOLLYWOOD GLAMOUR PORTRAITS, edited by John Kobal. 145 photos capture the stars from 1926-49, the high point in portrait photography. Gable, Harlow, Bogart, Bacall, Hedy Lamarr, Marlene Dietrich, Robert Montgomery, Marlon Brando, Veronica Lake; 94 stars in all. Full background on photographers, technical aspects, much more. Total of 160pp. 8⅜ x 11¼. 23352-9 Pa. $6.00

THE NEW YORK STAGE: FAMOUS PRODUCTIONS IN PHOTOGRAPHS, edited by Stanley Appelbaum. 148 photographs from Museum of City of New York show 142 plays, 1883-1939. *Peter Pan, The Front Page, Dead End, Our Town,* O'Neill, hundreds of actors and actresses, etc. Full indexes. 154pp. 9½ x 10. 23241-7 Pa. $6.00

DIALOGUES CONCERNING TWO NEW SCIENCES, Galileo Galilei. Encompassing 30 years of experiment and thought, these dialogues deal with geometric demonstrations of fracture of solid bodies, cohesion, leverage, speed of light and sound, pendulums, falling bodies, accelerated motion, etc. 300pp. 5⅜ x 8½. 60099-8 Pa. $4.00

THE GREAT OPERA STARS IN HISTORIC PHOTOGRAPHS, edited by James Camner. 343 portraits from the 1850s to the 1940s: Tamburini, Mario, Caliapin, Jeritza, Melchior, Melba, Patti, Pinza, Schipa, Caruso, Farrar, Steber, Gobbi, and many more—270 performers in all. Index. 199pp. 8⅜ x 11¼. 23575-0 Pa. $7.50

J. S. BACH, Albert Schweitzer. Great full-length study of Bach, life, background to music, music, by foremost modern scholar. Ernest Newman translation. 650 musical examples. Total of 928pp. 5⅜ x 8½. (Available in U.S. only) 21631-4, 21632-2 Pa., Two-vol. set $11.00

COMPLETE PIANO SONATAS, Ludwig van Beethoven. All sonatas in the fine Schenker edition, with fingering, analytical material. One of best modern editions. Total of 615pp. 9 x 12. (Available in U.S. only) 23134-8, 23135-6 Pa., Two-vol. set $15.50

KEYBOARD MUSIC, J. S. Bach. Bach-Gesellschaft edition. For harpsichord, piano, other keyboard instruments. English Suites, French Suites, Six Partitas, Goldberg Variations, Two-Part Inventions, Three-Part Sinfonias. 312pp. 8⅛ x 11. (Available in U.S. only) 22360-4 Pa. $6.95

FOUR SYMPHONIES IN FULL SCORE, Franz Schubert. Schubert's four most popular symphonies: No. 4 in C Minor ("Tragic"); No. 5 in B-flat Major; No. 8 in B Minor ("Unfinished"); No. 9 in C Major ("Great"). Breitkopf & Hartel edition. Study score. 261pp. 9⅜ x 12¼. 23681-1 Pa. $6.50

THE AUTHENTIC GILBERT & SULLIVAN SONGBOOK, W. S. Gilbert, A. S. Sullivan. Largest selection available; 92 songs, uncut, original keys, in piano rendering approved by Sullivan. Favorites and lesser-known fine numbers. Edited with plot synopses by James Spero. 3 illustrations. 399pp. 9 x 12. 23482-7 Pa. $9.95

AMERICAN ANTIQUE FURNITURE, Edgar G. Miller, Jr. The basic coverage of all American furniture before 1840: chapters per item chronologically cover all types of furniture, with more than 2100 photos. Total of 1106pp. 7⅞ x 10¾. 21599-7, 21600-4 Pa., Two-vol. set $17.90

ILLUSTRATED GUIDE TO SHAKER FURNITURE, Robert Meader. Director, Shaker Museum, Old Chatham, presents up-to-date coverage of all furniture and appurtenances, with much on local styles not available elsewhere. 235 photos. 146pp. 9 x 12. 22819-3 Pa. $6.00

ORIENTAL RUGS, ANTIQUE AND MODERN, Walter A. Hawley. Persia, Turkey, Caucasus, Central Asia, China, other traditions. Best general survey of all aspects: styles and periods, manufacture, uses, symbols and their interpretation, and identification. 96 illustrations, 11 in color. 320pp. 6⅛ x 9¼. 22366-3 Pa. $6.95

CHINESE POTTERY AND PORCELAIN, R. L. Hobson. Detailed descriptions and analyses by former Keeper of the Department of Oriental Antiquities and Ethnography at the British Museum. Covers hundreds of pieces from primitive times to 1915. Still the standard text for most periods. 136 plates, 40 in full color. Total of 750pp. 5⅜ x 8½. 23253-0 Pa. $10.00

THE WARES OF THE MING DYNASTY, R. L. Hobson. Foremost scholar examines and illustrates many varieties of Ming (1368-1644). Famous blue and white, polychrome, lesser-known styles and shapes. 117 illustrations, 9 full color, of outstanding pieces. Total of 263pp. 6⅛ x 9¼. (Available in U.S. only) 23652-8 Pa. $6.00

Prices subject to change without notice.

Available at your book dealer or write for free catalogue to Dept. GI, Dover Publications, Inc., 180 Varick St., N.Y., N.Y. 10014. Dover publishes more than 175 books each year on science, elementary and advanced mathematics, biology, music, art, literary history, social sciences and other areas.

252 *Index*

Purvis, Arthur, 27, 61, 62, 64, 67–68, 98

P.W.B. (Psychological Warfare Branch), 170, 198

P.W.E. (Political Warfare Executive), 151, 170

Qadir, Major Altaf, 209
Quebec Conference (1944), 179, 210
Queen Elizabeth, s.s., 65
Queen Mary, s.s., 65

Ramirez, President, of Argentina, 202
Rath, Ernest vom, 126
Rath, William vom, 126
R.C.M.P. (Royal Canadian Mounted Police), 51, 135, 212, 229–235
Recollections of a Picture Dealer (Vollard), 97 *n.*
Red Sea, 47
Rekowski, —— (German agent), 69
Repulse, H.M.S., 110
Research and Analysis Branch, O.S.S., 169, 178–179
Reynaud, Paul, 32, 103
Ribbentrop, Joachim von, 69, 75, 76, 78, 126
Richtofen, Lothar Von, 8
Rieth, Dr. Kurt Heinrich, 127–128
Rintelen, Captain Von, 69
Rio de Janeiro, 53, 131, 132, 133, 145, 146–147, 221; Conference (Jan. 1942), 139, 144, 147, 163
Road to Safety, The (Willert), 63 *n.*
Robert, Admiral Georges, 111, 113, 190–191
Robertson, Norman, 229–230, 234
Rockfort, Jamaica, 239
Roosevelt, Franklin D., 4, 26–27, 30, 31, 32–36, 37–40, 41–43, 45–47, 49–50, 54, 67, 72, 94, 99, 100, 115, 128, 134, 140, 142, 150, 152, 153–154, 159, 164, 178, 179, 186, 191–194, 197, 201, 202, 203, 204, 206–207, 208 *n.*, 210, 213
Roosevelt, James, 213
Roosevelt in Retrospect (Gunther), 192 *n.*

Roosevelt Letters, The, 35 *n.*
Rose, Fred, 233, 235
Rosenman, Judge Samuel, 194
Rothermere, Lord, 76, 78
Royal Canadian Engineers, 7
Royal Canadian Flying Corps, 7–9
Royal Canadian Mounted Police (R.C.M.P.), 51, 135, 212, 229–235
Royal Flying Corps, 7, 8
Russia, 45, 58, 61, 77, 132, 166, 191, 192, 206, 230–235

St. Lucia, 113
St. Pierre, 98–99, 113–115
Salerno, 228
San Francisco, 74, 76–77, 160
Sandstede, Gottfried, 150
Santa Cruz, 142
Saratoga, U.S.S., 214
Scheer (German battleship), 43
Schering, A. G., 122–124
Schering Corporation of Bloomfield, 121, 122–124
Schneider Trophy Race (1929), 14
Schwarz, Dr. Paul, 92
Scientific Astrologers, American Federation of, 191
Sealy, Theodore, 239
Seamen, National Union of, 66
Sebold, William, 84, 219, 221
Second World War, The (Churchill), 16
Secret Intelligence Service—*see* S.I.S.
Secret War, The (De Gramont), 178 *n.*
Security Division, B.S.C., 62–67, 69
Seiferheld, David, 193
Sequel to the Apocalypse, 125–126
Seven Major Decisions (Welles), 67 *n.*
Shaw, Bernard, 92
Shepardson, Whitney, 152
Sherwood, Robert, 5, 31 *n.*, 114 *n.*, 152, 154, 169–170, 191, 197, 204 *n.*, 208 *n.*, 236, 237–238
Ships' Observer Scheme, 131
Sichel, Herbert, 181